THE BROOKLYN NOVELS

Also by Daniel Fuchs

Summer in Williamsburg (1934)

Homage to Blenholt (1936)

Low Company (1937)

Stories (1956)
(with Jean Stafford, John Cheever,
and William Maxwell)

West of the Rockies (1971)

The Apathetic Bookie Joint (1979)

The Golden West: Hollywood Stories (2005)
(selected by Christopher Carduff)

DANIEL FUCHS

THE BROOKLYN NOVELS

Summer in Williamsburg

Homage to Blenholt

Low Company

Introduction by Jonathan Lethem

A BLACK SPARROW BOOK
David R. Godine · *Publisher*
BOSTON

This is
A Black Sparrow Book
published in 2006 by
David R. Godine · *Publisher*
Post Office Box 450
Jaffrey, New Hampshire 03452
www.blacksparrowbooks.com

The contents of this volume were selected, edited, and arranged by Christopher Carduff in consultation with the Estate of Daniel Fuchs.

Book design and composition by Carl W. Scarbrough.
The Black Sparrow Books pressmark is by Julian Waters
www.waterslettering.com.

LIBRARY OF CONGRESS CATALOGING-IN-PUBLICATION DATA
Fuchs, Daniel, 1909–1993.
[Three novels]
The Brooklyn novels : Summer in Williamsburg, Homage to Blenholt, Low company / Daniel Fuchs ; introduction by Jonathan Lethem. — 1st ed.
p. cm.
Originally published: Three novels. New York : Basic Books, 1961.
"A Black Sparrow book"—T.p. verso.
ISBN 1-57423-211-8 (alk. paper) — ISBN 1-57423-210-X (pbk. : alk. paper)
1. Brooklyn (New York, N.Y.)—Fiction. I. Title.
PS3511.U27A6 2006
813'.52—dc22
2006023170

First Edition

PRINTED IN CANADA

CONTENTS

INTRODUCTION

Six years ago I wrote:

> There's nothing on my shelf I flip open for inspiration as often these days as Daniel Fuchs's three novels about Brooklyn, set and written in the 1930s . . . reprinted in 1961 in one volume as *Three Novels*, then separately in paperback in 1965—a moment of rediscovery now as forgotten as the original publication. Fuchs published in *The New Yorker*, was a buddy of Cheever's at Yaddo, and somewhere Irving Howe compared him to Willie Mays for the ease of his effects, but unlike Willie Mays he's nearly vanished from the record books . . .

Today, thanks to Black Sparrow's superb one-volume distillation of the latter part of Fuchs's career—in which our hero flees Brooklyn and, for the most part, fiction, in favor of Hollywood and an uncommonly serene career as a studio screenwriter—contemporary readers are likely to come to Fuchs's grittily enchanted vision of Brooklyn backward. That moderately scaled volume, *The Golden West*, published in 2005, gathered essays and a trickle of fiction on the theme of Hollywood, produced over five decades. However lovely—and any paragraph Fuchs put to paper is lovely—*The Golden West* records a disconcerting abandonment. The present bulging volume, *The Brooklyn Novels*, three books produced in little over five years, presents the commitment—to fictional voice and fictional form—that was to be abandoned. And, since Fuchs was a man of compulsive scruples, the book also records the dilemmas, artistic and personal, that made Fuchs's flight from the material of his splendid early fiction so needed, as well as the terms by which abandonment was to be enacted.

I discovered Fuchs at Yaddo, while browsing idly on the shelves reserved for the works of previous occupants of the place. I was there trying to find a way to write about Brooklyn. You can imagine my surprise at opening *Summer in Williamsburg* and discovering Fuchs's secret Dickensian tapestry depicting a coming of age among immigrant dreamers and scoundrels. Fuchs's voice—tender, embracing, antic, vernacular—seemed to me immediately essential, a compass for my own work, and his collected works a missing piece in my interior bookshelf. Here was something like the milieu I'd glimpsed in Malamud's earliest fiction, in Vivian Gornick's memoir *Fierce Attachments*, in the tenement stories of Will Eisner, depicted in full and from the inside, with absolute and sometimes claustrophobic authority, yet without the air of decrepitude and undropped grudges, of mingled bitterness and sentimentality, which had so often discouraged my curiosity about Jewish Proletarian fiction—material which lay so near at hand to my experience of my mother's family (my uncle Fred, a numismatist, author of several volumes on American coins, who tattled on a mobster and lived in fear of reprisal, was, just for instance, a perfect Fuchs character). In fact, Fuchs's voice was so fresh and enticing, I felt a disbelief at the 1930s copyright dates—yet if I could accept the sense of contemporaneity I located in the dialogue in Fitzgerald and in Howard Hawks movies, maybe I should accept Fuchs's.

Summer in Williamsburg ("written," Fuchs said, "in a state of terror") is a first novel if ever there was one: a "dictionary" or "encyclopedia" of the Brooklyn precinct that formed Fuchs's awareness, and encapsulating almost despite itself the writer's meditation on the development of his own puzzling sensibility, despite the fact that the central figure, Philip Hayman, never declares himself a writer-to-be. Rather, he seems to accept the collapse of any dream of escape from the pragmatic logic of Depression life. Suffused with forgiving humor, the tone is one of endurance, but never stoical, always yearning. *Homage to Blenholt* reapproaches the same turf with new writerly tools: comic compression, ironic distance, and rattletrap dialogue. Fuchs's characters jabber in poetry, compressed and glinting, warmer than Don DeLillo's Bronx argot in *Underworld* but worthy of the comparison. *Low Company* (set not in Williamsburg but in Brighton Beach) distills Fuchs's instinct for the comic-grotesque even further from the earlier tone of autobiographical reminiscence. Here it's schemer versus schemer, with nary a dreamer in sight. Or rather, dreams have been now sublimated in schemes, a perfect model of American arrival. *Low Company*, of the three, might even be called a crime novel (and in fact, *Summer*'s little plot concerns Catskill bus-route gangsters), except that Fuchs's tone is resolutely soft-boiled, and his bullies' brief outbursts of violence tend to fall like weather, or fate.

This third novel, so chewily grim, exasperated at least one critic who might have wished Fuchs to go on exemplifying if not exalting the Proletarian dilemma: Irving Howe, who called it "slick." It may also have somewhat exasperated another, peculiarly harsh critic: Fuchs. "I was tired of making fun of the people in my stories, hitting them off, as I did, easily and without conscience. I was, in the end, in the peculiar position of a writer whose forte was a quality he secretly disliked and wanted to lean on less and less and not at all, and who, on the other hand, had no other special talent or great idea to offer in its place."

All this was in long retrospect: those comments come from a 1987 autobiographical essay, extensively and seductively justifying his migration from fiction to screenwriting. One could also point out that all the vernacular elements that attracted him to Hollywood (and vice versa), abundantly present in the fiction from the start, found culmination in *Low Company*: the rapidly sketched milieus of tawdry Americana, the scraped wit, the ferociously humane dialogue, the unfussy emotionality, the love of "types." Soon enough Fuchs would become one of the myriad voices expanding, if not originating, what would later be called Film Noir. In the Hollywood sun and in the scenarist's craft he seems to have found the escapes he desired: out of the guilty traps of a Jewish-ghetto cultural inheritance; out of the political duties of a Proletarian novelist, from which he instinctively flinched, to the great benefit of his prose, but which he nevertheless seems to have felt weighing on him implicitly; from the solitary woes of a public-school substitute teacher writing novels on the side and measuring his value by "four hundred copies sold." The movies, which he plainly loved—and why not?—presented him with his own American arrival. The dream-turned-scheme out west was the greatest scheme of all: the production of dreams.

Perhaps it's defensiveness on Fuchs's behalf, but I find myself eager to provide comparisons for the vigor and sorrow and drollness of Fuchs's style that point beyond the orbit of Malamud and Bellow. Not that John Updike was anything but wholly right to identify Fuchs's "admiration of energy, however ill expended," and his "acceptance of people as the troublesome, messy spirits they are" as Bellovian. There's little doubt that had Fuchs stuck around the fiction game he coulda been a contender for that Jewish-American pantheon, a founding father. Another inevitable point of reference is Henry Roth, Joycean poet of Yiddish-American childhood, whose own famous early-sixties republication certainly suggested to some editor the attempt, not nearly so successful, to reintroduce Fuchs shortly thereafter—yet Fuchs is so much less neurotically Modernist than Roth. It may even be fair, oddly enough, that 1930s critics groping to explain the energy of Fuchs's tragic farces compared him to the Marx Brothers: Fuchs's characters draw on that same reservoir of panic, that clawing for attention, that fueled comedians who never completely left the vaudeville stage no matter what fame they attained.

Yet what's Jewish about a writer when he only happens to be a Jew? Unlike, say, Philip Roth, Fuchs never toils in Talmudic consideration of his immigrant families' dual allegiances, Old World piety versus New World secularism. For Fuchs, as for so many others, that's what running to California was for, guiltless escape from entrenched identity (California being in this sense America, squared). Blenholt, the commissioner of sewers in *Homage*, is celebrated for his ethnic mutability: he plays to the expectations of whatever constituency he addresses, his only religion being power, and money. Setting aside cultural particulars (we're all from *somewhere*), the apt comparison for Fuchs's affectionate nightmares of underclass striving may be Thomas Berger's roiling Midwestern small-town farces *The Feud* and *Sneaky People* (and Thomas Berger, despite the affection, also fled from his Midwest). Like Berger, Fuchs touches every character with sympathetic irony and, while suffusing his depiction of the human sphere with a visionary wholeness, eschews redemption in favor of a benign shrug.

Describing *Homage to Blenholt*, Fuchs said "I devoted myself simply to the life in the hallways, the commotion at the dumbwaiters, the assortment of characters in the building, the tenement scholar, the horse-bettor, the tenement æsthete, their strivings and preoccupations, their troubles in the interplay of the sexes. There was always a ferment, slums or no slums." Fuchs is as native a voice as we've got, at least in Brooklyn, where it was not only during the Great Depression that the American dream uncovered a choice between surrender to the grind or to collusion with the grinder, between aspiring to the murderous practicality of Fuchs's mobsters or the hunger-artist sublimity of Philip Hayman's father in *Summer in Williamsburg*: "honest, good, and kind, but poor . . . he's old, he's so skinny, and all he has after all the years is a cigarette and a window." Deliverance from this punishing axis, if it comes, may only be in a storyteller's craft: "the timing; the devices and felicities; the insistence on style, to throw the story according to the guise that properly belonged to it; the instinct for material and content, to choose what would ensnare; the instinct for form, to give the piece its full workout so that at the end everything has been said and exhausted," wrote Fuchs in 1990. "The best is when you write and *know* what you're doing, that you've got it." Of course, he was by then speaking of his work in Hollywood. That he'd gotten it right fifty-odd years earlier he was never to allow himself fully to know.

JONATHAN LETHEM
Brooklyn, New York
June 2006

PREFACE

WE MOVED INTO WILLIAMSBURG the summer I was five. I remember the troop of us going past the elementary school; my oldest brother said to me, "That's where you'll be going to school." The kitchen had a pair of washtubs in it, and the first night my mother put me to sleep on top of the tin covers. The rooms were lit by gas jets, gas mantels; Welsbach. The world was new.

The tenement, 366 South Second Street, was just completed but it was called a tenement from the start. We lived in five small rooms, cubicles. That building, the number 366, have a magic for me which can make me tremble. It was amazing how industriously we combed the building. We were everywhere, the halls, the yards, the cellars, the roofs. Everything people do they did in those places. Outside on the street were great wide bins of white plaster; I watched the laborers slice into the plaster, pack it in slabs on their hods, and then carry the hods in files up into the new tenements still building around us. I became lost and couldn't find my way back to my apartment. I remember once running in panic through the halls, opening doors: a woman looked up at me from the floor, cleaning a gas range. I took long walks as I grew older. In one direction were low-lying wooden structures; the airy expanse of the sky and clouds; a storybook idleness; store windows with odd, faraway-sounding names on them, Faulkner, Brown, and Jones. I had an image in my mind, in connection with this place, of a hangman's noose. I don't know why, never did; I mention it. In another direction, going into Greenpoint, there were small red-brick factories; the smells of dyes; pony carts with Shetland ponies hitched to them, standing in the sun; Italian cafés, men inside smoking cigarettes and staring out at the bright patchwork of sunshine on the pavements. *Pinocchio*. Above us, cutting across the numbered streets—South Second, South Third, South Fourth—and putting an end to them, was a street called Union Avenue. Trolley cars ran here; nearby lived a wonderful girl whose name was Dorothy Kirschenbaum. Beyond Union Avenue began a new maze of streets, and this limitless stretch of territory became, in my mind, Greenland, Norway, and Sweden—don't ask me why, the hangman's noose again. Nor can I really explain why in time I was impelled to write pieces about these long walks I took, the things I saw on them and the things I liked to make up and imagine. One of these pieces, a forty-page account, was submitted to *The New Republic*. They accepted two thousand words of it and the editor there kindly suggested that I expand the account into a novel.

Summer in Williamsburg was written in a state of sheer terror. I didn't understand what I was doing and had read somewhere that authors often wrote books not understanding what they were writing but hoping that the reader would. This is really as it should be and no offense. But I didn't know it then. I was determined to write fairly. I wanted to be like the man from Mars. I wanted to examine everything with an absolutely clear view, unencumbered and unaffected. Everyone's adolescence is no doubt precious and important to him, but I don't think it was Williamsburg or my adolescence there which caused my terror; although years later, driving through Williamsburg, I found myself shaking all over. No, what caused my trouble was that I was trying to find a design. A seed is put into the ground, the plant and flower emerge—everything directed from the beginning, according to a plan and purpose, with nothing left to vagary. I was trying to find a similar direction and plan to the life I had witnessed in Williamsburg. I was struggling with form. I was struggling with mystery. I was young and intent and met my problem head-on. And what I didn't know was that if I was successful, I would not come up with meaning but with fantasy. The material in *Summer in Williamsburg* is in many ways dear to me. I often thought of rewriting the novel, but then I realized that this would be tampering and wrong. The book, such as it is, has value perhaps only because of my ignorance or innocence at the time I wrote it, and I am led to offer it again without apologies for these reasons.

The books were failures. Nobody seemed to care for them when they came out. I saw a man once on the subway, reading *Homage to Blenholt* and chuckling aloud; that was the only clean appreciation I can remember—unsolicited, true. A friend told me regretfully he could read my novels while he was reading them, but that when he put them down, there was nothing to make him go back to them. The books didn't sell—four hundred copies, four hundred, twelve hundred. The reviews were scanty, immaterial. The books became odious to me. My young wife and I were living at Saratoga Springs then and I remember fussing and complaining, asking who wanted stories, who really read them. It suddenly occurred to me that great numbers of people read *The Saturday Evening Post* each week. Right then and there I undertook to write a short story for the *Post.* Ten days or two weeks later they sent me a check for six hundred dollars. I decided to become rich. I was in the middle of a fourth novel but broke it up and swiftly turned it into three or four short stories. I worked away all spring, one story after the other—perhaps a dozen or fifteen in all. I rested. It was July. Nothing happened. I had a lovely young lady as my agent but didn't know her very well at that time and was too uncertain and abashed to disturb her with my inquiries. I assumed the stories were rejected. It was August now and the racing season had begun. My wife and I went to the track every day. We bicycled out for the early morning workouts, were often given tips, and won—sixty dollars one day, a hundred dollars, one day two hundred. I had visions of spending the rest of our lives at the races, traveling from track to track with the seasons. Suddenly I heard from my agent. The editors had simply been away on their summer vacations, that was all. They took the stories, all of them—one afternoon three acceptances in the same mail. I had my racetrack winnings in cash all over me in different pockets; I had checks from the magazines laid away in envelopes. The stories began to appear. Promptly a barrage fell upon me, friends and strangers and well-wishers, wondering what had become of me, why I had sold out, and so on.

How fast the time goes. We are given only a few decades apiece. I didn't become rich. I went to Hollywood. The popular notions about the movies aren't true. It takes a good deal of energy and hard sense to write stories over an extended period of time, and it would be foolish to expect writers not to want to be paid a livelihood for what they do. But we are engaged here on the same problems that perplex writers everywhere. We grapple with the daily mystery. We struggle with form, with chimera, and to seize upon the elusive, fast-gliding image of Dorothy Kirschenbaum. "Poesy," my father used to call it, and I know I will keep at it for as long as I can, because surely there is nothing else to do. Of course I am always flattered when people ask about me and I am sincerely grateful for their kindness and interest.

I want to acknowledge the help I have received, in the writing of these novels and everything, from the one who has been with me all the years, the one who is part of me, my talisman, my love, my wife.

DANIEL FUCHS
Hollywood, California
April 1961

SUMMER IN WILLIAMSBURG

PROLOGUE

THE THUNDERSTORM BROKE very suddenly. With the first drops excited women's voices were heard, windows opened and wash was hastily taken off the clotheslines. It was one of those hard, mad rains that come down as if with deliberate fury. Standing in the basement doorway, Mahler, the cobbler, smoked a cigarette and quietly contemplated the downpour, his face wrinkled into a grin at the sight of it. Philip Hayman, a young man on the first floor, looked down at him. "Just watch it rain," he said. "Just watch it." "Yeah," said Mahler, "maybe God is mad about something." They both smiled, and the cobbler went into the cellar, worrying a little over the joke on God.

Soon the yard became flooded. The sewer in the middle was clogged, and the water swirled and gurgled on top of it in white foam. A boy on the third floor, eating peaches, amused himself by throwing down the stones. He was Davey. He aimed carefully for the center of the swirl and was visibly pleased when he made a hit. In a minute he finished with the peaches, and, having no more stones to throw, leaned far out of the window and began to spit. Davey let thick drops of saliva slip from his lips, fascinated as he watched their mysterious descent into the pool. Now the rain came down so fast the drains on the roof were overfilled and were unable to convey all the water down the pipes at once. Here it shot out in a wide arc and splashed six stories below with a loud noise.

Then abruptly the storm lost its force; the downpour diminished to a drizzle and in a minute or two stopped altogether. The sun came out brightly.

The boy on the third floor regarded the sky incredulously. Mahler came running to the basement doorway for he liked the sun to sleep in, but on the other hand Philip, who had been relishing the wild fury of the rainstorm, regretted its passing.

Two or three women arched their necks to look at the sky and, satisfied, began to hang out wash again. All together for some reason there broke out a wild confusion of music from different windows—radios, player pianos, phonographs, and someone practicing on a saxophone. The man with the sax was playing "A Russian Lullaby" in a choppy way, and he played it interminably. At the same time a man and woman were heard arguing heatedly, their words too blurred to be distinguished. The Russian lullaby and the blurred argument filled the yard in fierce competition. Then the man's voice rang out dominatingly. "Listen," he shouted, "I don't care if she is my sister-in-law, the next time I see her I'm going to spit straight into her eye!"

Suddenly a woman screamed. She screamed hard, fiercely. Startled, Philip Hayman immediately visualized the creased expression of her face, the jutting jaw, her teeth revealed. It was like an alarm. Women could be heard leaving their different flats and running through the tiled hallways, their wooden heels clicking sharply on the stone. As they ran they were accompanied by waves of hubbub that grew heavier and heavier as they began to meet. In another moment it was a roar of noise, question, answer, sigh, protestation, all mixed. One woman wept in a thin, wailing voice that pierced through the confusion and seemed to move upward like a thin line of smoke.

Philip rushed through the halls. On a landing he met the kid of the peach pits, scared, but nevertheless enjoying the excitement hugely.

"What's up, Davey?"

"Nothing, nothing. I don't know. I could only see a man sitting on the floor with a basketball bladder."

Philip walked up. The knot of people were talking violently but in a steady stream. Mrs. Linck stood in a circle of women, big and sloppy, dressed in a rose wrapper, her face swimming in sweat as she passionately told them the story. Mahler, the cobbler, was there, scared and pale. Mrs. Miller, even, the old miser's wife, hung on with her eyes to every word as it came from Mrs. Linck's mouth. Everyone was there. Philip pushed his way politely through and saw the pulmotor squad working over the man on the floor who sat in his underwear, his legs crossed, resting comfortably on pillows. Nearby lay the basketball bladder. Its tongue had been connected to a rubber gas pipe and part of it had been cut away so that it might be worn as a mask. The windows had been open all the time, and there was little odor of gas.

Now the young doctor walked out with an authoritative air in spite of his wilted white uniform. As the women clustered about him anxiously, he shook his head with self-conscious impatience. No, no, the head said, the man can't be helped. The men carried out the pulmotor apparatus and soon the crowd began to break. In pairs, in small groups, the women went back to their flats, to finish cleaning up, to make lunch. It was all over. They would talk about it for a few days and then it would be all over. Philip was pushed with the crowd down the steps. He returned to his flat, wondering over poor Meyer Sussman. Why had he done it? No matter how hard he tried, Philip could not understand it. He remembered the butcher's red cheeks, his hearty laughter, the kind, joking manner he had had with customers as he cajoled them into waiting quietly for their turn. This man, Philip marveled, this man; and he waited for his friend, Old Miller, to explain the riddle. Miller knew everything.

The yard became quiet again. Three little girls came back and resumed their game of potsy, kicking a thick slob of folded banana skin into the different boxes. A window above opened, and a housewife, irritable and tired from the excitement, leaned far out and yelled to one of the girls playing. "Ella, Ella, what'll you have for lunch, potatoes in milk, or rice?"

Ella, poised on one foot, thought it over carefully for a minute. "I think I'll have potatoes," she finally said.

"Then," said her mother, "I'll have you under the ground. I have only rice."

Meyer Sussman. Butcher to the fat housewives of Ripple Street waddling in loose kimonos, Meyer, hazy-eyed and tender-minded, gentle creature, sometimes called half-wit, perhaps because you contrasted so oddly with the bloodstains of your trade—why did you commit suicide? The autopsies of the housewives who were so fond of you were many and doubtless entirely wrong. They all began by saying that there was no reason for the suicide, and then they said it was your wife (impossible), money (you had enough, you never complained), insanity (in these things where does sanity end and insanity begin?), some disastrous secret (you lived the simplest, most even life). They all agreed that you were a fine, kindly man, and that it was a great pity, and that no one could ever have foreseen it. And this was all true.

When you meet God, Meyer Sussman, ask Him for me what made you squeeze the basketball bladder over your face. Little God in Heaven, sitting somewhere on a cloud, where are You?

ONE

OLD MILLER, PHILIP'S FRIEND, stood near his bedroom door gingerly listening to the housewives as they discussed the suicide, careful to avoid meeting his wife's eye. Once again the janitress, Mrs. Linck, was going over the details of the first sight of the poor man, and the ladies grouped about heard her avidly, punctuating the recital with eager contributions of their own, which they could not restrain. The women talked in absorbed concern until abruptly Mrs. Miller noticed her husband's interest and, irritated, slammed his bedroom door shut.

"Stay by yourself, miser!" she muttered angrily, and pushed the women out of the flat onto the landing so that the old man would hear nothing of the gossip. The little crowd of women, taking no time from their chatter, followed Mrs. Linck down to her rooms. Old Miller went to his bed and sat down, smiling wryly. When he would die, the thought occurred to him with great amusement, his wife would have to put on a show of grief to satisfy those same neighbors. Miller rubbed the slippers off his feet against the bed and prepared for his day's work.

He had a peculiar job. At Greenwood Cemetery he spent the day reciting prayers over graves. Relatives of the dead would pay him from fifty cents to five dollars for these services. His big beard and somber clothes made him look very religious, as indeed he was in the formal way, so that it was easy for him to attract mourners.

What a pleasurable tickle of nervous excitement to appraise a customer, to pocket the fee, to await the next.

Mrs. Miller, who confided considerably in Philip's mother, said that when they had lived in Russia he had never provided sufficiently for the seven children. Once it had happened that a neighbor took pity on them and tried to carry some of Mrs. Miller's produce to town, intending to sell it secretly and bring back supplies. The plan miscarried. When her husband discovered it, he beat her severely in cold anger.

Now Old Miller never spoke to his wife or children in their tenement flat. He had his own bedroom, which was directly at the left of the brown metallic door that led to the hallway. When he came in, with the mud of the cemetery still on his shoes, he passed immediately into his own room. For furniture there was an old-fashioned metal bed, which had been painted in white enamel, now peeling. There was also a bird's-eye maple dresser, the mirror of which was cracked. A wood chair, painted blue, was at the window. There was nothing on the floor or on the yellow walls. Miller rarely left this room when he was indoors.

He did not contribute any money to the expenses of the household. He prepared his own food, mended his own clothes, washed his shirts. His children insulted him or tried to coax money out of him. His wife, who was now a pious little woman with a white linen kerchief over her thinned hair, cursed him all the time in a mumble because he would not give her any money. Old Miller ignored them in a detached way. They weren't there.

Once neighbors saw Old Miller mend his shoes, in laborious, deep-breathing concentration, by tearing down the wood of his window slats and tacking it on for soles.

Miller was old and sick and his pleasures were few. It was already long past his usual hour for leaving, but he remained, locking the bedroom door against interruption. Between his floor and the ceiling of the flat below was an empty space about a half-foot deep. When electricians had ripped up the boards some years ago to install wires, replacing gaslights, Old Miller had noted the space. Later he cleverly sawed one of the planks and made himself a good hiding place. Here he concealed eight bankbooks. Now Old Miller pried the board up with his penknife and took out his bankbooks. He handled them fondly, as some people like to feel their pet dogs. Some of the books had leather covers. These Old Miller enjoyed bringing close to his face for they had a wonderful smell for him. He turned the pages, blowing at the thin lines of black dirt between the leaves. From his pockets he took brown paper bags that he had picked up on the streets, and he covered these with big round figures. For a long time he pondered over them in a haze, hardly distinguishing the numbers, for he knew exactly how much money he carried in each bank.

At last Old Miller crumpled the bags carefully and threw them out the window so that Mrs. Miller would suspect nothing. He unlocked the door and walked down to the yard. He was already so late he would indulge himself a few minutes further and see what he could find to chat about with his serious young friend, Philip Hayman. Besides, and he was careful to make the mental reservation, he would make up the loss by staying at the cemetery later tonight or by coming earlier tomorrow morning.

Philip Hayman had a vague distaste for Old Miller. The oily side curls, the splotched-up face with veins purple and red, the shiny black garments he wore, his ankles so thin that they seemed abnormal. Somehow he reminded Philip repellently of clinics and dispensaries for the red-eyed sick. Nevertheless they were often together, Philip drawn in some way by this strange old miser.

In the evenings they sat at the foot of the long wooden planked stairway that led down to the yard, talking occasionally, but for the most part silent. Miller had a sly, sardonic humor. He would tell Philip in a cool voice that at bottom everything in the world was flat and common mud. The rhythmic tumbling of the surf, he said through smiling lips that laid bare his two or three brown teeth, was upon sober investigation no thing of beauty but an impersonal natural phenomenon, and the moon was a scientific fact. Folk moved about in the dinginess immersing themselves continuously in a sedative warm bath of ideals and dreams, but these were artificial and delusory as a soft waltz.

"What about the moving pictures?" Philip said, laughing, and the old man stopped talking, smiling with his eyes and shaking his head.

Miller told Philip there was one truth, one meaning in life, and this was money. "Let them talk, let them write, that is it and the only thing." All smiles and half-smiles, sharp and good-natured, he interpreted the quality of the activity around them. People spent all their effort in work, he pointed out (going, like an old man, to generalities), and everything that was big and vital in their lives was intimately connected with money. The other things were unimportant, they didn't really count. Once the two of them had happened to see a tired man, bald and sweated, shot to death while he held a glass of soda water in his hand at a candy stand. He was murdered, they later learned, because he employed non-union men at his cap shop. Another time a man and his four sons were taken bloody to the hospital in a small fleet of ambulances. They had been severely cut up in a knife fight with chicken-market competitors. Philip often walked down to Wallabout Market about a mile from his home. He went to see the long lines of trucks that waited there to load up from the fruit cargoes of the ships docked there. The wait took hours, sometimes days. Meanwhile the fruit decayed. To avoid these losses, a number of gorillas were hired by individual owners to beat their way through the lines. Bloody tussles occurred when some driver was rash enough to try to stop them. These things Miller, patiently, in slow discussion, pointed out to Philip with his everlasting quiet smiles. "That's it and all there is," he would wind up in a sort of chant.

That was Old Miller, he knew everything; and this morning Philip, wondering over poor Sussman and perplexed no matter how hard he tried to understand the suicide, anxiously waited for his friend of the long beard to give him the answers. What would the old man say? And when Philip spied him on the basement stairway he ran down to meet him.

"You're late, Mr. Miller. I thought you were already at the cemetery."

"I'm old and sick and my pleasures are few," Miller said, smiling. "What do you want to hurry me for?"

"Well, Mr. Miller," Philip said, "what do you say made him do it?"

Miller shrugged his shoulders. "How should I know? People usually don't kill themselves. Perhaps he lost money."

"He never was occupied with money. Sussman was not like that at all."

Miller stopped. Hayman waited a moment, and when he saw the old man had no intention of prolonging the discussion, he grew impatient and annoyed with him.

"Come, Mr. Miller," he said. "I've been expecting much more."

"Why does a man kill himself?" he asked very slowly. "You ask me that as though I might be God, only you are kidding with me, to find out what I will say. But I don't mind, my young friend, it is all the same to me. You could say it was some single thing, like a bad marriage or money, but Sussman seems to have been an extraordinary man, a simple man, and this, you insist, will not do. So you might say that it was some small thing that happened years ago when Sussman was a child perhaps, some small thing that altered the progression of his days so that it led at this time to this catastrophe. You could say it was the working of fate, warped by some misstep long ago; yes, you could say that, but what terrible nonsense you would be saying.

"To find out properly you must first understand Meyer Sussman, and this, of course, is the most difficult thing to do. Even if I were God, I am afraid I might not be able to do this, there are so many persons. But even when you know Sussman you are only at the beginning of the problem, for then you must make a laboratory out of Williamsburg to find out what touched him here, why these details affected him and in what manner. This is a tremendous task, but you insist, young gentleman. If you would really discover the reason, you must pick Williamsburg to pieces until you have them all spread out on your table before you, a dictionary of Williamsburg. And then select. Pick and discard. Take, with intelligence you have not and with a patience that would consume a number of lifetimes, the different aspects that are pertinent. Collect and then analyze to understand the quality of each detail. Perhaps then you might know why Sussman died, but granting everything I do not guarantee the process.

"Certain men are the sum of a million infinitesimal phenomena and experiences. A million atoms of a certain type produce, in the end, wood, just as a million of another type make stone, others iron, and others gold. The same is true of these men, only here the atoms are no physical substance but psychical, and, further, they do not belong to any one type but are variously commingled. The ultimate product, man, therefore moves mysteriously, but he is a scientific outcome of cause and effect."

Hayman waited for the old man to finish his slow-moving homily and then said, "Mr. Miller, Mr. Miller, that almost might be poetry!"

Miller reflected. "Yes, you may be right. You see, I say all this and yet another man might come along and tell me this is nonsense, and how just he might be."

The old man rose heavily from the wood plank of the stairway and climbed the steps, back to work at last, to say prayers for the dead at the cemetery. Philip, having had his answer, was not satisfied. He followed Miller outside the tenement, pausing at the stoop. The street seemed deserted. It was Sunday and hot. An old woman with a brown face wrinkled into a baked apple trudged down the middle of the street, sucking a paper cup of lemon ice; but what was remarkable about her was her air of complete indifference to the world. Well, said Philip, that is the privilege of age.

Mrs. Linck, in the rose wrapper, big and sloppy, sought solace on the cool stone steps of the stoop, shifting her place periodically. She fanned her face with a handkerchief as she sat, a monumental image, tired and depressed after the excitement with poor Sussman.

"Well, Mrs. Linck," Philip said because it was necessary to greet her, "someone must have turned on the heat."

She rubbed her throat with her handkerchief, erasing the black lines. Mrs. Linck could make only blurred noises in answer. "My goodness," she said finally, struggling, "it's so hot I can hardly talk loud enough these days." She rose and left for the cool dimness of her dirty flat where she might sit in her rocker in peace and talk to the guinea pigs she had roaming the floors.

Philip walked down the street clinging close to the tenement houses for the shade. If you would really discover the reason, you must pick Williamsburg to pieces until you have them all spread out on your table, a dictionary of Williamsburg. And then select. Pick and discard. Take, with intelligence you have not and with a patience that would consume a number of lifetimes, the different aspects that are pertinent. Collect and then analyze. Collect and then analyze. So spoke the sage in the long beard.

That means Mrs. Linck and her guinea pigs, said Philip; my uncle Papravel, and my father, Mahler, and even Old Miller himself. It means my lovely friend Cohen and his pimples. A million things. That means the raw metallic tunes of a player piano that come out of a window and paint the buildings with drabness; it means the horse rippling the skin of his rump; that couple, fat and perspiring, in holiday clothes with bathing-suit bags at their sides, drinking vanilla soda water at the candy stand. You must even include the awkward way they bend their bodies at the hips from caution lest they stain their new clothes. Collect. That includes people who suck air through the cracks in their teeth, people who tap regularly with their fingers, people whose own growing baldness causes them to inspect their friends' scalps as they talk with them; it means children shrieking as they play in the streets. Collect. This means the sickly colors horses' urine creates on the wet asphalt, Halper's Stable with its warm manure smells and the hanger-on bums; it means Yozowitz's laundry with the curtains stretched on the tall racks as they dry in the sun. Collect and analyze. Collect. Listen, said Philip, even God took a day off. Passing by the dark window of a funeral parlor Philip turned his head to observe his appearance in the glass as he walked.

Out of nowhere the procession suddenly came down the street in a hum of noise. Frantically a small, dead-looking man held the wrist of the fat woman who barged ahead, absorbed in grief and anger to the point of hysteria. She spoke from excitement in a constant stream while the little man tagged along in jerky hops and skips, all the time pleading energetically. Somehow the briefcase he held under his arm with such care seemed out of place under the circumstances and altogether he was a ridiculous figure as he tried to calm her. As for the woman, she was wholly insensible to the scandal she was creating. And this added to his discomfort probably more than anything else, for he was continually looking back at the long chattering train of boys and girls who were following them, enjoying the situation with unconcealed relish.

In a sudden outburst the woman tugged and wrenched free into the gutter. The man, undecided, paused on the sidewalk, his face set with the ugliness of the scene. Then he rushed to her vigorously, shouted something, and compelled her to stop. The children encircled them, quiet with expectation in the face of this new twist. While they argued in painfully restrained tones a taxicab drove up the street. The little man hailed it and pushed the woman in roughly. The last Philip saw of her was her faded green blouse sticking to her broad back in curves where it was plastered by perspiration.

As the cab pulled out and the crowd broke up, a bald-headed old Jew was yelling down the street in anxious tones, "Moishe, Moishe, what's the matter? Moishe, come here and let me know what's the matter."

Collect, said Philip. That includes the fat woman and the little man. Even the green blouse sticking to her back and the bald-headed Jew. Philip entered the depot to wait for his uncle's arrival from Havers Falls.

The streets were still wet from the thundershower when Papravel arrived at the bus terminal. Hayman had to wait until his uncle had finished some business in the office. He was a busy man, had begun to smoke cigars religiously now, and with time was getting fatter and more important. Philip went up to him as he came out.

"What was all the excitement here? Somebody hurt himself?" Papravel asked, still straightening his knees and stretching.

"A man called Sussman took gas. Where did you hear about it?"

"They mentioned it inside. What was the matter with him? Why should a man go and kill himself?"

"I don't know. They say he was kind of nuts."

"Oh. Well, that's too bad," Papravel said. He threw away his cigar. He had just started it, but in spite of the prestige cigars afforded he could not get used to them. The truth was they made him sick at the stomach.

Philip turned his eyes down and decided to be looking at his uncle's collar while he spoke. That would make it easier.

"Listen, Uncle, let me tell you why I'm meeting you here. Now, you know Pop. I don't want to say anything unpleasant, it's got nothing to do with you, but you know how the old man is. Every time you come around to the house and give Momma money it hurts him. It makes him feel bad for days. Momma really doesn't need the money. You know she wouldn't spend it on herself. All that happens is that the old man feels bad. I wish you'd tell me you'd cut it out."

"What's the old man always sore about? Philip, I tell you, that man never liked me from the first. He thinks he's a king or something. A prince in Williamsburg."

"It's not that, Uncle," Philip said quietly. He didn't like to hear Papravel mock his father. "You know it's not that."

"What's the matter? Isn't the bus business honest enough for him? I work hard for my money. It's good money. If I want to give it to my own sister, why should he have something to say? If I want to fix up your brother Harry in a nice position that's my business, and if I want to give you a good, easy job with a big salary I don't see where he's got a kick coming."

"Listen, Uncle, don't get excited about it. You know how Pop is about this, and that's all there is to it. Why can't you tell me you'll cut it out?"

"We'll see, we'll see," he said. "And, listen, Philip, you can tell your aristocratic father for me, you tell him, he's no rabbi himself."

An hour later Papravel, in a double-breasted suit, tab collar, and derby, walked into the Silver Eagle bus station. Behind him were Harry Hayman and a heavy-jowled Irishman called Gilhooley. Hands in pockets, these two leaned against the walls of the narrow store, surveyed the streamers advertising round trips to Oshkosh, and waited. Behind the ticket counter a stumpy man in suspenders had been talking to a customer, but he stopped and looked at the three anxiously, for the brisk entrance had been something of a sensation.

Papravel rapped his fist on the ticket counter with deliberation.

"Who is the boss here, please?" he asked.

"Yes?" said the stumpy individual. "Yes?"

"Are you Mr. Pomerantz?"

"Morand. My name is Morand. What can I do for you, gentlemen?"

"I'm a representative of the Williamsburg Business Board," said Papravel, and thereupon began the comedy. "What we try to do always is not only to help business in Williamsburg but also to help the businessman too. Because we always say if the Williamsburg businessman loses, Williamsburg loses. That's a slogan."

"Yes?" said Mr. Morand, sweating a little. "Yes?"

"When the businessman loses, Williamsburg business loses. And now, Mr. Morantz, I don't like to say it, but you made a mistake. Everyone makes a mistake sometimes, and what we try to do is to hurry up and help out before it's too late. If you catch it in time you don't lose everything. And while you still got a shirt on your back listen to me, Morantz, I know what I'm saying: get out of Williamsburg because you can't make money here."

Morand went white. He stared at Gilhooley and Hayman against the wall and then back again at Papravel. The customer to whom Morand had been talking grew worried and wondered whether the bus owner wasn't going to have a stroke.

"Who sent you?" Morand asked very quietly.

"Who sent me? Listen, Morantz, you don't understand my

meaning. I'm your best friend. We got an organization and all we want to do is to help. All I'm saying is you'll lose less if you get out of Williamsburg now before it's too late."

"Never mind," Morand said rapidly. He drew himself up to indicate that he knew with whom he was dealing, comprehended the situation, and was able to handle it. "I know you and I know who sent you. Your name is Papravel, and it was Rubin of the Empire Lines who told you to stick your rotten nose in here. But listen to me, because I mean every word of it. So long as Rubin does an honest business I'll do business honest too. But if he fights with fire I'll strike with fire also. And listen, Papravel, remember you're not the only louse, the only snotnose, the only lowlife in Williamsburg, for every one like you there's a hundred more bumming the streets. And you can tell Rubin for me, you can tell him, I said he will burn like in hell before I get out!"

Morand stopped, almost bouncing from the nervous excitement. The customer, aghast at these proceedings, touched his arm to quiet him. Hayman at the wall stood erect alertly. Gilhooley said, "Here's where I lunk that potbelly," and set off, but Hayman held him back. "Not now, you kluck, not now." As for Papravel and Morand, it was a climax, and neither could think of anything to say.

"Listen, my friend," began the customer timidly. His voice was very thin. "I don't like to go where I don't belong, but let me tell you something. What I say is that a man can't be successful unless he's got a warm heart and is willing to give the other fellow a chance."

"Well, what am I saying?" Papravel almost wept at him. "I come to this man from a public service organization to give him advice free. All I want to do is to help and that in the nicest way, but he roars at me like a lion and insults me left and right."

"See," the customer went on with a little more conviction, establishing himself properly, "I've traveled everywhere: Paraguay, Chile, Peru, Argentina, Brazil, Mexico, everywhere. I always say I don't like to go where I don't belong, but maybe I can tell you something, and if you like it take it, and if you don't, leave it alone and we're still friends."

Harry now came up. "Mister," he said kindly, taking him by the elbow, "I think your wife wants you outside." Papravel wiped his nose in two movements and returned to Morand. It wasn't proving so easy, Morand was being stubborn and he would have to give him the works complete.

"Listen, Mr. Morantz," he said conciliatingly, "let there be no hard feeling. Believe me, I wish you all the luck and all the money in the world. Only, if business goes bad remember, Morantz, remember I gave you advice and you wouldn't take it."

"Never mind," Mr. Morand said coldly. "Never mind."

"All right," said Papravel, and he said it with a sigh for he really did not enjoy the work he had before him.

Besides Harry Hayman and the Irishman Gilhooley, two Jews, one Negro, and three Italians were the actors in the sequel to Papravel's visit. As they barged into the Silver Eagle bus station Hayman walked up rapidly to Morand.

"Listen, Morand, and shut up. All you have to do is stay where you are and not make a move. What we will do here we'll do, and it's no good to worry about it now. Just stay and wait, but above all things, Morand, keep quiet." He nodded to Gilhooley and returned to the business at hand. The Irishman took his place beside Morand.

"Open your mouth," he said with seriousness, "and I will knock out every tooth, one after the other."

Morand stood as though he were paralyzed.

The six men proceeded then to strip the place bare. They worked with a methodical nonchalance, a businesslike coolness that was particularly disheartening. One of the Italians went behind the ticket counter and with one rip of his monkey wrench unhinged the ticket box. Like a confetti cascade the blue and white slips showered to the floor. Then he smacked the cash register four or five times until it became a jumble of screws and springs. The counter, wrenched from its supports, clattered down. Morand's hands moved nervously but Gilhooley caught his eye.

The Negro, an elegant gentleman named Fleurie O'Johnson, made a running leap for the modernistic chandelier. He swung the length of the room like a monkey until it gave, dropping him on the floor with a loud boom. O'Johnson looked up at the hole in the ceiling ruefully and rubbed his backside. Hayman, supervising the job from the wall, had to laugh.

"That reminds me," he reflected pleasantly. "Did you ever go to the zoo? Once I saw a baboon there and he had no hair on his can at all."

"Why?" Gilhooley wanted to know perplexed. What was the point?

"Why?" repeated Hayman, discountenanced by the failure of his joke. "Why? Kiss my ass, why. How should I know?"

In the meantime the Italian with the monkey wrench was walking around cracking windows, mirrors, wall fixtures, and signs. He did not even spare the telephones. Others were laboriously occupied with benches, hacking away at them until the legs caved in and the bench was smashed together like a bridge table.

All this time Morand had contained himself with frozen attention, but when they started to rip the rich red carpet, he could hold himself no longer. He opened his mouth to protest and immediately Gilhooley brought his palm stiffly against it. Gilhooley slapped his face repeatedly and he did it with passion.

"Enough," Hayman finally called out. "Do you want to keep on massaging his face all night?" In the recess Morand sucked in his breath, broke down and cried with extravagance. Hayman disliked the Irishman's treatment. There was something ugly about physical violence.

The Italian with the monkey wrench stopped and wiped his forehead. Outside the hot sun poured down over the pavements.

TWO

WHEN PHILIP HAYMAN ENTERED the room Cohen immediately began to talk of Meyer Sussman. He was immensely interested in the subject of suicide, it was an old favorite. "Sussman had a delicate soul, a sensitive disposition. Anyone could have seen that, Hayman," he said. "A man reacts to his environment. He is depressed, overwhelmed."

"Cut it out," Philip said. "This is serious, you ought to keep your filthy hands out. A man does not kill himself to give you the chance to pass some rotten wisecracks."

Cohen's eyes lifted in protest. "Please," he said. "Please."

There was a pause while he walked preoccupied about the room. He was wearing an intern's jacket and a pair of white ducks. It was a costume of a sort, but he always insisted that this was the coolest combination for the weather. Philip settled himself comfortably in the chair and dropped his feet on the bed. He had not relished his errand with Papravel.

"Are you going to Tessie's party tonight?" Cohen asked suddenly, trying to keep from giggling.

"I don't know. I suppose so. What's so funny about it?"

"Nothing. Well, you know. I heard Tessie's making this party just for you, something about you having an argument with her. You know." Cohen was tremendously fascinated by girls, perhaps because he was so helplessly shy with them.

Philip waved his hand in disgust and wouldn't talk about it.

"I'm invited, Philip," Cohen said proudly. "She asked me to come too."

"She's nuts on you. Didn't you know that? She thinks you're the Sheik of Araby."

Cohen drew himself up in great affront. "Never mind," he said, his whole manner instantly changing. "We can do without that sort of business." He walked away stiffly into the kitchen and wouldn't come out for five minutes.

But finally Cohen returned to Sussman's suicide. The subject was a favorite with him and he couldn't resist it. This time he began by deploring Sussman's choice of instrument. "Really," he said, in a serious manner, "gas is vulgar. Gas should not be used." Cohen went on to declare himself all in favor of the ancients' method of slashing the wrists. It was deliberate, he pointed out, civilized, Hellenic.

Philip refused to be disturbed. He thought of Edgar Saltus and said to himself, it's the usual crap.

"As for me," Philip announced solemnly, "I proclaim my unflinching loyalty to potassium cyanide. I mention the scientific despatch, the neatness, the absence of bloody mess."

"But, Hayman," he perspired at Philip with sincerity and desire to convince, "all you do is fill a bowl with warm water, slit the wrist, and lie back. You smoke a cigarette, read a poem, and then—it is all over."

Hayman really did not care. He was lying comfortably in the overstuffed chair drinking Mrs. Miller's sweet wine. Every year the old lady put away a keg or two in the cellar to ferment. Cohen waited a while and then made periodic trips with a flower vase, his manner so detached and cheerful it was sometimes difficult to remember that he was stealing. So Philip let Cohen go on peripatetically, supporting his method over the cyanide, until in the end he grew bored with the subject and turned again to Mahler, the man who loved the noonday sun to sleep in.

Now Mahler——. In one of the two stores of the house in which they lived there dwelt the cobbler, Mahler. He was a big man with big hands, but the immediate impression was one of barrenness; to quote Cohen, he resembled an old tenement house standing with all its rooms untenanted and its windows black. Considering his background, that huge face, kneaded in a thousand wrinkles, meant something in its very blankness, for, Cohen again, "He is a living corpse, that's all, Hayman, the soul and life extinguished through the years by fire, flame, and the knout." Mahler had one of those fascinating histories, rich in incident, meaty in detail, and therefore full of appealing flavor for those of us who know only the flat dishwater of reality.

Mahler had been born in Russia, along with a million other wailing Jews, had been persecuted for religious and political reasons, sent by his government to exile in Siberia, escaped, traveled through China to Peking, across the Pacific to San Francisco, until, out of Egypt and the wilderness, he finally had made his way to Williamsburg and his shoe shop. A full life, for from all accounts he had known on the way poverty and plenty, pleasure and pain, jail and the bawdy house, the whip on his back and the sun, cold, hunger, the soul's torment—and all on intimate, elementary terms. One meets disconcertingly too many like him, but except for that fact he was really a character out of a book, and Cohen's delight.

Cohen's delight, because Cohen had reached the time when a young man with temperament recognizes for himself a spiritual kinship with Byron and Shelley in their more purple moments, with certain of the Oriental poets and all of the decadents. And here was Mahler himself, with his elegant career, appropriately esoteric in his way, and above all an actual ornament to Cohen's daily existence. As for Philip, he was eager, too, to know metropolitan life in all its strange and foreign complexities. Yet, try as he would to overcome what might have been a natural stubbornness in these matters, Mahler never seemed to him to be more than an old man who had spent his time in gaudy adventures, the histories of most of them adulterated with time, and who had in the end established this comfortable routine of mending soles and heels for a living. When Cohen interpreted Mahler's vacant stare in terms of heroic adjectives, Philip used to think an innocent stupidity was more likely indicated. Or if he pointed with feeling to the wrinkles on his face, Philip would refer to the skin on his own knuckles and beg for an appreciative explanation.

Their disagreement over Mahler was a lively thing for them because it expressed concretely the entire disparity in their characters. Cohen was given to wild mental extravagance that broke out in the manner of tropical foliage. As for Philip, "What you need, Hayman," he would say to him, "is a little insanity." Cohen felt acutely a personal divinity and it was a source of considerable inner distress. Consequently, he spoke with just enough trace of quiet fine suffering, of the beauty, poetry, and poignant pathos of existence.

Now he had turned from Mahler and was relating one of his wistfully tragic episodes. "I was walking through the park, Hayman, and abruptly I saw a girl sitting on a bench, so pale, so slight, I might have thought for a moment she was a leaf that had drifted from a tree." Followed a long, intricate tale, compounded with innumerable digressions on the philosophy of love, epigrammatic observations on the behavior of ladies, and, especially, charming self-revelations of Cohen in a delicate mood. He approached her, they conversed, she was lovely in her sadness, they ended up in her apartment with the usual, they parted forever, having suddenly discovered the essential flaw somewhere within themselves.

It was, of course, Philip thought, all lies. When Cohen sensed Philip's suspicions, he was unbelievably offended. "You think I am making this up?" he said with quiet rage.

"No, Cohen, no," Philip humored him. "Why should I think you are lying?"

Finally, to save himself and also because it had the proper dramatic twist, he confessed boldly, and forthwith Philip received a complicated argument in defense of the imagination over reality. "It does not matter whether a story is true or not. The thing is, is it amusing?"

Philip put the pan of wine on the table and got out of the chair. He was leaving.

"You're going?" Cohen asked, a little sorrowful over the loss of his audience, such as it was.

"I got enough," Philip said and went to the door.

"But I'll see you tonight, Hayman? You'll be there, won't you? Tessie's making the party especially for you."

"I know," Philip said and closed the door.

In the Ripple Street backyard the afternoon sun now descends the arc, but it beams down strongly, still covering the yard with force but nevertheless already moribund. And Mahler, Cohen's hero, tilted against the wall, sleeps, he lazily sleeps. This is so because for three years Mahler, the cobbler, a simple man without guile and untroubled with a metaphysical conscience, takes his nap in the yard every afternoon there is a warm sun. He closes his store, walks around through the cellar to the yard, and nothing stops it, not even the apparition of death.

Directly above him, at a window on the third floor, is Davey, whose hair, parted in the middle, hangs over the sides of his head like curtains draping a stage. The coiffure, together with his sharp eyes and high cheekbones, gives him a diabolical expression, and surely, in his way, he is an agent of the Devil.

At five-thirty he has a rendezvous with Yetta, the girl of his dreams, but there is still time, achingly there is still time, and to divert his mind he has been regarding the appearance of Mahler sleeping in the sun. Inspiration has seized him in her imperious grasp and now carefully, with caution and tremendously absorbed, he fills an eyedropper, and after the fashion of a Chinese Torquemada presses down intermittent drops on poor Mahler's nose. One. Two. Three. Four. Mahler stirs, the soul gently awakening. The Devil's agent ducks behind the windowsill. Later he reappears furtively and surveys the scene. A preoccupied cat moves along the top of the wood fence. Mute black fire escapes, having no place to go, patiently adhere to the walls of the tenement. The tenement itself, ignored so blandly, has by this time forgotten its chagrin and simply rests in its indifference like a very old woman. Lines of wash, some still dripping, hang the length of the yard, floor above floor, until at the end a quadrilateral sky is revealed. As for Mahler, he is sleeping, his mouth slightly ajar.

Davey now jiggles the clothesline at his window so that drops of water fall down on Mahler. This operation is fascinating, calling as it does for a high order of concentrated skill. First the water must be watched as it collects into a globule at the end of the pillowslip so that when the time comes to shake it deftly on its passage it is not too light and therefore meaningless. Nor will it do if one waits too long since then the drop of water falls without benefit of direction, and this has the defect of being inartistic, producing no true joy. The critical moment, which arrives after forty, or perhaps fifty, seconds, may be designated the moment of suspense. As moments go this is a difficult one, for not only must it be promptly seized when it finally occurs, but simultaneously the proper aim must be taken. Three or four times in all Davey succeeds, and three or four times trickles explore the somber crevices of Mahler's face.

Mahler does not answer; his face is set and still, effecting a rebuke. Davey, not so much displeased as angered by the failure of normal reactions in selected individuals, subsequently dismisses him. When he next appears he holds a mirror in his hand and with it redirects the rays of the sun. The sphere of light traverses the opposite walls of the tenements, discovers the interiors of assorted kitchens and bedrooms, a new Columbus. Abruptly a housewife sticks her head through the window, her expression belligerently searching. She has the soft, plump femininity of ladies of thirty-two. The yard once again is virginal in its stillness. Davey has ducked. The housewife looks up and down, rests briefly on Mahler, but passes on without having begun to question. One thing about persons like Mahler, they are above the possibilities of sexual suspicion.

The soft, plump lady has gone, back to the dimness of her bedroom. Now the yard seems truly forsaken. Just as, after the winter, the sight of an opened window sometimes creates the sensation of the new spring, bright sunshine over an empty yard may connote complete desolation. A player piano drowsily floods the area with its metallic music. The aforementioned alley cat has rolled up in the sun for a wary nap. A bedsheet on the third floor slowly bellies out with the breeze and then falls flat. The sunshine lights the walls in squares, in odd triangles, in long slits, and in sudden, wide splashes. Is the performance over?

But at this point the Devil's agent appears with his most ingenious contrivance. All anticipation and all delight, he has fastened a clothespin to invisible tungsten wire. Lowering it gently, he dangles the wooden pin, suspended mysteriously without support, before the eyes of Mahler. The clothespin bobs up and down, again and again, to no effect. Mahler is asleep. Slightly impatient, Davey then lightly taps him on the head. He awakes, the lids slowly moving apart a fraction of an inch. He regards the pin, marveling at its detached presence. O the wonder! Meanwhile the earth keeps spinning at the rate of twenty-four hours per revolution, passes on its orbit 365¼ days per cycle. A star up high waits for nightfall so that its light, already on the way a hundred years, may be apparent to those who care to look. Winds from Capricorn and Cancer round capes and peninsulas, bringing weather fair and warmer. Mahler remains, his eyes transfixed. At last, overpowered, he resigns himself to a peculiar world of phenomena he can never hope to understand. Here he is affected to the extent of concrete response, to wit, he shakes his head. Then, yielding, as he has yielded all his life, he goes back to sleep again, the mouth slightly ajar.

Directly above, on the third floor, a window slams. In some neighborhoods this is a token of disgust. As for Mahler, the simple man, he has done his duty and deserves his rest. For some time after they had found poor Meyer Sussman he had gone about with his mouth open wide in mute wonder. But the moment for his afternoon nap had come, he had tilted his chair against the wall in the sun and, in spite of Davey, in spite of death, Mahler sleeps.

There was still time, achingly there was still time, for his rendezvous with Yetta, and Davey, enduring a major disappointment in Mahler, walked slowly to Rodney and Ripple streets, where his gang had their hangout. The air was full of yells. All the kids on the block were running around in a wild exhibition of energy, playing ball or tag, or else chasing one another purposelessly. But Davey, disregarding them, went to screw himself into one of those odd seats boys find. This was a disused doorway, now covered by a tin billboard exclaiming the attractions at the Republic Theater. Wedged below this, in a space perhaps four feet by three, Davey sat with a film on his face. In the past he had utilized those precious moments before falling asleep to think and dream of indescribably lovely ladies in organdy. Now he found himself leaving his gang during the day to roll himself in the sleepy bath of his fancy. It was Yetta. Davey loved her.

The characters in moving-picture romances are men and women, and grown-ups claim love as an adult privilege. Davey disagreed. He knew his love for Yetta was as profound and genuine as any man's might have been. He liked the cleanness that was always about her, and the freshness. He liked the odd way she had of holding her second finger to her lips. Her complexion was pink and clear. What was love? Davey knew. It was a sucking emptiness in his belly when she passed him on the street. It was a gasping sensation that took away his wind. It brought the flush to his cheek and a shiver to his scalp. Only children, who are inexperienced, true unsophisticates lacking the balance of humor, can lose themselves in passion so completely.

For a long time Davey had worshiped Yetta from a distance. It was difficult to speak to any girl, and his feeling for Yetta made it impossible for him to approach her. Once, and he treasured the memory, he was playing punchball. As she came walking down the street, straight and clean, the ball happened to be traveling in her direction. Davey ran to catch it. "Keep your head up!" he had called, and snared the ball. Those were his first words to her and it was an important event. Keep your head up, he said again and again, wondering how the words in that particular combination sounded. He even tried to recapture the way he had said them, the pronunciation of the different words, the quality of his voice, the inflections. He must have presented a handsome picture, dashing masterfully in front of her, shielding her from harm, pulling down the ball. But as time passed he managed to talk with her, starting a brief conversation casually one day and developing it gradually, until he had taken courage in both hands and gone on walks with her. They even had become sweethearts of a sort, but when her friends wrote on walls in chalk that she loved Davey, Yetta always denied it with a show of virtue. That meant, and Davey understood it, that his courtship was not officially recognized.

That afternoon under the Republic Theater billboard Davey pondered the proper procedure to clinch his affections with her. That was love, gaspingly uncertain. He was preparing the position of his hands, the eyes, his expression when he was to talk to her. Davey, the Devil's agent, scourge of Mr. Yozowitz, and his laundry, leader of the Ripple Street gang, Davey thought of Yetta and of his love, and his belly swam with apprehension.

At this moment Natie the Buller came up to him. He was Davey's right-hand man, his lieutenant, and sympathetic, "What's the matter you ain't playing?" he asked. He looked at Davey's face and asked him whether he got hurt, did he have a toothache or something? Davey, rudely awakened and off his guard, forgot himself.

"You'll think it's funny," he said softly. "Natie, this sounds funny. I'm in love."

The Buller surprised him. "Why should I think that's funny?" he protested with respect. Understanding, he looked at Davey with tenderness. Davey was seriously involved in a grand passion; he was, therefore, suffering, and it followed that he was already an adult. Natie was left to admire him. "Why should I think that's funny? You sound as though I'm a kid. I've been in love too. Only, with you it's Yetta, and I can't have my girl. I know about it better than you."

"What's the matter with your girl?" Davey asked. "Who is she?"

"Marion Davies."

"I don't know any girl around here called Marion Davies," he said.

"I mean the moving-picture actress."

"Oh. Marion Davies. You mean you're actually in love with her?"

Natie nodded his head. His own passion rendered him helpless, ashamed and dumb.

"Well. That's certainly funny. I mean, I'm not making fun of you. Only, how can you be in love with Marion Davies? She's so old."

"The difference looks big now because I'm still young," Natie said. "Later on the difference wouldn't look so much."

"Oh, no, Natie. It is big," he insisted gently.

"No," said Natie. "You often hear of men marrying women ten years younger than them."

"I know, but it's different when the man is younger."

"Why should it be different? Take my Aunt Lillie. She's six years older than my Uncle Joe."

"They used to do those things, our fathers and mothers. But people don't get married like that anymore."

"Why?" Natie asked with all his heart. "Why?"

Davey did not answer. Although he could understand Natie, the comparison with his emotion somehow made his own feeling for Yetta slightly ridiculous. Besides, it was half-past five, and at that hour Yetta always passed Cheap Simon's candy store. They had never arranged to meet, but at half-past five Davey was always there, as if by accident. They talked sparringly. Then, "Are you going my way?" Yetta always said, "Yes." That was always nice. They went off walking stiffly.

Today Davey had resolved to bring their affair to some kind of a head. He met her at the candy store, went through the ritual, and the two walked off. Their legs had no knees and they kept their eyes directly before them. Davey trembled a little at the prospect.

"I was thinking," he said, eager and restrained. "I was thinking."

"What about?" Yetta said.

"I mean. Here we've been going together, seeing each other, talking and going for walks together, and I was thinking, sometime I would like to ask you a question."

"There is no time like the present," Yetta assured him. She had sneaked some powder from her sister and her nose looked as though she had been caught in a blackboard-eraser fight.

"I mean ... It's this, only this ... Yetta, I want to know. Do you really love me?"

"That's a hard question," she said promptly. "Let me think."

Yetta thought and thought.

"It all depends," she finally said, "what you mean by love."

"Ah," said Davey sadly, remembering the words, "you are invading the issue."

"What?" asked Yetta immediately.

"I mean ... I asked you a question. That's no answer."

"All right," Yetta said with finality. "You asked a simple question; here's a simple answer: Next to my mother and father, my sister Essie and my uncle Max, I think I love you best."

Davey's heartbeat increased. He touched her hand, but he was careful to look dreamily into the distance at the other side.

In the evening after supper Davey sat in ecstasy on the fire escape. He had to keep his legs bent closely to him because his mother had put a glass gallon of wine outside to ferment, and he had to be careful not to push it. Below were the crowds enjoying their usual night session. The rays of the electric lamppost came directly into Davey's eyes in thin gauzy lines. The buzz of the street crowds came up to him like trees in the country bending with the wind. No matter. Davey was strolling serenely through a lovely garden. His face wore the movie hero's expression of vacant seriousness, adulterated a little by some invading sorrow like intestinal trouble. As Davey lifts the cigarette to his mouth, he sees Yetta. She is dressed in white organdy and is the very picture of innocence and prettiness. Davey's eyes pinpoint with delight, he flings the cigarette over the hedge. “My dear Susannah,” he says, and stretches out his arms for her.

There was a loud crash. A few women screamed. Everyone pushed his chair back and ran a short way from his place. Davey looked down in surprise. Faces, angry, grimacing, with holes in the center working savagely at him, returned his stare. He had kicked the gallon of wine through the fire escape. The purple mess, with scattered cherries and pieces of glass, formed a big splotch on the sidewalk. Davey’s mother ran up to him through the dark room. He was not so much afraid as startled. Davey did not have his bearings. His mother, bawling him out fiercely, swung her arm to slap him.

Davey rolled from the window to the floor and lay in a faint. His mother looked at him silently. “My God,” she began to cry, “the poor child was so scared he fainted with fright.” She held Davey’s head and said, all at once, everything was all right, she would not hit him. “Get up, Davey, my life. Don’t lay there like dead.” She ran to the kitchen for a glass of water. Davey’s eyes followed her as she left. He picked himself up quietly and stole out of the house.

It was an ugly incident in his life, Davey said, but it would pass, he would forget it, he would forget. He walked in the shadows of the buildings. “My dear Susannah,” he said, “my dear Susannah.”

THREE

MRS. LINCK, THE JANITRESS, went back to the dimness of her dirty flat and sat down in her rocker. It was all over, she sighed. The last obsequies over Sussman had been held in her rooms even though the guinea pigs running over the floor had made the women nervous. The ladies had left and with their departure the sense of excitement diminished and Mrs. Linck was experiencing a depressing letdown. When they had first found poor Meyer Sussman she had once again proved her energy in handling these situations. The women in her flat had all said that without her they would have been lost. She had been wonderful. Mrs. Linck had flopped around in a commanding manner, opened the windows wide, phoned for the pulmotor, the hospital, and had taken charge in general. She was a warm-hearted woman and capable. The housewives all admired her that sultry morning. Themselves, they had contained within themselves too much delicacy for the calamity.

Now Mrs. Linck sat vacantly in her rocker, waiting for the perspiration over her to dry. All over, she said, and rocked monotonously. Then she became aware of the girls playing potsy in the yard and this immediately infuriated her. Her greatest worry spent itself over the kids playing in the yard. Mrs. Linck banged the window open and yelled at the children madly. The girls, calloused by this time, went on serenely. Mrs. Linck twisted her head in exasperation as though she were on the way to a stroke. She left the window abruptly, and, reappearing, poured pitchers of water on the kids.

The girls scuttled through the yard-alley, shrieking at the tops of their voices, "Linck stinks! Linck stinks!" The rhyme always infuriated her almost to the point of frenzy for Mrs. Linck had a proud temperament. For a moment it seemed that the massive chunk of flesh, blown to excess, was about to explode.

Mrs. Linck, big and sloppy, her flesh perpetually escaping from her loose-fitting kimono, went back into the dimness of her flat. She walked about in the gloom, her red face dissolving in sweat, her jaws working constantly as she cursed the children. At a time like this, when he had been alive, poor Mr. Linck, cowed and half-dead, had kept his head down while she was in action. Once he had been a pants presser, but in his last years he had suffered from an assortment of ailments and had simply sat in the center of the kitchen quietly playing with the guinea pigs that ran over the cracked linoleum and uneven planks of the floor. His wife had imported these partly from a feeling of affection for the little beasts and partly because she believed they helped keep the house clean. Mr. Linck had been careful to do nothing to excite his wife. He had barely spoken to her in consequence. And when she was ignited he had muttered feebly, "A little peace, please. A little quiet." Unheeded, there was nothing for him to do but mumble, through the bread he was always munching, some wavering gem of wisdom, muffling his words in fear so that they might not aggravate his wife's condition.

The door opened and into the dimness came Mrs. Linck's daughter-in-law, walking rapidly and careful to pay no greeting to the woman in the rocker. Suddenly she skidded, tripped, shrieked, caught herself, and turned to the older woman belligerently. It was one of the guinea pigs.

"For God's sakes!" she stormed, choked with anger, "For God's sakes! Why in hell do you have to have those dirty things running all over the house?"

"Look at her!" Mrs. Linck screamed from the rocker. "It ain't fancy enough for her here! Hell yourself! Is it a fire you got to run into the house?"

"Aw, shut up, you make me good and sick. I can't stand the living sight of you!" Mrs. Linck's daughter-in-law walked into the bathroom, taking pains to slam the door, but this was hardly enough to stop the janitress. Mrs. Linck bombarded the ugly glass door of the bathroom with insults, curses, and protests. The door opened, the younger woman ran to the hall, said dispassionately "Go to hell," and fled.

Still mumbling, Mrs. Linck rocked furiously. Then a wave of self-pity swept over her and she cried softly to herself. Three daughters of her own she had and she had to be cursed with a devil like her. Mrs. Linck wept, rocked gently, and felt sorry for herself, and in another few minutes dozed off.

Three daughters and a son Mrs. Linck had, and while she and her corpse of a husband used to sit in the filth and gloom her children had gone out, having found life generous and inviting. And of them all only her son, Sam, together with his wife, was left at home. The son's more imaginative adventures were by this time at an end. He had had a series of minor jobs, became a truck driver, did not take to his mother's everlasting bawling and left. Four years later he returned with a wife and two children, dumped them on his mother, and went out to look for a job. Since Mr. Linck had died this domestic arrangement had become permanent.

But the daughters had flown from Williamsburg. Lillie, the oldest of the Linck girls, had been an unusually ugly girl to start with. It was her smashed-up nose that wrecked her features. In her childhood children had tortured her for it until once, sunk in a deep despondency, Lillie had planned suicide but had succeeded only in making a more ridiculous object of herself. She had arranged to hang herself from the gas chandelier, but as an afterthought decided to turn on the gas as well. Then when the experience was beginning to prove painful, she had had to scream for help.

Lillie left grade school in the sixth term, hopelessly outwitted by the intricacies of elementary education. The usual small jobs followed until one day she burst in with the news that she was getting married. The women all wondered, it didn't seem possible, some actually felt resentful. Mrs. Linck, unbelieving at first, soon grew happier and happier as the full meaning of the prospect soaked in. Lillie had seemed such a difficult case. Mrs. Linck walked around in a gibberish of joy, not knowing whether it was appropriate to cry or whether it was etiquette to show how glad she really was. For two months she retailed the news, told stories of Lillie when she was a baby, and shed sad tears because she was now losing her daughter.

The bubble broke cruelly. It was a hoax. Mrs. Linck repeatedly asked to see Lillie's fiancé until in the end she screwed out the truth. Poor Lillie howled, her mother cursed like a witch, and the tenement laughed for a week.

Julie was the youngest, really pretty and a consolation to Mrs. Linck for she had actually been graduated from elementary school. She lived on the tabloids and the movie fan magazines. The surest access to her favors was to take her to a show. Lillie allowed the boys to be free with her because she imagined she would catch one in that manner. But Julie found her encounters with boys a source of tantalizing enjoyment, a chance to tease them, to make manifest her charms. The boys on the block had a name for her.

Julie's disappearance was a sensation that lasted for a week. Abruptly she was gone. Mrs. Linck cracked her knuckles, wept, and asked everyone what could she do. Daily she expected word from her, but with the days the excitement diminished, Mrs. Linck ceased running to meet the postman in the mornings, the matter died.

Philip's brother Harry had unexpectedly met Julie in a brothel on Division Street, Albany, but had found it difficult to mention the news to her mother.

The level-headed one of the sisters, the sensible one, was Bertha. She was a capable girl, strongly built, and she handled the boys shrewdly. Bertie alone of the three sisters was properly married, but this was where she had made a mistake. When she picked up her Bridgeport, Conn., sailor, a Christian, and he offered to marry her, she glibly waived the material considerations every housewife in the tenement never stopped mentioning. But after two months of wedded bliss she discovered her husband was a drug addict. When this came up, she told the housewives, she immediately went to the doctor to see whether she had caught "it" also.

After he had lived on her for three years and had made life exciting in other ways she finally managed to divorce him. Sporadically he sent her telegrams, collect, threatening to kill her if she did not return to him. When someone once asked her why she had had to marry him, she rolled her eyes, and protested loudly, "He was so good, he was so good when I first met him, if you went to the cemetery and dug up a grave you couldn't find a better man than him."

Now Bertie and Lillie danced in a burlesque show that trouped the lesser towns. Julie was half-forgotten. Mrs. Linck waddled in the gloom and filth and had a daughter-in-law to curse, and they were at their quarrels interminably. The son worked grimly, prolonging in the evenings a love life that was already moribund. Occasionally he took time to rise in his masculine wrath and bawl them out lavishly for their incessant bickering.

Poor Mr. Linck was dead and in his grave these many years, but his two unkempt grandchildren still played with the guinea pigs, running through the rooms after them and sometimes barely distinguishable from them in the dinginess.

Now Mrs. Linck's two grandchildren came bawling into the house, dragged from their play in the streets for supper.

"Shut up already, you rotten kids," their mother yelled at them. "You got to eat, don't you? What do you want from my life?"

Mrs. Linck rose from her rocker. She was still sleepy and her mouth had a distressing acid taste. "Shah!" she shouted at them and went to the kitchen sink. She rinsed loudly and then slapped her wet hands over her face.

"Well," said her daughter-in-law, "what I would like to know is where is that wonderful son of yours? It's after seven already."

"What's the matter? I'm your servant? I should go looking for him? How should I know where he is?"

"You're his mother, ain't it? You always tell me what a wonderful husband I got, ain't it? Well? Maybe you think I don't know he's chasing around with some dirty tramp?"

"Go to hell," Mrs. Linck said softly, concluding the argument. The evening had come on and it was time to collect the garbage on the landings. After that Sam would be home, her daughter-in-law would fight with her over his supper because he was late, the children would be put to bed howling, and the day would be over. That was how it went, and, looking forward to the night when she might go to sleep again, she went to the cellar.

Over in a South Fifth Street rooming house Mrs. Linck's son, Sam, lay in bed, with the sheet up to his chin, smoking a cigarette in the gentle afterglow of passion.

"Say son of a bitch."

"What for? Are you crazy."

"Say it, Marge. It's always so damn funny to hear a girl say dirty words. I was just thinking maybe you'd come out with it, and I kept on waiting for it. All you did was begin to snore."

"Do I snore?" Marge asked. "Well, I can't help it. I'm all knocked out after a day like this."

"Don't get mad, baby. I like you."

Marge, alongside of him, smelled a little of unwashed clothing, but Sam Linck didn't mind. After all, he had picked her up out of a blue sky, she had turned into such a good thing he couldn't kick.

"Come on, baby. Say son of a bitch."

"You're a goddam son of a bitch."

"That's fine. Now say bastid."

"You're a goddam bastid. Will you leave me alone?"

"Listen, Marge, you're a good kid. I like you. I think we'll get along very fine."

"Sure," she said. "In another week you'll be calling me whore."

"That was swell, Marge. I mean the way you said that. I never heard a girl get out with those dirty words the way you do."

Linck congratulated himself. Marge was a Polish girl of eighteen, with a fair figure and good-looking face except for a pug nose. He had been walking home early in the morning after putting the truck in the garage when Marge had busted out on him from a store hallway. Linck had bought her a cup of coffee and some doughnuts. The next day he had fixed her up with the room here.

"Listen, kid, we'll get along fine. I got an idea what you think, but I'm all right. I'll treat you fine," he said.

"You can't tell me anything about that. That's all people have been doing to me, treating me fine. I know the words and music by this time. When I was up in Willimantic, making sometimes five dollars a day with the overtime, a guy told me he'd treat me something fine. He brought me to New York on a joy ride and brought all his pals into the bed the first night."

"Honest, Marge, you got me wrong. I don't blame you, but I'm different about these things."

"You bet," Marge said. "I can see that right now. Can you imagine it? He takes me out to Coney Island in a Mack truck and spends sixty cents on me for hot dogs and root beer and then he tells me he's all right, he's treating me something fine."

"All right. The hell with it. Forget it. Just hang around and see how it works out," Linck said. He reached over and squeezed the cigarette in the heel of his shoe.

"Maybe I shouldn't talk like that," Marge said. After all he was paying her room rent. "Only, you see how it is right now. I've been hanging around with that red bastid up on the houseboat in the Harlem River. It was swell on the river, especially in the evenings. We used to walk around all day in bathing suits, and in the evening the sun got red as hell. And I fell for that red bastid. God," she wailed, "how I loved that red bastid! 'Marge,' he used to tell me, 'one kiss from you gives me a bigger kick than seven times with any other broad.' He bought me a ring even. He told me it was genuine white gold but I knew it came from Woolworth's, but I was so nuts on that red bastid I didn't say nothing. And then one fine day one of his pals tells me he's been going to the clinic for weeks already. He had it and here he was telling me all along about getting married."

By God, thought Linck, if I get it from her I'll push in her goddam pug nose.

"I got to beat it," he said.

"Any girl who trusts a man is a sucker," Marge said.

"I said I got to be going."

"Don't rupture yourself. What do you want me to do?"

Linck got out of the bed and began to dress drowsily. By God, I'll push in her goddam pug nose.

"Say, big boy, while I think of it. I need underwear. You ought to leave me a couple of dollars."

"You better get a job behind somebody's counter. I ain't Vanderbilt."

"I know, you kike, I know that."

Marge jumped up, punched the pillow and rolled over. Linck went on dressing, admiring her little round bottom. He'd tell the wife the boss had sent him out on a special job to New Haven. Hell, he'd tell her to go to hell. It wasn't that late. Linck pulled his pants over the shirttails, stamped his legs to smooth the clothing, and went to the door.

"Marge," he called softly. "Marge, say bitch-bastid."

"Go on home, you goddam bitch-bastid," she said.

Linck smiled. He took out a dollar and laid it on the dresser.

"Who turned off the radio?" Sam Linck asked. "Listen, if I get home and my only enjoyment is to listen to the radio, you have to shut it off."

"It's in my ears all day. Can't I get a little rest too? My head is ringing."

"Turn it on." He opened the pink pages of the *Journal* to the comic section. His wife put a plate of roast meat before him. Her housedress was soiled with food stains and wet in spots from the sink. Sitting at the opposite end of the table, she began complaining about her mother-in-law.

"I'll go crazy one of these days," she said. "That woman is driving me out of my mind. I put a pot on the stove and she takes it off and puts her pot on the stove. If I go into the bathroom for a minute she bangs on the door and yells, hurry up. She won't even let me move my bowels in peace. She put your father in the grave with her nagging and she'll do the same with me. You'll see."

Linck kept his eyes on the comics while his fingers pushed food in his mouth. From the blank expression on his face he might have been asleep. The stink of wet clothes drying filled the room. Dirty rags lay on every chair. The floor was dirty, and the electric bulb, too small for the room, distributed its depressing yellowness. The house was always in a mess.

"All you do is read the paper," his wife went on. "If I sat here dying you wouldn't know the difference."

"For God's sakes," he said, "are you at it again? I work all the time, Sunday or no Sunday, like a horse. I drive that goddam truck until my can feels like it's on fire. And when I get home for a little rest you won't let me listen to the radio. I can't read the jokes. All I must do is listen to you shoot your goddam mouth off about my old lady. Why don't you lay off me for a change?"

"I'm sick and tired. I've never had a good day in my life yet. Do you think I want to live in this filthy hole until I'm dead?"

"Please," Linck begged. "I work all day and all night, like a nigger. I'm tired. I want rest. I work from seven to nine in the night. Have a heart."

"Yare! Now you come to me and cry you work all night! As if I don't know what goes on, as if you think I ain't got ears. Listen to me, I know how you work all night!"

"What's the matter with you? Are you crazy? Is it my fault the boss sends me out on jobs at night. What do you want from me?"

"Jobs the boss sends you out on at night! I'm a dumbbell—I ain't got eyes, I ain't got ears. I don't know how you carry on with that Polack tramp!"

Linck gathered himself together for the explosion. "Shut up!" he yelled as hard as he could.

"I won't shut up. I've had enough. When I married you you didn't tell me I was marrying into your whole goddam family with its whores and burlesque dancers and your filthy mother. I won't shut up! I won't live in this rotten hole with your mother nagging the life out of me all the time. I'm not going to stand it while you go into every filthy whore's bed. I won't shut up!" she screamed, shaking her head with fury.

"You dirty slob!" Linck said. "You dirty slob!"

"Slob? Slob?" she yipped. She picked up a kettle of water from the stove. "Slob? Just say another word and I'll burn you to death!"

"Put down that pot or I'll brain you, you lousy slob!" The guinea pigs scurried with fright. They were upset by the commotion. Sam's wife broke out in a frenzy, awkwardly swinging the kettle so that streams of hot water scalded her husband. He jumped and tried to skip out of the way. "God *damn* you!" he cried. "God *damn* you!" The kettle caught him across the face. Linck stopped dancing. He held his face in his hands and sat down on the floor. The pain was so great he disregarded his wife altogether.

She held the pot over him suspended, her fury gone cold.

"What's the matter?" she said weakly. "Did it get into your eyes? What's the matter?"

Linck stood up. His face was patched with red. "Here," his wife said, "put butter on it." She tried to smear it but he pushed her away. He sat down at the table and picked up the funny paper again. Mrs. Linck moved the plate of meat up to him.

"Eat, Sam," she said, "eat."

One really remembers, said Philip, not a narrative of incidents but more often an isolated picture standing apart from the stream of experience like a snapshot. These images are not clearly defined but they remain with their peculiar flavor in the mind for years. Nevertheless, it is difficult to account for their particular selection or their durability. Philip, for the moment, recalled the scene at the foot of South Second Street when once, as a boy, he had been taken for a walk. He recalled the sun-splashed picture, some boys diving off the pier and from the tug anchored to it. He remembered the green, oily water and the quiet. This must have been a long time ago, but now Philip remembered it.

His awkward errand with his uncle Papravel still disturbed him, Cohen in his silliness had irritated him further, but primarily the inexplicable death of Sussman was having a vaguely unsettling effect on him. Why, Philip asked himself again, had the butcher done it? What did Miller mean to say was wrong with Williamsburg? And, above all, why was it that Sussman's suicide seemed to affect Philip so intimately? Philip felt troubled, and, trying to lose his mood of uncertainty and dissatisfaction, he was walking to the dock again.

On Sunday the sun floats down tranquilly to cover with its glaring brightness the pavements and the buildings. The streets are deserted, their inhabitants jamming the subways for Coney Island or else seeking the dark coolness of moving-picture houses. Williamsburg becomes for the day like a bright painting in its motionlessness, and somehow this creates an atmosphere in which you may like to bathe sleepily.

No boys were to be seen diving now. The dock was completely deserted. A ferry boat patiently paddled across, one of the few signs of life along the waterfront. The huge cranes of the Domino Sugar plant hung suspended in midair; black factories, their windows barred by iron shutters, rested inanimate; and freightliners wearied from long trips slept in the sun. Desultorily in the distance and far overhead the subway train rattled over the bridge.

Inland the tenements seemed abandoned and resembled for the day ruins of an early time. On summer weekdays and nights there were always hundreds of people thronging the streets and a constant flow of traffic. The emptiness now took on all a stranger significance by contrast. The grocery and butcher stores, closed by municipal law, had their green blinds drawn in front of their windows. A candy store here and there dozed in the mid-afternoon heat until the subways restored its customers. A pair of ice picks, hanging neglected over the iron railing of a tenement basement, indicated that here at other times Italian icemen did a noisy, open-air business. A few sleepy cats nosed deliberately in cans of garbage for scraps. An old woman shuffled down the street, and this completed the effect of lifelessness.

Philip walked across Bedford Avenue, down again to the riverfront, but this time to the other side, at Wallabout Market. The Market off the bay on the East River was picturesque, and this was especially striking for Philip for he remembered its aspect during the week. Now the atmosphere was pervaded with a profound stillness as unnatural as the silence in a subway train when it comes to a full stop waiting between stations for a signal. The machinery of activity and noise was everywhere visible but the wheels on Sunday did not turn.

The buildings here were old, quaint in their architecture and mellow in appearance from age. The storehouses of fruit jobbers had no doors and the merchandise lay exposed to the sidewalk. Watchmen were seen napping off in the corners. Anchored at the docks ancient steamers with half their paint gone rested from trips to tropical ports, carrying cargoes of fruit. They were like sleeping old men. In the shade of a shed an artist was painting the fire-engine building for the sake of its tower.

A wide cobbled street ran through the Market. At one end it was squeezed into a narrow, short drawbridge over a greasy canal. Over the bridge Philip proceeded to the academic quiet of Pratt Institute and the Library. In this neighborhood the air was one of respectability becoming impoverished. The houses were low, but a few mansions, remnants of a former time, occasionally showed their broken windows to the street.

Philip sat down on a bench in the park. Now he took from his pocket the letter his brother Harry had sent him from Havers Falls and, thinking of Sussman and what Old Miller had said about him, he read it again.

> Williamsburg is for people like Pop, Old Miller, the shoe-cobbler Mahler, and everyone else who wants to let himself be played for a sucker, or doesn't know better. Get out. The trouble with you is too much school. You don't know how things really are when you try to hand out any of this ethical

baloney. Who cares about ethics? While you're worrying about treating the other fellow right, somebody will be stepping all over your neck and you'll end up with a dead look in your eyes. You'll work all your life at some rotten job you hate, you'll get paid enough to take three swell rooms in a Ripple Street flat, and you'll finish like Pop, whom you admire so much, worn, poor, and dead before you die.

Listen, kid, I want to give you a shove. You don't want to go around refusing Papravel's offer on the bus job. He'll give you everything you'll need. You can make plenty of money with Papravel's bunch. The life is easy, the work may be dangerous sometimes, but it's easy by and large. We don't keep regular hours, no one bosses us, and there's travel. Women are everywhere. I want you to tell Papravel you've changed your mind.

I suppose it's better not to let Pop see this, of course, but it's about time he layed off Papravel. Tell him even Morgan and Rockefeller didn't make all their money honestly.

Philip slipped the letter in his pocket. Money, women, money. You'll have a good time. Well, said Philip, that's something.

It was pleasant always to sit on the benches here and watch the empty streets through half-closed eyes, to daydream, to think. Suddenly a vague and sleepy nostalgia permeated him, but it was a nostalgia for places he had never seen for they did not exist; it was a longing for people and experiences that, also nonexistent, were impossible.

Philip walked off, but this mild sense of sadness accompanied him back, as he smoked cigarettes in a rootless reverie, to the quiet streets of his high school and the Williamsburg Library where he sat on the steps waiting for a friend to pass by. It followed him into an empty delicatessen restaurant, over meat sandwiches and glasses of tea. And finally Philip felt compelled to lose it and his loneliness in the darkness of a movie theater.

High up, a million miles into the sky, God sits on a big cloud. He looks absentmindedly about. His beard is long and very white, the flesh of His face is gnarled. Now He peers down and for a moment His gaze rests on Williamsburg and He says to Himself, How are things going down there, I wonder? And He looks. It is as though you had supernatural eyes and were a mile above Manhattan, and all the subway streets were open and you saw the trains moving at their different points.

God wonders and looks. Everything is just as it always has been and as it will be. Mrs. Linck's flesh moves in rhythm to the count of the rocker while the guinea pigs scurry beneath her. Papravel wears a derby and is in his vest and shirtsleeves washing his hands, Mr. Miller is now waiting at the cemetery entrance expectantly eyeing a middle-aged couple in dark clothes, Cohen lies in a purple dressing gown reading an unexpurgated copy of *Minnie the Moocha* in a tooled-leather, privately printed edition. Mahler, now awake, is creakingly performing the operations incidental to cleaning his nose, and Philip with a half-conscious expression is gazing at Gloria Swanson, whose long, black eyelashes murmur an innocent guilt to the hero's question, "Do you mean, dot, dot, dot, question mark?"

For this is life, not as a novelist sees it but as God in His all-knowing wisdom does, and we are all children of God, even Gloria Swanson, and it is good. Now God perceives Mr. Meyer Sussman bouncing on the clouds as he runs to meet Him.

O Meyer Sussman! As a favor to a young writer, will you ask God for me what made you squeeze the basketball bladder over your face?

FOUR

THE LIGHT FROM THE LAMPPOST flooded the bedroom window. The two boys bounced upon the bed, struggling to get away from their mother as she forced them into nightclothes.

"I want to make a horse's head," one said. Mrs. Sussman patiently waited at the edge of the bed as the children fixed their fingers in odd positions to cast figures of shadows on the wall. They jumped with glee. Mrs. Sussman sat with her hands in her lap, dreamily waiting until they finished their repertory, a sort of numb blankness in her mind. Finally she pushed the boys under the blankets.

"Hush, little mothers," she whispered, caressing their heads and pressing them to her bosom with great feeling tonight, "go to sleep, go to sleep."

Mrs. Sussman, her hair plaited, in a cotton nightgown, sat on a box and looked out the window, gazing at the people in the street. It was the same. The children made pictures on the wall from the light, only Meyer wasn't here to pat their bottoms with his big hands. Mrs. Sussman thought of Meyer and the tears welled in her eyes. She sniffed and rubbed her eye with a finger. They wouldn't let him stay a day, his body was still warm when they put him in his box. Alive and healthy in the morning, at night under a pile of yellow earth with a little stick on top. At the funeral all the neighbors followed the hearse through the streets and there had been crying wholesale. The men, home because it was Sunday, attended to the details with businesslike sobriety. After the trip to the cemetery every house on the block had pitchers of water and glasses outside for the mourners to wash their hands according to the ritual. It took so little time. Dead at ten, buried by one, and resting in his grave forever already. The people downstairs on the sidewalk went on talking and laughing. A few hours ago they were crying at the funeral and saying it was such a great pity. How can they talk and drink soda water as though nothing has happened, Mrs. Sussman thought, how can they do it? Is it still the same? Meyer is dead and everything goes on just the same. A person is alone in the world, always alone.

"What will I do now?" she said, and quietly at the window, while the women peddled gossip downstairs and the men smoked their cigars, Mrs. Sussman wept from her heart.

In the synagogue a dozen old men leaned on their elbows over a bare-board table studying the Talmud like a bunch of college boys working on Kant. An old man read three or four lines aloud.

"Rabbi ben Onz said this is to mean this, Rabbi ben Twoz, of a later generation, said it is to mean that, while here, nearer to our own time, Rabbi ben Threez said that in spite of the opinions of these venerated rabbis, it means neither this nor that, but, if the word 'fourz' is properly understood, the passage clearly means part of this and part of that together but neither this nor that in themselves, but in part, together, and also the other thing added. All these have been the words of the learned, and what say you now?"

"Hichle," said a little, wizened man, clearing his throat, and for fifteen minutes in phlegmatic deliberation the man solemnly argued the point and finally dispensed with it.

"Pichle," said another. The old gentlemen shifted the positions of their heads and elbows and set to work on the new theory.

"Schmichle," said another, introducing a third interpretation.

"Hichle, pichle, schmichle," said Old Miller, the ultimate sage, the man who contained within his skinny body all the cold, clinical wisdom. "Let us go again to the Talmud, the Good Book. It says, 'Va-cha-choo-loo, va-cha-choo-loo.' And this means, when the wind will blow, the cradle will rock." And for a half-hour Miller held the discussion in his cool, slow voice, expounding gently, parrying objections skillfully, using logic both ways. Oh, these mysterious men in their black, shiny caftans, in their skullcaps, these old men who come together in the evenings to play tic-tac-toe with the great Talmud, itself brought down miraculously through the centuries. In our time we must admire and respect this fervor, this tradition. They are true heroes in a world of puppets and therefore we do not understand them. These old men who find synagogues in a tenement basement store with the terrible toilets facing the backyards. These old men nodding over the yellow, holy-odored volumes, arguing in a straight line of tradition that extends over the world in width, in depth to the earliest times, in length to God himself. What dimensions, what awful dimensions, what wonderful men as they spit generously on the dirty floor.

"There are the earth and the heavens," said Miller the miser, "there are two worlds, the one we inhabit and the other. And the secret in both is activity. What a man may do in one is divorced from his path in the other, but in both he must be active or he dies. Observe all forms of life, it is constantly in movement. The ants, the mice, the dogs, and the fish in the seas. Even in zoos and aquaria the beasts do not stay in inaction, they move in endless circles. The dog chases his tail and he is content, for he does. As for man, there are two tasks. There are the heavens and the earth. In the one he must take care of his soul, and in the other, the meaning is, he must nourish his body. He must find food and study truths. And this is the meaning of the passage."

Miller finished and the old men cleared their throats, turning pages. The flush of the toilet tinkled musically in the night

The old men finished arguing over the Talmud. Someone put a plate of cake on the table and a bottle of homemade cherry brandy, and they dabbled in the lighter news of the day. Some told Jewish witticisms, and old men laughed in rasping sounds. The janitor turned off the lights in the two big globes outside the synagogue. The day was over.

A thin-necked, redheaded Jew in a derby pulled Miller's sleeve. "Mister," he said, "step outside a minute. We want to talk a piece of business. Maybe you can help us and help yourself at the same time."

Miller had never seen this man before but he followed him outside the store. A second stranger stated the case:

"We speak for kinsmen, people who have just come from the old country, and we come to you because your name is a good one in this synagogue. What we have with you is this: these people are in trouble, the husband is sickly, they can't make a living. We do what we can to help them, after all they are kinsmen, but they are a great burden."

Miller broke in impatiently. They were trying to get at his money again. "Listen," he said, "you waste time. Whoever gave you my name told you wrong. I am very sorry for these people, but I am a poor man too. Indeed, do I look so prosperous that you pick me out for charity?"

"Just a minute, mister," the redhead said soothingly. "You run too fast. The least you can do is hear this man out."

"These people were not always poor, but what the times have been on the other side these last years I don't have to tell you. They were rich folk once, they had estates, servants, and beasts."

"What is it?" Miller said. "Well, what is it?"

"In short, they have diamonds."

Miller was suspicious. "I don't understand," he said.

"What is there to understand? They have diamonds."

"What has that to do with me?"

"Diamonds are like gold. They are better than gold. They always keep their value."

"There are pawnshops," Miller said. "Why do you want to sell me diamonds?"

The thin-necked redhead spoke up. "There are pawnshops, only they will not buy these diamonds. The duty hasn't been paid."

"Smuggled?" said Miller, shaking his head. "Well, let me hear the wonderful bargain."

The man spoke rapidly. "These people were rich and the diamonds are no trinkets. You can see them for yourself, of course. But if you can find anyone who says they are not worth ten thousand dollars, I'll give you that much money out of my own pocket."

"How much do they ask?"

"This is not a business deal. The family needs money quickly and they will sell for almost nothing if you will give cash. Can you pay two thousand dollars in cash?"

"Two thousand dollars in cash!" Miller said. "Are these the family diamonds of the Czar?"

"Let's not joke, mister. The family starves and needs money by the minute."

"Two thousand dollars," Miller said. He stopped and went over the deal in his mind. He once knew a man who had crossed the ocean fourteen times successfully smuggling jewels until someone, grown envious, informed. There was certainly money to be made here. At the same time he would be doing a holy good deed to a family in need. Miller, bargaining carefully, said:

"I will examine the diamonds in the morning, if this pleases you. But two thousand dollars is out of the question."

The next day Miller met the two men, inspected the jewels, and was brought by them to a jeweler who appraised their worth above ten thousand dollars. Upon this Miller went to his bank accompanied by the two strangers and withdrew sixteen hundred dollars in payment.

⸺⸺⸺

At the window in the darkness Mrs. Sussman wept quietly over her calamity and feared for the future. Old Miller, the sage in the long beard, forgetting the cool dignity of philosophy (business before pleasure), bargained craftily for smuggled diamonds. But at Tessie's apartment, a hefty stone's throw from Ripple Street, soft music played and the young bloods of Williamsburg, dismissing sad care from their souls, flung roses with the throng. It was a great night for Cohen, but the company of ladies was too much for him. Giggling in his nervous uncertainty before them, Cohen took the speediest way out and with conscientious gaiety was drinking gin rapidly even if he drank ostentatiously. It was a great night too for Tessie, and as she walked from kitchen to bedroom to living room performing the imperative rites of hostess, her arch glance strayed again and again to the figure of Philip Hayman.

In the stiffly upholstered chair Philip sat, the perspiration covered his body with its stickiness as though someone were plastering his back with wet lollipops. He wriggled restlessly until his underwear, yanked and screwed, cut into his crotch. Parties on July nights and sweat. Dim lights and a red board floor losing its wax in a crazy design from dancers' heels. Blue river, blue river, blue river, the radio kept on playing. "Please keep your hands off me, Eddie," said a lassie at an elementary breach of rules. "I mean I just can't stand it when anybody touches me." The wet-lined hair of the boys was beginning to lose its silly, combed grandeur; their faces, still smelling of shaving cream, burned from the sweat at points where the razor had nicked the skin. When they rubbed their foreheads with their handkerchiefs their skin smarted and they cursed. Shirts, newly ironed, were losing the starch, and the tails coming out were jabbed from time to time under the belts, while their hips, irritated by this treatment, protested. This was the era of gaudy socks. Between stiffly creased trousers and shoes losing five-cent shines under the red dirt, the socks flashed their brilliance for an admiring feminine world. The feminine world, however, had its own affairs to consider and made a constant pilgrimage to Tessie's bedroom where it fixed its hair amid a profusion of cosmetic odor.

Collect, said Philip, and the radio said, Did you mean it when you said you loved me? Did you mean it when you said you cared?

The dancers pressed their unlovely moist bodies against one another, a decorous substitute for what the blurred forms were doing in the corners. In these matters there were two schools of tactics in Williamsburg. The first held that an introductory session was to be spent in dancing in order to ascertain the eventual compatibility of the couple. The second school believed that this was nonsense and urged the elimination of this first step, encouraging a prompt retreat to the corners for the preliminaries. (1. Embrace lady, kiss face, kiss mouth, long and with passion. You mean this, throw yourself into it. 2. The embrace is developed, hands move, but from the waist up only. 3. Rub the breasts gently, with the palms, not the fingers, concentrating on the nipples. 4. Slip hands through throat of dress.) The next step took the pair into the bedroom where they made themselves cozy among the wraps and hats and there they might languorously wrestle. An ultimate possibility, the gentleman was always to keep in mind, was the hallway of the lady's home where she might, dot, dot, dot, a broad h'm—but this depended entirely upon the lady's caprice of the moment.

The gathering had been arranged by Tessie expressly for Philip. "If you don't come, it's all off. It's for you only," she had said, and he had promised to come. A month ago she had told him she was marrying Schlausser, thirty-two and solid, salesman of ladies' sundries, corsets and brassieres, and it had irritated Philip keenly. It was one of those experiences that do not quit the mind, that refuse to be forgotten but return again and again to torment. "Do you mean to tell me," he had said, choked with indignation, "that when I used to be on the sofa and said all those dopey things to you and you took it all in and I thought you were with me all the way, what you mean to say is that you didn't mean any of it, you had Schlausser in the back of your head all the time? Well, that makes me a fine-looking dope." "I'm sorry," she kept on saying. "Oh, you don't know how sorry I am about the whole business." But it did no good, Philip felt awkward and angry with the situation. "I'm not angry with you, Tessie. Naturally," he said. "Only what gets me a little sore is that after all I am me. See, I am I. I feel that a funny I lives in my body and in that way I am so separate and, let us say, different from you, who are only something outside of me. I mean I get sore when you do this kind of thing with me." He had grown disgusted with himself and the muddled paste he had been saying. That time Philip had grabbed his hat and walked out while Tessie called after him that there was no reason why they couldn't remain good friends. There was no good reason why she couldn't go to hell, he wanted to yell back, but he had resolved to keep his mouth shut once for all.

That was a month ago, and all month Tessie had struggled with her eternal soul in an effort to discover truth, which in this instance was clouded by the shadowy influence of the movies. And now she was great love, recklessly forgoing, like the lady in the green hat, the material considerations, and going back to Philip. Schlausser was a purveyor of women's sundries, corsets and brassieres, he was stout and set, a good husband for the having. Philip had dizzy spells but she, ah, loved him, and love would always out. "About Schlausser," she had been saying with traces of tearful sorrow in her eyes, "about Schlausser, he is nothing to me. I've been thinking it over. A girl has to marry, you can see that, Philip. And that was why it was that way with me. But just for the moment, because as soon as I had definitely decided to marry him, the prospect became real and I knew immediately I couldn't do it. Let us both forget about it, Philip, it means nothing to me now."

Ah, Tessie, Tessie, who studies the amorous postures of movie stars and tries them out on me, Philip thought; Tessie, who even borrows the subtitles and says them as if they meant something. Once she rode on top of a Fifth Avenue bus and saw the signs, the well-dressed people, Maison Blanc, Lazar Frères et Cie, Black, Starr, Frost, and Gorham, and she could not elude the effect. "What are you saying?" Philip had drawled, as though he hadn't the slightest idea what it was all about. His awkwardness a month ago still nettled and he was determined to carry this off finely. "Don't be a baby, Tessie. Everything's all right. Forget all about it," he had said, and then casually, as though everything was of a piece, he rushed across the room to greet a friend and to leave Tessie hanging in midair, barely having completed reel one.

A piece of the membrane of the apple core squeezed itself between Philip's front teeth. While he sucked air vainly to dislodge it, Cohen came up shakily with a bottle of gin. Cohen liked to fake drunkenness upon the least provocation but this evening he was really half gone. However, he was capitalizing upon the authenticity of his inebriety and was experiencing a great emotion.

"Have a drink." He swayed over Philip. "It shuts the eye, Hayman, it destroys Gehenna, obliterates the Everlasting Nay, and relieves the soul's torment."

Philip placidly held the bottle in his hand. Gin always made him feel as though he had been etherized. He examined the square-edged bottle carefully.

"Someone must be playing a joke on you, Cohen," he said finally. "This isn't gin, it's ordinary urine."

Cohen seized the bottle from his hand, sniffed it, and held it to the light. He wagged his finger at Philip. "Oh, my brother, my brother," he wept. "Oh, my brother."

The radio's cracked music poured out. As the girls danced Philip could see the bare knees where the stockings stopped. He looked for the little soft roll of flesh above the rubber garters. It was an amusing pastime. Some fellows lifted Cohen up from the floor and took the bottle away from him. "The evening's young yet," they protested.

Tessie stopped Philip at the door. She was big-eyed with solitary sorrow.

"You're going?" she asked.

"It's getting late," Philip said, "and it's hot as hell."

Tessie's eyes softly pinpointed reproach. Why do you torture me? they whispered. Am I not sufficiently humiliated? Forgive me, love me. At a Park Avenue penthouse the lovely gentlemen glide over the carpets with their hands nonchalantly in their pockets while their heads stick out above high wing collars like chrysanthemums. Fascinating women in liquid gowns flow and ebb as they move from group to group of men. Wafting through the still summer night air the far-off dim music murmurs its sad melodies. Tessie, glorious and devastating, haunts the terraces alone in her grief. Why do you torture me? Am I not sufficiently humiliated? Forgive me, love me.

"Well," said Philip, "I'll see you later."

"I'll be waiting tonight, Philip," she said in a low tone, her eyes on the floor, "after they go."

"I can't say whether I can be here tonight."

"I'll be waiting, anyhow. Come to my room and walk in. The way we used to."

"I don't know," repeated Philip.

"I'll be waiting."

"I don't know."

Philip went down the stairs. After the heat in the house the evening breeze was a relief and he decided to walk home.

Philip met his brother hanging around the house on Ripple Street.

"Hello," Philip said warmly, surprised. "What are you doing here? I thought you were in Havers Falls now."

"I got in the next bus after Papravel. We've been doing some work at the Williamsburg office but I have to get right back. How's it been?"

"All right," said Philip. "Come on up. Mom would like to see you."

"It's Pop. I don't like to get him bothered. I was around and I thought I'd like to see Mom, but I didn't know how it would strike the old man."

"Come on up," said Philip. He liked the way his brother was afraid of his father. It meant he liked the old man in spite of his letters and what he said. There was something in the old man. This was not his time nor world, but given the proper setting his father was a man. "Come on up. There's no sense in hanging around the street this way."

"All right," Harry said. "I can only stay a minute." He was glad he had bunked into the kid. It would make it easier now.

Harry's mother immediately rushed to him. "Look, Max," she cried, "look who's here."

"A guest. Truly a guest," the old man said, sour, but nevertheless trying to bring some feeling into his voice. While Mrs. Hayman fussed over him, asking a hundred questions, seeking to make him comfortable, Harry could feel his father's disapproval as he smoked a cigarette in the corner to cover the pretense that he was unaffected by his son's homecoming.

"I was in the neighborhood for a minute and I thought I'd drop in to see you," Harry said. He spoke rapidly, feeling uncomfortable before the old man. "We're doing a little work here tonight but I got to rush back in a minute. It's a good season. Everybody's going away this summer. Why don't you and Pop get out of here and go up the mountains yourselves?"

Mrs. Hayman set a small glass of whiskey and a piece of bread in front of him on the table. "It's a holiday, you come so seldom," she laughed. Harry held up the glass and fumbled the toast. Philip noticed the way his father's hand trembled as he brought the thimble of whiskey to his lips. He's getting old, Philip thought, and abruptly a rush of feeling for the old man filled him. He's getting old and Momma's worn and Harry's on his way, already a stranger, while I, of course, I move along the moonlit paths like a moving-picture star untouched by life, detached and above. It has happened a million times, they will say, it is an old story, we are not the first to inhabit this world. But this is the first world we have inhabited and these old stories mean something new and fresh to us. A man is born, grows and grows, and dies, and here is Pop getting on and nearer his time and it is an old story, they will tell him, but death is always new.

"I must be going," Harry was saying. "I just dropped in for a minute. I've got to get back on the job."

When he left there was an empty silence. Philip's mother knew there was nothing to be said but she resented the old man's coolness. "He's your son," she said quietly. "He's your son." The old man would not say anything until she had gone to her bedroom.

"Put the cigarette in the sink," he said to Philip. He had done this when the boys were young and now it made no difference that Philip was grown. He took the butt from his father's hand and dropped it into the sink.

"I just left a party, Pa," he said. "I don't know, maybe I'm getting too old for parties. What did you do when you were kids?"

"Oh, then it was different, everything was different," his father said. "It was like a different world."

"Tell me," said Philip. "What do you mean?"

"Ah, in the old days, in the old country, people were, you know, friends, brothers. A man did not have to work all the time, money wasn't so important. Life was easier, more pleasant. In the old days people came down to the village to town to dance as though it were a religious law to be merry. And the music they made! You'll never hear it, Philip. It's gone, you know, gone. Zither and fiddles, fifes. What music they made! And, you know, they did not even know how to read the notes!" He laughed from the fun, walking up and down the room, absentmindedly going through the motions of playing a fife until he remembered Philip and stopped, embarrassed.

"Yes, it is nice to think of those days, the zither and fiddles," he said. "Of course, maybe that's how it feels now, it is so many years away. But no, I remember, I remember, for example, when there was to be a wedding. My, you should have seen it. It doesn't happen anymore. When a man was going to get married his friends went with him to buy the cloth. If he was a rich man, the tailor, the tailor's whole establishment, moved into the groom's house to make the suit. Oh, what a time! They laughed. They cried. Years and years later, he would wear the suit, or perhaps only the coat, and he would always say, very proud, 'This suit, now, I made it at my wedding.'

"Now they go into a store and hire it. 'Say, what do you want to get married for?' the dealer wisecracks. 'I'll tell you, George, I never wore a full dress. I want to feel how swallow tails are and I guess this is the only chance I'll ever have.' Ah, people aren't honest with themselves or with one another anymore."

The old man, lost in reverie, hummed as he undressed for bed. It was after eleven o'clock and past his bedtime. He removed his collar and slipped down the suspenders to take off his shirt, and again, as upon how many other evenings, he spread his legs in that odd posture to keep his trousers from falling. Philip had to smile at it, he never changed.

"When a daughter was to be married," the old man went on, "what a noise in the house! You know, for months they planned. And the wedding week—it took a week to get married in those days—the wedding week, oh, my!"

As he went to bed, he snorted happily, coughed, and cleared his throat. Then his face clouded. For the moment he had forgotten Harry and his sharp disappointment over him because, against his wishes, he had gone to work for Papravel.

"Have you got it? Again?" Philip couldn't believe it. Where could Mahler have gotten the money for such a lovely drunk?

"Sure I got it. I got it something fine." Cohen's hero giggled in high spirits. "Look, I got it all the way up here." Mahler saluted at his Adam's apple. His hands were bony and resembled an X-ray. "All the time we drank and drank the wine."

"You can't get drunk on wine. You only drown," said Philip.

"Sharrap!" the drunk snapped. "Cohen, too, he's got it."

"Cohen, too, he's got it? Well, that's fine. When did he get here?"

"Hah!" screamed Mahler. A huge face with a thousand wrinkles, each and every one of them signifying the soul's oppression, quoth Cohen, but inspecting him now all Philip could see was an old skinny man with a tremendous purple-veined nose. "Hah! Cohen took me down to Mrs. Miller's barrel and we both got it. Good. Up to here!" The X-ray went to his throat again. He stamped his feet in a paroxysm of glee.

"Where's Cohen?" Philip wanted to know.

"He went away. He got sick and cried. He said it was torturing him. Cohen, he's got it too."

"I know," said Philip. "I'll be back in a minute." He looked at his watch and went off.

"Sharrap!" snapped the old man to his back.

Philip ran up to Cohen's room and found it neat and empty. A few pictures, cut out from *transition* and backed with beaverboard, hung above the bed. They were some reprints of Picasso, the long faces and wavy guitars, a print of Epstein's *Mother and Child*, and, placed among them, a cover of *The Saturday Evening Post* by Norman Rockwell. An oval hooked rug lay neatly on the floor.

Philip wondered what had happened to Cohen. Seeing the light in the boiler room he had thought Cohen had gone to sleep there, but he had found only Mahler. Some day Cohen would play a little too hard with his beautiful soul and get banged up. Philip worried because this time he had been drunk. He went back to the cobbler.

"Cohen's fine," he said. "Who told you he was stiff? Cohen's upstairs eating an Eskimo Pie and reading the *Ladies' Home Journal*."

"Keep quiet!" Mahler squeaked, angry because Philip had left him alone so long.

"Oh, say, Mahler," Philip said. "Cohen says he just won the Irish Sweepstakes."

"Don't believe it!" Mahler drew within himself.

"Cohen just won the Irish Sweepstakes. He's got $125,000."

"*Don't believe it!*" the old man almost cried. With all his soul he didn't believe it.

"I don't know. Cohen says he just won the Irish Sweepstakes. You think he's fooling?"

"Don't believe it!" shrieked the old man. He made so much noise that he scared himself. "What'll he do with all the money anyhow?" he asked quietly.

"He'll go off, I suppose. Cohen says he's going to stop hanging around here in this flat because Mrs. Linck never takes away the garbage cans and the stink comes straight up to his room. Cohen says God didn't make people like him to live with such stinks. He says he's going to quit. Cohen says he's going to get himself a flock of chorus girls and go off to China with seven of them on each lap. Cohen says he's sick and tired about those garbage cans under his window all the time. Cohen, he's got it."

"Oh, yes," said Mahler with a shy smile. "He's got it. Good."

Philip yanked him on top of his bed, opened his collar and pulled off his shoes. Mahler protested feebly. "Go to sleep, you bum," Philip said kindly. "Keep quiet now and sleep here." He looked around the room to see that everything was all right and snapped off the light. Mahler was left suspended. He was just beginning. "Put on the light," he ordered Philip. "Put it on, I say!"

"Go to sleep," Philip said, and closed the door.

"Put on the light!" Mahler called after him. "Put on the light!" he pleaded. Slowly, as water soaks into bread, his face filled with infinite sadness and self-pity.

"Put on the light," he begged. And then realizing that Philip was too far off to hear him and that he had gone for the evening, his lip trembled, and in another moment he was crying brokenheartedly.

Philip came up the basement steps. Across the street it was a big night at the Auburn S.C. The top-floor windows were dark while the members, nervously silent, smoked cigarettes on the front porch, and Philip knew that meant surely the lineup. From time to time a man came down awkwardly, and forthwith another jerkily flipped his butt into the street, hitched his belt grimly, and hurried on. Ripple Street, too, had its social club. It occupied one of the few remaining shacks that were being torn down one after the other to make room for genteel apartment houses. In the daytime the young bloods shot pool in the basement or played punchball in the street. On gala Friday evenings dances were held on the parlor floor. In the backyard was a tastefully appointed garden, with suggestive stone love seats and a symbolic statue representing the tender joys of Cupid. It was a beautiful statue, and on Friday nights the members walked their partners self-consciously amid the beauty. But the great nights occurred when a lady—a prostitute or some gracious one of the girls—entertained the club en masse. Then there was an air of restrained feverish excitement. The members sent out boys far and wide to summon their absent friends. One by one they went up the stairs, dallied for five minutes, and returned chastened. As for the lady, she lay half drunk over the bedspread, giggling, filthy, sometimes asleep.

Collect, said Philip. This was the Auburn Social Club, and it had its advantages. Non-members were reduced to the more hazardous expediencies of seeking their lights o' love for themselves and utilizing rendezvous less ornate. Nearby was a lot where Halper's Stable stored wagons, and here gentle liaisons were consummated, although the floors of the wagons were hard and the appearance of kids, too old for their age, was a constant risk. Much more suitable, perhaps, were the roofs, especially on hot nights. Cool breezes blew from the East River, the roofs had a canopy of stars and the moon. Ledges and chimneys formed appropriate shadows. But for those who desired cloistered privacy the cellar was always available. Here were to be found the odd corners and out-of-the-way nooks cozily hidden in the labyrinth the stalls and foundation walls created. Further, in case of extreme necessity, there was always a convenient avenue of escape by way of the dumbwaiter. One could always kick up the middle shelf, squeeze in, hoist oneself to the second or third floor, and then walk respectably down through the halls.

"Shall I see Tessie tonight?" asked Philip, walking from the basement stairs. Through the streets, lighted brightly from the candy store, which rigged up for the evenings enormous electric bulbs, Italians drove their wagons, hawking watermelon in the unusually strident yells that were traditionally part of their trade. "Waw-de-melo, melo, melo, melo," they cried, prolonging the "melo"s into a soft diminuendo, and taking great pride in their talent. The constant merry-go-rounds added to the din with their horny music. Every summer for some reason the gas or electric or telephone company ripped open the pavements in trenches that ran for blocks, and now the yellow, lifeless earth dirtied the whole street, giving out an overpowering gassy odor.

In summer Williamsburg lived in the open, on fire escapes, on roofs, in lots, and on the sidewalks. The men sat late into the night without shirts cooling off from the heat of the day, waiting for their rooms to air in the night breeze. The women talked loudly in a social world of their own, drinking soda water and fanning themselves incessantly with strips of cardboard. Periodically a gale of noisy laughter rose to the heavens, which were above the lights of the lamppost.

A group of children ran around deviously, smoking punks to keep off flies and mosquitoes, chasing one another through the chairs that cluttered the sidewalk, or playing games on the street. When they wanted to say something they did not talk, but screamed and shrieked from enthusiasm.

Now they play games, Philip said, various with the season, adapted to gutters and city streets. Kick-the-can, using the four corners at the intersections; Ringolevio, the elaborate form of hide-and-seek played over lots and yards; Johnnie-on-the-pony, a favorite at night, watched by groups of middle-aged men wondering at the agility of the children and at the same time sighing over their own lost spryness; one-foot-off on the street curb, and the other games. Now they play games for diversion and soon it will be the old thing all over again. They will be noticing cats lying on their sides in the yard with litters of kittens, and their wonder and awe will develop into the dirty jokes. Nights they will begin to haunt the roofs, hiding behind chimneys to spy upon the strangely agonizing movements of couples in the shadows. They will peek into cellars and parade up and down the streets with a rubber contraceptive on top of a pole as a standard.

They will grow bolder, said Philip. It is the same thing, the same old thing, only we are new in our lifetimes and it is again new. They will seek the breasts of little girls as they jam the wardrobes at school when the teachers send them for their clothes. The adventurous with their companions will explore the staircase on the top floor, leading to the roof and secluded. Occasionally an overaged pupil will walk into the classroom to be told she is pregnant.

Itching with curiosity they will go to the burlesque shows on

Throop Avenue and be disappointed. Under the guise of play they will wrestle with girls on the dark parts of South First Street, and they will take them out for bicycle rides to McCarren Park, there to embrace. Their turn will come for the business in the cellars, on the roofs, in the wagons in Halper's lot. They will join the Auburn Social Club and flip cigarette ends over the dirty lawn as they wait nervously. It is the old thing, said Philip, it is the old thing all over again. They do not stop doing it, it goes on.

"Shall I see Tessie tonight?" Philip asked, although he knew.

⁓⁓⁓

Davey, little Davey who had been so successful with Yetta, the girl of his dreams, Davey had a vision in his sleep. On certain occasions he dreamt of watermelon, fat, juicy slices of cool watermelon. Once Philip had saved a rotten melon that had turned vinegary solely to see what effect it would have on Davey. While the boy was asleep he broke the fruit into rough, inviting chunks, placed it before Davey, and then gently waked him. Davey opened his eyes with irritation, perceived the chunks, and in the fogginess of sleep rushed headlong into the juicy mess. Philip would prize for a long time the recollection of his face as Davey pulled it out of the watermelon.

A day ago, however, he had been to the movies where he had seen Adolphe Menjou wearing evening clothes exclusively in a picture called *The Ace of Cads*. It was a moving idyll and it was set among the fascinating rich of London, people who always impressed Davey acutely because he wondered invariably, do these people go to the bathroom too? In the picture Adolphe Menjou is very much in love with a beautiful lady who wears organdy all the time and is the very picture of maidenly innocence. Somewhere between the cocktails and the flashy automobiles a social mishap occurs and in the ensuing developments Adolphe Menjou takes the blame. "What?" says the father of the organdy. "You, a cad, would marry my daughter?" He is flabbergasted. Adolphe Menjou shifts his eyes weariedly and takes a long cigarette from a silver case. "Oh, goodness gracious," murmurs the organdy, and she runs weeping to her bedroom, which means, you're out. Adolphe Menjou looks as though somebody has pushed him in the chest, his eyebrows say, Dear me, dear me, this is terrible, and he takes out another long cigarette from the case. Now he is smoking two long cigarettes simultaneously and he is overwhelmed with grief and there is nothing more to do. The old man says, "There is the door" or something, and Adolphe Menjou puts on his cape and walks out, his eyes looking as though they have gone blind suddenly; if you passed your hands in front of them they would not flicker. Outside it is raining, and he walks in the rain, walks slowly, smoking the cigarettes, in his misery unconscious of the rain. Suddenly there is the patter of small feet. "Oh, my darling, my poor darling." It is the organdy. The eyes grow good again, Adolphe Menjou throws away the two cigarettes, he smiles and grabs her in his arms, and this means, the picture is over, please walk out quietly, no yelling, no whistling, please.

Davey had left the movie house, his eyes blank and weak. Boy, said Davey, that's it, I wish I grow up fast. Every time he would put his hands in his pockets there would be nickels and dimes, he could go to the icebox for watermelon whenever he wished. He would have affairs with exciting ladies in organdy and smoke long cigarettes. Boy, sighed Davey, hoping for man's estate, there's love for you. And now he dreams a lady in organdy is coming down to him, only he can't make out whether it is organdy, she is so indistinct, and her face is so wonderful he can hardly see it. Everything is dark and mysterious. She plucks him to her as though they are swimming in water, and she clasps him to her bosom. Davey grows drowsy with love and from the look on her face it must be the same with her. They go down, down, down, their forms slowly revolving, embraced in sleepy concentration. Now she is above him, now he is above her, their figures entwined so that they resemble a Siamese twin mermaid. And this goes on and on.

Mahler, the cobbler, has a dream too. He is lying in his dirty underwear on the dirty bed in the boiler room, but he is in Paradise also. In Mahler's vision there is a bathtub, three or four times larger than usual, Mahler sees it and he makes his way to it but there are obstructions everywhere. It is like walking up endless stairs. He walks and there is always a heavy door to be swung open or a rock to be shoved aside. He goes on until in the end he is in the bathroom. There is the enormous bathtub and in it is wine. Mahler flops in and he opens his mouth. His nose becomes a mouth and he drinks with it. His ears become mouths, his eyes, his cheekbones. With his whole head, Mahler drinks the wine until finally the tub is empty. He stands up in the bathtub looking for more wine. There is no more. He gathers his long beard in his hands, pulls it over his face and slowly wrings the wine out of it.

Finally Mahler is finished and with a huge hole in his face he lies down and sleeps.

At her window sat Tessie, and she wondered, will he come tonight? Or should I go to sleep? She sat alone in darkness, detecting a pleasant unreality in the night. The party was over, they had all left, and she mused alone. My God, she said, am I suffering? Is this really how it is? Tessie tried to recall one of Mr. Hergesheimer's characters, a woman in similar straits, frigidly burning with sorrow, and wondered how she compared. She didn't know exactly, but it was being a little disappointing.

Cohen had been having a great time with his soul but now he was sober-minded, with a slight headache from the gin and wine, and he wondered how exactly he had come to the Canal Street station. He mixed himself mechanically with the stream of persons, walked around the tunnels to make his change, and stepped into a train.

A heavy person next to him said, "Mister, does this train go to Coney Island?"

"Oh, no," he said politely. "This is a Canarsie train."

"Beg pardon," chirped a stringy body at his other side. "This is a Sea Beach train."

"My error, I thought this was a Canarsie train."

The stringy individual began to tell him how he could make the appropriate changes to get back on the Canarsie local. Cohen tried to follow him but it was too complicated.

"Never mind," he said. "It doesn't matter. I'll go to Coney Island."

"Beg pardon?" said the stringy one, all amazed. From time to time he looked over his paper to inspect Cohen.

It was a long ride to Coney Island. Cohen sat back in a sleepy haze trying to forget his headache. The jumping, jerking train, the dull lightness with the filter-patches of darkishness, the other persons hiding behind the *Daily News* and the *Journal* as they picked their noses, the dirty, red clay floor with swills of mouse-colored dirt, the enameled hand supporters, the signs above: All tea is economical . . . here's the finest . . . keep your hands soft and white . . . in crowds . . . in dusty streets . . . GUARD——. . . year in and year out . . . always the same flavor . . . PLEASE keep hands off doors. . . .

Now they were entering the long stretches of rail where the express thundered along without irritating stops. Cohen was conscious of the pleasant pull beneath him. The jumping rhythm of steel wheels, gulping silvery rails, spitting them out again, crushed in white foam . . . Cohen liked it. Part by part, his body went to sleep, first his legs, then his arms, then the trunk. There was no sap in his body, as though he had been asleep.

What was the matter with him? Cohen asked himself. His head felt numb as he left the train at the Stillwell Avenue station. A disagreeable odor of bathing suits wet with salt water plus the odor of the thousands who had lived all day on the beaches, hit him as he stepped out. The restless, excited noise of the mælstrom came up to the elevated station. Numb, he went up the street to the boardwalk. From where he walked he could see into the flats, which sweaty persons from the East Side, Williamsburg, and the Bronx, come to the seashore for the summer, occupied. A life, that, thought Cohen: bedrooms and fried food and dripping bathing suits, and sand all the time.

On the boardwalk there came to him the confused din, petering out and dying. He heard the clumping of heels moving steadily, never pausing. He felt or saw the heat of the evening in the noise. From his right came the lights and the smells of concessionaires. Oh, you must come over, they besought him, you must come over . . . waw-haw-whooppee, hatta-patta chips fried in mah-zo-lah.

To his left was the blackness studded with weak, dead lights, and the whimper and moan of the buoys, and quiet.

His mind was still asleep from the train ride. Trying to escape his mood, he inexplicably grew furious with himself. As he walked his dissatisfaction increased in violence. He began to screw his head from side to side in hot desperation. The roar of a car, thundering down the rails of a scenic railway, filled his ears. Cohen recalled in a blurred way a newspaper story about a woman who had stood up in the excitement of the ride and consequently smashed her head when she hit a beam above.

He rushed to the entrance in a stimulated burst, wondering what it was he was doing and at the same time afraid to hesitate lest he lose courage. He slapped the quarter on the board and settled himself in the wooden car. There was something of a wait until the barker outside cajoled more customers. Cohen's uncertainty and yet his impatience to be off formed a mixture torturing and melting, but the wait was making him feel ridiculous. Then the car went and the wind rushed up.

There is a difference between killing yourself and actually doing it. It is hard, it is hard when all that is necessary to die is the act itself; just as, say, when at morning you try to get out of bed on a cold dark day: in your mind you order yourself to throw off the blankets, but your body, another's, not your own, remains in bed. Cohen saw the beam before him. Stand up! he cried to himself, soon you will be passing the beam, the opportunity will be lost. *Stand up!* His mind, his spirit rose; his body was still sweating on the wooden seat.

The experience sobered him, taking away the fierceness. Out of the thriller, he rested weakly against a wall while the gluey stream of people sluggishly flowed past him. He got the feeling that he was sitting on one of the bulbed half-moons of Luna Park, looking down at the stream from the sky. From his perch aloft he gazed stupidly down. He lost himself in the feeling for some minutes. Then, as if in a dream, he felt that terrible, gasping, speechless sensation of falling through the air from his half-moon. Cohen at the wall shook himself awake. He mustn't stop moving, he told himself. Slowly he made his way back to the boardwalk. Say, he asked himself, am I really dreaming all this? He tried to think about it and find out. Finally he said, no, I guess I'm not. He was conscious of a little pimple at the tip of his tongue that was beginning to burn. I'd never feel that in a dream, he said.

Cohen was moving up to the thirties. Distantly, like your mother's voice in the morning breaking into your consciousness when she awakes you, it was occurring to him that there was a crowd down below on the beach. It took a minute before he understood clearly that two persons in bathing suits were fighting in the sand.

Then Cohen suddenly jumped over the railing. He hadn't thought the beach was so far below and was stunned somewhat when he landed. Spitting out sand, he got his feet under him and began to run madly into the crowd. As he ran he brushed the sand off his clothes. As he ran he was telling himself it was crazy for him to be brushing his clothes just then. But he plunged through, the crowd making way for him because it was impressed by his rushing importance.

Cohen began to hit both fighters fiercely, wildly. They said, "Jesus, what the hell is this?" Cohen had come up with such a rush that he knocked them down. Then he began to strike out at the crowd. The people drew back, stumbling over one another and crying out scared, panicky noises in fright.

He was having his own crazy way when one of the fighters came up behind him and smashed him on the head. The crowd looked at his still form very much puzzled and interested.

After a minute one of the fighters began looking at the other, wondering whether to go on with the scrap. All interest in the fight had gone, but according to his code he had to continue fighting or else he'd be yellow. He tried to work himself into anger. You could see him egging himself on.

"Damn you," he finally said. "Crazy guy or no crazy guy, you can't say what you said to me and get away with it." He rushed in.

"Yay," yelled the crowd. "Give it to him so's he'll know it."

The fighters jumped about and moved off. The circling crowd moved along with them as they danced; after a few minutes they were all some distance away from Cohen.

Cohen had come to in a little while, but he lay with his head sunk into the sand until the heat left him. His blood raced dizzily around him. Crazily he saw again in his mind the image of two Chinamen whom he had once seen in a vaudeville house swinging through the air by their queues. Carefully now Cohen's mind followed them as they swung from side to side, from side to side.

When he arose he felt singularly cold and satisfied.

Late that night Papravel finally got Morand on the telephone. He was talking from Havers Falls and the operator had told Morand it was long distance calling.

"Morantz," he said kindly, "this is from a friend. You're going to have trouble. Be smart. You know already what happened today. Listen to me, I'm talking like a father, get out of Williamsburg because it's no good to you."

"Who's talking? Who's talking?" Morand's cracked voice came through the earpiece.

"What difference does it make who's talking, Morantz? It's the best friend you have in the world, believe me. Listen to me, get out and get out in a hurry. Because all that's happened already is only the prologue, and if you insist on being stubborn, may Heaven help you."

"I know who it is, you cutthroat!" the voice screamed in a fury. "I want you to know this and I'll say it with the last breath in my body. I'm no ninny, I'm not afraid. I'll fight you and Rubin with my last penny and until I'm in my grave, may you both rot in hell. May your bones be twisted in their sockets, may your eyes be screwed to the back of your skull, may God strike you with a bolt of lightning! Till I'm dead and buried in my grave I'll fight you, and tell Rubin for me, tell him may his belly foster cancers and ulcers, may his tongue grow swollen and hang from his mouth like a beard, may a subway train run over his stinking body, Goddamit!"

From the other end came a sharp click. Papravel hung up.

"Goddamit yourself!" he bellowed at the telephone on the wall, and then it was that he first began to grow angry with Morand.

Philip felt a little chilled walking down the street to the trolley so late at night, but on top of that feeling he was aware all the time of a soothing new sense of power. He put his hands into his pockets and walked with jaunty step until he reached the street corner. "Don't come back any more," she had said. To beguile the wait for the trolley Philip began jigging and dancing because he was satisfied with himself and sure.

Streets at night are gray and ghostly. Are there no ghosts in Williamsburg? The lamppost lights were shining stupidly in the emptiness of the streets. A man hurried by in the shadows and the two eyed each other suspiciously. On the building across the way were reflected the telephone wires above him. They looked like long, black fingers of a skeleton. "Go home, Philip," she had said. "Go home, Philip." When he had risen from the couch she held him close and would not let him go. "Go home, Philip, go home, Philip." Philip, my boy, oo Philip mon gar, je vouzem, je touzen.... It was late as hell. Philip was half dead from sleep.

"Cab?" It made him feel a little self-conscious when he had to shake his head at taxi drivers. The cabs scuttled around the corners like scared mice. Like Moishe. A little mouse that used to come out of the holes. When he was up late at night cramming or reading books, Philip got to look forward to seeing him, and he called him Moishe. Well, well, well, here is little Moishe again. How's it been with you, my young friend. Here, don't get scared. Come here, Moishe, old boy. P'sst, p'sst, p'sst, Moishe. "Don't come back," she had said.

Why wouldn't the trolley come? Philip stepped off the curb and looked down the street. One headlight in the center would mean that the car was coming. Philip saw only the double lights of the autos. By putting his ear to the rails it would be possible to hear whether a trolley was on its way. It would look strange if anyone saw him doing that. Philip stepped back to the curb. For a moment he thought of walking the distance home, but he was too sleepy.

Chase the blues away . . . he stopped. It annoyed him considerably that he was singing a popular tune in his mind. That went back to the party tonight, back to waxed floors with dancer's lines, to *True Story* magazine and the *Daily Mirror*. He switched to Tchaikovsky's Fourth, going over the sad little melody. It took some time before he recalled it, but he got there. If you got to hum, hum something classical, he said. "I'm helpless, Philip. Go home, Philip," Tessie said. "For the love of Pete, cut it out," he replied gently. She held him close and wouldn't let him go. Her hair got into his mouth. "I'm chewing your hair." "Oh, go home, Philip." He got up but she held on so that he had to lift her from the couch. She weighed his head down as they stood. "You've got a swell pair of shoes on," he had said. That had been all he could see in that position. "Oh, go home, Philip, go home." My old Kentucky home, good night. Weep no mo', my lady, Oh, weep no mo'. . . .

He was very sleepy when the trolley finally came. On the ride home he dozed off, but the conductor promised to wake him when they came to his corner.

FIVE

TWO ITALIANS, ONE NEGRO, and three Jews, besides Harry Hayman and Gilhooley, were installed in a farmhouse off Aligerville. Aligerville is a tiny town near Havers Falls, and Papravel had installed his boys there because he wanted people in Williamsburg to forget their faces until the excitement over the wrecking of the Silver Eagle office had passed. They had slept all morning coming up on the bus and were mildly belligerent when they first viewed the house. But it turned out later that they were going to have a good time, and at the expense of Papravel.

Mrs. Van Curen, who owned the place, was a shriveled little lady past ninety, the last of the Van Curens who had first come to the mountains in the eighteenth century and who had a private cemetery to establish that fact. She had the odor of piety, but that is natural for people her age. Nevertheless, when Papravel offered her thirty dollars a day for the men she thought the sky had fallen out of the heavens. The old lady was tremendously grateful, and after a while it began to grow a little trying. But the men soon came to hold a sort of affection for her.

It was an old house, perhaps a hundred years old, and it was filled with a thousand and one gimcracks, the accumulation of generations. Also, with a smell, neither pleasant nor unpleasant but definitely a part of the place. At night these hoodlums slept under elaborately decorated panels that said gaudily "Home, Sweet,

Home." The quilts were many and soft, and they would lie in a bath of warmth listening to the country night noises, and they were awed with the strangeness.

For a lady of her years, Mrs. Van Curen was remarkably sound in mind. All day, while the men sat on the old-fashioned chairs, whose stuffings escaped at the ends, and while the cigarette smoke piled to an almost solid substance underneath the ceiling, she dispensed in a cracked voice stories of the old days to entertain the visitors. How the country was seventy and eighty years ago, the wild animals that had roamed the forests, the Indians who used to scalp the girls when they went out on the hills. She was a spry individual. Mrs. Van Curen read the *Literary Digest* and was installing a hot-water boiler. In the end the men were obliged to spend their time elsewhere, and then it was that they first discovered the mountains.

Originally, as everyone knows, the mountains were settled by the Dutch, but for the most part they are now tenanted by the Jews. In the winter the countryside still manages to retain a rural aspect, but all this is changed with the summer months. The state highway becomes a Broadway, there are dance halls, casinos, even chop-suey joints, canoes on the lake, couples in the brush, and whiskey bottles strew every path. Hayman went for the girls. He was in his element, telegraphed home for a trunk of clothes, and was having a great time. Gilhooley confined himself to the liquor. He was an unreliable man, had once belonged to the Hooper Street gang, a notorious hooligan outfit, and had no head for business. Papravel often worried over him. Gilhooley had found an Italian place where the liquor was plentiful, and he was satisfied with the mountains. The others, with two Nashes at their disposal, distributed their attentions widely and variously.

Papravel alone had his nose to the grindstone. In a short time he had created for himself a great reputation for goodness. It is remarkable how a few random acts of kindness build a legend. Papravel had once helped a man, stuck for gas, by going to the trouble of drawing it from his own car through a pipe. But, in addition, noting that one of the stranger's tires was going flat,

Papravel had insisted he accept a tube and refused payment. Mrs. Van Curen, who considered the city gentlemen little short of princes, circulated the story widely, and Papravel's fame grew. Everywhere he went he carried with him that air of importance that is tempered with the milk of kindness. Local politicians and drugstore hangers-on grew to like him enormously. The state troopers in their kiddie cars never failed to greet him cordially as they drove past. And Rubin, who grumbled from time to time at the sums of money be had to hand him, nevertheless was secretly proud and pleased with his new assistant manager.

Harry Hayman wrote to his brother:

> If you knew what a sap you are! You stay in Williamsburg, rolling in the sweat and dirt, while here I am in Havers Falls having the time of my life. Papravel knows how to take care of his boys. He's no piker. We live in a house that's run by some Gentile dimwit, and she takes care of everything for us. When it's hot we go swimming. And at night, Philip, you never saw women like these. In the canoes, off the roads, and in the houses. I suppose they're the same kind you see home, but when they get up here, they feel it's a holiday, they can get away with anything they like, and you have a hard time keeping up with them. Maybe it's the air.
>
> Why don't you think over Papravel's offer? I suppose he'll give you a job whenever you ask for it. Don't be a fool. Pop may have his principles, but where does it get him? A flat in a dirty tenement, the subway in the rush hour, and an early death. Look ahead. That's exactly what you can expect if you keep on with your ideas. But you won't. Sooner or later you'll break away from your crazy ideals, and you may as well start early. Money is everything, remember that, and nobody can make a living honestly.
>
> You're a schlemiel. Anyhow I'd like to have you come up and spend some time here. The change will do you good and perhaps you'll decide to stay with the boys.

The crowd collected in knots under the circular wooden signs that indicated where the doors of the different trains opened. As time went on, the knot grew larger and became more compact. Philip and Cohen were beginning to grow a little uncomfortable, but both smiled and retained their good humor. A man next to Philip continually looked up at the sign to see if he wasn't being pushed too far away. He was skinny and small and seemed sour. Cohen smiled. "Look, he's worried," he said. It was the first time Cohen had been in a rush hour with Philip and for his benefit he was professing a great poetic interest in the phenomenon.

From the other end the Canarsie train slowly came out of the darkness and lumbered on its rails up to the platform. Cohen was considerably affected by the sight. He reduced himself to awe.

"Like the head of some enormous monster, Hayman," he said. "With those green and red lights in this darkness, with its bulk and its sinister silence, it has a certain majesty, a certain—you get what I mean, Hayman."

Philip, who used the B.M.T. frequently and knew Cohen used it frequently, said, "What's the matter with you? Are you pulling that stuff on me again?" He was a little tired, and disinclined to bear with Cohen. He wished he would shut up.

Just then the train slowed down and the knot of people became suddenly animated. There was a tremendous push to the doors although everyone knew they wouldn't be opened for a full minute. Some of the people were turned sideways and lost their footing. Clothes were yanked out of order. A man's hat was knocked askew and fell over his eyes. He had some difficulty before he could free a hand to fix it. In the squeeze a girl cried out in a thin, tearful voice, "Please, please." The man who was pressed against her was apologetic but couldn't help himself. "I'm sorry, miss. It's not me who's doing the shoving." His face was flushed and moist with perspiration. A woman with red eyes and a big mouth became violent in the stress of the moment. "For cri' sakes," she said in an outraged tone, "why don't you have a heart?" Few paid any attention to her and she lapsed into self-conscious quiet. Then three Italian girls in black clothes suddenly broke out into excited giggles that soon grew into screams. There were always Italian girls in black dresses who screamed, Philip thought.

When the doors opened there was a wild race for the seats. They half fell in the rush, caught themselves and darted for a place as though they were all playing some child's game. A foreign-looking man, his face full of anxiety, ran to a seat and missed. "Goddam," he muttered deeply. "Goddammit." He almost cried from vexation.

Cohen had been jammed against the door and had had a struggle before he was able to get in. When he finally rejoined Philip his breath was pretty much gone but he remained triumphant. "Did you see them squeeze me against the door?" he asked. "I thought they'd crack something." He drew his jacket in place and composed himself. "I knew I'd lose something. A button got pulled off. And yet," he said exultantly, "how vital, how living, these people are. What force, what—how dynamic—the surge of the crowd. Essentially it is a poetic thing, Hayman. Believe me."

Philip was tired. It had started to rain and the air in the subway car was thick with mugginess. His throat was dry and it was hard for him to speak. He mumbled something about horse excrement and when Cohen said, "What?" Philip said, "Never mind. Let it go, only stop blowing the bull in my direction." Soon the train pulled out around the curve and was on the bridge. It settled down to a steady run. Philip liked the sensation of the movement and lost himself in it. As for Cohen, with his goggling eyes he continued to feed upon the wonders of the scene.

Philip and Cohen walked down the street from the elevated station. After the crowded train Philip welcomed the fresh air even though the rain kept dripping.

"Say, Cohen," he said, "what happened after you left the party? I found Mahler pickled and he said the two of you had been working on Mrs. Miller's wine. But after that what happened to you?"

Behind the glasses Cohen's eyes assumed a look of profundity. Cohen was really passably built but he held himself so peculiarly at the hips and knees that the effect of his physique was at once comic. His face was red in blotches from acne. Through the pimples and the red patches protruded a thick pair of lips, and above, over the big round spectacles, strings of his oily hair were plastered down over his forehead in a weird arrangement. Lips, eyeglasses, and hair, thought Philip, that's my lovely friend Cohen. Cohen's eyes welled with the blankness that denotes wisdom. He was giving the impression of reluctance.

"You wouldn't understand, Hayman," he said. "You'd only laugh. For a time I wandered. I walked and rode all over New York. It was mystical. I had no idea where I was going, yet all the time I felt impelled by some mysterious force to keep myself in constant movement. I saw strange sights, met with strange people, and ran through the gamut of extraordinary sensations. Everything was cloudy and filled with mist. In some way I finally came to Coney Island, to its beaches. There was a fight, I was beaten, I forget. There was always the ocean and the fog. That night was unreal. No man, I am certain, ever experienced its like."

"Cohen," Philip said, "let me tell you something like an old friend. What you need is a good woman. Don't you ever run around with girls? You should find one and play parchesi with her. Otherwise, some fine day you will be playing with that great mind of yours and get yourself in serious trouble. That's a prophecy."

"Hayman," Cohen said, "you don't understand. What do I need girls for? In the flesh they are a care and a nuisance. If you have the necessary imagination reality is unnecessary. I have a powerful capacity to visualize, and that is enough. Seriously, let me tell you about an experience I had. Once I lay on my bed, willing myself to think of one thing. In my intense absorption, utilizing every bit of imagination I possessed, I created for myself a beautiful lady. Everything was to my order. I wooed her, I slept with her, and so powerful was my illusion it was real."

"Dear me," said Philip, "that's the best one yet."

Mahler, that gaunt silent corpse from the Siberian wastes, Mahler, Cohen's hero, was sick with bronchial disorders. Today there would be no nap in the sun for him. Every time he took a deep breath it sounded like a soft breeze blowing through the treetops. Cohen and Philip dropped in on the old man in his bedroom behind the shoe store. In the store itself a half-dozen kids were playing a newly invented game. There were lemons all over the floor and they skated gaily on them. The kids whooped with delight as they skidded and rolled over the floor.

Inside, the sick man lay on his back, a blanket up to his rusty beard. He held his hand to his head.

"Go away, Yente Maldick," he wept at a brown old woman over him, "Why don't you go away?"

When he saw Philip and Cohen, he turned to them for salvation. "Some enemy I have told this old fool I was sick, and she came to see that I don't escape the grave. Will you put her out for me? I'm a sick man, I can't get out of the bed. Do me that favor." He was overcome and collapsed.

"I told her, since she was here already, she might make me some tea with lemon," Mahler sobbed. "What does she do? I give her a dollar to buy a lemon and she goes out and brings back a whole sack of them. She buys lemons with the whole dollar. Now the children all over the neighborhood come here to skate."

Cohen left the dingy bedroom to shoo the kids out of the store.

"Yente Maldick," Philip said, "why don't you go to Havemeyer Street? You're late. You'll miss the rush."

She was a very old, bent woman, who kept herself alive by peddling pretzels at Havemeyer Street. Here pushcarts and open-air stores did a sort of bazaar business at bargain prices. Yente Maldick sold her pretzels without ever having taken the trouble to secure the proper license. She simply squatted on a convenient stoop, listlessly croaking inducement to the passing shoppers while her head, under her kerchief, steamed with perspiration.

"Business can wait," Yente said, preoccupied. "The poor man has no one to help him. No one is too old to do a holy good deed. He's sick, poor man. Don't mind what he raves."

"What are you doing now?" Philip said. She was continually shuffling over the room, getting into the kitchen and back.

"I'm making a little oatmeal for the sick man. He hasn't had a drop of water."

"I don't want oatmeal!" Mahler suddenly shrieked with all his strength.

Philip quieted the old man. Yente Maldick went back to the stove. She herself lived in the basement of an old shack, and her perpetual torment was the stray men of the neighborhood. These in passing often mistook the gloom and filth of her quarters for an abandoned cellar and appropriated the space for a convenient toilet. Yente was always on the lookout for them, running up to them in the midst of their delicate operations. She held a chamber pot and yelled, "Not here, not here, please. Here's something, my child. Not here." But helpless as she was, Yente Maldick felt herself appointed to take care of the old man and she was everlastingly at him.

As Cohen came out of the store he felt a wave of excitement coming from the kitchen. Philip and he ran in. There was Yente Maldick in a panic, running about in her worn slippers as she seized pots and pans, saucers and cups. She had dumped the whole box of oatmeal into a pot. Now it was expanding and spreading all over the stove. Further, Yente didn't like to see any of it going to waste, and she ran around furiously trying to catch the overflow. Chairs and tables held the pots of oatmeal as though they were vases of flowers.

Philip left Cohen to wrestle with Yente Maldick and to do what he could for the old man. As he walked out of the store he saw women and children running down to the street. It was some mishap again and no one in Williamsburg would miss it. Philip went with the stream of people down the block.

In one of the remaining small houses in the neighborhood, a middle-aged man had committed suicide by hanging himself in the cellar of his house. A neighbor going down on some errand was the first to see the terrible spectacle. She screamed. The ambulance had come and was already leaving. Now the suicide's wife walked up. She had been to the market at Havemeyer Street, her paper bags were full, and she was tired.

"What's happened?" she asked. "What's the matter?"

No one had the heart to tell her the sad news. A woman finally spoke up and said some man had hanged himself in the cellar.

"The rotten bum," the wife said, "he had to use my cellar?"

Everyone felt sorry for the suicide and his family, but it was a good story. They would keep on telling it for a week. Somebody in the crowd suddenly remembered about Meyer Sussman and said, "What's the matter, is there an epidemic?"

Philip remained in the drizzle for some time after most of the others had left. Was it an epidemic? He tried to find out what had led the man to kill himself. Everyone who spoke had another reason and Philip had to give it up in the end.

As he went home, he thought of Old Miller and his discussion with him over Sussman. "Certain men are the sum of a million infinitesimal phenomena and experiences. A million atoms of a certain type produce, in the end, wood, just as a million of another produce stone, others iron, others gold. The same is true of these men, only here the atoms are no physical substance but psychical, and further they do not belong to any one type but are variously commingled." So spake the sage in the long beard. Well, thought Philip, collect. He stopped at the cleaning store on the corner and took home with him the extra pair of trousers of his suit. They were pressed with a crease to dazzle a girl's eye (fifteen cents) and he shielded them carefully from the rain. Philip had a date with Tessie.

Schlausser was back, Schlausser was back. He had, in the warm days of his courtship, given Tessie a set of Eugene O'Neill's *Collected Plays*, and subsequently had brought her additions to the set as that gentleman produced more works. By accident, misguided or not, the latest volume had coincided with her decision to give him up for Philip, and the O'Neill book, finely printed and impressive, once again signified respectability, solidness, and marriage. She loved Philip, but he was so dippy sometimes, and a girl had to get married, that was how it was. Tessie reconsidered, and in the meantime Schlausser was back. Now they were interminable at the cold, glass-topped dinner table. He and Tessie said nothing in the delicious, sentimental tones of genteel wooing, their figures tightened and balled up close to the table top in warmth, in the gladness.

Interminable they were, sentence and sentence, phrase and phrase, laugh and laugh. Outside the rain dripped. Philip stood at the window, romantically postured, to contemplate it, and it dripped, one of those lifeless rains that struggle through a whole day monotonously, ceaselessly. Well, he asked himself very seriously and very hopelessly, what could you do about it on a day like this? When he had walked in and discovered Schlausser there, he had been surprised for a moment, but then he had grasped the situation completely. He might have expected it. There was nothing to do, and he kept on smoking cigarettes one after the other until they made him feel dizzy. Philip went off toward the bedroom.

"Where are you going?" Tessie asked with tender attention to him. She was letting him down, she was talking with Schlausser, she had to be sweet with him.

"I'll be back in two minutes," Philip said. "I'm going to lie down."

"What's the matter?" Schlausser asked with earnest kindness. "You got a headache?"

"No," Philip said. "I just feel like lying down."

He went to the bedroom and stretched out in the dark. Why was he staying? Why didn't he leave? Let me tell you, my lovely Tessie, he said to himself, let me remind you in my most dispassionate manner how wildly I love you. However, here is Schlausser. Gather ye rosebuds, et cetera. How much of a jackass am I? Philip asked himself. He could hear their laughter as it rose above a monotone. He could see them smiling into each other's eyes. Philip rolled over and lay on his face.

My dear darling Sonia, my love, where are you? Oh, yes. In my dreams it always seems I kiss your little hand. Sonia, my love, I love you, I love you, you are the sweetheart of all my dreams. I'm crazy about you. Say, baby, just say the word and I'll hop atop the Empire State mooring mast and such love bear I for thee, I would right merrily float down to the pavement for you. What do you think of that, Sonia, my love? And this is a great deal for a man to say even though he might be kidding. Not twenty flights, not forty, not sixty, but think of it, one hundred and two flights for you and that, of course, does not include the mast itself.

But what is still unclear, Sonia, my love, is who the hell are you? Philip roused himself, the dizziness in his head was clearing, and he felt a good deal like a fool. All right, he said, I'm a dope, I fall in love with movie stars and there isn't even a great emotion for Tessie to turn down.

He went into the kitchen and hunted around familiarly in the wall closets for cocoa.

"Hey, kid, what are you doing?" Tessie asked with her tender attention.

"I'm making a cup of cocoa. You and Schlausser go to the movies too much, goosing into each other's eyes that way. Why don't you people make love like men?"

Schlausser giggled nervously, and then they were interminable again. A pan of water boiling, a pan of milk simmering, two teaspoonfuls of cocoa mixed with two of sugar, pour some boiling water in, make a paste, dump everything into the simmering milk, stir, stir, stir dreamily. Philip stirred dreamily. He liked Schlausser too, after a fashion. They made a logical pair, and even though Tessie might still be wavering, Philip knew that they would be married. Schlausser was all right. Do you take this man for your legally wedded husband? Da da dada, da da dada. The cocoa was hot. Philip fixed himself on two chairs and poured the cocoa into a saucer, sipping it cool. Was he not, if she looked at him, lovable in this manner?

Tessie's oldest sister, Bertha, came in. She was thirty-one and taught French and Spanish in a junior high school. As she removed her galoshes she looked tired and depressed.

"Say," she said, perceiving Schlausser and Tessie in the unlighted dining room, "I didn't think you would give up so easily. I wouldn't let anybody grab off my girl that way if I were a man."

"I send her to Schlausser's bed and board with my compliments," Philip said, hunched over his saucer of cocoa, and really very smooth. "I am a fickle young adolescent. Women, ach, women, I never love them, they love me. As the little ladies I go out with say, there's a hell of a lot of the Byron in me. What do you think?"

Bertha was in no mood for kidding. "All right," she said. "You kids can clear out of here. It's late, and I want to go to sleep."

"Bertie's sore," Tessie said, coming out of the dining room. "She's just been to the wedding of an old friend."

"I'll hit you with something," Bertha said calmly. She was almost bitter.

"Don't lose hope, baby," Philip said. "There's lots of chances yet. Millions believe in reincarnation."

"Oh, yare?" Bertha said.

"Poor kid," Philip said. "Here I'm only twenty and I'm beginning to know what it is to be without a woman now that Tessie is deserting me. It must be like hell to be thirty-one without a man."

"Oh, go to hell!" Bertie said savagely.

"I know it's pretty difficult to get one, even with all this loose talk going around. But on the level, Bert, don't be bashful. I'm in the same boat, what's the matter with me? I'll tell you what I'll do. Call me up any time you wish. Tessie's got my number."

Schlausser and Tessie laughed at this, and in the noise Bertha shoved them out into the hall.

Schlausser was beginning to take an interest in the proceedings. He had just started his conversation with Tessie and there was a great deal he had to say. "Do we have to go home now?" he asked with unmistakable regret.

"I got enough," Philip said. "I'm going to beat it."

"Well," said Tessie, "we can all go down to the cellar."

"Oh, that will be nice," Schlausser said joyfully.

"What are you thinking about?" Philip asked him.

"You know what?" Schlausser said. "I'd like some hot dogs."

"Me too," Tessie said. "Krauss keeps open all night if you want to walk to Rodney Street for them."

"I don't want to walk to Rodney Street for them," Philip said.

"Nobody said you, Philip," Tessie said.

Schlausser became a sport. He took out a nickel. "Heads I go and you foot the damage. Tails you go and I foot the damage."

"That is O.K. with me, Mr. Schlausser," Philip said.

It was heads. Philip gave him three quarters. "A pastrami club sandwich for me if the meat's hot. Otherwise I don't want it. Two pickles also."

Schlausser, sighing over lost opportunities, made his way to the door. Philip led Tessie down to the basement.

Tessie's folks had fixed up the boiler room with a superannuated couch, some chairs and mats. Forty watts and dust make a mellow light. It was like the boiler room in Philip's house where Cohen and his friend Mahler liked to get drunk on Mrs. Miller's wine, but here it was warmer, almost hot.

"What a day," said Tessie uncertainly, "what a day."

"What's the matter with the day?" Philip asked, noting immediately a feeling of antagonism toward her and trying to repress it. "God made this day, just like you and me, and it's got a momma and a poppa."

"Don't be ridiculous. I mean, when it rains and rains, it makes you feel morbid and depressed. I hate it."

"It's remarkable. For you and me existence is a soup of details the effect of which is sedative. Whatever of an ache there is, it is easily suffocated into a sort of anesthesia. Yet all it needs is a day like this to expose the soul's nerves to the cold."

"Soul? You sound like Cohen, talking about soul." She was beginning to worry and tried to think of something to change the subject.

"I knew a man once," Philip said, "who declared that the only people who had souls were middle-aged Russian-American women, Yiddish intellectuals, and all others with perpetual colds in the nose. Nevertheless, that man was wrong. Everyone to greater or smaller degree has soul, but they are perhaps ashamed of it and kid around with it just as perhaps I am doing right now."

"Are you kidding me?" Tessie said, wishing Schlausser were back. "Don't kid me, please. I got chapped lips."

"And you also have, as you have been told countless times no doubt, very, very beautiful eyes." Philip bowed. He took a banana from the fruit bowl and peeled it thoughtfully. It would be out of place to mention that her legs were a little too fat, her neck too short, and her complexion uncertain. She was, poor kid, no dream baby.

"My darling," he murmured to her, "my dream baby, don't you like what I say?"

"Don't get disgusting, Philip. If there's one thing I cannot stand, it's a person who has no respect for a woman."

Philip held up a palm. "Please," he protested. "Only I am afraid I have no illusions about you. Can I help it if I have no illusions about you?"

"I like that," Tessie said. "I suppose I'm getting this treat on account of Schlausser. Well, why don't you make a speech?"

Philip jumped up on a chair. He held the banana stiffly before him. "My dear madame," he said, "—a good beginning, like Schlausser peddling corsets and brassieres. Why should I be mad about Schlausser? He's all right and the chances are that in the end you'll be married to him. All we're doing now is hastening a natural process."

"Oh, don't get disgusting," Tessie said. "Who mentioned anything about marrying Schlausser? What makes you think I'm marrying Schlausser? He just came off the road and I didn't have the heart to send him away."

"My dear madame," Philip went on from the chair, the banana still before him, "the inventions on love exist in our heads long before you appear, and what happens is that we really compress you within them like squeezing putty to hold a windowpane. The first time, it is altogether wonderful, you are Gloria Swanson, it is the Heavenly Kiss, but the abrupt tragedy is the inescapable contemplation that these things don't last."

"Oh, shut up, Philip. You're ridiculous. You have no right to hold Schlausser against me this way. Who mentioned anything about marrying?"

"That's the tragedy, madame, we have such elaborate ideas on the subject, when you appear you couldn't possibly fill the bill. And when we kid ourselves into thinking that you do, it does not take long for the illusion to break. And it is painful. It hurts you and it hurts us more. Yea, by the East River we sit on the banks and weep." Why was he so stupid? Philip asked himself.

"Don't be mean, Philip," Tessie said, angry. "Just because you and I have had relations, it's no reason for you to try to make a holy show of me. If there's anything I can't stand it's a fellow who has no respect for a woman."

"Madame," Philip floundered. He was feeling thickheaded and ashamed. "Madame, Tessie. . . ." He was suddenly feeling desolate. Philip stepped off the chair and began walking around the room.

Tessie was giving the impression that she was terribly hurt. After all the noise, Philip continued walking and she said nothing. Tessie finally crossed her legs and looked fixedly at the carpet.

"I never thought you were that kind of a fellow, Philip," she said with a very quiet sadness. "Do you think I'd throw myself at a fellow just for a good time? I'm not that kind of a girl and I think you ought to know it. I can't stand it when a fellow gets disrespectful, especially after what we've been through together. Sometimes a fellow thinks he can do or say anything to a girl, but I can't stand that."

All right, baby, all right. Philip was feeling ridiculous. Why hadn't he left on the landing when he had said he was going. I'm sorry, dear, so sorry, dear, I'm sorry I made you cry. Can't you forgive, can't you forget? Madame, a man lays his life on the floor before you for you to spit at or accept. Can't you forgive? Can't you forget? "All right," Philip said to Tessie. "All right. Stop."

"If it's Schlausser you're sore about, that's ridiculous. I hope you didn't make a scene just on account of Schlausser. Nobody mentioned anything about marrying him."

"All right," Philip said. "Keep quiet, will you?"

"Well," she said, "you certainly get half dippy sometimes." She kept quiet, and in time Schlausser came back with the delicatessen.

Philip took his pastrami sandwich and went over to the window. Schlausser sat down beside Tessie on the couch and the two politely munched their dogs. They were interminable all over again.

Philip ate busily for some minutes and dropped his feet on the windowsill. That was love and that was all you could get and don't be a pig. The trouble was, he thought, he was still a kid and needed time to get over poetry highly seasoned like wurst. It was adolescent and anything adolescent wasn't mature. Mature was good and adolescent was bad. You got over it. I'll get over it, Philip thought, and then everything will be hotsy-totsy again. He slumped in his chair and grew drowsy.

In his brown warm mental mist a machine gun began pumping bullets into his heart, his face full of surprise at the unexpected attack. Ta ta ta, rra, traa, ta ta ta. The belt of lead sluiced through the gun. Boomp, boomp, boomp. The bullets sank into his flesh, each impact individually shaking his body. The movies. One hand at his heart. The absorption on his face, the complete absence of any effort to effect some facial expression. Music. Ah, dear Philip. Ten thousand lovely maidens all grow sad in contemplation. A field of hay bends in the cool wind. Five million violins weep. Philip shook himself out of his reverie.

He heard the bony patter of cold, hard feet somewhere. Mice were running around seeking something to nibble. Cats, doubtless, were tracking them down, hunched up and patient. Here he was on his spine. At this moment somewhere a man was dying in the yellow light of the electric bulbs, his family grouped about him with anxious faces, wishing it were day already. At this moment a couple was sleeping in bed, arms thrown over each other. Somewhere at this moment a baby was being born in the nervous excitement. A man was sleepily putting on his coat and saying he guessed he'd got to go. A man was stretching and yawning in the bathroom. All these things were happening, and at this moment Philip was slumped in his chair, a witness to a romance in full bloom.

Then, remembering that he should have left hours ago, Philip felt humiliated by his stupidity and rose abruptly.

"Good night," he said. "I'm going."

"Ah," said Schlausser, anticipation creeping into his voice, "you're leaving?"

"There's no reason for you to go, Philip, unless you don't want to stay," Tessie said. "It's really not very late."

"No," said Philip very normally, "I guess I'll run along."

The cool air hit him as he left the house. Philip shivered. Once again the streets were abandoned. The electric lampposts, standing on the same spots, were shining superfluously. The wind played all the way down the street with a piece of the *News*. It was like the other time, it was like all the other times, but this was going to be the last time and Philip did not feel jaunty. It was over, Tessie would marry Schlausser, but Philip had no tears for his sorrow. His mind was re-creating the features of Irene Lubya, the movie star, trying to draw with its fingertips the strands of vapor that, interwoven and blended marvelously, produced her face. Philip turned up his coat collar. Outside the rain still dripped, but captured in his mind was the countenance of Irene Lubya and she was indeed wonderful to behold.

"Say, you! Hey, you!"

Marge turned her pug-nosed face around. It was Sam Linck's wife. She wore a gingham housedress with an exotic flower design. Her eyes protruded, and finally the skin of her face, unwashed and uncared for, gave her away. She was going to stringiness and seed rapidly. My God, said Marge, no wonder, what can you expect?

"What's the matter with you?" Marge said in great astonishment. "What's eating you, missus?"

"Listen," Sam's wife said, talking through choked-up anger, "I know you and I know what you are. You don't have to make believe you don't know what it's all about. Do you think I'm a dope? I've got ears, I've got eyes. I know what you've been doing in that room on South Fifth Street and I know my husband don't stay there till three in the morning only to play checkers with you."

"Lady," Marge said, looking around, "you must be crazy. I'm sure I haven't got the slightest idea what you're talking about."

"I'm crazy? I'm crazy?" Sam's wife cried. She was raising her voice and a crowd of women and boys were beginning to gather around the two. "Isn't it bad enough you take him away in the nights? Aren't there enough boys, you have to twist a married man? Do you have to parade up and down here where he lives so that you can have more satisfaction? Listen, you bum, get away from here or I'll put your lousy eyes out!"

"Don't you call me a bum, you cheap slob," Marge said coldly. "Who do you think you are anyway?"

"Bum, whore, streetwalker!" Sam's wife shrieked at the top of her voice. She began to cry and talked through her wailing. Women left their flats, boys ran up from street to street as word passed. All Ripple Street and its environs stood about, taking in the performance. This was one of the advantages of Williamsburg, and they watched the show as by right. They made no effort to interfere. Sam's wife turned weeping to the crowd, hysterically explaining her troubles and Marge's part in them. "She won't leave me alone in my hole, even. She comes in front of me to show off what a filthy tramp she is and she's proud of it."

"Who is she?" Marge asked the crowd. "Is she always like that? Why don't somebody keep an eye on her? Some day she'll hurt herself this way."

Mrs. Linck herself came panting out of the house. Her bosom lifted and fell in long swings. Her face was red.

"What is it? Tell me quick, what's the matter?" she gasped, catching her breath.

"There she is, the whore," Sam's wife wept. "That's the one."

"Bitch!" shrieked Mrs. Linck, using all her teeth. She shrieked it like a prayer to God and she wanted to make sure He heard it. The veins on her neck bulged. "Get away from here before I pull your goddam hair out!" She worked herself into anger and now was going on like a motor engine hitting the cylinders. "Get out, I say, get out or I'll send you out in an ambulance!"

"You dirty cow!" Marge said, moving out of the crowd.

"Get out, illegitimate!" Mrs. Linck screamed fiercely, and she pushed Marge.

"Stop pushing, stop pushing, you sheeny slob," Marge said.

Mrs. Linck slapped the Polish girl with her fat hand. The crowd gasped. Here it came. Marge slammed the old lady's jaw with a hard shot from the shoulder. The crowd distinctly heard the bony sound of her knuckles against Mrs. Linck's face. "You whore!" Mrs. Linck gasped grimly and dug her fingers into her hair, pulling the girl over the gutter this way and that like a cat playing with a dead mouse. Marge yelped from pain. She sank her nails into Mrs. Linck's face and ripped. The blood streamed in lines. The old woman cracked her over the head, both her hands working on her ears as though she were patting potato pancakes into shape. Now Sam's wife came up with a long-handled aluminum pot. She edged herself between the two women and belabored Marge's head. A boy suddenly vomited, causing a small flurry of excitement in the crowd. A short, potbellied man in a wilted striped shirt began to yell in a hoarse voice, "Call a policeman! Call a policeman!" Marge kicked, working silently but with skill, furiously. Mrs. Linck mauled, and cursed as she mauled. Sam's wife kept on bouncing the pan on Marge's head to the count of "Whore! Tramp! Streetwalker!"

In the end Marge got her fingernails into Mrs. Linck's kimono. With one pull the back part of it was torn away. Mrs. Linck's round buttocks, huge and ruddy, presented themselves to the crowd. The fight ended. Mrs. Linck had to hurry back to the privacy of her flat.

That evening Sam Linck broke into the room on South Fifth Street in a rage.

"What's the idea?" he said, glaring. "Will you tell me what the bright idea was? You've certainly done your best to get me into one fine hell of a stink."

Marge, puffed, scratched, and swollen, looked up at him with silent hate. This was what they had been fighting over.

"That's the trouble with you sheenies. You've always got your old ladies and wives hanging around. When a girl goes out with a sheeny, she's got to figure on his whole goddam family," she said bitterly.

"What's that got to do with it?" Linck demanded. "What were you hanging around my house for? You knew that would get me into a fine fix."

"I needed money. I didn't eat since the morning. I was broke and I figured I'd see you on your way home for lunch."

Sam Linck drew himself up in his rage. "What makes you think I'm your meal ticket? Listen, you pug-nosed Polack, if I take you out on a good time, that's my look out. If I want to pay your room rent, I'm doing it, but don't get the idea I'm supporting you. What kind of a sucker are you playing me for anyhow? Do you think I'm taking care of all the bums in the neighborhood? Listen, if I catch you hanging around my old lady's house again, I'll break every single bone in your body."

"Go to hell, you Jew bastard," Marge said, astonished at the outburst. "Where do you get off bawling me out like that anyway? Who do you think you are?"

"I'll show you," Linck said. He beat her black and blue.

The rusty-looking kitten moved its lean body and mewed piteously. Mrs. Sussman had been watching it from her yard window until in the end she had felt compelled to bring down to it an ashtray with milk. She placed it before the kitten, coaxing gently, but it refused the milk. The kitten took a halfhearted lick, submitted to Mrs. Sussman's petting, and walked away slowly with a pained expression on its face.

"Poor kitty," murmured Mrs. Sussman and worrying over it, she went back to her flat. The house was spotlessly clean for Mrs. Sussman kept her home with almost religious feeling. Cathedrally dim, it always smelled of varnish and cleansing agents. Heavy lace curtains hung and even in the hot summer the windows were kept shut tight to keep out the dust. Perhaps that was why it was oppressive; as soon as she entered the rooms she felt a wave of despondence. The cleanliness became a bareness, it emphasized her solitude.

Meyer Sussman had been dead a week and he had been dead forever. Mrs. Sussman's tears had dried. The lodge had buried him and given her six hundred dollars. She remained a widow with two children. What now?

She smoothed the airmail letter from her sister in Butte on the windowsill before her.

Dear Anna,

The telegram you sent brought terrible news, but you can't cry your life away. There are your two boys, you must be a mother to them. You, yourself, you're a young woman yet. You must not kill yourself with grief. I can say that, but when Joey read the telegram to me, believe me, my head went dizzy and I felt as though something was cutting my heart to pieces. What a terrible, terrible thing, Anna. Meyer always had such red cheeks, he was such a healthy man, he was always laughing, who would have thought he could do such a terrible thing to himself?

You write, dear little sister, what can you do now? From us, as you already can imagine, you cannot expect great things. Sam is still unwell and the grocery store pays a poor living. Nevertheless, if you wish to come here, to be with your own flesh and blood in a world of strangers, it will be a burden, but come, you will be always welcome.

This is a small town and the life here is not easy. However, there is a man here called Silberstein, a good Jew in early middle age, and he wants to get married. I have been thinking it would be a good match. Silberstein owns a clothing store and he is a settled solid man. I know it will be hard for you to think of this so soon after your sorrow, but you must provide for the children. I think Silberstein would make a good husband, he is such a steady man, and if you come soon the marriage can take place before the Holidays.

Otherwise, what the future holds in store, only God knows. Write me soon. . . .

What now? thought Mrs. Sussman. The prospect of going to far-off Montana, to live with a strange man, to start altogether anew, was achingly distressing. "You are a young woman yet, Anna, you must not kill yourself with grief." It was so much trouble to live in this life. I wish I were old, Mrs. Sussman thought. Then it would be over soon. "I know it is hard to think of these things, but you must provide for your children." There was the six hundred dollars. How long could it last? To whom in Williamsburg could she turn? People lived so close together, they were warm-hearted and sympathetic, but all alone a person was, alone.

One of her boys ran up to Mrs. Sussman and looked out of the window.

"Look, Momma," he said. "Somebody threw down a bag of garbage and it looks so funny, like a little cat."

It was the rusty kitten, balled up in a corner of the yard and motionless.

"That's not garbage, little mother," she said. "It's a kitten. Run down and see if it will drink the milk now."

The child called to the kitchen, holding the ashtray with the milk in it. "Here pussie, pussie," he called. "Here pussie, pussie." But the kitten did not move.

"Oh, Momma," the child called up, "it's dead."

SIX

LIKE A THREAD OF CHEWING GUM a child stretches in idle play from her mouth, the state road picked its dainty way through the hills. The morning sun beamed down in yellow brightness cheering the countryside. Through the quiet roared the huge Empire Lines bus on its way up to Havers Falls. Nature and power, God's majesty and Rubin's.

"Already," said Rubin, speaking almost poetically, "the railroads are giving in. Yesterday they cut their rates again and still they can't touch Empire fares."

Papravel lay contentedly against the over-upholstered leather cushions. Expansively he smoked a cigar because it always gave him a sensation of opulence even though it frequently made him sick at the stomach.

"It's America," he said softly, his eyes almost closed. "Where but in America could a man do so well by himself?"

"When we began," Rubin continued, full of honest enthusiasm, "the railroads, they said we were a bunch of snotnoses, we would be thrown on our behinds in six months. You should have heard them, Papravel. Big speeches, big shots. Big bellies with cigars all the time stuck in their faces. 'Transportation is the backbone of the Nation.' 'American Industry and American Imagination will find no serious rival in foreign competition.' Now they come to me and give me, 'Mr. Rubin,' until I tell Louie, 'Louie, throw these bums out, they're taking up my time.'" Mr. Rubin laughed and in harmony Papravel smiled pleasantly.

"Listen to me, Papravel, and I'll show you how a man can work himself up in this country. Four years ago I was a jobber in candy. I made fifty dollars a week, sometimes sixty. I worked like a nigger but I thought I was getting rich like Rockefeller or Charlie Schwab. And now, look at me, knock wood. President, Empire Lines, Inc., with regular service to the mountains five times a day in the summer and twice daily in the winter, with a coast-to-coast connection. Fourteen Superba buses, seven Nashes and four Buicks, four offices, and a payroll of sixty-six. And it is just the beginning.

"Four lines there are to Havers Falls: The Empire, the Green Hawk, the Excellent, and the Silver Eagle. The Green Hawk is a fancy outfit operated by goyish dopes, catering to Gentiles strictly, and tell me, Papravel, how many Gentiles come to the Mountains? They'll go out of business the first bad winter, but it's all the same to me, they don't hurt my business. As for the Excellent, did you ever hear what happened? It's a funny story. Moss and Reinhardt were partners until one day Moss says he's got enough, he wants to get out. And who buys him out, Papravel? So all that's left is the Silver Eagle, and now with God's will and your help they will move out of Williamsburg, and without a station in Williamsburg they too can't hurt me."

Rubin stopped. It was a long speech, but he had relished every word of it. His cigar had gone out and now Rubin took time to relight it with the air of self-satisfaction that this operation alone makes possible.

"Yes, yes," murmured Papravel, awakening from his mild slumber. "Did you hear what happened to the Silver Eagle, Rubin? Eight bandits, eight bums, eight lowlifes, the rottenest kind of people in the world, you and I should never have anything to do with them, they walked into the bus station at Havers Falls. With no pity, no heart, they knock down the furniture, rip the carpets, and smash up the place. And poor Morantz, he comes running up to me. I swear to him, Morantz, I'm no roughneck, it isn't my business, why should he come to me? I think he will have to get out of Williamsburg after all."

Rubin looked sideways at the innocence of Papravel. They rocked gently with the motion of the bus. It was a pleasant sensation.

"Poor Morantz," Rubin sighed. He leaned back, grew lost in thought while the smoke rose and circled in the bus. With the Excellent crippled and the Silver Eagle out of Williamsburg, a man could make in the summer, let me see, eight hundred, nine hundred dollars a day. Maybe a thousand. Rubin crossed his legs. One thousand dollars! If God would only be good.

Through the window could be seen the lifting dew now rising in mist from the fields. A vari-colored cow, taking no time from her chewing and looking no less stupid for it, stared dumbly at the speeding bus. What hath God wrought? The hills extending upward on either side revealed squares of blue, green, and yellow acres. Now the sun had grown richer, resembling the yolk of an egg medium boiled. Far off came the shrill whistle of a speeding train. Rubin awoke abruptly from his reverie. "Hey, Mike!" he commanded the driver. "Press the button!" Through the still air in answer sounded the soft melodious note of the bus horn and it floated above the car like a plume.

The arrival at Havers Falls was like cold water. The news greeted them from Williamsburg that Morand, determined to fight, had reopened with the help of a Detroit combination. Rubin was stunned. After all, he had a wife and four children.

"Listen, Rubin," Papravel said, speaking carefully and slowly, "trust me and everything will be all right. Don't cry like a baby. Your place in Williamsburg I guarantee they won't touch. Every day I'll have three men to watch it with more waiting near the telephone. And as for Morantz's place, leave that to me. Not in a month did I learn my business, and only God knows how many ways there are to make trouble. Import! Let Morantz import gangsters from today until tomorrow. What difference does it make if a bum comes from Detroit, Chicago, or New York? He's still a stinker and let there be an end to it."

Moreover, Morantz meant business. That very night his men broke into the Empire Lines Havers Falls' office and wrecked it with a thoroughness and regard for detail that rivaled in every respect the despatch that was Papravel's trademark. Rubin howled. He was scared and saw the fortune of a lifetime going to ruin. Papravel brushed him aside roughly.

"I'm busy," he said. "In the end everything will be all right."

But Harry Hayman had to leave the little ladies at the resort hotels, Gilhooley had to pass up the Italians and their drinks, and the two Nashes went out now on business only. Papravel wired instructions home, left Harry in charge of the men in the mountains, and drove back to Williamsburg.

> "There are two worlds and the secret in both is activity. He must be active or he dies. Observe all forms of life, it is constantly in movement. The ants, the mice, the dogs, and the fish in the seas. Even in zoos and aquaria, they move in endless circles. And that is the meaning of the passage."
>
> —The Sage in the Long Beard

Mr. Yozowitz, also called Skinny Shanner, carefully leaned in lines against the windows of his laundry store eight racks of curtains stretched on pins to dry in the sun. It had rained all day before, now he seized the sun. Yozowitz's Adam's apple moved tremulously as he swallowed, surveying the layout with satisfaction. But hereupon he spied Davey, the Devil's agent at such moments when the enchanted fingers of love released his mind from thoughts of Yetta, the girl of his dreams. Davey came strolling down the street, a rubber ball bouncing in his hand. It had happened so often before that the curtains were soiled by boys playing in the nearby street, he had had to wash again so many times before. Yozowitz waved his fist at Davey. They knew each other well.

"Stay away with the ball," he warned. "You hear what I'm saying, stay away with the ball."

Davey retreated, bowing close to the ground. "Yassem, yassem," he said but already he was licking his upper lip with his tongue in anticipation.

Five minutes later he was back with his gang. Yozowitz was out of the store like a shot. He sputtered curses in a wild spasm, chasing the kids down the block with a long bamboo stick waving in his hand. His wife always went around begging the boys' mothers to control them, wailing that her husband would some day die of apoplexy, and his fury was so enormous now that sad day seemed imminent.

"Get away from here, you illegitimates," he yelled, spitting out saliva. "I'll break your rotten heads if you ever get close enough for me to put my hands on you."

The boys listened stolidly, a hundred respectful yards before him. Mrs. Yozowitz came out in front of the store, wringing her hands in her apron from anxiety and to get them dry. Skinny Shanner went on with his harangue, which resembled a series of small explosions. He pointed out the unsuitability of his store as a play area, the nearness of other more apt spaces, the general blackness of their hearts.

In the pause while Yozowitz was sucking in his breath Davey gave the signal and the boys began chanting solemnly and evenly:

> "A fly flew in
> In Yozowitz' store,
> He s'sst on the window,
> He s'sst on the floor,
> He s'sst on the curtains
> That hung by the door.
> And when the fly
> Got Yozowitz sore,
> The fly, he s'sst
> On Yozowitz' jaw."

Yozowitz tried to restrain himself, but in an inevitable burst finally charged the gang. They receded like a wave falling back, and when Yozowitz stopped, they stopped, placid and tantalizing. The laundryman fumed until his anger was spent and his voice hoarse. Now his wife was plucking him by the elbow, pleading with him to calm himself. Yozowitz made his way back to the curtain racks in jerky backsteps, still addressing the boys.

"The secret of life is activity. Man must be active or he dies."

Underneath the Williamsburg Bridge there were some improvised playgrounds, so-called because there was no pavement, but dirt. An excursion here netted a black eye more often than a good time, for the local Irish boys resented sheeny invasion. Nevertheless, Davey had had one triumph, there might be another.

The crowd walked down to the Bridge Plaza looking for dimes and nickels at the curbs. The playgrounds were empty, dark except where thin slits of light cut through the floor of the bridge. Some children were riding bicycles and roller-skating. A hot-dog-and-lemonade stand waited for trade, and Davey regretted he had no nickels.

"Let's lift rides over the Bridge," he commanded to keep going. The boys arranged themselves in pairs at the auto entrance. Some of them, however, declined. Instead, they went up to the footpaths of the bridge to explore the delights there. They examined the great rivets of the structure at close hand, looked up at the towers and admired the cool run of the cables. They leaned over the railings to spit, visited the lavatories with signs in four languages, and watched the movements of tugs and barges below on the dirty river.

As for Davey and the rest, they hitched across with little trouble, but there was nothing to do at Delancey Street and they immediately hitched back. The gang assembled and set out for new streets.

They went in the opposite direction, toward Newtown Creek, and here too the local Irish boys were inhospitable. But a trip in any direction was something of an adventure. As they went up Maujer Street they grew tense and kept closely together. The Maujer gang was comparatively a weak crew, but when its terrain was invaded it usually recruited aid from older individuals of the neighborhood. However, everything today seemed quiet and dead; St. Catherine's Hospital set the tone of silence for the wooden, half-painted shacks, but Davey feared an ambuscade at any minute. He sent Natie the Buller to scout ahead and told his boys he was just itching for a good fight, this place was so dead.

Newtown Creek stank with a beautiful overpowering stink that impregnated the general vicinity. The boys stood at the shore, watching the sun reflected in the greasy water in dancing flashes, in curves and swirls. They had little to say to each other and felt uncomfortable. Suddenly Natie rushed back. He had seen some boys up the street, they had better beat it, there were too many of them.

Everyone knew this was a lie but it was welcome news. Relieved, they broke up and headed in pairs north for Metropolitan Avenue. Scared of meeting hostile gangs, and because they were scared, they now entered the most vicious of all neighborhoods, the Italians'. These were severe in their methods, seldom willing to fight with their fists or stones but resorting unethically to knives and guns. After all, the Irish might be said to fight almost for the fun of it; with the Jews it was most often a case of self-defense. But the Italians went out definitely to hurt and maim.

Davey and his gang walked the foreign-looking streets apprehensively. The section drowsed in a hot sun and, together with the strongly Italian atmosphere, this produced an effect of faraway places with faraway customs. It was like a strange country altogether. Metropolitan Avenue, too, had its distinctive smell. This was one of garlic, old cheeses, and the nauseating odors from the dye factories located there. The gang looked, as they passed, into the strange windows of Italian grocery stores where green, odd-shaped cheeses hung from strings, cans of olive oil bore peculiar labels and pictures, and the vegetables appeared fascinatingly foreign.

The Italian men with their red faces and big bellies, smoking thin cords for cigars, sat in the cafés and interested Davey's gang because they refused to regard themselves as in any way unusual, a proper subject for tourists. The cafés themselves, apathetic in the sun, were painted green and ornamented by calendars and murals, the themes of both of which were invariably ladies with big, overflowing breasts. Davey's gang inspected the breasts, marveling. A fat Italian perched in a little wicker carriage came riding down the street behind a Shetland pony. It was so unreal the sight resembled an illustration in a third-grade elementary-school reader.

A festive-looking funeral, gaily decked and preceded by two carriages that contained only flowers, swept down the street like a gorgeous lamentation. The wailing flutes and brasses poured out loud, sad melodies. The hearse was white and intricately ornate. "That means it's a kid," Davey said, and the boys lined the curb to watch the procession. Down the long line a carriage door opened. Davey could see the people inside eating and drinking. A woman of the party stuck her head out and called to someone on the sidewalk. "Come in, Luigi, come in," she shouted. She did not want him to miss the ride.

Back on Ripple Street the boys climbed into the backyard of the Auburn Social Club. They were always fascinated by the lovely stone statue and the garden seats that reminded them of the movies. Davey had organized a jumping club. In the neighborhood there were many lots where the brick foundations of buildings still remained. Davey used to lead his gang from lot to lot, jumping in rotation from the different heights available. A small clique of the most hardy jumpers was evolved, but in the process they had learned to use the broad blade of a kitchen knife to press down head bumps.

Now Davey took them on top of a shack outside the clubhouse. From one side there was a jump to the basement yard of the tenement adjoining. It was a long jump, but it was broken in the middle by a slender ledge formed by the top of the stone wall of the tenement yard.

The boys debated. It was an easy jump, Davey said, but the gang said anybody who tried it would get his head broken. Even the hardy clique faltered. Davey resolved the discussion like a true leader. He went grimly to the edge of the shack. Everyone watched silently. “You better drop it,” Natie the Buller said. That meant holding on to the top of the shack with the hands and slipping down instead of jumping feet first.

“I’ll jump it,” Davey said. “It’s easy.”

Davey jumped, landed on the stone ledge, wavered, lost his balance, and went down. He lay on his back, his head had been banged. For a moment Davey looked up at the sky and then he gazed into the anxious eyes of the gang. Was he killed? Davey determined to play the hero, but at that moment he drew his hand from his head and discovered blood. He thought his brains were leaking and he howled.

Halfway between Utseck and Middletown they stopped the screaming Silver Eagle bus. Two Jews, one Negro, three Italians. The driver, a big man with long arms, leaped out ready for a fight, but when he saw the guns he stopped short.

“All right,” he said. “What’s the game?”

“Shut your mouth,” Gilhooley said, and the first thing he did was to pull the driver’s pants down so that he couldn’t move his legs. In the early morning the cool air struck him disagreeably and the driver protested. “Shut your mouth,” Gilhooley said. The driver with long arms reflected for a minute and shut his mouth.

It was an early mid-week trip and there were few passengers. However, Harry Hayman went through the car to calm them. “Gentlemen,” he announced, “everything is all right, keep your seats and stay quiet. Because if anyone will make a noise it certainly will go hard on him.” He sat down in the driver’s seat. Half the time he kept his eyes on the passengers, half the time he surveyed the work his men were doing.

Neatly they slashed the big expensive shoes at the side. This took some time but they accomplished it, pausing each time as a corner of the car settled gently to the asphalt. The Negro, Fleurie O’Johnson, opened the hood with relish. He spat on his hands.

Expertly he crumpled the fan, ripped the wires from their places, and smashed the magneto, in that order. He moved deftly, and one could see easily that he enjoyed his work. In the meantime the Italians had been knocking holes into the huge gas tank and the liquid gurgled out in streams, giving a strong smell to the atmosphere. Two men, Hayman helping, unscrewed the shift cover and with skillfully aimed blows mashed the teeth of the gears.

It was a cold morning, anyone might be coming down the road, and the men worked rapidly. All in all, the job did not take more than nine minutes from the time they stopped the Silver Eagle bus to the moment they piled back into the Nashes. The bus was not a complete wreck, but it would serve as an example. Actually Hayman was highly satisfied. He would have something to tell the boss. Hayman had held a watch in his hand all the while, timing the boys.

"Not bad," he said. "Not bad. You did that one in nine minutes."

Fleurie O'Johnson showed his white teeth. He had had a good time.

As they went off down the highway the driver with the long arms forgot to pull up his pants but looked after them, almost blue with cold. "The dirty bastards," he said quietly, in a kind of astonishment recollected in tranquility, "the dirty bastards."

Hayman and Gilhooley drove through the mountains looking for trouble. Two Italians, one Negro, three Jews. By this time Morand was sending a Detroit gunman with every bus and they had to work carefully because Papravel's orders were to stay clear of cops. They could get away with skillfully inflicted damage, but shooting, open conflict, might lead to murder and that meant the courts, judges, cops, and heavy graft. Rubin would quit on him cold. No one could make a living if he had to hand over 50 percent of the proceeds to the police. Papravel didn't blame Rubin. And he told Hayman to be careful.

The boys had to pick their spots, swiftly slashing shoes or punching holes in Silver Eagle gas tanks, and then they had to duck out of sight immediately. Morand's men retaliated in kind, so that Hayman was compelled to split his men, half protecting, half attacking. He sent telegrams home asking for more men and he got them. Rubin groaned.

The Maujer Street gang came out of nowhere, armed with onion bags of stones and helmeted with milkcan covers, ready for battle. Davey saw them a block off and he had little time to marshal his gang at full strength and run for the ammunition caches they had planted in yards and lots for emergencies like this. Davey lined the best men up in front, protected behind washkettle and ash-can covers for shields and supplied with little piles of rocks at the sides. The younger boys had the menial job of picking up stones as they fell from the enemy and rushing them forward to their own front-line men.

The fight began at the corner of Hooper Street and at the outset looked like an easy conquest for the Maujers. They had taken Davey's men by surprise, had given them little time to build up an effective morale for the battle. Davey's gang were being pushed back steadily, some of the more timid were already deserting into hallways, and the worst of it was that they were soon lacking ammunition. For the further they retreated the more they fell on territory that had not been visited by the enemy's hail of stones. Then Natie the Buller, next in command, a highly imaginative fellow who owed his importance to the gaudy stories he told, conferred with Davey on a plan of action. They decided to surround the Maujers. Davey remained fast at the front while Natie dived down the cellar steps of the nearest house. Gradually the boys at the rear slipped down after him, one at a time to attract no attention, until about fifteen were gone. They climbed over fences, reached South Third Street through the opposite tenement and marched down Hooper. There was a short wait until Natie had gathered all his men. Then with a concerted whoop they fell upon the back of the enemy. With the Maujers thrown into confusion the rest was simple. They ran off in panic, scattering through the yards and scuttling over fences while Davey's men relentlessly pegged away at them until they were out of sight.

In the calm of victory Natie's group and Davey's division walked slowly up to one another in the middle of the street.

"One thing about these goyim," Davey said with the triumph that marks the strong, "they never got no brains."

He enjoyed the victory. The Maujers were comparatively a weak outfit but he hated them particularly for one nasty trick they alone used. When one of his gang, usually to get to the Leonard Street library, entered their territory they would not jump on him and give him his beating forthwith. Instead they would send a kid of four or five who would start a fight with him. Naturally the Rippler would hit back, only to find himself instantly surrounded by Maujers popping out of hallways. "You dirty Jew kike," they would say with painful deliberation, "you cheap Jew bastard, hitting a kid below your size. Well, we'll show you." The dozen or so true defenders of proper sportsmanship would proceed to show him.

Actually, Davey's gang was a pretty anemic bunch, never venturing on any attack, often declining to accept battle when it was proffered. Instead they ran up to the roofs of their houses. Davey, a recent importation from the East Side, owed his leadership to his vigor, his swagger, and the bold tales he narrated of his former neighborhood. He came to displace one called Coke, whose frail body was the subject of fascinating shivers and jerky movements. Davey had refused to be impressed by this boy's talents, provoked a fistfight, and established himself within his first week. Coke languished until his family delivered him by removing themselves to the swell elegance of Brownsville.

The only Jewish gang of importance was the Havemeyer Streeters, all newcomers from the East Side. They furnished fierce opposition, to the Italians especially, and as more Jews settled in the neighborhood the Havemeyers often boasted that it was they who had compelled the Italian migration to Bensonhurst and Bay Ridge. One of the Havemeyers' specialties was to smash repeatedly the windows of the Williamsburg Mission for Jews. This was an organization on the Bridge Plaza for converting Jews to Christianity, and anathema to every Jewish mother. The worst Davey's gang had done in this connection was to parade inside of the meeting house in a rapid snake dance, chanting:

"We'll all stand up for Jesus,
We'll all stand up for Jesus,
We'll all stand up for Jesus,
For the love of Christ sit down!"

Natie the Buller and Davey swaggered up and down the street.

"Well," said Natie, "I guess that showed 'em."

But Davey was not listening. Once again he was miles distant, walking in the gentle paths of his mind's creation. He wished Yetta had been there to witness the battle. "You're so strong," she would be saying with a shy look in her eyes. "It was wonderful, wonderful . . ." Natie kept tagging after his leader, enthusiastic, with loyal praises after the victory, but Davey did not listen.

"It was nothing," he was saying in his mind, at the same time fervently impatient for man's estate and an adult's privilege to love, "nothing at all." My dear Susannah, my dear Susannah . . .

⁓⁓⁓

Sam Linck walked into the café, a little drunk, sullen, and hankering for trouble. Three truck-driver friends accompanied him, soothing and talking him down. They held their hands in their pockets and were worried because people already were looking at them.

"I'm not going to take this standing up," Sam muttered. "That little skirt can't make a sucker out of me and get away with it."

His friends sat him down at a table with a red-checkered cloth. They ordered coffee and sandwiches and tried to blend with the other diners.

"Tell Marge I want to see her," Linck told the waitress. "Tell her it's all right. I just want to talk things over." He took out a bottle of rye, held it on the table for a while, and gulped a shot. His friends told him to put that thing away, why didn't he cut it out?

The orders came. The waitress placed a cup of coffee and a ham sandwich on the table before Linck. "Marge isn't here," she said. "She worked here only a couple of nights. She isn't here now."

"You had to go back into the kitchen before you knew that, didn't you?" Linck said. "That's what she told you to say?"

The waitress looked scared. "She isn't here," she repeated and placed a mug of mustard on the table. Linck got up resolutely, brushed his friends away, and walked to the kitchen. He found Marge cringing in the corner near the swivel door. He spoke to her in a quiet, calm voice, even coaxingly.

"What did you want to leave the room for?"

"I got a job. Cut this out, Sam. I'll lose my job."

"What difference does that make? Why don't you come back?" he said. "I'll treat you fine. It'll be like before. Just quit hanging around my old lady's house and we'll get along fine."

"I can't, Sam. I'm working now." She spoke in hushed tones.

"Come back," Sam said. "You're coming back right now."

"I can't. I'll lose my job."

"You're coming back. Get your coat on." He tried to push her toward her coat hanging on the wall nearby.

Marge lost patience. Their forced restrained tones were difficult. She broke. "Leave me alone," she said raising her voice hysterically. "I got friends. They'll take care of you if you don't quit bothering me."

"I know you got friends," Linck shouted. "Every whore's got friends. Wherever you peddle your music box you got friends." He went for her.

"Keep your hands off me, you kike!" she screamed. "If you put a hand on me I'll kill you, you sheeny bastid."

Linck's friends pulled him away and sat him down at the table. He was soberly silent. Linck began to paddle mustard on a slice of rye bread. He kept on smearing the stuff until it was an inch thick on the bread. The boss came out and told Marge he couldn't have this disturbance, all the customers were looking, would she get her coat and get out?

Marge said in a trembling voice, "I can't help it. If he comes here it isn't my fault."

"I'm sorry," said the boss. "Look at it my way. It doesn't make any difference whose fault it is. I can't have all this going on here."

Marge threw her apron on the floor angrily and seized her wrap. She stormed through the café to the door. As she passed Linck he stood up hastily to seize her, overturning the table. The vinegar bottle spilled all over the floor. He spotted his pants with ketchup. The other patrons had a trying time pretending to notice that nothing was happening.

Marge turned her face full on Linck. "I'll get even with you for this, you dirty sheeny!"

Linck took careful aim with the slice of rye bread he had been so heavily paddling with mustard. It smacked her flush on her pug nose.

"How's that?" he asked as if he really wanted to know. He was satisfied.

⌣⌣⌣

Before the end of that week four events took place on Ripple Street. To begin with, Old Miller had discovered he had been swindled with the diamonds. They had been paste, the jeweler planted, the strangers fakers. When he discovered this he was both overwhelmed and furious. With remarkable energy for an old man who spoke little English he had had the two men arrested. However, the money had been spent. It was a heavy blow.

His wife and children cursed him ceaselessly now and said that God was punishing him for his sins.

Soon after, Miller was brought up from the cemetery in a taxicab. Everyone knew immediately this meant he was sick. Miller was unable to move his arms or to speak. His eyes were wide open in scared wonder. Mrs. Miller wrung her hands, cried, and put him to bed. The doctor said it was a stroke, he might get over it, it might take a week or a month. In the end he would be all right again.

Mrs. Miller stopped crying. She cursed him again and said she would never get rid of that ulcer on her flesh.

Marge's friends waited one night outside the garage where Sam Linck stored his truck. They were three men and they beat Linck mercilessly. He went to the hospital with a slight concussion of the skull, disorders in the abdominal region together with lesser wounds, cuts, and bruises. He was away two days. When he came back his head was bandaged and he had difficulty in moving. Linck kept pretty close to his flat.

Mrs. Sussman packed her belongings in apple barrels and wicker baskets. Her boys were dressed in neat serge suits with Buster Brown collars and big bowties. The younger child felt awe-stricken at the commotion and began to weep. Mrs. Sussman kissed all the neighbors, cried, and said good-bye. She went to Butte, to her sister and her grocery store, to Silberstein who was waiting to marry her. Everyone said it was a pity for such a nice young woman.

The invitations for Tessie's marriage to Schlausser came through the mail as Philip had expected. It depressed him although he had thought it would not. Somehow, he suddenly hankered after grass, trees, and the countryside. Philip had also received a letter from his friend Charles Nagleman who was spending the summer at a camp in Maine. Nagleman came of a well-to-do family, lived on Eighty-sixth Street in Manhattan, and always impressed Hayman because of his well-furnished home, the pictures, the books, the decorous ways of living that his father's money made possible. Nagleman now wrote of nights in the country, canoes, lakes, the woods, and in comparison Philip's ugly tenement and the summer heat oppressed him. Abruptly, the hot pavements of Williamsburg became intolerable. Philip wired ahead to his brother Harry and left to spend some time at Havers Falls.

SEVEN

PHILIP REACHED HAVERS FALLS early in the evening. He was beginning to resemble his father, resenting change, insisting only on the same conditions. Now he experienced a kind of homesickness, and, seeking something to occupy him, he found some paper and immediately wrote in answer to the letter he had received from Charles Nagleman:

> You send your letter from Maine and it is neatly characteristic of the two of us that I answer you from the Catskill Mountains. Eighty-sixth Street and Ripple Street, Skowhegan and Havers Falls, I cannot seem to escape my destiny. I mention this because on the way up here I had been thinking about you and our lovely friendship. And thinking of you, I suddenly discovered myself envying you. Why? I wondered at it until it occurred to me that what I admired in your fancy home, the furniture and the costly gewgaws was simply its style. For about two miles I was something like ashamed of myself because this seemed shallow and I was admiring these things too deeply for that. But as we pulled out of Middletown it seemed to me that I was looking too hard.
>
> In my maudlin moments I have already wept on your shoulder proclaiming the extraordinary virtues of my father,

his ethics, and his delicate life. Well, partly it is the sentimental feeling I have for the old man, but also, I have always told myself, it was that I respected his elementary honesty, truth and goodness. Certainly these are strange characteristics to find in our time. Further, he seemed like an Oriental of some old age, living within himself, calm and collected, shell-proofed. And this is a good thing.

But on this trip up, I felt this was not enough. It was too inactive. I looked about for some force of action, some direction of energy, that seemed strong enough in itself to occupy the space. I am afraid my philosophy is, as Overstreet, whose genial mind and soft manner you love so much, says, rotten. At any rate here I found myself with a hole and nothing to put into it, although it seemed to me very important to fill it.

Perhaps it was a kind of rationalization, but I next said, if there was no great task to perform, the valuable thing was to stick to the minutiæ, to move decorously, with style, notwithstanding the fact that we were moving nowhere. And now I thought of you and felt less ashamed. To surround myself with good-looking people, clean and wholesome, to live in handsome homes, to follow a smooth, pretty routine, all this, so presented, may spell for you Magnolia. You are, more or less, accustomed to it and may find yourself growing self-conscious as you read these nice tributes, but as for me, as I peek through the ash cans and the garbage on Ripple Street, it has a lively meaning.

Philip read the letter, wondering how to continue. To surround oneself with good-looking people, to live in handsome homes, to follow a decorous routine, all that meant money. Thinking of his father, of Papravel and Miller, Philip recognized that what he had written was completely negated by the logical conclusion. Money was a dirty business in itself, it meant everything contrary, and he wished he had been blessed, as had been his friend Nagleman, with a father who had made a small fortune out of manufacturing vanity cases. These problems were not for Charlie, they would have touched Philip only indirectly, and in these things it was so easy to ignore and sidetrack them. The letter itself seemed formal and academic. Disconcerted by his reflections, Philip determined not to mail it. Charlie would think he was trying to imitate the literary correspondence to be found in collections. You must be monosyllabic in your communications to friends, Philip thought, or else you begin to feel funny with yourself. He opened his bag and unpacked.

When Harry Hayman came in he ran up the stairs to greet him. He really liked the kid.

"Well, you're here. How do you like it?"

"I just got in," Philip replied. "It's the country."

"You'll like it. What's the news home? How's the old man and Momma?"

"Everything's the same. The old man walks around pretty satisfied with himself and Momma clucks anxiously after him. You remember Miller? That old skinflint saved his nickels and got taken in by swindlers. They sold him paste and now he's sick in bed from the excitement."

"That's what I call poetic," Harry said. "Come on down and meet the gentlemen. You'll find them all learned and scholarly boys. The dinge, as a matter of fact, is three legs up on a Ph.D., and if there's anything you've been wanting to know about Chaucer or Elizabethan drama, ask Gilhooley."

Harry introduced his brother as Professor Ginsberg. They all knew about him and held him in respect. He had not only completed high school, he was finishing college. They offered him a chair.

Three Italians, one Negro, and two Jews. They sat over the round dinner table playing five-cent stud poker, talking, smoking, and drinking wine like respectable businessmen after work. Call them what you want, Philip said, they're grown-ups. He, feeling himself still a kid, admired their matter-of-fact ways. They had been around.

One of the Italians, a powerful, muscular man, was talking about the war. Gilhooley, trying to get a rise out of him, had said the wops were the dirtiest fighters.

"You bet," the Italian said frankly. "I never saw such dirty fighting. If I told you some of the things you wouldn't believe me. The wops were dirty, but the Armenians and the Greeks were even lousier. We could always tell when they had been around by looking at the stiffs in the mud."

The Italian described the horrible thing the Armenians and Greeks did. Philip shuddered and wondered whether the man was kidding, but the others believed him too. Impressed, they kept silent. Gilhooley said reflectively, "By God, I'd like to shove a pile of manure down their throats."

The Italian tried to change the subject. He told of a time he was on a forty-day leave and returned to his home. His mother was a devout lady about whom he spoke respectfully, almost distantly, as though she had been someone else's mother. She had given him five hundred lira to make a pilgrimage to a mountain saint and pray for safety when he went back. He took the money, picked up a friend, and the two of them went off to make their prayers. Every cathouse, every café on the way, they stopped at, making a great time of it. After seven days they ran through the money and started home. "It took us seven days to go and one day to come back. We came home and told the old lady, you bet, we went to the saint and made our prayers. That was fine, but some old excrement-pot sees us lying in the gutters in one of the towns, and he tells my mother. By God, then the old lady called us every name but the good one. Maybe she was right because the first day back in the trenches I got hit with shrapnel. I got hit good. She sent me letters saying I got hurt because I lied to her and didn't pray."

This started off one of the Jews. He too had been hit by shrapnel, on the leg. He said he lay in the hospital for weeks and wouldn't let them put him out. "I'd rather lose the goddam leg than go back and get killed altogether." As soon as the wound healed and closed, he said, he smacked it with his palm, one big, sharp, hard crack. "'You son of a bitch, you pulled him open again,' the doctor said, 'No, Doc, no, so help me. She opened herself.'"

Gilhooley called out to another of the Italians. "Where were you in the war, Ferd?"

"Oh," said Ferd, "didn't you know? I got flat feet and bum eyes."

Everyone laughed. They went on with the poker until Philip grew dizzy following the cards. He told Harry he was going to sleep. In the room with them, Philip forgot they were racketeers, hold-up men, and gangsters. He even liked them. Philip took off his clothes. They, too, are children of God, he said, and they make money in their own fashion.

In bed, the whistle of the crickets, the tearing sounds of automobiles speeding past on the state road, the noises of the country at night brought him the feeling of strangeness and he found it hard to fall asleep. Philip looked out of the window and saw the stars, and it seemed to him that it was the first time he had ever seen them. In the city, perhaps, there were no stars and no moon. One grew calloused to them and disregarded them. They became no wonder, but stale from time. It took a change of scene for the perceptions to become alive again. The stars now appeared like beads of mercury and the moon was sickly in its pale, metallic color. The wind blowing into the room was cold and Philip drew the blanket up to his chin.

He thought of the letter he had written to Charlie Nagleman, wondering why he would not mail it. That was what he believed, why was he ashamed of it? There was always something uncertain about reasoning on general principles. It was all right in a philosophy class, but outside, theory was so easy to laugh at. And, above all things, Philip did not want to be laughed at. Logic was all you had to go by, yet, Philip thought, it did not satisfy, a cigarette did. What was wrong with Papravel, his boys and their ways? By all reason Philip ought to join them. He knew there was nothing more important than money—that was what the old sage in the long beard kept on reminding him and it was true. And there was nothing loathsome in his brother Harry, or in the Italians, or Gilhooley. Actually, at the poker game he had been growing to like them as real, warm persons. For a moment Philip seriously considered telling his uncle Papravel that he would join them, but at the next instant the picture of his father, pained and broken, stopped him.

Philip turned over in the bed. He always had trouble sleeping the first night in a strange place. As he grew drowsy he began to think of Ripple Street. He thought of the first day he had lived in Williamsburg. The tenement was new, smelling of paint and mortar. The gas in their flat had not been turned on, and his mother, young then and strong, had had to burn candles for light. In this strange place with its dim lighting Philip remembered he had cried—sleepy, tired, depressed. There was no bed for him, the furniture had not arrived, and his mother had rolled up her coat for a pillow on top of the tin covers of the washtubs in the kitchen.

The next morning, Philip recalled, he had run down eagerly to explore the streets. That was the first of his many walks through the section. How many times, Philip said, how many times. In the main the buildings then were dirty brown-colored shacks, empty and waiting for the wreckers. Construction was proceeding swiftly everywhere. In front of the sidewalks were the bags of cement neatly piled under a spread of tarpaper. Alongside were the wide rectangular bins of white plaster for the ceilings, and the screens to sift fine sand. Philip walked along watching laborers slice the ceiling plaster with shovels and pack it on their hods like whipped cream. The choo-choo which operated the unusual lift, the men rhythmically relaying floor planks from window to window like boys playing a game, the bricklayers aloft smoking cigarettes as they casually built new walls, these were the first things to interest Philip on Ripple Street.

It was time for him to go back for lunch and then he discovered that he had forgotten which apartment he lived in. With mounting terror he ran from flat to flat, throwing open doors and examining staring faces for his mother. He forgot which floor he lived on. He even forgot which house. His excitement ran with time almost to hysteria. Philip, lying in bed at Havers Falls, could still visualize the scenes, now stationary like tableaux, which he had encountered fifteen years ago when he had opened those doors in his frenzy. A woman with safety pins in her mouth diapering a baby whose legs stuck up in the air; another, a big woman, wet with perspiration, energetically poking a sawed-off broomstick into a steaming tub of wash; a third on the floor, a handkerchief over her head, cleaning a gas stove.

In time he had managed to flop into his own house. He was exhausted by his gasping, fear, and Philip remembered how there was nothing for him to do but sit on the floor and bawl extravagantly in relief.

Soon after his brother Harry got into the bed Philip fell asleep. Just before leaving home he had received the news that Tessie was getting married within the month. He had told himself this meant nothing to him, but now he dreamed he was in his room at home, embracing and caressing Tessie, who lay on his bed. He was going over her as he had done so many times that it was a ritual, and even in his dream he went laboriously through the many phases. At the same time there was something going on in a room to his left, which he identified vaguely as Cohen's room. He paid no attention to it for a while but the noise grew almost violent. Actually, it must have been a truck outside heavily going up the hill. In the dream, Philip finally left Tessie and went into Cohen's room where he discovered him standing in front of his bed, squirming, his face flushed with the embarrassment of his predicament, and evidently trying to worm his way out of a hole. His head resembled a gorgeous, red, angry plant. When he saw Philip he talked to him stiltedly of small unrelated matters. Philip looked on the bed. It was a girl with the loose features of an idiot. She was lying in a quilted bathrobe, her legs sticking crazily into the air so that she resembled a fowl hanging from a butcher's hook in the window. She was an idiot girl, but looking more closely Philip now noticed that her face was red, splotched and pimply. She had Cohen's face on.

Philip spoke to her softly, trying to calm her. He said she was making too much of a racket, the neighbors would hear her. She looked at him and said, "I'm in trouble. I don't know what to do. I'm in trouble." Then the dream ended.

When Philip awoke in the morning he heard the sharp chirping of the birds and at first he mistook it for the piercing noise boys make when they rub peach stones flat against the curb. At home the kids, using saliva generously, worked for hours to flatten the pits so that they might bore holes through them and wear them for rings. Harry woke as Philip stirred. The room was cold.

"Is it always as cold as this?" Philip asked,

"Yep. It gets warmer as the day gets on. Why don't you get out of bed and warm up the room a little?"

"The mountain air is certainly wonderful," Philip said. "I never had such dreams. They were almost nightmares."

"Get yourself a good girl and then all your nightmares will be little ones."

Philip applauded, clapping his hands. "You're so bright in the mornings it will be a wonderful break for your wife."

They went down for breakfast, talking and smoking the first cigarette. The dog, newly christened Goulash, lay on Philip's feet and he enjoyed the warmth. He felt a little more used to the country. Afterward the two went out exploring the hills. They were off the state highways, far from the hotels and summer cottages. It was real country. They followed the dog through the brambles and over cow pastures, wherever he took them as he chased rabbits. It was a cold day for the summer and the wind was strong.

They came upon a farmer alone in the field lifting hay into a wagon. He was a little startled when he first caught sight of them but he waved to them cordially and asked them how they were.

"Fine," Harry shouted. "How are you?"

"Fine," said he.

"That's fine," Harry answered. "Everything's fine."

By this time they were getting back to the house again. Harry told his brother not to play with any girls he might find around. "I'll take you to the fair some time," he said. "That's just what a nice, clean boy like you would enjoy. I'll buy you all the popcorn and lollipops you want."

Philip smiled at him. "Go to hell," he said.

The man in the policeman's uniform beat on the garage door with his stick. "Open up in there," he called. "Open the door or I'll break it down."

The night watchman peered through the crack of the doors at the cop. "What's the matter?" he said. "What's wrong?" He had been sleeping.

The policeman edged his stick between the doors and pushed himself in.

"Who do you fellows think you are anyway, trying to pull a stunt like that and get away with it? Do you think we're blind or something? You can't run a brewery here and stick a couple of trucks around the place to make it look like a garage. It's been done too often before."

"Officer," the watchman said anxiously, "there must be a mistake. This is no booze joint. This is the Silver Eagle bus garage. We keep buses here. Look around and see for yourself."

At this point a dozen men walked into the place. One of them flashed a detective badge at the watchman, sat him down and said everything was all right, they were handling this, don't make no noise or you'll get your funny face bashed in. The men went immediately to the buses. They wasted no time. The watchman's face was pale with fear. "I'm only the night man around here," he said. "I got nothing to do with the bunch that runs this business. You can't do nothing to me." The detective told him to shut up, he knew all about it. The men went immediately to the buses. They wasted no time. With the despatch and thoroughness that were the trademark of Papravel's organization they set about putting the big cars out of commission. For the most part they worked on the huge tires and the gasoline tanks. The stench of gas and the stale air from the tires filled the garage.

At the end the men surveyed the ruins and slipped out without hurry in pairs. The policeman wagged his stick at the watchman.

"You can tell your boss," he said, "this is just a sample. Tell him if he keeps on with his monkey business we'll run his whole goddam outfit out of town."

"There must be a mistake, officer," the watchman said eagerly.

"This is the first time I ever heard of booze being pulled off around here. You must have got the wrong place, officer."

"Yare?" asked the cop, and he walked through the doors.

So skillfully had they done their work that for a day and a half Morand had no cars on the road and his schedule was thrown awry for a week. The damage was terrific but he was stubborn and held on, although he wondered, how long, O Lord, how long? Morand had put so much money into the business, a station in Williamsburg was so indispensable, that he had gone into the fight with Rubin and Papravel although these tactics distressed him. He had calculated the storm would spend itself, but Rubin was being inhuman. As the struggle went on Morand disliked with increasing trepidation the tenacity, the grimness, that characterized the other side, but it had gone this far and he could not drop out. At night he prayed to God to strike his enemies.

Papravel wiped the sweat and dirt under his eyes although he knew the cloth only irritated his skin.

"Rubin," he said energetically through the heat, "this much I want you to know before another penny is turned over. What I want to do is always the right thing. I come from a good family in the old country and there is no one in Williamsburg more honest than me. It is true people here call me a crook, but I work hard for a living and no one can ever say I cheated a customer. Besides, would you have come to me in the first place if you hadn't heard them say those things about me? But trust me, Rubin, and everything will be all right.

"Only sometimes a man makes a mistake. Everyone makes mistakes, and what I want with you now, Rubin, is, in case it happens, you must promise to help."

Rubin stared angrily, bewildered. He was a skinny, middle-aged man in a brown suit and a turned-down hat that were both too large for him. It was a difficult situation and he was showing it. Morand might be worrying and praying, but Rubin too groaned through it all. He had also thought this would be a temporary encounter. With the passage of time he grew frightened to his marrow and regretted every day that hot afternoon in July when he had first bargained with Papravel. There was no getting rid of him. He had nothing to lose, while Rubin's life's earnings and prospects were involved. He would be ruined. A hundred times he was on the verge of quitting but always Papravel forbade it. He kept pointing to his swelling army of men and calling for more money, more money.

"You're sucking me dry," Rubin wept at him. "There's a limit to everything. A man can't go on like this forever."

"Give in," Papravel argued. "You can't afford to back out now. After all they've been through they won't quit if you do. Morantz will walk off with your shirt if you take it into your head to stop now. Hold on a little longer and trust me, Rubin. Everything will be all right in the end. Imagine how Morantz must be worrying if you yourself have it on your mind so much. He won't last forever. You can't get something for nothing, I don't have to tell you that, Rubin. If you want an exclusive station in Williamsburg you must work for it."

"What are you talking about?" Rubin burst out. "All I wanted was one simple job and you begin to grow on me like a wife."

"Listen," argued Papravel swiftly, "these things are not managed, one, two, three. I can't go to the Silver Eagle and say, 'Look here, mister, you can't have a bus station in Williamsburg. Go on, beat it.' They will go all right, and you will pay me, it is finished. But listen, Rubin, this is what will happen, and believe me I know what I'm talking about. The next day they will open again and you will have to start the same business all over again. Now, I'm talking to you as a businessman—does it make sense?"

"All right, all right," Rubin exclaimed impatiently. "Then what do you want me to do?"

"Just what everyone does. You should put me on the payroll, that's how it's done everywhere."

"Yes, yes," Rubin cried, his voice approaching a crescendo. "And how long does this keep going on?"

"Don't worry! For every nickel you give me, you'll get a dime and maybe a quarter."

Rubin stopped to think. Papravel lit a cigarette carefully and waited.

"Well?" he kept on saying. He was confident. "Well?"

"I don't know, I don't know, we'll see. Meanwhile, what do you mean, a man makes mistakes, in case anything should happen I got to help?"

"Oh," said Papravel. "That's a small item, but I want you to know everything from the start. I mean, in case one of the boys gets into trouble—everyone makes mistakes sometimes, Rubin, remember that—you got to help. But who besides God can tell whether something like that will happen?"

"Listen," said Rubin, greatly perturbed. This was getting to be too much. "What do you mean? Lawyers, graft, politicians?"

"Who can tell?" Papravel repeated. "Leave everything to me. I'll take care of everything. Only it takes a little money to do everything the right way and that's what I want you to know first. Rubin, I'm an honest man. I don't tell you lies at the beginning and then bother you later. I want you to know everything from the start and then if anything turns up later on you will know that I didn't cheat you."

Rubin calculated. He could make so much with a bus monopoly in Williamsburg, these bandits would cost him so much, was it worth it? Rubin calculated.

"Well?" said Papravel. "Well?"

Rubin's neck itched with the pimply heat and he scratched it. "I'll let you know," he said with calm resignation and ended the discussion.

But Papravel won out. He was given his funds, for it was true that Rubin could hardly stop now. He realized how hopeless it would be to drop everything at this stage; he gave Papravel the money and tried to gather strength from the other's enthusiasm. But at night he slept badly. Mrs. Van Curen alone was overjoyed. For every new man Papravel sent up to her boarding house the little lady received an extra three dollars per day. She had never made so much money at one time. It was such a sudden burst of riches. Papravel, she swore devoutly, was her benefactor, a straight, stalwart man who honestly paid his bills and would never cheat an old woman. He had a warm heart. Even though he was a Jew, the pious old lady said, it would be hard to find a better man.

And the struggle went on like an epic.

On the ride to the fairgrounds the Italian kept telling Philip stories of his experiences in the war. It was dark and cold. Auto rides always made Philip sleepy, and as they sped through the empty towns or forsaken fields he felt the strangeness of the country at night. There was too much of Williamsburg in him, the country always seemed an unnatural setting. His brother Harry and Gilhooley sat in the front seats, smoking cigars. They were silent, but Philip could see the red ends of their cigars reflected in the windshield.

The Italian was the one who had told about his trip to the mountain saint. In the darkness of the car he was talking this time about the revolution at Torino. Philip had been a baby when this had taken place. Nevertheless he was surprised to hear there had been a revolution there. He should have known something about it. It was a long story the Italian was telling, and at times Philip was startled to realize he wasn't following. The Italian had been home on a leave when the revolution came. He said he took no time about it but grabbed his bicycle and rode back to his division. He had always wanted the revolution.

The Italian said it was one fine time. He never saw such dirty fighting, even admitting that the wops were the dirtiest fighters. It was a combination of fierce riots that terminated only when the town was knocked wide open. They broke store windows and helped themselves. When it was all over half the men were on the floor good and drunk. Only, Milan failed to come through. That was too bad and it still disgusted him. Milan failed to come through in time and he would never forget it or forgive them.

"What happened then?" Philip said.

"They got our whole division together, sixteen thousand men maybe, they lined us up in a big plaza in the middle of the town. Every tenth man was marked off. Myself, I was eighth. They picked out every tenth, walked him down to the valley, and machine guns hidden in the bush went dra-da-da. Fini. The whole goddam valley was choked up with the dead bodies. It was one grand sight. Then they flooded the place with some kind of burning acid and after a while nothing was left."

"That must have been over fifteen hundred men." Philip said. He was impressed. "Do you mean to tell me the rest of you just took it?"

"They got us all lined up again in the plaza and made us listen to big speeches about a new Italy—all was to be forgotten; patriots, die for the mother soil—a fat load of horse manure," the Italian said. "What could we do about it with the machine guns waiting to do dra-da-da? But we got the bastard, we got the general later in the trenches. While the battle went on I was with a machine-gun crew of six men. The general, who had given the orders, passed by, and the six of us pointed our guns at him all together. The general fell down. We all looked at the machine gun as though it was a sick baby."

He knew who had shot down the general. The man had gathered the rest of them, placed his finger vertically across his mouth, and patted his holster. That was enough. The Italian would say nothing further about the killer. He told Philip the man now lived in New York, he still saw him, and he wouldn't say anything more about it. He didn't want anything to get around even at this time, in America.

Harry Hayman reached over the seat and turned his head at them. "Lay off the kid, Louie," he said. "He's too young for that kind of bull. You'll give him nightmares and I've got to sleep in the same bed with him."

Louie wanted to go on with his stories but they hit the town. Although it was only eleven the store windows were dark and the streets empty.

Two or three lamplights shone bleakly. They drove swiftly through to the fairgrounds, which were some distance outside of the town. Here it was quiet also. The carnival for the day was getting over. Philip felt he had never seen such a large hunk of sky at one time in his life. There were no stars, no moon tonight. In the blackness the little lights attached to the great Ferris wheel blinked weakly, suspended in air. Few people walked about. Nailing boards, the countermen were shutting up for the night.

"They certainly hit the hay early in these towns," Gilhooley said. He was disappointed.

"It's the middle of the week," Harry explained. The four of them stood before the huge Ferris wheel, grasping for something to do. Two couples were having a hilarious time. They were dressed in bright clothes that didn't fit well, the boys wearing flannels that had shrunk, and they kept on going around in the wheel. When their carriages were at the top, the girls' screams rudely broke the stillness. Philip guessed at what was going on up there. Mentally he compared the carriages with the cellars, Halper's wagon lot, and the Auburn S.C. Well, he said, it's certainly healthier. It keeps you out in the open.

Gilhooley insisted on going up in the wheel. It was kind of kiddish but there was nothing else to do. Hayman and Louis accompanied him while Philip remained below. He had a fear of going up in these contraptions and refused. As night crept over the fair, as the men continued busily closing for the day, Philip saw the discarded candy boxes, the trampled grass, and the crowd's garbage, and he felt lonely. In the country he was always a stranger and uneasy.

Off to his right were the big tents where prize poultry and choice cattle were kept for the contests. Philip opened a flap and went in. The lights hanging high up near the roof of the tent cast dim rays through the big space. The floor was lightly padded with straw and hay. Philip could see a few farmers sleeping near their stock.

The cows, silent and with big stupid eyes, lay on their bellies, their legs folded, solemnly inspecting Philip as they went on chewing their cuds. The warm smells of the cows' bodies, the cow manure, and the hay hung heavily in the air. Philip's eye caught a couple moving delicately in a corner. He deliberated and left the scene.

Back at the Ferris wheel the three others were laughing and having a great time. They were talking and gesticulating to a huge woman in a dirty black party dress of cheap chiffon. It was evident that she wore nothing underneath for her body protruded frankly. The skirt was too short and the woman looked ludicrous. She resembled a bulky piano resting on thin, insufficient legs.

"There he is," Gilhooley said, pointing to Philip as he came up. "That's the one you've been looking for, girlie."

Harry Hayman said, "Cut it out, you lummox. What's the fat idea?"

She went to Philip immediately. Gilhooley had said they couldn't use her but a friend of theirs was just the right article. She kicked her legs awkwardly after the manner of a chorus girl. Philip wondered what it was all about. From her face he thought she might be demented. "She's deaf and dumb," Harry said. "Pay no attention to her. This is Gilhooley's fat idea of a good joke."

The woman began patting Philip's hand and making noises that, together with the grimaces on her face and the gestures at her heart, indicated that she loved him. "I love you, I love you," she said silently for Philip to get the idea. She kissed her fingers like the barber in the hair-tonic picture, and pointed to the big tent where the prize cows lay chewing their cuds.

She was the ugliest object Philip had ever seen. At the prospect of accepting her invitation he felt for a moment on the point of vomiting. She was such a tremendous hulk of flesh, flabby, almost unlike a human being.

"Get out of here," he said in a low tone. "Beat it. This fellow's been playing a trick on you."

He joined the others and walked to the car, but the prostitute grew violently angry. She pulled Gilhooley's sleeve. He had cheated her. Her face went through a series of grimaces that brought back to Philip's mind an illustration in a psychology textbook showing facial expressions registering different emotions. Gilhooley's eyelids closed and he told her curtly to take a walk.

She took out a police whistle from her bag. "I'll blow it," she said and waited for an answer. I'll blow it, her fingers went. You better pay me or I'll blow it. Gilhooley stepped back, grabbed the whistle and shoved it into her mouth.

"Go ahead," he said. "Blow it."

She smiled weakly. Only kidding, she said, and replaced it in the bag. Give me money, her fingers were saying. Give me money. Gilhooley didn't even look back at her. They went to the parked car. The prostitute took out a pad of paper, wrote on it in a scribble, and ran in front of the Irishman waving the pad before his eyes. She had written, "Dunce! Dumbbell!" She stuck it in front of him and pointed violently at him. You, this, her lips said. You, this. Dunce! Dumbbell!

As they piled into the car she began writing again. "I wish you are dumb!" the pad said in a loose scrawl. "I wish you are deaf!" she had written. She waved the pad in front of them, her face red and wet with anger. She felt that she had been swindled and she was passionately excited. The car pulled out and she watched it, still wildly waving the pad. At this point the engine backfired two or three times in sharp, exploding sounds. Gilhooley leaned back against the seat and roared with laughter.

Home in Williamsburg, Miller was dying. In the dinginess of the dark room the old man lay on the bed, motionless, the blanket over his arms, his beard resting on the quilt, the great face set, the eyes opened in a meaningless stare. The room was bare and hushed with the proximity of death. Miller, the sage with the long beard, in whose skinny body dwelt the cold wisdom of the world, Miller lay dying, and he knew they would come and tell him it was an old story, it happened every day and to everyone, but he was not comforted.

In the haze of these last days, for the first time Miller recognized the futility of reason. The intellect was a fraud, logic a false device, for man, reduced to the individual, did not go by these things. Here Miller understood the logic of death, it was clear to him as two and two, yet he was dying in the same fashion as an ignorant clod. For a moment he went back through the years to the time when as a boy he had cried because he had lost some coins. He remembered someone had tried to console him, saying the money was inconsequential in amount, he would forget it, there would be more later when he grew up. Miller remembered how clearly he had understood the man's arguments; he had paused, hiccupping, because of their truth. Nevertheless the tears had come, he had still bewailed his lost coins. Now Miller did not like to die.

A man had a sense of humor, Miller thought, until things became serious. To tell the truth, he was chagrined with himself, with his state of feelings. He had always been so cool, impersonal, that had always been his way of living. He had flattered himself on being a genuine sophisticate. What would that youngster Philip say, smiled the old man, if he could read the obscene quake in my mind now? Miller was ashamed of himself, and chagrined. How much had he truly known? What was wisdom? It was a pose to be put on like a cloak, the sly grin, the all-knowing taciturnity, the hunched-up shoulders, the laughing eyes. Miller kidded with himself, but that was to hide his regret at the prospect of death.

Miller thought and thought as he lay dying, but he said nothing. Mrs. Miller shuffled into his room from time to time, caring for him. It had to be done. Her attitude toward him in the past now made her clumsy as she fixed his bed, gave him food, and washed his face with vinegar and witch hazel. The sons, fearing what neighbors might say, were energetic. They visited the house regularly, giving advice and passing comment, calling doctors one after the other. Secretly they wondered the amount of the old man's wealth and the manner of its distribution. How long would he lie dying? They asked, and they were not hard-hearted sons, only impatient. As for Miller, he continued until the last days to disregard his family thoroughly.

The doctors his sons brought came bristling with professional assurance a little stronger because actually they did not know the exact cause of the old man's illness. They were certain of its outcome, he was an old man, why take the trouble? The first man said it was a stroke and let it go at that. Others said Miller was an old man, an automobile lasted so long, this was to be expected. An eminent specialist, at a fee of twenty-five dollars, pronounced Miller sick with an embolism that was traveling and would be fatal within a short period. He packed his bag, washed his hands, surveyed the gloomy surroundings, and left in a Packard motorcar. Still another specialist said it was acute ascending paralysis. This was a rare disease and generally fatal. He had never treated a case of Landry's disease in his personal practice and he was eager to observe Miller. Mrs. Miller let him visit the old man subsequently but told him not to return when she discovered he was interested in securing the corpse for postmortem examination. The specialist patiently argued the sacrifices necessary for medical progress, but Mrs. Miller refused. It was against Jewish law and the neighbors would have made a misery of her life.

Whatever it was, embolism, paralysis, or general debilitation, Miller knew he was dying and he did not like it.

The neighbors, too, knew the old man was near his end. As they passed the door of his apartment they gazed at it with awe. It was an ordinary brown, heavy metal door but in its mute way it had assumed the grim properties of death. Children ran past it, genuinely fearful of the strange phenomenon it was shielding. Mrs. Hayman alone, in her time the witness of many deaths, was not afraid. She visited the flat three and four times a day to pass the time with Mrs. Miller. Then they talked and sighed and said everyone had to expect it, it always came.

Philip's mother was intrigued by the old man's stolidity. She wanted to ask him whether he wasn't afraid. How did he feel, so near the finish? Possessed of death he became an extraordinary man, and she wanted to discuss his condition with him, but she had to forbear.

Once she went into his room. Straightening the blanket, she

spoke to him kindly, saying with a show of humor he ought to be getting up. "A man can't lie in bed all the time," she said.

The old man smiled and said, "Thanks. Thanks for fixing the quilt and thanks for pretending I'm a man who is still alive."

"Nonsense," Mrs. Hayman scolded. "It's a sin to talk like that."

In a voice that Mrs. Hayman later said sounded as though it came from a cave, the old man with his smile said wryly, "I've lived my time, now it is getting finished. It's true no one likes to die and everyone likes to eat, to drink, and to feel the warm sun on his back. But, after all, what do we lose? Food, drink, and the warm sun. That's all. Be well, they tell me, even my sons and their wives who will later fight among themselves over the division of my poor dollars. Be well, they say, but what difference does it all make?"

When Mrs. Hayman left, Miller said to himself he wished he felt as he talked. What a faker he was, he said, how he liked to fool these people even to the last. Sometimes nothing destroys affectation, not even death. While he was trembling, he was making Mrs. Hayman believe that he was moving to his end nonchalantly so that she might pass the news on in conversation and the housewives would all set him up in their meaningless gossip as a wonderful man, a heroic figure in spite of his many faults.

No one likes to die, said Miller. A man is born, he grows and grows, and dies. We must expect that, everyone says, but we who say it never do. We expect death in others, to ourselves it is always remote and impossible. A man grows and grows, not understanding time, getting up day after day, not noticing the street number on his door, and he expects this series of days to go on forever. Time measured by chronological days and weeks is an invention of reason and a fraud. When a man dies it makes no difference whether he has lived eighty years or eight weeks. The days that have slipped by mean nothing, for the past is dead. The days that are to come deceive because a man does not live them in a lump sense. The future dribbles itself away in minute parts. Divide an hour into minutes, minutes into seconds, and seconds by sixty. The products are the true intervals during which he lives, and they pass so rapidly that we cannot know them as they go. Finally they all pour away, like fine sand through a child's fingers. The supply has been exhausted, the man has been deceived and he is asked to die. You have lived your time, they will say, and he will wonder, what time have I lived if I am to die now?

Miller lay dying, and he lamented the days that were gone. From the yard he could hear someone practicing on a saxophone. Women were feeding lunch to their children at the windows in forced spoonfuls. Downstairs a group of girls were playing a game and singing:

"How do you do, my partner?
How do you do today?
We will dance in a circle,
I will show you the way."

EIGHT

Cohen, waiting for evening and Tessie's wedding, had been reading a Russian novel in which the characters, fascinatingly foreign, had been discussing the melancholy in their souls, the huge lamentation that was life, and the burdens they endured. He marveled at their rich lives and envied them. Here the people lived with strong emotions. They felt keenly, and they did not restrain themselves when it came to action. What conversation, Cohen gagged to himself from respect, what talk! And the things they did! Their movements had a beginning and an end, there were so many adventures life was constantly in meaningful flux. Take Dostoevsky. That was life, turbulent, profound, meaty, as it should be.

Cohen read Russian novels and he regretted the condition of existence in Williamsburg. People were commonplace, either going to the movies or returning. Conversation concerned the price of pot cheese. And, worst of all, nothing ever happened. Cohen examined his own life. Nothing had ever happened to him, he had to admit. In spite of his reading and culture how many cuts was he in the essential richness of existence above Davey, the kid who ran through the streets with his gang? The reflection distressed him, but then the thought of Mahler came to cheer him.

When Cohen entered the shoe store, the old man was sitting before his iron shoe gigantically engaged in clearing his chest. He nodded to him and went on with his duties, this time pushing his nose into a big dirty rag. The stool on which he sat was a chair with its back knocked off. Around it on the floor was a dusty mess of leather scraps, paper, and worn ladies' heels, the collection of months. Cohen sat down near the wall of the store. He liked the smell of the glue the old man used to paste on the soles. Mahler came out of the rag and asked Cohen for a cigarette.

"What are you doing out of bed so soon?" Cohen said, giving him one. "You're a sick man."

"To tell the truth, I'd stay in bed another day, but I had to get up or else Yente Maldick would have come again. Another day with her and I would be dead for sure."

"Listen," said Cohen, "isn't it funny? Here I know you so long and I still don't know your first name."

"I'll tell you, young gentleman," Mahler said slowly. "At my naming ceremony a funny thing happened. The guests were all present, the rabbi was saying the words, and the man who was to circumcize me already took out the blade. Just then in rushes a stranger with a yell. 'What are you filthy Jews doing here?' he cries. 'Are you sacrificing an innocent babe so that your filthy God will have something to eat?' And the next thing that happened a bunch of Cossacks swarm into the room and slaughter the people right and left until everyone is lying with his bowels on the floor. So all my life I have to go through torment not only because I am not properly circumcized but also because I have never been given a first name."

Mahler had given the tale with a straight face, solemnly continuing all the time with his work. Nevertheless, Cohen was incredulous.

"Is that a true story?" he said.

"Listen, young gentleman," Mahler said, putting the shoe down and rising to his feet, "there doesn't have to be another word said. If you have any doubt, let me prove it right now."

Cohen protested hurriedly. All right, he believed him. The bell on the top of the door tinkled and in walked Yente Maldick carrying a tin cup.

"All right," the shoemaker said, returning to his stool. "There's a woman in the store now, but any time you think I have been lying let there not be two words and I'll be happy to show you." He turned to the old woman. "What do you want, missus?" he said, pretending not to recognize her.

"How are you, Mr. Mahler?" she said. "Look, I brought you some hot milk with butter. It will do you good."

"What's the matter with you, woman?" Mahler asked. He looked at Cohen. "What's the matter with this woman? Maybe you know her, mister? Missus, don't you know poor Mahler died last night? He didn't have any bread, so he died."

"It can't happen," Yente said firmly. "America has enough bread for everyone."

"He was eating herring, missus, and a bone got stuck in his throat. 'If I had a piece of bread,' he said, 'I would be able to get rid of the bone. But I have no bread.' So he sat down and waited until he choked to death."

"That's terrible," Yente said. She began crackling her fingers. "What a calamity! What will we do? What will we do?"

"And what's more," Mahler said, "did you hear what happened to poor Yente Maldick? She went to a Turkish bath to get ready for the Holidays. She knew that when she had all her clothes off there would be no way of telling Yente apart from the others, so she tied a piece of red ribbon around her ankle. Everything went well until a terrible thing happened while she was bathing. The red ribbon fell off and Yente Maldick was lost." It was an old trick, but Yente Maldick had never heard of it.

"Oh, woe, oh, woe," said the old woman, uncertain and wondering whether to believe him. "Woe is me."

"Yes," said Mahler, "terrible things are happening all the time because there is no more a God over America. But look, missus, the milk is getting cold. You better go home with it before it gets like ice."

"Yes, yes, my child," she told the old man. "You're right." The wrinkles on her brow multiplied as she considered what Mahler had said, but finally, finding the problem too difficult, she solved it by dismissing it, and, relieved, carried the tin cup out of the door.

Cohen, who had paid no attention while all this was going on, had been thinking. He had hired a tuxedo for Tessie's wedding and it was to be the first time he would be wearing evening clothes, a stiff shirt, and a wing collar. The prospect exhilarated him, made him feel expansive and urbane.

"Listen, Mahler," he said smoothly, "I'm a writer. You did not know that perhaps, but this was because I never mention it."

"Don't be ashamed of it, young gentleman. At your age everyone is a writer. Even me, although I can't tell you what I wrote. Tell me, what have you written?"

"For the present, I am collecting notes, observations on life and general principles of behavior. Just now, however, I intend working on a play. What I want to do, Mahler, is to talk it over with you. A play should reflect life, and certainly you should know life. After all, I realize I am young and there are many things about which I do not know. Now, the plot of this play goes like this. A certain woman spends the night sleeping with three different men."

"All in the same bed?" Miller asked, aghast.

"No, no. One after the other. There are three scenes. This is the first act."

"But all in one night. Wonderful, wonderful."

"Here is the problem of the play. The second act opens some months later. The woman knows she is going to have a baby, and the problem of the play is to discover which man is the father of the child. Remember, the three men have been carefully portrayed in the first act. They have different temperaments and they are in different conditions of society. You can see how interesting the problem becomes. Can you imagine what a riot the third act will turn into?"

Mahler rose. "Excuse me," he said, "there is something I have to do." He went to the rear of the store.

When he came back, Cohen was on top of him. "Well, what do you think of it? Did you ever hear of a thing like that?"

"I never heard of such a thing," Mahler said.

"Isn't it original? I told the plot to some friends of mine and they all said they never heard of an idea like that either." He was jubilant. Here was Mahler, the man who had lived all over the world, who had lived intensely, even Mahler recognized the uniqueness of his theme.

"What are you calling this thing?" Mahler wanted to know. He sat before the iron shoe and began hammering small nails, taking them one by one from his gums.

"Well, it's a long story," Cohen said, his face very serious. "At first I wanted to call it 'The Whoremonger,' but I thought that would be too raw for prurient New York audiences, so I changed it to 'The Harlot-Master.' I was thinking of calling it that for some time, but then I had an inspiration. I finally decided to call it 'Green Gods in Yellow.'"

"In what?" Mahler shot back, his face wrinkled with surprise.

"You know, yellow. Like in the war, when a man had too much sense to fight, they called him yellow."

"Oh, that's a pity. With a beautiful idea like that you should never burden the play with a title 'Green Gods in Yellow.' Of course you young gentlemen won't listen to an old man, but, if I may say so, I think a better title would be 'Green Gods in Yellow Tights.'"

Cohen thought it over. "Never mind," he said uneasily. "Never mind."

He hated to admit it to himself, in fact he failed to, but often his favorite was a little disappointing. Was he really kidding him? Cohen sat dejected.

"Cheer up," Mahler said. "Don't look so glum. Look, I'll tell you a joke that will make you happy. It's guaranteed. A fat man was running down the street to catch a trolley car. On his back he was carrying a heavy sack and he was so fat it was hard for him to run. But the trolley was going to leave and he had to run to catch it. So he runs and runs. Just when he comes to the street corner the trolley car begins to ride away. He stands in the middle of the tracks, looks at the car, and says, disgusted, 'A joke!'"

"What's the point?" Cohen said. "I don't see anything funny."

"Ah, you young American gentlemen," Mahler said sadly. "In spite of all your learning you still know nothing."

Cohen walked out. What kind of a joke was it, where was the point? He went over Mahler's exact words as well as he could recall them. Where was the point? He was not so much angry with the old man as disappointed. Was Mahler kidding him? Cohen would not admit it, but in spite of himself he was suspicious. He tried to think of the tuxedo. He would be fascinating tonight and already had composed the postures he would assume.

As he passed Yente Maldick's shack he saw her standing outside, still holding the tin cup and reflecting.

"What's the matter?" he asked. He had forgotten all about it.

She looked at him with grief in her eyes. "Tell me, mister," she begged. "Please, young gentleman, did Mahler choke on a herring bone? Did he really die?" Her eyes were wide and tearful. She wanted earnestly to know.

The bums at Halper's Stable, together with Willie Bernstein and his pals, were having a sham fight. On Keap Street there was a great lot, parts of which had already been excavated for the cellars of apartment houses. The men from the stable had divided themselves into two groups that proceeded to do battle against one another. Cohen, on the sidewalk, wiped his spectacles with his handkerchief and watched them ardently. They were grown men, but they fought for fun like kids, and it was a great sight, but so meaningless, so American in its stupidity.

The men slashed long whips to keep the enemy at bay. Others prepared pails, filling them with water from a hose. They sent the pails up and the frontline men swished the water in thick waves. No one minded getting wet. They rubbed the water from their eyes and dug into piles of horse manure. They seized it, rounding the lumps with their hands like snowballs, and flung them, aiming carefully for the faces. Bernstein suddenly grabbed the hose and played it full force into a friend's mouth. They were having a riotous time.

Out of the stable Halper came running down to break up the

game. He waved a blank-cartridge pistol, fired into the air, and chased the men with his whip. He cursed hotly at them as they scrambled out of reach. Halper was the only one among them who had any sense of responsibility. The fight was over. Halper stormed at the men at the threshold of the stable while they wrung the water out of their clothes. They cleaned off the manure with sticks. A few went inside to wash. The smell and the filth made little difference with the stable bums. The place was quiet again, and dim.

Cohen shook his head and disapproved, but Davey kept hanging around. It was the high spot for boys, an odorous spot where the atmosphere hung rich in adventure, cowboys and the Wild West. There was always something doing if one waited long enough to watch it break. The stable was owned by an old family of American Jews, cigar smokers, brandy drinkers, and fast livers who in the winter never failed to appear in expensive fur-lined coats. Halper, a stout, solidly built man, ran the place and worried. The trade had fallen off. It was not like the old times when a horse dealer engaged in a fast-moving business. Halper had to squeeze out the work, no longer trading exclusively in workhorses but having to handle saddlehorses and ponies. His face was fat and florid, and he was always to be seen in a big hat, a cigar working between his teeth and a long whip in his hand. Wherever he went he smelled warmly of the stable. Willie Bernstein, his nephew, was a wild youngster who would never settle down. He had his uncle in a perpetual state of worry over him. Willie had been a successful lightweight prizefighter until his uncle heard of it and made him quit the game. A memento of those times, he still had a broken nose.

From the West, Halper was shipped horses that were often only half-broken. All day he had his men ride them up and down the street pulling wagons to accustom them to harness. When a horse was being exhibited for a customer the back wheels were chained to show the horse's strength. Sometimes all four wheels were tied. Then the men ran alongside shouting wildly, and Willie, who generally drove on these occasions, cracked his whip madly to urge the beast forward. In the great din, the animal dug his hind legs into the asphalt and the muscles on his rump trembled with effort.

Almost every other month Halper exchanged stables with some other dealer. As many as thirty and forty horses were to be seen parading through the streets.

There was always something to see here. Often a horse broke through the wood grating over the cellar and fell through. The boys flocked to see the sight, the news traveling rapidly. A beam was put in place on the roof, block and pulley were set up, and the horse was pulled out by his belly, the stiff legs hanging helplessly, his eyes glazed in an empty, scared stare. The boys admired the activity of the men as they went through the tasks.

The greatest treat occurred when a horse died. Then the bloated body was dragged outside and Davey stood about with his gang contemplating death and the sickly colors the horse's urine produced on the wet pavement. In a few hours the horse's wagon pulled up for it. The van was big, closed, strange with its mission of death. Chains were fastened to the neck or hindquarters of the beast, and huge dirty men in black workclothes drew it up. Inside the wagon Davey could see the corpses of other horses in odd postures, among whom the new arrival was economically squeezed. The horse undertakers, busy men who disregarded their audiences, were marked by tattooed pictures on their arms. Davey assured his gang that these were vaccinations against disease.

The men who collected at Halper's Stable held great attraction for Davey and the boys of the street. They paid no attention to the stable bums whom Halper took in and fed in return for the work they did about the stable until they wandered off somewhere. These were sorry specimens, lacking color and resembling the garbage scows in flat hues of gray and brown carrying cargoes of nondescript refuse to sea. On the other hand, there was Scotty, a faithful little man who was a mute and could only manage to mumble out things in thin gasps that were unintelligible. He followed Willie Bernstein with devotion. Rusty, a grinning, cheerful Irishman, periodically got drunk every Saturday night, and kind friends made it a point to look for him and toss him into an opened bale of hay. There were others; a short, dark-faced man chiefly interesting because of the scars on his face; another who attracted

Davey because the three fingers between his thumb and little finger on his right hand were missing; and a constantly changing group of cowboys, some tremendously robust and big, bulls.

Willie was easily the most popular of the lot. He was a great hero with the boys. Bernstein was whole-spirited, reckless with himself and carefully considerate of others. Moreover he was the champion of the Jews in a difficult neighborhood. Once an Italian, in the course of some argument, was smacking skinny Yozowitz, the laundryman. Willie rushed out of the stable, yanked the heavier Italian to the gutter, and then neatly cut him up with his fists.

Further, in one of the few frame buildings there lived an old Civil War veteran. He was creaky and witless. Sporadically the veteran would run out to the top of his wooden stoop, brandish his sword in the air, and cry out crazily. Willie seemed to be the only one who had any influence with the old man. He would go up the steps, gently take the sword from his hand, and lead the soldier back into the house.

A year ago he had married; a chorus girl, people said. Halper waited to see his nephew settle down, but when a boy was born Willie promptly named him Mustang and went out roistering.

The stable remained quiet and dim. There was nothing for this afternoon. Davey went across the street to play shooters on a piece of unpaved sidewalk in front of the lot Halper used to store his wagons. Scotty, tilted against the brick wall in the round-backed barrel chair, slept with his hat over his eyes. Within, the horses' hoofs punctuated the silence as they changed position. The strong smell of manure mingled with the softer one of hay.

A half-hour later Davey had an exciting adventure. He was glad he had waited for something to happen. Three men rode up to the stable. Willie took out a horse for them and went running up the street freely to show the horse's form. Coming back, the beast suddenly went wild and galloped off to the sidewalk at full speed. The horse was almost on top of Davey. Bernstein managed somehow to pull the animal high up on his hind legs. Davey saw Willie struggling back with the reins, his body almost parallel to the floor of the wagon. Scotty dashed out of the stable, swung up at the bridle of the horse and twisted him to one side so that he fell, breaking the shaft.

It was a miraculous escape. At half-past five, when he met Yetta at Cheap Simon's, he narrated the story in faithful detail. "Geezus," he kept on saying, having only admiration for Willie Bernstein and forgetting all concern for himself, "Geezus." Yetta, however, made a show of displeasure. The story did not impress her. "Please," she said, "I wish you'd take care of yourself." She was angry with him, but tender in her anger, and Davey was happy.

Cohen found the conversation going badly. It was the tuxedo. He held his neck stiffly above the wing collar, the girl was wearing a flowing red dress that swept the floor, and this was a strange sight to behold in the Canal Street subway station. Cohen made a passing remark about the gaping people in an effort to be superior, but even he recognized the failure of the attempt. In addition, there was the complex etiquette of handling a young lady. It was like walking on eggs. Cohen felt constrained all the time, and tight. He never knew exactly when to hop and skip in front of her to hold open doors and let her pass. Often he had to grope awkwardly to express the appropriately smiling sentiments. Cohen regretted his lack of experience with girls.

The lady herself was disgruntled. She was a plump individual, with wide hips and an oily face. Her hair was ornate. It had waves, bangs, and dips, all on one head; she had been to the beauty parlor and had spared no expense. She was disgruntled because Cohen had led her to the subway, disregarding the taxi drivers who had spotted his tuxedo and hailed him repeatedly, to his discomfiture. Her attitude was inconsiderate. Cohen had already gone to the trouble of hiring a tuxedo when a dark business suit would have done just as well. She lived in Bensonhurst. Tessie was getting married in Williamsburg. What could she expect? Besides, and he mentioned it, the subway was faster.

Cohen in his tuxedo tried to overlook the skinny fit of the

trouser legs, the way his vest creased out at the sides, and the cut of the collar around his neck and shoulders. He knew his tie made him appear funny. A boy holding his mother's hand stopped flat-footed and nearly tripped in astonishment as he stared directly into the faces of the pair.

Cohen tried to swing easily into stride beside his companion. "Did Tessie mention perhaps that I am a playwright?" he asked, beginning a conversation to kill time until the train came. They couldn't just stand there.

"You write plays?" she said, frozen in her finery. "What did you say your name was?"

He told her.

"Cohen?" she said. "I don't think I ever heard of you."

A train roared in. Cohen felt so discountenanced that he actually said that he wasn't famous as yet. The doors opened and in his embarrassment he entered.

"Not this train," the girl said, standing on the platform. "That's the wrong train. It's an express."

"Come in," Cohen said. "Come in. This train's all right."

"No, get out. You want a Canarsie local. This is an express. Get out." She stood outside, her face screwed with impatience and irritation.

While Cohen stood there thinking, the doors closed. He pushed to open them, but they closed with too much force. He began yelling instructions, but stopped. He didn't know exactly what to tell her and he couldn't think fast enough. She stood magnificent in her cold anger, her eyes glaring terribly to the last.

Cohen was disgusted. The evening was turning out poorly. He had set so much store by it. Here he had a wedding, and for once in his life the opportunity to get dressed up, to wear evening clothes, to stick his handsome head on top of a high wing collar, to have his chest gleaming proudly with whiteness. There were to be potted palms and soft music. Lovely ladies, each looking like a different flower, would sigh at him because he was so unapproachable. He would walk on the tips of his toes, wafting about the palatial halls like the soft music itself. Cohen would seek a secluded corner, slip his hand urbanely into his pocket, pensively light a cigarette. As the train beat the rails Cohen took heart. The evening was just beginning.

At the hall he burst in while the marriage performer was in the middle of his address to Schlausser and Tessie. Cohen's entrance created a disturbance. Everybody had been listening to the speech and welcomed the interruption. The rabbi, a young man combining the smooth traditions of America with those of Judea, smiled kindly and went on. He had a greasy voice and was all smiles, speaking with the corners of his mouth constantly upturned. He referred to Tessie and Schlausser as dear bride and groom, at each occasion presenting them with a flash of gold teeth as he smiled a little more sweetly. A tender allegory concerning birds and newlyweds was being unfolded. The marriage performer said nest, lovemaking, billing and cooing, and, of course (a big golden flash), fledglings. He depicted the course of married life, gently warning that there would inevitably be brief storms. "But where there is such love as I see in your smiling countenances I know the compromises will be easy to make. The groom will take his wife into his embrace, kiss away her tears, and the sweet calm that follows a storm will be doubly welcome because you have cleared away anger that has been long pent up." Finally he mixed his metaphors a bit, said something about twin oaks rearing their branches to the great heavens and growing old entwined, and Schlausser smashed the wine glass on the floor with his heel. Schlausser had been sagging at the end. He had shifted weight repeatedly from leg to leg.

The group broke out of its trance. Everybody kissed Tessie, who tried to get over the veil. Her eyes were a little moist, and she hugged her mother with passion. People pumped Schlausser's hand. He was in a hurry and had a difficult time breaking away. He went to the bathroom. As he came out the marriage performer was there to meet him. He congratulated the groom, complimented him on his choice, and said with a wide smile that Schlausser was not to hesitate very long in calling him again. He performed circumcisions as well as marriage ceremonies. Finally the holy man came to the point, seeing Schlausser was holding back. He said that in these cases the groom generally expressed his appreciation in some tangible way to the man who had bound him to such a lovely wife. Of course, he wouldn't be expected to know the custom, this being the first time he was getting married. They laughed, "Hah, hah," but Schlausser was ready for him. He said just then he hadn't his wallet with him. He'd see him later in the evening some time.

A five-piece band, mostly brass, began a foxtrot with snap. A few couples went out on the floor. The man with the cornet stood up and wagged the horn. Somebody yelled out, "Hot-cha," and the dance was on. The old folks sat stiffly on the chairs which lined the walls and told stories about the couple when they were young. They all said time flew, they could remember when.

The girl in the flaming red dress, whom Cohen was to have escorted, would not favor him with a glance. Nevertheless, he was having a great time. He had found a group of girls, and in the general excitement at the close of the address he too had unloosened and was talking abundantly. Cohen discovered there was nothing particularly different about girls. He told a few amusing anecdotes about himself. The girls giggled in appreciation. It was easy, it was like talking to Philip. Cohen was carried away with himself. He was feeling brilliant, suave, and self-assured.

Tessie's father became loudly perplexed. He had forgotten the pickled herring. Thereupon Cohen stepped in and offered his services. "Don't bother," he said, stopping the man's protests. "It's no trouble at all. Just give me the key and I'll fetch it. It'll take me a minute." He was off, gallant and dashing. Cohen wondered what kind of an impression he had left with the girls.

He walked to Tessie's home in a few minutes. Now the streets were empty and he walked unmolested. It was late. In the cool breeze, swinging along in his evening clothes, Cohen played with his tie and began to feel like the movies. To have style, to live with grace and elegance, that was the thing. He found the jar of pickled herring and lugged it down to the street with some effort. Cohen stood at the curb and debated with himself. The jug was large, of earthenware, half brown and half white. How would he look dragging that jar through the streets in his tuxedo and wing collar? He calculated the cost of a taxi and his mood won. He lit a cigarette, lifted his arm, and yelled smartly, "Taxi!" He piled in with the herring.

As they came to the wedding hall Cohen opened the door while the cab was still in motion. He bounced out and worked snappily on the brown-and-white jar. His hand slipped, the jar fell to the sidewalk, the pickled fish slipping over Cohen's trousers and sliding onto the ground. Cohen smelled the overpowering stench of herring all over him. He thought of his awkward time with the girl he was taking to the wedding from Bensonhurst, the mishap when they changed trains at Canal Street, and now this. He was just beginning to have a good time, he had been so happy and exultant, that wonderful mood had passed already and it all came back. He almost wept from disappointment and misery. What would he do about the tuxedo? It was stained, ruined, the man who rented them would demand full payment for it. Cohen's heart ached with his unhappiness and he worried about the tuxedo he had rented.

It was late at night. The street cats with bulky faces, crude, like fists, and chewed-up from fights, crept among the garbage cans seeking food. They slinked nervously. Here one jumped up, pawed stonily about, and ripped open a bag of chicken intestines. She gobbled it up, her sharp teeth going all the time while she looked from side to side to ward off possible attacks from other cats. An unhappy group sat crouched in the center of the street, having the light of the lamppost all to themselves. They cried and whined, and their sounds had a strangely human quality. From time to time there was a long wail, slow and full, unfolding the misery of the world.

In the desolation of the night a baby woke somewhere and began crying. It cried with all its soul, "E-yah, e-yah." It made a deep gasp for breath and sent it all out on the "yah." The cats in the cold went "Ya-ow, ya-ow," and the baby in answer said sharply, "E-yah."

Suddenly an alarm clock went off with its harsh clatter. The cats and the baby stopped.

Cohen, condemned to men's laughter, a frustrated human, Cohen the poor simp, walked the lonely streets at night, seeking peace for his soul. He looked at the houses before him. Out of a canvas, it seemed, he saw the tenement buildings erect before him with their yellow and red brick, with an occasional square of light in a window, with the mournful black fire escapes. He saw the garbage cans forming uneven designs on the sidewalk, which was marked up with the colored chalk of kids who had been playing there. In the gutters were newspapers and bags, banana skins, orange peels, and watermelon rinds. Whatever meaning he read in the picture coincided with his own: a biting sadness. He was ugly with his pimples. His hair was thin, and he had to oil it and plaster it over the bald spots. Girls laughed at him, Hayman laughed at him, Mahler laughed at him. He knew now that in speaking of his play he was a liar. He would never write. Cohen verged on a condition of self-pity, and the feeling consumed him with bitter tenderness.

A Mary Sugar bum competed with the cats for scraps at the garbage can. She was old, rickety, and seemed put together with safety pins. A gray bristling mustache protruded from a face lined with dirt. The seams running from her cheekbones to her mouth were deeply folded. Cohen stopped, observing her. Nothing was strange. She walked past him, her body bent, unseeing, clutching her oilcloth bag filled with choice refuse.

Cohen stood under the lamplight. He suddenly took it into his head to make a speech to the cats, the garbage cans, the mute fire escapes. It was his last testament. He stated that the world as he knew it was futile, vain, and lying. He had sought industriously for beauty and poetry and had found only ugliness. He had sought something good that would have the power to interest his mind since the world had failed, interest his mind singly, to the exclusion of all else. Therein too he had failed. Life was senseless, it had no dignity. The manifesto was long-winded, turgid in spots, often trite. Cohen spoke and looked up at the stars. He walked off to the

Williamsburg Bridge and to his death. He was determined this time.

Cohen saw a tall, very thin man leaning up against the wall of a chicken market. His clothes were black and damp. Cohen was impressed by the color of his face. It was not flesh-like, but ink black, sickly black. Sweat increased it. He wondered whether the wretch was drunk or dying. He had urinated in his trousers and now held his legs apart while a thin thread ran to the gutter. A cop down the street saw him. The policeman wheeled and walked in a long circle to avoid the bother. In a sick gesture of greeting the thin man held up his hand, the fingers spread, and feebly rolled it. He grinned at the cop. The hand fell to his side.

That was life, Cohen said, a man so thin that the legs ran up to his shoulders, leaning against the wall, urinating as he died. Life was Mary Sugar bums groping among the garbage, hungry cats wailing in the cold, and an alarm clock going off sharply. I am no part of this life, Cohen said, therefore people laugh at me. I have pimples on my face and tears in my eyes. My head is almost bald. Girls ridicule me almost to my face. Everything I say is ludicrous, for mankind is cruel. Not one of my actions goes unheeded and not one is unmocked.

By this time he had reached the deserted bridge. Cohen walked through the lonely lights. Looking from a distance, he saw the lamp bulbs suspended on the cables like a string of pearls. The sky was a million miles up. Cohen walked in the center of the setting, facing the huge towers, the cables coming down to meet him, the lights at the sides shutting out the world. He was alone, and amid these surroundings in spite of his profound emotion he thought he resembled a woodcut.

Cohen climbed down from the pedestrian walks to the paths for the automobiles. He scaled the railing here. Below was the East River, somber, undulatingly fearsome. The red and green lights of the tugs and barges looked up at him. What are you doing? they blinked, like children in their wonder. What's the matter with you?

Cohen jumped. His legs were outspread, his face covered with his arms. This was a terrible moment. In it Cohen saw reality. He became a speck in the air. His feet churned furiously, he waved his arms like a mechanical toy released. The air rushed up to meet him. Cohen slipped into the water easily. He had struck the river feet first and entered smoothly. Down, down he went. His eyes were opened and he cried with fear at the black desolation of the water. Now he came up, pushing with his arms and kicking. He rose interminably. Finally he bobbed above the water. His eyes were blinded with light.

A tugboat with all its compartments lit rested near him. A man threw a coil of thick twine to him.

"Grab it," he called. "Grab it."

Cohen held on and the men pulled him through the water. He was dazed. The oily smell of the tug, the heat from the boiler, the gleaming brass filled his head.

"Thanks, buddies. Thanks," he said breathless. "It was an accident. I don't know what happened."

"Accident, my old lady, accident," a man said. He had a fat face, and Cohen noticed the way his dirty sailor hat was stretched over his skull. "You were spread out on the railing like Jesus Christ crucified, thinking about your accident."

Cohen meant to sit down, but the deck rushed up to hit him. The bones in his behind hurt. He was exhausted.

Tessie with characteristic consideration and kindness sent Schlausser to visit Cohen at the hospital. This was four days after the wedding, when Schlausser was on his way to his upper New York State tour.

"Why did you want to do a thing like that for?" he asked. He held his grip, ladies' sundries, corsets and brassieres, and the flush of getting married had already worn off. Business was business. "Why?" Schlausser asked a little impatiently. "Why should a man do a thing like this?"

"I don't know," Cohen mumbled. "It was like this. My head was getting bald and I got to thinking. It was just the way it happened. Then the tuxedo got ruined and I didn't know what to do about it. Everything gets mixed up and sometimes a fellow gets crazy."

Schlausser looked at his watch, unable to fathom the enigma that was Cohen. "Well, I guess I got to be running along. Is there anything I can do for you?"

Cohen was still worried about the tuxedo. "What should I do about the suit?" Cohen asked. "I don't know what to do yet. I can't pay him."

"Forget all about it," Schlausser said. "What can the man do to you? He can't kill you, and if he's crazy enough to sue you, let him sue. He can't do anything to you. Is there anything you want?"

Cohen squinted through his weak eyes. His spectacles had been broken and he had not had an opportunity to replace them. However, he forgot about that now and asked Schlausser if he could get him something to read, something interesting, like *Lady Chatterley's Lover* or Rabelais. It was very dull at the hospital.

"You mean those dirty books?" Schlausser asked, for some reason astonished at the request. "Well, I certainly can't understand some of you fellows, the way you do things. I don't know about the books. I'll write to Tessie when I get to Albany."

NINE

All Williamsburg stood in array to witness the end of one of its oldest institutions. Certain corners here retained their popularity as hangouts over periods of fifteen and twenty years, the legacy having been handed down from one generation of bad eggs to the other. Such was Hooper and Ripple, once toughest, lately degenerate, now in its death throes. This bright afternoon the folk gathered from blocks around to watch the Hooper gang indulge in their last orgy and fold up as a unit forever more.

The entire thoroughfare between Ripple and South Fifth was closed. Within, two-dozen adult members of the Hooper gang performed the last rites. They were all drunk on gin, violent, ripping, tearing, and fighting with one another. In the free space they had unencumbered play, while at either end the crowds solemnly watched the performance like an audience in a theater. It was a wild time. No one dared walk through the street at the risk of a broken head. The Hoopers, young men between nineteen and twenty-five, ran crazily up and down the street, from sidewalk to sidewalk. They flung empty whiskey bottles at one another. For no reason discernible, two men would take their stand in the middle of the street, trading savage blows grimly. Occasionally, a group of them would run down in a concerted rush and swoop on a fellow member. He sank to the ground fighting, but like a lump of sugar melting.

Originally the Hoopers had been a reckless, fearless crowd of Irish boys, roaming the streets at will, masters among the many gangs. Their name was dreaded the length and width of the section. But with the immigration of the Jews, who soon dwarfed them with their numbers, they were won over and their strength was diluted. Their wildest adventure at this stage was centered in the election-night celebrations when they built gigantic fires from stray wagons and ripped-down fences. These were held at the corner of Ripple and Hooper and were ended only by the fire engines and a detail of cops. The pavement was scarred for months afterward in deep, crisscrossing lines. In time they found the Jewish influence fatal to their morale. Their spirit was fast ruined by the complicated allegiance to their own brothers in Christianity and to the Jews. Members of the gang moved elsewhere to their greater glory, returning periodically for affectionate visits. Organized activity faltered. This afternoon was their swan song.

All at once the entire group engaged in a general melee in the center of the block. Twenty men fought terribly in a mad mix-up. Fists flayed. Blood streamed and spurted. Some had their clothes ripped off and they battled half-naked. Others had their faces messed with blood. Two or three men hit the pavement, rolled into the gutters, and lay still. One man ran around with a great smear of blood on the back of his shirt. The fighting could not last much longer at this pace. The brawl thinned. Men walked off with little streams from their noses. Two men were abruptly seen swinging alone and they soon parted. They walked slowly to the curb, their heads held low, oddly trying to fix their clothing. There was a pause. The Hoopers sat at the curbs gathering their strength.

On the corner of South Fifth and Hooper stood the Colonial Theater. Now a fellow was seen climbing up the brick wall, clinging painfully to the cement cracks with his fingers, inserting the ends of his shoe soles. The crowd watched him in his insane struggle, wondering whether he would make it. Momentarily they expected to see him smash to the sidewalk. They gasped with relief, and expectation freshened as he swung his leg over the stone ledge. What would he do now? They wondered and looked.

He was a short man, with wide, strong shoulders. His shirt had been ripped at the back and flapped with the breeze. For a moment they lost sight of him. Then he returned with hands full of pebbles. He threw them down like buckshot and laughed. Below the men ran for cover, holding their hands over their heads. They tossed back stones and pieces of the whiskey bottles. The big-shouldered man now wrenched with profound concentration at the stone slab that rested on top of the brick wall. He pulled and pulled. Finally it gave, slipped from his fingers, and slammed down to the sidewalk with a crash. The slab broke and the pieces flew in the air. The proprietor of the movie house ran out. He was a little, nervous man. His courage was heroic. He ran straight into the Hoopers. The crowd gasped. His shrill protests were cut short as one of the Hoopers went up to him and slammed him in the face. His body lay still on the sidewalk, face downward, one arm trailing in the gutter. He was such a little man.

A cop, passing at a distance, saw the riot. He ran out of sight immediately. The crowd perceived another man break through at the other end and walk down the street. It was Sam Linck. He walked resolutely and was untouched until he reached the middle. Two drunks stopped him. He tried to brush past them. One grabbed his necktie tightly and began pushing his fist into Linck's nose. Blood spurted. Linck opened his mouth for air. The fist smashed repeatedly. It was like an automatic machine. When the man let go of the necktie Linck slumped to the ground. He lay stretched out.

Three patrol wagons came shrieking to the scene. The policemen ran out energetically. The Hoopers scurried to the other end. The cops appeared now from the other corner. The hoodlums ran in circles, trapped. The policemen rushed after them, running on fat legs, the chests with the buttons low to the ground. They pressed the drunks heartlessly, banging the sticks on their heads. One by one the Hoopers fell. The cops pushed them together with their feet. Satisfied, they walked around the battle area and scattered the crowd.

Thus ended the Hoopers. As for Sam Linck, this was the second time that he had been beaten. Everybody said he just was having bad luck.

At the end of July, during Philip Hayman's visit to Havers Falls, Gilhooley failed to restrain himself and got into a jam. With him hooliganism was no colorless business adjunct but a career appropriate to a sporting temperament. When Papravel had picked him up he had been a member of the Hoopers, and despite Papravel's influence the Irishman retained the signs of his early training. Near Batick he had the lack of discernment to get mixed up in a fistfight with two of Morand's men. Forgetting himself and Papravel's orders, the Irishman was having a great time until a state trooper drove by.

Harry Hayman, getting the news, rushed to the scene barely in time to prevent Gilhooley from working on the trooper. Hayman smelled the odor of gin and was for slapping his face right there and then. He gave Gilhooley a look of contempt and disgust.

"I'll take care of everything," he said, presenting himself to the state trooper. He made a show of authority and tried to bluff his way through. "This man works for me, officer, and this is the first time he ever got into any trouble. He's a good man. A drop of the old stuff was a little too much for him and he lost his head. There must have been some kind of a misunderstanding with the bus driver. I'll straighten it out, and the whole thing can be taken care of without bothering you."

The trooper looked at Hayman briefly. "Shut up, you little rabbi," he said curtly. "I'm taking care of this in my own way."

Hayman bounced back at him so hard that he grew afraid.

"What?" he exclaimed. "What was that you said to me? Listen, mister, if you want to try any fresh business with me you'll find yourself broken out of a good job. Don't think just because you've got a uniform on you can get away with that stuff on me."

"Who are you?" the trooper wanted to know, feeling his way cautiously. "Who do you know? What's your name?"

"Never mind," Harry Hayman said. "My name is Cohen and I don't know anybody. Not a soul. But what I'd like to know is, why don't you leave this Irish fool go? What the hell! He got mixed up in a fight, but that happens to everybody at one time or another. You don't see a cop every time a man starts scrapping. It was his bad luck you happened to come along. Let him go, officer, and forget it."

"Oh, no," said the trooper, still dubious, but holding on. "This bird goes with me to the judge."

"No, sir," Hayman said calmly. "He goes to no judge."

The trooper said, "Say, who do you think you are anyway?" But he stopped to think it over. Finally, he drew Hayman aside and lectured him gently on the necessity of peace and order on the state highways. He wound up, "All right, I'll let it go this time, but I've filled out the forms in my book." There was always a lot of red tape in these cases and it would come to fifty dollars.

"Fifty dollars!" Hayman said in amazement. "All right, we'll go to the judge. It's cheaper."

When Papravel, in Williamsburg, received the news, he swore. He was at this time busily engaged on the final effort, which was to crown the month's work, and he could scarcely afford to spare the time. Nevertheless, he made the trip up in three hours. The judge had been put off until his arrival, but in the meantime Morand's lawyer had been at work and had built the case against Gilhooley to serious proportions, charging in the tropical foliage of legal language an imposing assortment of offenses, civil and criminal. Papravel walked into the courtroom directly from the car.

"Guilty or not guilty?" asked the judge for the sake of form. He was a wizened man with a red, scrubbed face and white hair.

"Not guilty," said Papravel without a ripple. He had just arrived and was barely acquainted with the facts. Everyone wondered.

"What?" said the scrubbed face. "The evidence and witnesses seem very strong for the prosecution. Are you sure you want to enter a plea of not guilty?"

Papravel brought the situation to a speedy finish. "Not guilty," he repeated firmly, "and, what's more, I want a trial by jury for this man."

"Very well. You'll have to wait until bail is set."

"Not necessary," pronounced Papravel. "I have my jurymen right here."

Twelve six-foot bruisers walked silently into the room. They faced the judge with the dumb expression of animals. Their massive arms hung at their sides. The judge looked at them and at Papravel.

"What does all this mean?" he sputtered. "Who are these men?"

Papravel protested. "You're the judge," he said. "Why ask me questions? All I say is that this man is innocent and that I want a jury trial. That's my right, ain't it, Judge?"

The scrubbed face with the white hair thought it over. He was thinking fast. It was just an ordinary brawl. He looked at the twelve men.

"Very well," he said. "Case dismissed."

Prompted by Papravel, who had a taste for etiquette, Gilhooley seriously shook the judge's hand and thanked him. He even took the trouble to promise that he would behave himself in the future.

Afterward Papravel bawled out Gilhooley extravagantly. He said he was a dumb Irish kluck, the next time this happened he could expect no help, why didn't he listen to his orders? Gilhooley took the berating good-naturedly. After all, Papravel was his boss. "One thing about that sheeny," he told the others, "you can always depend upon him to come to the bat for a fellow when you get into a jam."

Papravel made the most of his trip to the mountains. He saw Rubin, cut short his protests concerning expenses, and administered a few shots of courage.

"Rubin," he said and positively glowed with the prospect of his latest venture, "this is good. In a week there will be no more Silver Eagle in Williamsburg."

Rubin couldn't believe it. This was going to keep on forever. Every possible wrinkle in his face was blossoming with worry.

"What are you talking about now?" he said. "How much will it cost this time?"

"Listen, Rubin, did you ever hear of the United Bus Drivers

Association? Well, it's a fine organization, and you ought to make all your boys join it if you're a real boss to them. The United Bus Drivers Association, yes. It was my idea. With an organization, the bus drivers can help themselves. Better pay, shorter hours, good working conditions. In union there is strength."

"What?" gasped Rubin. He did not see the point. "Is this a joke? I haven't time to listen to jokes."

"Jokes?" Papravel said. "What jokes? It turns out like this. Morantz will soon discover that he is underpaying his men and not meeting union demands."

"Well?" Rubin said, still perplexed. "What do I care what he does?"

"Well, Morantz is fighting the union. His workers are scabs. By court order two men with big signs on their backs will picket the place in Williamsburg. And if anyone wants to go in to buy tickets they will give him a pretty good idea that maybe with all these strikes and business fights it might be better to travel on a safe line."

Rubin relaxed. This was clever. He liked these tactics. No blood would ever be shed if people did business by using their brains.

"All right, Papravel," he grumbled. "You're ruining me so far, go ahead. You know what's best."

Philip Hayman was in Havers Falls, but even though he was not there to watch, Williamsburg went on as usual. It was night again. The women sat in their chairs on the sidewalks retailing the day's gossip.

"My, oh my," gasped one, and the thought of it alone was enough to make her shake helplessly with laughter, "listen to this, it's good. There was once a woman, Mrs. Rand. Well, her boy Leonard was playing with the, excuse me, chamber pot, and ended up by squeezing it on his head. When he couldn't get it off, it was so tight, he began to cry and worry. His mother was away, so he rushed into my house with the pot on his head like a king's crown. Well, naturally, we all laughed to beat the band, it was so funny, but then we couldn't get the pot off neither, and we worried. Mrs. Rand, the boy's mother was still away. Another lady called, let me see, oh yes, Mrs. Troy said, 'try oil, it would make it easier, you know, smoother.' So we took out a bottle of Rokeach's frying oil and tried to get the pot off with that, but it wouldn't work. Just then in rushed Mrs. Rand. 'My God,' she screams, 'Help me, God. It's a filthy business.'

"She almost turned away from disgust, she thought Leonard had made number two in it on account of the oil. My, my, how we laughed. Well, what do you think? We couldn't get that pot off until we called the plumber and he had to use his tools for nearly an hour."

In the daytime the women kept their babies on the good side of the street, which received the sunshine. The carriages formed lines in an exhibition. In the afternoon they went to the delicatessen stores for hot pastrami sandwiches and tea and then to the movies. The management took care of the babies crying outside. These were the two positive institutions of Williamsburg. Every corner had its delicatessen store, and within a radius of seven blocks of Ripple Street, there were no fewer than eight movie houses, three of them pretentious palaces, the rest of the dump variety.

Later, at six and seven, the men came home in unbroken lines from the elevated stations. They marched tired, in the uncomfortable clothes of workers, their faces blank. There was a pause while they had their suppers. Now the entire community spent the evening on the sidewalk, the women telling the day's stories.

"That reminds me," said another. "Did I ever tell you about the robbery that happened to my husband's married sister? You never heard such a thing. A man with a gun came into the house. He stuck the gun into my husband's sister's husband's belly. The husband yelled to his wife to run out of the house—she had diamond earrings on. My husband's sister ran into the yard. My husband's sister and her husband, I give you my word for it, they lived together for fourteen years like two babies, they never had a fight, they never even had a bad word. Well, when my husband's sister went out in the yard and screamed for help not one of the neighbors paid any attention to her. They thought her husband was beating her!"

"See," said another with great wisdom, "you can never tell. A family doesn't always get on well together. Take my brother-in-law. When he got rich my husband's other brother, his own brother Moe, walked down the street one day and said, 'Hello, Millionaire.' 'What's the matter,' my brother-in-law said, 'you want a fight?' He is strong, you never saw such a strong one. One of his hands is like my two. Well, my brother-in-law Moe was crippled. Right in the street, in front of the whole neighborhood, the two brothers started to fight. You can imagine how my husband felt. I was hysterical."

The group of women pondered the truth of the parable in silence. A young woman with a pretty face but very stout figure passed by, greeting each of them warmly. "Isn't it a pity?" a fourth woman in her chair said with great regret. "She was so nice and slim when she was a girl. Ever since she got married she started to get fat. It's a pity. I remember when she was a girl. It wasn't so long ago. She used to draw. Make pictures. You know, when she was cleaning the windows with Bon Ami she made pictures on the windows with her finger. And she's so fat now. Oh, yes, Esther, she's much stouter than you."

A swarm of gnats proceeded maddeningly in front of Philip's head. No matter which way he set out or how he twisted his face, the little insects flew crazily before him. Once or twice he struck out at them with his hands, but it did no good. He straggled off the dirt road, through fields that contained high bushes. Breaking his way through the branches and leaves he ran into the swarm of gnats. They persisted, taking him away from his thoughts. Then Philip came to a wide, shallow brook. It was suddenly refreshing. The water ran over a stone bed and transmitted the sensation of coolness and peace. He noticed the moss, and because he saw it so rarely the sight was meaningful. Moss was moss, not an unperceived blur. Something slipped into the water with a sharp flip instead of a splash, and Philip realized how alone he was. He surveyed the picture. Hidden between the tall bushes the brook ran steadily. A few yellow butterflies played in the sun. How still it was. Even the clouds, like fine marble, hung suspended in the air, moving so slowly they seemed to be stationary. Philip felt he could hold up a frame and say this was a painting.

He followed the brook, walking carefully at the side, clinging to the bushes and trees as he made his way past them. A white-painted railing came into view. Philip climbed over it and was again on the dirt road. Of all his pleasures walking was the best. A bit afraid of the country quiet, he nevertheless relished keenly the time spent among these new surroundings. Occasionally he passed a farmer standing against the sky in blue overalls as he held the reins of his healthy horses drawing the flat hay wagons. The man said, "Howdy," and Philip returned, "Howdy." Once he saw a man with a big, tattered straw hat sleeping in the brush that ran up from the road.

Now he came to the summit of the hill. He felt exultant. It was a clear, cool day with a breeze. Below, spread out, were the little houses, the miniature cows, the squares of the acres with the colors of hay and oats. On the sides of the rolling hills in the distance, Philip saw the great shadows made by clouds. At the top of the hill Philip felt close to them, the clouds, close to the sky, and high in the air. He paused to watch the scene.

Going down the hill, in forced, halting steps, knees bent, Philip thought of cold nights in Williamsburg when he walked home from the Leonard Street library with an armful of books. He remembered the calm days when Leibel the Meshugenuh told his insanely fantastic stories to a group of kids sitting about him on the stone steps of a tenement stoop, their cheeks red and their mouths open with interest. On the country road his mood brought him back to those fresh spring days in Ripple Street when everything for a day seemed to be joyously alive. He thought of the snow in winter when boys played in streets and ate hot sweet potatoes, and of the sad quality of autumn. Philip thought of these things and each memory had deep meaning for him. He felt homesick for Williamsburg.

What is happening to Old Miller, he wondered, and who's hearing Cohen's nutty stories? In Philip's mind Ripple Street passed in a procession: Mrs. Linck and the guinea pigs, Halper's Stable, the Auburn S.C., Mahler, his mother, his old, smiling father, and skinny Yozowitz. He tried deliberately to bring back those names and the images. He tried to re-create for himself the picture of Ripple Street. This is the country, it all seems so far away, he thought. I have been here a short time and it feels so distant.

Gasoline pumps and the big signs awoke Philip from his reverie. He was coming to a town. He looked at the signpost. Aligerville was eleven miles off. He suddenly realized he was tired. There was a square plot of grass, neat and closely mowed. He lay down with his hands under his head, looking at the clouds. Perhaps one of Papravel's boys would drive past and give him a lift. Philip did not like the prospect of tramping eleven miles of dusty hills. He sprawled on the common, chewed grass and looked at the sky. Philip tried to see how far up in a direct line his gaze would go. It went up, up, true and unbroken. Abruptly, he could see no further. It was an amusing pastime. He attempted the trick many times but it always failed.

His body creaked as he swung again into his stride. He worked the stiffness away in time, but as it left the sweat came in spite of the cool weather. He was moving rapidly. At first he couldn't get used to the perspiration all over his body with its sticky feeling. But when he caught the hang of it, after the first mile, he didn't mind it. There was even a sort of pleasure in moving in the juicy syrup that covered his skin. That was, no doubt, because he was wearing old clothes. But after the physical side of eleven miles was mastered the mind lay open, grasping at things to keep it occupied. He tried to think of Williamsburg, but the throbbing of blood in his head overcame the effort. Instead he sang in his mind an old camp tune that he now remembered. The tune repeated itself interminably. Philip wanted to spit it out to get rid of it, but it sang obstinately in spite of all he could do. He started to sing it aloud to lose it, but the dust in his throat gave out weak, rasping noises. Besides, it seemed so strange to sing there alone that he stopped abruptly.

For a while he watched the red earth in front of him. Here the color of dirt roads was red, a dull red. Philip thought the color should have been brownish; well, here it was red. The fact became enigma. His mind seized it, played with it, and would not let it go. It was like the song.

Almost fiercely he forced his mind away. In time he grew fascinated by the movement of his legs. He took pleasure in the action of their muscles and put a hand on his thigh to feel it as it worked. His legs moved as though they did not belong to him. He looked down at them, seeing at the sides how the road slipped past. In the middle of the road the earth was soft and turned up by the hoofs of horses. At the sides it was hard from the iron rims of buggies and the tires of flivvers. Philip walked along at the sides as a matter of efficiency. Or else he walked in the middle of the road kicking up little dust storms to amuse his empty mind. The shoes were old and didn't worry him.

When the day is windy in the country the tall trees bend their backs, and the paleness of the undersides of the leaves shows. The trees sway and rustle in a murmur as if they are praying or beseeching for some gift by their shaking fervor. The road broke off from the open hay fields on either side of it and entered into a wood. The sun no longer shone on Philip's head and shoulders, and he missed its friendly warmth. The trees made odd noises in the wind. It was cool and dark. It made Philip afraid. Of what? he asked himself, but he was afraid.

When he was a kid his father used to send him down the street for seltzer late at night. The lights in the long hall through which he had had to pass were turned out at eleven, and Philip had run through the darkness as though hell were behind him, spilling thick splashes of the soda water from the pitcher. The same dumb fear now. It filled his mind completely. As he went on, it worried him cruelly. He longed to see Mrs. Van Curen's house and end the whole foolish business. He looked behind him frequently, scared and ashamed of himself for his fear.

At a distance ahead the dirt road was joined at a fork by another. Philip saw a man on his way down. Inside he almost cried with fear. His stomach went sick. It was as though this were the whole world and they were the only two men inhabiting it. Hastening his pace, he hoped he might be far ahead when the man reached the crossing but the distance was too short for that. Instead he stopped, busying himself with his shoestrings so that the man might get ahead. He tied his laces and untied them again and again, but when he turned his head up, the man was at the crossing waiting for him to come up. He said:

"Dry weather we're having. We need rain." He meant to be friendly.

"Yes," Philip said. "Rain."

They walked together. "You from Mrs. Van Curen's place?"

"Oh, yes."

"You come from New York?"

"Yes," Philip said. The fear was really torturing him. It was exhausting him. This was like the last lap in a swimming race. Philip wanted to cry out at the man and run away.

"I've never been to New York," the stranger said. "It must be quite a town."

"Oh, yes. It's a town all right."

"I'll run down this winter. That's what I always say about this time of the year, though. But I guess I'll take the trip this winter."

Philip did not answer, and they walked in silence. He couldn't stand it. His mind was making weird stories about the man, making them, and simultaneously realizing that they were artificial and false. He reasoned with his fear and was ashamed of it, but it was conquering him.

Finally he choked, hiding the cries of fear he was unable to suppress.

The man looked at him and said kindly, "Is anything wrong?"

"Nothing," Philip cried. Before the stranger could say anything further he broke away in a sudden burst. He ran with all the speed fear and terror gave him. The man was left wondering. His mouth opened as he stood.

Philip ran until his breath left him and the strength petered away. Stopping, he looked back: the man was hidden by the hills. As he rested, the fear went away as stupidly and slowly as it had come. It died out like the light in a gas heater when the tap connection is turned off. Philip felt overwhelmingly foolish.

When he reached the house he kept silent until long past dinner. Harry asked whether he wasn't feeling well, but he said, no, he was just tired from his long walk. The shame troubled him. He couldn't get rid of it. He concentrated his whole mind on forgetting it as soon as he could.

"I'm thinking of leaving," he said to Harry. "I've been hanging around here long enough."

TEN

Philip reached Williamsburg late that Friday afternoon. First his mother sat him down to dinner. After the flat smells and lifeless, unspiced Gentile cooking, he looked forward to his mother's warm tasty foods and juicy meats. She set before him chopped liver mixed with onions, cold borscht with cream, and then the brown, soft, roasted duck surrounded by peas, carrots, and applesauce. On the table were sweet wine and seltzer. Philip picked up the plate of delicious flesh close to his nose and sniffed it. His mother sat with her hands folded, looking carefully at his face after so long an absence and observing his satisfaction as he ate. Philip examined the roast suspiciously, gingerly brought a morsel to his mouth, and chewed it critically. His eyes suddenly opened wide. His face twisted into grimaces, the muscles worked as if in convulsions, he grabbed his throat and slipped off the chair to the floor. He rolled in pain.

Mrs. Hayman laughed, rocking in her chair helplessly. That was Philip's favorite trick. Whenever children came into the house while he was eating, she always made him go through the performance for their benefit. Philip looked at her from the floor with a bitter expression. "My God," he gasped, "you've poisoned me."

Then he jumped up eagerly, seized the fork, and began eating as though he were administering an antidote.

"Eat with bread, Philip," she said. "Don't eat only the fancy stuff."

"Bread she wants me to eat," he muttered. "Bread. As if I don't know she ground glass into the flour." He sizzled seltzer into the glass of wine.

"How is it, Philip? Do you still like my cooking?"

He rose formally, held the glass and toasted. "To the worst cook in the world. To the lady who doesn't know the difference between a boiled egg and a herring."

Mrs. Hayman brought him a large cut of cold watermelon. "Here, you with your funny business, fill your monkey face with this."

Philip leaned back in his chair and held his stomach. "I'm waterlogged. I feel as though all I've got is a belly with arms and legs stuck on."

As he cut the melon into neat geometric shapes, Mrs. Hayman began to talk. How was Harry?

"Don't worry," Philip said. "He's getting fatter and fatter every day. Even though Pop's down on him he's so fat he'll be a great success some day."

"Poppa," Mrs. Hayman said. She had been having trouble with the old man. For the last few years she had been coaxing him to sell his business, and now a man had offered him five thousand dollars for it. She regarded the offer as little short of providential, but the old man refused to sell. He claimed the place wasn't worth the money, wasn't worth anything. "It would be a swindle," he said, and that was the end of it.

Philip smiled at the news. It was in character. Philip knew his mother would continue the argument for days until her strength gave out and she dropped it. Knowing his father as he did, he felt that the old man would not fail himself and that he would hold to principle. If his father sold, it would be finally rest and a respite. He was old and worn; it would make things easier for him. Philip wanted it for his father, but he admired his refusal to sell because he thought the man would lose by the transaction. His father was thoroughly a man.

"Well," Philip said, "that's Pop. You can't make him over. Tell me, what's happening to Miller?"

"The old man won't die so easily, he fools them. You don't know. It was a whole business, and when you left everybody thought he would be all right soon, and then doctors came and they said he would die any minute. He's paralyzed and has a blood clot and God knows how many other sicknesses, but he keeps on stretching his life along."

"Miller is as bad as that? I thought he'd get over it. It's too bad. I'll have to see him," Philip said. "What else happened while I was away?"

"What should happen? Nothing, and everything. It keeps on going and everything is still the same. Tessie was married. You know that. Look," she said, "I almost forgot. She sent you a letter."

"She did? That was nice. It must be a wedding announcement." He pocketed the letter casually. "And how is my schlemiel, Cohen?"

Mrs. Hayman told him about the bridge. "Go on," Philip said. "I can't believe it. I know he's a nut, but to go ahead and do something like that! Somebody's got to keep an eye on him all the time. It's a miracle he wasn't killed. What else, Mom?"

"What else? I could sit here telling you grandmother's tales all night. A great deal happens all the time and it's nothing. You get excited, and then it passes. It's all over and you forget about it. Things keep on rushing like water boiling in a pot, and when you're all through there's nothing left. I've lived so long there's nothing to expect."

Philip contemplated his mother over his cigarette. "See, Mom," he said, "you're a regular philosopher. Why don't you go up to the college, kick out Overstreet and Cohen, and give the boys the real lowdown?" He looked at her. She was old and tired but her face had a gentle loveliness. She was sympathetic and human, yet existence was an old story to her, and she remained placid with the world. Philip remembered how she always came to him with her needle. "Thread it for me," she said. "Everything gets old and useless, even my eyes are no good anymore."

"Before I forget," Mrs. Hayman said, "Charlie called up two or three times on the telephone. He's home from camp and he said you should call him back when you came home."

"That's nice," Philip said. The news of Charlie Nagleman's return pleased him and helped to round out the pleasantness of his homecoming. At Havers Falls he had always felt an outsider, as though he did not belong to the country, and as his mother gave him the news he felt at home with people he knew. There were many things for him to do. Philip wanted to see the old sage in the long beard, Miller, on his deathbed. He was eager to see Cohen and discover what the latest adventure meant. The letter from Tessie exhilarated him with its warm possibilities. And he always enjoyed the time he spent with Charlie. Meanwhile he waited for his father. The evening grew.

On Friday nights the yellow stars on top of the three candles shed their soft light through the dim room with the gentleness of enchanted fingers. The tablecloth still showed the fresh creases, and on it, in a long oval dish, rested the knotted challee shining from egg yolk Mrs. Hayman's palms had patted on the dough. Philip's family was not very orthodox, but on Friday night a special air of quiet and peace pervaded the rooms, and it was in this atmosphere on those nights that Philip enjoyed lulling his mind into a kind of warm sleepiness.

Earlier, when the dark had first come, over his book he watched, without seeming to watch, his mother light one candle with a match and use this as a taper for the other two. This was, perhaps, a simple thing, but he always observed the ritual, and it affected him. She would soften the heels of the other candles with the flame, press them into the sockets of the candlesticks, and light them one after the other. Then she covered her head with a napkin, placed her fingertips to her eyelids, and moving her lips in a murmur, withdrawn for the moment and apart from the world, she recited the ancient prayer. There was always something strange, a little awesome, in the spectacle.

At eight o'clock Philip's father came home from his shop. He walked with the tired tread of a worker, and the expression on his face was as if glazed, the lips were dry and cracked. But he greeted

Mrs. Hayman warmly, to her "Good Sabbath," he answered, "Good year."

"Home already?" he asked as he noticed Philip. He was pleased, and smiled, but there was little ceremony. At the broom closet, where he kept his coat and slippers, he changed shoes. This was one of his customs, performed regularly as he entered the house every night. It was the first thing he did, but it no longer attracted notice. Then Philip had to leave the chair he was sitting in, for it happened to be "Poppa's chair." When he was home he sat only in this chair and it was given up to him, as a matter of course, whenever he appeared. Now he sat down for his evening meal. He dipped a piece of the white bread into the salty sauce on his fish plate, wetting his throat as he ate. Then slowly, chatting with Philip's mother as she served him, he ate the Friday dinner—the chopped fish, noodle soup, chicken, and applesauce.

"That man, Coblenz, he was here again today," he said. "I don't know why he's looking for trouble."

"Well," asked Philip's mother, "are you going to let him buy the business?" She was upon him at once.

"It's ridiculous. He wants to give five thousand dollars. The place isn't worth it. If I let him have it, it would be a swindle pure and simple." He rustled his newspaper. "Besides," he added, "what would I do with myself?"

"Sell it," she said. "Don't be silly. See, Philip, it's just like I told you."

His father read, and his mother, with the marvelous serenity of older people, cleared the table and washed the dishes. She was finished with the week's work, had bathed, and her long black hair, washed and combed, hung on her nape in a neat, shining knot. Philip too was reading, but the pages remained unturned. Philip supposed it often happened that children had no intimate knowledge of their parents. His also were distant. That was because he did not understand them; they were strange to him and often even unreal. What had they been when they were my age? he speculated. Was it possible that they had been once boy and girl? What had their courtship been when they were young? And what would happen when the time came for them to die? It was difficult to imagine that they had been young once, or indeed that they had ever been other than as he saw them now. He was, of course, young himself and had no vivid understanding of the remarkable phenomenon of growth, but especially with his father and mother it was not easily possible for him to think of them as young, lively, and fresh.

And yet there was an old picture of his mother, taken over thirty years ago. It was a large picture with a heavy, ornate, old-fashioned frame, and his mother kept it hidden in the cellar because at a certain age not only is there no affectation but honest sentiment becomes a little pretentious. Often Philip gazed at his mother as she was years ago, deeply impressed and wondering at the young, fine face with the sad, innocent eyes. He could never picture his mother as a girl, and here she was, soft, feminine, and really very lovely. At those times too, Philip thought of earlier days when he himself had been younger and watched his mother in her bedroom brush her hair or powder her face. Even then the performance affected him strangely. Once he examined her box of face powder. The cover was printed in soft, gray-blue colors, the design was of blossoms and leaves delicately intermingled, and the French words held a mysterious charm. Pussy Willow, the box said, and, fascinated, he used to say to himself, pussy willow, pussy willow, hardly knowing what exactly those silky syllables meant. Later, as often happens in such cases, walking, or at a theater, thinking of other matters, the chance scent of powder would bring back in a sudden nostalgic wave the memory of his mother in those days and his wondering about her.

On the other hand, even this much could not be said for his father. He had always been, as Philip remembered him, old, and this was something his mother confirmed. Even when she married him, she said, his hair had been white and he had had the appearance of an old man. He was bent now, drier and skinnier, shriveling with age, but except for those changes Philip supposed he was the same. The old pictures sustained this impression. There was one of his father and mother at the tombstone of his older brother.

This had been twenty years before, when Philip was born, for while his mother was in bed with him his brother George was pushed off a roof. The picture, rusty-yellow from time, showed his mother still young and slender, but his father with his big mustaches was almost exactly as he was now. He might have been her father.

However, just as Philip remembered his mother's box of face powder and its effect on him, so he could recall his father ten years back. In the summer months he wore a Palm Beach suit, a Panama hat, and he carried a cane, walking with the jaunty step of a young man. And when Philip walked with him, accompanying him along Grand Street where he shopped on Sundays, it was Philip's practice to walk, not alongside of him, but some paces to the rear. Mr. Hayman would enter a shop, pick his article, and lay the money on the counter, point at Philip with the stick to indicate that he was to be given the package, and walk out, leaving him to follow. In the warm sun Philip would come after him down the street, holding his purchases, waiting until his father felt ready to return home and never thinking of questioning this odd little custom. At that time Philip held great respect for his father because of his dignity, his years, and his noble presence.

While Philip might have had difficulty in visualizing his parents' younger days, they had had them, of course, and it was this realization, as he contemplated them over his book on that Friday evening, that saddened him. For their youth was gone, they were old now, and when something was gone it made no difference whether you had ever had it in the first place or not. It was truly as though it had never been. A memory was unsatisfying solace. His mother, in speaking of herself, would often say with wry humor, "Downhill. We're going down the hill now." They had been young, they would soon come to die, and it would be all finished, a drop of water losing its identity in a sea.

Philip was saddened not only for his parents but for himself. He knew that time was a subtle thief, and even though he was only twenty years old he felt that his own life was running through its rapid course. He had lived a fourth, or even a third, of his life already, and how fast it had gone! Philip remembered how astonished he had been when he was graduated from elementary school. Seven years, measured neatly for him so that he could notice it, had already passed. This was also true of high school, and when he entered college Philip thought: four years, they would be over in no time; and it was true, for already his senior year had come; in a year he would be leaving college.

Time was a sly, deceitful companion; it slipped away in a minute, unsuspected divisions, like a group of boys trying to escape from a classroom, leaving one by one to attract no notice. As he thought of his father it came to him with great force what a pity it was that this sham had been put over on him too. He had worked so hard and honestly, he was old and tired, his life was passing, and it seemed to Philip that in some way his father had been tricked. Further, the calm acceptance, or the resignation, at any rate, the aloof disregard of what seemed to Philip a tragedy, rendered him a noble figure. With the candlelight softly outlining his white head, his father read his newspaper, knowing that tomorrow he would be going to work, that on Sunday he would buy breakfast and spend the day resting, that on Monday he would be going back to his shop again, and that week would follow week and he would leave the house every morning not noticing the street number on the door.

"Max," Mrs. Hayman said to him across the table, "Max, do it for me. I can't understand why you don't sell the place. You ought to stop already and take a rest."

Philip's father looked at her over his newspaper. "I say it would be a swindle, a plain, ordinary swindle, to take money from that man Coblenz. The place isn't worth the money."

"How do you come to say that? The man isn't a baby. He knows what he wants. If he wants to pay five thousand dollars it's not your place to tell him no."

Mr. Hayman exclaimed his impatience in a syllable of a sort, shook his head, and returned to his newspaper.

Philip laughed. "You can't make him over, Mom," he said. "That's the way he is." He rose and fixed his tie.

"You just came home," Mr. Hayman said. "Where are you running?"

"I've got to see some people." The old man had made no fuss over Philip's homecoming, but it was difficult to leave. Philip fingered the letter from Tessie in his pocket. "I'll try to get in early," he said, "but I guess it'll be late."

"Go in good health," his mother said. "Don't listen to him, he's topsy-turvy in his old age. Go, have a good time. You're young."

In the dinginess of the dark room Mr. Miller lay on his bed, motionless, the blanket over his arms, his beard resting on the quilt, the great face set, the eyes closed, for all the world like a death mask. It was night. The lights from rooms across the yard sent their rays into the dark room. Shadows sat on the chair. Mr. Miller's yellow face lay in a spot of light. He was sleeping, and in his dream also he was sleeping. He had pondered much and long and he was tired, feeling through with thinking and the world.

There was a light slapping sound, rhythmic and regular, annoying him in his sleep in the dream because he did not want to leave his bed and shut out the night air. In his dream or half-dream he was already walking to the window; he eliminated the noise, he was back in the bed again, but of course the slapping continued, he had not moved. Miller dreamed that lately he had been troubled at night. The old superstition was that the bed should not face the door because that was a bad portent, signifying death. Now, Miller understood this, but at night it always appeared that the bed had moved itself of its own accord out of position and that his feet were pointing to the door. Miller had the uncomfortable sensation of being worried, but for vague, undetermined reasons. And the flapping continued. Soon the sound grew stronger, communicating an almost human quality of impatience. The slapping became insistent. It was no cloth disturbed by the wind—it was tapping! Miller opened his eyes.

The faces of these old men were inarticulate, composed of shadows. But there he was, the old man, sitting on the chair, in black shiny clothes, with the strange bulbous shoes. His small body was bent over his stick, which he held with both hands, tapping with it on the wooden floor until he had awakened Miller. For years now Miller had been expecting him, although he had never admitted this, even to himself. Recently he had even forgotten about him completely. Seeing him there exposing his self-conceit, Miller had to smile. At this he smiled back, although surely this was an old story with him. The little black man lifted his stick, poking it gently in the air at Miller as if to say in all good nature, come, come, get over with it.

As Miller rose, he left. Miller saw him move ahead, move until he became a black blur, a dot, dissolved into the horizon.

There was time enough. Miller walked with his hands in his pockets, his face set. He knew what to do. As the night progressed the white light from the stars became suffused grayishly by the rising mist. He could hear no sound. The mist thickened until it was a fog. He was alone. The universe was bounded by his fingertips, and now he knew the answers to all the questions.

Miller walked until he reached the top of the hill. Down below him was the town, which revealed itself by four or five gauzy lights. It was in every respect a usual town but Miller did not like it, for once he had been standing on this very hilltop looking at the town, and this was during those sun-tinted days of his early youth when he saw it and the people in it as in dreams, water-blue, like reflections in a big soap bubble. This had been illusion, and a long time ago, and all these things appeared now to Miller as he dreamt, but he did not like the town.

Down below, the misty lights of the town blinked. Miller lifted his hands high above his head, pressing the little fingers against the thumbs, and as he pressed the hilltops moved together, the one upon which he was standing and the one opposite, they closed together, destroying the valley and the town within it. There were no lights, no people, no town. It was all over. Miller smoothed the earth with his foot where the two hilltops met.

A man does not die, he said. He lives. The whole world dies, he lives.

In the morning Miller woke up smiling. He was almost hearty.

For the first time he took notice of his wife and sons. He looked at them regarding his face for the morning inspection of death, and he laughed at their expressions because he read them. They wondered at him.

"Open the windows," he cried. "Pull the curtains over the chair. Let the light come in. Who's going to die today in Golus?"

When Mrs. Hayman came in he greeted her cordially. They had a spirited conversation.

"You're all right, Mr. Miller," she said at the close. "You should be getting out of bed."

"Soon. I will not be in this bed much longer."

In the kitchen. Mrs. Miller complained and said it was all a trick. Miller had never been sick, he was shamming so that they wouldn't nag him about the swindle. He wanted to have an excuse for lying in bed all day and having attention. He had such a terrible disposition, he had used his devil's brains to devise this torment for them. Mrs. Hayman asked her what she was talking about, she shouldn't say those things, it was a sin.

"Tomorrow, sick or not sick, the old sore gets out of bed." She felt as though she had been tricked, and was angry with the old man.

"What is love?" Tessie asked, her eyes big and round with sadness. "Sometimes I think there just isn't anything like it at all. And then again, I think I have been very unfortunate. These things never happen to me. Everyone else has good luck, but nothing ever happens to me."

"What's the matter?" Philip asked. "What's it all about? Here I get home and my mother gives me a letter from a married woman saying: Is everything over? Can't you come and see me? I need you now, perhaps for the first time I really need you. Marriage should not break old friendships. What's wrong?"

Philip sat on a great chair with a rose design, respectably, at a distance. He was drinking a rye highball and his legs were crossed.

While he made his speech he was handling a bronze bookend showing a girl with breasts reaching to the sky for light. It was a particularly apt sentiment. All this new furniture, the baby grand, the etchings on the walls from Liggett's Drug Store, they all looked clean, and it was something to make a good housewife worry wondering how soon these objects would lose their freshness and turn into the junk one saw in longer-established homes.

"Schlausser has done very well by you. What are you complaining about? You're a lady, you serve rye highballs, you lie on a couch reading a book and playing delicately, when nobody is looking, with your nose."

"Are you going to be impossible, Philip?" Tessie asked. "We're not children any longer. We're grown-up people. Please don't become silly and smart, because I need your help so badly. You're my oldest friend, you're my closest friend, Philip, don't make fun of things now."

Philip tried to hide his resentment, but he was having little success. He took out a cigarette and lit it with careful nonchalance. "Well, what is it? What can I do when Schlausser stands stretched manfully to shield you from harm?"

"Philip, you're angry with me for what I've done to you. You resent him. You still don't understand."

"Don't be foolish," Philip said. "A girl has got to get married. I understand that. She can kid around with boys, but there must be a finish to it, and she has to get married. Only, where does that put me in the picture now?"

"You won't understand, Philip. It's clear you can't miss seeing it, but you're stubborn, you're refusing to let yourself see it. Can't you see that I can't live with him? Can't you see he means nothing to me? I've made a terrible mistake. What have I in common with a man I see three or four times a month? A man who is always on the road peddling lingerie to lady buyers in Rochester and Buffalo? He thinks he's intellectual when he goes to the movies. Books and concerts mean nothing to him. Can't you see how mismated I am? How miserable I am?" Her voice broke.

"Listen, Tessie, are you kidding me? Do you mean to say that you've been married to such a nice fellow like Schlausser for such a short time and you're already beginning to think you're wasting your life on him?"

"Philip," she said, and closed her eyes with pain. She walked to one of the lamps and clicked off the light. The radio dispensed a soft waltz, but she softened it further. She lay down on the couch to be alone with her unhappiness.

She had been reading an English novel of manners in which the heroine spent her time going through mental soliloquies as she decided yes and no over the fates of her husband and her contemplated lover. Eric was solid, dependable, and in his way lovable. He left each morning for the city where he was engrossed in his business. He had many interests, his wife was an accessory to him. Vivian walked through the garden desiring a life of her own. She did not want to be a casual part of her husband, comforting, serving, an incidental receptacle of his affections in stray moments. She thought of Hugh Baden-Thwyte-Baden and wondered. He was madly in love with her. Hugh's profession was love, not business; life with him would have a separate, important part for the woman. Tessie had reached the climax and wondered which way Vivian would turn. Would she remain with the rugged qualities of Eric, or would she courageously break for love and romance? How true to life it was. How easily one might substitute living people for Eric, Vivian, and Baden-Thwyte-Baden. Tessie wondered how it would all turn out, but in stepped Philip and she had had to put the book down. Nevertheless, Tessie had resolved the problem for herself.

"I think I'll be getting along," Philip said. He was still sitting on the big rose, fingering the bookend. Tessie was ridiculous. She was making him ridiculous. It was clear, and Philip saw it. Tessie, who worried about her weight and the styles of next year's clothes, who had studied the amorous postures of movie stars and read the manners of English society, Tessie who once rode on top of a Fifth Avenue bus and saw the signs that would not release her, who would rather have a milkshake at Sherry's than a full meal at Foltis-Fischer's, Tessie had grown up, married, and was ready for the next of life's experiences. Tessie wanted an affair.

"I think I'll be getting along," Philip said. He understood her.

"Philip," she murmured, "Philip."

"What?"

"Come here."

He looked at the bookend, the lady with the breasts that reached to the modernistic chandelier for light, and he sat down on the couch.

"Philip, if you knew what you mean to me. A moment ago I said I didn't know the meaning of love. That was a lie. I wish it were true. I'm so miserable. I know this is wrong, but I am so alone. Schlausser is gone for a month."

"I know about Schlausser."

"It makes no difference whether he's gone or here," she went on. "It's the same. I always have the feeling of being alone. I'm wretched with unhappiness, Philip. It was a big mistake. You cannot fool yourself in these things, Philip," she said, stroking his face and his head, "Philip."

"I know," he said, "I know." The radio began playing a lively jazz tune. He reached out to turn it off.

Philip woke up late the next day. It was almost twelve. His mother looked into the bedroom and brought him a glass of orange juice.

"I was around to see some friends last night," he said. "I got in late."

Mrs. Hayman sat on the bed watching him drink. "Philip," she said, "what do you think? It's so funny. This morning Mr. Miller looked so well I thought he would get out of bed and be back at his place in the cemetery. He laughed and talked and moved instead of lying in a lump."

"Well," said Philip, "what happened?"

"It was such a surprise to me. I just saw him. He died an hour ago."

"Oh," said Philip. He had meant to see the old man and regretted he had delayed his visit. He really should have seen the old man once again. If he had only known Miller was on the point of death he wouldn't have missed it. That was to have been the final touch to the old man's wryly piercing homilies, the skinny sage with the long beard slowly saying the last smiling pronouncements on his deathbed.

Mrs. Hayman sat on the bed and narrated the details of Mr. Miller's passing.

ELEVEN

It was one of those dripping days when the clothes feel uncomfortably warm and sticky, the shoes lose all their luster and the scalp is itchy. The pavement in the yard gleamed black and gloom pervaded the tenements. Listlessly the rain fell down in anemic straight lines, moving from the dirty-gray heavens with deliberate slowness until abruptly in the descent it hit the yard with a little smacking noise. It was like the sound a woman makes with her lips when she is busy eating herring.

A boy stood in the yard, calling up to his mother in a flat, expressionless voice. Unmindful of the rain, he stubbornly yawped, "Ma, Ma," at intervals until she was obliged to answer in a fit of irritation from her flat.

"What do you want?" she yelled.

"Stick your head out of the window."

"Well, what do you want?"

"Ma. Throw me down a penny?"

"No!" The window slammed. She had been disturbed under false pretenses.

"Ma!" the boy screamed, overwhelmed with anger. "Ma! Stick your head out of the window! Ma! Every kid on the block gets three cents a day. If I ask you for an extra cent, I don't see what you have to be so stingy about. Ma! Ma! I hate you! I don't see why I've got to have a mother like you for anyhow. I hate you, Momma, you're a dirty Litvack."

Does it always rain at funerals? Philip wondered. Across the yard he could see one of Miller's sons sitting on a box while he waited for the old women to finish washing the dead man and get him ready for the coffin. The son had a big face, with both the color and lumpy texture of Swiss cheese, marked and lined from rashes of pimples he must have had as a youngster. He sat on an egg crate, in his shirtsleeves, with the collar detached, the expression of his face showing that he was waiting, waiting for things to get over. He had been unable to find a black skullcap, and for this solemn occasion he now wore a boy's orange-and-black-colored bean hat. Miller had died on a Saturday morning, postponing the funeral until Sunday, and his son regretted another day of waste, and waited, tired.

Mahler, the cobbler, came out of the doorway of the cellar and sadly looked at the interminable rain.

"That finishes your nap," Philip said down to him. "Your nap's all washed out."

"Maybe it'll stop," Mahler said hopefully. "Sometimes it keeps on going like this and then the sun comes out and it stops. You can never tell."

"No, Mahler. I don't like to tell you this, but I was having a conference with God. He says it's going to rain like this forever. It won't stop for the rest of the summer."

Mahler looked up at him suspiciously. "Listen," he said, "do you think I've got it again? What's the matter with you?"

"I'm not kidding. It always rains on funerals. According to the Good Book, if an old man dies on a Saturday and gets buried on a Sunday and it rains on that day, well, it means we're all finished. It just keeps on raining."

"Who's getting buried today?" Mahler asked gently, the grim finger of Death already wagging him into a state of respectable awe.

"The old man, Miller. The one who ripped up the windowsills to fix his shoes."

"Oh," said Mahler. His eyes were opened wide and he nodded to indicate his comprehension of the sorrowful law of life. After two minutes of nodding and contemplation, however, he looked up at the dark sky. There would be no sun for a bit of sleep in Williamsburg this afternoon.

Philip's mother asked him to go into Miller's flat with her because there was so much excitement and rush. As they walked in, two sons were in the midst of a heated argument. They talked in restrained tones because the mute corpse in the bedroom said, quiet, gentlemen, quiet, but the globular beads of sweat on their foreheads showed how earnestly they felt. One waited, holding himself silent by almost physical force, until the other got through arguing his side. He explained with great labor and desire to convince, but as soon as he stopped the other began. They changed roles like acrobats waiting for their cues on the trapeze. Mrs. Miller sat at the dining table dressed in her good black garments, ready for the ride to the cemetery. She cried a little and looked out of the window. That was easiest in this time when she didn't know exactly what to do with herself.

Mr. Miller, it had been discovered, had left almost two thousand dollars. One of the sons argued that the money should be given in its entirety to the old lady, who was to live on it until it was all gone. In this way she would be taken care of, and, more, the sons would no longer be required to contribute money for her support. It would be a release for both sides and seemed eminently satisfactory. However, the other son said that the lump sum was an unnecessary temptation. The old lady would be fooled by some trick and swindled just as Miller had been. "Give everybody a piece and it will be safer. No one will have to worry," he said. They argued with increasing violence, their enthusiasm even overpowering the commanding influence from the dark bedroom.

"My God," one of them exclaimed finally. "Argue with him! Try and talk to him. It's like talking to the wall."

The other picked up a seltzer bottle in a spasm of anger. "I got half a mind," he said threateningly, "right here and now."

Mrs. Hayman stepped in for the sake of peace. "Children," she said tearfully, "it isn't at all nice. Is it decent for sons to fight while the father waits to be buried? You can settle this later, the money isn't flying away."

The sons glared at each other and walked sullenly to opposite ends of the room. Off in the yard somewhere a child began practicing on the piano. Laboriously, heavily, came the clipped notes of the Minuet in G. For a while everyone sat in the dingy room saying nothing and listening attentively to the piano. There was nothing else to do while they were waiting. Suddenly a hot quarrel broke out into the yard from the fourth floor of the building opposite. From the voices it was apparent that two couples were involved. The angry murmur of their discourse rested on top of the gentle patter of the smacking noises the rain was making. One man now yelled in a tone that filled the yard, "That's a nasty habit, mister. Don't think you can attract my wife by standing naked in front of the window."

"Please," a woman's voice begged. "Don't shout. Everyone can hear you."

"I don't care who hears," said the other man defiantly. "If your wife didn't have a filthy mind she wouldn't twist her neck until it almost breaks to look at me."

Philip didn't know whether it was disrespectful to show his interest in the proceedings. He looked at the bedroom door where they were laying out the old man, combing his beard and dressing him. Thus went the sage with the long beard, amid dirty arguments, while Mahler regretted the falling rain and a child jerked out Beethoven's minuet into the gloom.

The undertaker strode into the dining room importantly. "All right," he said in a subdued tone that was nevertheless authoritative. "Are you ready here?"

Six men lifted the coffin and squeezed it around the sharp corners of the doors. They moved their legs delicately and watched the big box with their eyes, like a mother bringing a full bowl of soup to the table. The coffin might have been made of thin glass. The staircase running down in squares gave trouble, but in the end they managed to reach the long hall. As they passed, neighbors stuck their heads silently out of their doors to view the strange spectacle. Children leaned over banisters to watch the procession. They were filled frankly with awe. As the pallbearers carried the box through the hall, an unhappy boy was caught against the wall. He stood back stiffly, as though paralyzed, and as they finally passed him, he could control himself no longer, broke wildly into a spasm of tears and dashed madly up the steps. The sight of death is sometimes terrible, especially when it is covered plainly by greenish new boards.

Outside, the crowd, attracted by the hearse, waited under umbrellas. In spite of the rain all the windows were open. Two and three persons squeezed through a ledge and pushed their eyes toward the scene of the show. Some boys sat pensively on the fire escapes directly overlooking the entrance to the house. They had vantage seats. This too was one of the privileges of Williamsburg, and the neighbors would not miss it, they took it in as by right. Yente Maldick sat on the stone stoop, folded up like an Oriental statue in the image of lamentation. She cried wantonly, cracked her fingers and sporadically thought it was time to scream piercingly with grief. The steam rose from the kerchief over her head.

There was the black ugly hearse with its intricate carvings for ornamentation. Two automobiles, black, long, and shiny, waited for the mourners. Mrs. Miller walked between two sons and saw the crowd. She was weeping, but the size of the crowd impressed her. She was a little old woman and here were so many people to witness the funeral of her husband. As her sons were lifting her through the car door she began to wail frantically, shaking her head with torment and bouncing up and down. Everyone noticed how her head beat against the roof of the auto and how she disregarded the pain. He had been a louse, a miser, they all said afterward, but spite of all a man's faults and the terrible life he might have given his wife, she was always true and she bewailed him.

The ride to the cemetery was long and dull. They had intended to hold a ceremony at the synagogue but it was raining and the undertaker had taken so much time. There would be prayers enough at the cemetery, the holy men said. Philip sat cooped up in the limousine. He had not wanted to go. When his mother had told him his friend Charlie Nagleman was in town he had phoned and arranged to spend all of Sunday with him. He was anxious to see Charlie again, but his mother had begged him to accompany her and he did not know how to refuse her. She asked so little of him. As they drew into the cemetery Philip saw the old men waiting at the gates in the rain for customers. He wondered whether these professional prayer makers knew that it was their colleague who needed their prayers today.

The yellow earth surrounded the grave in mounds. It was a dismal morning. They grouped around the wet hole, seeking dry spots for their feet. The rabbi stood at the head and went through the form. It was, Philip had to admit, an impressive sight. Nothing stopped these old Jews and their rituals, not even a nasty day. Before the black sky, in that peculiar scene where white gravestones listened respectfully, the holy man was upright, the downpour soaking his clothes until they were heavy and sodden, the water forming in the crown of his hat a little pool that dripped unattended over his nose, his shoes sucking in the mud, the water penetrating until he must have felt cold and wet and miserable, but he went on stolidly uttering eenie-meenie-miney-mo to God who might have been listening but who sent down the fine rain nevertheless.

Mrs. Miller cried. The sons clasped their hands together and looked without positive expression into the grave. The first spadeful of earth hit the wooden box. Philip heard the pebbles as they struck. This was the last of the sage. He tried to deny it to himself, but the sight affected him considerably. This was the end of the sage, he said, but actually he was impressed. Sometimes a boy will find grief contagious and cry himself, and so Philip felt now oppressed, sad, and wondering. He took out a pad and began writing. His mother edged up to him.

"What are you doing, Philip?" she whispered reproachfully.

"Nothing. It was an idea, it came to me when I heard the sound of the earth on the box, and I wanted to write it down so I wouldn't forget."

Mrs. Hayman looked at him chidingly. "Do you bother with that when a man dies?" she said.

The old sage was dead and in his grave, but Philip, sitting in Charlie Nagleman's living room, remembered his words. There was one truth, one meaning, and it was money. Twenty was a young age. At twenty a young man might feel rather that purposeful work and love were the important goals, but nevertheless Philip recognized intimately that there was much in what Miller said. The room in which he was sitting was in its way proof. The pictures on the walls, the tasteful furniture, the tall bookshelves that went up to the ceiling, all this made a difference, subtly projecting its influence in a hundred ways, softening the lives of the people who dwelt there. These people lived decorous lives, they rode in Central Park, played tennis and golf, and they attended the various resorts of reputation.

Charlie came into the room. He had been changing his shirt and was now adjusting the suspender buckles.

"I almost sent you the goddammedest letter while I was at Havers Falls," Philip said. "I still don't know why exactly I held it back."

"What was it all about?"

"All about money and love among the ash cans of Williamsburg. The terrific importance of a clean shirt and why it is a great thing to have a father who's made a fortune out of vanity cases."

Charlie smiled and went into the bedroom for his jacket. He was tall, blond, and good-looking. Philip had met him one day through college friends and somehow a friendship had developed, although Philip knew it would have to break with time. They were too far apart. Much as Charlie liked him, a difference in settings often proved too great a handicap. Actually, and Philip knew it, the Naglemans weren't very wealthy; there was no great fortune in this home, but it wasn't Williamsburg. The large room, the grand piano, the furniture in neat, handsome summer covers, the cream-colored walls, the drapes, the atmosphere of comfortable living, these were simply not to be seen on Ripple Street, and Philip was appreciative, all the more because of the contrast.

For some time Philip had been a little ashamed of his admiration for these things, thinking they were shallow and stupid. Compared to the more serious properties of living they were, he had felt, superficial. But in fact, and he grew bolder in admitting it, the ornaments were often most important. Just as the great disease of pellagra was discovered curable, not by some complicated toxin or treatment but by the simple addition of fresh meat and milk, or yeast, to the diet, so the texture of existence might be enriched by furniture, books, and surroundings. Philip remembered when the gas connections in his tenement house had been taken out of the chandeliers and electric light installed. He saw the white light reflected in the porcelain tops of the washtubs in the kitchen and said, how could there be misery now with all this wonderful clean light? Philip felt that he could see for himself the softening effect that had been caused by the few improvements already instituted in Williamsburg. They were few and rudimentary but their effect was discernible nevertheless. As backyard toilets were succeeded by more adequate plumbing, as hot water was added as a usual service, as tenements were built with greater concern for light and air, it seemed to him that the brutality, the coarseness lessened.

Charlie returned. "Let's go," he said. "It's almost nine."

"I think I'll be going home," Philip said. Charlie was going to a party on Madison Avenue and had asked Philip to accompany him.

"Come along," Charlie said. "You've got nothing else to do."

Philip always felt a little like an intruder when Charlie brought him into these homes. They were not meant for him, he did not belong there, and he tried to dissuade Charlie from taking him there. Tonight, however, his friend insisted. These smart youngsters, in well-fitting suits of white linen or in gay chiffons, lived in the restricted residential sections, they went to expensive summer camps and attended the fashionable schools. Philip was not deluded into a state of awe by these facts, but it was true that he could not match their background, that he could not meet them on their own ground. He felt uncomfortable before them, as if he were an imposter. When he had to mention that he attended City College or that he lived in Williamsburg, he always flinched at their considerate acknowledgment.

"Come on," Charlie said. Philip picked up his hat and they went to the door.

It was at this party that Philip met Ruth Kelman. He noticed her immediately and kept his eyes on her. She wore a plaid guimpe with a white organdy blouse, was pretty, and what impressed him particularly was her grace and charm. He kept watching her. Once or twice her eyes met his, and in that embarrassed pause she smiled uncertainly. When she came to him with a bowl of cherries he felt he could talk to her familiarly.

"My name's Hayman," he said. "These people are terrible. I've been watching you ever since I got into this place, but no one tried to do anything about it."

"Well, that's over. Here, eat these cherries."

"I like cherries, only I never know how to handle the pits. I'm sick and tired of swallowing cherry pits just because there are people in the room."

Ruth laughed. Philip, placing the cherry in his mouth, had to smile at her as she laughed.

"What a lovely girl," he said. "In all my life I have never seen such a lovely girl."

Philip asked Charlie Nagleman about her.

"You mean Ruth?" he said. "She's a kid. I didn't know you liked them that young." Charlie told him her name, that her father was a doctor, that he lived on Eighty-eighth Street. "Listen," he said, "I got my own troubles."

That night Philip walked with Ruth to her home. The streets were cool after the hot day and a pleasant breeze blew. At her door he confessed to her that he was quite taken in. "How soon can I see you again?" he asked. He felt exultant with his discovery.

My dear Susannah, Davey said, lost in the gentle waltzes of his dreams, my dear Susannah. He wore a hairpin bent over his nose to resemble eyeglasses, and he sat on the shaft of one of the wagons in Halper's yard. There she came down the country lane in white organdy. He stretched forth his arms to receive her. My dear Susannah, my dear— What next? He could go no further in his reverie. From that point the motion picture jammed and stuck like a magic-lantern slide. There he was, his mouth opened, his arms outstretched. He couldn't go ahead.

"All right," he yelled. "What do you want?"

"How many times do I have to call you?" Natie the Buller asked. "Are you deaf or something?"

"Cut the baloney. What do you want?"

"Let's go down to Cheap Simon's and get some junk."

"I like that. With what? I'm broke."

"That's all right. We can work the yards and pick up the change."

"All right," said Davey. "Get the gang."

This summer they had hit upon a simple stunt for getting pocket money. Davey always claimed the credit, but actually it was Natie the Buller who had devised it. He had a rich mind. In the past Italian guitar players and stray bums had made a practice of going through the yards singing sentimental tunes for the fat housewives getting dinner ready. The rusty-looking tramps generally sang ballads of hard luck with tender passages to the memories of their mothers. The Italians, professionals, accompanied themselves on guitars and violins, offering a finished article. Always the Jewish housewives, easily made to capitulate, sent down a light rain of pennies wrapped in newspaper. Natie had been following these minstrels from yard to yard, running to pick up the paper pellets as they showered over the yard and handing them to musicians. Then it had occurred to him: why not go into business for himself? The gang tried it, and although housewives were suspicious it was nevertheless a success. Once they had netted as much as twenty-four cents in one afternoon.

Davey stepped out first into the center of the courtyard. He specialized in Italian tunes and rendered:

"O, Mardi, O, Mardi,
Da da, la la, boom boom,
O-wo-O, Mardi,
Ala-fung-ulator-iodi."

The boys gave full performances and knew how to sing loudly. They gave "Ole King Cole" and "Rock-a-Bye-Baby." Davey, who had a nasally soprano voice developed in choir singing ever since he had been six, now sang "My Bonnie Lies Over the Ocean" with appropriate interpolations by the group.

"My Bonnie lies over the ocean, (Dead drunk)
My Bonnie lies over the sea, (De-he-d drunk)
My Bonnie lies over the ocean (Dead drunk)
O, bring back my bonnie to me. (De-he-d drunk)"

Finally Natie came forth with the last one. This was easily the most effective of all the repertoire. It was sad, done in Yiddish, and autobiographical. Natie wailed he was an orphan and he missed his mother. He was very good at it. The paper-wrapped coins never failed. "Where is my mother?" Natie asked, with soft sobs in his throat. "I have no mother, what shall I do?" The ballad ended in a great cry. They collected twelve cents in that yard alone.

At Cheap Simon's, that establishment renowned throughout Williamsburg for the variety of its candies and the cut-rate prices, Davey and his gang bought a mess of Three-X gum, marshmallow bananas, sixteen-to-ones, licorice (both the stringy kind and the plump brown sticks), jellybeans, and soft chocolates with pineapple cubes inside. It was enough for the afternoon. They sat down in the yard alley, dividing the candy and chewing on it carefully, arguing which pieces to eat first or save for the end and whether it was better to eat rapidly in full mouthfuls or slowly, making the sweet stuff last.

My dear Susannah, Davey said, blowing the Three-X gum into small bubbles and balloons. He rose with a start. It was almost half-past five, Yetta would be passing Cheap Simon's, and here he still was.

"I got to be going," he said, but just then in ran Natie the Buller, breathless with excitement.

"The Maujers are going to raid us tonight. My cousin who lives on Meserole Street came down and warned me."

"What of it?" Davey said. "We licked those yellow-bellies once, we can do it again."

"My cousin says they've joined up with the Staggs and the Throops. The big guys are coming down too. They're piling stockings with rocks and getting pails of ammunition ready. They'll murder us."

"All right," Davey said. "We can handle them anyhow."

They set off for Havemeyer Street to seek an alliance for the battle. After all, they were all Jews in Golus together. If the Goyim were uniting, they could do the same. But at the Market they could find no one about. Natie ran up one of the tenements and returned with a fellow called Ikey the Kikey. He was a rosy-cheeked individual with a luxuriant mop of curly hair growing forth in all directions like the subway sun. In between were pale blue, watery eyes, which were mysteriously strabismic. The Havemeyers listened seriously to the discussion. "We can't hitch up with a cheap outfit like yours," he finally said. "Do you think the Havemeyers would join up with the Ripples? Don't make me laugh. We got troubles of our own anyway."

However, he outlined at length a plan of tactics that had been used extensively on the East Side when the opposition was too strong. "That ought to help you muggs," he ended. "Go on home and grow up."

"Don't talk like that," Davey said. "I got a good mind to take a smack out of you for that wisecrack."

"Oh, yare?" the curly-headed kid asked.

"Come on," Natie said. "We got to get going."

Back on Ripple Street they worked industriously. Detachments were sent out to look for bottles, stones, and pieces of wood. Natie loaded his air rifle with BB's and kept it at a vantage point. They stored the roofs on both sides of the street with piles of ammunition. The streets themselves they left empty.

Then the wait began for the Maujers. It was distressing. After all their work, they experienced a let-down as the enemy refused to put in an appearance. Some of the boys rolled in the pebbles on the roof and began fighting against one another in sham battles. Davey feared the weakening of his gang's morale. He inspected the different positions in tours, instructing, reprimanding, and encouraging. He felt like a general awaiting a siege.

"Keep quiet until Natie goes bam-bam-stop-bam. Then let it go," he reminded them with important secrecy. That was the signal.

The night came on. Davey kept looking up the street toward Union Avenue, but there was nothing. He was disappointed and wondered how much longer he and his gang would be able to hold out. Natie was busy pulling away at a scab on his knee. He was tremendously absorbed in the delicate operation. In his irritation Davey bawled out his lieutenant for his negligence. "How do you think the rest of them will act if you're supposed to be the lookout and you don't keep your eyes peeled? You make me sick and disgusted."

"Look," Natie said quietly. It was really impressive. The Maujers had profited from their previous experience. One group came swinging down from Union Avenue, their numbers swollen, carrying blatantly the implements of war. Confidently they swished the long stockings through the air, filled with ashes and stones. From his perch Davey could see the whole show. Down at the opposite end of the street, toward the Extension, another group waited. The intention was to trap the Ripples, to drub them in severe crossfire, to make up for the humiliation of their own defeat by giving them a dose of their own medicine. Davey shuddered at the thought of what would have happened had he not been forewarned.

"Keep your heads back," he whispered savagely to his men. They were peering over the cornices in their eagerness. He pulled them back by their pants. "Keep back, you klucks. Wait for the bam-bam-stop-bam and then let them have it for all you're worth."

The Maujers and their allies swooped down the street, joyously expecting easy victories. Davey restrained himself with terrible control until they came plumb within the range. Down below, the two divisions met and stormed about looking for the enemy. "All right," Davey said. Bam-bam-stop-bam went the BB gun. The bottles fell out of the sky like rain.

It was the most satisfactory encounter Davey could remember. The streets were cleaned in less than five minutes. Davey went down to his supper, reconciled in his jubilation to the bawling out he would get from his mother for being late. As he passed down through the halls, he suddenly remembered. In the excitement he had forgotten all about Yetta and his tryst with her at Cheap Simon's. She would not understand and he feared her wrath.

Cohen had solved the riddle of the world. Ever since his attempted suicide he had left the hospital and carried himself grim-faced, satisfied, and cool. Neighbors pointed him out in the streets. "That's the one," they said, and shook their heads wisely. "He looks happier because he knows that no matter how terrible life is it's better than to be dead." Cohen disregarded them. He did not even speak to Mahler. Philip was back, he knew, but he took special pains to avoid him. Alone, within himself, Cohen pondered, running his fingers through his oily hair and taking time to look at them carefully for more fallen hairs. He had solved the riddle of the world.

It was a huge fake. He remembered when he was a boy he had always had the feeling that all people were liars. Actually, the entire world existed as far as he could see. That was all. People said the world was large in a concerted effort to give coming generations confidence. Great seas, foreign countries, pictures, ocean liners were all accessories to the fraud and part of the deception. At this time Cohen's greatest desire was to walk in a straight line and to walk endlessly until he saw what there was of the world. He didn't believe them. Often, even now, he had a momentary feeling that history was manufactured fiction and that the physical properties of the world had been deliberately exaggerated to give people the feeling of dignity.

It was a matter of proportion. To an ant an inch might be a block, a mile, the universe. In ratio to man the earth was big and a lifetime great. But in truth what was known? We could not think of limitless things, Cohen argued, and yet they told us the universe had no bounds. They said the cosmos had no beginning in time, but we could not imagine matter growing from no origin. Nor could we picture the eternality of the universe. Actually, Cohen affirmed, man did not know. He was as ignorant as the ant. At bottom there was complete blank and everything man said, no matter with what authority and self-assurance, was based on a complete want of knowledge.

These were fundamental truths. Cohen pondered long into the night while the big tenements slept, and in passing he wondered whether he would not die of a cerebral hemorrhage, which would have its romantic advantages. Cohen would erase this perpetual laughing, he would show them. In preparation he was working on what was to be a gigantic outline for a book. This was not to be one of the season's output, but revolutionary. It would change the reasoning habits of thousands, dim into silliness the effect of any other man or work. Cohen.

He lay back on his bed to consider the pleasant possibilities. He put his hands over his eyes to keep out the light. They would come to him, Mahler, Philip, and the girl in the sweeping red gown, respectful with awe at his fame. The rotogravure sections would print his casual presence photographed in Paris, Madrid, Budapest. Every morning there would be a fat handful of letters for him. He was the man, Cohen, the world would say, and never take its eyes from him. All the world would drive him to the civilized capitals to do him homage, but Cohen, tormented by a restless soul, would travel interminably alone, scorning women, men, and diversions. With his money he would build fantastic houses in Tibet and gratify every chance whim. And with equal nonchalance he would discard them as soon as they bored him. To have fame, fortune, and to be loved, those are what all men desire most, and Cohen, dreaming on his bed, took sharp delight because he would be able to have them by opening his hand but he would be too world-worn to stretch for them. Then they would say how in the old days he had lived in his miserable room, how he had stridden the streets mysteriously at night absorbed in himself and the stupendous projects he was always dreaming of. They would recount his attempted suicide and its miraculous escape. The tugboat that had fished him out would be sought and photographed. Tourists would fill Ripple Street looking for the marks of the master, his poor room, the modest writing table, and the fountain pen he had used.

Cohen rose and stared at the empty white page. His idea was, briefly—he would put it down on paper. His brain was still fogged from his dreams on the bed. To start with, briefly, to get it into words, his idea was—corpuscles. Corpuscles raced through a human body. There were millions of them, like the number of people on the earth, and they formed a perfect society of their own. The man was their universe. Briefly, the idea was, just as corpuscles inhabit the universe of man, racing through him, living long ages of days or of minutes, traveling from organ to organ which they call capes, continents, peninsulas, and oceans, so in proportion do we lead our lives, ignorant as the corpuscles and creating a great universe after the same fashion as they, but in proportion. We disregard the society within us but they too have the equivalents of all kinds of phenomena, arts and sciences, experiences and consciousnesses, individuals who sniff through heavy nose colds and anemic youngsters with dull feelings in their bellies and pimples on their faces, all after their own fashion, valid fashions and worthy of tolerance and respect. Cohen squeezed his pen, and in a burst of effort wrote: "We follow our dark paths in the same fashion as corpuscles in a human body. Really, we are all—peoples, houses, land—minute parts of some great body who walks nonchalantly with no concern for our desperate ignorance. We occupy our days senselessly, like waterbugs sliding over the smooth surface of a pond."

That was all. Cohen gripped his pen until his knuckles hurt. He stared at the white sheet of paper. The three lines stood at the top waiting patiently. More, they said, more. Cohen pressed the pen with his fingers and struggled within himself. His intention had been to do a mixed book, fantasy and realism, revealing satirically, creating the life of the corpuscles paralleled by the life of humans. This was to be a piercing, illuminating thing. The three lines at the top silently begged, more, please, more. He reread them and was distressed by the reference to the waterbugs. He liked that very much, but it was bad. This was a mixed metaphor. You had to cross it out. Cohen threw the pen down in a fit of disgust and walked from the table. He returned, the fit had worn off immediately, and carefully he screwed the cap over the point so that the ink wouldn't dry. He lay down.

Cohen was heartbroken. He knew again that this was going to be a humiliating flop. It was "Green Gods in Yellow" all over again. Cohen felt almost like crying. He rolled over to hide his face in the bed but his spectacles pushed into his eyebrows. He took them off and dropped them on the floor, and this little incident complicated his grief because it made him feel a little ridiculous again. His great idea now sounded flat, the daydreams were a joke, he knew he would never write.

What had started him off that day was the recollection of that line he had read in a Russian novel, that line everlastingly with him, interminably repeating itself: "I am, as you know, an employee of the post office, but I have always wanted to be a poet." There was something pathetic about it, it might be his own epitaph it applied so accurately to him. Cohen's mood might also have been caused by his persistent dwelling on his appearance, the ridicule he always met, his growing baldness, and the flat, even way of his life in spite of all the dust storms he tried to kick up for himself. He thought of Barbellion, whose *Portrait of a Disappointed Man* the librarian had given him in an effort to stabilize the excitable creature she always saw hanging around the bookshelves. Now it seemed to outline with trenchant meaning for Cohen the dreariness of days succeeding one another with petty misfortune, absence of achievement, and in addition his own special heritage of the always-present laughter. Cohen thought again of his trip to the Williamsburg Bridge. That too, meant as a dignified conclusion, escape from misery, was epitome, for he succeeded here only in making himself more ridiculous and more laughable.

Cohen lay long in the sticky bath of self-pity. Then it became monotonous. When he rose he pulled up his pants. The shirt always rubbed out at the hips and his suits fitted poorly. The vest and trousers never met, and when he was with company he was always obliged to button his jacket in order to hide the white breach. As he cleared his eyes he saw the three lines on the top of the sheet asking for more. He grabbed his hat and walked out of the room.

Among the passers-by he felt an outcast. He walked toward the elevated pillars of Broadway, pulled the lapels of his jacket up, and pushed his hat down. He was sullen with himself. Cohen now pictured himself homeless, unwanted, rejected by his fellow men. He was no better than a bum. A man turned the corner briskly, smoking a cigarette. Cohen stopped him.

"Can you spare a butt, buddy?" he asked, keeping his head down.

The man looked him over, took out a pack while his eyes still surveyed him, and gave him three cigarettes.

"Here," he said, "take as many as you want. It's all right."

"Thanks, bud," Cohen said, and smiled to him the gratitude of a generation of homeless bums. The man with the breezy walk moved ahead, warm in the solace that he had done humanity a good turn.

Now Cohen turned down toward the Fourteenth Street subway, moving in the shadows of the buildings as he sulked mysteriously in his fit of depression. He was, in fact, beginning to enjoy it. It was a stage. It was a purge. Carlyle had it, Mill had it, it was the catharsis a sensitive temperament had to undergo. The Italian ditchdiggers on Metropolitan Avenue resting on the sidewalks after the day's work looked up at this strange Jew walking defiantly in his private cloud of gloom. Cohen stopped at a candy stand. He pointed to an inverted bottle of lemon-lime.

"You want five-cent drink?" the man inside the store asked.

Cohen pointed to the jar again and gestured that he could not hear or talk, reluctant to waste conversation on the man.

"Oh," he said. He filled the glass with the syrup carefully, out of respect.

Cohen drank it critically. "Too sweet," he muttered and the candy-stand man looked at him in surprise.

The speedy train ride under the river was cool and soothing. Cohen always sought out the subways for his periods of despondency because the mechanical clatter and jangling metals gave him sustenance. Here he felt among heroic proportions and it seemed fitting to him. More, he relished the presence of the people in subways for then he felt his savage despair was at least observed.

Cohen threaded his way through the moving throngs on Fourteenth Street to his favorite corner. This was where the models in the dress shop above the cigar store walked their coy bodies carrying wraps and dresses. Cohen bought an apple from a pushcart and settled to watch the models as he chewed. His neck grew stiff, but there was a fascination about it. It was like the zoo. Here were humans walking, swaying, pirouetting for the express purpose of having people on the street, like Cohen, look upon them and admire. They kept going around with the frozen expressions on their faces, one foot being placed in front of the other in their elegant strides. From time to time a model slipped through the curtain at the rear, and when she reappeared, lo! she was more radiant than ever. Cohen grew to recognize them in spite of the new coats they wore. He threw the apple core away. His neck ached and he was getting a little dizzy following their movements in the circle.

Across the street on the Square a shirtsleeved man spoke forcefully from a wooden platform. He waved his arms to emphasize his point while the spittle gathered unheeded at the corners of his mouth. "Well," he shouted, swaying back, "what did Henry Ford do? I'll tell you, my good friends." He had to wait, stopped full in his fury, before he could tell them. A trolley car was taking the curve screechingly. He waited patiently. "I'll tell you what he did," he said, turning on his fury to its former intensity, and he told them.

Cohen stood at the fringe of the crowd. This was always a good show. He admired the passion with which these men spoke, their entire absorption in their work. The man was small, skinny, and sweated. He spoke in the sharp, clipped pronunciations of New England dialect but his accent was also unmistakably Jewish. Occasionally an unfortunate inflection escaped, giving him away disastrously. "Take me," he cried vehemently. "I've been slaving twenty years. I know my trade, fellow-workers, not that I want to boast, but I can work hard. What do I get? I am a married man with three small children, and they threw me out like I was the dirt on the floor. I ask you, should we go on with a way where one man gets the fruits of my labor, and of your labor, too, my friends, and we get no accident insurance, no unemployment insurance, no pension?" He paused for breath.

The crowd listened to him with open mouths. The speaker gave a solid story of his own life. He had worked in a dress shop as a cutter, he had suffered various injustices, and under a more equitable system of government he felt he would have received better treatment. "I come here tonight," he said, the calm tone indicating that he was winding up, "not to bellyache in this hot weather, but with one thought in my mind. If the people understood, if they took an interest in their government, they would all work together for their common good and do something. I come here night after night, I tell you no fancy stories, I give you fact after fact. You stand there and listen to me for half an hour. What are you going to do?"

He climbed down from the platform. A half-dozen younger members of his party walked through the crowd with copies of the *Daily Worker* and kindred literature. They broke into knots. One man with a triangular face calmly smoked cigarettes as he held the center of discussion. He had shaved so carefully that his jaws were greenish and he spoke with the casual wisdom of the ages. Patiently he explained how they did it in Russia.

"Any of you who are interested can come along with me to our room. We can talk there." He moved off. Of the small group about him Cohen alone followed.

"I'd like to hear a little more about this business," he said.

The man with the triangular face inspected Cohen critically. "Come on," he said. "We've got a basement dump, but you're welcome."

On the way down to the basement dump he explained the life to Cohen. He said you had to be altogether serious about it, they didn't want any kidders around. It was a rigorous discipline. "You can't look at it like any other political club. We don't go in for that. We know what we're fighting here. It's everything, we demand sacrifices from you, and you've got to expect it from us."

In the room on Ninth Avenue, a dark basement under the elevated structure, cigarette smoke circled in a blue haze around the single electric bulb. The discussion going on was almost violent. Cohen's friend with the triangular face left him suddenly to shift for himself. He leaned against the wall, taking it in. The young men and women said "Comrade" and "Party" and uttered their arguments with intestinal sincerity. It was wonderful, Cohen said. How these people gave themselves! That was the answer, to lose oneself in a cause greater than oneself, to become part of some great movement. A man who lived within himself and for himself was rotten and three-quarters dead. Cohen gasped with excitement. This was it.

A heavy girl with a loose face and big lips came up to him wielding a cigarette.

"My name is Shura," she said point-blank and with dreadful solemnity. "Who are you?"

TWELVE

"Hurry up," Sam Linck said. "We'll never get there."

There was a group of women on the sidewalk. Sam's wife, in a black satin dress with the sleeves shortened and in a white straw hat modishly pressed on her head, clutched her bundles and her two children as she said perspired farewells. She was going off to Fallsburgh, to the country, for three weeks, and now she had to kiss all the neighbors good-bye.

"Take care of the children," Mrs. Linck called out.

One of the boys broke away and ran down the street to the candy store. Sam's wife interrupted her duties to the housewives and yelled shrilly. "Come back, I'll break your neck!" She turned again to her neighbors. "What's all the fuss?" she said modestly. "Someone would think I'm going to Europe."

"Hurry up," Linck said. "Do you want me to wait all year?"

He had borrowed the Ford coupe from a friend and was taking his wife and kids to the country. He was doing her a great favor, and as he waited for her to get through he felt sorry for himself. While she lived the life of Riley in the mountains, among trees and away from the hot city, he would have to keep on burning his can in his truck.

The Ford was old and stiff in the joints. Sam got his wife and kids packed in among the baggage and closed the doors tightly. As the motor raced and knocked, the women raised a flurry of farewells. Sam's wife stuck her head out of the window and waved.

"Take good care of the children," Mrs. Linck commanded with matriarchal importance.

"Don't worry yourself," Sam's wife said resentfully. She looked sweetly at her friends and waved her hand vigorously.

The Ford backfired, Linck released the clutch, and the car started staggering up the street in jerks before it got going, leaving the smell of gasoline to overpower the neighbors. They walked back to their flats. Mrs. Linck was very proud. The incident showed that her son was a steady husband and gave his wife luxuries. "When I married," she said, "no one ever heard of a wife leaving her husband by himself and wandering over the country."

Linck said nothing as they drove out of the city traffic. His face was glum. You're going off for a good time, the glum face said, but I'm stuck in this hole. His wife glanced at him from time to time through the corners of her eyes and she was apprehensive. The children snuggled against the big sack into which she had sewn the blankets, sheets, pillows, clothing, pots and pans. One of the kids began working on a sharp edge where the handle of a pan protruded. He was intent on wearing a hole through the sack. Sam's wife caught him just in time. She bawled him out savagely, and after that it was like a release. She could talk to her husband.

"Why do you look so grouchy?" she asked. "I'm not going for a good time. It's the children. They need the country. They're so skinny."

"Who's complaining?" Sam said belligerently. "I know it's for the children. When you go to the movies it's for the children."

"Sam," she said positively, "if that's the way you feel, you can turn right back. It's no pleasure for me."

Linck went on driving. They had crossed the Hudson River now and the green countryside showed itself through the windows. It was really a vacation for himself too. With his wife and her perpetual nagging out of the way for three weeks there were joyous possibilities. He began perking up. His wife looked at his face and worried.

"You'll take care of yourself when I'm away?" she asked.

"What's the matter with you? I'll be home with my mother. She cooked my meals before I knew you and she can do it when you're away."

"I mean, Sam. You know. I'll be away for three weeks and I was wondering how you would spend your time by yourself."

"Don't worry about me," Linck said angrily. "I'll have a good time. I can go to the movies, and if it gets too hot I can always go to Coney Island and sleep on the beaches."

"I didn't mean that," his wife said in a low voice.

"What's on your mind?" he asked impatiently. Then he understood. "Jesus, that's good. That's hot. It's the reward I get. I put together seventy dollars and send you for a good time to the mountains. I even borrow a car and take you up myself so you won't have to travel in a crowded bus, and what do I get for it? Jesus Christ," Linck said as if to himself, "I certainly like that."

"Don't get mad. I didn't mean anything. After all, you can't blame me if I worry, Sam," she said. "Everyone has his troubles and all married couples have a fight once in a while, but after all you're my husband, you're all I got."

"All right. All right. Stop crying over me. You're not going away for a year. I'm not dead yet."

The Ford rattled along in silence. Linck wanted to get to the boarding house before eight, but he couldn't get the four-cylindered car to move faster than thirty-five.

"We've got to step on it," he said. The children fell asleep on the back seat, using the sack for pillows. Sam's wife grew drowsy with the rocking motion of the car. From Fallsburgh they bumped over the dirt road to the house. It was an ugly new wooden structure dumped on top of a hill. Linck manipulated the Ford under the arched doorway on which was printed Villa Caprice, and his wife, rubbing her eyes, said, "We're here already? I can't believe it."

The proprietor, a healthy bearded man smelling of sweat, greeted them effusively and sat them down to a supper of pot cheese, sour cream, and bread. Linck saw his family fixed in the unpainted boardroom and waited until his wife put the kids into the bed. It was a metal one, and she wondered whether it would be comfortable when the three of them slept in it. The farmer helped Sam haul the heavy sack up the hill and they dropped it on the floor of her room. The place smelled strangely, not of the country but of fresh lumber, nails, and sawdust.

Mrs. Linck felt lonely and desolate. She was tired from the ride.

"You can open up the sack tomorrow," Linck said. "Go to sleep early and get a good rest."

He stood awkwardly facing her. "Well, I'll be seeing you before we know it, the time will pass so soon."

"Sam," she said tearfully, "I feel so lonely."

"It'll be all right in the morning. I guess I'll be going. I've got to get to work tomorrow."

They stood clumsily and didn't know how to kiss. The last time had been so long ago they felt as though kissing was nonsense and ridiculous, but now they knew they should be kissing each other good-bye and it was difficult to do it.

"Good-bye, Sam," she finally said. "Take good care of yourself and remember what I said, you're all I got."

"Don't worry. I'll be all right." He patted her on the shoulder and went out of the room.

As the cool breeze of the country night blew into his face Linck looked at the sky from the high porch on the hill, wiped his nose, and pulled up his pants. He was happy at the prospect. It was as though a weight had been lifted. Three weeks, he said with zest, three weeks.

"Bread and butter! Say bread and butter!" Ruth Kelman cried. That was for crowds, when some one walked between them. It would drive away bad luck, keep them together always. "Say bread and butter!" she demanded.

"Bread and butter," Philip said.

"I'll go limp! If you don't watch out, I'll go limp!"

"What for, you nitwit?"

"Just to embarrass you."

"Now? Right here? You'll be embarrassing yourself." He could see her eyes from the side, threatening, and yet questioning and in play.

"I don't care. I'll go limp."

"That's a silly stunt. Go ahead. I'll let you fall to the ground and I'll walk away. I won't know you, you won't be walking with me." He was sober and spoke with adult seriousness.

"You mean it? You mean it?"

"Of course."

"All right. Here I go. I'm going limp."

And surely, in that ridiculous way of hers, she was dissolving herself to the pavement until Philip had to pull her up by the arm. If he had really walked off he knew she would have been sitting on the ground by this time. People were already looking at them, and he grabbed her so tightly by the elbow that she had to half-stumble before him.

"All right," he said roughly. "Come along."

Philip pretended he was annoyed with her. He walked steadfastly ahead, keeping his eyes before him.

"I told you I don't like to have people looking at me in the street," he said.

"Don't get mad at me. I'll show you what I can do if you want to get nasty with me."

"You couldn't do a thing. You're a chirp in the breeze."

"I'll show you, you big mutt."

She ducked behind him, put her hands on his hips, and suddenly began pushing him up the street. He was caught off his guard. The two of them went running while people stopped to look at them.

"Cut it out, you idiot," Philip called over his shoulder at her. He had begun by laughing but grew genuinely uncomfortable at the stares of passers-by.

"Listen, you nitwit, you walk with me like a lady or I'll leave you flat."

"Shut up, you big stiff," she said, and grabbed his arm.

"I mean it, Ruth. I'm serious now. I don't like to make a holy show of myself like this. Cut it out."

"All right. Fingers." She was contrite.

The streets were wet from rain, reflecting the lights of the store windows and passing cars. The autos dashed up and down, the lights beamed, store windows either cast their rays over their faces or returned their walking pictures, people kept looking at them because they almost danced as they walked, from un-uttered laughter. At times Philip's eyes met hers and then they smiled in surprise. And at darkened street corners he bent down, putting his lips on her forehead to feel the warmth and smoothness of her skin. They were bubbling with gladness because they had found each other.

Philip had met her in the afternoon. They had walked up Fifth Avenue and across to the ferry pier at Forty-second Street, taken the trip to New Jersey and back, ended up in a movie, all the while delighting in the discoveries they were making of each other. Ruth was like a child, lovely and unaffected, moving without regard to whatever impression she might be creating. That was what Philip liked so much about her, her spontaneity, her natural charm and grace. Here is a lovely thing, he told himself repeatedly, here is something to love. On their walks and on the ferry they had talked of a million subjects, revealing themselves, and now they felt as though it was an old friendship, there had been a long time in between, and they were close to each other. He liked her softness, the big eyes, the chestnut hair massing in curls and waves above her head. As they went along Lexington Avenue on their way to her home he took pains to pause before every letterbox so she could jangle it.

"On Lexington Avenue? Here? All right," he said. "I'm game, but you're it."

The streets at Eighty-fourth Street were dark and empty. He ran off to a store doorway to hide while Ruth put her head over folded arms against a street lamppost. She counted loudly so that he would hear and know she wasn't cheating. Philip watched her look for him as she went cautiously up and down a few yards from the base. Finally he stretched too far beyond the window and she spied him. She ran up in glee, threw her arms about his shoulders and yelled, "You're it!"

"Look," said Philip, "here's a stunt you never learned. Stay over there and watch." He pressed one side of his body against the end of the store window and began waving his arm and leg to the side. From Ruth's position the reflection of his one side made it seem as though his entire body was off the pavement, floating and moving in the air like a monkey-on-a-string.

"I know that trick," Ruth cried. "Watch me do it."

She improved on Philip's performance, puffing her cheek and wagging her leg and arm, producing weird effects.

"Hey," she said, "I want my turn. You're it."

Philip felt silly at the lamppost counting aloud. He hoped no one passed by, but there she was back again before he had reached thirty, quiet and a little scared.

"What's the matter, baby?" Philip asked.

"I ran into a doorway and a man was there."

"He must have thought you were crazy." They laughed. Philip put his arm around her and said it was good for her. She felt very warm and alive in his arms.

"Hey," she said, starting away, "after all, I just know you a day."

"That's all right. We're old friends now. I've got clean habits, there's nothing to worry about."

Nevertheless, Philip was a little sobered too by the realization. They were very fast for such a short time.

"We're certainly not wasting time," he said with a laugh.

At her home they found no one in. Ruth's younger sister was at camp, her father and mother were out for the evening. "That's a convenience," Philip said. Then they discovered they were both hungry. He had forgotten all about buying her dinner. At her well-furnished home he felt apologetic for it.

"I guess I forgot all about it," he said. "I'm a dope."

Ruth said she had too. They went through the icebox and found a can of tomato juice, some cold chicken, bread, and ketchup. At the kitchen table they made their meal long, talked, and smoked cigarettes. It was pleasant to be hungry and to have food, she said, and Philip had to laugh as he recognized with fresh clearness how true the simple fact was. He played phonograph records while Ruth cleaned up the plates. Philip found some Strauss waltzes, *Tales from the Vienna Woods*, and played them, repeating the records. He was chagrined at his pleasure in them, it was the movies, but his mood was so strong he surrendered to them.

Ruth was sitting on the davenport and Philip went to her. He held her to his chest. "We fit nicely," he said. The needle scratched as it reached the end of the disc. He found a tango with the dreamiest falls and rises he had ever heard, and put it on. "It's beautiful," he said to Ruth. "This is the wonderful music of love. It has depth, understanding, and murmurs the sad pathos of life."

"Don't be ashamed of it," she said. "Have a good time. You think too much about these things. Don't be a prig."

Philip sat down, but just when they had got comfortably mixed together the record finished. "The hell with it," he said. "We'll burn candles for atmosphere. There's less wear and tear."

He closed the phonograph lid, and they sat together on the davenport in the darkness, Ruth lying drowsily on his chest. They were both tired from their walk, the rides across the river, and the air. It had been a long day. As they sat together Philip was conscious of the warm smell of her hair, the life in her soft body, and the deliciousness of her presence so near him.

"Come on," he said finally, "let's get up. We'll go to sleep this way. What would your esteemed parents say upon finding us sleeping together already?"

Ruth did not move. He pulled her gently by the wrists to her feet, but she kept her eyes still closed and her arms were outstretched as he had left them.

"Look," he said, "you like games. Keep your eyes closed and see if you can find me."

He went off to hide in a corner. She soon found him, he couldn't restrain the chuckles of amusement at the sight of her, sleepily blundering.

"Now I'm it," he said. "I'll look for you."

Ruth went to hide behind a chair. Philip had a hard time finding her. She was quiet, tired, and sleepy. He went around the room and around. It was a peculiar sensation. "Where are you anyway?" he said as if to himself. "It's funny as anything, the way I feel looking for you now. It must be terrible to be blind. I'd hate to look like this and grope all the time. Where are you anyway?"

Then she ran out, put her arms around him, and cried a bit.

"What's the matter, baby?" Philip asked with concern. "What's the matter?"

"Nothing. Only, I can't see you stumble with your eyes closed and your hands stretched out."

They sat on the davenport again and she tried to hide her head in his shoulder, ashamed. Philip felt tender toward her. There was something strangely good and natural in her. He felt he could trust her all the time, trust her in everything, all thoughts and hopes and daydreams, as if with himself.

"Look," he said sincerely, "we're kids, Ruth. We're young and all that. But, honestly, I'm loving you with everything I have. I never really believed in this. I'll probably change in my feeling toward you, but now it makes me feel helpless in a way and dependent on you. Before I had you I was all right with myself. I could feel satisfied and whole. Now I find I'm incomplete in myself."

Philip stopped himself abruptly. He considered what he had been saying. "By God," he swore with determination, "that leaves me open for a fine kick in the pants. I know you for a day and just listen to this swill I'm throwing at you." He felt ashamed of the Strauss waltzes, the darkness in the room, and his feelings.

Energetically the begrimed man with the bald head worked on his knees over the pot. It was a big, shallow copper pan used for boiling fish on Fridays, but its style was so old it probably was owned by a woman who had been given it as a wedding gift twenty years ago. The rims were leaky, and the man blew his torch hot to melt the lead. Davey and his gang sat on the curb watching with absorption the way he worked and followed with especial wonder the smoothness with which he soldered the pan. It was like the hypnotized stare that follows a man who sweeps a given square with a broom. The gray circle ran evenly around the pan. Davey marveled at the chunky fingers of the man, their nails black and broken, the flesh seamed in an intricate pattern of myriad dirty lines.

This too was one of the legitimate spectacles of Williamsburg, the man who came in his homemade pushcart to fix pots and pans. He was an infrequent visitor and Davey had to watch out for his appearance. The umbrella fixer with his oilcloth bag of black rags and spokes did an even more spasmodic business. Most frequent were the junkies in their pushcarts with the two bells suspended overhead. As for the old-clothes men, these came every day after nine in the morning because then housewives were tempted by pocket money and sold their husband's old suits more freely.

Davey gazed from the curb in peaceful contemplation, but Yetta, appearing from nowhere, created a minor disturbance. She touched Davey on the shoulder. "Can I see you for a minute?" she said, and every kid turned his head to look at her. Even the pot fixer raised his eyes for it was a great thing when a girl talked to a fellow in this fashion.

"I'll be seeing you kids," Davey said nonchalantly, and brushed his pants. He turned to Yetta.

"Do you have to talk to me here?" he said with annoyance.

"I was just passing by and I happened to see you," Yetta said. She was stiff and formal and possessed. "There's something I want to say to you, and I thought I'd do it now being that you were there."

"I would have been at Cheap Simon's at five-thirty. Couldn't you wait? These fellows are kids, they don't understand about you and me. They got filthy minds. It makes it bad for you, and I get the razzberry."

"If that's the way you feel," Yetta said. She had turned to ice and was heartbreaking.

"Well, what's on your mind?" Davey asked, but he knew.

"I've got a bone to pick with you." She didn't know how well this fitted in now, but she had prepared the line for her opening and it would have to do anyhow. "If there's anything I can't stand it's a person who makes an appointment and then doesn't keep it."

"You mean about Cheap Simon's? Didn't you hear about it? We had a raid, Yetta. The Maujers hitched up with the Staggs and the Throops and came down against my gang. I realize I broke my appointment, but I knew you would understand."

"I said," Yetta said, "if there's one thing I can't stand it's a person who makes an appointment and then doesn't keep it."

"Yetta! I don't blame you for being sore, but after all, what did you expect me to do? Did you want me to leave my gang and turn yellow on them just because the Maujers hitched up with the Staggs and Throops? There's a time when a person can't keep an appointment with a person no matter how fond he is of her. I thought you would understand."

"Tell me, David," she said darkly, "is a street fight more important than our love?"

Even he was surprised. But he recovered quickly, he remembered the passage in the movies. It was like *The Ace of Cads* with Adolphe Menjou when his girl thought he had been unfaithful to her but he hadn't, only he couldn't say anything on account of honor. "I can't help it," Davey said. "There are certain times when a person can't do what he wants. It's not that one thing is more important than the other thing. I thought you would see it. It's not like I purposely give you a stand-up."

"If that's the way you feel," she said, waiting for capitulation. There was something about her stance that suddenly infuriated Davey. Who did she think she was anyway? Greta Garbo?

"Yes," he shouted, once and for all, "that's the way I feel. Who do you think you are anyway?"

"Well, in that case," Yetta said with enormous disdain, "I better say good-bye."

"Good-bye!"

He turned his back swiftly so that he would have the satisfaction of letting her see him walk away. After the first rush of independence, however, Davey reconsidered and doubted whether he had acted wisely. This meant the end. He would never speak to her again. Now, this was important to him. He had loved, enshrined her image in his heart, this was the end, and no one could say his passion was a silly thing just because Davey was young. What made him talk to her like that at the end? he asked himself. It would have blown over, like in *The Ace of Cads*, it was a small quarrel. Then his anger toward her returned and he repeated the question, who was she anyway? The answer was, a fat load of nothing in his life!

What is love? Davey asked with the air of a man who had just left prison. He wasn't a kid any longer. What did he want to suck around that kid for? What could he get out of her? A kiss. What was a kiss? He was no baby. The movies were a load of hooey. He went back to the curb. The potman was putting on his sweat-soaked cap over the bald head and surveying the finished job.

"You like it, boys?" he asked them nastily. "Get the hell out of here. What are you hanging around my neck for?"

The kids scrambled out of his reach. Natie drew Davey aside. "What did Yetta want?" he asked with interest. Ever since Davey's confession to him at the sawed-off doorway weeks ago, he felt they had a special bond in common and that he was privileged to ask these intimate questions.

"She had a nerve," Davey said. "Can you imagine her stopping me on the street?"

"She certainly had a nerve. I'd never let my girl do that to me in front of my gang."

"Who's your girl?" Davey asked, wanting to know. "You don't mean Marion Davies? Don't be crazy."

"Oh, I don't mean her. Naturally. I mean if I had a girl like Yetta, I'd never let her pull that off on me."

"I'd like to see her try it again. I told her where she got off."

"You can't let a girl think too much of herself or the first thing you know she'll be swinging you by the nose. That's what my old man says."

"Listen, Nate, what's love? That's for kids. I don't say we're grown up, but we're not kids no more. Listen, I mean, you know about Solly Leparbow? He's not so old and he had that broad Ida down in the cellar for half an hour. On the level. Solly said he felt like he was swinging around in the air like a wheel on fire. How old do you think he is? He's only twelve."

Natie broke out into giggles but at Davey's show of disgust he stopped and felt foolish.

"You're a kid. Don't act like a kid."

"The way you talk!" Natie the Buller rushed in to explain. He had to establish himself with Davey again. "Listen, I know more about that business than you'll ever know. Did I ever tell you about the time I was living on Broome Street? I was walking near the river when a rowboat passes by. There was an old man with whiskers and a young fellow in the boat. I saw them both doing something at the bottom and I looked, and Jesus, if you only saw it. It was a naked woman and she was lying like dead on the bottom of the boat."

"That's a load of crap," Davey said, straight out. "I know you and your load of bull."

Natie or no Natie, Davey resolved to spend his evenings near Cheap Simon's at South Third Street, where the candy-store lights beamed mightily, where the boys ran wildly with the mad jitters of love, the girls dangled their favors tantalizingly, and Ida the young cow, Ida was glorious on display. He wasn't a kid.

Philip was home by ten in the evening. His mother was ready to meet him, worried and a little angry because he had failed to appear for his supper and because he hadn't told her he would be late.

"All day you went without anything in your mouth," she said. "Where were you anyhow, trumbinick?"

"Didn't you know, Mom? I'm married, and my wife, she says she likes to see me sometime."

"Who would marry you with your funny nose? You're so thin the light comes through. Here, sit down and eat."

"Listen, my sage, you don't know everything. There's plenty that would marry the handsome likes o' me."

"Don't talk so much. Eat. Tessie sent you another letter. What kind of business is this with a woman who's married? And why does she have to write letters? Can't she telephone?"

"Oh, it's a long story, Mom. Tessie and me were sweethearts until the news came out about my wife and three children. That broke everything, but love is love and you can't say stop."

He was annoyed with the letter. Philip never liked to have his mother know what he did with his time. She worried too much. He recalled the time she told him of a discussion she had had with their family doctor. The doctor had been saying how it was almost like yesterday he had delivered Philip, and here he was a big boy, ready to make babies himself. And at this point Mrs. Hayman had said, "Oh, doctor, he's a good boy."

Philip glanced at Tessie's note. It was what he expected. "What has happened? Why don't I hear from you? If you knew how lonely I am in my apartment with my husband gone for weeks at a time, you'd come to see me more often." It was the usual. Complaint, protestation, the delicate vicissitudes of love as they were portrayed in certain English novels.

"It says Tessie's going to have a baby, Mom," Philip said.

"Don't be foolish. How can she have a baby? She just got married."

"Well," said Philip, "sometimes it doesn't come the way it should. On the level, she and Schlausser are going to have a son. She wrote to tell me what they're going to call him. Anthony Sherrick Van Twillinger Schlausser. Isn't that a beautiful name?"

"Quiet, quiet, you talk in bunches," she said. "Here, eat with bread."

"Well," said Philip, "how is it going with Pop and the man who wants to buy his place? Coblenz? Will Pop sell?"

"Sell!" said Mrs. Hayman. "Try and make him over. If he makes up his mind it's easier to push a building out of the way. He was always peculiar, but he's getting topsy-turvy in his old age like Yente Maldick. I can't do anything with him."

Philip smiled. "Don't give up hope, Mom."

"I gave up hope a long time already," she said. "You can't change him. Just like before I was worrying over you because I didn't know what happened to you without anything in your mouth all day. So I worry and walk around, and Poppa sits in his chair reading the paper until it comes half past nine o'clock and, Philip or no Philip, he goes to sleep."

Philip wiped his mouth and rose. "I'm going to run down for a newspaper."

He walked around the corner, went into a drugstore, and called up Tessie. He could feel her powdered presence through the earpiece.

"This is Philip," he said. "Did I wake you?"

"Who? I can't hear you."

"Philip."

"Oh, Philip. I thought you said Willie." Her voice softened. "What's wrong, Philip? Why don't I ever see you?"

"I'm kind of busy lately. Tessie, I hope you won't take offense, I know you'll understand me. It's simply that you oughtn't to send me letters. It doesn't look well for you, and my mother thinks it's odd. I don't like to upset her."

"You're a stranger," she said. "I can't get in touch with you at all and you never call. Don't you want to see me?"

"It's not that. Why put it that way? It's simply that I don't want to worry my mother. Besides, I can't see much point in making any permanent arrangement out of this. It'll lead us into trouble and we'll have to stop sooner or later. We can't get any place going the way we are."

"We can't talk about this on the telephone. Why don't you drop in tomorrow?"

"Of course. Perhaps we'll go for a walk in the park some afternoon soon."

"Tomorrow?"

"I can't say," Philip said. "Some day soon."

Ever since he had met Ruth Kelman Philip had found it hard to think of Tessie. His relationship with her now became disagreeable and made him feel uncomfortable. Like Mrs. Linck's son Sam and his lovely amorous adventures, Philip thought, and then uneasily he tried to drive the problem from his mind. He went around the block looking for a newspaper. It was late and the candy stores here carried few papers. He ended up with the next morning's *American* and walked back to his home.

"Well, I'll be goddammed," Sam Linck said quietly, with real surprise. "I don't know whether to take a good sock out of you or not."

He looked at Marge. It was the same black dress with the scalloped satin collar she had worn when Sam had first met her, but now it was dirty and wrinkled. Linck couldn't remember seeing her wear anything else. Her legs were bare and the hair showed. Her shoes, once of modish lizard skin, had lost all shape. A delicate curlicue of sweated dirt moved down from her eyebrow.

"Look at you," Linck said with disgust. "Just look at you. I got a good mind to take a sock out of you right now and leave you laying in the gutter."

"Don't be like that," she said with a little defiance. "If you want to be like that there's no law that says I got to stay here and take it."

"What's the matter? All your fine friends walked out on you?"

"What friends are you talking about? I got no friends."

"I know," Sam said with anger. "I know all about those friends you ain't got."

"Say, listen, Sam, you got me wrong. I don't know what's on your mind but I got no friends."

"That's hot," Linck said bitterly. "You don't know anything about it. I got a good mind right now."

"Do you think I'd come around here and be tagging you if anything like that happened? Why don't you use your head? Figure it out. You know it don't make sense."

Linck looked at her nastily. She wasn't worth his time. "On

your way, bum," he said curtly, and began walking away. Marge ran after him.

"Sam," she begged, "have a heart. I'm broke. I ain't eaten a thing all day."

"Go on back to your friends. Since when am I your sucker?"

"I got no friends, I told you. I got a job down at that café until you came in that night and made a scene and I got fired. Then I went to live with some girl friends, but they left town. I can't get a job, Sam. I'm broke. Sam, I'll starve."

Linck said nothing but he let Marge walk alongside of him. It was after work, just as on the first time when Marge had picked him up outside the garage. She had been waiting for him to pass by and her dependence upon him, her return, brought Linck the sensation of power and it felt good. At first Linck was angry with her, he had sworn if he ever saw her again to break every bone in her body. She had stood him up, made a sucker out of him, and finally set the men to beating him. He would break every bone in her body. But now his wife was gone for three weeks, he was looking around for company, and Marge appeared conveniently. I'll show you, you tramp, he said to himself, I'll show you. He was planning to work her for a week or two and then dump her out into the street again. He'd have his fun and at the same time he would be getting even with her. I'll show you, he thought, and was pleased.

"Come on," he said at last without looking at her. He was entering a bean wagon. Marge hoisted herself immediately on top of the stool and looked at the menus above the coffee boilers.

"Give me soup and some hamburgers," Marge said. She ate rapidly. In spite of her prettiness there was something about her that reminded Sam of his mother's guinea pigs in the way she held her head close to the plate and the fast movement of her sharp teeth chewing at the food. Linck had an idea and deliberated over it. No one had seen them talk to each other since they came in. He would let Marge finish her pie à la mode and then refuse to pay her check, claiming he didn't know her, that she was just a street bum working a new racket. The piquancy of the situation appealed to him. It would be goddam funny. But in the end Linck had to relinquish the project. That don't give me nookie, he said, but I'll show that slob. He waited for Marge to finish.

"Who's paying for all this?" he asked coolly. "You just told me you were broke."

She looked at him uncomprehendingly. "You said . . ." she faltered. "Didn't you just tell me before to come in?"

"You didn't hear me say nothing about buying you a feed. Did I say anything about all this grub?"

"Have a heart, Sam. For Christ's sakes, don't be a mean bastid."

He liked her, and the smile escaped. Marge felt more sure of herself.

"Give me a smoke," she said. "You and your funny tricks. How about going down to the Island and cooling off?"

On the ride to the beach Sam's pose broke. The smile gave him away. He wanted nookie and he couldn't keep on being stiff and angry at the same time.

"On the level, Marge," he said intimately, "what happened to your pals?"

"Say, you ain't sore no more?"

"No," Sam said. He was philosophical and detached. "That's the way it goes. It's like a game. When you get it, that's fine. And when it's going against you, you can't bellyache. It's the way it goes. I got no hard feelings."

"Hell, Sam. I always liked you. But a girl's got to take care of herself. And Jesus, you certainly got me sore. I certainly was hopping, the way you acted. God Almighty, I didn't lose those black-and-blue spots for a month."

"What happened to your pals, Marge? I know that business about your girl friends was a load of bull."

"Don't remind me," Marge said, speaking with pain. "It was fierce, simply fierce. I always said you sheenies were the worst pikers, but those shanty Irish bastids were the limit. All they wanted was a good time. They never gave me a dollar. They wouldn't even pay my room rent. The landlady walked in on me while I was sleeping yesterday and threw me out."

"Listen, Marge," Linck said, speaking with sincerity, "I said this before and I'm saying it again. You stick around with me and you'll never regret it. You'll have a good time. I'll treat you fine. I'm not one of those wise guys."

"I know, Sam." She was skeptical. "It's all O.K., but how about your wife?"

"You leave her alone and she'll leave you alone. All you have to do is stay out of her way and we'll get along fine."

As they left the subway station the blare of Surf Avenue immediately heightened their senses. Linck wanted a good time. Ever since he had been mauled the second time by the Hooper Street gang on their drunken spree he had been quiet and hanging around the house. He went to work, and in the evenings he stayed home with his wife. He was tired of the dirty flat, of his mother's curses, and his wife's constant nagging and complaints. It was getting so he didn't know what a good time was anymore.

"Come on, kid," he said as they plunged into the crowd. "I'll show you a good time. I guess you need it and it's about time I had a little sport myself."

They went laughing and pushing each other down the street, stopping to take in all the sights with their eyes and pausing for the street performances of the sideshows. The commingled noises of Coney Island, barkers' cries, speeding autos, trolley cars, the rolling fall of the surf, the zooms of the scenic railways, these noises struck their ears like an invitation to gaiety. They knew these sounds and were comfortable among them.

Linck stopped at Nathan's where they had five-cent frankfurters and root beer. Marge plastered on the mustard thickly.

"Here's where I get back on you, you bastid," she laughed.

"No hard feelings, Marge. I was drunk then. You know that."

She shoved the end of the roll into her mouth. "That was fine," she said through the food, laughing as she remembered the scene. "Even though the joke was on me and you were taking a shot at me, it certainly was grand the way you threw that slop. Boy, you should have seen yourself."

"Is that so?" Linck said, pleased. "It's funny, I don't remember it at all. Well, that's over. Let bygones be bygones."

He bought tickets for the Thunderbolt. Marge clutched at his coat as they roared down the chutes. She couldn't talk but gestured with her hands at her stomach and throat to indicate that the frankfurter was on its way. Linck grew worried and calculated the distance remaining. He yelled to her to hold on, it would be over in a minute.

Out on the street again they waited expectantly at the curb. Linck watched Marge's dumb look on her face as she probed within herself.

"Well?" he asked. "How is it?"

"I don't know." Her face was blank as she pondered.

"Oh," Linck said, and shook his head.

"Don't look so disappointed," she said angrily. "Somebody would think you're sorry."

Linck grabbed her arm and walked again, part of the thronging crowds that pushed up and down the streets in a constant procession. They came to the Tunnel of Love. Here, over soft water, wide boats were gently propelled through the caverns that were dark and suggestive. "This ought to cool you off," he said. He went up to the ticket booth. It cost thirty-five cents a head. Linck wanted to renege, but, hell, he'd show her he was no piker. They took their seats and waited for the boat to fill up. As they started off, the couples rearranged themselves for the trip, and a great silence overtook them.

As for the ride itself, it was too short. You barely got started. "For seventy cents," Linck said, feeling cheated, "you'd expect them to give you something for your money. They're just a bunch of highway robbers."

"What do you expect?" said Marge, belligerent because he had been too rough and she was still protesting. "A bed with a woman in it?"

Who the hell did she think she was anyway? Linck was disgruntled and angry with her. He counted up the money he had already spent. Twenty cents for the dogs and drinks, fifty cents for the Thunderbolt, and seventy cents now. Also, twenty cents carfare, counting the trip back. By God, who did she think she was anyhow? Greta Garbo?

"Come on," he said, and went directly for the boardwalk. Linck took her below, and they walked past the cement pillars on the beach sand while he sought out a spot that was quiet, removed, and away from any light.

"Here on the wet sand?" Marge said. "Who do you think I am anyway?"

"It's not wet. Only a little damp. You'll get used to it. Hell, you've been in worse places." He was still angry over the seventy-cent boat fare. They embraced rapidly on the sand. It was cozy there, their bodies' warmth transmitting a pleasant sensation as though they were lying in a hot bath together. Overhead they could hear the steady tramp of heels on the boards, all those people were walking over them, and at the side they could see the dark outlines of the waves and the glitter of the lights on the water from the concessions. Linck felt all the more hidden and secluded. He liked it. She had a nerve, complaining. Hell, the first time with her it had been in a store doorway. Linck reached over and kissed her violently, and then they began to wrestle.

Linck lay on his back in the darkness. He would have his fun with her, treat her rough, and then when he got finished he'd dump her out into the gutter. He'd show that slob she couldn't put anything over him, he thought, but he was wondering. He glanced at her. Marge was half-sleeping, her mouth opened a little. She was a neat piece. He'd buy her some clothes, get her a room, and fix her up. Excepting for the pug nose she certainly was a pretty baby.

"Marge," he said softly, nudging her, "Marge, say son of a bitch."

THIRTEEN

AT HAVERS FALLS a terrible calamity had happened. Two Italians, one Negro, three Jews. Gilhooley sat in the center of the room wearing off a drunk, rebellious and stubborn.

Harry Hayman glared above him. "You goddam ox," he said bitterly.

"I never liked that cop. He stuck his nose in my way that time and he tried it again today."

"You goddam kiyoodle!"

"Say, listen here, Hayman, you can't talk to me that way. I don't care who you are, you can't get away with it."

"Shut up!" Hayman said. "You goddam crazy shanty-Irish lummox, now you've gone and smacked up the whole works for us. As for yourself, I promise you, for this you'll surely burn. When Papravel gave you a gun he meant you should use it only to scare. But if you had to kill someone, why, you filthy blockhead, tell me why you had to pick out a state trooper? They'll get you for this as sure as you're born."

Gilhooley, still heavy with drunkenness, was beginning to understand the seriousness of the situation. The blustering expression on his face was cracking and revealing his fear. He had shot the state trooper in a rush of violence it had been impossible for him to suppress. The trooper, meeting him on the road, had begun to bawl him out for no good reason. He wanted to show the

Irishman that he still wasn't afraid of him in spite of the ease with which he had gotten out of the courtroom. Gilhooley had gone back at him like a kid. He wasn't afraid of a uniform and he wasn't yellow.

"I never liked that guy's face anyhow," he said.

Hayman considered, and he considered hard. Until this moment he had always regarded himself as a legitimate businessman. He was working for a living, others did the same kind of work he did, he was not concerned over his job. Gilhooley's murder made his position different. There was danger, this was definitely breaking the law. Hayman wondered whether the proper move for him was to get out of sight before he was mixed into the mess. But Papravel, Papravel . . . through the darkness came the gleam of Papravel for a consolation. "Come on," he said to the boys, "we've got a lot to do."

Gilhooley looked at the men leaving the room. "Wait a minute," he said. "You fellows ain't going to leave me in a hole?"

They all stopped and stared stonily at him.

"Listen," Gilhooley said, his arrogance vanished, "you can't leave me in a fix like this. I wouldn't walk out on you."

No one said anything. Hayman said, "Let's go," and they continued out of the room.

"All right," Gilhooley ranted. "Go ahead, you dirty rats. Go ahead and walk out on me, you cheap yellow-bellies!"

It was in this crisis that the true quality of Papravel was revealed. A lesser man might have been inclined, like Harry Hayman, to clear out, but to Papravel the emergency presented a challenge to his energy and resourcefulness. And if Papravel had anything, it was a vast confidence in himself. Besides, it was alien to his nature to leave Gilhooley stuck, for essentially Papravel was a simple man.

Nevertheless, he roundly bawled out the Irishman for his want of business sense. Gilhooley, who resembled in the excitement a man with a heavy nose cold, stared dumbly, accepting abuse and asking monotonously, "What'll I do? What'll I do?" Papravel was disgusted with him.

He went directly to Rubin. "Remember, Rubin," he said carefully, "remember long ago I told you sometimes mistakes happen? Well, a terrible mistake happened and now we've got to help."

"What happened?"

When he heard the word "murder," Rubin shivered.

"No!" he almost screamed. He was blown up with resentment. "No! Once for all I made my mind up. No! For a month already you've bled me until I'm sucked dry. Let Morantz have his bus station in Williamsburg. It's cheaper."

"This has nothing to do with Morantz, Rubin," Papravel said patiently. "The bus station is all finished. The Silver Eagle will be getting out in no time now. About this, I'm telling you, I'm positive. But this has nothing to do with Morantz. Don't be stubborn now, Rubin, because, if you wanted to be stubborn, this is the worst time you could pick."

"No!" Rubin's voice rose to a wail from persecution. "Every night I ask myself, why did I ever get mixed up with you, Papravel? You've never done me any good. You've been like a leech on my flesh, sucking blood, sucking blood until I'm sucked dry. Not another cent will I give, Papravel, and you can know it right now. These things can't go on forever and let there be an end to it right now!"

In the face of this unexpected resistance Papravel sharply changed his tactics. He had expected trouble from him because the cost of the defense would be huge, but he thought he would be able to convince Rubin that the profits would make up for it soon. He was disgusted with Rubin's cowardice. He expected everything for nothing. The only way to make money was to work hard, plan, and see the plan through. Papravel never lost courage midway. He was especially angry with Rubin. The man acted as though Papravel had intended to swindle him, to take money under false pretenses and not in return for his services.

"An end?" Papravel repeated with terrible calm.

"Cutthroat!" screamed Rubin. He was enormously afraid of Papravel's tone. "Get out, you robber! I'm an honest businessman and won't have dealings with gangsters like you!"

"Don't call names," said Papravel imperturbably. "It won't do any good. Besides, have you forgotten already the business you ran twenty years ago when you told the poor yiddles in the old country what a wonderful place America was? And then when they came over you put them to work in sweatshops at four dollars a week and collected a weekly commission on their wages. You even took the dumbbells to board in a railroad flat with no windows and the toilet in the backyard so you could make more money on them. You're no rabbi yourself, Rubin, and from candy jobbing alone a man does not make a fortune. But what will be, will be. Only listen, Rubin, there is no end yet, because I'm coming back."

"Get out, bloodsucker!" Rubin shrieked. But already his whole body was wet with the sweat of fear.

From Williamsburg appeared one Anschele B. Nussbaum, and concerning him as a lawyer the legend was great. He was a stoutish man whose shirttails were always coming out in folds through his vest, and in some neighborhoods this is held to be a mark of importance. From the way in which he shoved the cloth back into place within his trousers one could perceive Nussbaum's satisfaction with himself, his confidence in his ability, and his pleasure with his growing fame and fortune. He was an energetic man. Papravel could have chosen none better.

Papravel faced three problems: Morand and the Silver Eagle, Gilhooley, and Rubin's stubbornness. However, in this time of stress, his first concern was with the Irishman. There were many reasons for this, but chiefly, Gilhooley's case couldn't wait. It was murder. In spite of everything Papravel did as a matter of practice in his business, murder was still murder. He was no ordinary, run-of-the-gutter cutthroat. From the first moment of any deal to the last he always impressed customers with his fundamental solidity. Papravel was a businessman. He performed certain services and expected to be paid strictly for them, in his way he was honest and had his ethics. Often he had been impelled to print stationery with a trademark and a slogan: In Business Since —— Without a Single Dissatisfied Customer. This was America where customs were different but people still had to make their livings. And now he would regard his organization tarnished, its reputation damaged in the community, if it was to be associated with the signs of common thuggery and gangsterism.

Besides, Papravel had always reminded his boys that he stood firmly behind them. Gilhooley was no example, but Papravel had always tried to attract within his group men of responsibility, not hoodlums. They were settled men, with few exceptions, and he had to tell them there was no danger, in any emergency he and all his resources would take care of them. Papravel knew at once that every man on his payroll was watching him now. If he did not suspect the uneasiness in Harry Hayman's mind, he felt sure that there were others who might be considering a bolt. Papravel knew that if Gilhooley was convicted, or if he deserted the Irishman now, his organization would melt like butter in a hot sun, and that he with his rapid rise and work of years would find himself in the gutter in no time.

Papravel was a busy man. Anschele B. Nussbaum held him in conference together with Harry Hayman for over an hour. Thoroughly, detail after detail, they went through the case. Gilhooley had met the trooper on the road, the likelihood was that no one had seen them, and if some chance witness claimed that he had sped past them in his car it would not take long to discredit his testimony. Of course, there was strong circumstantial evidence, and a possibility of some chance destructive factor always existed. Nussbaum pulled up his pants and said, "All right, all right." He reasoned with skill and from experience.

"Who might have seen your Irishman afterward?" he asked Hayman.

"Outside of our boys, Mrs. Van Curen is the only one I can think of. But wait a minute. Gilhooley was drunk when I saw him. There's no telling what he might have been doing afterward."

"Call him in," Papravel said. "Let's not waste time."

Gilhooley swore violently that right after the crime he had been careful to keep himself out of sight. He had gone straight back to the house. "Jesus," he said, offended, "give me credit for a little brains."

"How about Mrs. Van Curen?" Hayman asked.

"I don't know. I guess the old lady did see me maybe. What difference does it make?"

"Never mind," Nussbaum said, speaking to Papravel. "Never mind about the old lady." Mentally he reviewed the case, asking Gilhooley and Hayman questions from time to time. "All right," he said with importance finally, "all right."

Nussbaum instructed Gilhooley to go to Rochester as quickly and quietly as possible. There were three men already prepared to assert with the protesting conviction of solid truth behind them that they had seen the Irishman in town for more than a week. "Get around," the lawyer said. "Let people see you. Let them think you've been there all the time with those three boys. Keep your mouth shut, take it easy, and whatever you hear from us, you do."

"What's it all about?" Gilhooley asked. "I don't see the idea. Let me in on it. They've got nothing on me, nobody saw me."

"We keep quiet here," Nussbaum said. "We don't know anything about it. When the cops get after us we fight the case all the way, claiming it's circumstantial evidence, he's innocent, and we stall for time. Then after six months or so, when the trial is almost over, we jump in the witnesses from Rochester, and if Gilhooley watches himself there it ought to be easy to make out a good alibi for him. Of course, everything depends on God knows what, but that's the best we can do and maybe it will be enough."

Papravel told the Irishman to get going.

"Watch it," Hayman said. "We'll take care of the money you'll need. Take the Nash and get out of here. Don't stop to talk to cops."

Papravel felt relieved. This was going to cost heavy money, Nussbaum's expenses, funds to Rochester, the witnesses, and the trial. He would have to dig into his own pockets, dig down, but on the whole he relished the incident and the way it was turning out. Particularly was he glad Rubin had failed to kick in.

"What do you think, Anschele?" he asked the lawyer. "What do you really think?"

Nussbaum lit his cigar carefully and shrugged his shoulders. "What are you worrying about? We'll see. This isn't the first time I am doing work like this. Let's go down to the old Gentile."

In the dining room Mrs. Van Curen was helping the girl with the plates and silver. "What happened to Gilhooley?" Nussbaum said loudly. "I don't seem to see that Irish fellow you used to have around."

"Oh, he left," Harry Hayman said. "We sent him to Rochester some time ago. When was it Mr. Gilhooley left, Mrs. Van Curen? Do you happen to remember?"

"Mr. Gilhooley?" the old lady said. "Is he gone?"

"Oh, yes. Don't you remember? He must have left about a week ago."

"Well, that's strange. I could have sworn I've been seeing him around the place. There's so much coming and going here all the time," she explained apologetically, "I can never keep track of all the boys."

Papravel stepped vigorously into the room.

"How are you, Mrs. Van Curen?" he asked kindly. "Tell me, do the boys make you much trouble?"

Harry Hayman went faithfully through his part of the act, but ever since he had received the news about the state trooper his position with Papravel had begun to trouble him. He had become too lax in his mind, he had accepted conditions too readily, without thinking, without scruple. For the first time, perhaps, he saw his work clearly and without self-deception. He had vaguely supposed that business went this way, that it was all right to be dishonest. The question, what would any other man do in his place? always had been easy solace and balm for him when he had doubted himself. But now he felt that something was wrong. Was he really meaning to be a crook, a racketeer, a gangster? Harry Hayman, feeling foolish, at the same time thought of his father.

That evening he had no desire to go out with the girls at the hotel resorts. Instead he went up to his room and wrote a letter home to Philip.

⁓⁓⁓

On Sunday morning Philip Hayman's father rose perhaps as much as half an hour later than usual. There was no necessity for the early hour, but this, as was almost everything else with him, was habit, and he obeyed it. While Philip and his mother were still asleep he went out to the stores to buy breakfast, and later, as the two waited to begin, the food came in spasmodic deliveries. Bundle after bundle piled up, Mrs. Hayman greeting each arrival with exclamations at the waste, but the old man failed to appear until the very last. Then he came, pink with the air, and smiling hesitantly to ward off Mrs. Hayman's protests, which he knew were forthcoming. "Next Sunday," she always said, "next Sunday I'll do the buying. You throw away money like water."

"Pish, pish," he burlesqued at the excitement. He took off his coat and passed the Sunday newspaper to Philip.

Mrs. Hayman unpacked the bags with a show of anger for the old man made a point of buying unfamiliar delicacies, which she considered ridiculous. He came home one Sunday with a strange fruit, another time with some unusual pastry. They seldom ate these exotic articles, and it angered Philip's mother that money was thrown out week after week on stuff that went directly into the garbage can. The Sunday-morning breakfast at its normal was a hodgepodge affair consisting mainly of preserved fish: carp, sturgeon, butterfish, and whitefish. Then there were olives, the black and the fresh; pickles, figs, dates, black radishes. The cheeses were many, but each week one in particular among the assortment Mr. Hayman favored and urged upon Philip. "Eat it," he would say earnestly. "It's really good. Just take a taste and see." "Yes, and what did you pay for it?" Mrs. Hayman would ask belligerently. "This? Let me see . . . I don't know." His eyes were helpless. "How should I know?" Like the cheeses, the breads were varied, chosen for the odd shapes or curious arrangements of seeds, and Mr. Hayman would chuckle with delight at his success if Philip noticed some special distinction in a roll.

While Philip ate and talked and read, while his mother served him, simultaneously prolonging the stream of abuse at his father, the old man paid no attention to her but busied himself making a salad in a huge bowl. This brought him near to silent rapture; he peeled, cut, and sliced with great concentration, mixing radishes, cucumbers, and tomatoes. When he finished, he recommended the concoction to Philip ardently, and beamed as his son ate. Looking at Philip at the table, he smoothed his mustache with his fingers or held his hands in a pausing clasp, satisfied with the scene, with the success of his morning industry, and content. After Philip and his mother finished, he himself had a glass of milk, a nibble or two at the carp, and some cheesecake.

In the afternoon Mr. Hayman leans back in the big chair in the living room, pushes his spectacles up on his forehead, sighs, and looks out the window. There is nothing to do. He turns to Philip. At various times his son has displeased him, for Philip, twenty years old, active with sports, girls, and other occupations, he is America. Philip's father does not understand America. Although he has been in this country almost fifty years he disapproves of it, often with strong feeling, with heartfelt indignation. So many times Philip has heard him say "Humbug!" or, noting some unpleasant condition, protest "Miserable! It shouldn't be!" He says that there is no friendship, no brotherhood, no genuine feeling, pity, or charity. The New York subway, for instance, depresses him because he does not like the savagery with which people push, shove, and fight. One winter night he came home, eyes wide, with a great story. Could Philip imagine it? he asked. He had entered a lavatory at a subway entrance and seen a tramp sleeping there, for the warmth, on the shelf on top of the urinal slabs.

"People here," he says, "remind me of the green, deformed,

uneatable apples you find in a neglected orchard. No taste. No character."

Philip's father tells him stories of weddings in the old country where people were simple and honest and it was like a religious law to be merry and glad. He talks fondly of his grandmother who was such a wonderful cook and such a fine soul. He says there was more leisure there, no hurry as here. "The way people live in New York it is shiny and speedy, but you miss a great deal. It takes you a long time to grow and live. You don't grow very much. Everybody here makes a living, and there is no rest or quiet."

Philip's father sits in the big chair, sighs, and turns to his son. There is nothing to do. "Here's a story for you," he says, his eyes lighting up at the recollection. Philip knows the story but he listens to it again. "This is something I did see with my own eyes. I heard it myself. You can believe it. Long ago, oh, it was very long ago, in the time of Nicholas, they picked up a boy in the streets for military service and sent him away for twenty or thirty years, according to the practice in those days. He was a Jewish boy, but naturally he was taken away so early that when he came back he had forgotten most of his boyhood and his Jewishness. When I was a boy in the old country he was back already, a man, a Christian, but still he worried over his lost Jewishness because one after the other his children fell ill with mysterious sicknesses. And he thought it was God punishing him for letting himself be baptized. So every once in a while he would go to the town synagogue, not in the small schul downstairs but in the big schul we used only for important holidays. All alone in the empty room he would open wide the doors of the Holy Altar and cry to God. 'God!' he screamed at the top of his lungs to make sure God heard him. 'God! It wasn't my fault! How could I help it? It wasn't my fault!'"

Mr. Hayman laughs warmly at the story. "I did see it with my own eyes. Many times I heard him. Often, you know, a stranger would come to the town and see what was going on and we had to explain it to him. Everybody in our town knew about him. 'God!' he would yell so loud. 'It wasn't my fault, God!'"

Philip's mother comes running into the living room. "What are you shrieking about?" she cries at him. "You're topsy-turvy in your old age. Somebody would think God knows what's happening to you."

"Sh!" Mr. Hayman mutters, waving his hand behind him to silence her. A little disconcerted, he picks up his paper, climbs the steps, and makes ready for his Sunday-afternoon nap. All Philip's life, on Sundays his father has taken a nap in the afternoon. If there were an earthquake or a war, Mrs. Hayman says, and it happened on Sunday, it would make no difference, he would be going to sleep. Mr. Hayman arranges himself in the bed, reads for a minute, and then opens the newspaper, spreading it over his face to keep out the sunlight. He sleeps. Two or three times he dreams of something he doesn't like for Philip hears him spit in his sleep to break the evil charm.

Now the peculiar thing about his father's story of the man who cried to God was that for some reason it reminded Philip of him. Every time Philip heard it, he promptly thought of his father and vaguely felt that it applied to him. Like the boy in the story, his father had been snatched from the old country, and while he could not be considered to have lost faith, there was here too a resemblance, for the change was detrimental. Perhaps it was not, as he affirmed, the change in countries that was at fault, but rather the clean demarcation between his inexperienced youth, which he could be said to have left in Russia, and the harsh responsibilities of manhood. At any rate, whether it was America or increasing perception, his ideals were questioned and shaken; perhaps, although Philip could not remember ever witnessing an instance of it, he had even been obliged for one urgent reason or another to debase himself before his ideals, to commit some petty act of dishonesty or meanness or selfishness. And when he was perpetually crying for kindness and goodness in people Philip felt that it was like the man crying to God for forgiveness.

Philip supposed the old man felt that he was failing himself, but to Philip, thinking of Papravel and his brother, Harry, the way of living his father embodied seemed, compared with the reality he knew, beautiful and heroic. Philip remembered the countless examples of his goodness, his unvarying gentleness and conscientiousness. Especially what impressed him was his age, that he had lived so long without material reward and that he had kept steadfast to his maxims. Philip had often been told the story of his father's earlier days in America, the miserable voyage in steerage, his struggles in a new world as he sought to find a way of providing for himself. Mr. Hayman used to talk to him about his trips to the Middle West, telling him casual reminiscences of his adventures, but Philip could sense in his recital the confused, worried time he must have had to place himself.

When he married Philip's mother he had had a grocery store, but as his first children came the income here proved insufficient and he was compelled to return to his old trade, fur. Apparently he had a kind of love for this business, for later, in examining Mrs. Hayman's coat or the coats of friends who visited the home, he would speak with quiet pride and smooth the fur fondly. He had left this trade in the beginning because the skins and dust in these shops affected his lungs. Now he had gone back to it, but after a few years he had become very sick. His mother told Philip (it was before he was born) that in those days it looked very black. There were little children then, no savings, and it appeared that his father would never be strong enough to work again. Those must have been hard, gloomy weeks, and yet Philip had never heard his father complain of them, or, indeed, mention them at all.

One of the first skyscrapers was then being completed in the downtown section of Manhattan, and here his father stood selling newspapers to the construction engineers and officials of the building. Through their help, probably, he managed to obtain a concession in the building when it was opened, and ever since he had been there. He had spent a lifetime there, retracing his dull footsteps for years.

To Philip this waste of life seemed appalling. He felt then that if he had to face a similar prospect he would do everything imaginable to get free. This was another reason why Philip loved and respected so deeply this man who, with no bitterness of spirit but rather with still faithful obedience to his principles, accepted his fortune and minded not that it was bad. On coldest days, no matter how sick or indisposed he might feel, he always rose before six to open his shop. Philip remembered what a shock he had received on one occasion when, entering a friend's home one school day, he saw the boy's father there. It had always seemed so completely impossible for his own father to be away from work that it startled him to see his friend's parent idle. Even when there had been a death in the family, at the time of his brother George's accident, although he left the shop in the daytime during that week of mourning he nevertheless opened and closed the shop himself.

With him this was not, of course, a matter of money involved, but principle and conscience. From the same sense of obligation he was a particularly soft victim for those who wanted money whether they deserved his help or not. If the man told a straightforward story and Philip's father felt he was sincere the money was given. His charity did much genuine good, but often he was imposed upon. In one instance—concerning a man named Ginsberg who made a regular practice of borrowing without returning the loans—Mrs. Hayman was finally obliged to move out of the neighborhood. Principle meant everything to him. Philip remembered one time he had seen him given a husky boor a lecture on politeness, not at all intimidated by the man's bulk. For another example, during the war in Europe their name impressed many as being German and so caused Mr. Hayman some inconvenience. But he never defended himself by saying he was Russian. He felt there was as much to be said for Germany as for any other nation, and argued on those points, disdaining the easy self-defense, which he considered a cheap escape. Philip could think of many stories and examples, but possibly the greatest tribute to the intensity of his father's spirit lay in the painful efforts he made in concern for his sons' upbringing. They had lived most of their lives in slums and semi-slums, the East Side, New Lots, and Williamsburg. Life for children here might be treacherous, but in those days as well as now Philip's father refused to accept the conditions as they were and dumbly submit. Many foreign parents in these localities, feeling perhaps that this was America, overlooked their children's defections, helplessly allowing them to coarsen. But Philip's father was everlasting in his lectures on character and proper behavior, and by his home life, by his own example, he tried to help his sons retain a sense of integrity. That was why he had always regarded his wife's brother, Papravel, with such unfriendliness and distaste. When his son Harry had gone over to Papravel the old man had been bitter and would not permit himself to lose his hard feeling. It was more important to be good, to be honest, to have pity and benevolence, and it had pained him deeply that Papravel and his easy money had won, at least in Harry's eyes.

So Philip sat, that Sunday afternoon in his mother's living room, hearing his father's heavy breathing from his bedroom and thinking of his life. He was a man, it was important to be a man, but Philip could not blame his brother Harry or Papravel. What was the use of denying it? Old Miller was right, money was important too. Was it not possible to think of his father as a schlemiel, a dreamer, a fool who had no common sense?

Philip's mind reverted to Ruth Kelman, and once again he recognized the difficulty that lack of money caused. Just as Philip realized that sooner or later he and his friend Charlie Nagleman would separate, finding the difference in matters of money insurmountable, so it would be difficult for him to continue for any great length of time his relationship with Ruth. Already he had noticed a feeling of restraint and coolness whenever he met her mother or father, and he feared that if anything would turn her away from him it would be the poverty of his background and the thousand subtle effects this had had upon him. She would notice it in some mannerism, some casual gesture or statement, and it would make him different, it would set him apart and away from her.

"Philip," his father was calling him from the bedroom, "Philip, a little seltzer, please."

That was his job. Every Sunday he had to wait until his father awoke and called for the seltzer. Philip supposed the old man would not have been able to leave his bed unless he brought the glass and carried it up to him.

When Papravel left Havers Falls he was satisfied that the situation with Gilhooley was on its way to solution. Anschele B. Nussbaum was one to be trusted. Just as Papravel was eager to maintain his reputation of solidity and reliability in the community as well as with his hired men, so Nussbaum was solicitously building up a name for himself as a lawyer who could handle ticklish cases and win them. Nevertheless, Papravel did not fool himself, and he worked carefully. He was excited by the developments of the past week and a little apprehensive of the future. But his apprehension was strongly mixed with confidence so that actually he relished his position. This was a fight, he was moving, progressing, and alive. He smoked cigars now habitually. The plan in his head was an ambitious one, but to him it was a test. Through it he meant definitely to clinch his destiny as a big man, a made man, and not a petty racketeer. Papravel was moving to the top.

Strictly speaking, he was no longer on the payroll of the Empire Lines and Rubin, but it was necessary for him to go on with the work. He outlined for himself a program. First, he must settle Gilhooley in order to establish himself once and for all with his organization. That was on its way. Before Nussbaum left the Van Curen house all the men were brought together in the living room for a conference. Papravel explained exactly and in detail what was being done for the Irishman. He cautioned them against extravagant behavior, asserting that Gilhooley had automatically deprived himself of any support from him because of his rashness. Notwithstanding, however, he took this opportunity to indicate the strength of the backing he would give them if they fulfilled their legitimate duties, by spending money generously and hiring the best legal brains available for Gilhooley. Nussbaum himself got up, pushed the folds of his shirt into his pants, and made a short speech of general advice to the boys. But he took particular pains to refer, as if incidentally, to the yearly arrangement for service that Papravel had with him. "Watch your step," he wound up, "but always remember, when the time comes we'll take care of you." The cigars were passed out and everyone said, one thing about Papravel, he was like a father, he always came through for you in a pinch, he was a great little guy.

Papravel felt solid with his men. The second point on his program concerned Morand and the Silver Eagle. Morand would have to be completely defeated before he could go ahead. Unless he won here, his importance as a strong man, as an aid to be considered in competitive business, would be lost. Rubin would have no respect for him, and this would be just, Papravel was the first to admit, because that was his stock in trade. If he could not perform his services satisfactorily he had no justification.

However, Papravel had no fears. His pickets, the organization of the United Bus Drivers Association, were proving the final straw on Morand's back. Simultaneously with the synthetic bus strike the Empire Lines went down to still lower fares. Rubin had concurred in this step before the break and he had too little courage to make any move now. He knew Papravel was still working on the Silver Eagle, felt confused at the nature of his own action, and hoped weakly that in the end a painless reconciliation would be effected.

In the beginning a round trip to Havers Falls was six dollars. It had been reduced in gradual stages to four-fifty, but now Rubin and Papravel went down to three dollars flat for the ride. People left the hot city and went up to the mountains as though it were an excursion. The townsfolk at Havers Falls, taking advantage of the rate war, started for the city in the morning, took in a moving picture, and came back for supper at home. When Morand failed to meet the new fare Papravel knew it for a sign that he was reaching the end of his resources and was near the finish.

As for Williamsburg, the people there had strong feeling for the cause of labor. When they saw the picket signs they would not enter Morand's place from principle. Indeed, one misguided liberal, a stout, aggressive man, made it a practice to assist the pickets voluntarily from a feeling of social duty. He harangued the passing crowd, made Morand's employees uncomfortable, and proved a disagreeable nuisance. If a chance customer tried to enter the station the liberal pounced upon him and lectured him severely.

The device was simple, entirely legal, and inexpensive. Papravel admired his own wisdom and wished he had thought of it sooner. There was no risk, no bloodshed, no interference from the police. Morand stuck up posters in the windows angrily repudiating the United Bus Drivers Association, but the people of Williamsburg, familiar with capitalistic tactics, sneered at the signs.

Besides, there was always the possibility of an accident. Strikers, on the point of starvation, with helpless wives and children to support, were not to be expected to control themselves with scabs. And finally, the Empire Lines ran a lower fare.

Morand grew bitter and desperate, Papravel beamed, and Rubin observed his line's growing prosperity with misgivings. He felt that Papravel's success with the Silver Eagle would make him relentless. He worried terribly and his night's rest was broken. In his bones he was dreading with an awful, gasping fear the visitation of Papravel.

These were the first and second problems. The third was Rubin himself. Papravel felt warm within himself at the prospect. He would wait until the time was ripe, until he was ready, wait without calling to Rubin in the meantime or getting in touch with him in any way. Suddenly, he would descend. Papravel rolled the cigar between his teeth and dreamed with the pleasures of sure anticipation.

His satisfaction was broken momentarily by the appearance of Harry Hayman in Williamsburg.

"What are you doing here, Harry? What's the matter?"

"Everything's all right, Uncle," Harry said. "I just came down to talk to you. There's something I want to say." He was serious and spoke as though he did not like the task facing him.

"It's like this, Uncle. Don't get me wrong, I don't like to do this but I have to. I'll have to quit."

Papravel was surprised. "Harry," he said, "I like you. You know that. Tell me what's the matter and I'll take care of it."

"There's nothing wrong. Only I can't stay in business with you. It's time I got out."

"Listen, Harry, if you're worried about Gilhooley or Rubin going yellow on me, don't be silly. Everything right now is fine. I never felt so optimistic. You heard what Anschele Nussbaum will do about Gilhooley, you know Morantz is finished, and as for Rubin, only God will be able to take care of him when I get through with him. There's going to be good times now. Why do you want to get out just when we're getting everything we want?"

"It's not that. I know how things are going, Uncle. I would have dropped out sooner but I didn't want you to think I was quitting on you. I know everything's fine, and you don't need me. That's why I'm leaving now. Louis the Italian can do my work. He's a good man. You can trust him."

"I'm not thinking about that, Harry. It's not that. I like you like a son. With my plans, I had a big place for you. You were going to be my general manager. Big salary, bonuses, and maybe even a share in the business later on. I like you, Harry. I want to see you fixed and well off. What's got into you?"

"It's not that. It's hard to tell you because it sounds so foolish. Any man's a fool who turns down a good job with big money. That's why it's hard to explain. It's not that I'm like Pop or Philip, Uncle, but there's something to what they say. A man should be honest. It's like a sin to make a living by forcing other people against the wall. Take Morand. I don't have to fool myself about him. I know exactly what we're doing to him. We're ruining that man just because we got to make money. I don't like to think about Morand. A man got killed because of us. That's what started me off in the first place, I suppose. It seemed terrible to me that just because we want money a man has to be killed and Morand ruined. I want to get out, Uncle."

Papravel dropped the cigar to the floor and stepped on it although it was barely begun. Harry could tell that his uncle did not like the news. He appreciated the affection, he liked the man, but Harry knew he had to get out.

"All right," his uncle said, his feeling of buoyancy gone for the day, "if you want to get out I won't say no. It's not nice to hear what you said about the cop and about Morand, but that doesn't worry me. I don't think about those things. That's why I can work in this business and keep at it. Harry, you went to school, I don't know anything about fancy things, what I know only is, a man's got to make money. Everybody who makes money hurts people. Sometimes you can't see the people you are hurting, but you can be sure all the time there is always somebody who gets squeezed if he is not ruined. That's the kind of a world it is, and who am I to change it? Only, in my business you can see the people you hurt and that's what makes you hate it. I don't blame you, you're not like me maybe. But remember this, Harry, no matter where you go, no matter what business you'll be in, remember there will always be people who will live in rotten houses, who will have no money for a good time, and who will die ten years earlier on account of you."

Harry Hayman listened unhappily to the homily. He couldn't think of anything to say. His uncle, too, sat for a minute without looking at him, staring out of the window. It was a long speech, and he was resting. Finally Papravel shrugged his shoulders and rose from the chair. He took out a fresh cigar and pared it carefully with a penknife.

"Have you seen Momma yet?" he asked in a casual tone.

Children have a crazy way of making clumsy round lines with yellow or pink or green chalk on tenement stoops. This delights them, but sometimes when you see it it is a melancholy thing. Harry Hayman felt wretched when he met his father standing at the stoop. The old man was smoking a cigarette, watching a group of children playing potsy on the sidewalk. Harry had not expected to meet his father this way. It was harder. He had hoped to run into Philip first, perhaps, or at any rate to have his mother in the room. She would have made his homecoming smooth; before her warm fuss over him his father's presence would not have been so oppressive. The cold disapproval implied in his father's silence rendered Harry empty-mouthed and awkward. He was a grown man, but there was something about the old man that always reduced him to childhood again. Perhaps it was because his father had kept himself distant, self-contained, and had withdrawn from any form of intimacy with his children. Harry, coming up to his father at the tenement stoop, felt wretched and worried about the trouble he had given him by his disobedience and the irregular type of business in which he had been engaged.

"Hello, Pa," he said, trying to smile. He searched for something to say. "I'm back now . . ." He had to finish in an unintelligible mumble.

"You're back? It's about time," Mr. Hayman said dryly. "But what do you mean you're back? How soon will you leave again?"

"I mean for good. I'm not working for Papravel anymore. I quit."

The old man considered as he looked at his son. "I don't understand," he mused. "I don't see how a man changes his mind like this."

The meeting was raw, cruelly raw. Father and son, they had never been an affectionate pair. In other homes Harry had seen families embrace and kiss after long absences as a matter of habit. It would have made things easier now. They never had in his house and his relations with his father were further strained.

"Where's Momma?" Harry asked.

"She went to the movies. Come on upstairs. You must be hungry."

In the kitchen the old man went about the closets looking for something to give him while Harry protested that he wasn't hungry, he wasn't to bother. Mr. Hayman found some cheese, bread, a box of dried prunes, and a can of salmon. Harry sat down at the table. The bread was hard, dry pumpernickel, but he opened the can of salmon in order to avoid displeasing his father. Sitting at the window, the old man was self-absorbed and silent as ever, his son's homecoming made no difference to him.

Harry found it hard to make conversation. He wished his mother or Philip would come. Now he took up the box of prunes and he read the labels carefully. He read every line of printed matter on the box. Tree-ripened California Prunes, medium-sized, net contents 2 pounds. Do not soak in water or wash these tender clean prunes and do not overcook. Simply cover with warm water (allowing for evaporation during cooking), simmer for *one half hour*, stirring occasionally. Then bring to a boil— Harry broke off, irritated with himself. What am I reading that damn thing for? he said, half aloud.

"What?" his father asked.

"Nothing. I didn't say anything." Harry looked out of the window. Directly in his view, hanging on a clothesline from the floor above, were a dress, two brassieres, and some panties.

Harry turned his eyes away. There was nothing to say. He was dismayed with the hopelessness that he saw in his father's droop. As he sat by the window in the dimness he seemed older and drier and thinner. It seemed as though he wasn't made of flesh but was an illusion, hollow, formed in some mysterious accident by air and dust. All at once a rush of sorrow swept Harry, then sorrow and pain. He seemed to understand his father and his meaning with sudden clarity and sharpness. In a wave of tenderness he wanted to put his arms around his father, tell him he was right, hug him, and shout out cheerful sounds. At the moment he loved his father more than he had ever loved anything in his life. Harry, disliking outbursts of emotion, was afraid to talk lest he cry. Perhaps he would not have been dominated so completely by his mood if the man in the yard had stopped singing "Yearning Just for You."

When his mother came she fussed over him and scolded because he had not prepared her for his homecoming. She took the news of his separation from Papravel with silent relief, but it was tinctured a bit with regret, for after all Papravel was her brother and she took him for a good man in spite of everything that could be said against him. However, Mrs. Hayman did not think of her brother at this time. Harry was home for good and she was happy.

"Then I'll have you both home, you and Philip?" she said as though it were unbelievable.

"I suppose so, Mom. Anyhow for a while. I can't stay here all the time. I've got to get a job."

He had been wishing for his mother to come home, and now she was here but it made no difference. His father still had possession of his mind. That night Harry Hayman wept in his bed for his father. Unable to sleep, he abruptly discovered that he was crying, and it seemed so strange, he had cried last so long ago, Harry was startled by himself. But he felt himself being gradually relieved as the hot, strange drops came. Instead of brushing them off he let them roll over his face. It had an extremely soothing effect.

Outside, the streets had grown quiet. There were still some boys and girls sitting on a grocer's bread bin, and from time to time their laughter came to him. Occasionally a horn sounded. The street trembled a little whenever a speeding auto fled past. A man's voice across the yard grew audible. He kept talking in a deep, sleepy tone, seldom pausing or making any inflection. A passer-by hurried on his way home, his heels producing sharp clicks on the sidewalk. The laughter of the youths in the street ceased. It was getting late. Harry turned on the other side and tried to force himself to sleep. It was more tempting to think and dream than to keep his mind blank for sleep.

What had they wanted from him? The picture came to him of his father asserting with quiet force, after his manner, that a man must be honest, must do no harm to anyone, but work at his trade justly and honorably. A man must be upright, the old man said repeatedly. Let those who had no character turn to speedy, unscrupulous ways of making money, but as for his sons, he wanted them always to follow a straight path or they might just as well never have been born. "There's too much meanness in the world already. People no longer have good hearts. It is not like the old days when friendship and brotherhood meant everything. These times people care only about making money, and they don't care who gets ruined or hurt so long as they make it."

Even when Harry had been a youngster he had been sharp enough to find fault with his father's argument. All he said was true, but when Harry saw the boys just graduated from high school, or even grade school, troop home from the subway exits in a line, with the dried perspiration and irritating clothes of workers, swinging their folded newspapers at their sides as a symbol, he grew firm in his resolution never to be one of them. Williamsburg and the squalid life here oppressed him. He wanted to get out, to live freely and luxuriously as they did in the movies, and he was old enough to know that only money could deliver him. In those days Harry had argued with his father. He said most of the people he knew had to live this way until the time came for them to die, and it seemed a great pity. This was anesthesia, it was death in spite of life. He wanted to live for the fun of it. "When I get going," he used to say, "I'm going to try to make money hand over fist. I'll get out of here as fast as I can. I'll live only once and I want to enjoy myself." And in those days his father, with a Hebraic sense of propriety, lectured him everlastingly, with patience, with pain.

Harry Hayman, lying in the bed, wondered at the diversity of human beings. The deep emotion he felt now contrasted sharply with his general attitude on these matters. Take a hundred men and he was sure a hundred of them would have done exactly as he had, given the opportunity. Honor, truth, ethical behavior, everyone recognized these things and said they were good, but in practice they made money as fast as they could, that was the important thing, the rest was mental affectation or luxury of the soul, similar to music, or art, or charity. Harry wondered at himself, at his break from Papravel and his change of viewpoint. Then again he wondered at himself for the feelings he was experiencing toward his father. How could all these emotions, actions, and thoughts, spread over different hours of the day, over different days of the week, how could these all belong to one man?

In those days his father had lectured him, but in the last few years the old man was silent and cynical because he was aware of the fruitlessness of his sermons. Once his father had been an inch short of six feet. When Harry looked at him he saw a small, shrunken man. There was no strength or dominance in him, only a contemplative isolation to protect himself. Harry realized that his father had no more hope and that he was bitter in his hopelessness, overcome with the failure of his ideals and gone sour because he had to accept conditions as they were. The tenderness for his father returned. Harry saw him now as some great noble figure who was good and true, who had had some illusions of kind will among people, and who in the end had had to wrench himself free of them. This brought to his father a touch of romance. Harry gave himself completely to the feeling of the moment. He promised himself that he would stay with his father, do as he directed, and be a comfort to him. The sobs came back. Perhaps it was the trip, his talk with Papravel, and the fatigue.

It ended when the water on his pillow, grown warm and sticky, began to irritate his nose. After he scratched it a while he muttered the weary sigh people make when they have been crying for a long time, and he turned the pillow over. In time he slept.

Harry was awakened early in the morning. Someone was persistently ringing an electric bell in short nervous dashes. In the early-morning rawness his mouth felt sour, and he moved among the bedclothes with irritation. What vexed him especially was that his ears strained to catch the bell after each brief intermittent pause. After some time a hallway window was opened noisily on its chains. Harry heard a woman call softly, "Open the door, Sammy. Sammy, I won't go away until you open the door." Then the ringing went on. Harry twisted his face in grimaces.

Suddenly a woman began to scream. Doors could be heard opening as women left their flats to run to her. Someone began crying out in a shrill voice, "Send for a doctor. Send for a doctor." Harry rushed out into the hallway. Half-dressed, he caught a boy.

"What's up, kid?"

"Nothing, nothing," he said. It was an old story to him and the accident itself was minor. "Mrs. Glickner put her kid into the bathtub in cold water on account of its being hot. The kid got up and turned the hot water on. He burned himself."

A doctor came up the stairs, two steps at a time, disregarding in his importance the questions of housewives. The noise diminished. Harry went back to his flat. He felt tired. Last night in his bed was very distant, like a dream, and he was trying to forget it. In spite of his affection for his father he knew he couldn't remain in Williamsburg. He wondered how he could arrange his departure in a week or two. The odor of lox, frying in onions, filled his nostrils.

FOURTEEN

Two red sores, hot, itching, and sensitive, burned at the sides of Cohen's nostrils. He knew he should not irritate them further, but he could not help himself, he had to deliver his nose again and again. He was having a terrible cold in the face, which meant his nose, eyes, head, and even his teeth. Cohen lay on the bed with a handkerchief over his face, weak and exhausted, but nevertheless he was exultant.

"That is the only way," he pronounced thickly through outraged membranes. "It is the essential secret of life, to move in meaningful, significant activity. There comes a time, Philip, when all the world's ornamentation turns into dross. We are kids no longer. We are men, part of life, and our mission is to accept our heritage and to serve humanity. To serve only yourself, to wallow in the pleasures of your mind no matter how refined, is decayed and a kind of masturbation."

"All this is news to me," Philip said. He was in a good mood, and was having a great time with Cohen, although he resisted his impulses and tried not to rub him. "I had heard something about what was going on with you, but I didn't know this was included. Are you actually telling me that you're becoming a useful animal?"

"Philip, I can speak frankly with you. When I jumped off that bridge, it was no sudden, random feeling. I had been deliberating over it for months. What had there been in my life? I asked myself.

Small, petty occupations, poetry, books, and the nervous twitchings of a quest for beauty. I meant with all my heart to end my existence because I recognized how futile it was, how worthless. At the same time I was killing myself I knew that my passing would make not the slightest difference, it would not affect the world in the least detail, and that was an indictment. And then it came to me. Philip, you like to laugh at me and you can laugh at me now, but if I was ever earnest in my life I am that now. It was like a renascence. I came to think of the miserable conditions of men. I saw what work I could do to help and how great the need for it was. It seemed to me a sin for me to waste my life when it could be used so well. Suddenly, I became important to myself and to the world. Philip, you will never know what it is like until you go through it yourself."

"I can't make anything of it. Here, you, Cohen, sing the joys of a socially useful life. I don't want to be indelicate at this time, forgive me, but you're the most cockeyed humanitarian I have ever seen. Tell me, just between friends, what is this? Another stage?"

"Philip," he cried, and it was like the wail through a saxophone reed, "all that part of me is over. Don't you believe a man grows and matures? I realize what I have been in the past. That is why I turn so eagerly to the work of the Party. It's so different, it's what I need. Believe me, Philip, I am interested only in genuine feeling. I want no affectation."

He stopped to examine his handkerchief for a dry spot. "Gee whiz," he muttered, "I use these rags up fast." Folding the hem tenderly around his bruised nose, he blew and wiped in careful dabs.

"I remember," he resumed with a burning light in his eyes, "I remember something I once saw when I was a boy. Do you know that old synagogue on Rodney Street near the school? Once I saw a woman in the wintertime walking past the tall iron railing slowly, weeping by herself. I shall never forget the image, the huge brick synagogue, the tall railings, the winter gray sky, and the way that poor woman wept. I knew it was real, no fake, some real heartache. Do you know what I mean, Philip? It was something you never forget."

Philip knew, only there was no image, no winter gray sky, no tall iron railings, it was no picture. Philip remembered the time he had been watching telephone-company laborers draw a cable under the pavements. A man was down in a hole in the street guiding the cable while the truck at the end of the block pulled it through by a rope. The man in the street hole jammed his finger against the wall. Philip knew it was no fake then. All the laborer did was groan, that was all, groan with the burning pain, waiting for the men with grim concentration on their faces slashing the thick rope and yelling hoarsely to the truck driver to stop. That was it.

"I know," Philip said. "It's like *Roses of Picardy*. Come on, I'll take you and your suffering nose for a walk."

Outside on the streets the evening air was cool and Cohen was grateful for it. He nursed his nose and felt a little relieved. His head was clearing. "If I stopped blowing my nose," he said, "it wouldn't be so bad."

When Philip had been small he used to think he could always tell whether he really loved a girl by trying to remember her face. If he could make an image of her in his mind, if the features were clearly distinguishable, that meant his feeling was not very deep for her. It was hard to tell in these matters, and Philip as a boy used this device for a deciding oracle. If the image was blurred in his mind, misty and unformed, he could be sure. And now, although he knew it was ridiculous, he was disturbed because when he thought of Ruth her smiling face came so easily into his head. He saw her with the round, rosy cheeks, the big eyes, and the curling, soft hair, even the prim, childlike expression on her face when she was thinking. Philip thought of her, he thought of the life in her body, the warmth, and her smooth, soft flesh.

"The work I do is fascinating. Really, you don't know how it draws all your interest."

It was Cohen. "Well," Philip said, "what is your share in the great humanitarian work?"

"I always thought of writing, but writing for its own sake exists in a vacuum. It has no spark. Literature should have substance, solidity, and meaning. In short, a book that has no definite moral for people, a book that does not communicate a lesson for a better way of living, is dead. I am for propaganda. What we do goes directly to the masses. There's no half way about our work. We know what we're after, and we're doing it. I'm with the Agitprop section. We write plays, one-act and full-length, put them on in cellars, in halls, in regular theaters, and in street lots. The idea is to reach the people directly, to teach them by concrete image and the story of the play."

"I know," Philip said, "but what's your share? What have you done?"

"Oh, I don't want to look ridiculous, after all this it sounds ridiculous, but actually all I've done so far is to attend the meetings, read the literature of the group, and get the general tone. I expect to get to work on a one-act play for a starter. No fancy stuff, no involved plot, just a straight, hard-hitting piece of realism."

"What's it about?" Philip asked. He was eager to know exactly what Cohen was doing, whether he was actually at work or whether it was talk.

"It's about a man who loses his job. He begins by going through the usual hard-luck story of being thrown out of his flat, his wife leaves him, and he's all alone. He's broke. What can he do? He hits it out on the road, hitchhiking and riding the freights. I depict his experiences, the life on the rods, and the bums he meets. He goes all over, Texas, Oklahoma, Florida, and Canada. The point of the play is this: he was an ordinary wage slave until he got busted, but in his travels he gets to see things and begins to think. He reads a whole lot and thinks a whole lot. Then he joins the Party in San Francisco and becomes a leader. There's a strike, and in the end he gets killed. There's no fancy stuff here, but you see what tremendous force the simple narrative has."

"All this goes into a one-act play?" Philip said dryly. The old bull thrower had made the story up as he talked.

Cohen thought it over but refused to be nonplused. "Well, I've just begun thinking about it. I haven't even drawn up an outline or worked on a plan, but all those things will be ironed out with time.

We're not interested in technique. We don't care a damn about craftsmanship and that kind of æsthetic hooey. All we want is matter, substance, reality."

"Listen, Cohen, I'm an old friend of yours. I can give you advice. Why don't you go to a good cat house and get over with it?"

"What do you mean?"

"What I always say is a fellow like you needs a good girl. Here you hand me out a load of crap about a bum. What do you know about bums? I'm not kidding with you, Cohen, I mean this. What are you yapping about Texas and Oklahoma for? What do you know about the life on the rods? Do you know what a rod is? I've never seen one, and you probably haven't either. Why don't you cut the crap and get a good girl? Get yourself a broad, be like everybody else, take her out to Coney Island and go home for a good night's rest. Don't try to make a freak out of yourself. Don't juggle so much with your soul."

"That's unimportant," Cohen said reflectively. Philip could see his indecision as he thought about it. "You're still a kid about those things. They don't mean so much once you get used to them. Take my friend Shura. She certainly has been through the mill in her time. She knows what it's like. Shura says it's like eating or drinking or going to the toilet. You don't talk about those things all the time."

"Shura," Philip said.

"She's with the Agitprop with me. She's a funny girl, Philip," Cohen's voice broke and he had to restrain the giggles. He spoke in a low tone. His face grew flushed and his troubled nose sniffed with the excitement. "You know what she says, Philip? She says I don't know life. She says she's going to do something for me some day and wake me up. You know what I mean? Do you think she's kidding me, Philip?"

"Are you adulterating the sharp quality of your work at the Agitprop with your relationship with Shura? I'm getting suspicious."

"Oh, Philip! You don't understand. I didn't expect anything so coarse and shallow from you. You ridicule the Party and my work in it. I'm disappointed in you."

They walked up toward Bedford Avenue. Here the wide street, the speeding automobiles, and the scattering of fine houses produced an air of gentility, and it was different from Ripple Street. Philip always liked to walk in the evenings on Bedford Avenue. The sidewalks were lined with young trees presented to the community by the American Legion in loving memory of the war dead. They looked pathetic and city-worn, but occasionally, at some street corner, a great oak or maple lifted its muscular trunk to the sky. They were planted in pavement and looked unreal. They came to a small circular park. The impressive, big Catholic Church set the tone for the neighborhood, and as they went up the street they looked casually into the softly lit homes for glimpses of the fine furnishings. One house, reputed to be owned by a politician who had to remain in the neighborhood for sectional voting reasons, was actually lavish, with twisted iron works and a coat of arms on the door pane. Cohen, in his new role, made a passing satirical reference to it. "He lives like a lord," he said with spirit, "and a few blocks down people crowd into dirty, dark rooms."

What a load of crap he was, Philip thought, but he had not expected this phase in him. Generally Cohen's poses had been more of the esthete and the dilettante. At times he wavered from the amusement of detached observation to lapses of sympathetic concern for humanity. His heart ached, really he felt these things very deeply, but before this condition was half-settled, before the week was over, Cohen might turn to something else, often women. He lied recklessly and proclaimed that a man who had not lived fully with a woman was not complete. At these times there were fantastic stories, laughable stories, rich and meaty, the details of which were thorough and exciting and indicated intensive reading in specialized fields. A virgin was not a complete man, he would cry, but actually, although at this time he probably hardly would have admitted it to himself, he himself was untarnished.

What was the matter with him? Philip asked, trying to understand Cohen. What made him go? There were millions of people, each acting differently, and Philip tried to discover why it was that Cohen was Cohen. Why was he so completely a liar, lying most of all to himself? Reality—the garbage cans, the dirty streets, and a wet, hot sun pouring suffocating heat over dark, close rooms in a Williamsburg tenement—reality was too much for him. Unable to find some girl to love as they loved in the nineteenth-century lyrics that Cohen memorized, Cohen lacked the energy and the confidence to avail himself of the pleasures to be found in Halper's Stable lots, the cellars, or the roofs. The world confused him, frightened him, and he set upon improving it and transforming it to suit his fancy.

And his fancy changed. That made changing worlds. Cohen would go storming away in self-inflicted fits of despair and bitterness. Then again he was apathetic, or else bursting with fresh emotion as he discovered a new enthusiasm. Unstable, bewildered, and affected, how would he end? Philip wondered. People, and this included Philip himself, laughed at Cohen and considered him a fool. But did the fault lie entirely with Cohen? Granted a certain amount of grace and smoothness, the ability to laugh ironically at himself, Cohen might even be respected as one who in his own fashion rebelled against the environment to which he was unable to adapt himself. Yes, Cohen was a schlemiel, but wasn't Philip's father also a schlemiel, wasn't poor Meyer Sussman who killed himself some weeks back a schlemiel, wasn't Philip himself? And was it supremely true that the only wise ones were people like his uncle Papravel, or Mrs, Linck's son Sam, people who accepted conditions as they were, without further thought, and made the most of them in their own ways?

At Bedford and Flushing Philip and Cohen suddenly came upon a horrible smash-up. A party of two couples in a smartly painted roadster had sped into one of the big oaks. Apparently they had been necking, the driver had lost control, and the roadster had swerved off the street. Cohen and Philip pressed with the crowd. The car was crumpled badly, and the twigs that had rained down from the tree with the impact recalled with terrible vividness the force of the smash and the shock.

Philip felt sick. The white uniform of the intern stood out in the darkness. He went from person to person, busily treating the injured youngsters. The crowd surged and ebbed as the cops pushed them back. The red taillight shone weakly and stupidly.

There were three cops. While one of them searched the car for identification or liquor the other two could be heard arguing over which one was to go with the ambulance to the hospital. They were both excited, but they tried to keep their raw faces impassive.

What impressed Philip most was the sight of one of the girls in the party who was still conscious. She sat mutely on the running board, her head resting heavily on her hands. On her forehead little streams of blood stood out as though they were opened veins. Her hair was wet, probably from the blood of the man who had been with her. In the coolness of the night Philip could almost feel for himself the naked sensation the wind must be producing on her head. She had thick lips and they trembled all the time. Her face had the twisted expression of one about to cry, but it remained twisted, she did not cry. It seemed as though she were so overwhelmed with grief that it was no time for tears. Tears were foolish, even they were affectation. That was it, Philip said, a person revealing herself to the raw. He looked at Cohen. His eyes peered through the goggles but he took no time from his nose, the handkerchief went on irritating the red sores.

"That must have been some accident," Cohen gasped. He shook his head. "Jesus, that must have been an accident. I bet that tree is killed."

They walked away from the scene. Cohen looked through the window of a barbershop and saw the time. It was after seven. "Gee whiz," he said, suddenly remembering. "I've got an appointment tonight."

"The Agitprop or Shura?" Philip asked.

"Both, in a way," Cohen said. "Let's walk faster. I don't want to keep her waiting." He said nothing further to Philip, but it was clear that the appointment was very important to him.

Later that night Cohen, with a clean shirt and his hair oiled heavily in place, sat with Shura in a café on West Fourth Street. He was trying to control the nervous excitement that two or three times, was on the point of overpowering him. In his agitation his head cold had even disappeared. The truth was he was having great plans for tonight. He polished his glasses masterfully with his handkerchief, failing to realize, however, that his weak eyes staring without the aid of spectacles were ruining the impression. He turned again to Shura.

"My idea for the Agitprop is this. I've talked it over with a friend of mine and he likes it. But after all I am interested in your opinion. I call the hero Joe Tenner. The title of the play is 'The Odyssey of Joe Tenner,' because it is through his travels over America that he learns the meaning of life."

Shura was definitely not interested, but Cohen refused to perceive it. It was an important evening to him and he went on with bland self-possession. She smoked a cigarette, surveyed the persons in the café, and took time off to show her annoyance with Cohen by the way she flipped the ash into the coffee saucer.

"No man can write anything about life until he knows it," she said positively.

"What do you mean?" Cohen said softly, trembling a little. "You yourself said that these things were unimportant, or aren't you talking about the same thing I'm thinking of?"

"Cohen," she said kindly, patting his hand to make him quiet, "Cohen."

She too had a cold but she ignored it thoroughly. Shura was a wondrously complacent individual, and she treated Cohen with wondrous condescension mixed with kind consideration. Her bulk did not form an impression of stark fatness as it would have with another, but of great inward satisfaction. Shura knew all the answers and she couldn't be bothered. The Greenwich Village café, a degenerate example abounding in derelict poets and gin-imbibing homosexuals, interested her, but it was a detached sort of amusement. In the small room a collegian acted pertly as master of ceremonies. He peered through the smoke and said, "We are very fortunate to have among us this evening the well-known poet Homer Quixby. Come up, Homer."

And Homer came, his face glazed with profundity and anemia. He took his stance seriously, forthwith breaking out into verse. His voice was very deep. Cohen marveled at it. Homer sat down. All in all it was a very abrupt performance, and four or five persons in the place caught their wind hurriedly and turned to their neighbors to say, "Homer is a so'n'so, did you know that? O yes it certainly shows too." Homer, very proud that he was a so'n'so, disregarded the applause, carried his hips wide and high, and took his place with three other so'n'soes.

Cohen cleared his throat and returned to Shura. This was wasting time. He was very sincere with his work and wanted to proceed with his outline. But quiet, she said with her lips, quiet, and she put a heavy hand on his arm. A goggle-eyed Chinaman was reading a poem in his native language, clacking off the odd syllables and restraining his laughter because he could imagine how extraordinarily funny the sounds were to his audience. "Now I will translate," he stuttered, his spirits high and uncertain. When he came to the word "concubine" it was over, he had to sit down, he could not stop giggling. It was like a fit.

The young collegian took advantage of the roaring confusion in the room to announce a real surprise. He bounced three fingers on the piano and held his hand up for silence. "A rare treat," he said. "We are very lucky tonight, very lucky indeed. The famous poet Herbert Fleishenhacker is with us tonight and he has been kind enough to promise us one of his latest poems." Cohen, too, was impressed. Herbert Fleishenhacker. At least this was a name he had heard before.

Then Fleishenhacker, a smooth, well-washed man of agreeable appearance, moved up front, humble before the applause in spite of his great fame. At first he seemed meek, but the fury of his poem grew upon him. The poem was about the designs dirt forms on city sidewalks, and in those designs the poet re-created life. An allegory, but vigorous, and when Fleishenhacker finished his head fell low with effort and he was exhausted. As he went back to his seat everyone turned to his neighbor and said, "Did you know about the scandal he was in two years ago, no, he's no so'n'so, he's a what-is-this, they do say he's constantly on the lookout for someone to revive his love life, that's why he got mixed up in that scandal two years ago, he thought maybe that would work."

A slight poet, product of the Midwestern soil, now spoke his lines, but Cohen was no longer to be hushed. He felt imperious.

"That's a joke," Shura said, looking at him for once. "I like your tone. Here you're bending my ear with all this crap about the Odyssey of Joe Tenner and I know what's exactly on your mind." She was omnipotent. One nostril was clogged from her cold and she exhaled magnificently, the smoke pouring out thickly from the one in working condition. Shura laughed at Cohen.

"Say," he said strongly, "what's got into you? If you think ... you're crazy. It was you who started this business in the first place anyhow. Didn't you say you wanted to do something for me? I like the way you act. As if I were going after you."

But the master of ceremonies was insistent. Shura hushed Cohen, and the collegian cried, "Here, here," with inspiration. "Take that poem. This is how Christopher Emanuel would do it." He recited the poem, rooted in Midwestern soil, in the lilting inflections and falsetto voice of Mr. Emanuel, who obviously was a so'n'so. But the Chinaman who giggled would not be restrained. He jumped up from his seat.

"Why take Christopher Emanuel?" he piped almost hysterically with excitement. "Why imitate him? What's the matter with Homer Quixby here?"

The crowd gasped. Homer, white but enjoying his prominence, flapped his hand at the Chinaman in a fret and cried, "Stop. Stop it. Don't be nasty." He shook his body with rage but everyone could see he was enjoying the incident and did not hold back the roars. The onlookers felt uplifted. They were present on the scene of a legend in the making. Later they would have to tell their neighbors, "Did you hear about what happened the other night et cetera?"

A waiter came through with a case of beer, and the master of ceremonies, with an eye to business, pointed significantly. There would be a pause, he announced, the time had come for three-point-two, a sandwich, and— a yew, "How'm I doing?" he asked gaily, and sat down for a while.

Cohen was upset by the proceedings. He wasn't getting on, he wasn't getting any place. "Listen, Shura," he said, "there must be some misunderstanding someplace. What's got into you?"

"I know all about it," Shura said, and indeed Cohen started wondering what this massive girl didn't know. "You think you can devirginate yourself tonight at my expense. Why don't you say so and cut out the crap?"

"Shura!" Cohen said. "That's an insult of the lowest kind. You take advantage of our intimacy. Perhaps you also think my interest in the Party is tied up with you as well."

"I don't doubt it. You've a Bronx idea that a radical is also a girl who is free with her charms. It's a common misconception. Just because I'm with the Party you think I'll be no trouble. I'm to be had for the asking or something. If it makes things any clearer for you, you can get it out of your head that I'm sleeping with you tonight."

All Cohen could say was, "Shura, Shura." It didn't make any sense, he was at a complete loss, and he ordered coffee and sandwiches again.

And now Herbert Fleishenhacker, moving carelessly about the room with the freedom of the great, came before their table. He eyed Shura, and she was not one to cast her gaze to the ground before him. Fleishenhacker, sensing invitations, began pirouetting in front of their table, going around in dainty circles on his toes, and making graceful curves in the air with his arms. The poet danced as if to himself, and as he danced he sang softly to create a rhythm. He was Fleishenhacker, and only Fleishenhacker could do these things without comment because he was Fleishenhacker.

"Won't you sit down?" Shura said. Cohen admired her composure. He himself was slightly in awe of the man. His name was in the papers. "Would you like some coffee? Cohen, order another cup."

Fleishenhacker sat, contributing to the conversation a noble profile. When the coffee came he made a ritual over it. "This is the way to drink coffee," he pronounced. "Just watch me." He poured seven spoonsful of sugar into the cup and waited until it formed a sticky layer at the bottom. Then he sipped the coffee slowly with great care not to stir the cup. "The hand must not tremble," he said. "The sugar is a base. It should not be excited and caused to rise so that, the nearer the end, the sweeter the taste."

He finished and smacked his lips with victory. "Poetry should be brought into life. That is my credo. Even the trifling matter of a cup of coffee can be rendered a poetic expression," he said.

Shura said it was very interesting. At this Fleishenhacker seized her hand with passion. Cohen was startled at the abruptness. "Let's get out of this hole," the poet said, his eyes thundering a thousand nothings into hers. "What are we wasting time for?" Shura gathered herself up, and, as she swept out of the room feeling the sharp looks of the people following them, she felt like Gertrude Stein collecting celebrities. And when the two had left everyone turned to his neighbor and said, "Didn't I tell you he's a what-is-this she's the latest some men favor fat women they think have a superior facility well well."

Cohen was left with the check. He waited a decent interval and walked out, disgusted with himself, the Party, and Shura. Once again he had been the buffoon. Cohen walked the dead, skinny streets of Greenwich Village, considering the possibility of a new renascence within himself, but the latest had been so recent he did not have the face to go on with it. Stubbornly, he would not relinquish all allegiance to the Party. This was not an enthusiasm among many, it was the true cause in his life, but he was getting dubious and tired of it. Shura was an ordinary bitch, he said with vigor. The hell with her, he said again and again until it became a chant.

Cohen had resolved to do one great thing tonight. With a rush of determination he asserted to himself that he would not let Shura stop him. The hell with her. His evening and his quest were not over. Philip used to tell him that any taxicab driver could show him a place. Cohen's fingers counted the bills in his pocket. What was this mysterious thing? What would it do to him? Why had he been waiting so long for it? It came to him now like a supernatural call: find out, Cohen, find out for yourself tonight, explore the vital maze. But Cohen did not know exactly how to word the phrases;

his traffic with hackmen and these matters had been limited, and the call failed to specify. Finally he brought himself to approach a parked cab. "Listen, buddy," he said, with nervous reserve, darkly, "I'd like to get fixed up tonight."

The cab driver lowered his *News* from the light of the street lamppost and looked at him. He saw Cohen's splotched face, the goggles, the plastered hair, and the strange expression. He must be one of these guys, the driver said to himself. "Are you making passes at me, dearie?" he said with hard sweetness. "Get the hell out of here before I slam my fist into your face."

What is love? Philip said. You get over it, it's hard and sharp sometimes, but then only for a while. A woman is nothing very important. Wife, mother, father, children, country, life, work, death—that's heroics, you get over it.

All this, said Philip with a smile to himself, is consolation in advance. Momentarily he expected his relationship with Ruth Kelman to break. She had said nothing to him; beyond the coolness he met with in her mother there was nothing to suggest it, but Philip, somehow sensing that he could not belong, felt that his intimacy with her was bound to be shortlived. And he was growing so completely involved with her that from pride he was preparing himself for the separation when it came.

"These things do not last, baby," he persisted in telling Ruth. "In the pleasurable tingle of the first weeks the inescapable tragedy is the contemplation that these things do not last."

The breeze blew cold on the steamer. The sky-blue day was almost like spring on the boat going down the Bay to the Atlantic Highlands. Ruth hugged his back with her arms for the warmth.

"Who would have ever thought it was going to be so cold," she said. "Oh, I'm so cold."

"Then hold tighter," he said, worried over it because it seemed to reflect on him that he could only take her on a boat ride. "Would you wear my jacket if I took it off?"

"No. It's all right."

They were passing Brooklyn. Philip had found a spot on the lower deck sheltered from the wind, and she was in the corner as far as she could push herself, looking at the shore where the big houses overlooked the water. "That's Brooklyn," she said. "Is that where you live?"

"Oh, no. Swells like you live there. That must be the Shore Drive. Where I live the view is hidden by garbage cans and boys swinging dead cats by their tails at tourists who come slumming. Do you mind sewer smells? They're terrible, but good for your soul. One must suffer. Through Purgatory to Paradise, like that guy Dostoevsky says. Some day I'll take you there, and then you'll come back uplifted."

He spoke almost bitterly from self-consciousness. They walked around the boat watching from different points the strange foreign tramps and the garbage barges with their cargoes of nondescript refuse. Once they saw a long, slim Japanese steamer going out to sea. It looked like a brilliant insect, clean, and newly painted black and yellow, but they saw no one aboard and it moved mysteriously past them. As they tried to light cigarettes the wind carried away the flame from the matches.

"It's cold," Ruth said. Her cheeks were red, her soft hair blew with the wind. "What are you looking at me for?"

"Can't I look at you, monkey-face?" he spoke sharply.

"What's the matter?" she said anxiously. "Is it dirty?"

"No," Philip said. What was the matter with him? "You look very nice."

In the end they came to the odd railroad, which stuck out from the shore, and they rode out toward Sandy Hook, wondering all the time whether they were on the right train. Here it was wonderful. After the dirty, sun-beaten streets of New York the quiet coolness and the blowing branches of the trees made them feel far away and refreshed.

It was a long climb to the lighthouse, but worth it to lie in the sun on the sloping grass looking down on the sea and Sandy Hook. The ocean liners, the toy railroad, the little automobiles from that distance gave an impression of unreality. It was like, Philip thought, the soft glazed colors and the dreamy pictures he had seen as a boy on hand-painted China vases his mother had placed for ornaments on the Dutch shelves in the dining room. There were many clouds.

"The trouble with you," she said suddenly, "is that you think too much about these things. About some things you shouldn't think too much. You must be Russian or something."

"No," said Philip. "Only, love is like that. It has a beginning, a middle, and an end."

"That's a nice thing to hear from a man who tells you lovely stories about yourself," she said calmly.

"Oh, please," said Philip, pained and confused. "You must try to understand the inconsistency, for really there is no inconsistency. You must try to understand it. After all, two people can't expect to love each other this way all their lives. This love is very fine, but it doesn't last. Besides, there very probably is something after it."

"Oh, let it go," Ruth said. "I never think of it. With all this beautiful background, what I'm wondering is, what are you wasting time for?"

"What do you mean?" said Philip. "Oh." He bent over on his elbow and kissed her mouth for a long time.

"What's the matter? What are you doing to her, mister?" It was a blond boy. He was magnificent, his legs apart, looking down upon them with half a reprimand.

"What's the matter?" asked Philip. "Don't you go to the movies here?"

In all his life he had never seen a boy like that. He did not belong to the earth. On his face was the unconscious ease of being that has a kinship with the sea, the wind, and the sky.

"Sit down," Ruth said, and offered him cake. "Do you live here?"

"I live there," he said, pointing to the lighthouse. "My father's the lighthouse keeper. You come from New York? I've never seen you before. What were you going to do to her, mister?"

"Eat your cake," Philip said. The blond boy sat down facing them, swiftly retailing an assortment of facts, local and personal, for their benefit. He was very lonely here and had few friends. All the time Ruth was feeding him cake and chocolate he talked and talked. Abruptly he rose. "I've got to go back now," he said. "Can I have a piece for my sister?"

"Surely," Ruth said. "Take what you like."

"That'll be fine. We always share what we find." And he was off.

Philip lay back. What was he worrying about? He was letting his imagination run away with him like an old woman. There was nothing to fear. Ruth was all right. He became suddenly happy. The mood of uncertainty that had clung to him on the boat left him. There was no reason to hold back, he told himself, he could love Ruth without reserve, without worry, and without thought. It must have been the blond boy. Philip laughed quietly.

"That's what I call stupid," Ruth said as she watched him. "What's there to be laughing about?"

"Nothing," Philip said gaily, drawing her shoulders to him, "I don't know. I'm a Russian who doesn't think. I'm a Russian, but I don't give a Russian hoorah."

⌢⌢⌢

Two days after Harry Hayman came home to Williamsburg from Havers Falls he decided to leave again. It was morning. Philip had walked into his older brother's room to give him a cigarette, and Harry said casually, "I guess I'll be leaving again. I think I'll go to Chicago and see what I can do there."

The news startled Philip. Occupied with Ruth Kelman, he had seen little of his brother and did not know why Harry had left Papravel.

"Why Chicago? You've just come home. What are you going to do there?"

"I know a man who's got a tie factory out there. After all, I've got to do something for a living."

"I don't want to say anything unpleasant," Philip said, sitting on his brother's bed, "but after all those letters you sent me I can't understand what made you bust with Papravel."

"You have a funny old man. All he does is sit at the window and smoke a cigarette, but that was what made me quit. I began to see the picture of Pop at the window wagging his finger at me. It's like a hoodoo."

"You're kidding," Philip said. "What was the matter? Don't you love your uncle anymore?"

"It's not Papravel. He's all right. You're like the old man, you don't give him credit for anything. Only, it was time I got out. Listen," Harry said, "I'm your older brother, I can tell you something, but I don't know exactly what to say. The trouble is I'm mixed up too. I'm not going to live like Pop. I don't like to use words like 'live' and 'talk' in this fancy way, but I'm not going to stay in this place, in the hot filth, squeezed in small dark rooms, one among a pack of dried-out, walking stiffs. When I think of Williamsburg, I always get the smell of vinegar. And the only way anybody can get out of this hole is to make money. I don't have to tell you by this time, you got an idea, but I am not sentimental about money. I know what it does and how much you need it. When you haven't got it you live in a place like this, three-quarters dead and the other quarter alive only because you can read the advertisements in *The New Yorker*. You see the swell women and the fine houses, the autos, the yachts, the red-and-brown colors, it is all very fast and gay, and it pricks you into wanting those things. So you dream, all the time you dream, about how you will be next year or in five years from now, hoping stupidly a fortune will fall down on your head and kiss you. You keep on going to the movies and you reach a point where you yourself actually believe in it. Ask the women on the streets drinking vanilla soda water what they're waiting for, and if they tell you the truth they'll say, next year, maybe, business will be better, we'll move to Flatbush or the Bronx, west side. Everyone wants to be rich and swell so much they get to expect it. They think it's real, it's coming. But the only way to get money is to go out and work for it. That's where Papravel comes in, Papravel and the rub. Philip, what jolted me was the time Gilhooley killed a cop. Then I began thinking about Morand. I've been getting heavy money to ruin that man, and it made me soft and sweet to think what I was doing to him. My delicate soul couldn't stand it and I quit. There's too much of the schlemiel in me. I guess I get it from the old man."

Philip concerned himself carefully with the cigarette because he knew the slightest movement on his part would cause his brother to feel ridiculous and shut up. To express audibly a personal philosophy, to talk with feeling, was a ticklish thing.

"Well," said Philip, "where does that put you now?"

"That's where I'm mixed up. You ought to hear your uncle Papravel on the subject of making money. Legitimately, I mean. He certainly can tell you all about it. The way he's got it figured out, if I open a haberdashery store in Grand Street three women and four kids will live stunted lives. I don't know what the hell I'm going to do. That is, that's what I say to you, but actually I know goddam well what I'm going to do. I'll wait until my soul stops backfiring and then it'll be the same old things again, but a little more decorous perhaps. Where's Momma?" he suddenly asked. "It's time we ate breakfast."

"She must be out schmoozing with the neighbors. I'll get her for you in a minute."

Harry began to dress. Philip went to the hall and paused outside of the neighbors' doors, one after the other. He could always tell whether his mother was inside because her voice was so familiar. He could distinguish it by its peculiar rise and fall. She was talking excitedly to Mrs. Miller. Something must be up, Philip said. He opened the door and stuck his head in. "Missus," he said, "J. P. Morgan wants you on the telephone. Hurry up." Mrs. Hayman broke off and excused herself.

"What's the rush?" she said. "Is there a fire?"

"Your oldest son wants breakfast."

She opened the door. "What good is breakfast," she asked Harry, "if you want to smoke first?" She put half a grapefruit on the table and began heating the oatmeal. "All morning you sleep, and when you want your breakfast you can't wait."

"Ma," Philip said, "did you hear the news? Harry's going to Chicago!"

"I heard the good news," Mrs. Hayman said. She had been excited, but now her face fell. "What are you going to do in Chicago?"

"I told you, Mom. I'm just taking a vacation, and maybe I'll find a job."

"Why must you always be running around? Can't you stay in New York? So many people can live here for years and you have to keep on moving. I never saw anybody like you. You've got pins in you. You just came."

"Say, Ma," Philip said, "what was all the noise going on inside? You were talking to Mrs. Miller as if there was a fire going on."

"That's funny," she said, breaking off from Harry. "I mean, Harry's going away now and you know who came back? You'll never guess. Mrs. Sussman."

"Mrs. Sussman?" Harry asked. "Who is she?"

"Mrs. Sussman?" Philip said. "Oh. Mrs. Sussman!" He turned to his brother. "You must have seen her husband around. He was the butcher. He took gas the beginning of the summer and she went to Montana and married a man there. That's right, Momma. What happened to her new husband?"

"She just came back," his mother said. She put the oatmeal on the table. "She wouldn't let anybody talk to her. She looks funny. I don't make anything out of it."

Mrs. Sussman was back. Philip wondered at the effect the news was having on him. It sent him back to poor Meyer Sussman and the questions he had set before Old Miller. It was odd, he had been at the time so much interested by the butcher's suicide, his strange death had occupied his mind so sharply. It was such a short time, but he had forgotten her completely. It was as his mother had once said. Things happened and nothing happened, it was an old story, you grew used to it and calloused, you forgot.

"What's funny about her? What do you mean?" Philip asked.

"I don't know. She looks funny. Mrs. Linck wants rent from her, but she stays in her old rooms. She won't talk to anybody and no one sees her. Why should she come back so soon? It's not even a month. There must be something the matter."

Philip considered for a moment. "It's probably nothing," he said. "You're just imagining it. You women like to find something to gab about."

"Momma," Harry said, "I don't like oatmeal. You know I don't like oatmeal, why must you always give it to me?"

FIFTEEN

AT THE VILLA CAPRICE housewives, delivered from the East Side, the Bronx, and Williamsburg, lead delightful lives. They rise after eight, wear anything that can be put on in a minute, and they wear it all day. Outside of sporadic washing and hastily-put-together meals there is little for them to do. Sam Linck's wife was having a good time. The two boys, dressed in blue overalls all the time, played in the grass without troubling her, intrigued by the novelty of country surroundings. They had found friends and the group of children took care of themselves, requiring little attention. All Mrs. Linck had to do was to take them into the big dining room for their meals. Soon after six they went to bed, tired and sleepy. The women always said that the country was the best place in the world for children. There were no automobiles or trolley cars, they could play all day in the fresh air and the sun, they lived like healthy animals in a wilderness. That was why they came to the mountains, they affirmed, for their children's sake, and the mothers went to their own diversions.

Sam's wife lay pleasurably in the hammock while the women recited their endless tales of birth, sickness, love, and man's infidelity. They were great themes in life and the women were perpetually concerned with them. Chiam, the ruddy-cheeked, bearded farmer with the smell of sweated clothing, had a dozen boarders in his ugly new wood house on the hill and they soon formed a society of their own, and in the cool evenings, as the sun moved away and the fragrant air came breezing through the apple orchard where they had their hammocks suspended, the women told in low voices the sad stories of strange confinements, abortions, of miscarried love affairs. Each presented, after the fashion of a contest, the virtues of her husband and referred to him always with regret and longing, as people remember the dead.

Later in the evening they went down the road for a walk because it was a healthful practice before going to sleep. You drank a glass of warm milk fresh from the cow's udder and you took a walk. They sang ribald songs, mainly in Yiddish, and they were always giggling. The country sights invariably set them off in wild spasms of surprised laughter, the people were so elementary and naïve. When they saw a bull with his head down, the eyes angrily staring at them and the tongue lolling heavily, each had simultaneously the same thought, and as they read it in each other's faces they broke out into screams at the coincidence.

It was a simple life, but Sam's wife liked it. After the stories in the hammock and the walks, she sat up in her room carefully spelling out letters to her husband under the kerosene lamp. While the moths flew madly at the light, she grew sentimental and worried. "You don't write me," she wrote in her letters home. "When I finally wait all day and get a letter you don't say anything. It's empty. The children are fine. They enjoy the country and I am glad they are here. But the time hangs heavy on my hands, there is nothing for me to do here, no place to go, no one to see. What do you do with yourself? Do you eat carefully? Are you losing weight? Is it hot? Tell me everything, I want to know."

In the bare room smelling of fresh lumber she felt strange at night and wondered, but in the morning the agreeable round began again. She ceased thinking of Sam and Williamsburg. Chiam started the huge black stove early, and the women said their good mornings as they boiled eggs and oatmeal in the kitchen. Two or three women began quarreling over space on the stove, but the breakfasts were made, the children ate impatiently and tore out of the room, and then the time of the women was theirs again and they could talk of what went on in the hospitals and the bedrooms.

Going from the pastures into the fields with low bushes they carried cans and pots for huckleberries, but they went on with their clinical tales. Sam's wife squatted with a friend on the ground, and as they picked the berries they seized these moments of privacy to discuss the others. This was an indelicate practice and they could only talk surreptitiously. Mrs. Linck's friend was a dried-out little woman named Mrs. Klein. They had struck up a common bond in the beginning because these two alone were slim among women who were laughingly submitting to increasing fatness as though it was a good joke on themselves. Unique, Mrs. Linck and her friend carried their light bodies proudly and said they ate anything they liked. Also, they both violently hated a woman whose only flaw actually was that she had lovely red hair. The red hair, painstakingly washed, combed, and dressed, offended them, and as they squatted before the huckleberry bushes Mrs. Linck said, "Klein, did you hear what that redheaded illegitimate said last night?" and Mrs. Klein said, "She thinks she's a raving beauty, don't she, Linck?"

"Excuse me a minute," Mrs. Klein said. "I have to sit down."

"What do you mean? Ain't you sitting already?" And then she understood. The two women broke into giggles.

"That reminds me," Mrs. Klein said, and she told a joke. Laughing, she left her friend and walked to the bushes below the hill. Mrs. Linck sat absentmindedly plucking the berries. The movement became automatic, occupying the eyes and the fingers but not the brain. She began putting the berries into her mouth instead of the pail. As she waited for her friend to return her mind fell into an idle haze.

Mrs. Klein came stumbling through the bushes with her face aglow in the tingling expectation of trouble.

"Linck," she said panting, "if you only knew what I heard! That woman is positively the lowest."

"Who?" she said. "You mean the redhead? Tell me quick. I want to know."

"While I was sitting in the bushes that redhead was talking to one of her Yente friends, and she had the nerve to say that you always took her pot off the stove and pushed it to the side and put your own on."

"The dirty liar!" Mrs. Linck said. "She's got a nerve."

"She certainly is looking for trouble."

"If that fat slob's looking for trouble she certainly came to the right place. I'll see that she gets it."

"Please, Linck. Don't do nothing on account of what I said. I don't want to make trouble. I just told you this because you're my friend."

"Don't worry," Mrs. Linck said confidently, but she began accumulating within her the bitter, silent venom in quantity. If that redheaded slob wanted to make trouble Mrs. Linck expected to be ready for it, aggressive and properly swollen with anger. "Come on, Klein," she said, "let's go back." Sam's wife took particular care to pass the redheaded woman on her way back to the road, and as she passed she gave her a look that would have killed if looks were daggers, and she said so later.

At the Villa Caprice news traveled rapidly. All the women eyed Mrs. Linck and the redhead expectantly. When the time came for dinner the tension at the stove was great, but the two scrupulously avoided each other, careful to keep their eyes down when they had to pass. They used opposite ends of the stove. But when the women went to the hammocks for the evening dissections and the stories, the atmosphere was so charged with restraint that it did not take long for the argument to break. It started when Mrs. Linck let a sharp tone creep in, and the redheaded woman, interpreting the remark personally and refusing to let any challenge no matter how small go unheeded, returned immediately. "Some people should keep their nasty mouths to themselves and they'd be better off," she said significantly, at pains to direct this statement to everyone but Mrs. Linck.

"I wonder what a person can mean by that smart crack," Sam's wife said with great lightness from her hammock.

"Some people can never be satisfied. They're always looking for trouble."

Hereupon Mrs. Linck rolled out of the swing. "Look here, missus," she said, "do you want to start something?"

"What if I do?" The redheaded woman was out of the hammock and surveyed her contemptuously, her hands firmly placed on her hips, the legs apart.

"If I was you," Sam's wife said, speaking with cool slowness, "I'd keep quiet or I'd find my hands full."

"Is that so? Tell me, lady, who do you think you are?"

"Listen, you raving beauty, I know all about the sweet remarks you pass about me to your friends about me pushing your pots off the stove and putting my own on. I know all about the filthy lies you tell everybody. Don't think I'm deaf and dumb."

"Nobody has to say you're dumb. God took care of that a long time ago."

"You must think you're smart, don't you?"

"Stop pushing me!" the redhead screamed. "Keep your goddam hands to yourself. I'll shove your funny face in if you try anything on me like that!"

The fight was on in earnest. The other ladies present had been listening anxiously from their hammocks, unwilling to intrude upon a private disagreement. But now they transcended the rules of polite behavior and climbed out boldly to behold the combatants more clearly. They were thrilled.

"Don't bother with that redheaded tramp, Linck," Mrs. Klein called out importantly. "Don't dirty your hands on her."

"Listen you, you better keep your goddam mouth out of this. Who asked you to stick yourself in here?" the redheaded woman asked belligerently. She knew there was no love lost between Mrs. Klein and herself too.

"Don't try anything on me," Mrs. Klein warned. "I won't take anything from you."

"Please, please," said a woman who always spoke of the professional people in her family. "It's not nice to fight like this."

"Leave me alone," Mrs. Linck said. "I'll show this redheaded bum where she gets off."

She rushed in and went immediately for the head of hair. Her arms were outstretched and she had to keep her own head back. The redhead was clawing at her face furiously. It was an odd posture. But at this turn of events the women sent up an appropriate cry in chorus and Chiam came waddling down the path to the apple orchard with his supper still sticking out of his mouth. He pushed himself between the women and suffered for it. "Like spitting cats," the farmer shouted. "What do you want from me? What are you scratching me for? I did you nothing. Stop, women, stop!"

Chiam pulled Mrs. Linck by the arm back to the house. The redhead began crying. She protested she was a refined woman, she had never had any trouble like this, the shame was too much. It was over and it had barely begun. The ladies went back to their hammocks disappointed, but the woman with professional people in her family disapproved and couldn't get over the fight. "It's not decent," she said, and shook her head. "It's not nice. How can people be like animals?"

Mrs. Linck, her passion half-spent and still hot, argued fiercely with Chiam. "What kind of a place do you keep if you let such tramps like her in? Do you take in anybody at all so long as they can pay the room rent?"

"Calm yourself, missus. Don't get excited." There had been many fights. He was used to them.

"Don't you tell me what to do," she screamed. "I won't stay in this house another night if you don't throw that bum out!"

"Go to sleep," Chiam said soothingly. "In the morning you'll forget all about it and become good friends again."

"Listen, Chiam, I'm telling it to you now, and I mean it. Either she goes or I go. I won't stay here another night."

He pushed her into her room and closed the door. The two boys were sleeping quietly, and as Sam's wife looked at them her rage went away and she began to feel wretched. It was too early to go to sleep and she could not bring herself to go back to the hammocks with all the other women still there. She hoped Mrs. Klein at least would be coming up to her room, and she listened for the footsteps on the wood floor of the hall. The longer she remained alone the more uncomfortable did she feel with the place and embarrassed with herself. Mrs. Linck could not see herself going back in the morning to the easy routine of the life here. She couldn't stay another day, she said to herself, it was miserable. She had to make sacrifices for the children's sake, but she'd die if she had to stay another day. She would take the next bus back to New York. Even Mrs. Klein was deserting her. Mrs. Linck put on her nightgown and crept into bed with the boys, feeling terribly alone. She wanted to go to the bathroom but she was so spiritless now she was afraid of meeting any of the other women in the halls and she would not risk the trip.

Davey's mother did not understand him. After supper he sat in his bedroom going carefully through the dictionary, and when she asked him what he was doing he said he was studying so that when he went back to school soon he wouldn't have forgotten all he had learned. "A blessing on your little head," his mother said fondly, and Davey went on searching through the dictionary with industrious zeal, looking for words like "womb," "bastard," and "bitch." Bastard, *n.*, was child begotten and born out of wedlock; an animal of inferior quality or breed; a kind of hawk formerly used in falconry; a coarse brown sugar made from syrup previously boiled. Was that right? Maybe he didn't have the right word. Bastard was a dirty word. He looked down the page. Bastard elm, the hackberry. Bastardize, *v.t.*, to make or prove to be a bastard. Well, that was a help. Bastard mahogany, an Australian tree of the myrtle family. Bastard type, bastardy, baste, bastile (or bastille), bastinado, bastion, basto. What did bastard mean anyhow? You're a dirty bastard. That wasn't right. Maybe it was bastid. No. Try womb. *N.*, the uterus of a female. What did that mean? Large or deep cavity. A cavity was a hole in your tooth. That was crazy. Bitch, *n.*, the female of the dog. What of it? Did this book have . . . ? Davey thumbed the pages anxiously. No. Maybe. . . ? No. Those were really dirty words. You could tell. Even the dictionary didn't have them.

Davey was disappointed. Once he had caught a glimpse of a small book of cartoons. It was ingenious. You held the pages in your fingers and flipped them rapidly. A man and a woman did strange things in a bathtub together. You could stop the action at interesting points and examine them carefully, as they did sometimes in the movies. Davey wished he had the book. The dictionary was nothing. All the kids on the block said there was a lot to find in it, but that was a lie.

"What time is it, Momma?" he called. He had almost forgotten.

"It's after seven, little son. Stop already," his mother said with glowing solicitude. "You studied enough for tonight. Go outside and play."

It was getting late. Davey ran down the steps and walked around the block to Cheap Simon's. It was still daylight and there was nothing doing. Across the street from Cheap Simon's another candy store had opened. The trade at this point was always so brisk that competitors were easily attracted, but they never lasted long. No matter how they cut their prices, no matter what tricks they used, Cheap Simon's always triumphed and drove them out in a month. Only Simon could present on the long counters that ran in a great L the delicious chocolates, the oozy fillers, black-and-whites, the varied assortment. If the candy man across the street started a contest with baseball pictures for souvenirs all Simon had to do was to sell black-and-whites three for a cent and the news traveled. It didn't make any difference what the trick was, or how good it was, the important thing was the candy itself.

The night grew and the darkness descended gently, but the streets remained unexciting. Davey bought two cents' worth of the rolls with the hard marshmallow centers. They were good. You chewed and chewed until the saliva in your mouth accumulated. Then you could spit as though it were tobacco juice. Davey walked around in the store until he bunked into Solly Leparbow. Solly was arrogant. His father gave him a great deal of spending money. He was rich. Last Christmas he had been given a Ranger bicycle with electric lamp, horn, and tool kit. Solly's teeth had sharp, rotten-brown points, and everyone said it was because he ate too much candy.

"Where's all the excitement?" Davey asked. "You guys are always talking about Cheap Simon's and the girls. I don't see nothing here."

"It's too early. What's the matter with you?" Solly knew the nightlife here and was an old-timer. His hair was slicked brilliantly back and he wore a purple-colored tie in a tight knot that must have been choking him. The skin at his neck was pushed up in wrinkles resting on the collar, for this was the fashion. "Nobody gets down here before nine," he confided generously, "and things don't get going until after ten."

"Say, listen, Solly, I don't know my way around here. I've been hanging around the bakery on South First Street. I was wondering, since you know everybody here, I was wondering whether you wouldn't sort of show me around."

"Sure," said Solly. "Only, don't expect me to do too much. I work fast." He smiled with self-assurance. "I don't hang around here all the time. You'll miss me soon."

"Oh, that's all right. All I need is a start and I can do the rest. Say, who's this broad, Ida, I been hearing so much about?"

"She's not half bad. Have you felt her tits yet?"

"I told you. I ain't been hanging around here."

"Yare, I forgot. Well, I certainly can tell you stories about Ida, but I got to get along. I'll see you later."

"Don't forget. I'll be looking for you."

Solly Leparbow, the gent with a flourishing past, moved off, working his gait after the approved fashion. The proper walk was a shuffle in which the hips rolled and the legs came out at tangents. Anyone who walked around that way was no kid, he knew the answers. The night came down, and Davey, waiting on the curb, was almost trembling with nervous excitement. This was going to be the first time, he was exploring altogether new territories, and the prospect made him shiver.

The great bulbs of Cheap Simon's sent white, dazzling light into the street, and in the candy store across the way the lamps were even larger. The whole area was lit brilliantly, but off to the right were the dark buildings of the public school. That was why South Third Street at Cheap Simon's was so popular. It had all the advantages, bright lights, the candy stores, and, most important, by going the short distance to the school one was alone and hidden by the darkness. To the left a big wagon now took its position and its radio filled the street with resounding jazz. This was one of the more progressive contraptions that were taking the place of the merry-go-rounds. A huge metal basket was pushed like a swing to the accompaniment of the radio and all the kids on the block nagged their mothers madly for money with which to buy rides. Davey felt as though it were a festival, the middle of the street growing alive with boys and girls, the white lights shining over the pavements, and the music emptying over the scenes. Davey walked to the center of the group of children, but he hesitated. They knew one another, played running games, and were busy. Davey was an outsider and found it difficult for him to intrude and take part in the activity. He wished Solly Leparbow was back to lead him.

A dozen boys began playing Johnnie-on-the-pony. Six of them served as the pony by bending forward and clasping knees tightly. Their backs made a straight line for the others to straddle. They were having a great time with the game for more reasons than one. Boy followed boy, taking running starts and leaping as far possible forward until the last jumper had barely enough room to hold on. The riders clutched fast to the boys in front of them. As they slipped off their perches, they swiftly chanted, "Johnnie-on-the-pony, one, two, three. Johnnie-on-the-pony, one, two, three. Johnnie-on-the-pony, one, two, three—all off!" And if no one had fallen off during this time the riders won, they could go on using the six other boys for the horse. The catch in the game was that the six boys who formed the pony began fighting among themselves for the privilege of being the first. This was because the first boy rested his head against a girl's belly for a pillow and it was an edifying experience. They all wanted to be first, and the game broke up. While they were fighting it out the pillow walked off, resenting the innuendo as it became more and more inescapable.

And now Ida, the glorious young cow, Ida took her stance directly in the middle of the street, in the cross radiance of the two candy-store lights, that she might show off her charms to greatest advantage. Everyone knew her here and it took little to tell. Her lips and cheeks were heavily rouged, her straight black hair was curled fiercely, but it protested, and she hobbled on high-heeled shoes like a cripple. Everyone here knew her, and for that reason the more adept bloods disregarded her as too easy game. But she held a coterie, mainly newcomers breaking in and swarms of kids. To the newcomers she spoke brazenly, with anger manifest in her tone no matter what they might be saying. Altogether she was a savage individual. The kids were like mosquitoes. Perhaps that was why she seemed so continuously belligerent for they ran around her in sudden sallies to catch her unawares, attacking the broad flesh of her behind in hasty pinches and smacks. The kids bubbled with joyous excitement, but Ida swore harshly she would break their little necks, those goddam dirty little rats. From time to time one of the newcomers thought the moment had come and he pushed her abruptly around to say something, and as if by accident his hand swept the delicate lines of her breast. It was the established technique for beginners, but Ida howled promptly.

"Don't try that on me!" she shot back. "I know those tricks. If you want to get funny I'll get my boyfriend around and he'll break your head open, you think you're so smart."

The boy protested with wide-eyed innocence, what was she talking about, he didn't have the slightest idea, it was an accident anyhow, but he was happy because a beginning had been made and now he was ready for the next step. Now he would select a girl, approach her, talk smoothly, suggest Cheap Simon's and a quiet retreat to the school to munch their candy. As for Ida, pinched and continually shoved around by the shoulder as if by accident, she felt vaguely that she wasn't getting anywhere, but there was excitement enough for her, and she was happy as she turned to the shy offerings of the next customer.

Davey, standing alone and forlorn, had forgotten all about the grander passions and Yetta. Natie the Buller was a kid who had a long way to go. All he knew now was that a girl's breast was a great thing, and he was intensely eager to begin. Where was Solly? It was getting late, and if he didn't get home soon his mother would be giving him Hail Columbia for staying out so late, but Davey couldn't leave. Where was Solly? Why didn't he show up? Davey trembled with the tickling sensations, he ached to be one of those complacent boys who talked and played so glibly with the girls. They knew what they wanted and they got it. Two fellows had bicycles. They sped up and down the block and went around in circles. One offered a girl a ride, persisted while she coyly deliberated. Finally he went off with the lassie of his choice sitting, not on the handlebars, but gallantly on the backbone shaft. As they passed out of sight down the block the girls on the sidewalk closed their eyes and smiled to themselves while the boys guffawed without restraint. Bicycles took girls to McCarren Park or the Bridge Plaza, to trees and secluded grassy spaces, and a fellow had a good time.

In the great light and in the din the boys started a new game. They went running after one another in a simple game of tag, but "it" was the girls. The fellows chased through the streets, careful that their paths took them through groups of girls where anything might be allowed because it was a game. They bumped and grabbed. The girls, however, were no fools; they understood the point and soon they were chasing in their turn. But this made the game better. Everyone went running around in mad circles, and Davey, standing at the side, trembled. Should he join them? Should he wait for Solly Leparbow? His hands were itching.

What the hell? said Davey in a spurt of determination. I can't stand here all night until my mother bawls hell out of me. He scrambled recklessly among them. And now, with the initial burst of spirit ebbing, the fine problem arose: did he have the nerve to make a pass at one of the girls? He had never been so excited before in all his life. Davey ran and ran but he could not bring himself to brush into the girls. The curves of their breasts protruded tantalizingly, he wanted to press them, and there it was, always holding him back. When he passed through a group of girls he drew his body sharply to the side and his hands were kept out and away. It was a test, a challenge. Davey had to get through with this part, and tonight. He had to screw up the courage somehow. A merry-go-round anchored a short distance down the block and the tinny melodies filled the air. The Italian with his loud watermelon cries moved slowly up the street. The lights beamed. Dazzled by the rays, their heads swimming with the great clatter of noise, the boys and girls ran over the pavements as though they had gone insane. Overhead the sky with a million star points gazed down upon them patient and unheeded. Davey's breath came fast. What the hell! he said. What the hell! But in spite of his defiance he carefully decided to pick on Ida first. She would be the easiest, she would make the least trouble. Davey ran with the others. He passed Ida once. Twice. What the hell! Davey cried, this time almost aloud, and he went straight for her. He pretended his foot stumbled, his hand went out and with unerring aim, he grabbed the ball of flesh. He pressed hard. Ida gasped. "You dirty pig!" she squealed, and went after him. Davey caught himself and she ran into his chest. As they struggled Davey's hands worked rapidly. It felt soft and it was hard to stop.

"What's the matter with you?" he asked with surprise.

"Listen," she panted, "you can't get away with that. I know what you were trying to do. Don't think I'm dumb."

"What's the matter? I know I bunked into you. All right, I bunked into you. It was an accident. I almost fell, but what of it?"

"You think you're smart, don't you?" Ida said. She was having trouble with her breath.

Davey felt masterly. It was easy, it was done, and now an inspiration came. "Take it easy, baby," he said like Adolphe Menjou in the movies. "Don't hurry. I can wait until you get your breath."

That left Ida stumped. She didn't know exactly what to say, no one had ever tried that on her before.

"Listen, girlie," Davey said, taking advantage of her confusion, "don't get mad at me. I'm not a bad fellow at all. We can have some fun together."

"Oh, yare? You should live so," she said weakly. "Oh, yare?"

"Yare," Davey said suavely.

He had to be going and he walked off, but on the way home he walked with a jaunty step. He felt sure of himself and confident. Once he broke the movement of his stride and started dancing with delight. He did it! He wasn't a kid. He knew what it was all about. Yetta made him laugh. She makes me laugh, he said as he thought of her. Who did she think she was anyway? Natie the Buller made him laugh too. He had to grow up. Could you imagine, he was in love with Marion Davies! Davey was a man at last, free to move in the adult circles of South Third Street at night, a connoisseur of women, a person done with childishness. What is love? Davey said as he turned into Ripple Street. What is love? A load of crap.

He tried to sneak into his bedroom without waking his mother, but as he opened the door there she was in her nightgown, waiting for him, pent up with worry and with anger. "Where have you been?" she asked through her teeth. "What were you doing all night?" She had forgotten all about his energetic studying before and now she bawled him out fiercely.

"What a darling girl, what a darling girl. I'm lucky to have a girl like you."

Ruth put her arms around Philip's neck because she didn't want him to see her smiling with the pleasure at what he said. But he saw her and teased.

"You like that, don't you, baby? You're a pig. You'd want me to say those things all day and all night."

"Shut up," she said. "Don't bother me. Look, you say another word and I'll never kiss you again."

Philip pressed her down on the bed, holding her face in his palms. She smiled at him and he shook her head.

"What are you looking at me for?" she asked.

Philip did not answer but smiled back. She was a lovely girl. Her shoulders were small like a child's, but the flesh was smooth, round, and warm. He kissed them in the hollows near the arms while she lost herself in dreaminess with the sensation. Her hands were in his hair as he went over her, kissing the delightful flesh. Her belly was soft and tender. He dug his head into it until she cried in protest. Philip turned her over. Her body was relaxed; she remained impassive to his every move. His hands felt big. She was his, he could enjoy himself with her in whatever fashion he wished. Now he examined with minute care the formation of her shoulder blades, the spine, the back running through the channel of her hips into her bottom. Her little buttocks were pink and round like a baby's. He was enormously pleased with them. He began by kissing and caressing the soft flesh, but soon his fingers grasped and pressed.

"Don't do that," she said. "Come on up here."

As their bodies pressed into one another she uttered a little gasp from the shivering sensations, and tickling waves ran down her body. She fitted neatly into his arms and shoulder.

"Some day I'm going to slice off a piece of your bottom. I'm going to fry it and have some for dinner."

"I'm sleepy," she said, her eyes closed. "Let's sleep."

They settled comfortably. The day had been hot, but with both the light and dark shades drawn the room was dim and cool. They lay on the bed with no cover. Philip had wondered whether she would come to the apartment, worrying whether he himself ought to be doing this to her. It was a little too much for her. Ruth was so young. But, in the end, he had been waiting in Charlie Nagleman's living room, going through the shelves for books to while away the time that passed in achingly slow seconds until she appeared. She was wearing a soft summer print, a dark background with a white flower design, with a bolero jacket. She carried her hat in her hand and in her hesitancy she resembled more than ever a startled child. "I'm scared," she had said, standing near the door for comfort. "I'm so scared. Can't you hear my heart?" Philip had embraced her. "Don't worry, baby." Her fear genuinely distressed him. "Don't worry. We won't do anything you don't like." "Not now," she had said. "I really shouldn't have come. Not today."

Waiting for her to recover herself, Philip had tried to talk casually. They drank ginger ale and smoked cigarettes. It was hot. Their clothes chafed their skin. "We'll lie on the bed. It'll be more comfortable." She had looked at him, her eyes big with apprehension. "I really shouldn't have come," she said, and fretted. "You can trust me," Philip had said. "It's just to be cool." But once their clothes were off and they lay on the bed, Ruth was again herself, simple and spontaneous. The bed was placed against the wall and she took delight in running her feet up in ridiculous postures until Philip scolded her. "You're a child," he had said. "Don't you realize that you're lying in bed with a man? This might be a great day in your life, you might be made into a woman. What dignity is there in a woman of affairs to be running her feet up the wall?" She laughed, disregarded him, and began singing. "Stop it," Philip said with real concern. "The people next door will get ideas in their heads and you'll get Charlie in a jam with his folks." "You're just a joy killer," Ruth said. "You've got no romance in you," Philip said. "You're a kid. You should be wearing a chemise that's rolled over your titties." "Don't be silly," she said. "Nobody wears chemises anymore."

Philip waked and listened to her regular breathing. He was still holding her and woke because his arm was growing a little numb. He pressed her close to him, feeling her breasts against his chest. Ruth stirred. "Can't breathe," she said, her eyes still closed. "What are you doing to me? I can't breathe." Her eyes opened. They lay apart now, side by side, looking into each other's eyes.

"Now," said Philip, and waited.

Ruth closed her eyes. "It won't be much," he said. "It's nothing." He could feel Ruth stiffening, and much as he wanted to have her, he knew he couldn't. There was too much responsibility attached to it. It was ridiculous to think of it in this way, Philip thought, but he loved her so much it was inconceivable for him to hurt her.

"Don't worry, baby," he said. "I'll get along without it."

She brought his hand to her face and rubbed it against her cheek, kissing it thoughtfully. "It's getting late," she said. "Let's get up or I'll be having a great time explaining."

"It's not late. What time is it?"

He liked the way she went fumbling through his trousers for his watch. She had trouble with the pockets. "I never heard of a man keeping his watch in his pants," she said. The watch said six-thirty. "Whoops," she said. "Here's where I get hell." She raced into her clothes.

"What's it all about? What's the hurry?"

Ruth waited until her face was hidden under the dress as she got into it. She didn't know how to tell him. "It's this way," she said. "I've got to go to Vermont tomorrow morning. This is a sort of family farewell dinner."

Philip, smoking a cigarette in bed, was stunned. After this . . .

"Vermont? You didn't say anything. How long?"

"Philip, I can't help it. You know how my folks are. They want me to spend the rest of the summer at my sister's camp."

"That means September," Philip said. It was going to be a long time. How could she do this to him? "That means September," he said.

"It can't be helped. Philip, you know how I feel about this. You don't think I want to go?"

"You never said anything about this trip. Has this anything to do with me?"

"Of course not. What makes you say that?"

"Your mother's doing this."

"Don't be foolish."

Philip sat up on the bed with sudden force and faced her. "Ruth," he said, "I want to know. Your mother knows I've been seeing you. Is this all her idea?"

"No," she said, protesting painfully. "What ever put that into your head?"

"You're lying. I can tell you're lying."

Ruth stopped and looked at him. "Don't be unreasonable," she said. "I'll hate you if you're going to be like this."

Philip was furious, but he spoke coldly. "Tell me this, Ruth. Will your lovely mother let me see you in September?"

"Philip, that's no way to talk. Of course we'll see each other again. Don't be so angry with me. I can't help it. It's not for long."

She held his head to her bosom. "Darling," she said. "Darling, don't be angry. I'll miss you just as much."

Philip knew his great romance was being finished. He had expected it, he thought, he had expected it, and already he was getting philosophical and humorous over its passing.

Tessie opened the baby grand piano for the first time in days. The Spanish shawl slipped off the polished wood but that did not worry her; the floor was clean. She adjusted the lights so that brown rays were washed against the walls. That was indirect lighting and it was very effective. For moods. Tessie picked up the shawl and draped it around her body. She took off her bathrobe, the shawl looked so funny with the bathrobe showing beneath. Now her legs under the shawl showed pleasantly. She went into the bedroom to get the whole picture at once in the vanity-table mirror. This was gorgeous. All her friends said it was gorgeous. You sat down on the chair and played the folding mirrors at the sides in all directions and you could see yourself simultaneously in three views.

Tessie stood in front of the table. She arched her neck and fixed her body in piquant postures. Was she really pretty? You could never tell by looking in a mirror. You never could really see how you looked in a mirror because then the face wore a strained unnatural expression. The shawl slipped over her shoulder. That was more interesting. Like the movies. With her dark complexion and her black hair combed back smoothly, she looked like a Spanish señorita. Like the ones on the calendar pictures. Tessie let the shawl slip further and arranged it becomingly so that the breast showed to advantage. She looked into the mirror, her face absorbed with interest. The shawl revealed a brassiere, not a breast. Tessie was on the point of loosening the brassiere when she caught herself suddenly. "What's the matter with me anyhow?" she said aloud, and dropped the shawl. She got into her bathrobe again.

Schlausser was coming back this evening. He had been away a long time. They had never even had a proper honeymoon. Just a three-day weekend at Atlantic City. Tessie went back to the living room. She fixed the books and magazines and arranged the sheets of music according to their impressiveness. No one could miss the French edition of Debussy. She couldn't play it very well, but the cover had the strange words with the peculiar accent marks. Tessie surveyed the room. It was warm, cozy, and yet refined. Not a vulgar note, she said to herself, thinking of the woman in Mr. Hergesheimer's novel and feeling like the lady in the mattress advertisement.

Schlausser.... At least he appreciated her. Tessie thought of Philip with softness but with reproach. He never seemed to have understood her. The truth was he resented her marriage, he was jealous. He didn't understand. A girl had to get married, but was marriage so important? Well, she said, I just won't think of it. Enough. I've had enough. She went briskly to the bedroom to change, and here the problem arose: should she wear pajamas or a dress? The print she liked so much? That was why she liked Schlausser. She really liked him, she told herself. He was appreciative and noticed everything she did. All Tessie had to do was to frown, perhaps, and immediately there he was asking whether anything was the matter. When she was with him she was conscious all the time of his eager gratitude if she was nice or his unhappiness when she became irritable with him and silent.

In a sudden wave of feeling Tessie resolved to become a good wife to him. He was, after all, so good to her. In her mind she pictured him after the image of the preoccupied businessman, hard and ruthless, the businessman who worked intensely all day to provide his wife with pleasures so that he might come home in the evenings to enjoy her gentleness, her culture, and her beauty. Those were the things that Schlausser missed in his own life, he was a hard and ruthless businessman, and he turned to her to provide him with the better things in life.

Tessie decided on the pajamas with the navy blue jacket, but on top of that she would wear an apron. Two in one. Like the shoe polish, she laughed. She liked Schlausser, she said. He was a dear. She took the pajamas out of the closet.

Schlausser's key turned in the door.

"Abie?" she called from the bedroom. "I'll be out in a minute. How are you, dear?"

"Fine, sweetheart, just fine and dandy." He beamed. Even in the bedroom Tessie felt it and began already to make allowances for his crudeness because tonight she felt so sympathetic. She strode out of the room with her arms outstretched to seize his hands. But the sight of Schlausser somewhat unnerved her. He was no businessman, hard and ruthless, and so on. She had almost forgotten he was such a short-sized man. He had loosened his collar on account of the heat. It was wilted and curled at the ends. Behind the brass collar button the unshaved hair of his throat stuck out against the moist whiteness. It was a little ugly.

"My, my," he said with enthusiasm. "What a lady I married. I never saw such a pretty one. Aren't you going to kiss me?"

"Of course," Tessie said, and gave him her cheek.

"Ah," said Schlausser with satisfaction. He stood off to look at her, and he shook his head with pleasure. "It certainly is good to see you again. Oh, I almost forgot." He brought out a box of candy and a copy of *Vanity Fair*. "I thought you would like these."

Tessie fussed over the presents. He was really so kind and well intentioned. "You shouldn't have gone to the trouble," she scolded. "A person might think you were still coming to see me as if we weren't married."

Schlausser laughed. "That's right. I feel as if I was still courting you or something."

"Come, Abie," she said. "You must be hungry."

"Oh, this is a surprise. I thought I would take you to a restaurant for supper and then we'd go to a show. I wanted to give you a good time. You're a darling."

"Don't be foolish," Tessie said. "Did you think I'd let you run around the hot city tonight right after you'd come home tired from the road? Come to dinner."

He took off his jacket. While he washed in the bathroom he did not interrupt the flow of conversation, there were so many things to say. He had missed her so much. What had happened to that fellow, what's his name, Cohen, the one who had jumped off the bridge? Business wasn't so good this trip but he couldn't kick. It was nice to get home to a clean, home-like home. "This is the life," he asserted as Tessie handed him the towel. "It's different from when I was a bachelor. Just a little different, ain't it?"

He went into the kitchen. He praised the tomato soup extravagantly.

"Don't be silly," Tessie said. "It's from a can."

"I don't believe it!"

"Everybody buys canned soup these days. In the morning just look at the garbage cans outside the incinerator. They're full of black soup cans."

When the pot roast came Schlausser could not be checked. "You can't tell me this comes from a can," he maintained with triumph. "In all my life I never ate such tasty pot roast, not even in the fanciest restaurants."

Tessie was pleased in spite of herself. "Everyone says it's hard for a newlywed to learn how to cook, but it's really nothing."

"Well," he said with determination, "I'd like to hear somebody say my wife can't cook."

After dinner they went into the softly lit living room. Schlausser sat down significantly on the couch but Tessie took her place in one of the chairs. He looked at the piano, the etchings on the wall, and the furniture. It was all his. He owned it, together with his refined wife who knew all about fixing up elegant homes. On the road he told all his friends about her. "She finished high school in three and a half years," he always boasted.

"Come here, Tessie darling," he said in a low voice.

She thought it over and finally came to sit next to him. She waited. She could feel his arms creeping around her shoulder. Not yet, Tessie said to herself, it was too early for that now. She stiffened a little to indicate that he was too hasty.

"Tessie," he said softly into her ear, "sometimes I feel like a stranger in my own house. I don't see you every night like the other husbands, and you can laugh at me, Tessie, but sometimes when I'm traveling all alone by myself on the road, from one hole to the next, I say to myself, I wonder what my wife is doing right this minute now. I try to make pictures in my head. Maybe you're walking to the movies with your sister Bertha. Maybe you're fixing up the house. Something like that. If you knew how I miss you, how I worry about you . . . Tessie." His hand rubbed her shoulder in regular movements.

"Why should you worry?" Tessie said. "What do you mean? Don't be foolish."

"I like you so much. You'll laugh, but when a man's by himself so much he gets to thinking all kinds of things. He worries about his wife. Of course, there's nothing to think about, but when I say to myself, you're so beautiful, I'm away so long, maybe, who can tell?"

"Listen," Tessie said in angry protest, "if you think anything like that about me, you ought to be ashamed of yourself. What kind of a girl do you think I am anyhow? Just to have those ideas about me is an insult."

"Oh, Tessie, Tessie, don't say another word about it. I wouldn't hurt your feelings for all the money in the world. I was just saying how I felt. You can realize how I feel about you when I'm so far away from you. I'm alone all the time, I miss you so much."

Tessie put her hand on his head and ran her fingers through his hair. It felt greasy, and when she withdrew her hand two or three hairs, curled and shiny, clung to her fingers. She brushed her hand on his shirt.

Schlausser drew her to him with force and started pressing. She laughed sharply and pulled herself away. "You hurt me," she said. "You're strong."

"Look, Tessie," he said, "look here." He pointed to the pillow at his knee, but there was nothing. But when she bent forward her breasts hung loosely down and he could see the nipples clearly. Schlausser put his hand inside the neck of the pajamas and his fat fingers pressed her breasts softly, one after the other. Tessie took his hand out and arose.

"It's all right," Schlausser protested. "I'm your husband."

"So soon after dinner?" she asked.

"What difference does that make?" Schlausser giggled uncertainly. He went to the closet where his coat was hung and came back puffing a cigar. All right, he was no pig, he could wait. Tessie walked to the piano and sat down on the bench. He was crude. Philip was not like that at all. For a moment her mind dwelt on Philip with regret but she forced herself not to think of him. She bent over the music on the rack. Schlausser was her husband, he was a little clumsy, but he was so kind. Now she meant to run her fingers casually and lightly over the piano keys for his benefit, and she hunted through the sheets of music for something she knew she could handle.

"Play something, darling," he said. He was sitting in a chair this time, his legs crossed, nonchalant and patient with his cigar. He was no pig, he could wait.

He should not have told her to play something, it destroyed the effect, but Tessie tried to blind her mind to it. She played Mendelssohn's "Songs Without Words." Her face grew sad and intense with the music. She played with feeling but the stiff choppiness of the notes made it seem as though a child were at the piano. Schlausser smoked his cigar, satisfied and completely content because his homecoming had been so carefully welcomed. She had taken care of every detail, the lights, the dinner, and now the piano. What a pretty picture she made, with the piano lid in the air. Schlausser enjoyed the music, but his mind was deliciously concerned with other prospects.

SIXTEEN

PHILIP'S MOTHER MADE A special visit to Mrs. Linck's flat as soon as she heard the report. When she opened the door the thick, stuffy janitress-smell rose up like a wave, but she stepped in resolutely. Actually she was a little afraid of the massive creature flopping in her gorgeous kimono and capable of such enormous wrath, but her task today was something she felt deeply and she couldn't postpone it. Mrs. Hayman invaded the dinginess strong with resolve, but suddenly she had the sickening sensation of stepping on soft flesh. She stumbled and could not restrain a small shriek. It was one of the guinea pigs.

"Watch out, please," the janitress said from her rocker. The jelly-like flesh shuddered in rhythm. "Everybody walks in here like it was a fire. Their days are numbered, the poor little beasts."

"Hello," said Mrs. Hayman uncertainly. "I just came in for a minute. There's something on my mind."

"All right!" the janitress exploded. It must have been a bad day for her. "What is it now? Everbody in the house has a complaint. Some people can never be satisfied. If it's not hot water, it's a window that needs to be fixed. All day they run to me like I am God. I can't do everything with two hands at the same time, but, no, I'm the janitor, they pay rent, and everyone is entitled to seize a piece of my meat."

Mrs. Hayman protested. "I got no complaint. Don't get so

excited. I came to ask a favor not for myself but for someone else. It's about Mrs. Sussman. Now, Mrs. Linck, it's none of my business, I can't tell you what to do, but really, Mrs. Linck, how can a person bother her now? You can wait a little while."

"So?" the janitress said savagely. "Already everybody knows I'm going to ask her for the rent. All you have to do here is to say one small word and in a minute everybody knows what's going on. In all my experience as a janitor in other houses I never saw such rotten people."

"Don't work yourself up. It's nothing. Only, you can see this for yourself," she begged. "Mrs. Sussman has had a great misfortune. She just came back from God knows what, she's had enough trouble already, why can't we give her a little peace for a minute? The poor woman never goes past the door, she's so afraid. We mustn't be like that."

Mrs. Linck arose from the rocker abruptly. The bulky figure stood up in front of Mrs. Hayman like a wall. "Listen," she said fiercely, "nobody's going to tell me how to run my business. Who does Mrs. Sussman think she is? Just because her husband took gas it's no reason why she shouldn't pay rent like anybody else. Let the street Yentes talk all they want to, I'll show them. I'm going up right this minute, and either she pays me the rent or out she goes."

Why doesn't she wash her face sometimes? Mrs. Hayman asked herself with disgust. "Please," she begged, "please. Can't you wait another day?"

Mrs. Linck marched, swollen with anger, up the steps. As she traveled, the curses and mutterings came from her ceaselessly. Everyone in the house thought she was a hard-hearted person because she tried to make her living. Who was Mrs. Sussman? A prima donna? What did she do? Just because her husband was in the grave, what kind of an excuse was it? Mrs. Linck's own husband lay dead but nobody lifted a finger to make her work easier. The people in this house were all flesh-grabbers. Everyone pinched flesh from her. They just wanted to tear her apart.

Mrs. Sussman lived high up on the fourth floor. As Philip's mother followed the janitress up the hallway she grew dizzy from the turns. Mrs. Linck's breath came now in hard-won gasps. She waddled to the door with ruthless defiance. Scorning the electric bell, she knocked on the door. Mrs. Hayman waited with her and said in a whisper, "Please, please, Mrs. Linck. It's a sin. You can't do it."

"Open the door, missus," Mrs. Linck shouted, disregarding Mrs. Hayman completely. "It's me. Open the door."

She listened, but there wasn't a sound from the flat.

"I know you're inside," she screamed. "Don't make believe. You can't fool me." She shifted her huge body and held her ear to the door carefully. Then one of Mrs. Sussman's boys began crying with fright. Mrs. Hayman could hear the way the child tried to restrain the sobs, but they came. The janitress had a spasm of anger.

"Open!" She screamed. "What's the matter inside? Open the door."

Now they heard the sharp clicks of Mrs. Sussman's heels on the wooden floor. Light and slow, the feet were bringing her to the door. It opened carefully. Mrs. Hayman hurried to beat the janitress to the first word. She smiled warmly and said with cordial feeling, "Mrs. Sussman! How are you? How are the children?" But she had to stop, Mrs. Sussman looked so haggard and sick. Mrs. Linck opened her mouth. Philip's mother, overcome by compassion, forgot her fear and shot her a fierce look of reproach, but it did no good.

"See here," Mrs. Linck said, speaking rapidly. "I'm sorry I have to talk like this, but a woman can't walk into a flat like you did and take rooms without saying as much as good morning to me. I'm the janitor. After all, troubles are troubles, everybody has his share, but the world can't go under just because you've had a misfortune. You must pay rent like everyone else, Mrs. Sussman."

The poor woman, thin, pale, and unsteady on her feet, simply stood in her confusion. Her long hair, well cared for even after her husband's death, was caught now in a hasty knot at the back and the strands escaped unattended. She looked as though she had just stepped from the grave herself. Mrs. Hayman couldn't endure the situation. She turned on the janitress bitterly.

"How can a person have such a black heart! Have you no feeling, woman, no pity? You should be ashamed, you should be ashamed of yourself! Why don't you go away and leave this poor woman alone? She's got enough misery on her heart, you shouldn't add to it. It's a sin, Mrs. Linck, God will never forgive you for this."

Coming from Mrs. Hayman, the outburst halted her. Mrs. Linck lamely muttered, "Never mind, never mind, I want the rent, and if it isn't here today the marshal will be here in the morning." She pushed her thick legs down the steps heavily, talking vigorously to herself for support. Mrs. Linck felt abashed.

"Thanks," Mrs. Sussman said tremulously. "I don't know what to do." Still holding the door by the knob, she looked into her rooms and then back again at Mrs. Hayman, and then she began to cry. Philip's mother put an arm around her and took her inside. She apologized brokenly for the state of disorder, it seemed to worry her even now, but Mrs. Hayman sat her down until the tears passed. What a contrast, she had to note. Mrs. Sussman used to keep her home cleaner than anyone else, she had a reputation all over the block for the carefully polished furniture, the curtains, and her tidiness. "You can eat off her floor," they used to say, and now the room was a disordered mess. It was bare, pathetically bare. She sat on a box and that was the only article of furniture in the room. Off in a corner the big trunk stood half-emptied, the lid opened against the wall, with odd pieces of clothing hanging over the top. The unpainted, cracked boards of the floor were uncovered by linoleum. The wall closets were empty and dirty. There wasn't a curtain at the windows. The two boys, unwashed and in dirty clothes, sat wondering on the mattress which had been placed crudely on the floor. They looked like little animals with the scared, uncomprehending wonder in their eyes.

"It's terrible," Mrs. Sussman sobbed. "It's terrible," that was all she could say, and she cried with painful sobs, her face wrenched with grief. Mrs. Hayman, seeing all this for the first time, was miserable.

"Come, Mrs. Sussman," she broke out, "this is no way to be. You can't do this. I can't see it." She held the woman's head on her shoulder and rocked to comfort her as though she were a child. It was wretched.

"Alone, all alone in the world, always alone," Mrs. Sussman wept. "It's terrible, it's terrible."

Mrs. Hayman became determined. It had to stop. She picked up a towel from the washtub and ran water over one end. "Here," she said soothingly, "wash your face and stop crying. It's bad, but we have to go on living. Come, Mrs. Sussman, a person mustn't do this to herself. You're still a young woman, you must still be a mother to your children."

Mrs. Sussman blew her nose and stared hopelessly before her. There was something wild in her desperation and it worried Mrs. Hayman. The two boys and their mother all looked like wild animals, hunted, frantic, and in torment. Mrs. Hayman tried to console her in a running stream of gentle rebuke and advice. She busied herself around the room trying to set things in order. God knows what they live on, she thought. The poor creatures, the poor things. The gas connection had not been made, there was only a loaf of hard rye bread and some cans of salmon.

Mrs. Hayman cleaned the bathtub, picked up the two boys, and gave them a wash together. She rummaged in the trunk for clean clothes. Dressed in fresh summer suits, they took heart and grew a little cheerful. As Mrs. Hayman combed their hair she hummed softly the old songs she had used for her sons.

"It's such a long time," she said to Mrs. Sussman. "I haven't sung these songs for fifteen years already. Now my boys are big. Time passes, everything goes. In my time terrible things happened too, they hurt deeply, but we went on living. You cannot keep them to heart all the time."

"Everything's upset. Look at my house," Mrs. Sussman said. It still worried her. She was calm now but her body still drooped with hopelessness. "I don't know what to do first. I haven't got the strength to make a beginning. My money I left over there, in Butte. The gas is turned off, Mrs. Linck wants rent, I got to fix up the house—it's too much. I don't know where to start. The night falls and there's no electric, so I sit in the dark until I go crazy. The mice run over the children on the mattress, and I can't go and get the beds and the furniture from storage. All day I sit and do nothing. It's too much to do, I don't know where to start." Mrs. Sussman shook her head with grief.

"Hush," Philip's mother said. "Don't worry. That's the least of your troubles. With a little help, everything will be all right in no time. In another day your house will be fixed up just like before. Only don't worry."

She went down to cook dinner in her kitchen for them. When she left Mrs. Sussman had seemed to have regained some courage. She had begun unpacking the trunk and was quiet. Nevertheless, Mrs. Hayman worried. It was strange, there was something strange about Mrs. Sussman, she couldn't understand the woman. It was the wild look of her face. Mrs. Hayman opened the door of her flat with a heavy feeling at her heart. Mrs. Sussman, the two boys on the mattress, the desolate house, it was truly terrible.

Philip Hayman said sharply, "Control yourself. What's all the excitement about? My God, Cohen, I've never seen you in such a state, and states are what you specialize in."

"You can say it," Cohen cried bitterly. "You've got the skin of a walrus. It's all the same to you. I'm sick and tired. I'm sick and tired. I wish I was dead, that's what. To hell with the whole world, to hell with you and your goddam smart-alecky cracks, to hell with everything. I'm through with the whole lot of you stinking goddam insensitive kiyoodles."

"Listen, Cohen," Philip said sympathetically, "I was just kidding. I didn't mean anything. When I came in here and asked you what made you go, I was interested in an academic problem in my mind. Perhaps I was taking advantage of you, but really, Cohen, I don't like to see you this way. We're all friends here. You ought to be able to take a joke from me."

He stopped weakly. What had made Cohen go off in such a tantrum tonight? Here he was, his pimply face screwed up in deep misery, his hands clenched at his sides with pain. Philip felt sorry he had provoked the outburst.

"Oh, dammit, dammit," Cohen said with despair, "I'm just sick and tired, the way everybody laughs at me. What am I anyway? The missing link? The perpetual joke?"

"Don't feel sorry for yourself," Philip said. "It's an ugly habit. Come on," he said, "we'll go to a beer garden. We'll sit in the evening breezes and you'll get over it." He felt repentant. Despondent himself and angry because of Ruth Kelman, Philip had walked into Cohen's room and had tried to relieve his stinging mood with biting questions about the Party and Shura. He had been nasty, but nevertheless Cohen's outburst had surprised him. In a wave of pity Philip now wanted to do something for Cohen, to cheer him up and set him in balance. Philip felt uncomfortable with himself because it was such a mean trick to mock a person like Cohen.

They sat in the cool backyard and Philip ordered dark beers. Cohen sulked, sufficient in his wretchedness unto himself. Profound depression, after a certain point, seizes the soul and renders a man imperturbable.

"What's the matter, Cohen?" Philip asked. "What is wrong, anyway? Don't you believe in the sacred duty of man anymore?"

"Mankind!" Cohen snorted with quiet bitterness. "What is mankind? The sum of the earth's asses. A composite great ass. The hell with them."

"How can a man change his point of view so rapidly?"

"Because it may happen that he learns rapidly. Listen, Hayman," Cohen said strongly, "humanitarian effort is concerned with unimportant things. It's an expression of sentimentality. Let's suppose the Party is successful and all social ideals have been reached. What happens then? A man has enough to eat and drink, and he has a place to sleep in. That takes care of his physical wants and goes no further. You may say that this stage, the Utopia, has not been reached and won't be for a long time, that there is so much good yet to do. Well, why should I excite myself doing something that is essentially unimportant? These people in the Party all give themselves, they have a wild full time with themselves, because it takes up all their energy and they are seriously occupied. But it has no meaning."

"Don't get violent," Philip said. "Take it easy."

Cohen, talking for a length of time, grew full of a feeling of power and self-confidence. He called to the waiter impressively.

"You got pickles here?" he asked. "Give me two pickles, round ones with warts all over them, you know."

The waiter was a kindly man. "Two pickles?" he said. "What do you want to eat pickles for? It don't go right, young man. Here you eat pretzels and drink beer. You'll get sick if you eat two pickles."

"Never mind," Cohen said. "I want pickles, I'll eat pickles. The hell with my stomach."

The waiter shrugged his shoulders and went to the kitchen.

"Now that's logical at least," Philip said. "I'm beginning to admire you. The waiter has a sense of social duty that you think is unimportant, and therefore you disregard it. I hope you eat the pickles and get good and sick. It completes the circle."

"Don't be clever," Cohen said resolutely. "You give me a stiff pain in the neck with your goddam smartness. I left the Party and its principles because a man learns. What do you expect me to do? Stagnate? Naturally I may seem to be erratic, but that is the by-product of progress. As I learn, I change."

"Progress, my eye. You move in circles. Two to one, I can tell you before you beat me to it, what the essential secret of life is now as you affirm it. It's poetry and beauty all over again, the indispensable endeavors of the civilized mind."

Cohen protested, but the waiter, cutting him off, placed the saucer with the pickles on the table. "I can still take them back if you changed your mind," he said.

"Listen," Cohen said impatiently, "I said pickles, and that's enough."

"All right, all right, don't get mad, young man. I only wanted to help."

Philip had to smile as he looked at Cohen. Witnessing Cohen's deep misery before, he felt that perhaps he had misunderstood Cohen, he had written him off too easily for a faker. But now it was the old Cohen, full of bull, and it was the old bull. When was Cohen ever sincere and how could anyone tell?

Cohen ate the pickles one after the other as if from urgent necessity. He would show the waiter, he would show Philip. He finished and sucked air through his teeth to clean them, and in a spirit of defiance loudly called down the garden for another two pickles. "Two more," he called with importance, "I want two more pickles." He felt masterly and turned to Philip.

"Poetry and beauty," he said. "Yes. Putting it like that, you think you've turned out another wisecrack. But wait a minute, Hayman. Let us suppose that Utopia has been realized, what would there be for men to do? There would be no need for social activity. There is no injustice, no suffering. What then? Well, you say, that's fine, those are the conditions for cultural activity. Truth and poetry and beauty. Yes, but I can't wait for Utopia, which won't be ever reached anyhow. I have a short time to live and I want my share of truth, poetry, and beauty. I want to occupy my mind in these things in which it is intimately interested, and I don't want to wait, building the understructure that will make these pursuits possible. I'll be dead by that time."

"'The pursuits of the mind, no matter how refined,'" Philip quoted maliciously, "'indicate a rotten character.' You said it."

Cohen had been raising his voice, the argument carrying him away. Everyone in the beer garden was looking at them. Now he almost exploded with irritation. "Can't you follow a line of reason? I said that before. I admit it. But I've changed my mind about these things. You make me sick."

"All right," Philip said. "Don't get violent all over again. Here, eat your pickles."

The waiter was still solicitous. "I don't like to say nothing, mister, but you're doing yourself no good. Don't come back here later and say you ate something bad in the food."

"Never mind," Cohen said. He was resentful and pushed the pickle into his mouth.

What had happened to Cohen? Philip asked himself. He had changed, sincere or insincere. Cohen seemed to be swollen with hurt and anger that burst out at the slightest prick. Within him he was raging with fierce bitterness. Philip even worried for him. He could easily picture Cohen going off in this state and doing himself serious harm. It was not a passing fit of despondency this time like the others. Cohen was pained, unsettled, and reckless. For one thing, he had never used such an aggressive tone to Philip personally. Cohen did not care, he was stung sharply, and he stormed without regard for anyone or for himself.

On the walk home Philip was careful not to start him off again. Philip tried to laugh it off. What mysterious springs were unwound in Cohen's head? he asked himself. What a strange mechanism he was, but Philip found it hard to think lightly of his condition. Actually, he recognized a deep change in his friend, an increase in intensity rather than change, and he worried because Cohen was too frail a person to contain such gigantic disorders without some disastrous consequences.

The waiter at the beer garden proved to be a true prophet. As soon as they reached his room Cohen lay on the bed face downward. His hands were helplessly at his forehead. He had flopped on the bed in gasping pain and now his legs stuck out over the cover in an awkward position.

"What's the matter?" Philip asked kindly. "Stomach kicking up?"

Cohen rubbed his chest to indicate he was having a heartburn. He lay stiff and waited for it to pass. There was nothing for Philip to do. He picked up a magazine and turned the pages, waiting for Cohen to recover. It was a copy of an artist-model sheet and it had the pictures.

After ten minutes Cohen rose silently and walked to the bathroom. Philip could hear him rinse his mouth. When he came back he looked shaken and his face was pale.

"How's it now?" Philip said. "You're all over with it?"

"Forget it," Cohen said in a subdued tone. "The hell with it."

Philip slapped the magazine against his knee. "By the way," he said, "what happened to your friend Shura? Did you have any luck?"

"The hell with her," Cohen cried, but he was too weak for

frenzy. "She's just an ordinary bitch. After this goddam heartburn all you have to do is mention her name and I'll puke."

After Philip left his room Cohen walked around while his despair welled within him until it grew savage. For a moment he had an insane impulse to destroy something, tear and break. He picked up a book and threw it to the floor with all his strength. He jumped on the book, stamping madly. There was no sense to it but he kept on. The woman in the flat below began knocking with a broomstick on her ceiling for quiet. The thumping made Cohen stop while he distinguished the noise and its meaning. He kicked the book into a corner. "Goddam," he wept, "Goddam." Even the waiter had pulled one on him, even the woman downstairs. Cohen took his glasses off, put them carefully on the dresser, and lay down on the bed and cried.

⁓⁓⁓

"Let's sit down, Tessie," Philip said. He chose a bench under a great tree on the little plaza that surrounded the park restaurant.

"What difference does it make whether we walk or sit?" Tessie asked. "You just keep quiet all the time. I can't say a word to you."

"That's ridiculous," he said. "You know it's ridiculous." He waited for Tessie to sit down and then joined her. He looked at the colors the setting sun produced on the lake. A duck with an aggressive bill proudly breasted the ripples as she swam, and a group of five ducklings followed in her wake. Four of them were sober and kept to the line, but the last was mischievously inclined. This one went off to the sides, examining with great curiosity floating twigs or pieces of Cracker Jack containers until a spasm of fright overtook him and he rushed back to the brood.

"Look at him. The little one at the end," Philip said. "He's comical."

"Philip," Tessie said, resolutely, refusing to look at the duckling, "I can't understand you. You know how lonely I am and yet I never see you." Her voice grew soft with reproach.

"Ah," said Philip, "let's not talk about that again. It gets tiresome."

He began to feel that Tessie was keeping after him in an odd sort of stubbornness. It was as though having once set herself into this position, she didn't know how to get out of it. Philip took out a pack of cigarettes.

"Will you smoke?" he asked.

Tessie took one, and he lit it for her with careful courtesy to show that he was meaning no offense. He leaned back. There were certain things that were said only to girls, and often they were ridiculous when you examined them in the cold light. He had told Ruth Kelman the story of the time he had first learned to put on his own shoes. It had been, of course, many years ago, but Philip remembered it because it had made such a sharp impression on him at the time. His mother had been busy washing clothes in the bathroom while he sat on the kitchen floor helplessly crying for her to hurry up. She had told him to wait, her hands were covered with suds, and in a fit of temper he had forced the shoes on, buttoned them laboriously, and finally stamped into the bathroom with defiant independence until his mother discovered he had the shoes on the wrong feet and laughed. "It's a precious story," Ruth had said, and later she would laugh to herself over it. "I keep on thinking of you standing in the bathroom with your shoes on the wrong feet," she said. Philip also told her of the time his mother was away and he had gone to the movies with his father. He was hungry and his father took him to a grocery store, bought him some cheese and a quarter of a loaf of rye bread, and gave it to him. Ruth had turned his face to her and kissed him when he told that story. "You must have been a sweet boy. I wish I could have seen you as you were as a boy," she said because the story made her feel tender toward him.

Philip told her about his father, how he had walked in his Palm Beach suit and Panama hat, with the white thick mustaches pointed up and curled. He had been a strong man then, and handsome. As long as Philip could remember his father he had had white hair, but it was full, in long waves, and beautiful. He used to go promenading on Sundays with a cane and observe the passing life with an aristocrat's detachment. Philip told her these intimate stories about his father, speaking fondly, and now he realized how foolish they might appear. A person acted differently at different times, and he felt foolish when he thought he might not have selected the proper part of him to suit the occasion. It was over, he felt, and Ruth had become an outsider, leaving him open to her ridicule if she was so disposed.

Philip felt his romance with Ruth was over, but he wasn't sure. He kept on revolving the chances in his mind until he grew annoyed with himself and his indecision. The letters will tell, he said, impatient with himself, I'll tell from her letters. He had deliberately said nothing about their correspondence while she was to be away, and he had been careful, too, not to note her address, so that she would have no excuse for failing to write him first. He wondered how soon she would write to him and what she would say.

The evening was passing. Most of the children had left the park, but the swills of peanut-shell dirt remained to line the paths. Young foreign-born men in shirtsleeves came down, singing to the accompaniment of guitars and mandolins as they sought girls. They were short and often pockmarked, but they had an air of gaiety. They had left their stifling close rooms to seek the cool air here and they felt they might as well combine pleasure with comfort. The sailors, on their night ashore unhappy in their lonely pairs, marched briskly, wistfully longing for dames. Here and there could be seen a couple engrossed in each other, for this was the preliminary stage and their thoughts were on the bush, and they waited impatiently for the night to grow old and dark.

"Let's go home," Tessie said sadly. "I'm tired of sitting here."

"Do you really want to go?" It was very pleasant and Philip was reluctant to leave.

"Philip," she said with determination, "I know you don't like to hear this but it's on my mind. I can't get rid of it, and there's no sense in sitting here like a couple of mummies when there is so much to say. I want to talk this over and get through with it."

"Well, the simple truth is that I've been going out with Greta Garbo lately. You can't expect me to handle two lovely ladies at the same time."

"Don't get smart. We can say good-bye right now if that's the way you want to act."

"Seriously," Philip said, "what do you expect? There's not much point in going on. This isn't right for you, and it does me no good. It's no confession to say that whatever we felt for each other doesn't amount to a great deal now. We're both grown up. I've got my own love life to continue, and you've got Schlausser. He's no fool, either. The way we're going now we're bound to finish off sooner or later, and then it will be with a nasty mess."

"Don't mention his name," Tessie said. "I can't stand the thought of him."

"You're being ridiculous. What's the matter with Schlausser? If you're going to let yourself treat him in this way and think of him as you do you're only making it more unpleasant for yourself in the long run. Marriages aren't made in heaven, Tessie. Schlausser isn't a bad fellow at all. We're grown up, Tessie. You're married."

Tessie blew her nose in the little ball of handkerchief, uncrossed her legs, and stood up. "There's nothing more to be said, I suppose," she said impressively. "I think I'd like to be going home."

On the long walk to her apartment house she was magnificently frozen. Philip found the time strained and was relieved when they finally reached her home. The parting was going to be awkward, the minor formalities of the occasion being complicated by what might or might not be a definite parting. What did you say at a time like this? Was she to ask him to her apartment? Were they to be gay, desperately gay? Or sad? This was, or was not, the last time, and neither knew what to say.

"Well," said Philip, breaking the silence as they reached the door, "I guess I'll be going."

"Good night," Tessie said.

"Good night."

It was over. On the walk to the trolley car Philip had to laugh at the speed and silliness with which they had left each other. It was as though they were children. Philip smiled and felt relieved. It was over until the next time.

Had anything come from Ruth in the afternoon mail?

At home, he immediately went to the mailboxes, which were hidden behind the steps in the hall. There was a letter in his box. He had lost his key and worked anxiously with a hairpin to force the letter up through the slot. Philip felt himself enlivened with a pleasant thrill of anticipation. He managed to push a corner of the envelope to the opening, and as his fingers seized it he prepared himself for disappointment by telling himself it was an advertisement, a bill, or a letter for his father.

He opened it and held it to the small electric bulb. It was from Ruth and he was elated. All four pages were covered but she wrote in a round childish scrawl.

Philip dearest,

Well, here I am in this hole in the woods and you can imagine how miserable I am. I never thought I would miss you so much. It's really pretty awful.

There is nothing to do here. I'm supposed to be a guest, and I live in the lodge with some mommas and poppas watching out that their children don't get poisoned or something. I have nothing to do all day. I go swimming and horseback riding every day. Then I read. I never stop reading. That's all I do.

My sister's fine. There are some girls here I know and we have some fun. Every night the boys come from the boys' camp across the lake in their canoes and take the girls out on dates. All the girls say I'm crazy because I refuse to go out with anybody. They must think I'm nuts.

The country is really lovely here. I suppose I shouldn't complain when there are so many people who have to swelter in the hot city. I guess it will be alright, but if you were here it would be simply grand. . . .

All right, Philip said as he put the letter into his pocket and went up the stairs, two l's, it's two words. He felt dissatisfied with the letter, but vaguely, and wondered what it was exactly that distressed him. The letter was affectionate enough.

Later that night Philip went to see Charles Nagleman off. He was going back to Skowhegan to finish the summer with his parents in Maine. They rode down in the subway to Grand Central.

"I want to thank you for the loan of the room," Philip said. "It didn't do much good. I guess your friend is a little hard to reach."

"You mean Ruth Kelman? You're peculiar. You're the kind of a kluck that meets a girl and first thing you think of is marriage."

"What are you talking about? You know I'm in no position to get married. My God," Philip said laughing, "how she would love a three-room flat on Ripple Street!"

"As a matter of fact the garbage cans of Williamsburg and your fortune have nothing to do with it. There's a funny situation about the Kelmans. They're related to a family called Rappaport, and between the two families, there's a lot of people. When a Kelman marries it's to a Rappaport, and vice versa. That's how they keep the money in the family, I suppose."

"You're kidding, Charlie. I never heard of anything like that. Besides, who's talking about getting married? I just liked the kid."

"Well, that's how it goes."

Grinding and screaming on the rails the train made the sharp turn and pulled into speed. Suddenly a butterfly appeared. It was a small white one, but it caused excitement throughout the car. Everyone lowered his newspaper, couples ceased their conversations, to regard the butterfly. The conductor forgot to close the door, he was so amused by its appearance. In the meantime the butterfly flew about in crazy lines, panic-stricken by its dilemma. Philip wondered whether it would manage to get out and how long it would take. Then, abruptly as it had entered, the butterfly made a sharp swoop and disappeared through the window. Everyone returned to his newspaper and the thread of his conversation. There was a general feeling of relief.

"What I can't understand," Charlie said, "is where a butterfly would come from into this train?"

The train rumbled along to Forty-second Street, maintaining a steady motion, and they were both silent. That was how it went, Philip said, and once again he thought of Ruth. Her image sought him out, it was constantly with him. Was it really over? he asked himself, was this the end? These things were ridiculous, Philip said, you had to save them only for daydreams and forget them as soon as you were up. But while he had been with Ruth the atmosphere was always pervaded with a gentle softness. It was like the pleasant, dreamy unreality he used to meet in the novels by Stockton. It was like a waltz. It was a romance. It was a hot joke. Ruth's image entwined itself into his brain and sought him out, begging him to stop everything and think only of her. He remembered the big eyes, the face with the childlike expression of goodness and gladness. Philip remembered the soft skin and the warm flesh. He saw her in a hundred and one postures while she said a hundred and one things. What was this nonsense he always used to say to her about love ending? What was love? It had nothing to do with him. All he wanted was once more to run his lips over her forehead, the curves of her cheeks, her mouth, her throat and shoulders, to feel the scent and the warmth, to taste the delectable skin of her flesh, to feel the life in her. All he wanted was to read again and forever in the evenings with the body in which she lived lying drowsily on his chest. All right, he said to himself, take it easy, don't get excited, but Philip had to admit that he did not like to see it end, and it hurt.

"Listen," Charlie said, "forget it. What's the matter with you? Are you going to mope about an eighteen-year-old kid? Let her be a sweet memory, and when you grow up and become a real man you'll meet some nice Jewish girl and you'll get married."

"When you mention ages, you make things sound ridiculous. All right, Charlie, it will leave a scar upon my heart, but I'll get over it." Philip laughed. "You're taking the thing more seriously than I am myself."

Charlie meant well, but Philip resented the shabby consolation and lies. He was depressed. He knew Ruth. She was a child, and no matter how intensely she might seem to be involved with him she was only eighteen years old and her parents would have no trouble changing her mind. It was over, he said, still hoping, however, that he might be proved wrong. Gumbye, Philip said, gumbye, and he felt bitter because it hurt, it really hurt, even though they were both kids, and it made him feel foolish with himself.

As the train pulled into the Grand Central station the crowd pushed to the door. One woman shoved her way through the crush, worried that the door might close before she got out.

"Lemme off," she cried to Charlie, "lemme off. This is my station. I want to get off."

"Nevertheless," Charlie said coolly, "the fact creates in me no sense of obligation."

"Crazy! Crazy!" she cried at him over her shoulder as they walked from the train.

Charlie laughed in amusement. Philip helped him with his bag and they walked to his sleeper. As the train pulled out, they shook hands smiling.

"Forget it, kid," Charlie said. "Forget it."

Philip stood on the platform for a minute watching the train. He was now more depressed than ever before. Possibly because he envied Charlie Nagleman, he grew bitter toward him. The train taking him to Maine, the fortune his father had made out of vanity cases, his attendance at Syracuse, his casual attitude concerning Ruth Kelman. Forget it, Philip thought. Charlie had already forgotten it, it was easy for him.

That night Philip had a peculiar dream. He was walking down a crowded street with a girl, and at the same time a drunk in a sloppy hat and a winter overcoat followed him. Philip paid no attention to him until the drunk persisted in sticking his finger into his shoulder and the annoyance increased. He grabbed the drunk by the collar, but the man simply put his hand up to his face and thumbed his nose at him. Philip asked him why he did that. "Can't you see it?" the drunk said. "You ought to be ashamed.

Can't you see you're walking with a colored girl?" Philip looked back at her and he saw it was Ruth.

In the morning he was irritated with his dream, but as he left his bed he immediately thought of the mailbox. His exaggerated feeling for the mail and his repeated visits to the box were becoming an obsession with him. The sight of a letter carrier was enough to excite him. Philip had written her a surly note, omitting definite signs of affection, talking about general subjects in which neither of them had any great interest, and he was expecting a reply. He dressed rapidly.

Ruth's letter had come and with it he knew for sure it was over. After her time at the Vermont camp, she wrote, her parents wanted her to visit relatives in Boston until school opened. That meant the Christmas holidays. That meant never. "I can't help it," she wrote. "You know how my parents are. Don't get angry with me, darling. I can't help it."

SEVENTEEN

SAM'S WIFE CLUTCHED THE BUNDLES under her elbows and held her children by the hand at the same time as she rushed from the bus station to her home. Worrying over the irregularity at Chiam's rooming house and Sam's reproaches, she decided to tell her husband it was a surprise. She had felt homesick and came home suddenly because she wanted to surprise him. "I was so lonesome," she would say, "Sam, I had to come home. I know the children need the fresh air but I couldn't stay there another day."

One of the boys almost pulled her off her feet as he dashed to the side. There was something he wanted to see. A bundle dropped from her elbow and Sam's wife had the difficult job of picking it up while she held onto the boy. "Stay here, you nasty kid," she said, and took a moment to slap him on the head. He cried promptly. Sam's wife, in her best dress, the same one in which she had departed, perspired abundantly, but she was excited by the homecoming. It was New York again, people, autos, streets. As she turned the corner into Ripple Street, it was hard for her to keep from running. But then she passed Mahler's shoe shop and through the window she saw the clock on the wall. It was an old one, with Roman numerals and rusty-looking cardboard, and it always said twenty-five minutes after six. She was momentarily depressed. Nothing had changed. It was as though she had never left, because she remembered that the clock had shown the same time when she had gone to the mountains.

Sam's wife rushed through the hall, her boys banging her hips as they tried to keep up with her. The white straw hat, now bent a little and dirty, fell back over her head, but she did not take the time to fix it. She opened the door.

"Who's there? Who's there?" Mrs. Linck cried out. "What is it, a fire?"

It was almost night, but she hadn't turned on the lights and the room was dark. The creaking noise of the rocker established the source of the voice, but it was enough. Sam's wife didn't have to look at her. All she needed was the rasping, thick quality of her mother-in-law's voice and she could picture for herself the red, fat face with the angry opening.

"It's us. We're back again," she said. "My God, why do you have to be so stingy with the electric?" She pulled the cord vigorously and the weak light came down. The blue paint of the table was chipping, and on the porcelain top lay a chunk of bread and a knife still smeared with butter.

"Oh, it's you," Mrs. Linck said. "I have the treasure back again. What's the matter you're home so soon?"

"Where's Sam?" she asked with more force than she intended. "It's after eight. Where is he?"

"The devil knows where. What's the matter with you? Are you crazy all of a sudden, shouting where's Sam, where's Sam?"

Her daughter-in-law dumped the bundles on a chair. "I want to know," she said, speaking with ominous gravity, "where is Sam? Where is he now?"

"Go to hell," Mrs. Linck shouted impatiently. "A nerve! What's the matter with you? Are you really crazy?"

"Never mind if I'm crazy or not. You don't have to tell me where Sam is. I know. I'm not deaf and dumb. Neither am I blind."

As she left she took particular pains to slam the door as hard as she could. With bitter determination, she hurried through the streets up to South Fifth. My God, she said as she ran, who did they think she was anyway? Who did they think she was, who did they think she was? On South Fifth Street one block held a row of two-story red-brick rooming houses. Sam's wife pumped furiously up the steps of a high stone stoop. My God, she said, my God! She was no fool. She wasn't deaf, neither was she blind. Sam's wife threw open the door and bounced into the room angry like butter frying in a pan. It was as she thought.

Marge slept in bed with her mouth open, while Sam, sitting in his B.V.D.'s reading the *Journal*, had his feet on top of the table. He looked up and gasped for breath. It was a surprise. The tilted chair dropped heavily to the floor on its four legs.

"Well," Linck said calmly, "I'll be goddammed." He hadn't even locked the door. Who would have thought?

"Well?" howled his wife fiercely. "Well?"

Linck stood up and discovered he was undressed. He looked around for his pants and in his confusion had a hard time getting his legs through them. He tried not to look at his wife. She was magnificent, simply standing there glaring and puffing with tremendous anger. She just looked and looked, and for the time being it was enough.

"God!" she suddenly screamed looking at the ceiling. It was a great scream and lasted a full minute. "Why do I deserve this? What have I done, you should send this filthy mess on my head?"

Marge woke up with all the noise. "For Christ sakes," she muttered, "what the hell's all the noise about? Can't a person even sleep?"

"Bitch!" said Mrs. Linck. "Whore! Streetwalker! I'll kill you!" Linck grabbed her.

Marge opened her eyes immediately. She sat up in fear. She had been sleeping in her underwear, and now she desperately put on her shoes and slipped her dress over her head. She ran to the door while Linck held his wife away from her. Breathing hard from the haste, Marge pulled the dress over the bump of her bosom. "For God sakes," she said white-faced, "how did she get here?"

"Beat it," Sam said. "Go on. Get the hell out of here."

Now Mrs. Linck broke down. She sat on the bed, held her hand to her chest, and cried bitterly. Sam had regained something of his composure. He had been walking around in his pants without shoes and he sat down to lace them on. His wife went on crying and mumbling to herself. Linck took out a cigarette. It helped. He sat down and waited.

"Listen, Anna. It's not bad as it looks. As a matter of fact, you got me wrong here. I know how it looks, but she's nothing in my life. She's a bum. You don't think I'd have anything to do with an ordinary bum? The fellows at the garage help her out once in a while; I give her something myself because I feel sorry for her. I just dropped in for a while to cool off because it was so hot. Hell," he said, "she's just a kid."

"Leave me alone," his wife sobbed. "You've broken my heart. You've ruined my life. Go away and leave me alone."

"How can I leave you alone?" Linck asked. "What's the matter with you? You don't live here. Come on home. I want to see the kids."

She wouldn't move from the bed. Hell, said Linck, he couldn't stay there all night. He fixed his tie, put out the light, and walked down the stairs. At the top of the stoop he waited for her, and sure enough, after a minute or two he could hear her leaving the room. It would be all right, he said, the hell with it, forget it.

"Go away," she said when she reached him. "Go away. I haven't the strength to talk to you or to cry anymore. I'm sick and tired. I don't want to see you anymore. Go away."

"All right," he said, and began walking home. He cursed himself for a fool. He hadn't even locked the door. How had she known where to find him anyhow? Yentes, he said, every goddam woman in Williamsburg was a Yente who couldn't keep her trap shut. He looked over his shoulder. There she was, following him. It would be all right. What a sap he was. He even took the old room to make it easier for her. What was she doing home anyhow? Linck waited at the corner.

"Listen," he said, "is everything all right? Is there something the matter with the kids?"

"Nothing's the matter, only you," she sobbed.

"Then why did you come home for so soon?" He was angry. She had been trying to catch him. The dirty sneak.

"You don't like it, do you?" she said sadly and feeling sorry for herself. "See, this is my reward. I come home before because I don't want to stay away from my home, I'm homesick, I want to surprise my husband. Surprise!" she wailed. "Yes, it's a real surprise."

"Oh, forget it," Sam said with irritation. "It's enough already. How long is this going to keep up? Somebody would think I died or something."

They walked home together silently. When they reached the flat his mother was out getting the garbage cans ready for the collections next morning. Linck picked up his kids, held them in the air, and slapped their faces affectionately. He sat down at the table and took the *Journal* out of his pocket.

"I'm hungry," he said.

His wife took off her hat and looked around. "I don't know what there is in this house," she said tearfully. It was over. The same thing, an argument, tears, and it was over until the next time. She couldn't see the end of it. What could she do? She looked in the closets for a can of soup.

Sam Linck had an afterthought. "Look here," he said looking up from the paper, "you didn't spend all the seventy dollars I gave you, did you?"

It was Saturday afternoon, and on Saturday afternoon Natie the Buller went to the movies. This was one of the institutions of Williamsburg. Indeed, it was so strong with the young folk that it carried over into the summer months when with the closing of school there was naturally no reason for it. Generally, Natie enjoyed gangster pictures with George Raft, slick-haired and in tab collars. Boy, there was a movie actor. He knew how to act. When he said something he was so mean he didn't have to open his mouth. Natie liked it in the picture when George Raft walked out of the house, like it was any morning, expecting nothing. Suddenly a car comes driving around the corner. Trucks begin to backfire. George Raft holds his stomach and his neck. He falls down. Why? He's been passing a window and in a nice line you see a lot of holes. It's the machine guns. Natie felt sorry but he liked it. It certainly was some way to end a picture, it was good.

Natie liked gangster pictures with George Raft, but if the truth were known he really liked love pictures better. At night the image of Marion Davies of the liquid lips floated through his head until he fell asleep. The mysterious charms of lovely ladies in fragile gowns set him off open-mouthed in wonder. When a movie star suddenly jerked herself into frozen dazedness it meant the man she loved had just walked into the room, and Natie watched. Natie followed the story as it unfolded with intense interest while the bones of his bottom ached from the hard seats. Take Greta Garbo in *The Kiss.* That was a picture, especially the part where John Gilbert and Greta Garbo made love on the fur rug in front of the blazing fire. Natie still remembered the time. He had sat in the movie house long enough to see the picture three times and his mother had gone to every police station and firehouse in Williamsburg looking for him.

The day was dark, cold, and damp. Overhead, the clouds had a conspiracy to keep out the sun. Every time the light came through it lasted a minute and the sky rushed to cover it up. Natie waited outside the Colonial Theater hoping to meet a friend. It cost ten cents to get into the Colonial Theater. It addition, his mother had given him three cents for candy, but you couldn't get much for three cents. In the past Davey used to meet him and they would pool their money for a varied assortment of sweets. At those times they managed to buy enough stuff to last them the whole show. Natie waited, but he knew his old friend would not meet him today. All of a sudden Davey had got stuck up. "I don't know what's got into you," Natie had said, but his friend had not even taken the trouble to talk the disagreement out. "Go on and grow up," Davey had said over his shoulder. "I'm tired of hanging around listening to your bull stories."

The heck with him, Natie thought. I can get along without him,

I don't need him to live. To show his independence Natie went forthwith into the candy store to spend his three cents. He inspected the curved showcase with deliberation. At this point Yetta, clean as a pin this muggy day, walked into the store. Natie left the penny counter in a hurry and went up to the five-cent bars in the front of the store.

"Hello," he said airily. "You here too?"

Yetta peered at him. "Oh, it's you. How are you?"

"You going to the movies?"

"Well, it looks like it, don't it?"

Natie expanded. "I saw a good picture last week. *Bad Boy of Chicago*. It was swell. Did you see it?"

"I don't remember. Was it about guns and shooting? They disgust me. I can't stand them pictures."

They were walking across the street to the ticket box together. Natie felt self-conscious, thrilled even. He was going to the movies with Yetta. He examined the street up and down for friends of his.

"That's funny," he said. "Most fellows like gangster pictures. Girls don't. This picture was swell. I don't see how a person can forget it so soon. It had James Cagney in it. He was swell. Like in one part, see, he walks out of a poolroom with a violin case under his arm. A man says, 'Where are you going, Jeff?' See, James Cagney's name in the picture is Jeff. So he says, 'I'm going to give a guy a lesson.' See, the violin case ain't got a violin, that's what racketeers use to hold machine guns in. It was swell."

"Well, what's so funny?" Yetta said placidly. "Suppose he was going out of a poolroom with a violin case. So what?" That was a new one, so what. Everybody in the pictures now said, so what. It slayed them. She was very proud.

"Don't you see? It was a violin case but it had no fiddle inside. It had a machine gun. So a guy says, 'Where are you going, Jeff?' And James Cagney says, like he was a violin teacher, 'I'm going out to give a guy a lesson.'"

"So what? All right, he's giving a guy a lesson—oh, I see. Well, is that the joke? My heavens, I knew it all along but what's so funny about it? I thought you meant something else, that's why I didn't understand."

When the time came to give up her dime she fussed over her bag after the powdery fashion of ladies. Natie knew this wasn't right, the man always paid, but there he was, he simply didn't have the money. He went off to the stand with coming-attraction photographs and examined them carefully until Yetta had her ticket. Then he followed her into the movie house and helped her find a seat.

They entered in the middle of the comedy. Natie sat back in the darkness and his face assumed the proper expression for true cinema appreciation. It was a Laurel and Hardy comedy. They were some actors, they were good. Natie's face went blanker still with enjoyment.

"Do you really think they're so funny?" Yetta whispered. "They make me sick."

Natie, marveling at her sophistication, said, "Oh, they're not half bad."

He was a little disturbed and had trouble falling back to attention. It was the usual afternoon crowd on Saturdays. The place was full of kids, restless and whistling. When Laurel shoved Hardy, or maybe it was the other way around, into the bathtub full of water, the kids raised such a howl Natie missed some lines of dialogue and two men had to come running down the aisles and insist upon order. The uproar ceased, but now a baby of perhaps four was running up and down the aisles. She had no interest in the comedians and preferred to scream piercingly from inner joyousness. The baby's sister went after her, but as the child was lifted off her feet she let out a powerful yell of protest for one so small and thereupon commenced a fit of unbroken bawling. It was terrible. Yetta turned to Natie and said frankly, "I can't stand some people's children. This place is getting to be a regular dump."

Natie couldn't understand the force of her convictions. After all, what did she expect? However, there was nothing to say. Instead, he took the occasion to push down a kid who was standing up in his seat for a less obstructed view of the proceedings. "Sit down," he said impressively. "Do you think your father is a glazier?"

When the feature began showing the noise diminished, the children stopped stamping on the floor with their shoes, the whistles ceased. The picture, it soon developed, concerned two women and a man. It was lovely. Yetta leaned forward, dislodging Natie's elbow from the rest. This was her sort of picture. The ladies went around saying "Darling" to everyone, a butler took people's hats, and the actors were always smoking cigarettes. Yetta yearned for the time when she would be able to smoke. It was elegant. The man in the picture, always speaking in a drawling, innocent voice, looked tired. He looked as though somebody had just gotten him out of bed every time he came into the picture. He was a book publisher, and the two women were after him, his wife and a lady writer. It was some picture.

Natie liked love pictures, but all the people did in this one was talk. He was tired of it. A man played a piano. Another man drank from a high glass. The lady with the slanting eyes and screwed-up mouth said "Darling." There were no passionate scenes. Natie, losing interest, shifted his gaze and watched the faces of the other kids in the moving-picture house. The kids sat with their mouths half open, following the action on the screen with interest. On their faces were the same looks they had when they read the funny sheets. One girl kept scratching her head, but delicately, with one finger, and she didn't stop. The picture must have been too much for her. Natie looked up to watch the stream of rays change from black to white in different combinations as the action of the film moved. He tried to guess what was happening on the screen by watching the rays, but repeatedly looking up and then at the picture made him feel dizzy.

He went back to the picture. The scene takes place in a penthouse overlooking a river. The men sit on cane chairs on the terrace, and the ladies keep their hats on all the time and cross their legs neatly. Everyone is drinking and smoking. Some people are doing both at the same time. Then the lady with the screwed-up mouth says "Darling"—and Natie lost interest again. "Darling," he mimicked to himself from annoyance. "Darling, shmarling, parling. Ow air yew, muhdir?" It was a rotten picture.

Natie glanced sideways and looked at Yetta. She wasn't half bad. Natie looked at Yetta and wondered. She was pretty. Did he like her? In absorption she brought her hand to her mouth and began sucking her little finger. It was a funny thing for a girl to do, he thought. But what made it funny? After all. . . . Well, it was the funny way she did it. Did he like her? he wondered.

"What are you looking at, nosy?" Yetta asked suddenly.

He was caught. "Who's looking?" he demanded.

Natie went back to the picture. The wife of the publisher is meeting the lady writer, but neither knows who the other is. It is night, they are going to sleep, and they smoke cigarettes in their pajamas (but there are no high glasses) while they talk. Natie became interested in the situation. At last something was going to happen. He settled back into his seat and as his elbows went back he could feel that he was pushing Yetta's off the wooden bar.

"Excuse me," Natie said, and withdrew his elbow immediately.

"Oh, it's all right. Put your arm there."

"What about you? I don't really need it."

"Well, we can both keep our arms there."

It didn't work. Natie's attention was distracted from the picture. He was continuously conscious of the presence of Yetta's elbow. He was either pushing it off the wooden bar or falling off it himself.

"Here," said Yetta, "this will fix it once for all."

She boldly put her arm through his. Natie was shocked. For the next minute it made no difference what the screen showed. All he felt was the softness of flesh and the warm sensation. It was as though he was learning for the first time that a person's elbow could be soft and warm. It was a pleasant thing. Natie's scalp shivered with delight. He looked at the picture.

The two ladies have placed each other. They tilt their heads back, the lady writer sincere and serious, the wife hurt. At this time who should walk into the room but the publisher himself! He does not see his wife, she should not have been in the room, it is an accident, and he calls out from the door to the authoress. "I'm so sorry, darling, I just couldn't get away from the office," he says in a juicy, dead voice. He looks as though he just got out of bed and doesn't know exactly where he is. He walks into the room, sees his wife, and says, "Oh." He sits down and smokes a cigarette.

Natie followed the story with furious interest. Yetta was absorbed by the picture and therefore it meant a great deal to him. What would the husband do? Would the picture end with the wife or with the writer ahead? The publisher smokes a cigarette and fiddles around with his mustache. The wife and the writer are arguing it out. Yetta was wide-eyed. Natie said, what the hell, this will tell. He pressed his knee against hers. Yetta did not flinch. Knees too could be soft and warm. She really liked him, Natie thought, else she would have taken her leg away. Maybe she was too interested in the picture? Nevertheless, Natie, en rapport with this lovely girl beside him, elbows and knees touching, felt as though he were sitting next to Marion Davies and the picture couldn't be too long. With regret he watched the husband kissing his wife, and the picture was over. She'd won. As the reel ended the screen became brilliant with the dazzling whiteness and the black flecks jiggled up and down. The kids in the theater clapped their hands, stamped, and whistled. It was like a relief. The manager yelled, "Quiet! Quiet! I'll throw out each and every kid who wants to make a racket!"

A girl at Yetta's left began squeezing past the row to get to the aisle. She was in a fearful hurry.

"Please," said Yetta indignantly to her. "Walk on your own feet." The girl was in a hurry and ignored her, but Yetta felt satisfied.

The screen now presented glimpses of coming attractions. Then the newsreel. Natie was still elbow and knee with Yetta. It was going too fast. It would be over soon. The girl in the hurry now returned, pushing through the row to her seat but watching the screen all the time so that she wouldn't be missing anything. She had missed too much already. Yetta withdrew her legs under the seat and Natie worried. But when she settled again she moved back into the same position and it was all right. She likes me all right, Natie said with elation, she likes me. The newsreel passed. He felt gypped, it went so fast. Then Laurel and Hardy again. It was a matter of minutes.

"That's where we came in," Yetta said with a certain sense of propriety, and she rose.

When they walked out of the Colonial Theater the light hit their eyes, dark as the day was, and they had trouble getting used to it for a while.

"That reminds me," Yetta said. "What happened to your friend Davey? I never see him around any more. Did he move?"

"No, he didn't move," Natie said. This was a ticklish subject, all things considered. "He's no friend of mine, Yetta. He's altogether too stuck up, if you want to ask me."

"I never liked him myself," Yetta confided. "He's one of those kids who think they're all grown up or something." She hoped Natie would go back and tell him.

"He thinks he's smart. Just because he's the leader of the gang, he thinks he's a regular guy or something."

"I don't see why we should waste our time discussing him," she exclaimed. "He certainly isn't anything in my life."

Natie was satisfied. That finished Davey. She wasn't half bad. As they turned into Ripple Street, he decided to make the test. Gingerly he took her elbow in his hand and held it for a few minutes. Yetta walked on as though nothing had happened. That night, before falling to sleep in his bed, Natie the Buller exhausted the wealth of his imagination in making up stories about Yetta.

Why don't I hear from you? I've been writing to you every day and all you sent was one skinny letter. If you knew the way I run to the office for mail, you'd write me sometimes. I can't understand what's happened. Out of a clear sky you suddenly seem to have frozen on me. You're interfering with my digestion. We get mail here after our meals, and while I'm waiting for it I just can't eat anything.

Well, the season's about over. I talk as though I were a camper or a counsellor myself, but it's impossible to stay here any length of time without getting involved with the activities. The season's winding up and all the girls are just counting the days. When I used to be a camper, that was what I used to do, count days, even count meals. After each mess I used to chalk one off on my pad. It makes no difference now. It's all the same, camp, Boston, or school. If I can't be home in New York with you, I don't care where I am.

Well, I have to cut this short now. The Senior girls are putting on a new show and I've promised to give them a hand with the skits and things. Much fun, but it means a lot of work.

Love, Ruth.

Write!!!

Philip seized the letter to tear it, but he reconsidered, smoothed the envelope, and put it in his pocket. Forget it, Charlie had told him, forget it. "Write!!!" "I have to cut this short." Philip thought of the mysterious tearing sounds she used to make with water when he waited for her at her home while she bathed. It's no good, he said to himself, it's gone. The trolley came to the corner. He got off and walked to the apartment house.

"Hello," Tessie said graciously, opening the door. "You're early. I'm not ready yet."

"What's it all about?" he asked. She had telephoned and asked him to come that evening. She wanted to see him.

She went into the bedroom to slip on her dress. Philip had to note the casual air she affected and silently he congratulated her upon it. Besides being a great New York beauty, Mrs. Schlausser—who here wears a fashion success of the Paris season, Chanel's caterpillar-green hutcha-putcha suit—is a typical modern sportswoman, very keen on shooting and hunting and golf. On the other hand she spends most of her time at her Long Island residence where she conducts a country home noted for its atmosphere of conviviality and grace. She is the former Miss Tessie Averbusch. O,

Mrs. Schlausser, who reads *Vogue, Harper's Bazaar, Vanity Fair* while she waits for her turn in the beauty parlor. "What's it all about?" Philip asked, sitting as though today was Saturday, yesterday had been Friday, and tomorrow would be Sunday. He was no small shakes at this himself, he would have her understand.

"I was thinking it over," Tessie said from the other room. "It was really childish, the way we parted. I've been thinking about it. We can still be friends. There's no good reason for not seeing each other, is there?"

"Oh, I didn't mean that," Philip said quickly. Was that business going to start all over again? "I mean your letter. What's happening up at the Stadium?"

"One of my friends is in the concert group of Tashimura. Did you ever hear of her? I mean, Tashimura? She's a dancer and she's giving a recital tonight. I thought I'd like to go up and see her because I think I'll join her group in the fall. I'm very much interested in dancing."

"What kind of dancing? Tap?"

"Oh, no." Tessie walked into the living room. It was a little cool this evening and she wore a coat. As she pulled at the gloves she reprimanded Philip with a look and said, "What's wrong with you? Do I look the type who goes in for tap dancing? I mean the modern dance, Mary Wigman, Martha Graham, and Doris Humphrey." The names came off easily.

"So you've gotten the bug too. Everybody I meet is participating in the modern dance. It's like a new diet. You don't get fat."

"Don't be clever. Just because a girl gets married you can't expect her to settle down and grow old. It's a new age. We're not like our mothers. We want to go on living full lives."

"Nu, nu," said Philip.

Tessie went around turning off the lights. "Let's be going, shall we?" That was what they were saying in the movies. Dance, shall we? Drink, shall we? Let us be vurry, vurry classy, shall we?

"Shall we?" Philip said and went to the door.

The ride to the Stadium took an hour. The train hustled up Manhattan, rocking, and Philip, sitting next to Tessie, powdered, rouged, and perfumed, Tessie, smart in hat, coat, and gloves, Philip had to shake his head. This should really be ending and here he was, sitting next to her again. Things moved in circles, nothing happened. That made him ridiculous. There were too many partings.

In the cool breezes under the great sky at the Stadium Philip sat on the concrete step and watched the dancer. The new American dance it was, and it sprang from a Russian and Jewish background. Tashimura herself was a likely-looking woman, husky, with heavy legs and big feet. Her face was masked by expression. It might have meant suffering, profundity, or ecstasy. The dance itself (choreography by Tashimura, costumes designed by Tashimura, musical arrangement by Tashimura) was based on a ritual of South American Indian origin. It was called *Pichle-Pichle*, which was the symbol of the forces of the sun, the moon, and fire. It was gorgeous. The hefty dancer walked pigeon-toed and at certain moments jerked her pelvis forward, the knees bent. She worked up a sweat, but it made no difference: the face kept the mask, it didn't move a ripple. The strange discords from the piano and the nervous rhythms from the percussion instruments ceased. Tashimura held her arms tightly to the sides, her head fell low. Everyone applauded.

"It's marvelous," Tessie gasped.

"It looks like hell. Do you mean to say that you actually like that sort of business?"

"It's primitive. It's real. It's natural. Some people just don't have the appreciation for these things."

"What's natural about it? You never saw anyone walk around with her pelvis stuck forward and the hips flying out. Tell me, does she walk pigeon-toed all the time or is it just for recital purposes?"

Tessie disregarded the question. She was considering the theory of the dance. It was important to her, Philip ought to realize that it meant a great deal to her, it wasn't a passing fad. "I don't care what you say," she said finally, "I don't care how it looks. It feels good to do, and that's what counts, after all. Dancing is a way of self-expression."

The orchestra played, the crowd on the stone steps smoked

cigarettes, and Philip tried to make himself more comfortable by leaning back, but all he did was to get his jacket dirty from the shoes of the dance lovers in the higher row. There would be a tussle at the door tonight, Philip thought, there would be many arguments and nice mental footwork. "Won't you come in for a minute, there's no rush." There would be the arguments with the soft, sad-eyed pleading and the whispered entreaty, reluctance, and the hesitation; there would be the powerful pull because inside there it was, you could have it, and it was something for nothing. Now the fiddles of the orchestra handled the part by themselves and it felt as though a hundred kids in play were wildly pulling sticky lines from a lump of dough. The pathetic melody wrenched itself free from the sound boxes of the violins and it floated in the air. There would be many arguments and a wavering capitulation, Philip thought, and he wished that Schlausser had a permanent job in New York.

Linck threw open the door expansively.

"Christ, what a hole," Marge said with disgust.

It was a dark, airless room with a white enameled bed, profusely ornate with knobs, curlicues, and whorls. Altogether it reminded her of a hospital bed. The room was depressing. She opened the window and noticed that the cream-colored curtains were heavy with dust.

"We should have done this before," Linck said. "We were just a pair of saps."

"Christ," Marge said again, "this ain't no bargain. I never saw a dump like this."

"What's the matter with it?" he asked angrily. "Somebody would think you're a queen or something. You certainly have the nerve when you want to."

"Look, do you see where this window goes to?"

"Well, what's the matter with it? I don't see nothing wrong with a garage."

"Well, if it's all right with you, I can't kick, I suppose. But you know what'll happen. All those truck drivers and hackmen will be taking sunbaths and nagging hell out of me."

"Oh," said Linck savagely, "so that's it. I could have imagined you'd think of that."

"Don't be a dope." Marge decided to change the subject. "It's certainly a dark hole in the wall all right."

"What do I care about that? I don't need no light here."

"What about me? I got to live in this hole all day."

"Listen, are you looking for a fight or something? Why don't you shut up? You're getting to be as bad as my old lady."

"Your wife!" Marge said, seizing the opportunity with bitterness. "That's a hot one. Just stay out of her way and we'll get along fine. Oh, yare! She found you out like she could smell you or something."

"I don't see what you're kicking about. I got into a stink, not you. It's me who should be doing the bellyaching." Linck quieted down. After all, she had him there this time. "How was I to know she'd be coming home so soon? Besides, we made a mistake. We shouldn't have taken the same room back. It'll be all right now."

"Oh, yare?" Marge said. "If I know that slob of yours, she'll smell you out in no time again."

"Well," Linck shouted with exasperation, "if you don't like it, you know what you can do about it. I ain't forcing you or anyone else to stay here in this room, and you can do as you damn please any time you damn feel like it!"

"Go on and shut up," Marge said, retreating. "You can't talk to me like that."

"Oh, yare? Get this through your thick head: I'll talk to you any way I feel like. Understand? If you don't like it you know what you can do."

"Go jump in the river," Marge muttered.

She pushed the cane rocking chair to the corner, pulled down the shade, and went to the sink to wash. Linck flopped down on the bed. His legs were spread apart. This was the life. He took out a toothpick from his pants pocket and grew reflective over it.

"You should have heard what I gave my old lady for busting in on us, Marge," he said from the bed. "When I got her home, I laced it into her. I told her where she got off. 'Listen here,' I says, 'get this through your head: If I feel like fooling around with a dame, it's my business and nobody's going to tell me what to do.' I told her, Marge. She won't come around here again busting in like that. If she ever tries anything like that again on me, I'll fix her little wagon in a hurry, and that's what I told her."

"That's a fine load of bull," Marge said. "Don't think you can get away with that crap on me."

"On the level, Marge. That's what I told her, so help me."

Linck could hear her pulling her dress over her head. He grew interested immediately.

"What are you doing now?" he asked casually.

"I got to wash my underwear as soon as I can. It's dirty as hell."

"Come here, Marge, I want to tell you something."

"Wait a minute. I want to get my dress on first."

Linck bided his time. She was no dope.

"What do you want?" she said.

"Come on," Linck coaxed. "Don't be a kid. I ain't going to hurt you." He pulled her to the bed and she lay alongside of him in her dress. All the time he was conscious that she was wearing nothing underneath. Naked skin. It excited him. He squeezed her to him so that the pug nose pressed into his face.

"I can't breathe," she said, struggling away from him. "Why don't you take a shave once in a while? You cut my face all up."

"Take it easy. Don't get so hot and bothered." He lay with her, his fingers working on the soft flesh of her shoulders. Linck slipped his hand down to her knee. Marge suddenly shot up and walked to the washstand.

"Jesus," she said quietly, "that's all you think about."

"Every kiss, every hug seems to act just like a drug," Linck bawled. "It's getting to be a habit with me."

He rose from the bed and looked at his watch. It was almost eight o'clock. He had to be getting back to the house or else the old lady would be after him all over again.

"I got to be going," he said. "I'll be around tomorrow night."

"Just a minute, Sam," she said. "I know you don't like to hear this, but I need a new outfit. I'm falling out of this dress already and my shoes feel like paper. It's about time I got myself some clothes."

"Clothes?" Linck said. "What do you think I'm made of? Money? Christ, Marge, I ain't no millionaire. I don't make all the money you think. I got a wife and two kids to support."

"Cut the whining and shell out. You don't have to spend all your money on them. You got no rent to pay, and the old lady cooks all the meals for your kids. Don't be a piker."

"That's what you say. Listen, you, I don't need you to tell me where my money goes. If I say I can't afford it, I can't afford throwing out money on you, and that goes. Why don't you get yourself a job? I can't support you too."

"I need five bucks for a dress and shoes," Marge said.

"Five bucks," Linck laughed artificially. "That's a hot one."

"Listen you, what do you want? You can't get everything for nothing. What do you think I am anyhow?"

"I don't have to tell you. You want to get paid just like the rest of them. Why don't you go out on the streets and pick up your two bucks if that's the way you feel about it?"

"Never mind, you bastid, I don't want to hear that kind of crap from you. Either you give me five bucks or you can cut out coming around here."

"You can go to hell first, you dirty whore."

"You goddam sheeny bastid!"

Linck drew himself up and gazed at her. "Say, I got a good mind to take a sock out of you. You've got it coming to you for a long time." He looked at his watch. Time flew. "The hell with you, stinker." He banged the door and went down the steps.

His wife was waiting for him in the flat. As he came into the kitchen she was standing all ready, looking at him with questioning eyes. She was a little pop-eyed, he thought, or maybe it was because of the swollen rings under her eyes. Linck sat down at the table and picked up the newspaper. It came. He was expecting it.

"So late?" she said with reproach. "I've been waiting for you since six."

"I couldn't help it. The boss sent me out to Long Island. I got the phone call just after four o'clock."

"Sam," she begged tearfully, "Sam, I can't fight with you no more. I'm all worn out with arguments. Tell me the truth, Sam, did you go to see that bum again?"

He flattened the paper on the table with restrained irritation. "I told you a hundred times," he said with force but speaking slowly, "and I ain't going to say it again. I don't know that girl no more, I ain't going to see her no more. Can't I get some rest now? All day I drive that goddam truck until my can feels like it's on fire, and when I get home you're always ready to nag me and nag me. I'm just about sick and tired with the whole goddam business." He slammed the paper on the porcelain tabletop, went to the radio, and dialed for a dance orchestra. He turned the music on loud. That'll shut her up, he said to himself.

She went to the range to heat the soup. Had he gone, or was he really telling the truth? It was late. It was almost nine. On the other hand, he couldn't have gone to that tramp so soon after she came home. What was the difference? If it wasn't today, it would be soon. If it wasn't Marge, it would be somebody else. Mrs. Linck wiped her nose with her finger and wondered what the end would be. She thought of the older couples in the house. They had fought on and off. If it wasn't other women or men it was cards, liquor, relatives, or money. There was always something. She looked carefully into the plate of soup as she carried it to the table. There was no end.

EIGHTEEN

Morand and the Silver Eagle collapsed all at once. Morand had imported gunmen from Detroit to help him in his fight against Papravel and a disastrous accident overtook him. One of the Detroiters, known to parties in Brooklyn, met his death in spectacular fashion. The gangster was killed on business unrelated to the Silver Eagle, but unfortunately it had had to happen in the bus station. Specifically, the prospective victim was guarding the station by his lounging presence when a heavy Lincoln sedan drew up to the curb. Three men popped out of the doors promptly. As the gangster perceived them his face became absorbed completely with fear, his knees buckled, and he scrambled like one in a dream to the telephone booth. The three men, running with guns in their hands, broke the glass of the booth and emptied their revolvers into the crouching corpse. They then returned to the sedan and sped away. It took less than two minutes, but everyone on the block said he had witnessed the killing and there were many stories.

The news spread. Morand knew he was finished. Together with the pickets and the talk of strikes and scabs, this meant the end. No customer would dare use his line now. Morand locked the door to the station, told the help to go home, and he wondered, why, God, why do You send me so many burdens all at the same time, what did I do? He had fought valiantly, Papravel was too powerful, and there was no luck. Morand went home to cry with his wife. He was a broken man.

As for Papravel, let no one say that he was a man who took relish in another's misfortunes. In fact, he did not regard the accident as strictly fair, he regretted it, but after all he knew it had just had the effect of bringing affairs to a head, of hastening Morand's capitulation by the small difference of days. He was a pleased man because now he could chalk off two problems. Rubin alone remained, and Papravel wondered whether he shouldn't wait even longer before attacking him solely because the state of anticipation was so enjoyable. But at this point Rubin took it into his head to seek him out. In a way, he was elated, too. His biggest rival had been eliminated. In a rush of good feeling he included Papravel among the causes of his gladness and he went down to New York for the reconciliation, all smiles, cheerful and benign, about to grant favors.

He greeted Papravel with noisy welcome, half hoping to cover all animosity in the confusing racket of the welcome. But Papravel smiled.

"Listen," said Rubin, coughing with excitement and keeping his eyes on the floor. He talked in the familiar inflections, with the big rises and falls. "Listen, I know there was a little misunderstanding, but things have turned out so nicely I'm willing to forget. I'm not the man who likes to hold a grudge until the grave; and I'm not the kind of a man who wants to be a pig. What means good for me should mean good for you too. And nobody, even my worst enemies, can say that Rubin don't treat his men good. Papravel," he cried, "what do you think? I'm going to make you general manager in charge of all New York points."

Rubin's hands were at the sides of his chest, his head thrown back with delight at his own magnanimity. Well, the smile on his anxious face asked, what do you think of that? Papravel sought out the spittoon and dropped the ash in it with intense consideration for the floor. He smiled gently. Rubin grew cold.

"What's the matter?" he asked as if insulted. "Isn't it good enough for you? What do you expect? Just look what I'm doing for you. I take a man out of a dangerous business, I set him up in a good job with a high salary in an established concern, and for all it excites him somebody might think I'm asking him if he can change two nickels for a dime for me."

Papravel smiled.

"What's the matter?" Rubin almost shrieked with suspense. Now the little beads of sweat on his forehead glistened in the light. "Are you still mad because I didn't chip in when your Irisher—what's-his-name, Gilhooley—got in trouble? All right, say so. I was excited. I didn't know what I was saying. My head was filled with a hundred other worries. Tell me how much money I owe you and I'll put it in now. Tell me. Just tell me what you want!"

Papravel did not interrupt him. He exhaled the smoke without haste and said quietly, "All right. I'll tell you what I want." With inordinate calm he baldly proposed: 1.) that Rubin resign and accept the position of vice president; 2.) that he transfer his office together with 3.) two-thirds of the stock to Papravel.

Rubin had a stroke.

When he recovered, Papravel went on with his inexorable argument. He spoke quietly and with great confidence in every tone, presenting his points neatly, one after the other. He was familiar with his speech for he had worked over it and elaborated it in his mind many, many times in the last two weeks.

"Give in, Rubin," he said, "give in while you still have a shirt on your back. You know what I did to Morantz and the Silver Eagle, you know exactly what I can do in such cases, and the same party will be in store for you if you make up your mind to be nasty. You cannot beat me, Rubin. No. I tell you this like a father talks to his son. Fourteen Superba buses, seven Nashes and four Buicks, four offices, and a payroll of sixty-six, all this you will lose like a dream going away in the morning. The money you would make out of Morantz being out of the picture you will never see. Your wife won't know what a new fur coat looks like one winter after the other, and if you're a real father to your babies you won't make trouble. And from you personally, Rubin, if you don't like what I say, from you personally I will make such a sight for all Williamsburg to talk about for a month."

He brought the cigar to his lips and waited to see what Rubin might have to say. From the owner of the Empire Lines came gasping noises as though he were choking, and his face was shot with blood until it didn't seem possible. That was good.

"On the other hand," Papravel continued with marvelous composure even for him, "with me as your partner you'll have nothing to fear. In the daytime you can go to your office without a worry, like a bird flying in the air, and in the night you will sleep. Think, Rubin, in the night you will sleep. All the worrying there is, I'll do. All your competitors I'll drive away from the mountains, and we'll expand. I'll make the railroads give up altogether and let them carry only freight. I'll establish for you routes to all the big cities, and I'll chase every other line from the roads. You'll have, with me for a partner, not a stinking small business to the mountains, but a coast-to-coast organization. Listen, Rubin, what I say to you now is all true, and may God strike me dead right now if anything I said is a lie. You'll be a big man with your picture in the paper every Sunday. You'll be a philanthropist like Warburg and Untermyer, and you'll do good wholesale. They'll name orphan asylums and hospitals after you, and when you die, Rubin, I promise you you'll get a funeral that no one in America ever saw before."

And he succeeded, Papravel did.

Morand, once sole proprietor of the Silver Eagle Bus Lines to the mountains, with stations at important points in the East Side, Brownsville, and Williamsburg, Morand, just recently worth so many thousand dollars, so many buses, so much real estate, Morand walked with the setting sun as if it were a personal symbol. He was wiped out and bemoaned the catastrophe. "I was just a little too smart," he said to himself, "I'm too goddam smart for my own good." Again he cursed himself because at the very beginning, on that hot day when Papravel had walked into his office with his sly advice, Morand hadn't had sense enough to see which way the wind blew and to accept terms. A small thing, a little visit, he could have helped himself so much if only he had seized upon the moment in the proper fashion. It was too late, exasperatingly it was too late.

Now he had nothing, practically nothing. Had he listened to Papravel his business would have been damaged. But there was still money to be made without a bus station in Williamsburg. As it was he was almost ruined. The Detroit gangsters were expensive folk; he had never had any experience with them, and if he hadn't been so goddam smart he would have known enough to shy away from people like them. In a rage Morand cursed the gunman whose death in the telephone booth had been the final spark, but he stopped and worried a little. It wasn't right to think evil of a dead person.

The buses, needing extensive repairs, were in terrible condition. He owed money for garage bills, he needed money for repairs, for gas, for rent, for a thousand things. He needed money, and he was ruined. It was all over.

"Mr. Morand!" he said with bitter sarcasm. Pomerantz wasn't good enough for him. City College wasn't good enough for his son, he had to send him to N.Y.U. Even Williamsburg wasn't good enough. He had to move to President Street so that his wife could be a swell. Only three months ago he had had to buy her a lavalière for thirteen hundred dollars. Thirteen hundred dollars. He couldn't get eight for it now. That was why he had been ruined, Morand said vigorously. God sent Papravel down on his head for a punishment. What could he expect, showing off with his good fortune to the whole world? Morand, walking home from the subway station on Eastern Parkway, felt bitter toward his wife, his son, and N.Y.U.

Life was rotten. Business was rotten. In order to make a nickel you simply had to go out and cut the next man's throat before he cut yours. That was the only way to make money in this country. Morand cursed Papravel and Rubin, but actually he felt no profound resentment against them personally. It was like a game, and they had won, he had lost. If it hadn't been them, it would have been somebody else. Morand thought of his neat-looking buses driving out of the stations full of people, with the snappy drivers in breeches; Morand thought of his stations with the signs and the boxes of tickets; he thought of the garage with the buses all put to sleep at night like babies; he remembered the pleasure with which he had signed the payrolls and bank deposit slips; Morand remembered his past glory and had a hard time keeping from tears on the street. Goddam, he wept silently, goddam.

By God, Morand cried in a frenzy of determination, I'm not licked yet. If I was stubborn once before, this is not the time to quit. Who does Papravel think he is? God? I'll show those bums they can't throw me out of business so easy.

Morand turned the corner and walked down President Street with its long lawns and stylish one-family houses. First he needed money. He had to get started all over again, the buses had to go rolling over the hills, the stations be set in order, the hired people put back to work. He would stay out of Williamsburg until he got on his feet again. This season was finished, but by next spring he hoped to be ready. Then he would be back again, a real fight. Who was Papravel anyway? He wasn't God. Morand would show him! All right, business was like a game but this time he would cut Papravel's throat first! Morand felt new strength.

He walked grimly into his house and dropped his hat on the commode in the vestibule.

"Jennie," he called. "Where are you, Jennie? Listen, take out your lavalière, the earrings, and the diamond rings from the safety deposit. I need them."

"My God," his wife gasped. "What happened? Tell me quick, what happened?"

"Nothing and everything. I've got to have a lot of money quick, that's all. Your diamonds I'll have to take to a loan society. We'll take a second mortgage on the house. And you can tell Ira he goes to City College in the fall or he can go to work. I won't let that illegitimate Papravel give me a beating. I'm not finished yet. I'll show the dirty crooks!" His voice rose to a scream with increasing fury. He was defiant, and Mrs. Morand waited patiently for him to cool off.

But that night in bed she held his head and spoke soft words of caution and solace. "I'm afraid, Jake," she whispered. "I'm so afraid. I don't like to see you get mixed up with crooks and gangsters. What good is all the money in the world to me if something, God forbid, should happen to you? For my sake, Jake, get out. This filthy business is driving me out of my mind."

"I'll show the dirty crooks. They can't ruin me so easy," he said, but in the dark his eyes were open, and he wondered. He did not have the heart to go through the whole mess all over again. He had had enough. Most of his courage had disappeared.

"Jake," his wife went on, "what's the matter with you? You're not ruined yet. Do you want me to go crazy altogether? For weeks now I haven't slept a whole night. All the time you're away from the house I sit and worry. Money is not everything. You can't buy everything with money. I'll go crazy. Sell out, Jake, sell out for me, for my sake. You can still get plenty money for the business. You can start in again in some other line. For my sake," she pleaded, "for my sake."

And Jake, moving restlessly over the bedclothes, went over the possibilities in his mind with uncertainty, and he listened carefully to his wife's arguments.

"I just got a letter from Harry, Pop," Philip said.

The old man was at the window, smoking, but he looked up with interest.

"What does he write about? Is he coming home soon?"

"No, he's in business in Chicago already. He doesn't say much what it's about, but it's got something to do with ties. He's made a connection with a manufacturer in New York who sends him the stuff. He's a kind of jobber and sells the ties to pushcarts. You ought to like that business, it's honest enough."

"Listen, that boy doesn't fool me for a minute, and you should know it. Just because he went out of the bus business it doesn't mean it makes a difference with him. He still wants to make money in the worst way. I knew it from the first day he was born. I'll bet anything you want he's squeezing money out of those peddlers in Chicago already."

Mr. Hayman had a habit of sitting hunched up on his hands, or with his feet on the windowsill, like a boy holding his knees.

Philip thought of his brother and smiled because the prophecy he had made about himself had come true so rapidly. Ties were a little more decorous; Harry's soul had apparently quit backfiring. Philip, thinking about his brother, remembered his homily and wondered whether Harry wasn't right. Philip had forced his mind to forget about Ruth, but it still hurt and he was bitter. There was the choice, he thought, Papravel or his father. Papravel smoking cigars piled up money, and glowed with sweat and happiness, while his father sat with his feet on the windowsill in the dimness of a Williamsburg flat. How much of a schlemiel was he? Philip asked himself. The thing to do, and he saw it, was to follow Harry, to get to work. He was heading in his father's direction, honest, good, and kind, but poor, and money meant so much. Look at him, Philip said, he's old, he's so skinny, and all he has after all the years is a cigarette and a window.

"Where's Momma?" his father asked.

"She's probably up at Mrs. Sussman's again. She's always there these days. I guess she'll be down any minute now."

His father picked up the newspaper and read to while away the time. Philip sat watching him. Be good, he said to himself, treat everyone honestly, walk the steps of a good man, and when you grow old maybe you will have the peace and calm of a great detachment. That was one way out of the problem of living. You could sleep within yourself, assured and peaceful. How much better than Cohen, worrying in nervous flinches and spasms. For Cohen, living was a constant torment, reality was something he was unable to adapt himself to and yet he continued trying. Like his father, it occurred to him, he too avoided the perplexities by withdrawal and by standing. Compare, Philip thought, all right, compare. He always made fun of Cohen, but there was a resemblance.

His pimply-faced friend could not handle reality, and neither could he, Philip, different as their manners were. Philip was a schlemiel also, only with a little more grace because he had a sense of humor and it helped to pull him out of the ridiculous pits. Philip was annoyed because he realized how closely he might be compared to Cohen.

Mrs. Hayman came into the kitchen.

"Mazel tov," his father said drily. "The Madame is finally here."

"All kidding aside, Mom," Philip said. "You've got a family yourself."

"Don't joke," his mother said as she busied herself at the gas range. "You shouldn't make fun. It's a sad story."

"What's wrong now?" his father asked. "Is she still so bad?"

"Oh," said Mrs. Hayman, "I'm worried through and through. You ought to see that woman. You remember how nice and plump she was? She's fallen through, sunken, dried out. There's nothing to her. She aged twenty years this summer. She has no interest in her home no more, she doesn't care what happens to the boys. All poor Mrs. Sussman does is sit and think and worry. I'm afraid she'll go out of her mind soon. I tell you I worry. God only knows what can happen when a woman is in such a condition."

"What do you mean?" Philip asked quickly. "She's not going to have a baby?"

"What baby?" his mother said. "My heavens, that's all she needs now, a baby. That would about finish her off for good."

"What are you worrying about?" the old man said. "To hear you talk, somebody would think the world was going to fall down all of a sudden."

"Don't be foolish. I tell you it's terrible. If you saw the way that poor woman looks you wouldn't say such nonsense. She looks like a wild animal. All I pray to God is that she doesn't go ahead and do what her husband did."

"Pish, pish," Mr. Hayman went. He was superstitious about suicide and death, and always spat.

"Did you ever see such a fool?" Mrs. Hayman said to Philip. "He's topsy-turvy with age like Yente Maldick."

"All right," his father said with patient irritation, "Yente Maldick again. How many times will I hear that witticism?"

Mrs. Hayman put the soup on the table, but almost upset the plate. A wild shriek filled the hall. She stood as though paralyzed.

"My God," she said, paling. "I knew. My heart told me. It's Mrs. Sussman."

"Stop it," Philip said. "It's probably nothing."

The noise in the hall grew. People were running over the steps. Mrs. Hayman stood at the table, afraid to move. She couldn't go out and learn what the matter was. "It's my fault," she said in a moan, "it's all my fault. I knew it all the time, and I left her alone. I shouldn't have come downstairs. It's my fault." She rocked with grief and remorse.

"Stay here and don't worry," Philip said. "I'll run upstairs and find out what it's all about."

By the time he reached the hall the noise had subsided and the excitement had passed. One of the kids playing on the third-floor landing had fallen down a flight of steps and banged his head. He had been unconscious for a moment and his mother had set up a wail, crying that he was dead.

"See," Mr. Hayman said to quiet his wife, "all that fuss for nothing. I never saw a woman get excited so easily."

She went on rocking. "My heart still beats like a pump," she said in a thin voice. "I was sure Mrs. Sussman had jumped from the banister to the ground floor. I thought I even heard the sound of the body." She began crying.

"Get over with it," Philip said impatiently. "You women always think up crazy stories. People don't jump down four floors."

And now, high up a million miles into the sky, God sits in His trundle on a big cloud. He looks absentmindedly about, the beard long and very white, the flesh of His face gnarled because it has been such a very long time, such a very long time. And now He peers down, and for a moment His gaze rests again on Williamsburg, and He says to Himself, how are things going on down there, I wonder. And He looks. We must forgive God for His apathy; it has been a hot summer and He is a little tired of us, we never vary the show. So He sniffs to clear His nose and He returns to the task.

God wonders and looks. Everything is just as it always has been and as it will be. Mr. Sussman is gone and Mr. Miller is gone, but there are many men growing old to take their places. Mrs. Linck moves in heavy rhythm to the count of the rocker while the guinea pigs explore the dinginess for scraps of food. On Papravel's head rests a derby for a crown, and through the cigar he is chewing he is telling Mr. Rubin, "All right, all right, don't worry. I'll handle it." Little Yetta is making her first experiments with an eyebrow tweezer, her face all deep concentration. Natie the Buller, overcome by his reverie, dreams of ladies in Arcady as he sits screwed into the doorway underneath the Republic Theater billboard of coming attractions; while Davey, grown in a week to man's estate, is following the gutter with careful eye for cigarette butts of appropriate length.

Mahler, the cobbler, is arguing with Yente Maldick, asking her in three languages—namely, Yiddish, Russian, and English—to get the hell out of his shop, please. That's love, too.

In Tessie's apartment the blinds are drawn, but it does not matter for God can peer his way through men's skulls and windowshades. She is lying on a chaise longue of elegant style, reading a story in which a distinguished gentleman says, as he moves closer to the heroine, "You little liar, you little liar, I don't know why you talk like this when you know in your heart that you feel as I do. You said sweet things to me when you thought I was dying." Tessie reads. And Cohen in his room has a book on his chest as he takes times to rage. There is a little pimple inside his nostril and he is rubbing it while he controls his anger because the world is as it is.

As for Philip, God looks down and sees him too, and He says, is that fellow still pondering at the window? He's like a bird standing up on one leg all the time.

God wonders and looks. The sun covers Ripple Street with its warm brilliance, the men sit on the barrel chairs outside of Halper's

Stable, the tall racks in front of Yozowitz's laundry store hold the curtains stretched on pins and needles, and all the housewives seize the good side of the street for their baby carriages.

What, what, what? says God in surprise. He looks over the clouds and there He sees a regular crowd. My, my, God sighs, and He prepares to meet them.

NINETEEN

On that last evening Cohen was at it again, this time taking Philip to task for his want of imagination and his impulse to ferret out an unromantic actuality for everyone and everything. It had been another of those dark wet days. The damp air had probably entered both their beautiful souls, for Cohen was more peremptory with his speeches, and Philip, willing to make allowances for Cohen's condition but nettled by his insulting tone, felt less inclined to be indifferent, detached, and to put up with them. Cohen confused his mood with his chronic weltschmerz. He spoke at great length on the vicissitudes of a sensitive spirit, his dissatisfaction, the inadequacy of this sphere as far as he was concerned. If he had only given him at some time or another a hint, Philip had said, of what it was he did want, of the kind of world that would measure up to his temperament, he, Philip, would have been more patient with him. As it was, Philip had said, it was not weltschmerz but a grouch, not the soul aching in torment but the weather, and for him it was just as bad. Therefore he had no imagination, he ferreted.

"Ferret?" Philip said. "Oh, no. I do not ferret, I see what I see. The whole point is I don't embellish what I see with false ornamentation. Once it is false it no longer interests me. I'm willing to accept beauty and romance when I find it, but there's no necessity for kidding myself about it."

"In that case you will never find it. This is something that does not exist by itself. The individual must have the vision. In short, Hayman, your wisdom is undergraduate and cynical. I'm afraid you are just one of these wise gazabos."

"All right," he said impatiently, "haven't we had enough of it? Why don't you let me hear something about lilies in the cemetery bending with the wind like mourners weeping, or about pale girls sitting on park benches like leaves?"

"Please," said Cohen, tightening. "Don't get personal. An argument is an argument, don't mix everything."

Cohen walked around the room silent with disgust. You couldn't talk to a person like Philip. He opened the window, yelled down for Mahler, and told him to come up. The old man was a sustainingly pleasant companion, while Philip, contributing nothing to the atmosphere and actively detracting from it, adulterated its rich quality. Soon the cobbler lumbered in, huge and empty. Cohen was perceptibly enlivened.

"Perhaps you have a cigarette?" Mahler asked promptly. Cohen gave him a pack. "I can't get rid of that woman Yente Maldick. She lies on my head like a cloud that won't go away." The old man shook his head and sat down heavily on the bed, resting there without moving a muscle, like a huge lump of lead.

"See?" said Cohen with a returning note of triumph. "See? An epitomized expression of defeat and suffering through the centuries sits on the bed, and you can see nothing. What Epstein could do now if he saw Mahler!" The possibilities reduced him to inarticulation, practically choking him.

"Don't bother the old man," Philip said. "Can't you see he's sleepy?"

But there was no stopping Cohen now. "Mahler," he said with excitement. "Mahler, don't you agree with me there are certain things that break a man's soul?"

"Soul?" said the shoemaker. "What is soul?"

"Don't you know, Mahler?" Philip said. "A soul is fat juicy sauerkraut. Yiddish journalists and skinny poets with colds in their noses have soul. Cohen himself carries one around under his heart like mommas who carry their babies before they're born. All night Cohen stays up in bed and cries because his soul is so wonderful."

"Please!" Cohen besought him impatiently. "I said, Mahler, don't you agree with me there are certain things that break a man's soul? Take yourself in Russia, Siberia, and China. Weren't there some things in your life that broke your soul?"

"In Russia, in Siberia, in China," the old man said slowly, "they nearly broke my back. Even in America there's Yente Maldick to drive me out of my head with her pestering. Only, I am too strong and they will have to shoot me before I die. What's a soul, Cohen? Let them break my soul if this pleases them, just ask them to leave my back alone. Soul," he said, "I wouldn't give a rotten nickel for my soul."

"Mahler!" Cohen cried. "How can you say this to me? Are you kidding?"

"Don't get angry. What do I know? To me bread is good, and drink is good and warm, and sleep. That's all, Cohen."

"A man," Cohen pronounced with impressive slowness, "cannot live by bread alone."

"That's right," said Mahler, grinning foolishly. "Listen, young gentlemen, maybe you have a drop of whiskey in the place?"

Philip jumped up with a show of jubilation and poured the whole flask of Mrs. Miller's wine into an aluminum pan for Mahler. Cohen sat down in quiet reflection with a confused expression on his face. Perhaps he was wondering what attitude to strike next. Perhaps he was taking the conversation more seriously than Hayman supposed. It was impossible with Cohen to be certain about these things. For all Philip knew, Cohen might be seriously affected, but he doubted it. Philip watched Mahler's absorption with the pan of wine. The old man drank it up in a minute. "Wine is water," he said, simultaneously wiping his lips and cleaning his nose, "but have you got more?"

"Shall we go down to the cellar, Cohen?" Philip asked. Somehow he had begun to regard Mrs. Miller's barrel in the cellar as his property. At this point Cohen energetically woke from the fog of his reflection. He sprang from the chair and went into the kitchen without a word. He returned with a pan like the one Mahler held expectantly in his hand except that it was two or three times larger.

"Tonight," he announced with drama, "I'm going to get good and drunk." His face was seriously set and he looked at neither of them. The impression intended, perhaps, was that, having lost father, mother, wife, country, and home, nothing was left. If only for the sake of art, a complete disintegration was required and now, with God's help and the wine's, Cohen was going to see that this took place.

"Sure, Cohen," Philip said. "It's logical. Get drunk."

"On this?" Mahler asked incredulously. "You'll drown first."

Cohen marched ahead resolutely. Mahler did not understand the melodrama, indeed he was slightly perplexed by the entire situation, but he saw the possibility of more wine and that was enough for him. He grabbed his pan in his hand and followed.

"What's the matter with you, Hayman?" he asked. "Aren't you going to drink?"

"Sure," Philip said. "But from a pan? When I drink wine it's from the barrel itself."

The procession went down the steps. In the hallway on the ground floor they came upon Yente Maldick. She was wandering helplessly around with a jacket in her hand, crying with anxiety.

"What's the matter?" Philip asked her.

"Oh, woe," she sobbed. "Woe is me. I can't find Mahler. He's all alone in this world, there's nobody to look after him, and with his chest he goes out into the street without a jacket or a sweater."

Mahler himself spoke up. "Well, you can't find him now, missus. I just saw Mahler. He was going up to the roof. He wants to talk to God."

She looked at him suspiciously. "What can I do now?" she asked hopelessly, but still doubting a little.

"Go up to God yourself and find him," Mahler said.

Yente Maldick protested. "I can't climb the stairs. At my age, you can't walk five floors."

"Do what you want, then. Don't bother me."

"Sit down," Philip said. "You don't have to climb the stairs. Sit down and wait until Mahler comes down. He can't stay and talk to God all night. Or, better still, missus, go home and wait for Mahler in your own house. When I see Mahler I'll tell him you're looking for him."

Cohen was impatient and they had to leave her sitting on the hall stairs, resting her head against the banister and still holding the jacket on her knees.

Downstairs the huge water boiler filled the room with a cozy brown warmth. In the dust the small electric lamp filled the room with a pleasant glow. They rolled the barrel from Mrs. Miller's cellar compartment into the boiler room. Mahler settled down affectionately near the barrel on a pile of dirty but soft hall streamers. His beard was pressed contentedly against his chest, his legs sprawled over the floor; he was busy drinking the sweet stuff and he was happy.

As for Cohen, he had already begun to walk around the place like Hamlet, alternately smoking his cigarette, drinking from the pan, and declaiming the essential rottenness of the world it was his vast misfortune to inhabit.

"Hayman, he's broken me. You don't know what this means to me."

"Who?" Philip asked. "Who broke you?"

"Mahler. My whole spirit, everything I have done or thought for the past fifteen years, my intellectual spine has been broken. Like a thread of cigarette smoke suddenly bent by an unexpected breeze." He smoked and pondered the threads. That was a favorite, a thread of innocent smoke set upon by malicious breezes, the half-moon laying an egg on the Chrysler tower, the melancholy of autumn sunshine filtering through the leaves of trees. "Everything I have done or thought for the past fifteen years!" Cohen, the philosopher and doer, at eight.

Mahler, who was not troubled with a metaphysical conscience, gave complete concern to the wine after the fashion of puppies at their food. This world had drifted away from him, he was alone in paradise, there was an aluminum pan in his hand and in it was wine. In spite of the low opinion he had of the grape, it was beginning to unbalance him and he was unnaturally cheery. At times he had to stop guzzling and smoke a cigarette, allowing room for more wine. Mahler even squeaked out an old Russian tune in sandpaper tones.

"Wine is water," he said uncertainly, "but what a feast, what a party!" He clapped his hands with pleasure. Far away his eyes swam helplessly in the black face. "Like a czar, like a king. . . ."

"Even so, you're in luck, Mahler," Philip said. "Last year the wine turned into vinegar."

"What a calamity!" Mahler gasped. Suppose it had turned to vinegar this year! He rushed back to the pan as though the wine would turn into vinegar if he delayed. The liquid streamed down his beard in fine rivulets so that he resembled a thirsty man drinking water in the movies. Mahler drank, but it was too much for him and eventually he had to stop, lying inertly with a weak grin over his sleepy face.

By this time Cohen had grown slightly hysterical, from the wine and enthusiasm. The more or less momentary disturbance with which he had begun now gave way to the real heartsickness Philip thought he had detected before. This wasn't another fit of depression with him. It was lasting too long. Philip watched Cohen, wondered at his condition, and grew worried. How much of a faker was Cohen? Wasn't there some genuine base of unhappiness within him, something one couldn't laugh away? The wine was needed to bring it out, but that wasn't its whole reason. Cohen took Philip back as a brother and a friend with tears. He was not one-quarter dead, nor did he ferret. He had been holily right all the time and possessed a miraculous fund of patience to endure him as he had. It was Cohen who had slipped, who was wrong, who needed a friend and brother. Then he broke off, holding his hand to his forehead with great force. Philip had known this was on the way but it came with remarkable force, the revolution did.

"Hayman," he almost screamed, "it's a renascence of my soul. Can't you see it? I'm being reborn. The old life is leaving me. I shall be another man from this time on. Everything is strange, mysterious, the mist, like dreams—" he waved his hand to indicate the dust in the boiler room. "Tomorrow I shall start a new life."

"That's right," Philip said. Cohen was pretty drunk. "You're beginning a new life. Everything's swell."

"You still think I'm faking," Cohen protested with great earnestness, as if Philip's belief were the most important thing to him. "I'm not faking, Hayman. I used to, but no more. That's all over. I was such a faker, such a faker. But now it's entirely different. I see it. I want you to believe me. Hayman, you can tell from my voice, from the way I talk, from what I say. Do I look like a man who's a faker?"

"No, Cohen, no. Sure I believe you. Come on, Cohen, you'll go to sleep. Tomorrow, the new life." Philip wanted to get Cohen into his room and go to sleep. The night had gone sour on him. He wanted to finish it off.

Then abruptly Cohen grabbed Philip and pointed to Mahler, his eyes bright with a boy's sense of mischief. Even for Cohen the suddenness and completeness of the change was a surprising thing. Poor Mahler had in the meantime fallen asleep with a lighted cigarette between his lips. Hiccupping among his tears, Cohen was hilarious with glee.

"Let's watch him when the cigarette burns to his mouth and gets at his skin!" It seemed impossible that only a minute ago he had been crying so heartbrokenly over his new soul.

Philip woke Mahler. His first move was toward the barrel, from which he began filling the pan again.

"Go home," Philip said. "Go home, Mahler. The party's over."

The old man looked at him with a dead, happy expression. "If it's all the same to you," he said, "I'll spend the night in the cellar."

"All right, Mahler. But watch out with the cigarettes. You'll set everything on fire and then you'll roast like in hell."

"Listen, Hayman," he said, "don't you worry about me. In Kiev they gave me forty blows on the rump with a stick like a tree, every blow you could hear in Paris, and it didn't kill me."

Cohen was a little difficult. All the way up from the cellar he cried on Philip's shoulder, now because he had spoiled the fun by waking Mahler. Philip was tired. These parties always ended depressingly. On the hallway steps he saw Yente Maldick asleep, still clutching the jacket for Mahler. Philip shook the old lady until she opened her eyes.

"Go home, missus," he said. "Go home."

He had to repeat it many times, she didn't understand what he wanted. Cohen fell asleep, and while Philip worked on the old lady he had to support his friend. Finally he sat Cohen down on the steps and the two of them drowsed and resented Philip's interference. "I can't stay here all night," Philip finally said. He didn't like to leave the old woman there, he hoped someone else would take care of her, and he pulled Cohen to his feet.

In the room he undressed him and put him to sleep in his underwear, but at this point Cohen grew wide awake and began to protest.

"No pajamas?" he wept. "I always sleep in pajamas, Hayman. Wait and help me."

It was late. Philip didn't want to take the time and bother, but, fortunately, as soon as Cohen's head hit the pillow he fell asleep. And Philip, too, went to his flat to bed.

On that terrible night, when Ripple Street lay dead under the bright lamppost lights with its mute gray ash cans and the pieces of newspaper that the wind chased over the gutters, deep in the night while Mahler snored in the boiler room and Cohen slept drunkenly with sticky tears on his face, while Natie the Buller had strange dreams and Yetta in her sleep pulled the quilt closer to her chin, while cats wailed and wished they had never been born and a baby on the third floor cried in gasps, on that same night Mrs. Sussman said to herself that her burden was too much for her, and she gently woke her two boys on the mattress that lay on the floor. Grim-faced, composed, and determined, she cautioned the boys to silence. She led them resolutely through the dark halls, holding their hands tightly while their faces twisted and strained to keep back the tears of fright. Her beautiful long black hair was pushed over her ears by the wind. In bedroom slippers, she walked rapidly, knowing that if she paused once, if for only a moment, she would stop, and stop she would not. High up, a window blind, escaped outside, flapped furiously like a lamentation, and the boys, one following the other's example, broke and cried. Up Ripple Street, block after block, Mrs. Sussman rushed the boys, their little legs tripping as they tried to keep up with her rapid pace. They cried now in fierce terror, but their mother with the terribly fixed eyes did not heed their fear, nor did she stop. An ugly street cat paused in her howling to gaze upon the strange procession and was awed. As they came closer to the river Mrs. Sussman could not restrain herself and began to run. Later there were people who said that on the dock she screamed, and there were people who said the children pleaded with their mother and fought her. Later they found one of her bedroom slippers on the pier, lying lonely, the only thing left, and they handled it with silent respect. Eight weeks after her husband had squeezed the basketball bladder over his face, Mrs. Sussman pulled her two boys by the arms and jumped with them into the water.

Had the wine turned into vinegar? Philip had drunk less than Mahler or Cohen but sour fumes and an irritated stomach made him feel uncomfortably sick. He couldn't sleep but drowsed, sometimes more awake than asleep, sometimes almost asleep, but never entirely the one or the other. This must have gone on for two hours when suddenly he bounded out of bed. The house was on fire. Philip cursed Mahler, cursed Cohen, he cursed himself, but there was no time to lose.

He swiftly woke his father and mother. The heat rose from the cellar and Philip rushed his parents up to the roof. The old man, moving slowly, befogged with sleep, wanted to stay and help, but Philip forced him to follow Mrs. Hayman up the stairs. Philip remained. He banged on people's doors, while the air grew hotter. From below the smoke rose, first in stray wisps, soon in thick curls. For a moment he thought of Mahler. The cellar must be an inferno. Even in the excitement he couldn't help imagining Mahler's expression when he must have waked, drunk and besotted, and really believed he was roasting in hell. He rushed to Cohen's room. The racket in the hall was intense but he was snoring.

"Get up! The place is on fire!" Philip shook him violently.

"Fire!" Cohen asked in sleepy wonder. The realization broke through the mist. He sprang from the bed and rushed out of the room without another word.

"Up to the roof," Philip yelled. "Go up to the roof!" He went back to see what he could do.

On the landing Mrs. Miller was cracking her knuckles and wailing loudly. She stood in her cotton nightgown as though she was paralyzed to the spot, kept rolling her head from left to right as she surveyed the scene, and blubbered like a child, the tears rolling down thickly over the wrinkles of her face. How bald she was. It was the first time Philip had ever seen her without the kerchief she always wore. A tall, worried-looking man, who had somehow managed to put on a shirt before he left his room, took charge of the proceedings by roaring directions in a loud, authoritative voice. As he waved his hands the shirttails would flap up. And in spite of the gravity of the moment he always took time to smooth the cloth over his body respectably. One woman had managed to pull a clumsy buffet to the door of her apartment, bent on saving it. The tall man with the shirttails left his post in the center of the bedlam to argue with her. "My God, woman," he said, "how can you think of furniture when human lives have to be saved? You'll block the hall and then we'll all be killed." "Go away," she cried with controlled hysteria, "Go away if you won't help. You've got fire insurance. You've got nothing to worry about. If I want to save myself from complete ruin with this buffet, you won't stop me." The two stood there arguing. She pushed him out of her path, and then they began to wrestle. People jammed the stairs. And Mrs. Mahler in her nightgown wailed.

The doors to all the flats on the floor were left open. Philip noticed a woman running through the rooms, from one flat to the other. It was Yente Maldick. She wore a preoccupied expression on her face and was engaged in turning on full force every water tap she saw. He ran into her. She was on the point of stepping into a bathtub brimming with water. Philip pulled her elbow.

"Go up to the roof," he shouted. "Don't stay here. Go up to the roof!"

"No, mister, no," she said, pushing for the bathtub. "I can't climb the stairs. When a person gets to my age, it's too much to walk four flights. I can't do it." Philip tried to shove her to the door but the old woman offered remarkable resistance. "Let me alone," she shrieked. "You can't kill me. Help! Help! If I'm in a bathtub full of water, the fire can't touch me." She stumbled and Philip had to lift her up. He half-carried her to the hallway.

The landing was thick with people, pushing and shoving in confusion. Suddenly Philip spotted Cohen rushing back to his room.

"Cohen!" he yelled as hard as he could. "Are you still drunk? Go back!"

"Pajamas," he shouted back, barely pausing, but eager to have him understand. "Pajamas. . . ." He disappeared into the room.

Philip dropped Yente Maldick's arm and began shoving with his shoulder through the crowd, but he could make no headway. Everyone was insane with the excitement. The tall man with the shirttails and the woman were still fighting over the buffet. The landing grew hotter and hotter. The smell of fire was in everything, in the air, in the hallways, and in the people. It was difficult to breathe. Then the firemen came down from the roof and put an end to the confusion by shoving them all up the stairs and out of the building. But Cohen did not come out.

The air was soft and cool. It was one of those rare spring-like days that come in early September to relieve the hot monotony of summer. All the young women had their babies out sunning in carriages. The sun came into Philip's room like a flood, brightening the bed, the table, the book he was reading. Then it disappeared, hidden not behind clouds but behind the summer blankets airing on the clotheslines in the backyard, bellying with the breeze and then falling flat. The recurrence of the brightness and the dimness was a melancholy thing, and somehow, with the departure of the sweating heat, Philip longed for the cold winter times. He was impatient. The gray sky, the clouds like frozen water on the windowpane, the lonely walks in cold weather—Philip remembered the images and he longed for the winter because then life in Williamsburg grew less exposed, less crude, and a little gentle.

In Williamsburg the summer was getting over, but, on the other hand, in Tasmania it was the winter that was leaving for the soft winds of spring. Philip, waiting for his mother to give him his dinner, went to lie on the bed. The halls of the building were still marked with the black scars and everywhere one went the fire smell of smoke and damp wood persisted, but after the first days it was all the same, no one noticed those signs. The fire was beginning to be forgotten.

Mahler had been dug out of the debris in the cellar unrecognizable and all black like a charred pole. Cohen they found stiff, sitting on the bed with his hands drawing the pajama pants over his knees, fixed in that peculiar pose when the heated air had killed him. To read about a fire in a book was always an exciting thing, but actually Philip felt cheated. He regretted the passing of Cohen and Mahler as sincerely as a man could miss people he had known, but they had disappointed him. For Mahler was certainly an extraordinary man, and Cohen as well, if less honest. And the incident was unusual. Had Philip read about these characters and their situations in a book he would have been easily drawn by their romantic flavor. He would probably have been envious because his own life would have seemed so empty by comparison. Yet knowing these people in the flesh and going through the story with them, it was all, at the bottom, strikingly unremarkable, commonplace, and even flat. When you met people and lived there was no heroism, no romance, no poetry. Cohen, of course, would have objected, Philip thought, but that was how he felt. Or perhaps there was something wrong with him.

The scars and smell of smoke persisted, but the children running through the halls in play paid no attention. The fire was beginning to be forgotten. It was as his mother always said. Many things took place all the time but it was nothing. People grew excited, and then it passed. It was over, you forgot about it. In a book, Philip said, a fire could be an important event, it could be used to bind together a setting and a story, it offered a neat end. But actually there was no climax, no end. It went on. Here he was himself, lying on a bed. . . .

Philip had been sitting at his table reading a novel by Thackeray and marveling at the clean delineations of the people therein. How wonderfully crisp were the characters. The author knew all about them and said it. He knew everything. All authors knew everything because they were like God. Thackeray told you what the people did, and then he said what caused the action. Old Miller, God rest his wizened soul, used to say, in his funny, smiling fashion, "Va-cha-choo-loo, va-cha-choo-loo," and that meant, when the wind will blow, the cradle will rock. How marvelously writers were able to perceive, clear-cut and with sureness, the causes and the actions of their characters. In life no man was known, even to himself, but in these novels the authors were able to explain their people logically. What wonder-makers! What liars.

Someone had just begun to play chopsticks on the piano. Two women were talking across the yard, in scrappy, raw voices. Philip's book rested on a glass top. When the sun hit the glass there came colors of weak green, light brown, and lemon yellow. About four or five babies were crying miserably, and about four or five radios dispensed cracked music simultaneously.

"Va-cha-choo-loo, va-cha-choo-loo," Old Miller used to say. "Men are the sum of a million infinitesimal phenomena and experiences. A million atoms of a certain type produce, in the end, wood, just as a million of another make stone, and iron, and gold. The same is true of these men.

"To find out, you must make a laboratory out of Williamsburg to learn what touches people here, why these details affect, and in what manner. A tremendous task. If you would really discover the reason for people's actions you must pick Williamsburg to pieces until you have them all spread out before you on your table, a dictionary of Williamsburg. Then select. Pick and discard. Collect and analyze."

How were people revealed? How could one discover what made them go? In books like Thackeray's there was always pertinent dialogue, action developing logically, and the subtle, deftly inserted comment of description. Actually, people said "Good morning" or "It's a hot day"; they went to work and sat on the sidewalk in the evenings. People did small, inconsequential things, they crooked their small fingers becomingly as they drank vanilla seltzer, they wiped their noses in absentminded slow moments and they said "All right, all right, don't holler. I'll be up in a minute." Writers selected, but their imaginations insisted, and was their judgment divine? Why did they pick certain things and overlook others? To present a man honestly you would really have to give him entire.

Philip went to the parlor and looked out of the window. The sun shone brightly across the street. His side was dark because the building in which he lived was blotting out the light. Along his side of the street houses were of different heights and on the sidewalk opposite, the shadows of the buildings formed an uneven line. Philip looked at the group of women around the baby carriages. Mrs. Linck, heated and angry, was involved in fierce conversation. The eyes went up and down savagely, the mouth sawed, the floppy individual raged.

"I don't want children in the yard, missus," she stated with great positiveness and in a voice that carried. "It's my yard. If you don't like the way I take care of it you know what you can do."

"Never mind," said the woman. "I don't care what you do with your yard. You can put it somewhere I don't have to tell you. But nobody can curse my child. I don't need you to say such terrible things. After all, he's my boy. No mother likes to hear anybody curse her baby like that."

"Listen, missus, you like him so much, why don't you take good care of him? Why do you think I keep him out of the yard? Because I like to holler? I'm a mother too, I had children in my time. All the women keep bottles and God knows what else on the windowsills. Would you like it if a bottle fell down, God forbid, and hit your boy on the head?"

That ended the argument, Mrs. Linck certainly had the women there, and she stamped across the street back into her house with a defiantly triumphant air. Her kindness to the neighborhood's children was unappreciated? To hell with the woman.

Philip looked down the street. The carriages on the sidewalk formed an exhibition. A middle-aged woman was dancing in clumsy, hopping movements to please a baby hidden among its blankets. The woman popped up and down and clapped her hands. Her face was creased with joy, for babies were wonderful things, everyone loved them, they were simply adorable. The dancing lady spoke kindly to a pregnant woman to indicate the joys of motherhood. How often Philip had heard them tell their syrupy philosophy to an expectant woman. It was hard, they said, it was very hard, but once you had them a mother's heart et cetera. They grew up, they went away, they forgot the pain they had caused and the worry when they had been sick, they went on, selfish, ungrateful, and forgetting, but after all, a mother's heart et cetera. The pregnant woman sighed with proud resignation and shook her head in sad concurrence. Look, she as good as said, I suffer for humanity, the world owes me something for it. A woman lifted her breast out of her waist and placed it in position. For the sake of delicacy she partly covered the soft flesh with a handkerchief. The pregnant woman and the one with the breast exposed conversed in the sunshine. Before and after. But we must not be disrespectful.

These were people as God made them and as they were. They sat in the sunshine going through the stale operations of living, they were real, but a novelist did not write a book about them. No novel, no matter how seriously intentioned, was real. The progressive development, the delineated episodes, the artificial climax, the final conclusion, setting the characters at rest and out of the lives of the readers, these were logical devices and they were false. People did not live in dramatic situations. You might even isolate some event in their lives, extract its drama, and labor over it according to the rules, but in the end you would still have an incomplete portrait of them, it would be unfaithful to the whole. Even by isolating one episode there was exaggeration. The trouble with writers was that they knew too much. They made life too simple. They could say of the women at their carriages in the sunshine that they rose at ten, made their hurried breakfasts, tidied the rooms, went downstairs, bought candy and soda water, gossiped, went to the movies, and made delicatessen suppers for their husbands; a writer could say that and get away with it, but it wouldn't be the whole thing. They could say that Cohen was a nut who tried to commit suicide because his head was growing bald, that Philip's father was an old Chinaman who hadn't been around, that Tessie was one of those girls who live by *The New Yorker*; they could say that Philip himself was an adolescent in the agonies of awakening inquiry, in the stage when one was occupied with gaudy abstractions like life, meaning, and the grave. They could say that and be sufficiently understood, but it wasn't enough, it wasn't the whole thing. What was all the excitement about? Philip asked himself. Literature was not reality. That was all there was to it. Writers who said otherwise were fakers, claiming more than they could do. A book was an artificial synthesis, the product of a man's idea, to illustrate through his stress on characters and situations certain principles in which he was interested. Take Ripple Street, with Halper's Stable, Yozowitz's laundry, the Auburn S.C., the life on the roofs, in the cellars and in lots, Davey and his gang, Miller, Mrs. Linck and her family, Cohen, his own father and mother, Mahler and Yente Maldick, together with the hundreds of other persons who lived in the tenements on the block; take Ripple Street with the merry-go-rounds in the sunshine, the Italians coming down the street with cheap ice-cream bricks in the small carts; take the whole of Ripple Street from morning to night and back again; take it and reproduce it faithfully and you would have a great formless mass of petty incident, the stale product of people who were concerned completely with the tremendous job of making a living so that tomorrow they would be able to make a living another day. Everything here was petty. Love was a hot joke, a soiled business in worn bedsheets, a sedative interlude in the omnipresent struggle of making a living. There was never time enough. Poetry and heroism did not exist, but the movies did. People in tenements lived in a circle without significance, one day the duplicate of the next until the end, which occurred without meaning but accidentally, cutting the procession short as pointlessly as Cohen's life had been cut. People were born, grew tired and calloused, struggled and died. That was all, and no book was large enough to include the entire picture, to give the completely truthful impression, the exact feeling.

And what is to become of me? Philip asked. These problems we ask to wait a while, in good time we shall worry; these problems persist and never cease, in their inarticulate way, to torment. He remembered his brother Harry's advice. He remembered what Miller used to say. A man must be active, he must make money. What was Philip kidding around for, exploring the cavities of his teeth and pondering his eternal soul after the fashion of poor Cohen? This was something definite and concrete. It meant release and time for life. Money, thought Philip, and remembering Papravel he admired his father for his fine serenity. Was there no way out between the dirty preoccupations of fast money and the deadness of his father's example?

Vainly, said Philip (Lo! and also, Behold!), do I seek within me something magnificent, worth enthusiasm, worth labor, to guide me for the next forty or fifty years to come.

Shall I continue in my quiet anesthesia and contemplate myself imperturbably? Self-possessed, controlled, and analytical, above and indifferent to everything, but really dead years before my time?

Shall I continue to tramp the streets covered in a sunny tranquility while a vague and aching nostalgia permeates me, nostalgia for places I have never seen because they do not exist, for persons completely unaffected, warm and kind and unreal?

Shall I fool around with Tessie Schlausser and dream at the same time of unearthly women, fascinating and wonderful because at twenty I cannot have Ruth Kelman?

Shall I wallow in this gentle sadness in the darkness of moving-picture houses, over ruminative cigarettes, like one allowing warm water to run through one's fingers on a cold morning?

And shall I, too, continue to inspect my comb in the light before my eyes for fallen hairs?

Dammit, Philip almost cried aloud. He tried to rouse himself from his mood and went back to his table. He opened *Pendennis*, but it was hard to read. It was getting late already and the sun had moved upward on the tenement wall, beyond the reach of his window, and there would be no more light and the crazy colors on his glass top. The women were going upstairs one by one as their husbands came home from work. Someone began to play chopsticks on the piano. Two women were talking or arguing in raw scrappy tones from windows across the yard. Philip tried to read, but with the sun gone he felt alone and depressed. He thought of winter, the quiet and empty streets. About four or five babies were crying miserably and the radios kept on sending out the chirpingly cheerful music. Philip's head ached. He lay down again over the bed.

Mrs. Hayman came bustling in to give him his dinner.

"What do you think, Philip? They just found Mrs. Sussman's boy," she said at the gas range. "After all this time. I just heard the news. The poor baby, they found him all the way in Queens someplace. In all my life I never witnessed anything so terrible."

"That means they're all found now," Philip said from the bedroom.

"Yes, but what good does that do anybody?"

If you want to discover the reason, the sage in the long beard had said, the sage in whose skinny body all the cold wisdom of the world dwelt, if you want to discover the reason, you must pick

Williamsburg to pieces until you have them all spread out on the table before you, a dictionary. And then select, look for cause and effect.

"Come," Mrs. Hayman called. "Come, Philip, it's ready on the table."

And Philip, waiting for the years to come to see what would happen to him, went to his dinner.

"Eat," his mother said. "Eat with bread. Don't touch only the fancy stuff."

It was night at the boarding house in Aligerville where Papravel kept his boys. Outside the full-starred sky resembled a huge ceiling in a Brooklyn burlesque house. The summer was already leaving and in the coolness of the night air could be discerned the gentle sad quality of autumn. But Mrs. Van Curen had the big living room all lit, the boys half sat, half lay in the chairs, and everyone smoked cigars. After war came peace, quiet, and content.

"Listen, boys," said Papravel from a full heart and with exuberant satisfaction, "it's a party. Tonight we celebrate because all that comes, knock wood, is good news. Morantz, he's quit not only in Williamsburg but in the mountains altogether. We bought him out. As for Gilhooley, let no one say Papravel don't take good care of his boys for Anschele Nussbaum here has everything fixed right, only give us a little time and God's help. And just this morning the railroad company sent out an announcement they take no more passengers, only freight. And it is only a beginning, because, remember, there is still a God over America."

Papravel interrupted the monologue long enough to relight his cigar. The boys listened with their eyes almost closed, but Mrs. Van Curen, that pious old lady, watched him intensely, listening with awe. As he held the match, Papravel turned serious. His eyebrows became constricted, and he waved the match vigorously to kill the flame.

"America," he repeated with conviction through the smoke,

"I don't care what anybody says, America is a wonderful country. Seriously, seriously, I mean it. Look at me, look how I worked myself up in four short years. In America everyone has an equal chance. I don't know how things are in Russia now, even God Himself don't know what's going on there these days, but even so, where, I want to know, where in the world could a Jew make such a man of himself as right here in America?"

He had to say the last part quickly for most of his breath was gone and now Papravel waited with his eyes opened wide for an answer from him who dared. But in the pause Mrs. Van Curen suddenly took it into her head to cry. She was very sleepy and wept noiselessly but with many tears.

"What's the matter?" Papravel asked concerned. "What's the matter, what's the old lady crying about?"

Mrs. Van Curen looked up sadly. "I'm crying because you're such a fine, upstanding, kind young man, and yet when you die you won't go to Heaven."

"Why?" Papravel wanted to know. "Why should you say a thing like that?"

"You've never been baptized, Mr. Papravel."

"Oh," he said with great relief. "Don't you worry your little gray head over that." He didn't know whether this was a joke or what. "Just you leave this to me, Mrs. Van Curen, and everything will be all right," Papravel said, and he smiled happily.

HOMAGE TO BLENHOLT

ONE

Byron lay, lazily lay

Balkan strode through the heavy morning mist that tenderly covered the dirty streets of Williamsburg feeling mysteriously enveloped by unreality, like one who walks in dreams. This conception was occupying his mind with its pleasant strangeness, but it was possible only because at the same time he was overlooking the character of his gait. This was a peculiar one, involving a delaying, circular movement of the right hip, which had the effect of kicking his right foot sharply forward in order to maintain the necessary rhythm. No man with such a mortal manner of walking had the right to think of himself as walking through unreality, but Balkan strode on, bathing deliciously in the tepid waters of his illusion, even though the repeated recurrences of that hip movement with its ensuing foot-kick resembled, spiritually, at least, the constant snifflings of a nose-cold sufferer.

"A word, sir, with you," said Ali Baba and the forty thieves. "Could I, sir, have your ear a moment?" Yes, yes, answered Balkan, his eyes half closed, but that was as far as the reverie took him. Ali Baba melted away, he wouldn't say another word. High above like a magic carpet in the sky, a red banner proclaimed the picture of a lady, wonderfully beautiful, of magnificent dimensions, in a net bathing suit. "The sign of Orocono Oil," she said cheerily, "is the sign of Happy Motoring." "Pay-puh? Pay-puh?" a boy asked Balkan. It was a real boy.

Balkan took a moment. "No," he said judiciously.

"Pay-puh? Pay-puh?" the boy wailed. There was nobody else near him but he was not one to be affronted and the boy addressed the misty morning resolutely.

Balkan turned from the Bridge Plaza and walked up the Extension. The cobbled streets had begun to grow noisy with traffic speeding by to the bridge to beat the day's rush, but lumbering dispiritedly, the milkman's horse made his way through the fog. Who has seen the white horse? Balkan asked, his face drawn tensely in the attitude of the mysteries. Who rides the white horse? Where is the whosis? Where is the oompah-oompah? Balkan had to emerge to laugh ruefully at himself. Well, why not? he asked.

Delicious! This strange world, with the dimly seen men hurrying grimly to make subway and trolley connections—weird figures in the mist; the phantom autos fleeing past; the sight of the streets themselves at this time, dirty with newspapers in the gutters; the quiet tenements resting like old dogs before the day's sun came out; and overhead all the marvelous ladies on the bill posters, smiling and without clothes even though there was no one save Balkan to look up at them and be impressed. Delicious! said Balkan, and thinking of the sparrows, he breathed a blessing on that white old horse.

Balkan's luxury, and most mornings he rose before seven to walk the streets, for then he felt as though he were eight feet tall and weighed three hundred pounds. There were, in America, it was true, the proud and the meek, and in the mornings, alone in the mist, he too was with the mighty. Balkan glowed. At seven o'clock the streets of Williamsburg were barely awake, there was no humiliation, no indignity, and it was possible for him to feel a man, living in great times, with grandeur and significance. With himself, in the morning mist, there was no sister to call him kvetch and ridicule him. Ruth and his friends were not here to make fun of his projects and his theories. And the sweaty dinginess of Williamsburg became distant, lost, for Balkan strode in a world of his own in which all dreams grew real, all wishes fulfilled. At these times, his mind, unvexed by reality, was drowsy with hopes and plans for success. He would rise, one stage following promptly the other, he would lift himself out of Williamsburg and its deadness, the spirit would become magnificent and heroic—a beaming life. The daydreams tumbled in his head as he walked, and he was all the happier because he thought of them now with sureness. All his hopes would come true, he knew, he knew, and the gorgeous feeling of certainty welled within him almost beyond capacity. Even like Tamburlaine, like Tamburlaine . . . On Rodney Street the candy store was opening for business, the man removing the huge glass windows.

"Good morning!" cried Balkan with joy.

"Hah?"

He was a bald-headed man with a collar that curled like a cord. His eyes, still showing sleep, looked at Balkan with worried suspicion.

"I'll be your first customer," smiled Balkan, nothing fazed. "Lemon-lime, please."

"Hah? What is it?"

Balkan pointed to the inverted jar of syrup.

"Soda water?"

He raised a glass, frowning, pressed the button for the juice to trickle, poured seltzer, and placed the glass before Balkan. The dead dampness and dark of the morning covered the store dismally. Balkan drank without relish, for the candy-store man watched him gloomily all the time, with deep concern, his hands on his hips.

Not so good. Balkan walked up Ripple Street, his first contact with reality sobering him. Suddenly he stopped, his mouth opening. What could it be? Far down the street, through the deep mist, he saw the blurred shape of some impossible figure. Short it was, but round and bulky, resembling nothing human. Balkan, instead of going up to it, waited as the strange form floated up to meet him. Tensely he waited, with his mouth still open, his eyes peering through the thick spectacles.

Finally his mouth closed. The apparition was caused by two pregnant women walking arm in arm. Once again Balkan acknowledged with a sigh the unreliability of sense perception, and he pondered the early skeptics, the philosophical problem: reality vs. appearance, Cameades who held that there was no truth, Zeno who would not get out of the way of wagons, denying his eyes. Was it Zeno? There were two or three Zenos. The difficulty about the Zenos always perplexed his scholarly nature. The philosopher in question, he finally remembered, was not one of the Zenos, but another called Phyrro. However, this did not solve the problem of the Zenos, and he passed with a vague but unmistakable feeling of dissatisfaction. The mood of happy exhilaration passed.

In the confused laboratory of his mind, a bell rang, chidingly calling the session to a halt, so to say. With a definite degree of sadness, for he had enjoyed his morning's walk, Balkan relinquished his speculations and turned his odd gait to the house in which he lived. He had to clear his head, the mist would be lifting, the hot sun was already breaking through. Now he had to think of preparing himself for Blenholt's funeral. The thought stirred him. In conscientious order he listed his tasks: one, to stop at his friends' rooms reminding them of the occasion; two, to dress appropriately for the ceremonies; and three, to go with his friends to Blenholt's late residence. Balkan tried to concentrate on these immediate problems and he hoped sincerely that nothing would arise to distract him.

In time the unlovely red brick of his tenement house presented its stolid appearance. Somehow afraid and a little unhappy with apprehension, Balkan nevertheless took time to notice the inscription on the wall above the stoop. At other moments he had often regretted the neighborhood custom that numbered houses but did not, as elsewhere, give them a name. But this morning his building bore one. It was written in yellow chalk, crude, but all the same a name. YOU STINKE, it said, and, heartened a bit, Balkan entered the hall.

He made his way in the gloom through the groups of children who were running about in games skillfully improvised to suit the limitations of tenement corridors.

"Stay outside and go break a leg!" Heshey's mother said, pushing him as he balked. Balkan stopped to watch, pained already by the condition of life in Williamsburg.

"I don' wanna. I gotta make pippee."

"Liar! You a liar!" said Heshey's mother, still pushing, the perspiration running down her face in little streams. "You just made pippee. You only wanna stay in the house."

Heshey dug his heels and pushed back stubbornly with his rump. His mother struggled with him. "Why do you get up so early, you bandit? Only to torture me?" she asked. "Stay in bed or go in the hall. I can't make breakfast with you in the house."

She boosted him with her knee and he fell forward on his hands. "Strong like a nox!" she commented, and slammed the door.

"Momma! I hurt myself!" Heshey wept cagily. "You knocked me down and I hurt myself!"

"Go to hell and break a leg," she said peacefully. As if she would be taken in by a maneuver as simple as that! "I'm making breakfast."

"Am I a stinker?" Chink asked, coming up to Heshey immediately.

"Who? Me? You asking me?"

"Am I a stinker?"

"Wa-ah! Momma!"

"Am I a stinker?"

"Momma, Chink's socking me!"

"Am I a dope? Am I a stinker? I'm asking you for real."

"Momma!" Heshey shrieked in frenzy. "It's no kidding! I ain't fooling! Chink's socking me!"

"Go to hell and break a leg," her voice floated out placidly. "You ain't coming into the house if you die!"

"What's the matter, you can't talk?" Chink asked with a mean look on his face. "You tongue-tied? How would you like a kick in the belly?"

"Wa-ah!"

Balkan decided to intervene. "Listen here, sonny," he said, "why don't you leave him alone? He's not doing anything to you."

"Oh, yare? Who's asking you?"

Balkan searched for something appropriate to say. He pushed the kid away.

"You keep your lousy hands away from me, you louse, you get funny with me I'll drop a bottle on your rotten head from the roof, how you like that, you yellow-belly, hitting a kid below your size!"

A neighbor stuck her head out of the door. She had heard the noise and seeing Balkan, gathered that he had been hitting the boy.

"Keep your hands to yourself, mister!" she demanded. "A man like you, you ought to be good and ashamed!"

Balkan stopped. There was the woman, a protector of the young. How could he explain it? Chink looked hard and tough, and before him Balkan quailed. He was bound to lose in dignity.

"It's nothing, missus. He was hitting the other little boy. I only wanted to stop him. Come on," he almost begged Chink. "Why can't you leave him alone?"

"Oh, yare?" Chink said. "Nuts."

The woman glared at her doorstep.

"Heshey . . . you better go down in the street. If he bothers you, tell me."

"Yare? And what'll you do about it?" Chink wanted to know.

"I'll—you'll see. You want to be careful."

"Listen, mister," Chink said. "You know what?"

"What?" Balkan asked hopefully.

"You stink!"

"Good! Good! Give him. Don't let him hit you," the woman said at the door. "Just because he's bigger!"

"Oh, go away, you . . . you little . . ."

Balkan walked up the flight in sharp distress. Even a kid. Everyone and everything. No matter what he tried to do, he always ended somehow in a drop from grace. The picture of the woman, righteously glowering at him at her doorstep, remained in his mind to torment him. Unjust! Unjust! Humiliation, the source of deepest hurt to him, was his constant peril. "Gee whiz," Balkan muttered, thinking of his pleasant walk in the mist. "Gee whiz." He was at Coblenz's door.

Hesitating on the landing, Balkan first became aware of noise. When he took time to analyze it, he knew he was hearing the swishing metallic noises children produce when they roller-skate on a board floor. Then there was a regular thumping. What this was Balkan could not imagine, but the spasmodic curses he easily identified as Coblenz.

Balkan turned to go away but he remembered Blenholt and the funeral. Shaking his head and fearful of what might be to come, feeling very much his own height and weight, Balkan knocked softly.

TWO
Joan Crawford's at the Miramar

BALKAN KNOCKED SOFTLY but it did no good. Again and again he knocked. He would have rung the bell but he knew that Coblenz had long ago smothered the little metal ball with paper and that therefore the bell would be useless. Nevertheless he decided to try it and he pressed the button. Overhead the swishing noises of the skates persisted together with the thumping and the curses. No wonder Coblenz couldn't hear him. Balkan took to pounding on the door with great force. Then abruptly Coblenz himself was there, almost to be greeted by both of Balkan's fists in midair.

"What's the matter with you? You crazy?" he asked. "How many times do I have to yell, come in? You like to knock on the door so much?"

"Why do you have to stick paper in the bell?" Balkan countered feebly. "How can a person ring the . . ."

"Those damn kids!" Coblenz said. "Listen to them."

The skates screeched over the floor as though it were a washboard. Then Balkan was able to identify the thumping for at this moment Coblenz picked up the broom and resumed poking the ceiling with the handle end. With relentless vigor he poked, his face masked into rigidity in order to control the furious desperation that was in him. Coblenz stumped along in solemn exasperation and in return, like an answer, could be heard the regular tearing swishes of the kids above.

"Then people say I'm nuts," he moaned. "They don't even have ball-bearing skates. I wouldn't mind it so much, maybe, if they had ball bearings. As it is, I'm going crazy. Then people say, they say, 'Coblenz is nuts.'"

"In many ways," Balkan said with a pang, "kids are no good."

"Thanks. Thanks very much. You're a great help."

"Well," exclaimed Balkan in protest. "Don't take it out on me!"

The ceiling was mashed into a rich design, the central motif of which was, of course, the inlaid holes caused by the broomstick handle. There was nothing for Balkan to do but examine the holes, and the more he thought of it, the more he felt that this design was capable of artistic appreciation. For a moment he thought of mentioning this to Coblenz seriously but he recovered himself immediately. He said nothing but waited for his friend to stop and at length he did, abruptly and without a word. He threw the broom to the floor so that it danced for a moment on the straws and finally, capitulating, fell. Balkan took care to breathe softly. He was afraid. There was something about his friend, especially when he fell into these moods, that frightened Balkan in spite of all he could muster to strengthen himself. And the acknowledgment of this weakness on his part hurt him more than the weakness itself. Why should he be afraid of Coblenz?

"Coblenz," Balkan began aggressively, "I came to remind you. You know. Blenholt's funeral. You promised to come with us."

But here Coblenz went to the windowsill to pick up a bottle of whiskey. He sucked a mouthful of liquor over his teeth, wincing as he drank for the alcohol, in addition to killing the pain in his tooth, also entered the crevices of his tongue and inside cheek, providing burning sensations. In the end he swallowed the mouthful manfully and sat down to contemplate its possible effects.

"Toothache?" Balkan asked solicitously.

"So what?"

"Nothing. Only, of course, I'm sorry. It's too bad."

"The whiskey," Coblenz complained, "it hurts my mouth."

"Blenholt, you remember?" Balkan asked, encouraged. "We said we'd all go, Munves, you and me?"

"What?" Coblenz asked dreamily in pain. "Listen, I don't want to give you the impression I'm squawking today, but it all happens together, that's my luck. Listen, professor, let me tell you how it all happened so you can get an idea."

Balkan dared not interrupt. It was going to be hard.

"This morning," whined Coblenz like a baby, "I get up at five o'clock in the morning and right away I know I'm in for it. Because why did I get up so early? Something must have gotten me up, I said to myself, and I start worrying. I'm feeling fine, but I got a hunch, like picking a winner in the races, only, of course, the opposite. So right away I take no chances. I gargle my throat with aspirin, I apply yellow oxide to my eyelids, I syringe my ears with boric acid, and I clear my nose with menthol. I get all these things done and then fine! My tooth begins to hurt.

"Ho! Ho! Ho!" Coblenz laughed bitterly. "I am laughing. Indeed that gives me a laugh. Maybe the pain will go away, I'm imagining it. So I wait. I wait and I wait but I can't let it alone. First thing you know I'm sucking air through the teeth and then it gets worse. Leave it alone, I say to myself, but I can't, I got to make it worse and then I am drinking cold water over it to numb the tooth. You know. Then all the teeth on the side begin to hurt until I figure, it's no use kidding, I got a toothache. So I go outside to Yusselefsky and I wake him up. Sell me a bottle whiskey, please, and he says, 'Who? Coblenz, he's crazy, so early in the morning.' So I get the whiskey and the more I drink the worse it gets. For a second the tooth stops hurting and I say, fine! but then it starts all over again, only harder. I don't know, maybe people are right, maybe I am nuts, but I'm getting to think that God picked me out special and He's got a grudge against me."

This was the nearest Coblenz had ever reached toward a personal confession with Balkan. Balkan heard the long speech out, his posture one of complete sympathy, and he was gladdened. He wondered whether he ought to begin with that theory of pain he had. It was true that Coblenz's tone had been more intimate than ever before, but nevertheless he had delivered himself with terrible self-restraint. Balkan, considering his friend's distended condition, feared. But bravely dismissing any possibility of unpleasantness for himself he decided to risk his theory for the sake of whatever good it might do.

"For," said Balkan nervously, "there is nothing either good or bad but thinking makes it so."

"What?" Coblenz asked, his swollen eyes staring with wonder.

"Hamlet," Balkan explained.

"What are you talking about?"

"See, this may or may not help. It sometimes works with me. See . . ."

"Is this a theory?"

"Never mind," said Balkan, wincing. "Try . . ."

"I want to know. Is this one of your theories?"

"Well, it's not a theory exactly. It's what I do when something hurts."

"Oh," said Coblenz doubtfully. "All right. Shoot."

Balkan drew a breath. "See, try to localize the pain in your brain. That is to say, Coblenz, can you possibly manage to think of your toothache as one articulated ball of sensation?"

"All right," said Coblenz impatiently. "What are you kidding around for?"

"All right. You have it isolated. Examine it."

"What?"

"The pain." Balkan spoke rapidly. Now or never. "Think of it. Try to determine its properties. Regard it as a sensation devoid of good or evil in itself. Investigate it with scientific detachment and now ask yourself whether this particular sensation must be necessarily unpleasant."

"Aw," said Coblenz suspiciously. "What are you trying to kid me for? This is a theory."

"Go on, try it," Balkan urged. "Give it a chance."

Coblenz tried it solemnly, probing within himself while his face added a new shade of trouble to its expression. Balkan, holding his breath in fear, studied the face to detect in advance, if he could, a sign for better or worse. Time passed achingly and there was nothing said. He began to worry.

"For there is nothing either good or bad," Balkan faltered. "As it says . . . Hamlet . . ."

"You know," Coblenz pronounced after all, "I think there's something in what you say. It works a minute, then you say, what's the use of kidding yourself, you got a toothache. It's a theory, all right, don't try to throw any bull at me. Anyhow, thanks."

Coblenz walked around the room, determined at all costs not to touch the whiskey bottle again, but it was getting hard. Someone knocked at the door and Coblenz, glad at the distraction, yelled with feeling "Come in."

An old man, in worn clothes, entered the room. He was gray with age, fallen apart and pasty. He held a string of yellow pearls suspended from his forefinger in a graceful curve.

"For your sweetheart," he said hopefully. "Fifty cents. Worth a dollar, I should live so."

"Got no sweetheart," Coblenz said, annoyed.

"Then for your sister. Forty cents."

"Got no sister. Got no forty cents."

"Thirty cents. Twenty cents," the old man begged. "You got a mother, ain't it? Ten cents! Give a man a show."

Coblenz began tapping, first with his thumb, then the pinkie, and then the fourth finger. He kept on tapping faithfully in that order. The kids on the floor above started roller-skating in earnest now, and every swish of their skates cut into Balkan's flesh as he felt for his friend. Coblenz was now sucking air through the side of his mouth, his face screwed up, ready to cry. That terrible peddler had brought back his bad humor, said Balkan, and he discovered he had an enormous desire to get out before the explosion. But as he rose to leave, he changed his mind. Blenholt.

"Oh, yes, Coblenz," he said as though the thought had just by some strange coincidence struck him, "about Blenholt's funeral. I wanted to remind you . . ."

At this point the pearl peddler ventured to jiggle the string a bit, his face clouding as hope left. Coblenz went on tapping, thumb, pinkie, and fourth finger. And the kids skated across the floor like a shriek.

"Then people say I'm nuts," Coblenz wept, speaking in a low tone, his head nodding accompaniment. "Then they say I'm nuts. GOD DAMN!"

He rose, grabbed the green bottle, and was sucking whiskey over his teeth again.

"All right! All right!" exclaimed the peddler, insulted. "You don't have to get mad. Not only he don't buy," he muttered, "he has to get mad too in the bargain." And muttering indignantly he left.

Balkan wanted intensely to follow. He looked at his friend's face swollen with pain and exasperation and he trembled. I'm scared, he thought, his fear humiliating him; look, he's got me bulldozed. Who is he to get me bulldozed? What's the matter with me?

"Coblenz!" he blurted out. "What about Blenholt's funeral? You promised, remember?"

Coblenz picked up the broom and walked to him menacingly. Silently, his expression ominous, he approached with the slow, shuffling steps of a maniac. "*Oui, monsieur*," he said, almost calmly, his eyes fixing his prey. "*Oui, monsieur*. Is there anything monsieur likes this lovely morning? All I need is you pestering the life out of me and that will make everything fine and dandy."

Balkan was on the point of shrieking. "Now don't get . . ." Coblenz came on. Balkan gulped with misery, it was the last straw, but he could not restrain himself. He backed to the door and bolted out. Defeat complete.

Within the room Coblenz was now left to himself. First he looked at the door, then at the ceiling, then at the broom. His whole head seemed to ache with pain. Oh, God damn, he wept. Why me all the time? Why me?

Sadly, with tears at his eyelids, he moved methodically around the room, poking the ceiling, poking the ceiling.

"Nayting Hale
God put in jail

Ride-ding ga hoss
Widoud da tail."

"You like my song?" Heshey asked Balkan on the landing.

"A nice song," Balkan said, trying to smile. He was grateful. By this time of day he felt himself sunk already among the meek and Heshey was easily a compatriot.

"Maybe you want I should sing it again?" Heshey asked shyly.

"No, Hesh, not here. You'll bother Mr. Coblenz. He's got a toothache."

"Oh, it ain't no bodder. Nayting Hale God put . . ."

"Hesh."

"Wad?"

"Don't sing. Go in the street and sing."

"I can't. My mudder don' wanna I should go in street. I'll get run nover."

"Then go in the yard."

"Chink, he went in yard. He'll hit me."

Goldie came tearing down the steps, a bowlegged little girl with farina over her mouth. She held a rubber ball at Heshey.

"You wanna play?"

Play with girls!

"Who? Me?" Hesh asked shrilly. "Wadda you take me for?"

"Come on. Let's play Melvin, Melvin, Melvin. Melvin, Melvin, Melvin," she said, bouncing the ball in time under her leg. Hesh watched the ball, his mouth open. He wanted to play.

"I can't do nothing. He don' let," Hesh said, reproachful eyes at Balkan.

"Oh, go on. Play," Balkan said and started to go upstairs. He had to see Munves and then dress. Later on, perhaps, he'd manage to pick up Coblenz and then the three would be able to go to Blenholt's funeral. Perhaps everything would turn out all right, after all. And he was going to the funeral, he vowed, no matter what happened. If he made his mind up once, he ought to let nothing interfere. Spirit, like air inflating a bladder, was slowly filling him and he walked up the steps with his chest high again.

"Max? Is that you, Max?"

"Ruth," Max cried. "What are you doing here so early?"

"Nothing. I went for a walk and then I thought I would drop in on you on the way."

"Robert, Robert, Robert, a name beginning with R," Goldie said, giving the ball a higher last bounce. Hesh caught it in the air on his palm and bounced it under his leg without a break.

"Rosie, Rosie, Rosie," he chanted, his face seriously drawn. "A name beginning with L."

"I just came from Coblenz. Gee whiz," Balkan said, "what a fellow. Sometimes you can't even speak to him."

"Who?" Ruth asked. "Oh, Coblenz. He's nuts."

"You know, speaking frankly, he's got me bulldozed. I don't like to admit it but I'm sort of afraid of him."

"He's nuts," Ruth said, with maternal understanding for Balkan. "Don't pay no attention to him. He's morbid and pessimistic, saying crazy things and thinking he's so terribly smart. He isn't so smart as he thinks," she added knowingly. The smart ones, all they had was a veneer.

"Yes, I know, Ruth," Max said, appreciating her sympathy but unwilling to use it as an excuse. "But still in all there's something funny about me. Look, I go to see him, I have to tell him something and then he gets sore with a toothache and the kids skating on the next floor, and I walk out afraid to open my mouth."

"Well, if it's so important, go back and tell him now. He's still there."

"See, that's what I mean when I say there's something funny about me. I can't go back. I just don't feel like. It's like going into a drugstore to buy stamps. Only worse, of course."

A yawn rose in Ruth and she tried to stifle it. Her nostrils twitched delicately, the mouth became distorted with the struggle, and the eyes closed dreamily. "Here," she uttered on the tail of the yawn, dismissing Coblenz. "It's for you."

A letter.

"What is it?" Balkan asked, all excitement. "For me?"

"A letter. From the telephone company. I saw it sticking out of your letterbox, so I thought I'd bring it up and save you the trip."

"Please," Balkan said, seizing it. He tore at the envelope in nervous pulls, read with swimming eyes. His face fell.

> Dear Mr. Balkan:
>
> Thank you for keeping us in mind in connection with your project as described in your letter of recent date. While we feel that your movie service project has no doubt definite commercial possibilities, we regret that we feel unable to take advantage of it at this time.
>
> Yrs. Yrs. Yrs.

"It's nothing," said Balkan in a hurry. "Just an advertisement."

"Let me see it." Ruth had watched his face, had grown suspicious. "You and your crazy ideas, what are you trying to sell the telephone company now?"

"It's nothing!" Balkan protested painfully.

"Give it to me."

"Maura, Maura, Maura," said Hesh with great concentration. "A name beginning with S."

"Seymour, Seymour, Seymour," said Goldie triumphantly.

"Don't read it, Ruth. It's nothing. Please! It's got nothing to do with anything."

They struggled politely over the letter but in the end Ruth had pulled it from his hands.

"Don't read it," he begged futilely.

Ruth read and her face grew stony. "After all I tried to do with you," she said, and her quiet tone disturbed him. "And they call Coblenz nutty. Just look at it! Just look at it! Sometimes, I think you're really dippy yourself."

"Ah," said Max. "What's the matter with my idea, then? Just because the telephone company doesn't want it, that doesn't mean anything. Every great man would look ridiculous unless somebody used his genius. That's what Arthur Brisbane says, not that he knows everything. Until a great man succeeds he's a fool. Better men than me have gone unrecognized."

"Organizing a telephone service. Getting people to call up to find out what's playing at the movies in the neighborhood. What's the use of talking, Max? You're crazy."

"Sometimes you get my goat! What's so crazy with my idea? People want to find out what's playing and the telephone company would make a lot of money from the additional calls. As I said in my letter."

"Look at him," Ruth said contemptuously. "Look how excited he gets."

"Gee whiz!" Max cried. "What's wrong with you? Don't they have a time service? Don't people call up to find out the time? Is there anything crazy about that? Ideas pay big money these days. I know a fellow, a relation of his got the idea of inventing a non-flaming cigarette lighter. Made a quarter of a million dollars in no time. Take my idea about putting individual wrappers around toilet seats in public places. I suppose you'd call that crazy too if somebody didn't beat me to it and make a fortune before I could interest any paper company in the idea. What you don't know!"

"You and your ideas!" Ruth said, her eyes glistening with tears. "You've got a million ideas and you ain't even got a job. You wanted the subways to put in radio sets so that the people, they shouldn't get bored riding in the trains. You wanted to open a nationwide chain of soft-drink stands from coast to coast, only they should sell hot chicken soup. In cups. You wanted to invent a self-sustaining parachute for people to stay up in the air as long as they felt like. Every idea you got is going to make a million dollars apiece, but you ain't got a job, you ain't got a penny, all you got is a million ideas!"

She ended in tears. Balkan had to wince at the mention of each of his cherished projects, the ridicule overcoming him in a steady downpour. It was their old argument. And now she was crying.

"A million ideas, you can laugh," Max said gently. "But one of them will click. Ruth, as sure as my name is Max Balkan, sooner or later, you'll see the day when one of my ideas will go over big and then I'll be in the money and you'll eat up every one of those words you said, one after the other."

"Listen to him," Ruth wailed bitterly. "John Pierpont Morgan!"

"Ickey, Ickey, Ickey, a name beginning with I!" said Goldie, just in time to catch her breath.

Balkan reached over to put his hand on Ruth's shoulder when he suddenly became transfixed with terror. Coblenz's door opened and he was sticking his head out—a fearful head, with hair mussed up, wild eyes and a savage mouth.

"Why in hell don't you go away from here?" he besought them earnestly, as one who really wants to know. "Ain't I got trouble enough? Ain't the roller skates making enough noise? Ain't my teeth hurting, every one of them? Go away! Drop dead! Shut up!"

The door slammed.

All in the hallway remained quiet. The kids had stopped to look with wonder at the strange appearance of Coblenz. The color left Balkan's face and Ruth had stopped crying.

"Sophie, Sophie, Sophie," Heshey said. "A name beginning with G."

"George, George, George," Goldie answered. That had been easy.

"Look," said Balkan in a subdued tone. He was reading the letter. "It says, 'While we feel your project has commercial possibilities we regret we are unable to take advantage of it at this time.' See, they admit it's a good idea. They don't want it just at this time. Maybe they'll take it later."

"Oh, listen, Max," said Ruth wearily, all tears gone. "I don't want to fight with you. Let's drop the subject."

"All right, only sometimes you've got to admit you're—all right, forget it. But what I would like to tell you is—don't forget what I said, about as sure as my name is Max Balkan. . ."

"Listen, Max, you want to go to the movies?"

The movies. Always the movies.

"So early in the morning? They're not open yet," he said, hoping that that would be the end of it.

"I mean for later. I have to go get my hair set in the beauty parlor. I got an appointment for eleven-fifteen. After dinner we can go to the Miramar."

"I don't feel like," Max said. "How can a person go to the movies in the daytime?"

"What's the difference? It's cheaper in the day."

"I don't feel like, Ruth."

"Listen, you want to go to the movies or not?"

"I can't, Ruth," Balkan said gingerly. "I'm sorry."

"Why?"

Balkan hesitated, deliberating. He shrugged his shoulders, gave up all hope. "See, it's what I was supposed to tell Coblenz about. We're supposed to go to a funeral, Coblenz, Munves, and me."

"Who died?" Ruth asked in the small voice of respect.

"Nobody. Blenholt," Balkan said apologetically. "Only Coblenz promised to go with me. I don't know, maybe I'll be able to get him on my way down, but right now I got to get Munves and then get dressed. The funeral's at two o'clock. It was my idea. The three of us are supposed to go to the funeral."

"Who's Blenholt?" Ruth asked, her face resuming that stony look as suspicion stuck its fingers into her mind.

"Nobody. A man." Balkan smiled weakly.

"What's so important about going to his funeral? Did you know him?"

"No," Max laughed hopelessly. "I never even spoke to him."

"So?" She was mystified.

"Nothing! You wouldn't understand. It would sound kind of ridiculous to you, and maybe it is for all I know," he admitted. "But," he added seriously and with conviction, "somehow it is important for me, for all of us, to go to that funeral."

"What's the matter?" Ruth wanted to know. "I wouldn't understand?"

"Well, I mean, it would sound just crazy to you."

"I like that! What makes you think you're so superior than me? Just because you're sensitive et cetera, that makes me out a slob?"

"Oh! It's not you! It's not you! Don't get the impression I think there is anything wrong with you. You know how I feel when it comes to you! You're close to me, closer than anyone I know. As I said! You remember, sometimes I think of you as though you're even a part of me. Like another leg or an extra arm. I told you, Ruth."

"Yes, I know, I know. But why can't you come with me and see Joan Crawford?"

"It's not a question of you," Max explained. "If I told you why I had to go to Blenholt's funeral, you would think it was only ridiculous and then we'd have another fight."

"Coblenz won't go with you and Munves is going to be busy studying, so you might as well come with me. I want to see Joan Crawford."

"My heavens," Max exclaimed, "you're being unreasonable about such a little thing. We can go to the movies tonight. Joan Crawford can wait but Blenholt can't."

"I'm unreasonable? I like that. If I'm so unreasonable why must you go to Blenholt's funeral?"

"Well, you don't have to get nasty, Ruth. It's nothing to get mad about. Listen, I'll tell you what. You can come with me to the funeral and then we'll go to the Miramar."

"Crazy! As usual with you."

Balkan thought it over. "That's right, too. We couldn't do that. It would be hardly fitting. Disrespect. Ruth, let's go to the movies tonight."

"You make me sick and tired," Ruth said, exhausted.

Balkan did not know what to do. The argument was becoming interminable. If she could only understand.

"Why?" he asked. "Why should I make you sick and tired?"

"Because," Ruth said.

"That's silly," Max wheedled. "You know you're being silly now." He forced himself to laugh.

"Wa-ah!" cried Heshey suddenly. "You gypped!"

"Who? Me?" Goldie asked, her mouth like a snout. "I'll break your rotten head."

"Yes, you did, you did. You gypped. You said a girl's name."

"You stink out loud!"

"Aw," said Heshey timidly. "Go break a leg."

"You first."

"Go to hell then."

"Sissy!" said Goldie. "Playing with girls. I'm going to tell Chink!"

The injustice! "Go ahead and tell him," said Heshey, furious with her. "Tell him, see if I care. You made pippee in your draws yesterday."

Goldie stepped forward, sticking her hands into Heshey's face.

"Wa-ah!" Hesh cried and went for her head, keeping his own face beyond her fingernails.

Ruth looked at the kids and back again to Balkan. She made up her mind. The hell with him. They were all crazy here. She started walking down the steps. Balkan reached out to hold her back but Heshey and Goldie scrambled into his way.

"Ruth! You don't have to get mad at me. Where are you going? Ruth!"

"Nasty kids!" she said, trying to push her way past their legs and arms. She moved without a look back at Balkan, talking almost to herself. "You've got a crack in your head and so have I for wasting my time on a nut like you. You're nuts, that's what it is, all of you, Coblenz and Munves, too."

"Oh, don't talk like that," Max begged. "That's common, cheap. Come back and we can talk it over in a civilized way."

"Oh, go to hell and stop bothering me," Ruth said with disgust. She had broken past the kids and was now stumping down the steps.

"Go to hell and drop dead," Hesh cried, victorious, for he had managed to bang past Balkan's hips out of Goldie's reach. Max was knocked down to the steps. He tried to secure his glasses as he fell and at the same time Goldie struggled sticky-fingered over him.

"Ruth!" he called from the stairs. "Come back and I'll tell you why it's important for me to go to Blenholt's funeral. Come back, Ruth, don't be sore."

But Ruth was gone. To take her place, and Balkan noticed it now for the first time, there stood Coblenz tall as the door itself. He held the broom in one hand and the whiskey bottle in the other.

"You kidding me, Balkan?" he asked in a gasping thin voice. "This your idea of a hot joke?" He threw the broom on his friend. "One more peep out of you and you get the bottle in your head too."

Balkan lay sprawled over the steps, motionless until Coblenz closed the door. He tried to rise but just then Goldie managed to regain her own feet. She rose with a final push, which served to throw Balkan off balance and back again over the steps. To save his glasses from her heels, he had to jerk his head back at once. He banged sharply against the marble step.

"Whoo!" sighed Balkan.

Above him, crowing like a cock, was Goldie. "I'll get even," she yelped to the turn in the staircase beyond which Hesh was hiding. "I'll get even, Hesh. Remember, revenge is sweet! He who laughs last laughs best!"

"Is Marty available?" Ruth asked sadly. "I got an appointment for eleven-fifteen."

The manicurist, a large woman whose nurse's uniform struggled with her bust, looked officiously through the red book, taking ages while Ruth busied herself, to drown her sorrows, with the signs on the walls: ADORATION SHAMPOO, A New Way, No Soap to Remove the Natural Oils, 40 cents; Hutsi-de-puh—The Latest from Hollywood (illustrated by a full-length photo of Loretta Young, a young lady remarkable chiefly for her gleaming teeth); a gilt-edge diploma, framed: FRANCINE, The French Beauty Shoppe, Member NATIONAL BEAUTICIANS LEAGUE, Gold Badge of Merit.

"My appointment was for eleven-fifteen," Ruth said dolorously but impatiently.

"Well, go right into the second booth. It's available," the manicurist said with resentment. "Marty! Marty! The young lady wants a finger wave." She looked at Ruth, the nose wrinkling, the corners of her mouth dimpling. Barely discountenanced, Ruth sailed into the booth, presenting only her back to the manicurist. The war of the sex.

Marty followed briskly. He bent over Ruth professionally,

dangling the wrist to show his bracelet. "Finger wave," he affirmed, nodding. "Yes," said Ruth, the woes of a nation upon her brow. Marty smelled sweet, and smelling him Ruth promptly thought of Max Balkan. Max was still a kid and Marty was a regular man. What a difference. She looked at the odd-shaped ring on his pinkie, the stylish collar he wore, the respectable mustache, his smartly brushed hair. This man had . . . personality. A real man. He had a job, he didn't fool around with toilet-seat inventions and telephone companies. He didn't go around to crazy funerals. Ruth wanted to bet that Marty earned forty dollars, including tips. Maybe more. If Max made forty dollars, . . . she almost shook her head as she speculated. If Max made forty dollars a week. . . . Why did she ever start up with him in the first place? Marty sprayed her hair until it was soaked. "You want the lotion or just water?" he asked.

"Just water, please. A little lotion on the bottom, on the curls."

Outside Ruth could hear a lady bubbling in. "I need a manicure," she gasped. "I got to go to a bridge this afternoon." That'll keep the fat horse outside busy. Give it to her, lady, I hope you complain all over the place.

"You seem very quiet today," Marty said. "Anything on your mind?"

"Well, yes and no. You know how it is."

"Boyfriend?" he asked archly.

Polite banter between the sexes. Ruth smiled wanly at him, Greta Garbo on a hot day, too tired to battle the world. He stepped aside to turn on the radio. The booth grew filled with the murmurous melodies broadcast from a phonograph somewhere. The music was like a hot bath. Marty's fingertips gently worked over her head, her scalp tingling pleasantly to the touch as he combed and pushed her hair in place. Ruth half closed her eyes with a luxurious feeling. Far off came the melancholy voice of the lady who was hurrying off to a bridge. "After it was all over," she was saying with a great sigh, "the doctors, they said it was all new, I was like a virgin. Inside, like a new glove, Mrs. Wolsky, they said."

"Two waves here or three?" whispered Marty, unwilling to break the mood.

"Oh, I don't know."

"Just the way you want it!" he protested.

"Three waves."

Her head swayed beneath his hands, the scalp warm and trembling. "'Twas in the isle of Capri that I met her," the radio said, and Ruth in her mind sang, "Da da da da, dada da dada dum." Nice, nice. Her eyes closed more often now and she dozed. Ruth dozed. Ruth, Ruth, Ruth.

Bing Crosby, *The Voice of the Masked Tenor*, Don Novis, *Rudy Vallee's Hour*, Myrt and Marge, The Gibson Sisters, Block and Sully, The Showboat Hour, Hollywood on the Air. *True Stories, True Confessions, Love Story Magazine* (Shall I Tell My Husband? Twelve Nights in a Dope Fiend's Penthouse! I Married a Gay Lothario!). *Movie Classics, Photoplay, Modern Movie, Movie Allure* (Are There Any Happy Marriages in Hollywood? I Shall Always Be a Bachelor Girl Says Lovely Lili Modjeska! Myrna Loy—From Vamp to Modern Woman! I Kissed Valentino!). Silverman's Lending Library—The Latest Books No Deposit Required. (*Valerie Valencia, The Story of a Lustful Woman!* A young woman's battle between flesh and the spirit. Sensational reading that holds you spellbound. Charging it with being immoral, reformers tried in vain to prohibit its publication. They Tried to *Ban* This Book!!!), Walter Winchell, Louis Sobol, Mark Hellinger, Ed Sullivan, Beatrice Fairfax, Antoinette Perry, Donna Grace, Irene Thirer, Garbo, Marlene Dietrich, Carole Lombard, Joan Crawford, Jean Harlow, Clark Gable, Franchot Tone, Gary Cooper, and Robert Montgomery. Beauty Parlor, Monday to Thursday, Reduced Prices on All Service. Hindu brown stocking, 59¢, bought too often in spite of stopping all runs promptly with soap. Brassieres with points, glove-silk panties light green in color or else orchid or tea rose. Two-forty-eight girdles. Formflex (Slenderizes—But No Bulges! Reduce While You Wear It!). E-Z Hair-Removing Glove (New Shammy Touch—Works Better, Lasts Longer). Naturelle Lipstick; Blue Donna face powder, rachelle color; La Nuit Pour L'Amour perfume, mascara, cold cream, astringent, all applied faithfully night and day.

"All right," Marty said cheerfully. "You're done."

Drowsy, Ruth walked out of the booth, holding her bag with one hand and feeling her hair with the other to see if it was really in place. Had he really finished with her? Time flew.

"I must have dozed off," she said dreamily.

Ruth sat down while Marty adjusted the dryer around her head. The air blew on her wet hair, making her shiver for a moment. Then it grew warmer as the wetness left, her scalp tingled again, and she felt herself slipping off to sleep once again. She picked up a copy of *Screenplay*. Lovely picture of Rochelle Hudson in a bathing suit. June O'Dea in a bathing suit, looking coy this time instead of the big smile. Virginia Meyer impishly smiling in a black negligee that was about to fall off her any minute. Chatter of the month: Genuine American Indians are on the warpath against all pretenders seeking jobs in pictures as Indians . . . Lewis Stone, who has been in pictures over twenty years, intends to retire when his present M-G-M contract expires . . . Wendy Barrie has just had her tonsils removed . . . Ruth Chatterton is now a licensed air pilot . . .

Why was Max such a schlemiel? Ruth asked herself, dragging her attention from the movie magazine. She hunted in her bag and put a stick of Juicy Fruit into her mouth. All her life she had known him. She had never gone with other boys. He had made it impossible for her to have any other chances. She had given, in a way, her whole life to him, she thought tearfully, self-conscious because the line seemed a little too familiar. And now Max was no nearer marriage than he had ever been. She had listened to him, sympathized with him, tried to make a man out of him and what did it get her? Her head began to feel hot in the air bag.

Ruth remembered how it had been when they were children. At that time her father had owned a butcher store alongside the stone steps that led to Max's tenement, and on the stoop Max and Ruth used to sit close together in the evenings, sometimes holding hands while he told her strange stories about what he was going to do when he grew up. Bull, she thought, all bull he made up out of his crazy head and I sat there and told him fine, it was wonderful. I listened to him.

Max had fitted up a carpenter's shop in his cellar. He wanted to make a boat and go riding in Sheepshead Bay, maybe go to the Atlantic Highlands and the country. Ruth remembered how she had helped him pull down planks from fences in lots and carried them with him to the cellar. For ten weeks Max labored on the boat. The Flying Ruth, he was going to call it, and it became a beautiful boat. She was proud of it and of Max, until finally, when it was all finished and the time came to take it out, they discovered they couldn't get the boat through the doorway. It was too big. Even then a schlemiel, she thought. Oh, he gives me a pain.

For years they had been going together, walking the streets of Williamsburg from Newton Creek to the River, from Greenpoint to Wallabout Market. As a boy Max had always been different from the others and she had thought it was because he was so much better. He never played games, he never even read. All the time he was walking with her, telling of all the plans he had for the day when he would be grown up. A strange boy, she used to think, a wonderful boy, out of the ordinary. As it says in the prayer on Yom Kippur: May my children be neither too clever nor too stupid. If Max had been like the other boys, everything would have been all right by now. They would have had a baby three years old by this time. Looking back, Ruth hated all sensitive children.

In those days he had been afraid of the other boys and he ran to her for protection and consolation. Now it was to tell her his crazy stories of inventions and ideas. He was going to make a million dollars any day now, she thought bitterly. Mr. Rockefeller, look out, here comes Maxie. Only try and make him get a job. "I can't work, Ruthie," he said. "I get sick when I work, really sick. I mean sick, genuine sick, not like you say, 'It makes me sick.'" He couldn't get out of bed early enough in the mornings and instead he came to her with one contraption after another, one scheme after another, each and every one guaranteed to make a million dollars, he wasn't satisfied with less. A million ideas and he couldn't afford to get married.

Williamsburg wasn't good enough for him. All the time he was talking to her about how terrible it was to live here. He didn't like it. In Williamsburg they murdered people every day or something. Everyone else lived to a good old age here, but Maxie, he was John Pierpont Morgan, it wasn't good enough for him. "There's no greatness here, nothing high and strong," he was always saying. "Everything is small and mean and dirty. I want to live with poetry and beauty." Poetry and beauty! God knew what he was talking about. He wanted to live like kings and emperors, nothing else would satisfy him. Majesty, meaning, heroism! Bull! Bull! A kid he was, he never grew up. All the time he told her about the wonderful life he would live, how he would finally make a million dollars and have power and importance, but just the same he never had a cent. They'd never get married.

It was too late for her to do anything about it. Twenty-five she was already and the only boy she went out with was Max. Ruth remembered Prospect Park the first time. Everything, everything, she had given him and it would be hard to drop him and go look for somebody else. It had grown dark in the park early that evening, and they lay on the grass, on a little hill away from people and the paths. Soon, in his childish way, his hand was under her blouse groping for her right breast. Ruth remembered it was the right breast because he had petted it for an hour with his palm, laid it against his cheek, kissed it, playing with it like a potato pancake. A man, and for an hour he had played with her breast. Not that she would, she hastened to assure herself. And ever since she had been discouraging him properly, often slapping his hands away.

Too late! She sighed and opened the magazine to a new place. A darling picture of Joan Crawford in green on page 43. She was standing before a door, hands on hips, her legs spread apart, her head held cutely to the side. Big smile, eleven upper teeth showing. She was wearing sneakers, shorts with sailor laces and a dark blouse. "I look for that spark," she was saying, "that certain something that spells personality in a man." And off in another corner, Ruth read: "Aristocrat, sophisticate, innocent—one wanted romance, the other wanted excitement—but one wanted his heart—and got it! . . . Sparkling romance of an artist who dabbled with love as he dabbled with paints . . . and of a girl who hid behind a smile—

but could not hide her heart from the man she loved! Joan Crawford adds another brilliant characterization to her long list of successes . . . You must see her!"

Ruth's head burned in the dryer. Wasn't she finished? She wanted to get out.

"Marty," she called, "did you forget me?"

"Just a moment longer while I hold your hand," he sang back. "Just a moment—"

Aristocrat, sophisticate, innocent—she had to see Joan Crawford. I'll go back and get Max, she said. After lunch I'll talk him out of funerals. Whadda dope! Whadda dope!

He was hopeless, but what could she do? Her head felt as though it were on fire.

THREE

Hichle, pichle, schmichle

ON THE FOURTH FLOOR lived Mendel Munves, across the hall from Balkan's flat. Munves was an amateur etymologist of distinction. In addition he had some reputation as a linguist, knowing not only all the possible languages but also all the dialects of each. He had lived for months at a time in the foreign quarters of the city so that he might learn even the expressions of the face, the attitudes of the hands and the postures of the body that accompanied each of the dialects of the languages. A great scholar Munves was indeed, even though most of the housewives on the landing said that he didn't know enough to wipe his nose without being told. But in spite of honors, in spite of the visits from men high in academic circles who came to seek his instruction on difficult points, he had always remained unpretentious, humble in his work and unseeking, an innocent student.

A nut, said Balkan dryly, trudging past the door without knocking. He felt tired and in his own way he had put up with much this morning. He would stand for little from Munves. All he would say would be: "Munves, get ready. You're coming to the funeral." Then he would go upstairs to dress.

The scholar's room showed a bookish disorder. He had been working passionately at his table, his Skeats, his Krapp, his dictionaries all opened and surrounded by scraps of paper. Munves looked through his glasses to discern his visitor, then burst out enthusiastically, beaming in welcome.

"I'm glad you've come, Max. Really, I've just finished a fascinating piece of work and I daresay I need someone to talk to about it."

"Never mind, never mind," Balkan said. "Today is Blenholt's . . ."

"Well," said Munves, drawing breath and convincing himself of the truth in his mind, "that is the characteristic of beauty, isn't it, Max, that its enjoyment must be promptly shared to reach its full effect? I must tell Rita all about it as soon as I can. She seems to enjoy my little achievements almost as much as I do."

Rita was Max's sister.

"All right, never mind," he said. "Today . . ."

"Just look," Munves said like a flood, putting his hands into his pockets and looking at the floor so that nothing might mar his concentration. "Take the Latin *findo*. That is, of course, *findo, findere, fidi, fissus*. To cut, dissever. Why does the 'n' drop out?"

"What en? What's an en?"

"The 'n'! In *findo*. *Findo, fidi*. The 'n' disappears. Where? Is it really part of the stem?"

"Oh, what the dickens . . ." Max said.

"I know, I know," Munves returned rapidly, anxious to ward off all possible objections. "Very possibly this may be an old point which has escaped me. I have not run across it, but very possibly, very possibly—no matter, old point or new, the pleasure of discovery awaited me, and, you can laugh if you wish, Max, but in a small way I felt like a new Columbus. In fact, however, I have never run across the point."

"Listen," Max said with determination. There were strong people in the world who were able to withstand any sort of interruption. "You . . ."

"I sat myself down to find it, the 'n' in *findo*. To us findo comes to be the word bite from the Anglo-Saxon *bitan*, which of course is cognate with the Latin *findo*. That is to say, the 'f' changes to Anglo-Saxon 'b', the Latin 'd' to 't', and so we understand *findo* to equal bite. But—and this is the point—where is the 'n'?"

"TODAY," Balkan ground through his teeth, "IS BLENHOLT'S . . ."

"Max," Munves confided with ardor, "Max, I had to go through every one of the Indo-European languages, through every branch of the Celtic, Italic, and Teutonic divisions, through the whole lot of them, and nowhere could I find the 'n'. The 'n'," Munves pronounced with dramatic finality, "does not belong to *findo!*"

So it didn't. So what? "Munves," Max began weakly, "I . . ."

"Oh, I know, I know," Munves smiled disarmingly, repressing genteelly all appearance of gloating, "I know that all this may seem small to you, to spend an entire morning just to prove that 'n' does not belong to *findo*. But really it goes to show, it goes to show . . . Rita will be delighted when I show this to her."

She will stand on her head with joy. Balkan made the laughing polite sound in his throat that is used to indicate sympathetic comprehension and makes possible a shift to other subjects. Then he drew his breath with speed, to beat Munves, and said hopefully, "All right, Munves, now listen to me a minute. They are burying Blenholt today. Today is Blenholt's funeral." There it was out, delivered, wrapped up.

"Blenholt, Blenholt, Blenholt, don't tell me," said Munves, worry in his eyes at the unfamiliarity of the name. "Blenholt. Don't tell me. I know. He wrote a book on Icelandic roots?"

"No," said Balkan, shaking his head as frustration stared him in the face. "Blenholt. Commissioner of Sewers."

"Oh, Blenholt!" cried Munves, striking his head with his fist in chagrin. "Of course. Funny, a man with something the same name wrote a book on Icelandic roots. Holtzager! That's the one. Holtzager."

"All right. You promised me you would come to the funeral."

"Oh, yes, yes, of course. You want me to get dressed now? Is it time? I'll take a minute."

"Well . . . that's fine." Success. Balkan sat back wearily. He had been worried over Munves too, for a minute it looked like another case of Coblenz, but God had been good. He leaned back on the couch to rest his head against the wall, shutting his eyes, and some one knocked on the door, boding no good. Kee-ryst. Don't answer, Balkan prayed, make believe nobody's home.

"Come in," called Munves cheerily.

It was the pearl peddler Balkan had seen in Coblenz's flat. The old man stuck his head through the doorway, held the strings on his finger before Munves, smiled as he surveyed the possibilities and said brightly, "For your sweetheart. Fifty cents."

"Pearls!" Munves exclaimed joyously, for God was in His heaven and all was right with the world. "Pearls! Max, do you think your sister would like them?"

She would do a kazotsky in the street with happiness. "You know Rita doesn't like Woolworth jewelry," he pleaded, speaking for the particular benefit of the peddler whose eyes he met, begging him to leave, to go away before Munves grew lost in the maze again. Success had been so near. "Rita would throw you out with those pearls."

"Oh, please, mister!" said the peddler in hurt surprise. "How can a person be so mean? Genuine artificial pearls, worth a dollar in any store, I should drop dead right this minute!"

"Oh, Max," Munves said, "just for the sentiment. Do you really think Rita wouldn't be pleased?"

Balkan turned to the peddler. "He doesn't want any pearls, mister. Nothing doing. Munves, go and get dressed."

"All right, all right," said Munves, nettled by his friend's tone. "I'll get dressed, don't you worry."

The peddler looked daggers at Max, and sat down on the couch alongside of him.

"Could an old man sit down and rest a minute, please?" he asked, rubbing it in for Max's sake. "I work all day on my feet, up the stairs, down the stairs, and I can't make a single sale."

"Really?" Munves asked with great sympathy. He was fussing with the buttons on a newly laundered shirt, but his face wrinkled at the plight of the working classes. Munves took time and looked into the old man's face to see, if possible, the reflection of suffering and hardships. What wonderful people old men were! What creases on the old man's face, what lines! "By all means!" he hastened to say. "Sit down and take a rest!"

"Thanks, thanks, a great favor," muttered the old man, looking around the room. Balkan knew the peddler would bring him nothing but hard luck, for so it had been with Coblenz. "A student? A scholar?" queried the old man.

"Etymologist," said Munves, happy. "A lover of words and their destinies."

"Good, good, fine," said the old man, impressed.

"Munves," said Balkan anxiously, "get busy."

"That was good—a lover of words and their destinies, no, Max? One thing about me, I may be off in certain things, but I can always turn a phrase, if I say so myself."

"Books?" asked the peddler respectfully, rubbing his chin. "You know languages?"

"Ten, fifteen, twenty languages," replied Munves gaily. "God himself doesn't know how many languages, no bluff!"

"Twenty languages!" gasped the old man. "No bluff! Good, good!"

"Don't think I'm boasting," Munves hastened to assure him. "I don't boast. I'm not interested in a big name, something like that. Only, that's not all. I know the dialects, everything. Ask him. Isn't it true, Max?"

"I got a brother," said the peddler slowly with reflection, "in Cincinnati, he's got a daughter, very educated too. She knows four, five languages, Latin, French, Spanish—everything."

"Would you believe it?" interrupted Munves, secretly irked by the comparison with the girl in Cincinnati. "The biggest scholars from the universities come to see me for my opinions. No bluff!"

"No bluff!" the peddler affirmed. "You young men with your education—wonderful, wonderful."

"Perhaps," said Munves, uncontrollable with the true scholar's zeal, "perhaps you would be interested in a little piece of research I have just completed. Are you at all familiar with the Latin *findo? Findo, findere, fidi, fissus?*"

"For God's sakes," Balkan cried out, "what's the matter with you, Munves? Haven't you got any sense at all? Leave the old man alone and stop making a fool of yourself."

Munves stopped in midair as though someone had stuck a finger into his eye. Balkan had never spoken to him in quite this tone before. Coblenz, yes, but Coblenz was unfortunate and could be overlooked. Munves had expected more from his friend.

"Please!" he said with soft indignation, staring at him.

Before his stare Balkan had to flinch and, flinching, he recognized this kind of impotence as the essential flaw within him. Why flinch? Why not shout down Munves as Coblenz would have done? Kick out the peddler and haul off Munves to the funeral, if necessary, by the neck? Balkan thought of all this but of course he said nothing and the pause between the friends grew heavier and heavier.

"My brother," said the peddler gently, "in Cincinnati, his daughter made high school in three years."

An innocent remark but Balkan found it intolerable. "Listen, mister," he said, "good-bye please. My friend's in a hurry, he's got no time. Go on the fifth floor, they got lots of girls there. You'll do a business there and all that's happening here, you're wasting your time."

"All right! All right!" cried the peddler in a huff. He creaked as he rose hurriedly to leave. "I'm not so old yet boys have to holler at me and chase me away. Nobody has to drive me. If you don't want me, just say it nice and I wouldn't stay if you gave me a hundred dollars!" He gave Balkan one last bitter look and went for the door. But there he paused and turned to Munves, changing his tone. "For your sweetheart, no?" he asked pathetically, jiggling the pearls.

Munves shook his head, his lips firm. He would take care of Balkan when the old man left. Don't worry, old man, I'll take care of him, he won't say things like that to you again. For shame!

"All right, all right," the peddler murmured piteously. "Not a sale all day."

He closed the door and Munves promptly looked at his friend reprovingly. He shook his head sadly.

"You ought to be ashamed of yourself, Max," he said in measured tones. "That's no way to talk to an old man. And, if I say so myself, I didn't like the tone you used with me either."

"It's all right, it's all right," protested Max. There, he had laid himself open again to a wrong interpretation. Personally he was kindness itself to old men. How unjust the world was! "Here's the old man, tired, he doesn't know what you're talking to him about. All that happens is that you make a fool of yourself, explaining a Latin root to a pearl peddler."

But Munves' mind had already led him away from the thought of Balkan's indignities toward the old man. Light showed in his eyes.

"Do you know, Max, I can't imagine how the image came into my head, but do you know what the old man made me think of?"

"What?" asked Balkan with a sickening feeling.

"A pretzel."

A pretzel! "Oh," cried Balkan, "he didn't look like a pretzel, Munves!" Could you blame Ruth for calling them crazy? Could you blame anyone? Here he was trying to redeem them all by showing that they were realists enough to attend the funeral of a great man, a practical man, and all that occurred in return was—pretzels.

"No, really," Munves explained heartily. "You don't catch exactly just what I mean. A pretzel that you see in the morning after it has been out in the rain all night. Gray, pasty, fallen apart. Shapeless. You know what I mean, Max?"

Just look at that. Argue or not to argue? "Well, yes, in a way, I suppose so," said Balkan, resigned. "Hurry up and get dressed now."

"I still don't know how that image ever got into my head. I ought to keep a notebook to jot down these ideas as they come to me. I always forget them and they're really good. Don't you think so, Max?"

"Listen, Munves. For God's sakes, they're burying Blenholt today, not next year."

"Yes, yes, Blenholt," said Munves, feeling contrite. "Blenholt, Commissioner of Sewers."

"Commissioner of Sewers," mused Balkan with a sense of displeasure. "A great man," he corrected.

"Yes, I remember," said Munves. "I quite agree with you as I've always said to you."

Balkan, putting his hand over his eyes, thought of Ruth and thinking of her he remembered heartbreakingly Heshey and Goldie. These things—how could you tell people what you meant? Even Mencken, certainly a cynical enough realist, appreciated his dilemma. He had once written: "In such a country as this, with practically all human values reckoned in terms of dollars and cents, it is not only hopeless for a man to try to get on without money, but also a trifle absurd." Balkan had joyfully copied the excerpt down as soon as he had run across it. He had shown it to Ruth and to his surprise she agreed with it completely. "See," she had said, "that's what it says. It's crazy for anybody not to get a job. You got to make a living." Misunderstood it completely, Balkan thought. He had tried to show her that what Mencken meant was that it was wrong for the country to reckon everything in terms of dollars and cents, that there were other standards. "Then the whole country is wrong?" she had asked. "Everybody is out of step except Max Balkan?"

It was hopeless. Just because heroism, great feeling, high poetry, and a keen spirit of living were never wrapped up in bundles across a showcase, anyone who was guided by them became immediately a nut, a fool, a schlemiel.

"Try and explain it," Balkan said. "It's impossible. I just had an argument with Ruth over Blenholt and it was just impossible for me to tell her why it was so important for us to go to his funeral. Now, you know Ruth, she's not a common girl. I've known her all my life and she ought to understand things better than most people. And yet she was blind. There's something hard and cross about people; ignorance and malice that make them able only to ridicule and laugh. Sometimes it's . . . it's disheartening."

"I've discovered that, too," said Munves, meaning consolation for himself perhaps more than he did for his friend. "Very often people are so unresponsive. They seem to be impressed only by the tangibles. How much can you get for it? Can you make a living with it? That's what Mrs. Wohl always asks me when she comes in to clean. She sees the books and she says, 'Can you eat languages?' Materialism, that's what it is. Of course. You know, that's why Rita means so much to me," he confessed shyly. "She's different—soft, tender-hearted and understanding."

"People like to laugh and be hard-boiled," Balkan continued, disregarding Rita. Somehow Munves' agreement served only to make him feel ridiculous and he closed his mind to it the way he tried to avoid smelling an unpleasant odor. "Do you know what they call Blenholt? A racketeer."

"That's how people are, Max. It's true," Munves said, the wise look indicating that all this was an old story to him, he couldn't be surprised at it.

"A racketeer! They say there is no heroism in our generation, no poetry, no height and they call Blenholt a racketeer. Hamlet is a great figure because anyone who talks against Shakespeare gets his head knocked against a wall. People read about the Roman emperors and marvel. Lorenzo is an historical character of glamour and in Hollywood they make pictures about him. Heroism is all right for literature and history, but Blenholt was a racketeer. Blindness! Blindness! Let other people call him a gangster, but to me Blenholt was no racketeer, no politician, no sewers man, living on the money he forced from the storekeepers. He was a kind of king, like the ancient Romans and Greeks, like the glorious Renaissance tyrants, powerful and crushing, exacting tribute from those who were obliged to bow before him. That is what makes a hero in any time and any land, power, but in return a hero relieves his followers of responsibility for he is authority in all things and sets their poorer minds at rest. As it says in Carlyle! Do you know anything about Spengler and T. S. Eliot? People pick me out and say I'm a fool, that nobody but me would have such crazy ideas. And yet these people all have the same ideas, not only me. One person's ignorance has to be the other's insanity, according to them. Yes," said Balkan, heartened for at last he was among the pastures of his fancy, "a true hero was Blenholt. In our time he stands for Tamburlaine or Xerxes or Caesar and so will he be recognized in history whether our age views him correctly or not."

"Did you ever stop to think," asked Munves, waiting politely for his friend to finish, "did you ever stop to think that the left jaw is slightly lower than the right?"

Munves was feeling his jaw. He had not been listening to a word, the capricious strands of his mind's speculations tossing him this way and that with no regard for his will or his duty. Balkan, emerging as from a happy dream, let his head drop and cursed softly to himself.

"Seriously, seriously!" Munves protested, noting disapproval in his friend. "When you chew, your mouth is lopsided and the food is ground only on the right side. Did you ever notice that? Or does this possibly apply only with me?"

He went to the mirror, chewing intently as he examined the movement of his jaws.

"Geez, you're . . . you're . . ." Balkan almost wept. "Get dressed. Get dressed." Hopeless! Hopeless!

"Well, it's an unimportant observation, perhaps," replied Munves in defense. He walked away from the mirror and occupied himself in a book to hide a sense of guilt. He knew he had hurt Balkan's feelings. "It may be unimportant, but it goes to show, it goes to show . . ."

"It goes to show what?" Balkan asked point blank. "Go talk to him, talk to a wall. Listen, Munves, I'm going downstairs for a paper, then to my house to get dressed. Are you going to be ready in twenty minutes?"

"All right. All right. Don't holler at me," Munves said sulkily. He kept his eyes close to the page. "I'll be ready, don't make such a fuss."

At the door Balkan hesitated. Maybe he had been too rough. After all there was no point in being disagreeable with Munves just because he was weaker. He was on the point of saying something conciliatory but at this point he was startled by a sudden scream from Munves.

"Look!" his friend cried. He stood up before the table with the book held in his hands, his eyes blazing with excitement.

"What happened? What happened?" Balkan asked with real concern.

"This can't be right, Max! Sealwudu in Essex! In Essex! Impossible!"

He sat down, groping for his spectacles, more books and paper. It took a moment for Balkan to learn what it was all about. Apparently his friend was on the point of making another discovery.

"Munves!" he bawled. "In twenty minutes! Yes or no?"

"Yes, yes, of course," Munves answered, but absentmindedly, distantly, for already his hands were going through the pages of the books scattered on the table before him with feverish interest. "Of course," he said, his voice trailing off, for his mind had withdrawn him along its own imperious paths. And so absorbed had he become in the short time that he did not take pause to notice his friend's departure even though Balkan slammed the door as he left.

"Sealwudu," he murmured to the empty room, jittery with passion's fires. "Sealwudu. In Essex!"

FOUR
Mr. Fumfotch

ACROSS THE HALL FROM Munves' room was the establishment of the Balkans: kitchen, one bedroom for Mrs. Balkan and Rita, and the living room. The bath was between the last two. Three rooms originally intended for another design but that was how the Balkans used them. On a daybed in the living room Max and his father slept, but there were hopes, on the part of Mrs. Balkan and Max, that these conditions would be changed when Rita was married. Then, thought Max, his father and mother would use the bedroom and he could have the front room all to himself. A room for himself and he looked forward to it. Mrs. Balkan also looked forward to Rita's marriage. She had no concern with rooms, however. Rita's marriage was her burning ambition and there was no one in Williamsburg to blame her. As for Mr. Balkan's desires, he had reached the point where he didn't want anything. And, the sad truth was, nobody asked him in the first place.

Now he sat on the daybed, his head nodding over the *Tag*, a thin worn man in spite of his gaudy colors. He was dressed in a resplendent patched checker suit, and his shoes, easily ten sizes too large for him, were not only bulbous but lacquered red. Between them and the cuffs of his trousers, flaming socks showed. In keeping with the enormous size of his shoes and suit, the collar around his neck served merely as ornament for no giant would have found it small enough. His face was smeared with white powder, apostrophes of white paint punctuating the area about his eyes below the two black circumflexes which were drawn above them. A great big red-painted nose like a baloney sausage. The nose interfered with his reading, both its color and size distracting his attention. Mr. Balkan often wanted to push it away, his nose, but he dared not muss himself up and, a man easily given to resignation, he tried to ignore it as much as possible.

"Doo-di-doo-di-di-da-da," he sang happily in the great quiet of the room. His wife was busy in the kitchen making lukschen and there was peace in the house. "Dear Dr. Holstein," wrote a lady in the *Bintel Brief* column of the paper, "I am a widow with a wonderful son-in-law. I live with them in a wonderful house on President Street, with a car, a chauffeur, a radio and a maid. But my daughter . . ."

The bathroom door opened rudely, the window covered by green-spangled oilpaper banging against the wall. Rita, the confidante of Munves, stuck her angry head out.

"Listen here, Father," she said furiously. "There's going to be a new rule around this house! You can't read the paper in the bathroom!"

"Look at her!" Mrs. Balkan cried out pleasantly from the kitchen in mock surprise. "Fancy lady. Father."

Rita threw the newspaper on the floor and slammed the door, withdrawing majestically without deigning to answer her mother.

Aw, chee vitz! "Quiet, please, a little quiet," said Mr. Balkan, holding his head down.

"Shah! Shtill! The rabbi goes dancing," his wife sang with malicious humor.

"Sh. Please," Mr. Balkan begged gently.

Max entered with the paper, his woes heavy on his brow. Everything had gone badly today. Heshey, Goldie, Coblenz, the woman on the landing, the pearl peddler, Munves, and Chink—ah, all a mess, a mess. His face overcast with repeated failure and indignity, he nevertheless sat down without delay, opened the paper at the last page, and read about Benny. Today the comic showed Benny feeding his five kittens. After they have eaten, his little mouse comes out of its hole for its snack of food. That's nice, Max sighed sorrowfully. His gaze traveled to Alley Oop, all about Ooola and Foozy today.

"All he wants," shouted Mrs. Balkan in high derision, "is quiet. In the grave you'll have quiet enough."

Mr. Balkan was a very superstitious man, getting up three and four times a night to spit over bad dreams. "Nu! Nu!" he exclaimed wrathfully.

"E-yah! Hah! Hah!" She was uncontainable with laughter. Her shoulders bobbed madly and her whole body shook. "Look at him! Maxie, look at him! Such a superstitious old fool. Did you ever see? He's so afraid of the death. Mr. Fumfotch!" she yelled with glee.

Mr. Balkan's soul, even if hidden behind his clown's outfit, contracted like a turtle's head when touched. Somewhere the embers of his youth were fanned, and anger, like a hiccup, rose in him in spite of the pains he took never to excite himself. Mad clear through, shouting through his makeup, he rose with the paper in one hand. "Listen, here! I'm still the boss in this house and if I want quiet, I'll . . ." At the climax of the crescendo his voice had to break, leaving him suspended, the effect being totally ruined. He sat down meekly, vanquished. "All right," he grumbled, "the hell with it. I ain't got the strength no more. See, Maxie, that's what happens when you get old. I can't do it no more. No voice, no fire, weak. Yes . . . yes . . . I remember, when I was in Melbourne . . ."

"He remembers when he was in Melbourne," Mrs. Balkan mimicked, hilarious with the fun. "It's a sketch! If you saw it in the movies, people would laugh their insides out!"

"Oh, for God's sakes," muttered the old man. He shook his paper violently—at least he could do this—and swiftly hid his head behind it.

Maxie took no part in the fun, reading the funnies to the end with great absorption. Little Mary Mixup's wrestler had won the bout after all. "Mom," he said, like one awaking, "Rita's in the bathroom?"

"Rita's in the bathroom."

"Mom, do you think she'll let me get in for a minute?"

"Wait. Is it a fire?"

"I'm in a hurry," Max whined. "I got to go to a funeral."

Mrs. Balkan left the lump of dough and ran into the living room. "My God," she gasped with grief. "Who died?"

"Don't worry for nothing," Max assured her. "It's nobody. They're burying a man called Blenholt today. He's not a Jew."

"Still," she protested, relieved but broad-minded, "it's no picnic. Even a Christian is a person too."

"He's not even a Christian!" Rita chirped cheerfully from the bathroom.

"What is he, then?" Mrs. Balkan shouted at the door. "A dog? Still it's a person, ain't it?"

"Aw, Mom," Max whimpered. "I got to get washed. Tell Rita to hurry up."

"Who was your servant last year?" she asked him. "Are you mad at her, you can't tell her yourself?" She stamped out to the kitchen, back to her lukschen, a big broad woman with drops of perspiration on her forehead. She had suffered much with her family and her husband, and there was no end in Golus. The only sensible person in a crazy house, she often thought. God give her strength!

Max looked helplessly at his father. He had been reading peacefully all this time, resting his chin on top of the big collar and looking at the paper with his head held high because in that way he avoided his nose.

"Rita . . ." Max began tremulously.

"Go to hell, what do you want?" Prompt as a bullet.

"See, Momma?" he wailed triumphantly. "See?"

"Hock mir nit kein chinook!" The voice floated to him.

"Rita. I got to go to Blenholt's funeral. Munves is waiting for me. Could I get into the bathroom for a minute? Now, that's a polite request."

"Go to hell. I just got here myself. You can wait."

"Doo-di-doo-di-di-da-da," sang the old man happily.

"Ma!" Max wailed, his patience exhausted. "Tell her to hurry up. I don't want to fight with her but she always wants to start something whenever I speak to her."

"The funeral can wait. Don't bother me," his mother shouted angrily. "What are you going to a funeral for altogether? A brother, why can't you do something and find Munves a job or something? Rita, she ain't getting younger by the minute, how long can she wait?"

"For crying out loud, cut it out, Mother," Rita said like a machine gun. "What do you want from Munves? I ain't got a mortgage on him!"

"Mrs. Mackenzie," Max said. "The Great Campaigner."

Mrs. Balkan came out of the kitchen, her whole manner altered by those two words. They always reduced her helplessness.

"Maxie," she pleaded softly, "what is it, Mrs. Mackenzie? What does it mean?"

"Never mind, Mrs. Mackenzie. I want to wash."

"Rita," she called, "why does he always call me Mrs. Mackenzie? Is it a dirty name?"

"Go ask him yourself, he's such a lummox, next week he's going to make a million dollars showing Rockefeller how to make a new kind of sauerkraut. Einstein and his million-dollar ideas!"

"See?" asked Max, his head shaking with the ingratitude. "Go help her. Get Munves a job. Do her favors."

"Listen, Tarzan of the Grapes, you keep your rotten nose out of my affairs and it will be better for all concerned. And don't think you do me any favors with Munves. He's no Clark Gable to say the least."

"Pathé News, sees all, knows all, says all. Talks like a merry-go-round," Max said.

"Kvetch!"

Max winced within himself.

"Pathé News!" he yelled back.

"Shah!" yelled Mrs. Balkan, between him and the door. They both shut up. "All she wants," Mrs. Balkan wailed, "is Clark Gable. Nobody else is good enough for her, the prima donna. What's the matter with Munves? A nice boy, educated, knows a hundred languages?"

"Nothing!" Rita shrieked. "Nothing's the matter with him

except if you don't stop talking about him I won't be able to stand the living sight of him! For God's sakes, Mother, drop the subject if you know what's good for you."

"Mother, schmother," said Mrs. Balkan, returning to the kitchen, "For God's sakes yourself!"

"Quiet," begged Mr. Balkan timidly. "Please a little quiet."

His wife turned to glare at him and the *Tag* came up again to hide his face. "Mr. Fumfotch," she ground through her teeth.

"Ma," said Max plaintively, "I still want to get into the bathroom."

"Listen, Maxie," she reasoned with him angrily. "Do I stop you? Do I keep you? Is it me in the bathroom making the beauty? Listen, when you make a million dollars from Rockefeller like Rita says, then we'll take the money and have two bathrooms in the house. All right?"

"Aw, for crying out loud . . ." Max gave up. He took a shirt from a bureau and went to the wardrobe in his mother's room where he kept his other suit, hoping devoutly that Munves would get a job and marry Rita in a hurry.

Mrs. Balkan, loose, her figure gone forever out of shape, her face wet with perspiration, came into the front room with the dough, which she now rolled flat on the table, stretching it until it would be thin enough to dry.

"Read the paper," she muttered at the old man in his comical outfit. "All you know is to read the paper. Why don't they bother you? You're the father. Only me!"

"Shah. Quiet. Please."

Mrs. Balkan left the table, a savage look on her face, and came before him dancing. "Shah! Shtill! The rabbi goes dancing!" she sang grimly in time. "Mr. Fumfotch!"

He held the *Tag* firmly before him, muttering quietly but half hoping that she would not be able to hear his mutterings. "All over the world was I," he said. "Paris, London, Amsterdam, Copenhagen, Budapest, Chicago—everywhere, and I must end my days with this witch. When I was in Melbourne . . ."

"Again when he was in Melbourne."

But Ruth knocked and entered, her plastered hair looking like corrugated cardboard, and Mrs. Balkan had to stop to say hello.

"Yes, yes, Ruthie," Mr. Balkan said, glad of the protection of her presence, "when I was in Melbourne, what a sensation, what a success. My King Lear! Antique! You know, Shakespeare? A great writer?"

"Shah," said Mrs. Balkan, the heat going away. "Did you ever see such a fumfotch, Ruthie?"

"Is Max here?" Ruth asked. "I thought that maybe Max would be here."

At this point his voice could be heard calling from the bedroom. "Who came in, Ma?" he wanted to know, and in another second he himself appeared running into the room. He was in his underpants, his trousers in one hand. His shoes were long and ugly with his thin calves exposed. "Oh," he cried in pain, "excuse me!"

Awkward, awkward! Always whenever he wanted to make an impression on a girl he had to do something to bust everything up. If Greta Garbo herself walked in on him one day he'd probably discover that his fly was open or something. Max backed into the bedroom in anguish.

"What a sensation!" cried Mr. Balkan, happy as his mind roamed the daisy fields of his great glories. "What a success!"

"Go already," said his wife to him. "Don't make such a fool out of yourself in front of Ruthie. Go, you'll be late for Madame Clara."

"Tchuh, tchuh, tchuh," sighed the old man, rising. He reached for a pack of blue cards, which he had to distribute on the streets. He slipped his head between the straps of the sandwich boards for which he had been made up and costumed. Great boards and heavy. He sighed as the straps settled on his shoulders.

"Ruthie, my child," he said, "to look at me now, with these signs, you would never think that before you stands a man who was once upon a time a great actor. Balkan, the greatest Yiddish tragedian. You heard of me? Maybe your momma and poppa know me. Ask them do they know Balkan, the greatest Yiddish tragedian from Yudensky's People's Theater on the Bowery. Many, many years ago. All right, maybe not the greatest but not bad, certainly not bad.

Othello I was once, and King Lear, Macbeth, and Hamlet and Tamburlaine and Faustus. Classical roles, nothing but the best.

> "She should have died hereafter;
> There would have been time for such a word.
> Tomorrow and tomorrow and . . ."

"Go already," his wife shouted impatiently. "Bluffer, you want to make a show before Ruthie?"

"Macbeth," said Mr. Balkan, having learned by this time how to ignore his wife completely. "I remember, I remember, in Melbourne . . . well, what's the use talking . . . it's gone . . . all over . . ."

He straightened to leave, shifting the weight on his shoulders more comfortably. And suddenly he became frozen for the moment, the posture of a statue handing out cards, a stone image. Everything from his eyebrows to his fingertips remamed fixed as if petrified. There he was, that funny face with the paint under the silk top hat. Underneath the bulbous red shoes stuck out. Between the face and the shoes there was no skinny old body but, to take the place of his trunk, the signs which said:

MADAME CLARA

SCIENTIFIC BEAUTY TREATMENTS

By Skilled Experts

ANY THREE ITEMS FOR A DOLLAR

Manicure	*Eyebrows*
Shampoo	*Finger Waves*
Henna Rinse	*Facial*
Scalp Treatment	*Marcel*

Haircuts To Fit The Face

Permanent Wave—$3.50 and up
Given By Licensed Beautician

Tel. STagg 5-8324 298 Roebling St.

His thin arms hung out like the claws of a crab. "You want one?" the frozen image said, offering her a card.

"See, look at him!" Mrs. Balkan laughed affectionately. "Mr. Fumfotch!"

The old man relaxed like a snowman melted. He waved his hand at her in disgust, said, "Sh!" defiantly (when his back was turned) and walked out.

"It's a shame for me to say it," Mrs. Balkan said, almost crying with laughter, "but the older he gets he becomes a regular iver-buttle. It was bad enough when he was young but in his old age he's a real Charlie Chaplin."

"Mom," Max Balkan said with much dignity as he entered. He was dressed in his dark suit and dark tie, wore a jacket and his hair was neatly combed. However he was still unwashed. "Mom, I want to talk to Ruth in private. Please go into the kitchen."

"What do you want to talk in private?"

His mother could be impish. It was one of her most charming qualities, Max often said. Sometimes you could almost forget she was an aging woman who had seen much and had suffered more, so childish and innocent could her ways be. But the trouble was, she never knew when to stop.

"Momma—if I told you, it wouldn't be private! Go into the kitchen."

"Oh, don't chase your mother away," Ruth exclaimed virtuously. "Don't listen to him, Mrs. Balkan."

"All right, Mr. Private," his mother said. "I'll go on one condition."

"What?" A fine kind of impression this was making on Ruth.

"I won't go unless you tell me what Mrs. Mackenzie is."

"Aw, gee whiz. Ma! Go into the kitchen. I want to talk to Ruth."

He stamped around the room in a fit of anger, his fingers massaging his scalp with exasperation. "Gee witz," he muttered. "Gee witz. Gee witz."

"All right. All right," Mrs. Balkan said. What a fuss he made! "Be alone!"

But when she went out Balkan found himself with the perplexing problem of handling Ruth. Why had she come? He could have patched up his argument with her some other time. It certainly wasn't the first that they had had. Now he knew there would be more bickering, more explanations that he would wrench out of himself to no good, more abuse from her and again an unsatisfactory parting.

Balkan regarded Ruth as she stood with her purse in one hand, patting her hair with the other to make sure that the stiff lines were being maintained. She, too, at the mirror was killing time to postpone the opening shot. She always seemed to wear tight-fitting silk crocheted sweaters without a blouse underneath, giving a glimpse of the brassiere. A little too big for sweaters, not nice, thought Max. Suddenly she seemed remarkably homely to him. Perhaps it was the finger wave, which by plastering the hair close to her skull emphasized the lines of her nose and mouth. Looking at her, Balkan felt for the first time that it was a different Ruth, not his, and this person appeared unlovely, without sympathy, without tenderness. There was something mean and hard, selfish and small in the way the skin ran in the two lines from her upper lip to her nostrils. Balkan tried to force his mind away from these thoughts. It was impossible. After all these years, this abrupt loss of affection seemed disloyal and unfair.

In the meantime something was dying to be said.

"Please pardon my appearance a minute ago," Balkan said gravely. Very formal, so soon after a fight. It might set the desired tone.

"Pardon your appearance," Ruth said, her eyes looking at his shoe tips with nonchalance.

Well, try again. "Sit down, please."

"Oh, don't be so formal," Ruth broke out. "Somebody would think this was in a movie."

"My goodness, Ruth," Max said, "what's the matter with you today anyhow?"

"All right," she confessed ungraciously, her expression of nonchalance never letting up a minute. "I got a grouch on, I guess.

I was nasty to you before even if you are nuts. I admit it. I'm sorry."

"You don't seem sorry," Max maintained.

"Well, I admitted it, didn't I?" she snapped at him. "What more do you want me to do? Fall on my knees and beg forgiveness?"

A step too far. Max saw his error the moment the words were out of his mouth. What to say now? But fortunately, at this point, someone knocked on the door and with relief he called, "Come in."

It was the old pearl peddler. He was everywhere in that house today.

"Oh," he said with disappointment when he saw Max, "it's you. What house do you live in anyway? I asked you twice already."

The peddler, remembering Munves, was wasting no words and made to leave.

"Wait a minute. Wait a minute," cried Max, flushed with inspiration. This would settle the whole business with Ruth. "How much for those pearls?"

"Max! I don't want pearls. Never mind, mister, I don't want it."

"Have a heart, missus," the peddler wept, genuine tears in his eyes. "How can a person be so mean? A man, he walks on his feet all day, he's got to make a living just like everybody else, ain't it? I get a chance to make one sale all day and you want to spoil it? Don't be so mean, please!" He turned rapidly to Max. "Fifteen cents. A bargain. Worth a dollar."

Max tried to smile debonairly, looked at Ruth's unsmiling hard face, faltered, and finally decided to go through with it. Cheerfully, cheerfully, with the greatest ease, as though he walked on Fifth Avenue every day in the week, he paid the peddler one dime and one nickel, and Ruth knew that it was a decision of this sort that made Max so detestable to her at times. I could kill him, she thought, her teeth grinding because she felt she had better say nothing. He held the string toward her as though his name was Adolphe Menjou.

"Max!" she had to say even though it was too late. "I don't want them. I told you . . ."

"Please, missus, for God's sakes, have a heart," said the peddler, pocketing the coins.

Max smiled eagerly as he beamed at Ruth. "It's all right, Ruth," he urged as if she had been merely polite in refusing the pearls. "Here, take it. How do you like them?"

The peddler had gone to the door in a rush and from it, thrown in for good measure, he shouted, "Worth a dollar, missus. Genuine artificial pearls, my child should drop dead right this minute." And he rushed out.

Ruth held the pearls before her, holding back the angry words with difficulty. All right, she would put them with her jewelry and all the other junk she kept in the wooden candy box. Only it was like Max. That was how he always did things, she could die.

"They're all right," she said, after an effort. "But what in the world do I need them for? It's crazy, ridiculous. You get a notion in your head . . ." She stopped. She hadn't meant to say so much.

Balkan's smile faded and left. No imagination, no feeling. Why couldn't she take his gesture in the spirit he meant it, gay, a little gallant, and especially, smooth? Instead Ruth spoiled everything, rendering him an awkward person even to himself.

"Everything I do has to be ridiculous and crazy" he said hopelessly.

"Oh, Max," she said, suddenly feeling sorry for him, "there's nothing wrong with you except you're so impractical. You've simply made up your mind that you're different from other people and you don't want to be like them. If you could only change your mind to do what everybody else does, to act like a normal human being!"

To argue or not to argue? Max wanted to change the subject before they lost themselves in the morass of the old, old argument, but it was irresistible, the pattern was so grooved he had to follow its distressing paths, he had to talk. "That's it exactly," he said slowly for special force, but gently. "See, Ruth, I don't want to be like other people."

Id-ee-ut! "Look at him talking! You know what they do to people who don't want to be normal? They put them into lunatic asylums. Are you a kid? After all, Max, you're not sixteen, you're old enough, you're grown up and you talk just like when you were in high school. It's all right when you were in school, adolescence is the time for crazy ideas, but now you're a man! Any one of these days, you're so crazy, I wouldn't be surprised if you walked in and told me you decided to become a communist."

See, all communists were crazy. No idealism whatever. "Oh, Ruth, don't be common. Don't say things just to be spiteful. It's not like you."

"You get such crazy notions in your head! Telephone companies, movie service, radios in the subways, watermelon ice cream, parachutes—you're always going to make a million dollars and in the meantime you won't get yourself a job. After all," she said, her voice breaking into a wail as she stopped to catch her breath, "after all, Max, there comes a time, a time, when a man should think of getting married, of settling down and having a family . . ."

Ruth was now crying all over the room. Max had to halt awkwardly. How painful it was to have her crying in his own house. Suppose his mother walked in on them. Balkan sat down, digging his elbows into his knees and holding his head in his hands. He spoke intently to the linoleum on the floor, studying the designs, which were of castles and a crest duplicated in boxes the length of the room. "Look, Ruth," he begged, hoping to shush her. "Look at it my way. Try to be sympathetic. Try to understand what I'm doing. I'm not the only person in the world with the ideas I've got. There are lots of people, important famous people, who have the same ideas, and if you could only be sympathetic, you'd know what I'm trying to do and then everything would be all right."

"All right," she wept, tears streaming. "I'm sympathetic. So what?"

"If I could only get you to understand what I'm going for, if you could only understand," Max began, although he knew it was going to be a difficult task, "it would be all over. I bet you'd be glad I was the way I am. See—" Max paused. The wrong tack. He was on the point of talking about great literature. Take Homer, he wanted to say, any epic, take King Arthur, Shakespeare. In all great classical works, what made them classics was the distinguishing characteristic of heroism and nobility. In those days people lived with richness and glory. These qualities were gone in America in 1935, it was true, but to him this seemed an enormous pity. He wanted to say that he meant to look for heroism in his own life, to live with meaning and vigor, ridiculous and painful as this search might make him feel at times. Max was on the point of saying all these things, but he caught himself in time, for he knew immediately how irritated Ruth would have become. Literature had a particular significance for people and this was apart from reality, no just moral could be drawn from it. It was so hard to talk to her, Max thought.

"See," he began all over again, speaking carefully, "take Tamburlaine. Did you ever hear of Tamburlaine?"

"Who?" she asked impatiently, her puzzled voice coming like the sound of reeds. "Who is Tamburlaine?"

"It's a play. A man hundreds of years ago called Marlowe wrote it. Pop acted in it once, it's a great drama. In those days when Marlowe wrote it, it was the Elizabethan times, an age of great spirit. People then felt stronger and important, there was majesty and glory in life, even the common people, and they felt they were going to be more and more important and wonderful with the years. You know."

"So?" she wailed. "So? What's that got to do with the price of onions?"

"See, this play, Tamburlaine, it's about a peasant boy, a shepherd. That's his name. He didn't want to stay a shepherd all his life. He wanted to be a great man, a king, a ruler of kings. The idea of power and importance. Of course, that's only the bare idea. Telling it this way it kills the whole effect, it ruins the entire impression. But he wants to be a king and he tries and he conquers everyone."

Shepherds, peasants, kings. Fairy tales. Meshuggeh. "Well? Well?" Ruth asked.

"Well, I can't tell you, you really have to read the play. I'll get it for you." He ran to fetch the book, returning to hold it triumphantly before her as though this gesture explained everything and clinched his point completely. "See, the idea is—listen, I don't want to give you the idea that I think I'm Tamburlaine—but the same urge for power, for significance, for importance—I've got that too. In a way I am Tamburlaine, only in Williamsburg, now, not a shepherd in the olden days. I can't win out by conquering kings the way he did. I've got to get ahead by making money. That's the difference, but behind it it's all the same thing."

"Well?" exclaimed Ruth. "You want to make money? Then why don't you look for a job?"

"I don't want a job, twelve dollars a week, pushing hand trucks with dresses on Seventh Avenue. That's like staying a peasant, Ruth. See, you didn't understand. I got to make a lot of money, a fortune."

"See, Max," Ruth concluded sorrowfully, "I'm sympathetic, I listen patiently. What good does it do me? What good is there in a dopey story about a peasant boy and shepherd boys and kings and making a fortune one, two, three? What are you talking about? It's all right if you want to have an intellectual discussion with Munves over books, but where does it get you?"

"Look, Ruth, you don't get it," Max cried, panicky as failure rose before him again. "There's a part in Tamburlaine when he speaks while he still isn't as powerful as he wants to be. Here, look, I'll find it for you." He looked through the pages at a terrible speed for any minute Ruth might descend on him and his last chance would be gone. "Here, here. I got it:

"Both we will reign as consuls of the earth
And mighty kings shall be our senators.
Jove sometime masked in a shepherd's weed,
And by those steps that he hath scaled
 the heavens
May we become immortal like the gods.
Join with me now in this my mean estate
And when my name and honour shall be spread
As far as Boreas claps his brazen wings,
Or fair Boötes sends his cheerful light.
Then shall thou be competitor with me
And sit with Tamburlaine in all his majesty."

Balkan let himself out here in one last stab at reaching Ruth. He read the poetry with fire in his voice and for the time he felt as he had during his morning's walk: eight feet tall and three hundred pounds in weight. What could she do to him, after all? Exuberance blew him up, he felt strong and sure of himself. Ruth, who hadn't been able to follow a word of the quotation, its meaning lost forever with Jove, Boreas, and Boötes, nevertheless remained fixed in the respectful attitude of one exposed to the world's greatest literature. Why be afraid of her? Max asked himself. As Rita said of Munves, did she have a mortgage on him? The hell with it! He had a perfectly sound theory of living and there was no reason for him to be ashamed of it or afraid.

"Do you understand that, Ruth?" he cried. "Do you see what magnificence there is possible, what heroism, what high feeling? That's what I meant, to live with majesty, with dignified ambition, with the trumpets blowing all the time!"

What was he yelling about? Ruth asked herself, unable to make head or tail out of the whole exhibition. What's the matter with him? It was a profound mystery to her. Outside in the yard a man was spiritlessly yelling up: "Clo'. Clo'. Clo'." and Ruth listened intently to the mournful sounds, caught completely unawares by Max's outburst. He was crazy, altogether crazy.

"You know what I think, Max?" she finally said with all sincerity. "Sometimes I think you're half crazy. Sometimes I think you got a screw loose. I'm not making this up. I really mean it."

"Oh, Ruth, try to understand," he implored her. "You say I'm old enough to act like a man, to get settled, to have a family. You say I ought to live like everyone else. What does that mean? It means living in a flat like this with a bathroom on top of you, going to a job all day and to the movies twice a week. It means listening to the radio all day, sleeping until twelve o'clock on Sunday, going to Coney Island if it's hot. All right, maybe I'm impractical, maybe I'm crazy, I don't want to live that way. It's dirty, sour, ugly. You're dead years before your time. Your whole life becomes a hot joke. All you do is wait for the grave. I don't want it for you or for me. There's no glory, no exhilaration—diapers! That's what it always makes me think of—diapers and the smell of vinegar! Ruth, Ruth, don't you ever get a feeling for greatness, for heroism, for poetry? Like the music in a parade when it's so strong you can almost cry? Ruth, listen to me, have confidence in me, let others laugh and think I'm crazy. Not you! 'Join with me in this my mean estate.' As it says in the play. Then you'll sit with Tamburlaine in all his majesty. As it says . . ."

"All right, all right," Ruth protested. "Don't get so excited. It's not good for you."

"Aw," cried Max disconsolately. "The hell with it."

He went to the daybed and sat down. It was all wasted. Now, for once, he had tried to explain the whole thing to her as it was with him. He had risked it, told her what he was aiming for, why he refused to get a job, settle down, do only the normal and easy things. Theories were all right to have and to talk about when you wanted to kill time. But to consider a theory seriously, that was inexcusable, bad. You had to be a dope and a lemon. He scratched his head and looked out the window. The hell with it.

"Max," Ruth said kindly, "I'm not being unsympathetic. I think what you said—all that, the poetry and then later—I think that's fine and wonderful. It's wonderful for a fellow to have ideals and to believe in them. I would be the last person to say anything against that. I can't stand people who are vulgar and never have an idea in their head. But, as a matter of fact, you have to be practical."

Down in the yard Chink was writing on the fence, and at the moment it seemed to Balkan that there was nothing left in life for him to do except to watch the kid at work. Wallowing in disgust and self-pity, he followed the letters mouthing the syllables to himself as Chink produced them. HESHEY ISA, the boy was writing in yellow chalk, the letters round and clumsy. Where had Balkan seen those letters before? He remembered. On the stoop, the name on the house. Max thought of his morning's walk with a homesick feeling. ISA . . . BIGE . . . STINKER . . . HE . . .

"Max," Ruth said softly with tenderness. "I know how you feel.

I can put myself in your place. But that's the way it is. You can't live on ideals these days."

Don't bother me. STINKER ... HE ... PLAYS ... WID ... GOLDIE ...

"Max," Ruth said hesitantly.

DOKTER ...

"What?"

HESHEY ...

"Let's go to the movies."

STINKES WID A CRASHE.

"What?" Balkan turned from the yard and looked at Ruth. "I didn't hear you. What did you say?"

"Let's go to the movies. The way you feel, the best thing in the world for you would be a good movie."

Gpfghsic! "Oh, I told you, I told you! I can't! I have to go to Blenholt's funeral."

"Let's go to the movies, Max," she coaxed. Aristocrat, sophisticate, innocent—one wanted romance, the other wanted excitement—but one wanted his heart and got it! "Joan Crawford is excellent. What's the difference?"

He felt hopeless. "You didn't understand a word I said. If you did, you wouldn't talk like this now."

"What's Blenholt's funeral got to do with what you said?" she asked, really puzzled. What had he been talking about anyway? "Where's the connection?"

"Where's the connection? Don't you see, Ruth, that's the whole thing. Blenholt is Tamburlaine. He was what I want to be, Tamburlaine in New York, now, and I want to pay him homage if it's only for the sentiment."

"Who was Blenholt?" Ruth asked with deep curiosity.

"Oh, a hero," Max said, his annoyance making his voice sound like a whine. "I told you. Commissioner of Sewers."

"Don't believe a word he says, Ruth! He's crazy! Blenholt was a diabetic and he died a good ten years before his time!"

A voice out of nowhere. What, what, what? Ruth uttered a small shriek and Balkan jumped up impulsively, his eyes opening with wonder. Did he really hear it? Of course! He told his blood to slow down again. It was Rita. In the bathroom all this time. She had heard every word. His stomach felt a mild nausea as he thought of all the misery she would be able to make for him now.

"Who's asking you, you rotten snotnose?" he yelled at the bathroom, angry enough to cry.

"Blenholt was a diabetic, Ruth," the voice went on imperturbably. "Don't listen to a word he says, he's nuts as usual. The doctor said Blenholt, he shouldn't have no sweets, it would kill him. So when people went to see him for favors, they sneaked in candy and ices to get in good with him, and the great hero died in a hurry."

What pleasure she took in telling the story. "Shut up, Pathé News!"

"He was a racketeer, a dirty gangster, a grafter and a politician. Don't listen to him!"

"A hero in this flat age!" Max shouted back. "A racketeer, a gangster, a grafter, a politician, anything you want to say, but a hero! Like an emperor in the olden days! Tamburlaine in nineteen thirty-five! Blenholt was a hero! Who's asking you to stick your dirty nose into my affairs?"

"A bum! A grafter!" she chanted with glee behind the oil-papered door. She was having the time of her young life. "On Catholic Holy Days he went to church to get the Italians to vote for him, and on Yom Kippur and Rosh Hashanah he went to the synagogue for the Jews. That's how he became district leader."

"A hero!" Max screamed with rage. "Ruth, listen to me, she just wants to make trouble for me. Blenholt was so powerful there was a slogan about him. 'Not an artichoke leaves the dock without Blenholt getting his fair-and-square cut.' How is that for a man?"

"And listen, Ruth, when Blenholt dies," she went on, "they find out he's not Jewish, he's not Catholic, he's not even a Christian. He's a Turk or something."

"You—you—Pathé News! Knows all, sees all, tells all. That's what you are, Ruchel, Pathé News. You want to be swell, don't you? Ruchel isn't good enough for you. Everybody has to call you Rita!

Who asked you to butt in? Do you have to spoil everything I try to do? Go to hell, tell her about my inventions, make fun of me, go ahead! Ruchel! Pathé News! Go to hell!"

"A grafter!"

Why did he have to have such a rotten person for a sister? Max hated her. She was cheap, mean, and inhuman. The memories of twenty years of brother-and-sister fights all came back in a minute to distress him like a feather sticking in his throat. Everything that Max detested in the world could be found somewhere in Rita.

"A hero!" he shouted with all his strength, goaded to the point of fury. "And what's more, Munves is coming with me, Coblenz is coming, and you too, Ruth, you're coming with me too to pay homage to a hero in a flat age. What do you think of that, Pathé News? And as for you, yourself, you can stay in the bathroom all week for all I care!"

He had to start. It was already past two, the hour at which the funeral was scheduled. For a moment he ran about in a circle, thinking of what to do first. He ran to the door and yelled across the hallway, "Munves! Are you ready? We're coming!"

There was no answer but Max could not wait. He ran to the window and shouted down through the yard for Coblenz. "Get ready," he yelled. "We're coming down in a minute, Coblenz! Get ready!"

Nor was there any answer this time. Balkan, however, unwilling to accept defeat from either of these quarters, persisted in dashing from the doorway to the window calling his friends. He was growing hysterical, and, to make sure of something at least, he grabbed Ruth firmly by the wrist. And as he ran for his friends, he began dragging her with him. She protested indignantly, completely unaccustomed to treatment of this sort from Max, but he paid no attention.

"Stop it!" she cried sharply, hitting his arm with her free hand.

"You, too, shut up!" he said to her, and so firm did he look that the surprise alone made her capitulate, wondering what had suddenly possessed him.

Now the telephone rang. Simultaneously Mrs. Balkan popped

out of the kitchen and Rita threw open the bathroom door. All the shouting and the rumpus could not drag them forth but the magic ring of a little bell brought them out jumping. The expression on Mrs. Balkan's face was grim and determined. Rita flew, her hair in curlers, her face smeared with cold cream, her kimono flapping from her. The bell rang again and Mrs. Balkan grabbed it.

"It's for me, Mother, I'll answer it."

"It's all right, Rita, darling. It's all right. Shah!" she yelled at Max. "Hello? Oh, hello, Freddie?"

"It's for me," Rita whispered fiercely. "I told you it was for me. Give me the phone."

Freddie's father owned a meat market. A possibility, a hope, but definitely a meat market.

"How are you, young man?" Mrs. Balkan syruped into the telephone. "Who? Rita? Yes, I think she's here. I'll call her to the wire if you'll hold it a minute."

"Mother!" said Rita.

Mrs. Balkan smothered the mouthpiece with her palm. "Ask him to come to the house, Rita," she said savagely because there was no time.

"I told you it was for me," Rita said, blazing with anger. "Give me the phone."

"Wait a minute, Rita. It don't hurt to keep him waiting a minute. It makes a better impression."

"You make me sick," said Rita, pulling the telephone from her hands. Then composing her face to the semblance of calmness, she said, "Hell-oh?" in the fashionable, polite, querulous note that society demanded of young girls who pick up the telephone talking to God knows who might be on the other end of the wire. "Oh, Freddie!" she said as if she hadn't had the slightest idea.

"Let me go," Ruth gasped, recovering herself. "You're crazy, Max. You're absolutely out of your mind."

"For once I'm not crazy," he said, holding on. "I'll show you! Coblenz! We're coming!"

"Shah!" cried Mrs. Balkan anxiously at the telephone, trying to hear Freddie over Rita's shoulder.

"No, Freddie," Rita chirped, giving her pronunciation the correct touch of smart clipping and shading. "What did you say? I can't hear you. No, I'm not doing anything this minute. What? What?"

"Let me hear," Mrs. Balkan begged. "Say 'dear'! Say 'darling'! Don't be bashful. Go on, go on."

Rita covered the mouthpiece and turned to her mother. "Mother, please, for God's sakes! You'll embarrass me. He can hear you. Yes, Freddie," she cooed. "How about a picture? Joan Crawford's at the Miramar."

"Tell him to come to the house, Rita!" Mrs. Balkan whispered almost hysterically. "Say 'darling' to him. It don't pay to be bashful.—Shah!" she yelled full force at Max. "He owns a meat market. Give her a chance!"

"Coblenz!" Max yelled at the window. "Coblenz! What's the matter with you? Are you ready?" He ran to the door, still dragging Ruth, and called for Munves.

"A crazy house!" Mrs. Balkan said.

"No," said Rita, perspiring. "I said Joan Crawford's at the Miramar. Well, we can do anything you say, Freddie."

"Is he coming to the house?" her mother asked vehemently. "Tell him to come to the house!"

"Have a heart, Mother!" Rita whispered. "How can I talk to him when you're hanging on to my neck all the time?"

"All right, all right, darling. Don't get angry. Talk. Talk. You're making him wait. Say 'dear'! Does it cost you something to say 'dear'?"

"You're just hopeless," Rita exclaimed, giving up. "Just a minute, Freddie. There's too much of a racket here. Just hold on to the wire for a moment. Gee whiz, you make me sore," she said to her mother. "If you knew how good and mad I am this minute!" She carried the telephone into the bathroom with her and slammed the door.

Mrs. Balkan was left outside, defeated and pained. Her eyes looked wrinkled and she thought for a minute she might cry. "All I want is for you, Rita," she said tearfully. "Why must you always be so mean? All I have on my mind all day is for you."

"Coblenz!" shouted Max. "Are you dead?"

"Shah!" his mother yelled, the tears still on her face. "I've got what's my own troubles on my mind and he's yelling his head off! Sharrup!"

Max took time out from his labors to deal with his mother. "Mrs. Mackenzie!" he said poisonously, leaving her overcome.

At this point the pearl peddler came bursting through the door, pausing not a moment to knock. The strings of pearls swung wildly from his neck and his satchel banged his hips as he rushed.

"My God, mister, quick! Your friend on the first floor! Quick!"

"Who? Coblenz? What happened?"

"The crazy one with the broomstick! He's out of his mind. He's wild like an Indian. He's drunk and breaking up the whole house. In all my life I never saw anything like it. He's a devil!"

"Well," Max shouted at him, "what are you hanging around here for? Who needs you here? Go down and stop him."

"Me?" asked the peddler. "He's your friend!"

The old man stood at the door undecided, looked at Max, and finally scurried out of the room. A crazy house!

It was a blow to Balkan but the truth was he had been expecting it. That green bottle of whiskey! Intending to kill the pain in his tooth, Coblenz had grown drunk.

"See?" said Ruth, breathless. "What did I tell you? Coblenz can't come."

"The hell with him!" Max thrilled with power. It felt good! He was dominating this situation, all right. This was as it should be! Look, everybody, Balkan is no schlemiel. When he makes his mind up, he can act like a man. "The hell with him! We can go without him. Munves! Munves!" he screamed at the top of his voice.

Munves came trotting in with a book still in his hand. Through his spectacles his eyes proclaimed the indignation of a scholar interrupted at his work. "What do you want?" he asked petulantly. "Somebody would think the building was on fire!"

He had forgotten all about Blenholt. "The funeral!" Max cried. "Did you forget? Blenholt's funeral. Come on!"

"Well, I did forget," he retorted with frozen anger. "I admit it. But I can't leave my work. I know I promised but I can't possibly stop."

"What do you mean, you can't stop?" Balkan asked like George Raft in a hard movie. "You're coming with us."

"I can't. I should lose all thread and then it would be lost forever. You know how it is. Sometimes an idea hits you and if you don't get to work on it immediately, it leaves and that's the last you see of it."

"Yes, I know, Munves. Pretzels all over again. But it can wait. Put it down on paper and you won't forget. I'll remind you."

"This is big! It's important! I can't drop it. While you were in my room I was looking through the *Anglo-Saxon Chronicles*—the glossary of it, prepared by Kennedy under Krapp. Are you at all familiar with it? Well, you must have heard of Krapp anyhow? I noticed they placed Sealwudu in Essex. Can you imagine that? Sealwudu in Essex!" He turned to Ruth to make sure she caught the emphasis too. "In Essex!"

Somehow they all did not fall down with astonishment. Mrs. Balkan threw up her hands, forsaking all hope of hearing anything of Rita's conversation with Freddie. She went back to the kitchen. As for Max, he looked at Munves, his nostrils dilated with contempt.

"Munves," he said coolly, "do you know what you are? You're a lemon, a schlemiel. That's what you are. You're impractical with your nose stuck into a book all the time. You make me good and sick. The hell with you. How do you like that?"

"Well!" said Munves, shaken up considerably. What language! "If it means all that to you, why, all right, I'll go with you."

"You can stay right here where you are," Max replied, captain of his soul and master of his fate. "The hell with you. I don't want you. The hell with Coblenz too. The hell with everybody. All right, so nobody wants to go to Blenholt's funeral! That's fine. That's lovely. All right, then, come on, Ruth, we're going!"

"We are not!" she replied. "You crazy all of a sudden? I'm doing nothing of the kind. I'm going to the Miramar."

"Come on!" Balkan said in a low, strong voice. It was a new Balkan, a miraculous change. Power and will he had. He pulled her with him to the door, flung it open, and paused at the threshold.

"Go to hell," he cried gloriously to Munves. "You're—you're—small, anemic, unimportant. What am I wasting my time here for?"

They went forth.

Munves had barely time to close his mouth when Rita came hurtling out of the bathroom. She replaced the telephone on the end table and went directly into the kitchen to deal with her mother. "How," she demanded, "can a girl have a decent conversation with a fellow with you hanging on my neck all the time?"

"Sh!" whispered her mother, worrying over Munves. "Sh."

"You know what he said? Chances I get here? He said everybody here is crazy, now you know?"

"Sh," breathed Mrs. Balkan, twisting her cheeks in agony. "Munves is here."

"Oh!" said Rita cheerily, stepping into the front room. "Hello, Munves. I didn't even see you."

"Look, Rita," he said. "What do you think of Max? I know I promised him I'd go to Blenholt's funeral, but a chance turned up for a really original piece of work and I just wouldn't let it go. You know how it is. And you should have seen him!"

"Oh, don't mind him, Munves," she said blandly. "He's nuts three-quarters of the time."

"Rita!" Mrs. Balkan exclaimed. "Why don't you offer your friend some fruit or cake?"

"No, I don't care for any, thanks," said Munves, still worried.

"You been working hard, Munves?" Mrs. Balkan asked. "It don't pay. Education don't bring you bread and butter."

"Mother!" said Rita. "Go into the kitchen. What's this original work you've been doing?"

"I haven't finished but it's really fascinating." But Munves spoke heartlessly, for Balkan and his strange behavior persisted in troubling him. He held up the book and explained about Sealwudu. "It couldn't be in Essex. I knew immediately that something was wrong. From one clue and another I just had a hunch that something was wrong. So I brought down a gazetteer and started to check."

"You know, really, it's marvelous," Rita confessed, "the way you dig into those old things. I guess you really must have a genius for it."

"Wonderful!" exclaimed Mrs. Balkan who had been listening to every word. "Wonderful!"

A faint glow lit Munves' face. "Nothing of the kind," he said modestly. "You exaggerate."

"Munves," Mrs. Balkan said, wiping her hands in her apron with anxiety. "You're educated, you read books all the time, tell me. What is Mrs. Mackenzie? Max calls me it all the time and I don't know what it is, Mrs. Mackenzie."

"Mrs. Mackenzie, Mrs. Mackenzie," Munves said. "Don't tell me. I'll get it."

Mrs. Balkan stood poised, her mouth open. At last.

"Thackeray!" Munves cried. "*The Newcomes*. That's it. The Great Campaigner. One thing about me, and I'll say it myself, nobody's been able to trip me up yet on a name."

"Yes, yes, Munves, darling," Mrs. Balkan said. "The Great Campaigner. But why does Max call me that for?"

"Oh, she's the woman, she's the one who's always trying to marry off her daughter. Max calls you that?"

It was a mystery to him.

FIVE
In the lion's den

To rub peach stones in spit, making rings.
To stick cock-a-maimies.
To play with the soda water cap collection.
To make watermelon seed necklaces.
To play Dixie Cup pictures.

HESHEY HAD NOTHING TO DO AFTER LUNCH.

"Goldie," he asked shyly, "you still mad at me?"

"Kiss my ass."

"Dirty word!" he chortled, grinning. "You should get your mouth washed in soap."

"My heart is an open book," she sang, disregarding him with ease. "There's nothing concealed in it."

"Stick mad and see if I give a Russian hoorah."

They were on the landing near Coblenz's door. The storm from him was over and quiet descended muggily like a heavy feather-pillow blanket on a damp day. Chink was in the yard and Heshey's mother forbade him to go into the streets. It was dull.

"Momma," he cried to the closed door, "I want to go inside. I'm bored."

Absolutely no answer. That's what he was, bored.

"Hey, Goldie, come on! Don't be stuck up. Let's play Buck Rogers in the year 2540. I got a rocket pistol."

"You," she said, her eyebrows lifting, "can kiss my you know what."

Holl right, see if I care. She'd give in sooner or later, or what was she hanging around for? Heshey beguiled the time by looking through his eyelashes, a difficult feat but worth the effort. When he managed the trick just right, a new world opened to him: strange meshes of shadows and purple-colored bubbles shimmering as his eyelids pulsed.

"Can you make cockeyes?" he asked. No answer, but he could sense that Goldie was looking at him enviously. Hesh held a finger a foot in front of his nose, stared at it with concentration, drew the finger slowly to his face and lo! cockeyes! "That's nothing," he said aloud, speaking to himself. "I know plenty other tricks. The tricks I know! Boy, I could get hunnerds guys sucking around me just to learn him my tricks."

"Showoff," said Goldie, giving in.

"You want to feel good?" he asked promptly. "I got a trick."

He walked to her and bade her sit down on the step. "You comfortable? You got to be comfortable in this trick. Now close your eyes. Keep 'em closed, else no fish. Now sing: 'Lookie, lookie, lookie, here comes Cookie.' Sing low and dreamy."

"Lookie, lookie, lookie, here comes Cookie," sang Goldie.

Hesh held his ten fingers above her head like Dracula. The hands descended. He was massaging her scalp in slow rhythmic movements, occasionally varying this procedure to rub his fingers gently over her forehead and eyes. "You feel good," he whispered in a monotone. "You feel nice. You're having a very nice time. Ain't you having a very nice time?"

"Lookie, lookie, lookie," said Goldie distantly. "Here comes Cookie." He was right, his fingers felt nice, his fingers made her feel creepy all over until she could die.

"That's all," Hesh said sharply, clapping his hands like a real actor.

Goldie had to wet her lips to wake up.

"Hypnotism," Hesh said triumphantly, standing away to grasp his success from the expression on her face. "I could make you do anything I wanted you to." And Goldie could believe him.

Hesh sat down again alongside her on the step. He turned her about so that she was facing him and gazed steadfastly into her eyes. Goldie had to drop hers after a second and shifted her head away.

"What are you trying to do to me?" she asked uncomfortably, feeling completely at his mercy.

He grabbed her hands and turned her to him again. "Look into my eyes," he commanded, his face serious. "Let's see who can last the longest."

The two sat on the hallway step staring into each other's eyes. Goldie wanted to scream. She couldn't stand it another minute, but every time her eyelids began to droop, Heshey would jerk her wrists and force her to continue. The game went on and on. They were rapt.

Downstairs, approaching stealthily on his tiptoes, came Chink. He was Uncas, the Last of the Mohicans, trailing his quarry on his silent moccasins. Unheeded, he walked until he was directly at the side of the gazers. His shadow fell over them and reluctantly Hesh looked up. There was Chink, his fingers wiggling madly with the thumbs stuck into his ears, his eyes bulging unnaturally, his tongue stuck over his teeth to make him look like an ape.

"A-wah-a-wah-a-wah-a-wah," Chink gurgled ferociously.

"E-wa-ah!" gasped Hesh, finally catching his breath. He broke past him and ran wildly, just in the nick of time to catch Munves in the stomach and knock him off his feet. Munves was coming down the stairs with Rita to take care of Coblenz, but now he had to sit down over four steps.

"Kids," he explained intelligently as Rita picked him up.

They walked into Coblenz's room, leaving Chink alone on the landing, wahing magnificently at the top of his lungs and beating his chest after the manner of Tarzan in the moving pictures. Inside the room was a mess. Everything that had been standing on four legs now rested upside down. Like chickens on the hooks with their feet up in a butcher's window, thought Munves, marveling at the image and wondering how it had entered his head. Books and newspapers were scattered over the room, the results of one of Coblenz's favorite practices when in anger. For then he liked to throw things over his head, letting them drop where they would. This somehow made him feel that he was acting logically in a world of chaos, and, further, afforded him the sensation of opulence. As for Coblenz now, he was lying on the floor, half undressed, for he had jerked the clothes from his body in frenzy, asleep and snoring. The green whiskey bottle was kicked empty into a corner. Overhead the swishing noises of the roller skates persisted desultorily. And puttering around aimlessly, surveying the damage, was the pearl peddler himself, the strings around his throat like an African chief, his face composed in the expression of sad wisdom, as one looks at battlefields after the din has died away.

"See?" he said with reflection. "Just like I said. Everything, everything, busted. Smashed."

Munves bent cautiously over the still form lying among the overturned chairs and sniffed. "What a pity," he murmured, genuinely distressed. "Shameful, Rita. Just shameful." He turned to the peddler. "Why didn't you stop him? Why didn't you do something?"

"What could I do with a madman like him?" the peddler protested indignantly. "He was strong like a bull. Go move a house!"

"What he needs," said Rita, "is a sister. If he was my brother, I'd like to see him try to pull off that stuff and get away with it."

"Were, Rita, were," Munves corrected gently. "A pity. A really fine fellow like Coblenz. Essentially a capable boy. Animal-like. Brutish."

"Oh, you're exaggerating, Munves," she said. "It's really not so terrible. It isn't a pogrom."

"Yes, I'm afraid it really is bad." Lately Munves had heard definite reports about Coblenz. It seemed that for some time now, even though Munves had not been aware of it, Coblenz had been drinking, and, worse, betting on horse races with the cigar-store bookmaker. Munves did not condemn these dissipations for their intrinsic evil, although certainly he could not understand them, but what disturbed him most was that his friend was stepping down to low society. Especially at the cigar store. Hoodlums they were there. Whenever he passed by the store those boys—taxi drivers from the hackstand on the corner, mainly—called out all sorts of degrading abuse at him. Why, Munves often wondered, should it make them so happy to call him dirty names? "Mr. Pishteppel," they had named him, and once when he had stopped to remonstrate with a driver for calling him this, the roughneck had turned him about swiftly by the elbow and kicked him hard in the seat. A low crew, they were, and Coblenz was associating with them. Munves walked around the room, futilely setting two or three pieces to rights.

"Don't take it so bad," said Rita. "He'll sleep it off and then he'll be the same fine fellow all over again. He'll get over it."

"No, you don't understand it at all," Munves replied, loyally unwilling to tell her all about Coblenz. "A splendid chap like him. He could do a lot with himself and instead he wastes himself. Not a scholar, you know, but very practical in most things. A solid head."

"He had a toothache," said the peddler by way of mention.

"What?" asked Munves.

"What's that got to do with him now?" Rita asked.

"Nothing, nothing. All I said, he got a toothache. In my town long ago in the old country, there was a drunkard. My, my, you never saw such a drinker. The man, all the time he went around crying and crying he had a toothache, he needed a drop of whiskey. And if you opened his mouth, funny thing it was, he hadn't a tooth in his whole head."

If it had been only a toothache, Munves sighed sadly. Coblenz was getting worse and worse. Soon he'd be a bum just like the others at the cigar store. There were levels of society, Munves knew, and the best thing to do was to stay away, to keep a distance from the mob. That was one of the reasons he himself relished his studies so much. Some would say that they formed a way of escape for him from reality, but Munves knew that they served only as a barrier to its undesirable sides. His pursuits did not shut out life—for sordidness and cruelty, of course, were not all of life—but they made it possible for him to savor it at its best. All men, Munves admitted regretfully, could not very well be scholars. But it was Coblenz's duty not to allow himself to be tarnished and coarsened. A strange fellow he was altogether—bitter, rude, trying always to be sourly clever, and yet intelligent and capable of understanding.

"You young men, with all your education," muttered the peddler. "You study too much. The head can't stand it. You lose a screw. Look at the other one, upstairs . . ."

"Look here, mister," Munves said, rushing to his friend's defense, "you've gotten the wrong impression of that fellow. Not that it really matters what you think of him, but the truth is that in many ways that boy is remarkable. Don't you think ideals are important?"

"Ideals?" repeated the peddler, nonplused. "Who said anything?"

"Perhaps you too think ideals are laughable. In this country any man who is idealistic only suffers from misunderstanding and abuse," Munves said, speaking with feeling. "I admit, sometimes he's a little too enthusiastic, but after all, that's a fault on the side of the angels."

"Please!" begged the peddler, upset and almost in tears. "Mister, what did I say, it was so terrible? Did I say anything bad? I wouldn't say bad of nobody, not if you gave me a fortune! Listen, lady, did you hear me say something bad?"

"Oh, it's all right, mister," Rita said. "Don't get excited. Don't worry."

"I should say something bad!" he muttered, still warm with anger.

"An idealistic individual," said Munves, lost in thought, "has no real place in this calloused civilization."

"Please! Mister!" Was this crazy young scholar ever going to get over it? "What did I say?"

"This calloused civilization," repeated Munves happily. "Good phrase. No, Rita? Apt."

"Well," she drawled archly, "when you take into consideration your education, it's nothing for you to be proud of. Anybody with your education should know enough to talk like that."

"No, really, Rita . . ." said Munves, overcome.

"You know I dreamed of you last night, Munves. Guess what? I dreamed you died and, of course, you know how much you mean to me. Well—you know. But the funny thing was that instead of feeling sorry that you had died, I said to myself, in the dream, 'Gee whiz, now I'll have to go to a dictionary every time I want to find out something.'"

Munves smiled sheepishly, pleased at the flattery and yet unwilling to reveal his pleasure.

"Oh," Rita simpered. "My friend! My encyclopediac friend!"

"A funny dream," Munves admitted, smiling. "Encyclopedic, Rita, encyclopedic." Very pleasant, all this, but Munves had a vague feeling that these compliments were causing him to overlook his duty and his conscience bothered him. What had he been thinking of? Oh, yes, the defense of Max Balkan. "Many people fail to do Max simple justice," he said, magnanimously waving aside his laurels. "They misunderstand him all the more because he not only talks of his ideals—a practice that is passably harmless—but because he actually tries to live up to them in reality. A little impractical, quixotic. You know you just can't do that sometimes, but all the same, very creditable."

"What kind of ideals, Munves?" Rita asked him, nothing loath to enter an intellectual discussion. "He's got ideals to make a million dollars, that's his ideals?" She had finished two years in high school, but with all his education she certainly had Munves there. Education wasn't everything. Sometimes a lesson in the School of Experience was worth a year at college.

"You miss the point," Munves said gently. "I suppose he's never explained it to you. It's sometimes harder to talk to your own sister than to the motorman in a streetcar. The million dollars are only what we consider power and importance today, and those are the things Max really wants. He's not interested in the money for its own sake."

"Sure," said Rita wisely. "That's what they all say. It's not the money, it's the principle of the thing."

"You . . ." began Munves patiently.

"Oh, it's all right with me," she said. "Coblenz can get drunk and play the races, and my brother Max can think up schemes to make him a million dollars in a hurry. If it keeps them happy, I should worry."

"What a way of looking at it!" Munves exclaimed. "As though ideals were a form of narcotic, a way of escape. Why, Rita, if you take that point of view, you could easily say that my researches, my intense preoccupation with language, are only another kind of dodge from reality."

How difficult it was to make people understand that life was a kind of showcase. There were the good and the bad in it, and because a person selected only one of the good in it, it did not necessarily follow that he was shutting his eyes to the entire display. But what hurt Munves most was Rita's blithe dismissal of a philosophical system. From her, too!

"Oh, Munves," she said, protesting. "There's no comparison between you and Max. You actually do things, important things."

"Yes, yes, it is the same thing," he insisted. "I can imagine many people—the casual man in the street, truck drivers, street cleaners, taxi drivers ... (Mr. Pishteppel!)—I can imagine them thinking it strange and ridiculous for me to spend all my time on studies. You know, like the absentminded professor in the jokes." And in spite of the hints he had picked up hitherto, now for the first time the possibility struck him with any degree of intimacy. For once in his whole life he realized there might be something absurd in his wholehearted concentration. His life was much too bordered. He had to get variety into it. "Yes," he affirmed with force, never one to duck an unpleasant truth, "people might really think there is something funny and impractical about me, just as the peddler felt about your brother!"

"Oh, I know you, Munves. You're just fishing," Rita said, pointing her finger at him accusingly. "You just want me to say how important I think your work is. Digging into old words, thousands of years old, and finding out what happened to them."

"Do you really think so?" he asked, sincerely hoping he was wrong. "You're just kidding me."

"Of course I'm not kidding you!"

"Really?" He was still uncertain. She was just being polite and kind to him. Important as his work was, Munves now felt convinced, he really needed a change from it. Not, he hastened to reassure himself, that he would drop any part of his interests, but he would look about to find other diversions. Maybe a sampling of the showcase was necessary after all. Munves determined that at this point in his life there would be a change. "But," he told Rita gratefully, "it's charming of you to say that. Really, that was sweet of you." And he glowed at her bashfully as emotion revealed itself.

"What a pity," wailed the peddler among the ruins. "What a pity. All that furniture ruined. Busted. Worth good money and he breaks it like a crazy man. A sin, that's what it is."

"A shame," Munves agreed, quickly returning to his duty and regarding Coblenz. "A shame. Yes, yes, indeed."

"Not so much the value of the furniture as it stands," the old man mused. "Old pieces. But to buy new . . ." He shook his head. What a needless, forlorn pity.

"I'm going to talk to Coblenz," Munves declared to Rita. "I really shall. It may be none of my business but somebody ought to stop him before he gets much worse."

"No, seriously, seriously," insisted the peddler. "It's like you have an old chair in the kitchen. Worth maybe twenty cents, thirty cents, if you can find a buyer. Then by accident it breaks and you go to a store for a new one. They want two dollars, three, maybe. You see?" He held his wrinkled face to Munves, eagerness to convince shining among the lines of his other troubles.

"All right, all right, mister," Rita said. The old man was cramping her. "Enough is enough. Gum-bye, please, and thank you."

"Good, good, fine," said the old man, collecting himself and his pearls. "All I try to do is help. When I'm finished, nobody wants me, kick me out—good, good." At the door he remembered, took a string of pearls from his neck and jiggled them. "For your sweetheart, maybe? Twenty cents. A bargain."

"Why not?" Munves giggled. He smiled at Rita as the flush rose in his face, dug in his pockets for money and presented the string to Rita. "There you are!"

"Worth a dollar, my child should drop dead this minute," the peddler said with the calmness of one who delivers a benediction. And he walked out of the room humming.

"Now, that was really nice of you, Munves. I wonder what in the world made you do that."

"Oh," said Munves, jittery with excitement, "just for a joke. You know, sometimes you get a sudden impulse and on the spur of the moment you go ahead and do something."

"Well, anyhow, thanks," she said sweetly. "That was very lovely of you. Not, of course, that the pearls are valuable or anything, but for the sentiment, Munves."

"Rita ..." Munves said, struggling with himself. "Why do you always call me Munves?"

"Well, it's a nice name."

"You like it?" The giggles broke through. He wasn't able to restrain them.

"Yes." Coy.

"Ho! Ho! Ho!" cried Munves, busting in anticipation. "Well, how would you like to have it for your own name?"

Whoo, hoo, hoo! E-yah, hah, hah! The two of them broke into the wildest laughter. It was such a hot joke. "Is it a proposal?" Rita shrieked. "Is it a threat or a promise?" They laughed and laughed until water came into Munves' eyes and he had to stop and stopping, all at once he was sober, cold sober.

"But seriously," he said in a spent voice, "we know each other so well, Rita, you know it would really sound better if you could call me ... Mendel."

"Mendel ..." Rita said.

"You know," he gushed rapidly, "there's something essentially very sweet about you. Really ..."

Munves stopped, the muscles of his face paralyzed in the sweet arrangement of affection suddenly gone sour. Rita searched his face anxiously. What had happened? She turned around. The apparition of Coblenz had risen from the dead and was now confronting them. Their laughter had, most probably, awakened him, and now he glared, swollen, inhuman, and fearful. Their tender mood was gone like a gnat flicked to extinction.

"Look here," Munves found it in him to stutter. "You need someone . . . as your friend . . . I hope you won't feel offended if I . . . for your own good . . ."

"Look here, yourself," Coblenz said in an ordinary tone that frightened them more than shouts or screams would have. He was speaking with complete normalcy and Munves recognized something sinister and maniacal in his calm. "Munves, as your friend, you know what I'm going to do to you? Right now?"

Munves preferred not to reply, but Coblenz waited, evidently expecting one. "What?" he asked, doing all he could to keep from quaking outright.

"I'm going to cut your throat from ear to ear," Coblenz remarked dispassionately. "What do you think of that?"

"You're . . . you're joking!" Munves tried desperately to laugh.

Coblenz searched among the debris and somehow turned up a bread knife. "I'm joking?" he repeated. "All right, just watch and see if I'm joking. For three solid years," he mentioned casually, "I've been wanting to cut your throat, and now when I'm on the point of reaching my life's ambition, you stand there and tell me I'm joking."

He came forward. Rita jumped into action, for Munves was helpless, rooted to the floor. She pulled him by the arms, reached the door and hustled him out. "Crazy!" she yelled to Coblenz behind the closed door. "Nut! Lunatic!"

It was a terrible experience. Munves stood in the hall dumbly as though he had just suffered a sunstroke. Chink, the Last of the Mohicans, had been holding the landing all by himself. He sat on the steps, his knees widespread in the posture of an emperor. "Calling all cars. Calling all cars," he kept on announcing, hoping Heshey would open his door so that he could take a crack at him with his hunks of corncob. Chink had broken up two or three hot corns and had them ready in a neat pile at his side. This was war as always, but the tactics were different. Heshey, behind his mother's door for a fort, would open it suddenly, yell out, "Chink-stink," and slam it before the corncobs came flying. "Calling all cars. Calling all cars," Chink repeated hopefully but the door remained closed.

"He's crazy," Rita said. "They ought to put him in Kings County."

"See, Rita, now you understand what I meant when I said Coblenz is getting worse all the time," Munves pointed out weakly. "Decay. That's what it is. You'd hardly think it was Coblenz."

"Forget it," Rita urged him scornfully. "Don't you waste a minute on him."

Munves was never so much at loose ends as he was this moment. "It's all so upsetting," he complained, sad and worn out. "First Max and the funeral . . . Rita," he said, even in his own pain dutifully thinking of others, and this was typical of him. "Rita, do you really think I hurt your brother's feelings when I refused to go to the funeral? He seemed to be so engrossed in the passing of Holtzager."

"Blenholt, you mean," Rita said. "Don't pay any attention to Max. He's crazy, too, half the time."

"Such a peculiar interpretation of the man, he had," Munves said, speaking in a thin voice, for wheels were still whirring in his head. "A hero, your brother called him. Tamburlaine. The tyrants of olden days. Not anemic like us. You know, in spite of what I said to the peddler before, there's something impractical about Max. He's a dreamer, he needs a full life . . . life's a showcase . . . he's so impractical . . ."

"You feel all right, Munves?" asked Rita with concern.

"Nevertheless," said Munves slowly, "even if I couldn't understand his ardor, I think I offended him when I refused to go. Rita, do you think I ought to drop everything and go to the funeral? After all, as he said, I promised."

"Don't be silly," Rita exclaimed. "Your work is much more important than funerals. You ought to be getting busy. You're wasting time."

"Chinkstink!" The door slammed, the corncob bouncing off harmlessly, and inside Heshey could be heard jumping with glee.

"Calling all cars. Calling all cars," Chink said grimly.

"I've lost all track," said Munves, trying to catch hold of himself. "Such excitement. First Max and the funeral, and then Coblenz. Everything would happen on a day like this, just when I was on the track of something really important."

"You'll remember," Rita comforted him. "Essex or something."

"Such a full day. Everything happens at once. I can't even concentrate."

"You'll remember, Munves," Rita said imploringly. Sealwudu. Sealwudu in Essex. In Essex."

"Sealwudu! That's it!" he cried, heartened. "Sealwudu in Essex!"

"See, you'll remember," Rita said happily, leading him up the stairs. "I'll help you."

"Will you really? Really?" Munves grew warm at her kindness. "That's splendid of you. Really, Rita, that's very charming of you."

Hesh's door opened, he uttered his battle cry and ducked behind to wait for the corncob. It came. Then Hesh daringly reappeared at the door. He held a paper bag full of water raised above his head, ready to fling it at Chink who was to be caught off his guard when the door shut the first time. Too slow! Another corncob smashed the bag out of Hesh's grip. The water poured all over him like a deluge. He was drenched and he looked sick all of a moment. The meek get meeker.

"Wa-ah," began Hesh slowly.

"A-hahng, hahng, hahng," trumpeted Chink, beating his chest in victory.

"Why," protested Rita, "I'm fascinated by those words. If you let me, I'd be only too glad to help you . . . Mendel."

Munves was joyful but still incredulous. They proceeded to his room, eager for work.

SIX

The tenement without Balkan

WHILE BALKAN AND RUTH were running in the heat, arguing and quarreling as he sought the procession and worried that he would be too late, his friend Coblenz lay in a great field of daisies which the wind blew in graceful time to the music of a symphony orchestra playing the *Blue Danube*. Daisies, daisies for miles, and they dipped their cute little heads this way and that, smiling and cooing. And these daisies had long full soft thighs, for Coblenz perceived on looking more closely they were only young ladies dressed to simulate flowers after the fashion of the chorus girls at the Roxy Theater. Now they took to kicking and long V's of thighs appeared, the V's, of course, upside down. The breeze blew soft and fragrant, the music from the huge orchestra dripped over them, and there was much for the eyes to behold.

Coblenz himself is lying languorously amid the daisies, on the earth, in clothes that make him look like the Sheik of Araby. He has a beard, finely barbered to a point, his face is tanned and smiling, the teeth gleam, and his eyes are dark and mysterious pools. At each knee is a flock of chorus girls, the pick of the lot, regular lallapalloozas these, and nearby lies a thousand-page copy of *Popeye the Sailor Man*. Four hundred and fifty-nine high-stepping zebras prance majestically; there are peacocks in the courtyard and tigers in the forests; off to one side stands Munves, his eyes shining with the peculiar happy eagerness that generally lights up his face, even though at the present moment an ornamented, jewel-studded scimitar embraces his throat.

Zambina, Queen of the Zambesi, fair and like unto a willow tree, is sprawled out on her belly at his feet. She is reading from *Popeye* and as her perfumed words reach his ear, Coblenz inhales deeply on his cigarette and nods approval. Suddenly a cloud of dust is spied in the distance. It is Karatchka the Curt, dashing madly on his pureblooded white stallion. A wave of the hand. The music stops. The daisies stop. Zambina rises. Down from the saddle swings Karatchka. He kisses the ground before his master.

"Sire," he pants, "Latabelle won the fifth race at Empire City and she paid twelve to one."

"It is as nothing," drawls Sherif Coblenz, hitting Munves on the head with his scepter to remind him to make a note of it. A wave of the hand and the music, the daisies, Zambina continue.

But someone had to knock on the door awakening Coblenz. "Farewell, Zambina," Coblenz muttered aloud. The knock came again and Coblenz buried himself deeper into the pile of broken furniture. Finally Mrs. Wohl took matters into her own hands and entered the room. She was the cleaning woman who came every week, an old gray Yiddisher momma with a squint and shoulders hunched up from years of hard work. Mrs. Wohl took one look at the shambles, dropped her mop and dust cloths, cried, "Oh, woe is me," and a worried expression filled her face as she tried to puzzle out the scene.

"Nobody home?" she asked. "Nobody home?"

"Bong," said Coblenz from his hideaway, shutting the passages to his nostrils for the sake of resonance.

"Mr. Coblenz!" she called, sniffing anxiously for gas. "Where are you? What happened?"

"Bong," said Mr. Coblenz.

She hunted for him in the room, moving slowly as she turned the furniture away. Coblenz lay burrowed, enjoying the situation, and just when Mrs. Wohl was on the point of discovering him, he sang: "Yip I dee I die, yip I dee, yip I die."

She nearly fell over backward. "What happened here?" she cried. "Was it a revolution? A fire?"

"Bong," said Coblenz gravely, a vacant look in his stare. He still kept his position on the floor.

"He's crazy!" Mrs. Wohl gasped in a thin voice. She cracked her knuckles with anguish. "My God, it's terrible. The poor homeless orphan went crazy all of a sudden!"

"Cray-zee! Cray-zee! Cray-zee!" he clucked, trying to imitate a parrot.

Mrs. Wohl recovered herself and set about to tend him. She had to do something for the poor boy but she did not know what exactly to turn her hand to first. Holding him by the arms, she encouraged him to stand up, talking to him in a running stream of endearing terms. She called him her little boy, her poor innocent orphan, her wounded birdling. Coblenz allowed himself to rise from the floor and be led to a chair. He sat down with the harmless stare still in his eyes.

"Whu-hee-ee-ee," he uttered profoundly, attempting this time the whinny of a horse.

"Oh, woe. Oh, woe," cried Mrs. Wohl heartbrokenly. It was terrible. Such a fine young man. But she could have foretold this was going to happen. Often before in her trips to his room she had noticed symptoms of mental disorder. Why hadn't she done something then? She reproached herself. It was her fault. She should have made him go to a doctor. Now it was too late.

"Mrs. Wohl?"

"Yes, my child?" she said eagerly. He knew her. He could recognize her. "Yes?"

"You cut your fingernails?"

"Yes?"

"You cut your toenails?"

"Yes, with a knife." A pity! A pity!

"Shame on you!" Coblenz cried in a burst of tears. "Shame on you!"

"All right, darling. All right, little mother," she humored him. "No more. Mrs. Wohl don't cut her fingernails no more. Don't cry."

"You cut your fingernails," he sobbed. "You and you and you! Just think how many people there are in America and everybody cuts his fingernails. Think how many fingernail cuttings there are in America alone. Ten little fingers and ten little toes, and multiply by one hundred and twenty-five million."

"Oh, woe," said Mrs. Wohl, sniffling and shaking her head. "Terrible. Terrible."

"Matter," said Coblenz, suddenly speaking sternly, like a prophet, "is never destroyed. All these nail-cuttings accumulate and I see a time, verily, when all we humans will be pushed off the face of the earth because there will be no room. The oceans will be filled with fingernails and toenails, the lakes, the bays, the gulfs, all, all, all, by God, even the sky, no room, what was I saying?"

"Hot?" she asked, wiping his brow with a cloth. "Hot, my child?"

"Hot," he agreed soberly. "The day is hot, blue-streak hot, pin-point hot, by God, all the ice in Iceland is melting. Oh, Mrs. Wo-hull," he called, his eyes turning impish with delight. "Oh, Mrs. Wo-hull."

"Yes, my child," she purred, the tears running at her eyes with pity.

"If your ears were potatoes," he said in a sing-song tone, "there would be no famine in Ireland tonight."

Suddenly Mrs. Wohl understood and all sympathy fled from her face. The dirty bum was just playing a joke on her. All the time he played jokes on her, said crazy things and called her Mrs. Greta Garbo because she wore men's shoes to work in. Bummer! She found the empty green whiskey bottle and another, half full, on the windowsill. Drunk! A dirty lowdown louse! And she had felt so sorry for him. Now she called him every name but the good ones.

"Mrs. Wohl, please," he begged.

"I can't clean here no more. The hell with you! Look at your crazy house, all smashed and busted. You're a lunatic! I don't come back no more!"

"Mrs. Wohl," Coblenz wailed miserably, like Heshey talking to his mother. "Please, Mrs. Wohl."

"I'm calling a politzmann! A politzmann to take you to a crazy house! I don't clean here no more!"

"Please, Mrs. Wohl, just one question I want to ask you. One little question, you don't have to be so mean."

"Well, what? What?"

"Did you ever hear of Latabelle?"

This caught her in midair. Lottabelle? What was Lottabelle? Maybe she was wrong and unfair to him after all.

"See," he said, shaking his head sadly and choking a sob. "You don't know. Call me names, dirty names, and you don't even know who Latabelle is."

"What is Lottabelle?" she besought him.

All Coblenz would do to relieve her anxiety was to shake his head knowingly and pitifully. Mrs. Wohl looked at him suspiciously. It was another joke. But she could not be sure. After all, he was an orphan, homeless, he had nobody to look after him.

"Still in all," she said, "Lottabelle or no Lottabelle, I ain't cleaning here no more. You're crazy. You get somebody else to clean for you, I suffered long enough." She picked up her mop and dust cloths and shuffled in her men's shoes to the door. "Mr. Coblenz," she said softly, "you feel all right?"

He waved his hand in a weak gesture of assurance and sat limply in the chair. "Latabelle," he murmured with deep sorrow. "Latabelle."

"Does it hurt, Lottabelle? Is it a bad sickness?"

"My worst enemies shouldn't catch it," he said briefly.

"All right," she said, setting down the mop. "I'll clean."

"Tomorrow," Coblenz managed to utter. "Come back tomorrow. Go to Mr. Munves."

Mrs. Wohl asked him if she could do anything for him. He shook his head pathetically and with a great sigh of commiseration she left.

Latabelle, Coblenz said after the door shut, you're the horse of my dreams. Latabelle, I love you. Latabelle, where are you? He remembered his teeth and the tongue went fearfully out to reconnoiter. Ouch, it hurt. The whole left side of his upper jaw tingled with pain when he touched it. Anyhow it didn't hurt unless he touched it. The liquor was losing its force and Coblenz began to have a sinking feeling as he thought of what he had done to Mrs. Wohl. It had really been a cheap trick, he thought, genuinely distressed, for he liked the honest old woman and regretted the pain he had caused her. Rotten, I'm a louse, he said, feeling miserable. Why had he done it? He was drunk, that was it. He couldn't help himself.

"God," Coblenz said aloud expansively, "what a lousy world it is. I ought to commit suicide." Some day, the way he felt, he would write a great bitter work of literature that would immediately shame the race into wholesale self-slaughter. *Epitaphs and Epitaphs*, he would call it.

Chapter I: Life's a Bowl of Cherries—All Rotten.
Chapter II: Ninety-nine Out of a Hundred People Are Lice, The Hundredth, The Fattest Louse of All Because He Gets Away With It.
Chapter III: Go Fight City Hall.
Chapter IV: Fellow Passengers—To The Grave.
Chapter V: Any Guy Who Works For a Living Is a Nut.
Chapter VI: Heroism Stinks Out Loud.
Chapter VII: Latabelle, I Love You. If There Was a Horse Actually Called Latabelle, I'd Bet My Last Nickel on You.

The races! Coblenz had forgotten all about the races! The boys at the cigar store would be wondering what had happened to him, McCarthy would rub it in for a week if he didn't show up. And Louis XI had a strong tip for him in the third race! Coblenz rummaged feverishly in the wreckage for the *Morning Telegraph*, which he faithfully bought every night. The pages were screwed up and thrown all over the room but Coblenz managed to retrieve Hermis's Selections and the Empire City Charts. Post Time: 2:30, All Times New York City Time. What time was it? He searched through the pockets of his pants in the closet for his watch. Nearly four! They were running the fourth race. It was too late. The day was ruined for Coblenz. How had it ever reached four so soon? He had just gotten out of bed!

Then the whole day's events came back to him. Coblenz remembered waking with his bad hunch and his trip to Yusselefsky's for the whiskey. He remembered Balkan's visit and something about Blenholt with a pearl peddler mixed up with it. Who was Blenholt? The Commissioner of Sewers, he remembered. He had promised to go with Balkan to the funeral to pay his respects. He had thought it would be such a hot joke to do homage to a politician, a gangster and a racketeer. Too late for that too. Then visions appeared of Munves stuttering love nothings to Rita. It all came back to him in patches, experience screened into memory like the gauzed close-ups of movie actresses beyond their best years. Coblenz grew worried as he thought of the day's passage. Was he really going bugs? The last months of dissipation and racetrack betting returned to gnaw at his conscience. This kind of life was wrong for him—goyish—boozing, betting on horses, hanging around with driftwood like Louis XI, McCarthy, and the taxi drivers at the cigar store. Coblenz had long understood that he was a man who lived with careless disregard for his own welfare, but it had never entered into his calculations that he might go insane. He hastily formed plans in his mind for a more wholesome life. This was really getting to be bad.

He hadn't eaten all day. Sobered, Coblenz rose to wash and get dressed for a meal, but as he left the chair he nearly tripped and discovered that his shoelaces were undone. He knelt to fix them. A knot. He paused to call upon God for patience and help. With well-chewed fingernails he labored to undo the knot until the skin was rasped and bled at the cuticles. In that cramped position sweat covered him, his neck itched and his stomach felt slightly nauseous. "God damn!" he cried and yanked. The knot, grinning triumphantly, was only pulled tighter. In a frenzy Coblenz sawed and tugged at the laces for two minutes. Then he stopped, stood erect and wiped away the sweat. He tried desperately to be calm. Take it easy, he told himself, these goddam shoelaces aren't going to make a monkey out of me. He sat down again with patience that was each moment on the point of bursting. Slowly, methodically, he tried to undo the knot, studying carefully as he went along. It was war between Coblenz and the shoelaces. A nail caught in the knot. He pulled. The nail nearly came off and he wiggled his hand with pain. The knot grinned.

"All right, you louse," Coblenz said. "You win but you can't put anything over on me."

He hated those shoelaces. And after hunting about for the bread knife he cut them violently, panting with effort. "Now!" he taunted. "Well? How do you like that?"

The laces, cut, dirty, still retaining the shapes they had had when in the shoe, wept up at him.

"Hah-hah!" cried Coblenz, turning slowly to the ceiling, insanity brightening his eyes. "You're back! I had forgotten all about you, my love."

It was the roller skates without the ball bearings. The kids upstairs had caught their second wind and the metallic swishes came down to his ears like rain falling. He walked around the room, telling himself to be calm, to be calm, to be calm. All at once he discovered that his teeth were hurting him again. Too much, he cried, and hoped for a minute that he was imagining it. Coblenz strode from the door to the window and back again, pain and exasperation clouding his face. He looked at the ceiling and began sucking air through his teeth. The roller skates pounded and scraped. Coblenz gargled a glass of cold water over his teeth in spite of his better judgment. The teeth hurt now in earnest and upstairs the kids were whooping it up as they hit their stride. And the balloon burst with an explosion.

"Katy in her petticoat,
Katy in her draws.
Katy in her shimmy shirt,
Shame, shame, shame."

Coblenz bawled the song out at the top of his lungs. He reached for the bottle, which still contained whiskey, and swallowed.

Farewell, all thought of reform. In ten minutes it was the old Coblenz, his hair all mussed, the wildness in his eye. The silly song of Katy's immodesty, following the custom of songs like it at these occasions, went on repeating and repeating itself in his brain, keeping up with the throbbing in his teeth. He tried to lose the tune but it was hopeless. "My country, 'tis of thee," he shouted in despair but the national anthem was sung in the notes of "Katy in her petticoat."

"Whoa, Coblenz," he said. "Whoa." He contemplated the broom but found in his heart only derision for it. What good had it ever done him? The lady upstairs didn't mind brooms or else the skating drowned out the thumps. He sat down, his chin on his fist, and pondered. At last he rose, sought for a pin, announced to the empty room, "Trip to Oshkosh, or The Perilous Cave," and, except for the look in his eyes, he crept to the door with complete control over himself.

He opened it the length of a slit and peered out. A lady was walking down the steps, using the privacy of the hall to straighten her underwear where it caught between her buttocks. Coblenz waited for her to pass. Then he slunk out, like Bela Lugosi trailing Boris Karloff. He flattened himself against the wall and stole to the edge. Was the coast clear? He tiptoed up the staircase. Secret underground waterways of inestimable danger, burning deserts, pits of quicksand, the wild beasts of the jungle where the law was animal eat animal—all these waited for Coblenz and he moved warily to avoid them. On the third-floor landing a boy opened the door suddenly and went dashing down, but quick-wittedly Coblenz turned about, pretended he was a visitor, and, until the boy was well out of sight, absorbed himself by reading the sign on the dumbwaiter door:

GARBAGE COLLECTED
AT SIX O'CLOCK
Have a Heart and Get the Pails Ready
The Janitor Is a Human Being Too

The boy was gone, the hallway empty. So close to the flat, the skates screeched deafeningly. Coblenz approached the door, holding his breath, throwing all on one cast of the wheel. If luck would have it that someone open the door now, all would be lost and he would be handed over to the firing squad.

Coblenz held the pin in readiness, pressed the bell button, and wedged the pin in tightly to keep the bell ringing. That would fix them. As soon as the pin was secured, he scurried to the turn in the staircase, hugging the wall to be out of sight.

"Come in," called the lady in the flat.

No answer and Coblenz at the wall hunched his shoulders to his ears in order to suppress his delight.

"Come in," she called, her voice a shade higher and more indignant.

"Come in! Come in!" she screamed in anger. "What are you ringing the bell for? COME IN!"

Coblenz thought he would bust.

The lady swung the door open, fire in her eye for the visitor whoever he might be. There was no one. The bell went on ringing. What was it?

"Sammy, Sammy," she said to one of the boys, "take off the skates. Go downstairs and tell Mrs. Strudel the bell is busted, she should fix it."

"Aw," said Sammy, "why do you pick on me all the time? I'm always the goat."

The bell kept on ringing beautifully. Coblenz, squeezed against the wall, shook from his mussed-up head to his toes as he howled with noiseless laughter. "Why do I have to go?" Sammy still was protesting. "You always tell me. What's the matter with Itchy?" But he went to Mrs. Strudel, the janitor. The bell rang and rang.

"Who is it please?"

"Me. Balkan. The greatest Yiddish tragedian."

This was on the fourth floor, the establishment of the Balkans.

The old man moved in wearily, slipping off the straps of the sandwich boards (Madame Clara, Treatments By Experts), taking care not to smudge his red nose. The room was empty. Mr. Balkan sat down dispiritedly on the couch to rest his feet and dragged out the *Tag* from a pocket of the checkered suit. He rested his chin on the enormous collar (the nose again!) hoping for peace.

"When I was in Melbourne . . ." Mrs. Balkan said, coming in from the kitchen. She meant it in all kindness. It was her way of kidding with her husband.

Mr. Balkan rose and went off into another living statue, this time frozen in the appearance of one who was hunched up, his face twisted, everything to indicate mirthless, mock laughter in reaction to his wife's joke.

"Look at him," Mrs. Balkan gurgled with laughter, shaking all over. "Mister . . ."

"Fumfotch," he said, taking the word out of her mouth. "Again and again the same witticism. Over and over the same."

"If only Madame Clara should find you here instead of walking around in the streets on the corners!" she said.

Mr. Balkan's working hours were from eleven to seven, but he slyly dropped in for a half hour's rest, tossing an equivalent number of the advertisement cards down the sewer when nobody was looking. All day long he had to walk along Broadway and Roebling Street, seeking the crowds, and no matter how thickly he had the cobbler sole his shoes, the heat came through and burned his feet. Pavements he hated, claiming they were the inventions of the devil, the worst features of a mechanical civilization. Max Balkan felt the pangs of filial duty whenever he heard his father speak slowly, on Sundays, of the cool grassy earth of his native home in Lumsa Gubernia.

"What good do I do on the streets anyhow?" he asked guiltily, for he had been bred for scrupulous honesty. "Everybody goes in the movies or runs away to Cnu Island. All that happens, the children follow me. Baldy haircuts in the barbershops, no customers. And my feet, it hurts like a furnace."

"For blocks and blocks the children follow you," Mrs. Balkan cried in high good humor. She had once caught him in the streets and watched his performance. This was not required by Madame Clara but he gave it gratefully, happy to feel that he was somehow at his true profession even in this work. Mr. Balkan in his clown's get-up would freeze in the most comical postures for the children, would move his limbs in slow motion, jump straight at attention and click his heels, uttering odd noises. He had one special trick, a favorite with the kids who grew to know him well and look for his visits. Mr. Balkan would saw his arms up and down, starting with what seemed to be painful slowness. He would work gradually faster, all the time to the synchronized accompaniment of "Boom-choo-choo," until at the very end when he was going like a windmill in a gale. Then he would suddenly cry: "Boom-choo-choo, DOO!" And after this he straightened and bowed, counting the children's screams for applause.

"Sh, sh," he now said, smiling ruefully as his wife mentioned those performances.

"You give them a good time, hah?" she asked, clapping her hands and dancing in imitation of the children who followed him. "They have so much fun, eh, Mr. Fumfotch?"

"Believe me," he confessed wryly. "I don't feel it. I got it in my mind like to go dancing in a ballroom. My heart, you know, not in it. Played out. But the tricks, the tricks . . . I have the tricks. Yes, I still give the performance but there is no fire."

Mrs. Balkan adjusted the sandwich boards over herself, laughing hilariously with the fun. Madame Clara's virtues were spread out like a tent, for the straps were not intended for a stout frame. Mrs. Balkan moved around the room awkwardly, tripping over the boards. Before her husband she assumed one of his frozen comical postures and held it for some seconds. Then she had to break, she could not hold herself in, the great gusts of laughter made the boards bounce on her chest.

"Crazy!" she sobbed through her tears. "Did you ever see such a thing?"

"Bravo. Bravo," called Mr. Balkan gaily. "A perfect impersonation. Marvelous. You know something, Crenyella, I could have made a first-rate *comédienne* out of you. A wonderful actress. No, really, really, you have a flair."

"Shah!" she roared. "What are you talking about? Me?"

"Thirty years ago I should have done it. Too late. I should have taught you everything and then what a *comédienne* you would have been."

"Under the spreading chestnut tree," she recited, halting with the pain her laughter caused her, "the village smithy stands." She larruped with glee. "A wonderful actress? Me? People should pay money to see me on the stage! Madame Jeritza!"

"Thirty years ago I should have done it," he repeated sadly. "Old. Everything gets old and then there's no time left."

"Thirty years ago," Mrs. Balkan sighed softly. She sat on the chair with her toes gripping the legs, like a little girl, thinking of the years. She remembered the days at home in the old country and the pictures returned of apple blossoms and wide meadows of wild flowers, of horses racing without harness in the fields after the work was done, of the quiet nights when frost covered the winter while she sat gazing through iced windows wondering. Those old days returned to her, after thirty years of tenements and hard work in America, finely etched in sun and shade, vague because of time and memory, and also unreal, pervaded with gently spring sunshine, like dreams or images reflected on a bright day in a big water bubble. A little too rosy for truth, but Mrs. Balkan sitting on the chair longed for the old days, to be young again, to have one's life stretched before one like a country road.

Her eyes grew vacant with reflection and she remembered her husband when he was a wild boy in Lumsa Gubernia, skittish as a colt, strangely tempered and unpredictable. He ran away to America soon and at fourteen she followed him, alone, with an identification tag around her throat, traveling in the crude German boat that rocked sickeningly for sixteen days before it reached Ellis Island. At Hamburg, changing from the train, some German louts had frightened her dreadfully with their teasing and ever since the thought of boat trips came with a sense of terror. In all her time in America she had never set foot on a ferryboat.

Table, chair, horse, pot, mister, missus, dog, snot. The first years in America, a bewildering world, but with her great fund of cheerfulness she overlooked the slums of the East Side and went dancing in the halls, determined to be an Americaner, and singing songs to remember the new language more easily. Mr. Balkan had soon sought her out, a straight young man at twenty, with a little mustache and a black tie, full of enthusiasm and joy. He was an artist, loitered at all the Yiddish theaters on the Bowery and Second Avenue, and with passes he received from friends in the profession they sat in the orchestra, seeing Jennie Goldstein, the Tomashefskys, and the Adlers in terrible melodramas, in backside slapping operettas and comedies, and in the great tragedies.

Then the years when he went traveling with Yudensky's Troupe. All over the world they went, as he said, to Europe, Australia, South America, sometimes gone two and three years at a clip. Mrs. Balkan was left behind, to take care of Max and Ruchel and the grocery store, for times were always bad; everywhere they went the people had no money and Yudensky wailed that he could barely manage to feed the actors and carry them from place to place. Mr. Balkan sent little money home. The days then were long and hard, full of work with the children and all day at the counter. The milk in the cans turned sour on the hot days when the ice ran short, the herring barrels, with sales low, were held too long, the shelves overran untidily and the rats began to come up boldly from the cellars.

But time passed. The life flew. First she was singing to her children:

> "My mudder says
> I should not
> Go with the gypsies,
> If I should
> She would say
> Naughty girl, you ran away."

But in no time, when Ruchel reached the eighth grade with Mrs. Cassidy, Mrs. Balkan would recite with her the speeches required for memorization from *Julius Caesar*. "Friends, Romans, Countrymen, I come to *bury* Caesar, *not* to praise him," she declaimed in exaggerated accents, remembering Max as he gave the lines when he walked around the house preparing for Mrs. Cassidy, and she imitated the gestures and emphasis, putting them sing-song at the proper places.

The days passed. Mr. Balkan came home, played a few years on the Bowery, found no work, and idled about the house with a part turning up occasionally. And the money she had saved from the grocery store dwindled and dwindled, the cashier recognized her when she stepped into the bank for another withdrawal. Max grew up, crazy with funny ideas, now with Blenholt and funerals, and he wasn't even normal enough to get a job. Ruchel became Rita and a worry on her head in her old age. Mrs. Balkan sighed, awakening. What use these thoughts? Where did they get her?

"Vos taig der leiben," she sang with sad merriment, "der kotch-kas mit treynen? Ich hub nit kein mann, a cluck iz stu mir."

A silly song about life and geese and tears and sorrow. Mr. Balkan had been reading the paper but the tune made him lower it and he smiled, for it was his song, composed years, years ago when he was almost a boy.

"Oi, vay, oi, vay," he said, feeling his back. "Thirty years ago, thirty years ago."

"Thirty years ago. Ah, Label, thirty years ago what a crazy boy you was."

"Maybe I was crazy," he mused gently, "but such life, such fire. I'll never see it again. Everything was like a flame and the days were butter frying in a pan."

"Crazy, crazy," Mrs. Balkan chuckled, her reveries still on her mind like a haze. "You were such a crazy boy, Label."

"Do you remember, Crenyella," he said, his eyes brightening, "do you remember the spring it was in Lumsa Gubernia? How the apple blossoms were on every tree like a fine framed picture and the air gave such a pleasure to breathe? So sweet, so beautiful. On the hills, in the fields, we lay and watched the brook and the apple blossoms fell down like it was a shower, and in the sky the clouds looked like it was God's white beard himself."

Mrs. Balkan looked at the big red nose and the powdered face, the roomy checkered suit and the big shoes, and laughed because at her age, with perspiration drying in lines of dirt on her throat, with her loose wrapper over her neglected body, tenderness and sentiment made her feel self-conscious.

"What are you talking about, Label?" she asked. "What are you saying?"

"In the fields you were so small, Crenyella," he went on slowly, "and I was like a flame even though I was crazy maybe. Oi, vay, Crenyella, to be old and a fool, to be a Mr. Fumfotch for Madame Clara, but those times, those times . . ."

"I remember, Label. Like it was yesterday I remember, but what good does it do me? Mr. Fumfotch remembers when he was Rudolph Valentino," she laughed.

"Down the hill. Finished," he muttered, turning away and picking up the *Tag*. She tried to spoil everything and had no feeling for poetry and recollection. "All over, but in the valleys we used to run, in the hills you and me, and from an old broken-down tree stump I was Hamlet. In Yiddish. In a field of flowers, as far as a person could see, flowers like a lake, we ran like it was a moving picture because not only was I young but also a little crazy. Because I was crazy and wild and because in those days you did whatever I told you." He grew warm as he remembered his present condition and the insults. "Because in those days you didn't make fun out of me, you didn't make jokes and laugh all the time. Mr. Fumfotch and Mr. Fumfotch and Mr. Fumfotch, over and over again. When I was in Melbourne," he said mimicking her as she mimicked him, shaking his shoulders, his face drawn with anger.

He took out his handkerchief, held it oddly below his nostrils in order not to rub the red paint off, and blew his nose.

"Please, Mr. Fumfotch," she asked him hilariously. "Are you getting mad at me? Mr. Fumfotch is getting mad at me!"

"Sh," he said. "Leave me alone."

Mrs. Balkan grew mock solemn and contrite. "Mr. Fumfotch is mad at me," she chanted, rising an octave with each repetition. "Mr. Fumfotch is mad at me. Mr. Fumfotch is mad at me! What will I do? What will happen to me now? Mr. Fumfotch is mad at me. He won't talk to me for a week."

She went closely before him as he tried to hide his discomfiture behind the *Tag*, brushed it down and danced laughingly in a wide circle at his feet, clapping her hands and chanting of his wrath for her. But before she could indulge herself for any length of time, the telephone bell rang and fixed her into sobriety. She ran to it and at the same time Rita came rushing through the door. She had been with Munves investigating the hidden past of Sealwudu, but war was war and Freddie might be on the wire again. No one in these times could afford to sneeze at a meat market. "It's for me," she said as she came in. "I'll take it." Mrs. Balkan held the telephone out of reach, trying to keep off her daughter with her shoulder. "All right, darling. It's all right."

"Don't be a pest again, Mother," Rita cried. "Give it to me."

Mrs. Balkan held the phone at an angle of one hundred and sixty degrees, screwed her face into a smile, and said: "Hello."

"Give it to me," Rita thundered. "It's Freddie!"

"Yes?" said Mrs. Balkan, her cheeriness dropping and pushing off Rita brusquely. "Who do you want? Who?—Shah!" she said to Rita. "It ain't Freddie. Now I can live again?—Who? Mr. Balkan?" she asked the telephone, having a difficult time with it. "Which Mr. Balkan do you want? We got two Mr. Balkans. Mr. Max Balkan, he ain't here. Can I take a message? I don't know when to expect him. He can come in a minute and he can come tomorrow, whenever he takes it into his head. How should I know? I'm only his mother . . . All right . . . All right . . . Who? . . . All right, I got the name . . . I'll tell him . . . Good-bye . . . Good-bye . . ." She banged the earpiece on the hook with irritation and turned to Rita. She had her daughter this time. "Every telephone is for you! I can't even hear what a person says on the line, you and your hoorah!"

"Who was it?" Rita asked.

"How should I know? I can't make out a thing with you on my neck all the time."

"Who is it?" Mr. Balkan wanted to know, too. He always had a great curiosity about telephone calls and always insisted upon being told what was happening around the house. Any day now God might be calling up to offer him a fat part in *King Lear*.

"Mr. Fumfotch is here again," she announced, bending at the hips grotesquely and flicking her fingers at him in anger. "He's got to know everything otherwise the Williamsburg Bridge will fall down tomorrow."

"Well, who was it, Mother?" Rita asked impatiently.

"Hot Water! Mr. Hot Water! I don't know what. Don't holler at me!"

"Hot Water?" Rita repeated. Anyhow it wasn't Freddie. She turned to the door, noticed her father and wondered what he was doing there. "You ain't sick or something?" she asked.

"No," the old man said dolorously. "My feet—it hurts. I just sneaked in for a minute, Ruchel."

"Please call me Rita!" she snapped. "Madame Clara should see you now."

"Where are you going, Rita?" her mother asked. "What are you doing all the time?"

"None of your business. I'm going to Munves' room. I'm studying with him."

"What are you studying, Rita?" she asked, warm with hope.

"Sealwudu in Essex!" she answered tartly, resenting the implication. "Now you know?"

"Quiet," the old man said cautiously. "You don't have to holler at your mother."

"That's nice, Rita," Mrs. Balkan said, refusing to be offended. "He's such a nice, fine, refined boy. Educated, but he don't know nothing about girls, Rita. Don't be bashful, darling. Call him 'dear.' Call him 'honey,' like the other girls say. That's how the other girls catch . . ."

"Mother!" Rita cried, grinding her teeth and shaking her head with disgust. "For God's sakes, Mother, have a heart! Are you starting that business all over again? You make me sick and tired!"

She stamped to the door. The older generation was terrible when it came to girls and getting married. They had no romance, they were from the old country where a person went to a matchmaker in a dirty wig and ordered one husband, fat and juicy. All her mother thought about was getting her married off.

"It's not like the old days, Mother," she rebuked her. "We can't just go out and drag somebody off the streets to marry us. It's a new age. We girls don't marry unless we're in love. Can't you get that through your head?"

"Love, schmove," said Mrs. Balkan. "What's the matter with you? Who's asking you to drag somebody from the streets and marry him? All I'm saying is you shouldn't be so bashful. You can say 'dear' and 'darling' once in a while. It don't hurt to be nice. Does it cost you something?"

"Oh, leave me alone, for God's sakes, let me have a little peace!" Rita yelled.

"Love, schmove," Mrs. Balkan muttered bitterly. "Like Bing Crosby sings in the movies, love in bloom, is it the spring, oh, no, it isn't the spring! What is love?"

"Bing Crosby," said Mr. Balkan with professional jealousy. "A humbug. I wouldn't give two cents for Bing Crosby."

"See," said Rita, "that's the trouble with you old folks. You just don't know what love is or what romance means. Take Bing Crosby, you brought up the subject yourself. You know what he makes? Ten thousand dollars a week!"

"Fine!" Mrs. Balkan cried. "Bing Crosby, maybe you'll marry Bing Crosby!"

"For God's sakes, Mother," Rita exclaimed, "don't you stop at nothing?"

"Ten thousand dollars a week!" said Mr. Balkan, consumed with the injustice of the world. "America. A crazy country with the movies. Nu, Columbus, nu?"

"What are you burching about Columbus for?" his wife asked, turning on him savagely. "Mr. Fumfotch! Hold your mouth!"

"Gee whiz, Mother," Rita said. "What are you bawling him out for? What did he do?"

"All right. Stick up for him, do what he says, shah, shtill, everything happens by magic while you sleep! Stick up for him and stay an old maid all your life. A girl don't keep her looks forever. Pretty soon the years roll by and then you'll be thirty years old and then what? A woman falls apart if she don't get married and then no man wants her. Wait, Ruchel, wait, and then you'll see what I'm talking about."

"Don't call me Ruchel!" Rita shouted at the top of her voice. She was getting fat already! She had to go begging on her knees to get someone to marry her! What a mother. "I hate you!" Rita said venomously. "You make me sick and tired! Sometimes you make me feel so disgusted I could take gas!"

And she banged out, back to Munves and Sealwudu.

Mrs. Balkan was in tears. "Such a mean temper she has," she wept. "I never saw a girl so rotten like her."

"Shah, shah," said Mr. Balkan soothingly. "She don't mean nothing. She's only a girl."

"A girl?" Mrs. Balkan sniffled. "Twenty-five already and she ain't getting younger with the years. Other people, I don't know, they got luck. All their daughters get married. I got one girl only and it's like moving a house. Other people don't have no trouble, but me, I got to have a prima donna, a daughter like Rita, Clark Cable ain't good enough for her."

"Leave her alone," he said. "You're on her head every minute. Everything will be all right. She'll get married, she'll have a nice husband. Shah. Just a little time."

"Everything you should leave alone," said Mrs. Balkan, forgetting her tears. "Quiet, shah, don't touch. Like magic everything will happen. Mr. Fumfotch."

"All right, Mr. Fumfotch, the old story over and over again." He was resigned and rustled the *Tag*.

"A father," she said reproachfully. "If you wasn't such a schlemiel, you could do something. Other fathers . . ."

"What can I do?" he asked desperately. "Can I marry her myself?"

"What can he do? If you was a decent father to her, by this time you'd have some money in the bank. A girl can't find a fellow these days without something in the bank to help a young couple make a start unless maybe she's a schoolteacher with a permanent job. You find a nice boy, you put him in business."

"Money in the bank," Mr. Balkan repeated. "How much money does a girl need? Eight hundred dollars ain't enough?"

"Eight hundred dollars! What eight hundred dollars? Five years ago when I sold the grocery store, I put eight hundred dollars in the bank and the old iverbuttle still thinks it's there yet! We live on air, for five years we live on air. You bring fat paychecks every Saturday. Fool!"

"Shah, shah," he muttered and tried to read the *Bintel Brief* all over again.

"Look who I'm talking to. What's the use of talking? You were a schlemiel from the first day I saw you, you're a bigger schlemiel every day and you'll always be a schlemiel."

"Thank you, please."

"Just like Max," she said, rocking with her troubles. "Like the father the son and like the son the father. A fine pair!"

"Good, good, fine. Enough already."

"A brother," she went on. "Where is he now? Instead of bringing young gentlemen friends into the house for Rita to meet and get acquainted, he has to go to funerals. A Mr. Blenholt he's got on his mind and his own sister bothers him like last year's snow. Tomorrow he will make a million dollars from Rockefeller with sauerkraut. And Rita, Rita plays with a schlemiel like Munves. Oh, God," she suddenly screamed, talking to God, "what did I do I should deserve a daughter like Rita and a son like Max and on top of everything a Mr. Fumfotch like him?"

There was no answer and Mr. Balkan read his paper peacefully for a minute.

"What's the matter," he asked timidly, "with Munves? Everybody by you has to be a schlemiel?"

"A boy," she said, "a man, twenty-nine years old, all day he goes around with his nose in a book like a schoolchild. When will he finish studying? Can he make a living? Can he support a family?"

"So you help a couple in the beginning!" he exclaimed. "Like you said. You buy them a stationery store, a candy stand, and little by little they can work themselves up!"

"Fool!" she shouted at him. "Dope! Iverbuttle! Don't you know no more what goes around you? I talk to him and it's like talking to a wall. With what will we put a couple in business? With what will we buy a stationery store? A stationery store he's got it figured already! The eight hundred dollars ain't in the bank no more! We ate it up day after day!"

Oo, oo, he forgot. Mr. Balkan read the paper diligently. "All right," he muttered. "All right. Quiet."

"Quiet!" she screamed. "Please tell me one thing, Mr. Fumfotch. Why do I talk to you? Why do I argue with you? You got some sense in your head? You know what's going on?"

"Ps, ps," said Mr. Balkan through the crack between his two upper teeth and waited for the tempest to blow over. But Mrs. Balkan had much on her mind or perhaps it was the reaction to the sentimental talk she had had with him when he first entered the room, and to her memories of apple blossoms and the fields of wild flowers. Rita was a sore on her head and Max was a boil. Her children took the life from her, taking pieces of flesh every day. And what did he do to help her? All her life she had been the one to worry and work while he ran all over the world with actresses and dancers. And now he sat, reading the *Tag*, waiting for the Messiah to ride up to him on a white horse, tap him on the head and say: "Mr. Balkan, here's a million dollars, please. Sign here." She went on and on, unburdening her heart and giving him a large-sized piece of her mind. But Mr. Balkan would have been the last to object to this. The years of abuse and practice had trained him perfectly for these occasions. He sat and read the Questions and Answers column, impervious, unheeding and barely conscious that his wife was ranting before him like a cataract. Suddenly he thought of his son. He had gone somewhere, a funeral, a Mr. Blenholt, and the old man, who had to know everything that was happening in America, wondered where Max was.

"Crenyella," he interrupted her in her fury, "Crenyella, where's Max? Where did he go?"

He was hopeless and Mrs. Balkan caught herself like a horse rearing. What was the sense in yelling at him? She was only eating her heart out. "Go write a letter to Dr. Holstein in the *Bintel Brief* and you'll find out," she replied, and went into the kitchen.

Rita stamped out of the room leaving her mother in tears and she banged the door to show that she had had the last word. In the hallway she straightened her blue jersey over her hips, felt to see if her curls were all right and arranged the expression on her face. She walked in without knocking. Munves did not notice her. All she could see of him at the moment was his disheveled hair, the spectacles, and the nose on those occasions when the etymologist wiped it with the back of his hand. He was completely absorbed, the scholar at work, and his fingers flew over the books and pages.

"It was a telephone for Max," she said. "I was expecting a call . . ."

"What?" he asked, gazing at her blankly. "Were you out of the room?"

A lie, from beginning to end. Munves was trying his hardest to make an impression on her. He really wasn't so absorbed, the fingers didn't have to fly, and he had realized that she had left the room. While she was gone, indeed, Munves had waited for her impatiently, for her presence had been having a startling effect on him. As he worked, he knew she was there watching him and it was a warming feeling causing his scalp to shiver deliciously. He was hard at work, important work, the nations would be trembling soon, and there was Rita watching him. He wondered how he must look to her, bending devotedly over his table, his face rapt. She must be very fond of him indeed.

"Could you hand me that book, please?" he said, to show that neither rain nor storm, sleet nor hail could hinder him from his appointed task. "Bosworth's *Anglo-Saxon Dictionary*."

"Of course," she protested and fetched the book in a gallop, playing the same game with him.

"I'll look it up here as a further check," he commented. "I've hunted up almost every reference and checked about every lead, and nowhere is there the slightest indication that Sealwudu belongs in Essex. But," he said wisely, leaning back on his chair so that it rested on two legs, "research is valueless unless every possible item is accounted for."

Rita nodded in agreement, speechless.

"Do you know what this means, Rita? Really, this is a discovery of supreme importance. For years scholars have placed Sealwudu—that is, Selwood, to use its modern name—in Essex. This glossary, which contains what I believe to be the error, is a standard work on the *Anglo-Saxon Chronicle*. Prepared by Kennedy under Krapp. Did you ever hear of Krapp, Rita? Perhaps the greatest figure in the field in America today."

He took a moment to let that sink in. Munves, the man of importance, the man of action. Nations trembled when he frowned. Emperors ran to do him honor. The flower of the world's women offered him their charms.

"Well," said Munves, as though only yesterday he had been talking to Charles M. Schwab, "that's what Frank Vizetelly told me when he spoke to me some time ago. You know Vizetelly? *Literary Digest*? The way to break into any field, he told me, is to find the biggest man in it and to show him up."

Munves began a sigh but at that moment he lost his balance on the chair, which rested on only two legs. For ten seconds he groped in the air madly, tried to grip the underside of the table with his knees, opened his mouth to gasp with the fear of crashing to the floor. But Rita was quick and straightened him out. The chair banged on all four legs again.

"I'm wasting time," he muttered and opened Bosworth.

"What do you want me to do now?" Rita asked.

"Nothing. Get the gazetteer if you wish." Busy, busy, leave him alone, mind requires quiet.

Rita brought the gazetteer from the dresser. Maps, crazy maps. In a minute she exhausted the pleasures of its pages and went to look through the window into the yard. By twisting her neck a little she was able to peer into her own flat for the rooms had windows facing the same direction. There was her mother taking it out on Pop just as though it was a silent moving picture. She was terrible. Rita's face grew intense with anger. She thought of her mother's constant nagging, and Munves, stealing time from his work over the Bosworth and spying at her out of the corner of his eyes as his scalp shivered, marveled at the preoccupation in her expression. What a strange girl!

The inscription on the fence was now intriguing her curiosity and she worked out its meaning with effort. HESHEY IS A BIGE STINKER HE PLAYS WID GOLDIE DOKTER HESHEY STINKES WID A CRASHE, she finally deciphered the clumsy handwriting. A boy was playing at the cellar door, Chink. A bag of garbage lay burst in the middle of the yard. Three cats slept in the sun like balls of wool for crocheting. "When I grow too old to dream," she sang in an operatic soprano, enriching the quality of her voice by choking the muscles at her throat, "then I'll remember you." Max hated it when she sang that way. It made him furious. He couldn't stand it. "Sing in your natural voice. Please! I can die when you fake your voice like that!" he always shouted to her. But Rita seriously thought her voice had possibilities and disregarded him. Some day she was going to try for an audition with Major Bowes on the Amateur Hour. She once knew a girl whose cousin won the *Daily Mirror* Bathing Beauty Contest and was sent to Hollywood. All things were possible. Rita imagined herself singing over the radio for Major Bowes, a clamorous success, offers from Metro-Goldwyn-Mayer and Paramount, and finally she saw a grand close-up of herself, leaning over a bower of posies like Grace Moore, and singing: "Love, your magic spell is everywhere."

"Look," cried Munves, holding up the middle finger of his right hand. "A callus!"

"A callus!" exclaimed Rita. "Let me see."

A hard bump had developed on his writing finger from years of grasping the pencil. Munves, studying intently, had noticed it now for the first time and inspected his finger with secret pride. What a student! Rita took his hand and felt the callus gently.

"Oooh," she said with respectful wonder. "My! My!"

"Oh, it's nothing. It's nothing," Munves said, shuffling the pages with his free hand in pleased embarrassment.

"Does it hurt when you write?"

"Hurt!" he cried. "Of course not!"

The finger felt warm in her hand. What a nice, nice girl. Munves, so near to her, could smell the faint perfume of her body and it lulled his mind. Some strands of her hair brushed his face, the touch causing him to flinch inwardly. Had he ever taken the time really to see a girl? Munves slyly looked at her. Rita's mouth was opened charmingly as she worried over his callus. Surveying her, Munves felt strange and different. He followed the lines of her tight jersey. Soft, soft, and the curves. Her bosom. Mist filled his head. The presence of a girl was for once in his life exciting him into dreamy rapture. Where had he been all these years? he asked himself. The war was over. As he had said downstairs, in Coblenz's room, his life was too confined and he had to see what he could do to vary it. The vistas of girls opened to him, a new fascination, and he thought madly of *Mlle. de Maupin*, *The Red Lily*, Greta Garbo in *The Green Hat*, Valse Bleu and Argentine tangos. He didn't even know how to dance!

"Do you know, Rita," he said in a low voice, "you smell like a calf."

"A what?" Rita asked puzzled, but she decided to be flattered. The truth was that once Munves as a boy had played with a calf for a pet when he spent some time with his sister in Rochester. The flesh at the calf's neck ran in soft ripples and he used to enjoy feeling it, kneading it with his fingers. The calf, or so it seemed to him since, had had a sweet, milky smell and now he was certain the same smell came from Rita's body. Munves, in a haze, daringly imagined her body in the bathtub, under warm water, white and juicy, with gentle curves. The next thing Munves was in the bathtub himself, alongside her in the warm water. He embraced her, relishing the feel of her body on his. In his daydream Munves was kissing her and holding her, the core of his being seeking hers, his eyes closed, embracing, embracing, while the water remained marvelously warm and enervating. Oh, how lovely is the evening, is the evening, when the evening bells are ringing, bells are ringing . . .

Shame on you, Mendel Munves! he thought sternly, waking up, but he longed, he longed to hold the delectable mysteries of her body in his arms. And against his moral judgment he looked up at her and said:

"You know something? I can't dance."

"Really?" asked Rita. "That's surprising. I should think you'd have a good sense of rhythm."

"Do you dance much?"

"I should say so."

"Oh," said Munves, "I bet it's nice to know how to dance. You can't do much socially unless you dance these days."

"Would you want me to teach you?"

"Who? Me?" Munves exclaimed, in amazement. "Me? Me, dance?"

"Come on," she said. "Don't be silly. I bet I could teach you in a minute."

"Go on. I wouldn't think of it for a minute."

She held her arms out to him and smiled. "Don't be such a baby," she said, but he shook his head and wiggled like a child in a high-chair refusing spoonfuls of farina.

"Come on," Rita said coaxingly, picking him up by the elbows. He rose to his feet, sobered.

"All right," he said seriously, "but only for a minute."

Rita outlined a square on the floor. "We'll try a waltz first," she said. There were four points and the idea was to touch those points, using variations of foot movements to the corners.

"Look," she said. "I'll do it first by myself." Munves' eyes, heavy with mist, watched her ponderously. All you had to do was move your legs to the corners. It was really simple, the way Rita analyzed the essentials of dancing. It was easy, he could do it. He'd surprise Rita by being a rapid pupil. "All right," she said. "Now you hold me and I'll follow you wherever you lead. Don't you worry about me. Just make believe you're dancing by yourself and I'll follow." She held her arms open and walked into Munves' embrace. He stood paralyzed.

"Go on," she said. "Go on," and she hummed a Russian waltz for the time.

With a gigantic effort Munves pushed his feet forward. It was as though he were wearing deep-sea diving shoes, as though Rita were standing on his toes and he had to carry her as he moved. He groped for the corners, stiff-kneed, his head held back until there was a pain in his neck, shuffling on the soles of his feet. "One, two, three," instructed Rita. "Step, close, step. Da dam, da da dam, da da dam, da da dam . . ." Her voice wavered tremulously as she hummed in the high pitch and Munves thought that the essence of femininity was reached in her tones.

"I'll get it," he said solemnly. "I'll get it."

"Hold me tighter," she said. "I won't bite you, step, close, step."

"I'm close enough," he protested. He couldn't, he just couldn't.

"You're a mile away."

All right, then. Munves pressed her tightly to him and shivered. Ooooh, it felt good. Soft, soft. Women were originally built like a jackknife, like a Westchester roll, all one short round lump, he was thinking, and when God opened them up straight, the body protruded in round curved masses. He hugged her tighter and tighter, his skinny arm on her shoulders aching. His thigh felt her thigh, his chest pressed into her bosom, the sensation of her flesh on him occupied his mind completely.

"Step, close, step," sang Rita languorously. "Da da dam, da da dam . . ."

"I think I'm getting it," Munves said, stalking her around the square, his head held high, the feeling overpowering him. Her curls caught in his mouth and for some time he chewed on them unawares. His head was foggy and it seemed to him that he was floundering. The calf smell intoxicated him. All of a sudden Munves began to feel so strange he thought he was sick. His mind took him into the bathtub again and the waves of warm water washed over him. The jersey. He wanted to get his hand under her jersey and feel her breast with his hand instead of his chest. As he moved choppily from corner to corner of the imaginary square, his thoughts revolved endlessly on the unutterable necessity of slipping his hand through her jersey.

This had to stop at once, Munves said indignantly to himself. Indecent.

"We'll take a rest," he said, stopping. His whole body was swimming in sweat. "This gives you a regular workout."

"You dance divinely for a beginner," she said. "Is this really the first time you've ever danced?"

"Oh, of course it is!" he protested, happy but still feeling unsteady and extraordinary. "Don't you believe me?"

"Well, all I can say is you certainly have a sense of rhythm."

"Rita . . ." Munves said impulsively. "I . . . you . . ."

"What . . . Mendel?"

"Don't you think there's something wonderful in the companionship between a man and a woman? What I mean," he said, struggling, "is that I believe that women have certain qualities of character that complement those of a man and make for a beautiful union. Loneliness can be a truly terrible thing, for the beauty of life exposes itself in such a way that one person by himself can't savor it. Have you, too, ever felt that way?"

"Of course," Rita sighed. "Only, of course, I could never express myself so excellently."

"There is a quotation from Browning," he went on, soft and persuasive. "From 'Fra Lippo Lippi':

> "For, don't you mark? we're made so that we love
> First when we see them painted, things we
> have passed
> Perhaps a hundred times nor cared to see.

"And that is the essence of beauty, Rita, to have someone paint for you the things we have passed a hundred times so that we can first love them. To have someone with whom to share delights and ecstasies. I have been so much alone with my books and my work . . ."

"Mendel . . ." Rita said, barely touching his shoulder.

"Once I saw love," he said. "I was walking alone on Riverside Drive. The day was hot. Looking up at some skyscraper apartment building I saw a young couple on one of the terraces. They were gay and laughing. The wind blew her scarf. I saw them kiss high above, and down on the sidewalk I felt alone, unwanted, unloved . . ."

Munves passed a hand over his forehead, conscious in spite of his pain of the prettiness of the speech. He looked distantly into the yard. HESHEY ISA BIGE...

"Rita," he said, "could I ask you something . . . a bit bold, a little rash . . ."

"Mendel . . ."

"Will you . . . be my companion, my friend, my painter of things I pass a hundred times and do not see?"

"Of course, Mendel!" she said. "What a question!" But she was perplexed. Was he kidding her? Had Munves actually been making love to her all this time? What a line he carried, enough to knock a girl off her feet. Poetry he quoted at you, and they said he didn't know enough to wipe his nose! And what was this business of being a companion and a painter?

"Companionship," Rita said slowly, "is a wonderful thing. You don't have to tell me. I know, believe me. Companionship is why people get married and I think that it is the cornerstone of every successful marriage. Don't you?"

Yes, Munves did, he did, he did. But, marriage! Was she hinting? Mendel Munves getting married! For one thing, what would his sister Yetta in Rochester say? If he got married, the seven dollars her husband sent him every week would stop immediately. Yetta's husband wasn't supporting any strange girl in the bargain. Marriage! Munves thought, and as the prospect soaked in with full meaning he grew frightened. In all his life he had never had a thought of marriage with any degree of intimacy, contemplating it in the same fashion as he did death, as something that happened to other people not to him, as something that remained just as distant every day.

"You know," he said, "I enjoyed that lesson very much. Do you feel like giving me another one? I think I can get the hang of it better now."

"All right," Rita said with disappointment an inch thick. He took her into his arms with some ease now and to show further the nonchalance he felt with girls, he crooked his head fashionably as he led her around the square. "Da dam, da da dam, da da dam," sang Rita forlornly.

The door opened and Mrs. Wohl marched in with her mop and dust cloths. Munves and Rita stopped.

"Dancing?" Mrs. Wohl asked, beaming at the sight. "Dance, dance, children. Don't let me stop you."

"Mrs. Wohl," Rita said severely, "you got a door in your house?"

"Sure, I have a door. What a question. Who hasn't a door in America?"

"Do people walk in without knocking in your house too?"

Mrs. Wohl turned and rapped on the door with her mop. "All right," she said pleasantly. "Now I knocked. Mr. Munves, who learned you to dance? You dance nice. It's a pleasure to watch."

Munves stood awkwardly. He had gone to great pains to impress Mrs. Wohl with the grave importance of his scholarly calling, and here, with one swipe of the brush, all his effect was wiped out. She had caught him.

"See," she said, "that's what I like to see, a boy having a good time, dancing with a nice little girl instead of burying his nose in a book. Don't let him study all the time," she told Rita. "It's no good for the head. You study so long, you lose a screw."

"It's all right, Mrs. Wohl. It's all right," Munves said.

The old lady's eyes shone. "Her?" she asked, pointing to Rita, every matchmaking instinct aroused. "Your girl friend? She's going to get married with you?"

Rita could have dropped right through the floor, it was so embarrassing. "Puh-leeze!" she cried.

"Mrs. Wohl!" Munves said sharply.

"Never mind, never mind," Mrs. Wohl said smiling, nodding her head vigorously to show that she could see right through them. "It's all right. Don't be bashful with me. When I was her age

I had my first baby already. Yankele. Born black, without a breath. I thought I lost him for sure, good-bye Charlie. Mrs. Berman, the midwife who delivered me, held him by the feet in the air and smacked his little behind like he was a rug or something. 'Please, Mrs. Berman,' I shouted to her, sick as I was, 'give the little angel a chance, you're killing him." But he lived, thank God, Yankele has a family now. He lives in Bensonhurst and peddles fruit from a wagon for a living. In my time," Mrs. Wohl turned sternly to Rita, "I had seven children, every one in the house, the first three without a doctor, only a midwife. You young women have an easy life nowadays. Nothing, only in the hospital with a dozen doctors."

Rita turning to Munves, burning with embarrassment. "Well," she said, "you can imagine how I feel."

"Mrs. Wohl," said Munves.

"You young women," continued the old lady, "you go to the hospital with doctors and nurses, every improvement you have, and then you stay in bed ten days to two weeks before you'll move a finger in cold water. When I had my children, the next day I was on my knees scrubbing the floors."

"Mrs. Wohl . . ." said Munves.

"All right, all right," she said. "It's no crime for women to take it easy. My time made up for all the women already with plenty left over. They shouldn't be like horses like us. Good, good, let the men work for a change. Get married, make a living, raise a family and stay well."

"Thanks, thanks," said Rita.

For what? Munves wondered, and worried. "Mrs. Wohl," he said, "don't clean up today. Come back tomorrow."

"Why?"

"Because I said. I'm busy. I have a lot of work to do."

"Work," she said with some derision. "Dancing is work. All right. I'll come back tomorrow." And then she remembered poor Coblenz downstairs, sick and unhappy. "Your friend, Mr. Coblenz," she told them gravely, "he's sick. I worry for that poor orphan boy. Some day he'll go crazy."

"I know all about it," said Munves shortly.

"Sick," muttered Rita. "Then every drunken bum is sick."

"Oh, lady!" Mrs. Wohl reprimanded her. "Don't say that! Don't make fun from a sick man or God will give you his sickness and then how will you like it yourself? The poor boy is good and sick. He's got Lottabelle."

"Lottabelle," Rita asked contemptuously, "what's Lottabelle?"

"A terrible sickness. Don't ask." She turned to Munves. "If you was a good friend to him you'd go down every once in a while and see if he wants something."

"Never mind," he answered, remembering his friend and the bread knife. "Come back tomorrow."

"All right, all right," she said and picked up her mop and the rags. "We shouldn't talk of sickness when people are getting ready to be married. Pu, pu," she spat religiously for luck.

Who was getting married? Munves wept. She had it all settled.

"Anyhow," said Mrs. Wohl, closing the door behind her, "mazel tov."

"Well," said Rita, "this was certainly the most embarrassing moment of my life. I could send it to the *Daily News* and get two dollars for it. Honestly, I could have sunk right through the floor. She had us married already."

"Yes, yes," said Munves, feeling up to his ears in marriage and searching for a tactful way of informing Rita of his intentions. "Marriage, now, is a good thing. In fact when I'm in subway trains with nothing to occupy my mind, I often think of my sons with affection."

"What sons?" shrieked Rita.

"My unborn sons," Munves explained patiently, offset by her scream. What was the matter? "As I say, marriage is a good thing and I often wish I were able to afford it. Now, my sister Yetta who sends me money every week from Rochester would certainly get angry with me if I married without managing to get a job first. Sometimes I think the depression is hurting the younger generation the hardest."

"Who," said Rita with a proper show of offense, "is thinking of getting married?"

"I was only speaking in general," Munves said, and he sat down at the table careful to keep his eyes from meeting Rita's. He looked through Bosworth's *Anglo-Saxon Dictionary*. Mendel Munves getting married. And then Mrs. Wohl had to come in with her matchmaking. The most uncomfortable half hour he had had in days.

"Well, we've been wasting time," he said. "To get back to work. I think it's pretty well established by this time that Sealwudu can't be in Essex, but the trick now is to find out where it really belongs. With luck and hard work we may get at this in a few hours."

I'll sit right down here this minute and pray to God for luck, Rita thought. All I need in the world is to know where Sealwudu belongs and when I find out, the Statue of Liberty will get so excited with joy, she'll fall down and drown. Munves gave her a pain. When the thought of marriage came up he acted as though somebody had touched him with a red-hot poker. What was the trouble with marriage? Was it good enough only for niggers? Munves was a baby, he got scared too easily. Well, said Rita for solace, look at Ruth. She's got to run around with Max and he's even crazier, and a fine bargain she'll get in the end.

"Did you ever stop to think," Munves said from the table, "that the most outdated, cumbersome, stupid, illogical paradox of our civilization today is the alphabet? You know what the letters actually are? Pictures! Each letter was once a picture, of a cow or a house or something, drawn according to the way it occurred to some ancient Semite thousands of years ago. And we, a progressive civilization, use for an alphabet this system of time-taking, awkward, ambiguous pictures each of which may have as many as a dozen or more different pronunciations."

"Tsck, tsck," said Rita.

"I've been a member of the National Spelling Reform Society for years and no matter how hard we try to get it through people's heads that the alphabet ought to be, if not discarded altogether, at least simplified, people just refuse to take the time and effort to learn a better system. They're selfish. For the first thirty or forty years, it's true, it would be a little difficult to reeducate themselves, but because of this temporary obstacle the generations of the future will have to go on with an obsolete form of writing."

Just like that, out of a blue sky. Go, talk to him about marriage.

"I know men," Munves said, hoping the impression was of the best, "who have given up their lives for the ideals of the National Spelling Reform Society. They have met with rebuff after rebuff from people who are content to use the present awkward system. People, and even the most educated of them, are simply lazy. And the members at the Society have grown brokenhearted with time and lost hope. It was as though you tried to help a sick man and he not only refused your help but insulted you in the bargain. Became indignant!"

Munves halted with a pang. That was exactly how he had treated Balkan when he refused to go with him to Blenholt's funeral. Max was an idealist too. Munves had said so himself to the pearl peddler and it was true. For all Munves knew, Max might have been as earnest and purposeful a reformer as his friends at the Spelling Society. And Munves might very well have been the sick man who had not only refused help but had insulted in the bargain.

"I wonder," he asked penitently, "where Max is now?"

Driving Ruth crazy at Blenholt's funeral, Rita thought, but she restrained herself immediately. It wasn't over yet. Munves was just scared to think of marriage, he needed time, she didn't have to give up so easily.

"Don't worry about Max," she said. "He's crazy. Let's go and find out where Sealwudu really belongs. I'm dying to know."

"Really?" asked Munves pleased. She was a real helpmate, shared his enthusiasms and preoccupations. Companionship with her would mean its utmost. The idealist, Max Balkan, slipped from his mind and was sent off to take care of himself. Munves opened the gazetteer to a map of England. "Let's look together," he said. "If you're really interested." And that brought Rita to his shoulder again.

The calf smell . . . the scalp shivering with her closeness . . . Rita bent down to look more carefully at the map and her breast, resting loosely, lay on his shoulder. Oh, delicious! The point of her breast was an electric current going through him. In a second Munves was transported to the bathtub again. He saw the map of England in a blur, as though he read without his glasses. All he knew was that the water felt warm and he grew drowsy.

To be married! Actually to take baths with Rita! He remembered reading somewhere that this was the practice with some married couples. These things were possible. To sleep with Rita in the same bed every night, their naked bodies lying side by side! If some one could give Munves a guarantee that Rita would sleep without pajamas, he felt he could almost reconcile himself to the prospect of marriage, terrible as that was.

They worked hard trying to locate Sealwudu.

SEVEN
The funeral

THE AIR WAS HOT AND HEAVY. At three o'clock the sun poured over the streets like a flood. Max Balkan squinted to avoid the glare, wiped the perspiration from his glasses and looked for a shady spot. Across the street near the iron railings that led down to a cellar, a man sat on the sidewalk, resting against the building, his legs sprawled. Save for him the street was deserted. Balkan's strength was melting away from him with the perspiration, but he determined to ward off all weakness if it was at all humanly possible. A drop of sweat shivered from his nose tip like an icicle in the sun.

"They'll be here any minute now," Max said. "It'll just be a minute now."

"Sometimes you're aggravating. I could kill you," said Ruth with outraged feeling, wondering how she had ever let him drag her off. "After making me run all the way because you were afraid we'd be late."

The funeral was scheduled for two. Balkan, in panic because he was late, had decided not to go to Blenholt's late residence but to meet the procession at South Fourth and Rodney. And they were still not here. Or perhaps they had passed him by this time and were already at the hall? Steeling himself to the effort, Max walked across to the outsprawled man. He bent over him, trying to reach under the hat, which the man kept down to his nose.

“Excuse me,” Max said, “but did the funeral come yet?”

Standing close, Max could hear a gentle snore. He went back to Ruth.

“If you want to,” he suggested, “we could walk back to Blenholt’s house.”

“Yare, and by the time we’ll get there,” she answered viciously, “they’ll be started and we’ll have to run back looking for them somewheres. We might just as well stay right here.” She was furious. On a tin billboard nearby the sign announced the attractions at the Miramar. Joan Crawford, Thursday to Sunday. She could have cried. Ruth felt her head. He had rushed her and now it was still too early. Thirty-five cents and she had just had the hair set! She took a mirror from her handbag and started to fix her hair.

“Listen!” Balkan cried. “I can hear them. They’re coming. I can hear the music.”

He looked down the street, staring until the heat danced in waves before his eyes. There wasn’t a soul. He must have been mistaken.

“I don’t hear a thing,” Ruth said with all the meanness she could muster.

“Gee whiz, for a moment, I could have sworn I heard them. Didn’t you hear anything, Ruth?”

“They’ll come when they’ll come,” she shouted. “My God, my God! You’re such a . . . such a . . .”

It was too hot. She gave up. What kind of funeral was this anyway? Since when did people have to have parades?

Into the street rolled the mournful tones of an organ playing a sickly dirge. It was intolerable, and, Max hoped, at least someone might have the heart to shut the radio off. He hadn’t the strength to explain the strange circumstances that followed Blenholt’s passing but the truth was, as Rita had hinted from the bathroom door, that in spite of his attendance at church and synagogue, Blenholt belonged to neither denomination. This did not shock his followers, but what did inconvenience them was the obscurity of his extraction and the religion that went with it. Some said Turkish, but to his politician and thug followers the appropriate Turkish religion was puzzling and the facilities, certainly, were lacking. His old cronies, however, were not to be thwarted from giving the famous man a funeral in keeping. For this purpose they had hired McCarren Hall, arranged for elaborate exercises at which prominent citizens of the neighborhood, Catholic and Jewish, were to take part, and took all pains to see that the monster funeral parade through the important streets of Williamsburg would be lavish and suitable in every respect. Blenholt would get a funeral, they vowed, better than anyone living had ever seen.

In the meantime Balkan could hear the somber bongs from the radio as the announcer called the time. A hillbilly band promptly took the air with their brisk music, all of which sounded as though it was produced on a washboard. Then the rumbling drone of the announcer. A family in another flat began quarreling, their cracked voices reminding Balkan of a forest of crickets. Nothing went well, Balkan muttered to himself, aching in this dismal scene as he waited with Ruth on his hands. The radio was the last straw and he had to fight against breaking down. Someone must have had an evil eye on him. Everything he touched went sour immediately. Balkan always admired at the movies the ease and smoothness with which the petty events of life were accomplished, and it was an ambition in his life to be able at some time to achieve these acts as effortlessly and faultlessly. In a picture an actor said, "I am going to Monte Carlo," and in the next scene you saw him on the train, surveying the countryside with a detached air and smoking a cigarette. If Balkan prepared for a journey, he would break his trunk in packing, lose the key after it had been accidentally closed too soon, he would fall in a pool of mud, arrive breathlessly at the station only to find the train pulling out and that he had left his tickets at home. Somehow, perspiring in the heat, watching with pain Ruth's impatience from the corner of his eyes, that was all that Max could think of: the casual ease of movie actors in their routine actions, and Max envied them as the afternoon dragged and dragged. How long, O Lord, how long?

"Oh, you drive me crazy," Ruth muttered. "I'm going crazy with the heat."

"They'll be here in a minute, Ruth," he said, trying to make himself as unobjectionable as possible. Anything would set her off now. "You've waited so long, you might as well stick it out another few minutes."

"What am I hanging around here for?" she asked in an inevitable spasm. "I'm going home."

But Balkan was standing transfixed, as though someone had suddenly hurled a spear into his back. There it was, the funeral. He could really hear the music this time. "Listen, Ruth. Listen," he whispered electrically.

The music swelled. It was a flamboyant funeral march played by seventy flutes and brasses. The crying melody rose to the heavens as the procession approached, summoning housewives and children to their windows, rushing to take in the show. Balkan was overwhelmed. He forgot all his concern over Ruth, he forgot Ruth, and he stood in awe.

The former Commissioner's friends had indeed spared no expense. With black ribbons on their arms and their eyes alertly inspecting every detail, the lieutenants kept the procession moving efficiently and without a moment's delay, running up and down the lines to keep the marchers in respectful order. This was the last testimonial of the fondness they bore their dead leader and their bullet heads glared with desire to make it convincing. They were everywhere.

The hearse, a resplendent Cadillac, drove ahead in low. Directly following, eight Packards, empty of people save the drivers, bore the overflowing lavish assortments of flowers. Mountains of flowers and the perfume therefrom was enormous, filling the nostrils of the onlookers who came running up to the curbs and on the roofs, in addition to those squeezed three and four to the ledge at the windows. The heavy tubas and the horns mourned solemnly. The flutes pierced the air in tremendous overwhelming wails. A gorgeous lamentation and the great strains filled the hearts of the three full blocks of mourners who trudged behind, with tears, with pity, and with heroism.

How majestic! As the marchers came before them, Max and

Ruth filed into line. The music and the perfume of the flowers drenched his spirit, vanquishing him completely. This was as it should be, he nearly wept, a fitting ceremony for a great man. The difficult wait in the sun, the whole day's humiliating adventures were gone. It was gorgeous. Had the funerals of renaissance tyrants been any more ornate, more extravagant? he wondered, and the flutes set up a magnificent wail which swept over the procession like a tide. Balkan's heart jumped at the weeping sounds. How beautiful, how glorious, what dimensions! Balkan, trying to keep from slobbering, surrendered his soul completely and wallowed in emotion.

"What a funeral!" he gasped exultantly to Ruth. "What a procession! This is what I mean when I say that reality doesn't have to be dingy. This is heroic!"

"Look at him," Ruth said soberly. "Absolutely insane."

All the same, she was very much impressed, too.

A few blocks from McCarren Hall the procession was marred by an untoward incident. Automobiles at the cross streets had been considerately waiting for the funeral marchers to pass but in this case a lady driving a Buick sedan kept pressing the horn button and tried to creep through the crowd, inching her way. Balkan noticed, as they came near her, the two pinkish smudges near her nostrils and this in some way he always associated with cold, unlovely spinsterhood and all other women of petty, mean, and vindictive temperament. One of Blenholt's old hands immediately rushed up on her running board with a show of indignation. He was indeed a hard-looking gentleman and he wore his badge on his sleeve with distinct aggressiveness.

"Lady," he asked in great wonder, "what do you think you're trying to do?"

"I'm in a hurry," she said rapidly. "I want to cross. Tell them to move back a little, please, and I'll get through in a minute."

The hard-looking gent could not understand it. Some of his more forward companions had rushed up and were all for dealing directly with her, but his curiosity had been piqued and he brushed them back.

"What's the matter with you, lady?" he expostulated. "Don't you realize what this is?"

"I'm sorry, I'm very sorry," she answered briskly, knowing her rights and standing up for them, "but I'm in a hurry. I want to cross."

"You ought to be ashamed of yourself," he said, wagging his finger at her with reproach. "Ain't you got no respect for the dead?"

"I'm sorry," the lady glared in a burst of impatience. "I said I'm getting through and I mean it. I can't stand here all day arguing with you."

A small crowd had gathered around the car while the rest of the line proceeded forward. Balkan, standing by, struggled with himself. He felt that he could end the squabble and that, further, there was some necessity for him to inject himself into it. What was he standing idly by for? The spinster seemed to be a lady of some education and possibly could not understand Blenholt's crude assistants. All he had to do was to explain the situation to her intelligently. Balkan knew that his reluctance to intervene at these times indicated one of his more serious flaws and he rose to overcome it. And disregarding the pull on his sleeve from Ruth, he drew a breath and stepped forward.

"Look here, madam," he said sensibly. "This is no way to act. Why can't you wait? It's only fitting. The procession will be over in a minute and then you can go ahead."

Balkan, proud, hoped that Ruth was taking notice of his achievement, but before he could enjoy this luxury, the lady had spotted him and turned. "You," she said like a bombardment, "shut up. If you know what's good for you, you'll mind your own business."

"All right, kid," the hard-looking gent was adding unexpectedly. "You stay out of this. We'll take care of this in our own way."

"All I'm trying to do . . ." Balkan protested with hurt. But the gent shoved him aside without further ado, muttering softly, "Aw shaddap." In another minute he was swallowed up in the crowd until he stood outside on the fringe. He had even lost Ruth.

Within the crowd one of the men had told the spinster that she would proceed only when they got good and ready to let her. At this she said defiantly, "Oh, yare?" and meeting the challenge at once she started fumbling with the gearshift. Without another word Blenholt's former hired men took out long curved knives, such as are used in the oilcloth business, and slashed the tires of the Buick. They worked dispassionately and with collected faces, calmly watching the car sink to the pavement and wiping off the sweat with their coat sleeves. They heard the loud gasping noises as the air escaped, with satisfaction, noting it as a craftsman inspects his finished job. The lady at the wheel was practically choking. Balkan, still looking for Ruth at the border of the crowd, was disturbed by the violence and experienced an impulse to enter the quarrel again, but at the same time a strong feeling to hold back filled him and he obeyed it.

"Well?" asked a voice panting after the exertion. "How do you like that?"

"Don't think you're getting away with anything," the spinster cried, gagging. "You're going to pay for every cent these tires cost me. I'll . . . you'll . . ."

"Aw, shaddap," the voice said with great disgust. "You ought to be ashamed of yourself. What kind of a person are you anyhow?"

The crowd moved off, leaving the lady overcome. Balkan soon spotted Ruth by her plastered head and ran up to her.

"I want to go home," she fumed. "This is crazy."

She fired away at him. Why had he stuck his two cents into it? That was just like him and it was things like that that made him a schlemiel. He was lucky they had just shoved him away, it was a good thing he didn't get his head busted. Crazy! Crazy! A fool! Max pleaded with her firmly but in strained tones for fear of collecting a mob. Ruth started walking home and Max tagged after her, trying to detain her.

It took him a good fifteen minutes, but in the end he managed to convince her, and they had to hurry to the hall or miss the exercises.

On any other day Balkan would have quietly taken a seat

inconspicuously in the rear, but now, blown with the necessity of self-expression or else admitting the charge of cowardice, he walked all the way down the aisle to the front of the hall, to show that he was not afraid, that he could withstand the stares of people bored with eulogies. Ruth pulled at him but he persisted.

"I want to sit in the front where I can see everything," he whispered.

"The seats in the back are all right," she answered in the same whisper, fearful of the chairman now introducing a speaker. The ushers, who had been the hard-looking lieutenants of Blenholt, patrolled the aisle self-consciously with their badges and best suits and now several of them glared unpleasantly at Balkan and Ruth.

"Come on," he whispered uncomfortable.

"Stop pulling me. You don't have to drag me all the way to the front like a nut."

The chairman on the platform, distracted by their scuffling, looked down at them fiercely. "Please!" he uttered with contempt, and an usher ran over swiftly and pushed them into seats. "Ain't you got no sense of decency?" he glared. "Some people's children are certainly slobs." Balkan, chagrined and hurt, took his place. He was in one of the front rows but he would have preferred to be more in the center, and the usher's action constituted something of another defeat. The audience, regretting that the distraction was over, reluctantly shifted its gaze to the platform again. On it were an assortment of twenty men, some tall, some short, some fat, some thin, but they were all properly stiff and solemn, all held their palms on their thighs, showing their bootstraps and mercerized hosiery. The chairman, one of the short thin ones, his shiny hair, however, combed into an assertive pompadour, was still speaking. He introduced the first speaker in a deep voice of remarkable timbre, indeed having been chosen for the office on that account. A lay representative of the Catholic Church rose, coughed, and began to extol Blenholt as one of profound religious feeling, but his opening words were all but lost until he caught his bearings.

"This is no time," he intoned with his eyes closed to show that he was an experienced speaker, "to quibble over a man's denomination, his sect, or his race. In the Temple of God there is but one requirement and that is the true religious instinct and all that we usually associate with that quality. I refer to that wonderful saying: Nurture little children, shelter the old—and certainly Mr. Blenholt spent, as you all know, time and money to provide for them. Do you think, my friends who have gathered here this afternoon to pay homage to our worthy friend who has now passed to appear before the Final Judge, do you think that He would bar a man from Paradise just because he happened to be a Protestant instead of a Catholic, a Chinaman instead of a Frenchman? No, of course not, as you will easily enough realize upon a moment's reflection, my friends."

The representative paused to catch his breath, the last sentence being a tough one. How long? the audience wondered, looking up at him with glazed faces. He went on and on. The only times the audience perked up were those several occasions when they felt he must in all decency be finishing and a sigh filled the hall when it was discovered that the latest signal was only a false alarm.

"And so I say," droned the representative as though he would never stop, "that those who would for purposes of self-aggrandizement and motives of profit, malign a man for his individual faith, my friends—and I regret to state that there are some such—those despicable creatures who would do so, I say, are sorely mistaken, for the enlightened portion of the community will soon see through the fraud and the deception. Mr. Blenholt . . ."

The chairman of the magnificent pompadour had sidled up to him, whispering to him that the time had come for an end. Good, good, said the audience as one man, give it to him good. The speaker nodded vigorously five or six times to indicate his speedy demise, the audience brightened and he was off again. "And so I say, Mr. Blenholt had the true religious spirit which is one of neighborliness and he applied it not only in his social relations—as many of us do—but also in his business affairs—as many of us, I regret to be obliged to state, do not. I mean that if ever that wonder rule—I refer to the Golden Rule, which you all know well—if ever it were applied, Mr. Blenholt applied it. We can all recollect, I am sure, without too deep a search in the channels of memory, his many gifts of generosity to the less fortunate of us. His was a bright spirit of benevolence and so on and so on and so on."

False alarm? The audience grew worried. The chairman reluctantly but firmly whispered to the speaker who answered him with unconcealed annoyance. "And so I say in conclusion," he said, still glaring, "that in the passing of Mr. Blenholt to the Higher Sphere the community loses a great man, an inspired leader and a citizen distinguished for his kindness to one and all. And to his friends, Mr. Blenholt's passing is a great loss, a sad loss, an irreplaceable loss, I thank you."

The hell with it. They wouldn't let him finish. He had a real good ending all prepared and they made him go ahead and spoil it. He was disgusted and sat down sulkily, groping for his chair.

The chairman had rushed to the front of the stage in a hurry. "No applause, no applause," he cried anxiously. "It would be, as I am sure you will all agree on a moment's thought, hardly fitting at this time to applaud any speaker."

The possible catastrophe averted, he breathed more easily and got ready to introduce the next speaker. Balkan in his seat was being lulled by the barrage of words and he felt warm and drowsy in his mind, but Ruth still fidgeted with irritation. She just couldn't sit still and besides her finger wave was worrying her.

"I introduce to you," the chairman proclaimed with a flourish in that marvelous voice of his, "one who knew Mr. Blenholt, admired him and loved him. Mr. John T. Casporra, president of the Williamsburg Board of Business Trade, Mr. Casporra, no applause, no applause, please, as I mentioned before."

Mr. Casporra rose, a tall stringy man with a scrubbed face and graying hair. He spoke nasally and before many minutes had passed most of the people in the great hall were fervently hoping that he would take time out and blow his nose.

"I have in my time on one occasion or another," he said importantly, "made many speeches but I can truthfully say that never have I come upon the speaker's platform more heavily laden of heart than upon this sorrowful gathering. We have come together to pay homage to show our respect to that most worthy, dearly beloved and genuinely missed leader, I refer of course to Mr . . ."

A sharp commotion arose in the balcony. A woman, overcome by the humid closeness, had fainted and the audience turned in her direction gratefully. Balkan rose to go to her, determined to be a man of decision, a man of action, in spite of his experience with the Buick, but this time Ruth had secured a good hold on his coat and she managed to restrain him. And in short order smelling salts were applied and the woman was taken out of the building.

"Sit in your seats," the ushers were calling out nastily. "Everything's all right. Just sit tight and listen to what's going on up front."

"I might have been able to do something," Max said petulantly. "Why did you hold me back? What's the sense of sitting calmly while a woman faints?"

"I mean it," Ruth said, "if this is the way you're going to act today I'm going home by myself right now. What's got into you anyhow?"

"If I were asked," said the nasal voice, carrying on manfully. He paused until order was resumed. "If I were asked to select one outstanding characteristic that best described Mr. Blenholt I am sure my choice would be, as the previous speaker has so well mentioned, his quality of benevolence, His was a great good will toward his fellow man, and throughout the community of Williamsburg the name of Blenholt was synonymous with charity, kindness, and aid. How well we remember the late Commissioner of Sewers' gifts to the poor. As you all know, Mr. Blenholt provided the needy with coal in the bitter cold wintertime. Our less fortunate neighbors were supplied by him with baskets of good wholesome food on Thanksgiving and Christmas. Even though Mr. Blenholt himself was not a member of that fine race—I refer to the Jews—he nevertheless made it his custom to supply the needy of that race with matzoth on the Feast of Passover so that the Jews of Williamsburg, whether poor or rich, could be able to celebrate the High Holy Days in proper manner. Yes, my friends, I could go on for some time listing the number of Mr. Blenholt's philanthropies, his outings in the summer for the undernourished kiddies, the many, many rent bills he paid . . ."

"A philanthropist! The fine Mr. Blenholt a philanthropist! That makes me laugh right out loud!"

Who, who, who? The ushers gritted their teeth so that their jawbones stuck out below their ears. The voice, bitter and grating, had risen from the belly of the audience and everyone's head craned.

"My friends," shouted Mr. Casporra above the din, "if that gentleman will please stand up and show us his face."

A middle-aged man with a gray stubble rose bravely. Short and squat he was and as he got to his feet those about him could notice the pallor behind the lines of his face and the perspiration.

"Sure, Mr. Blenholt was a great charity giver," the man said staunchly. "Matzoh he gave and sacks of coal in the winter he gave. Sure he gave. Ask me! I know! I and many more just like me, only they're afraid to open up their mouths and get their noses busted, we, we gave for the fine Mr. Blenholt's philanthropies!"

"This is no time, my friend," interjected Mr. Casporra swiftly, hoping to save the situation. "My friend, have you no respect for the dead?"

"No!" shouted the man, hysterical with fear and excitement. "No, I ain't afraid! Who paid for it? All his outings and charities, who paid for it? Me! Me and every other little storekeeper and pushcart peddler on the block, every week we paid for it and for plenty more! Good money we made with sweat and blood we had to give out of our own pockets. Give, he said, and the bums with the pistols in their hands said give, and we gave like it was a hold-up, we gave! We gave until we got pushed out of business altogether. Like me!"

By this time the ushers had managed to push their way through the narrow rows of seats and had laid their hands upon him, slapping his face as he resisted.

"Communist!" murmured the audience hostilely. "Troublemaker! He ought to be lynched!"

"Go on, you bummers," shrieked the poor man, groveling in his frenzy, "kill me! Murder me! Butcher me! What do I care? I'm ruined already, finish the job altogether and shoot me! Murderers! Gangsters!"

He was being carried out crying and striking out feebly at the ushers. His wails and great sobs impressed the audience but they said forthwith that the man was a paid agitator, an actor, sent by the communists to make trouble, for that was what they always did at occasions like this. Some of the people in the hall had relatives who had given them inside information on the communists and that was how they always did things.

As the man was finally carried through the doors, a further catastrophe occurred. The hearse bearing Blenholt's remains lad been driven directly to the steps of McCarren Hall. The great doors of the hall were opened wide as were the portals of the hearse itself to the effect that Blenholt might better hear he eulogies. Now as the communist was carried writhing to he street, his head dangled for a moment toward the ornate silver casket that held Blenholt, and, passing, the man took to spitting great globs of saliva at the coffin, at the same time uttering horrible, foul curses.

"Whoo," murmured the crowd, appalled at the sacrilege.

"Just a minute, folks," the chairman begged. "Quiet, please. Quiet. Really it's a crying shame, a plain, common shame, that at a sacred time like this a lunatic should be left at large and be permitted to come into the hall and make a scene like this. It's disgraceful and I'm going to ask you to forget all about it and carry on. Mr. Casporra."

"My friends," said the nasal voice, clearing his throat, "the sad scene which you and I have just witnessed must be, as the chairman said so well, disregarded and forgotten. Pay no attention to it and do not condemn the poor unfortunate, I beg of you, for the man who was responsible for these scenes of disorder was of course insane. And just as we must not laugh at crazy people, so we must never permit ourselves to be angry with them, for they know not, poor mortals, what they do. Yet I am grieved at this painful happening and I trust that Mr. Blenholt is not deceived. For, as we all know, Mr. Blenholt hears everything that we are now saying, as any person of any religion, it does not matter what creed or sect, will be the first to agree. The doors are opened, the portals of his hearse are open wide. Mr. Blenholt," said Mr. Casporra, dramatically addressing the hearse at the end of the hall and looking up the center aisle, "do not be deceived. That horrible commotion represents only the ravings of some poor unfortunate. Look rather, Mr. Blenholt, at . . ."

Mr. Casporra stopped, his right hand still extended laterally. He stood transfixed. The men on the platform, too, sat paralyzed, their mouths agape. Was Blenholt himself walking down the aisle? The audience, taking its cue from the speaker, turned to see what it was.

It was the woman with the red smudges, the driver of the Buick sedan, the tires of which had been slashed. She was marching down the aisle in vicious determined strides, her hat askew, her face flushed and distorted. Her jaws were clamped together so tightly that they could hear her teeth grind. On she came resolutely, and the twenty men on the platform watched in anguish, unable to move a finger. She made the sharp turn at the stairs and pumped up to the stage. The house was enormously quiet. Straight up to Mr. Casporra she walked, set herself into position with her legs firmly apart, and slapped his face with great force twice, once on each side. Mr. Casporra's eyes flinched.

"I want my money for those ruined tires!" she shouted in a voice tempered to white heat, and she spoke with terrible clearness. "Don't you think for a single minute that you are going to get away with that on me! No bunch of gangsters can rip my tires and get away with it!"

The twenty men on the platform, awakened from their trance, came to life altogether. The chairman with the determined pompadour hurried over and put a quieting hand on her shoulder. She shook it off fiercely. "Who's asking you to stick your goddamed nose into this, you runt?" she asked. "You mind your own goddammed business! I want my money for those tires and I want it right now!"

"What are you hitting me for?" Mr. Casporra asked pitifully.

"What did I have to do with it?"

She did not answer but went on slapping him. The representatives of the churches approached, the others left their seats and they all surrounded the blazing woman, now wild with accumulated fury. The ushers were running up the aisles to the platform. The audience howled in an uproar. Outside the hearse of Blenholt, with the doors opened, was quite neglected. On the stage they all tried to put their hands on the woman, pushing and arguing, becoming a live chain of people, undulating, struggling and endless. The platform swayed threateningly, unused to these demands. A man's voice rose in the clamor. "Considering where we are and the circumstances," the voice boomed, "that's the only thing that keeps you from getting your head broken right this minute!"

Balkan in his seat looked on and writhed with internal conflict. He sweated with indecision and shame. He ought to be doing something. Why was he sitting there? Wasn't he a man? A man would get up and straighten this out.

"I've got to do something," he muttered unhappily to Ruth. "I can't just sit here."

"Don't you dare!" she shrieked. It was just like him, just like him. "What are you going to do up there? You stay right here and keep quiet!"

"I'm going right up there and straighten this mess out," he declared.

Fool! Fool! "Sit here!" she cried. "They'll take care of everything."

"No," he insisted. "I can't just sit here. I got to help."

"You're crazy today! Absolutely out of your mind! You take a step up that stage and I'll leave you flat in a minute! I'll walk out of here! I'll go home!"

Balkan wavered painfully, looking at Ruth and then again at the bedlam on the platform. The spinster was scratching and spitting. It was indecent. And at last, in spite of Ruth, determined to prove once and for all that he was not afraid, that when an emergency arose he could take his hand in it, Balkan rose for the stairs, his heart pounding.

"I'm going home!" Ruth called, and fled.

Balkan tried to call her back but it was too late. She was gone. He turned to the struggling boil of people and began wedging himself to the center of it.

A big man with a thick neck noticed him approach, detached himself and came to him. "Stay out of this, you," he said curtly. "We got enough people up here already."

"Perhaps I can do something," Balkan said earnestly, fixing his spectacles firmly so that they wouldn't fall off. He pushed forward.

"Stay away!" the big man said, irritated beyond endurance.

But Balkan paid no heed and moved ahead. The big man, impatient and wasting no more time, grabbed him by his tie and shoved him back. Max tripped and fell, his spectacles dropping from his ears to the floor. In a sudden lurch the circle about the raging woman took it into its head to swerve over Balkan. Three or four men stumbled heavily over him. Nevertheless, Balkan, worrying about his glasses, stretched out a hand to save them. Someone promptly stepped on his fingers, rasping the skin and crushing the bones, and groaning with pain Max was able at the same time to distinguish the noise of glass being crushed. The struggle continued over him. People kept digging their heels into all parts of his back, kept falling down on him with force every time he tried to raise himself to stand up, they mashed his face into the wooden planks until the skin was rubbed away and little dots of blood appeared. His breath was squeezed out of him. He couldn't get up. The stampede punished him as he choked for air. Balkan felt as miserable as a man has ever felt. The angry swirl went on like a nightmare.

In time the thugs managed to calm the woman. They carried her out, one hugging her about the middle, another at the feet, a third pressing her arms safely over her head. The ushers cursed discontentedly for they had been putting in a hard day. Balkan was picked up carefully. His clothes were jerked and torn, his tie pulled to a tight string. While they brushed his clothes for him, the big man with the thick neck who had first cautioned him said, not unkindly, "I told you to stay out of this. I told you."

"Don't bother," Max said weakly. "It's all right."

"How are you feeling, kid?' Thickneck asked. "Got the wind knocked out of you?"

"Oh, I'm all right. I'll be fine in a minute," Max protested.

But he could see only with great effort and then blurred powdery circles appeared. Max wondered whether this was due to his injuries or the loss of his spectacles. And where was Ruth? He was too stunned to cry, or else he very probably would have broken down and wept. He sat down, his mind numb, rested and tried to gather back his strength.

The audience had begun to compose itself for some very vigorous indignation. The chairman, patting his pompadour into place, tried to introduce the next speaker, a representative of the Ladies' Aid Auxiliary. It took him some minutes.

EIGHT
The tenement: Ta-ran-ta-ra

RUTH WAS SO MAD with Max Balkan that she ran all the way home to her house without a break, dashed straight to the vanity table in her room, and began combing out the finger wave into natural lines and curls. She fluffed and placed her hair, muttering angrily and bouncing the brush on the table. That took the cake!

"What's the matter with you today?" her mother asked her at the uproar. "She comes into the house like a pogrom. You got out of the bed on the wrong side this morning?"

"Leave me alone," Ruth cried. "I'm so mad I could scream."

Why did he have to go to the funeral in the first place? she asked, primping her hair before the mirror. Who was Blenholt in his life? And who did she kill, he had to drag her off to the funeral too? Heroism, personal dignity, poetry, Tamburlaine, Shmamburlaine. He was absolutely out of his head and if she didn't watch out he would drive her crazy too!

"Ma," she called irritably, "did you take my bobby pins again?"

"If you don't keep your mouth in a hurry," Ruth's mother said, "big as you are, I'll smack you good and hard."

"For crying out loud," Ruth said, "don't you start aggravating me too!"

But she quieted down. The pins were in the celluloid powder box she used to keep her junk in, and she stuck them into her hair savagely. The finger wave had turned out well, she had to note in spite of her exasperation with Max. Ruth brushed her hair neatly back from the forehead and the curls rolled at the nape in a golden mass. She patted the curls with affection. Ruth powdered her face for three minutes, dabbed the rouge on her cheeks and penciled her lips with lipstick until her mouth looked like a rosebud. Then she carefully tried to soften the effect of the powder, rouge, and lipstick, because if there was anything she couldn't stand, anything that was vile, it was a girl with too much makeup on.

Ruth's mother looked in admiringly. "Where are you going, Madame Galli-Curci? You're all dressed up," she said.

Ruth pushed her out and closed the door. "Don't be impossible," she said. "Please. I'm in no mood."

Ruth sat down on the rocker, leaned her head against the little red cushion that hung from the back, closed her eyes, and rubbed her fingers across her temples, an operation that produced a soothing feeling after a hard day in addition to preventing the formation of wrinkles, according to Antoinette Perry, Beauty Aids, in the *Daily News*. Max was absolutely the limit. For years now she had been trying to make a man out of him but it was hopeless. Ruth, in the rocking chair, saw herself a hardheaded, wise, farseeing woman of maternal omniscience. Max was a poet, daydreamer, romantic, and she, who was destined to suffer much, was laboring to make his way an easy one in a hard, material world. She saw Max a success in her vision, walking down Fifth Avenue in striped trousers and with a cane, his expression sure and capable, a little gray running over the ears. She saw rotogravure pictures of Max and herself on the beaches of the Mediterranean Sea. Mr. and Mrs. Max Balkan, et cetera, and people at home, reading the Sunday papers, were saying: "She made a man out of him. They all say he would be a nobody today if it wasn't for his wife."

Ruth rose and blinked her eyes to wake up. "I'm getting just as crazy as him," she mumbled. But now she thought of Max without anger, feeling indeed sorry for him, and tender. From her maternal elevation he became a small boy, puttering with silly schemes for making a fortune speedily, a boy moved by romantic ideals and illusions and silly as these illusions were, they disappointed him and he was heartbroken. An impulse came to Ruth to find him, protect him, and caress his troubles away.

He was crazy, she said, but she changed into another dress and went to his house.

When Ruth entered Mrs. Balkan greeted her and asked at once where Max was.

"Isn't he here yet?" Ruth asked. "I thought I'd find him here. He should be home by now."

"My God," cried Mrs. Balkan, immediately worrying. "What happened? Tell me quick, Ruthie, what happened?"

"Nothing, nothing," she said. "Don't get excited for nothing. Only he should be home by this time."

"Something happened," said Mrs. Balkan in the quiet voice of apprehension. "My heart tells me. Don't hide the truth from me, Ruthie darling. I'm his mother. Tell me quick. You look so funny. You went with him to the funeral, to Blenholt, God knows what, but you come back alone."

"It was nothing. I had a little argument with Max and then I went home by myself."

"Sh, sh," said Mr. Balkan, permitting himself to be a little angry. With all her fuss he had started worrying too. Subway, automobile accident, something, and it had been unnecessary. "Why should something be the matter? All these years you worried and did one accident happen yet?"

She turned to her husband. "Mr. Fumfotch!" she cried. "All these years I worried! How many accidents will I need? One will be plenty. Max lays God knows where, run over, maybe dead in a police station and all he wants is quiet, don't bodder, quiet, shah, shtill!"

"Dead, run over," he muttered, appalled at the way she invited bad luck. He spat to ward off the evil.

"Did you ever see such a superstitious old fool?" she asked Ruth. "Something is the matter? Don't worry, don't get excited. Spit on the floor and like magic everything will be all right."

The telephone bell rang. Mrs. Balkan clutched her heart and

stood stock still. Even the old man looked at the telephone with scared eyes. Why did it have to ring? Everything was all right and there would be quiet in the house. Now, perhaps, bad news would set everything awry. Mr. Balkan resented the telephone. If you didn't know of accidents, the accidents didn't happen.

"Oh, my God," Mrs. Balkan finally wailed softly. "It's Max. Something happened. A mother's heart knows."

She stood there, afraid to touch it, and the bell went on ringing. The door opened. Rita appeared but she did not rush for the phone. She looked at her father's face, fear and worry showing through the clown's makeup. She saw Ruth standing with her bag still in her hand and her mother transfixed, her eyes wide with worry.

"What's the matter?" she asked. "Was there an accident?"

"Take the receiver off the hook," the old man said anxiously to his wife. "What good is it to stand there?"

Mrs. Balkan handled the earpiece gingerly, shrinking from catastrophe. The old man shuffled over to her in his oversized shoes and tried to listen over her shoulder.

"Hello?" Mrs. Balkan said in a very scared small voice. "Mr. Max Balkan? Yes, yes, that's my boy, it's my child . . . Yes, yes, tell me quick what happened. Quick, I'm his mother, tell me what happened."

"Where is he?" Mr. Balkan asked. "Ask them where is he now?"

"What?" asked Mrs. Balkan, struggling with the earpiece. "What? What?" She turned to her husband. "Shah!" she yelled, irritated beyond endurance. "For God's sakes, how can I hear what's happening when you hang on my neck like a boil?—Yes," she said to the telephone in a tearful voice. "He's my son. Mr. Max Balkan is my son . . . From where are you talking, please? What happened to him? Just a minute, please. Hold the wire. Rita, I'm so excited I can't make out a word. Here, you speak to him."

"Rita, ask him where Max is now," Mr. Balkan pleaded eagerly as his daughter took the earpiece. "Ask him, Rita."

"Sharrup!" Mrs. Balkan shouted. "Sit down and read the paper. What are you mixing everybody up for?"

"Hello," said Rita professionally. They all stood around her. "What's the matter with Mr. Max Balkan? What happened . . . Oh!

Oh! I see. Well there's been a slight misunderstanding here and naturally my mother was slightly nervous . . . Well, he's not in now, but if you care to leave a message, I'll see that he gets it as soon as he gets in . . . We expect him in any minute now. All rightie, then . . . What name shall I tell him? All rightie . . . Good-bye . . . Thank *you*."

Rita turned from the telephone to the waiting eyes. The cheerful note on which she had ended her conversation melted promptly and now she looked at her mother with unconcealed disgust.

"Well, what was it?" Mrs. Balkan asked, sensing already that she had made a fuss for nothing. "Why are you standing there like a broken crutch?"

"Well, Rita, what?" asked her father.

"My God, Mother," Ruth said disdainfully, "you have to ball up everything. If you can't hear on the telephone, why must you always answer it? It's a man. He just wants to talk to Max. And that's all."

Mr. Balkan made a great business of his sigh of relief. "So long," he said triumphantly, returning to his couch with the *Tag*, "so long she raised a fuss like the house was on fire. Nu, nu." He opened the paper fearlessly.

"Who was it?" Mrs. Balkan asked in a subdued tone.

"Hot Water! His name is Atwater."

"Well," Mrs. Balkan said, "what did I say? Didn't I say Mr. Hot Water?"

"Did you ever see a mother like mine?" Rita asked Ruth. "All she does is worry. She enjoys it."

"It's foolish to worry. Really, Mrs. Balkan," Ruth said benevolently, "you shouldn't worry so much. You can wear yourself out like that."

"What can I do?" Mrs. Balkan asked, feeling sorry for herself. "It's my nature. I'm a nervous type. Other people, they're lucky, they wouldn't worry if the world turned over tomorrow. With me worry is a sickness. I should go to a doctor. I'm nervous, but what can I do? Can I change my nature?"

"Anybody who worries," Ruth said knowingly, "is foolish. It don't pay and there's nobody to thank you for your trouble."

"I know. Believe me, I know from experience."

"Didn't you go to the movies, Ruth?" Rita asked.

"No . . ."

"Why not?"

"I just couldn't get him to go. He was in one of his unreaonable moods today, I guess. We went to the funeral instead."

"Funerals," Rita said with contempt. "What a crazy brother I got. He takes his girl to funerals. That's his fat idea of showing a girl a good time."

"Well," Ruth said in all fairness, "he didn't take me there for a good time. That wasn't exactly the idea."

"Oh, don't stick up for him. He's hopeless. I don't know how you stand him."

"He's not so bad," Ruth said. "All he needs is some one to straighten him out and then he'll be all right. You just don't see his better qualities."

"Listen," Rita said very definitely, "you don't have to tell me nothing about Max. I know."

"Well," said Ruth, sighing, "you know how it is. Some fellows . . ."

"Some fellows . . ." Rita repeated. "I'm a fine one to be talking. You know what I've been doing all day? I'm looking for Sealwudu. Me and Munves, the world will come to an end in a week if we don't find Sealwudu. Can you imagine?"

They both remained silent, drawing closer, their thoughts in sad communion. They were allies in the war between the sexes. Rita and Ruth were women, they shared the same hopes and disappointments, they dwelt in a world of their own sex, full of feminine worry and suffering. The sad lot that mankind and history heartlessly gave women for their share in life loomed ahead of them: pregnancies, maternity hospitals, doctors, babies, children's sicknesses, erring husbands, money troubles . . . all these, all these in the years to come, and Ruth and Rita felt closer than sisters.

"Munves isn't so bad either," Ruth said sadly. "You just got to know them, both of them. Some day they'll grow up and then they'll be all right."

"When they grow up," Rita said. "They're kids. They just got out of diapers. When will they grow up? When they got beards?"

"Rita," Mrs. Balkan said finally, on pins and needles, "what are you staying here for? Go, darling, go and help Munves. Don't keep him waiting."

"Mother!" Rita shouted, as though a knife had been stuck into her. "Sometimes I could commit murder!"

"What did I say?" Mrs. Balkan asked. "The prima donna, you can't tell her a word."

"Shah!" said Mr. Balkan, feeling strong ever since the telephone. "I want quiet in the house."

"Look at him!" Mrs. Balkan cried. "Mr. Fumfotch wants quiet in the house. Everybody fall down dead and don't make a noise so long as Mr. Fumfotch has quiet."

"Ah," said the old man disgustedly, ducking behind the *Tag*. "Sh."

"Gee whiz," Rita said to Ruth. "If some mothers aren't impossible. She's the limit. Sometimes she gets on my nerves so I could almost scream from aggravation. You can imagine." She went to the door. "Sealwudu," she said with hopeless humor, "Sealwudu is calling me."

"Ruth," Mrs. Balkan begged after her daughter had left, "tell me, you're a girl too. What did I say to her, she should get so angry? Did I say something so terrible?"

"Well, Mrs. Balkan," Ruth said, "Rita is a sensitive girl. She isn't ignorant, you should understand that. You can't talk to her like to any ordinary girl. When you talk about fellows and marriage, naturally it hurts her. It makes her cry."

"Then what should I do?" Mrs. Balkan wailed. "I can't sit here and let her hang around the house. She ain't getting younger with the years."

"You have to leave her alone. That's what you should do, Mrs. Balkan. Rita is no fool, she can take care of herself."

Leave everything alone, don't touch, by magic Rita will get a husband. A girl, what did she know?

"Ruthie, Ruthie," Mr. Balkan suddenly called, laying down the paper. Worry showed earnestly through his powder and paint. He had just thought of it. "Where is Max?"

"Mr. Fumfotch!" Mrs. Balkan said. "He just woke up!"

It was late. Ruth wondered whether something had happened to him after all. She sat down and waited for him, worrying a little herself.

Balkan stumbled out of McCarren Hall, clinging close to the wall and shrinking from the stares of the audience. Anything to be outside and away. It had been a mess. He wanted to leave it forever, drive the memory from his mind. More than anything else in the world Balkan wanted to leave the scene, but at the big doors of the hall the gangster with the thick neck regarded him critically and grasped his elbow.

"You're pooped, kid," the thug said with compassion. "You can't go home like this."

"Oh, I'm all right, I'm fine," Max protested. "Don't bother."

"Never mind," he said. "You come with me."

It was too much trouble, really he didn't have to bother, but the thug led Balkan to a Lincoln sedan without wasting words. Even in his state of mind Balkan envied the man's assurance and his definite manner. A real man, he thought, not like himself, strong-willed and competent. You could see it in the way he walked and spoke. Alongside of him Max felt like a kid of ten.

"Here," said Thickneck, opening the door. "You lay down on the back seat and get your wind back. Where do you live?"

"Ripple Street. It's only a couple of blocks. I can walk it in no time."

"You just lay here," he said. "I'll get Firpo to drive you home."

Kindness from the thug at this moment choked Balkan with gratitude. With a rush of feeling he loved Thickneck. "Thanks, thanks," he stammered. "That's real nice of you. But I can walk it." He rose from the seat to get out of the car but the gangster shoved him back kindly.

"Lay down," he said. "Firpo can drive you home while they're still gassing inside and he can get back here in time to go to the cemetery. Lay down or I'll smack you one."

"Well, thanks, thanks," Max said. "But it's really unnecessary."

The thug went off to look for Firpo. Max arranged himself on the leather cushion and closed his eyes, but immediately he felt sick. Nausea swirled him about until he felt as though he were caught in a whirlpool. He opened his eyes at once and tried to sit up. The dizziness left in receding waves and he stared intently at the ceiling of the funeral car to prevent its return. And as he rested, staring, the musty smell rose from the upholstery of the sedan to meet his nostrils. Max associated the smell immediately with death and corpses. It made him feel uncomfortable and he raised his head swiftly from the elbow rest, hoping in this manner to avoid contaminating his hair with germs. Automatically he was breathing gingerly, trying to keep out the smell of death and disease. Soon Firpo would return to drive him home. Max looked out the window for Thickneck, opened the door on the street side and crept out. He moved as fast as he could in fear lest he be caught and returned to the sedan. But when he turned the corner and was out of sight, he slumped against the wall of a building, resting until his breath came more naturally. Counting the blocks in his mind he discovered that he had exactly eighteen to go. They piled one on top of the other into a mountain of a wall and he wondered if he would ever have the strength to climb it.

Balkan set out. Farewell to glory. There was something about physical violence, something about a punch in the nose bringing blood, that routed immediately all ideals and speculations. Before a punch or a kick, philosophy became unreal. What would Mr. Thickneck, Balkan asked himself, think of Tamburlaine and the urge for human dignity? He plodded homeward, aching and sore, in body and spirit. Suddenly on Rodney Street he felt that he had to stop or fall down. The knees refused to push forward. And it wasn't until too late that he discovered he was in the middle of a Squee-doo-gee game. The boys grouped about him angrily.

"Hey, mister, get out of the way," they yelled. "Have a heart and get a move on."

Eagerly Max went for the curb but motion caused him to dance unhappily on his heels as he sought to maintain balance. He tried to manage a grin for the boys to show that he was all right in spite of his clumsiness.

"Drunken bum!" they yelled with delight at their find. "Drunken bum!" And they started running around him in a circle, shouting taunts and insults. One boy daringly smacked him on the back of his head and, taking cue from him, the kids now took to pulling his coat, kicking him and pinching him on the behind. Max was helpless. He could think of nothing to do in defense of himself but cry, which he nearly did. Cruel, unjust, ignorant.

A fat housewife, taking pity from her window, ran out and chased the kids away, uttering curses.

"Thank you," Max said shakily. "I'm not feeling well. The heat."

She looked suspiciously at his scratched face, the silly expression caused by the loss of his glasses, his torn, soiled clothes. Max swayed before her glance.

"For shame," she cried. "A nice young Jewish boy like you. Getting drunk like a goy! Your poor mother could cry her eyes out if she caught a look at you now."

Max gathered strength and moved off, his back burning under the glare of the housewife. Unfair! Every intention, no matter how honest and noble, was carried through a series of heartrending disasters to failure. And there was no letup. It went on and on. What did heroism mean in Williamsburg? What did poetry mean anywhere? People were cruel and hard. Max stumbled along almost weeping with fatigue and humiliation. Nobility! It was possible only when you had power. A human being without money and influence became ridiculous if he possessed only dignity instead. Balkan's muddled mind took a minute to run over the list of his projects and enterprises, formed in his quick stabs at fortune. They were all good ideas. Why couldn't one of them go through for him, succeed, make money? With money he would immediately become a person to be considered seriously. The ridicule would end. Then pomp and splendor of the spirit would become fitting to him. If you were poor, people insisted that you drop into their steaming, sweaty life. Attempt anything on a grand scale, and they laughed at you, showered you with insults, abuse, ridicule, and laughter. Max was tired. At the moment the normal life to which Ruth was forever calling him, morass of vulgarities that it was, even seemed inviting. It would be so easy. There would be an end to struggle and humiliation. And people would even respect him as one of theirs. The thought of Ruth and her irritation with him returned to torment him.

Max plodded on. Two kids passed him, walking face to face as they solemnly produced the quack-quack noise made famous by Eddie Cantor. The sun was losing its force and the streets were thronged. Kids played Johnnie-on-the-pony and one-foot-off on the sidewalks, and swarmed over the streets in punchball games and Ringolevio. Through the block a huge auto crawled along powerfully amplifying the voice of a soprano who sang: "If I had a girl by the name of Kitty, I would take her with me to Atlantic City." The racket filled the street, the din must have soared to God Himself, but on the boards of the truck the coming attractions of the Miramar were advertised and it was good. An old lady sat hunched up on the stoop, her skirt making a shallow basin between her knees, gravely eating a piece of herring with her fingers. "Stop the radio!" a man's husky voice came yelling through a window. "Turn off the music! Another minute and I'll vomit!" The music stopped on the stroke but all the clearer came the woman's voice, cracking shrilly like a cuckoo clock: "What's the matter with the music? They got to make a living too."

Max's journey homeward to Ripple Street became nightmarish to him. It was as though he was remaining stationary and Williamsburg instead was moving before him like a procession. A pickle man brushed past him from a delicatessen store going to his truck and leaving the salt, pungent smell of his trade behind him. From one of the windows above came the sounds of a baby crying with conscientious steadiness, the wails interrupted by brief snatches of hiccups as it gaspingly recaptured its breath. "Good night bay-bee!" sang a girl, fiddling with her curls, "milkman's on his way . . ." "Go," shouted a boy to his friend, "take a flying French leap into the lake." The hot-corn man drew up to the curb with his steaming kettle of cobs. The heavy vapor smacked Max in the face and he gasped for breath. He went on, one foot laboriously preceding the other. "Wanna buy a duck?" a boy asked him, attracted by his appearance but darting away immediately. An old man sat smiling in the sun, squatting on an overturned egg box, calling out to the passersby in feeble tones: "A match. Please. Mister, a match." No one heeded him and the old man went on smiling and muttering. On the Extension where cars rumbled over cobblestones the billboards said: BECAUSE YOUR BAKER BAKES GOOD BREAD, showing a lady in a red bathing suit. I AM YOUR BEST FRIEND, said wisps of cigarette smoke, curling upward. NEWEST CAR IN YEARS $675, and underneath the slogan fashionable people dressed in polo uniforms affectionately regarded a shining car. Flies swarmed around the sugared, sticky marble of the soda counter of a candy stand. A girl of twelve came running down the street, gleefully yelling at the top of her lungs: "Davey loves Greta Garbo! Davey loves Greta Garbo!" Mother nursing her baby on the street; mother leading her three-year-old boy, anxiously overseeing his pee-pee lest he wet his rompers; a man in an undershirt, perspiration drying on his fat arms, calling: "Saura, Saura, throw me down the *Forvertz*"; a knot of sparrows feeding in the middle of the street, swirling in short curves and alighting again, as they avoided the cars; a girl reading *A Kiss in the Dark*, with all her concentration, stretching long strands of chewing gum from her mouth at the same time with the preoccupation; two boys matching Dixie-cup pictures, scratching their heads as they traded; garbage cans at the railings of the cellars, still left out after the collections had been made; swarms of flies; the smell of grapefruit rinds; of vinegar; of diapers drying . . .

Ripple Street! Four more blocks! Max thought of his morning walk that day, through the mist, alone in the streets. Max thought of Ali Baba and the forty thieves, the flying carpet in the sky, and the wonderful ladies in the bathing suits. That morning he had been so calm and happy with himself as he fondly pursued the rosy inventions of his mind. Now he was miserable, disappointed with Blenholt and himself, in despair. Munves was happily at home working on his eenie-meenie-miney-mo. Coblenz was joyously drunk and at peace with the world. Why, Balkan cried, why hadn't he stayed at home in the tenement with Munves and Coblenz? What had made him go to the funeral? In a sudden spasm of tears and gasps, he raged against the world. It was a nasty mess. Outside it was ugly, brutal, and evil in every respect. Balkan, keeping back the tears, hated it.

"Hey, Heshey, you know what?" said Goldie, intending to bring up a bitter subject, "Chink's in the dumbwaiter riding up and down for a good time."

"Don't believe it," he said nonchalantly. Joyriding in the dumbwaiter was great shakes in Williamsburg. You had to have nerve. You kicked up the centerboard of the three-foot box, squeezed your body into it tightly, and manipulated the ropes from a height as much as five stories. Further, Mrs. Strudel, the janitor, would positively break the neck of any boy she caught using the dumbwaiter for purposes other than collecting garbage. Riding the dumbwaiter was a feat of great courage and Heshey's shame was that he had never done it.

"Don't believe it!" Goldie exclaimed. "He asked me to go with him."

"Then why didn't you if he asked you to go with him? Hah?"

"My mudder's children," she said primly, "don't go riding in dumbwaiters."

"Ah," said Hesh, "so what?"

"You're jealous."

"Who? Me? I'm laughing out loud. Say, listen . . ."

It fell flat. On the third-floor hallway landing Goldie refused to be impressed by Hesh. Hesh hated Chink to the depth, breadth, and height his soul could reach. Chink always soaked him for no good reason at all, his lifework was to make Hesh continuously miserable, and every time Hesh tried to get even, something went wrong and he got the worst of it again. Take the time with the paper bag of water. His mother had bawled him out for a half-hour because he had had to change every stitch of clothing he had on.

Now Chink was trying to make a sap out of him in front of Goldie.

"Say, listen," Hesh said, "don't get the idea I'm scared of Chink. I got tricks, hunnerds tricks, you know yourself. If I wanna I could get a hunnerd guys they should shellac Chink good. Oney I don' wanna. Say, listen, I ask you, what's more important, strength or brains?"

Goldie couldn't say.

"See? See?" Hesh said. But just then the dumbwaiter door on the landing flew open and there was Chink, squatting like a Chinaman. Hesh ducked down the stairs like a shot.

"Hello, Toots," Chink said. "Come on, let's go for a ride."

"I should say not! The nerve of some people's children!"

"Don't get stuck-up on me. How's your boyfriend, Tarzan of the Apes?"

"Listen here, you dumb Chink," Goldie declared aggressively, "don't you think for one minute that I don't know you're the dope who wrote that dirty thing on the fence in the yard! You got a dirty, filthy mind!"

"What thing? Honest, I don't know what you're talking about." Chink was all innocence.

"You don't know nothing," she said with deep sarcasm. "It's too bad about you."

"What thing? Honest, Goldie, I ain't got the slightest idea."

"About Heshey playing doctor with me. You made it and don't think I don't know it."

"On the level, Goldie, I didn't write nothing of the kind. You want me to find out who did it? You want me to bust him one? Just tell me and I'll break his head in for him."

"You dirty, lousy liar! You stinker! As if I don't know you wrote it!" Goldie sputtered with anger. The ideeer! He was going to find the fellow and bust his head in for her benefit when she knew all the time for a positive fact that he was the one. "Listen," she concluded, "I wouldn't go riding the dumbwaiter with a filthy person like you if you was the last person on the world."

"Dry up! Dry up!" Chink closed the door in disgust. He pulled the ropes and went for a visit to the fifth floor, resuming his gay spirits. “One, two, three, four,” Goldie could hear him singing, “Greta Garbo went to war. Five, six, seven, eight, Goldie wets her draws each day.”

Goldie could have murdered him on the spot with the greatest of pleasure. She foamed with anger. But Hesh came back running with such a fierce light in his eyes, she had to stop.

“Listen, Goldie,” he said, panting with excitement. “I bet you thought I ran away because I was scared of Chink. Ain’t it? But I got tricks, hunnerds tricks. You wanna get even with Chink?”

“I wanna break every bone in his body,” she said, clipping each word poisonously. “Revenge is sweet.”

“All right. Then you do what I tell you. You go in the yard and pick up clothespins. Seven clothespins I need, unnerstand?”

“Clothespins?” Goldie asked.

“Do what I tell you. I’m in a hurry. If we don’t do this trick fast it’ll be too late.”

Goldie went running to the yard to collect clothespins dropped by housewives hanging wash on the lines from their windows. Hesh himself returned to his house, opened up the garbage pail and found two grapefruit rinds. Carefully, fastidiously, but with speed, he selected the juiciest pieces of garbage in the pail: tomatoes, lettuce, peas, farina, oatmeal, coffee grounds, banana peels. He stuffed the dripping mess into the grapefruits until they were each a luscious soft mass. Then he swiped the ketchup bottle from the closet and emptied it over the rinds, covering the goo with a thick rich red layer. Hesh ran back to the landing and found Goldie with the seven clothespins.

“For crying out loud,” she said, overcome with wonder. “What’s that?”

“Ammunition,” Hesh said briefly. “Wait and see. I got no time for explanations. Now listen, I want you should open the dumbwaiter door and call Chink. When he comes you have to make him stop and then you vamp him. Talk to him, say anything comes into your head, like Greta Garbo in *Mata Hari.* Keep him with you, unnerstand, don’t let him get away. Once he starts moving, the whole shooting-match don’t work. That’s important.”

"All right," Goldie said. "But I'm a Russian princess if I know what you're talking about."

"Listen," implored Hesh. "If you don't keep Chink and he wants to go down on the dumbwaiter, you laugh. See, for a signal. Laugh out loud like anything so I can hear you. But if everything is all right, cough. Cough to beat the band every once in a while so I can tell. Then when you hear me sneeze, you tell Chink you go for a ride with him only on one condition, he got to meet you in the basement, else you don't go riding the dumbwaiter with him."

"Me?" Goldie protested. "Nothing doing. I wouldn't go riding the dumbwaiter with that lousy Chink if you gave me a fortune."

"You don't have to! I don' wanna you should go riding the dumbwaiter wid him! All you have to do is say you wanna. Don't worry."

"All right. Why didn't you say so in the first place. I should call Chink now?"

"Yare, now. You know the passwords? Laugh, if bad. Cough, if good. When I sneeze you tell him the basement."

"Laugh if bad. Cough if good. You sneeze and I say the basement."

"All right. You got it."

Goldie opened the dumbwaiter door and yelled up the chute. "Hey, Chink! Hey, Chink, I wanna talk to you. I got a bone to pick with you."

Heshey hid the grapefruit bombs, waited for the ropes to start moving to indicate that Chink was on his way, picked up the clothespins, and ran down to the cellar. He opened the dumbwaiter door there and heard Chink and Goldie bantering. Good! Two rings had been screwed into each dumbwaiter door to serve as a hasp, but this arrangement was seldom used. Heshey stuck a clothespin through the rings. This was No. 1. Chink couldn't get out here if he stood on his head for a year. Hesh was jittery with anticipation. Six more and success. If only Chink stayed in the dumbwaiter long enough, if only he didn't smell something rotten too soon, if nothing happened to give the plan away, if only Goldie held him long enough . . . Hesh waited for the cough. It came. Too make-believe! Chink would get on to it! Hesh prayed for luck.

He ran to the ground-floor dumbwaiter. Mrs. Strudel, the janitor! She'd get on to something in a minute, she'd find Chink in the dumbwaiter, everything would be spoiled!

"Oh, Mrs. Strudel!" Hesh said. "You should know what's going on outside this minute. Those rotten kids, they got no idea what trouble they can make."

"Don't bodder me," Mrs. Strudel said majestically. "Stay out of the halls and it will be good enough for me."

"Oh, Mrs. Strudel!" said Hesh. "If you only knew! You know that rotten kid Chink? What do you thinking he's doing this minute?"

Of all the kids Chink was the greatest pest in Mrs. Strudel's life and Hesh well knew it. "The little illegitimate," the janitor cried prompdy. "He should only fall down and break a leg and stay in bed for a week!"

"Outside," Hesh went on, "he's chalking up the whole sidewalk to play potsy. YOU STINK he writes on the stoop too, all colors. It'll take a week for sure to wash them off."

"The illegitimate," the janitor gasped. She went to the stoop.

"Don't run," Hesh cried. "You go slow and catch him when he ain't looking. You run, he'll see you, you'll never catch him."

Mrs. Strudel was gone. In a moment Hesh pushed the clothespin through the rings and listened for Goldie.

"What's a matter you coughing so much today?" he could hear Chink ask, with altogether too much suspicion in his voice. "You got a cold?"

He'll catch on! Heshey ran in panic to the first floor, secured this door, and was shooting up the flight when he heard Goldie laugh. Yah! Hah! Hah! Too late! Chink smelled a rat! Heshey stopped, pinching his flesh cruelly at the chest with chagrin.

On the third-floor landing Goldie stood with her hand over her mouth, but she had covered it too late. She had forgotten all about the password and now she had gone and spoiled Hesh's scheme. Chink had been so funny, she couldn't restrain herself. He had shimmied the dumbwaiter until it spun like a top, and unawares she had let go of the signal.

"Boy! You're funny, Chink!" she yelled at the top of her voice, so that Heshey might hear her. "You're so funny I couldn't keep it in. Even though I'm sore at you, I had to laugh right out loud or bust. I didn't want to give you satisfaction but I couldn't keep it in. I had to laugh."

She coughed loudly. Chink squatting in the dumbwaiter was pleased with his success but all the same perplexed. Something fishy was going on. "Why you making such a holler?" he asked. "What's a matter with you today anyway?"

Hesh opened the second-floor dumbwaiter cautiously. The ropes were quiet, Chink was still there, it had been a false alarm. Good. He stuck the pin and fastened that door. Now he had to slink noiselessly along the hall up to Goldie. He sneezed.

"What's that?" asked Chink nervously.

Heshey stopped breathing.

"What?" Goldie asked.

"I just heard somebody sneeze. You hear something?" He didn't like the looks of things. Something fishy . . .

"You musta imagined it. I didn't hear a thing," she said. "Hey, Chink, it still goes you wanna give me a ride in the dumbwaiter?"

"You bet," he said. "Hop in."

"Oh, not here. I can't climb in here. It's too high."

"Come on! I'll give you a shove."

"No, down in the cellar. I'll meet you in the cellar."

"Come on! I'll jump out and give you a boost."

Boy, wept Hesh pasted against the wall, here's where the whole shooting-match goes busted. But Goldie kept her wits and made a dash for the cellar.

"I'll meet you in the basement," she cried, and Chink slammed the door and began lowering himself rapidly.

Hesh caught her as she made the turn in the staircase. "You stay here and watch the ammunition." She was certainly a kid who knew how to use her bean. You had to hand it to her. He galloped to the fourth and fifth floors, locked the dumbwaiter doors with the clothespins, and returned. And it was only when Goldie saw him peg the door on her landing that she first realized what Heshey's scheme was. He had Chink trapped in the shaft. Chink couldn't get out. Goldie had visions of Chink rotting in the dumbwaiter, traveling up and down, from the basement to the fifth floor, hopelessly pushing and pulling himself as he sought for the rest of his life a way out. She was aghast.

"For crying out loud," she said. "That's the limit. Gee, I hate him like poison too, but I wouldn't do a trick like that on a dog! He can die in there!"

"For all I care!" Hesh chortled. Let her see him as he really was, tough, heartless, as strong as Chink, stronger because he used his head which was always mightier than ordinary strength, a hunnerd times mightier. Horses had strength. What did it get them? "Let him rot!" Hesh said. "He's got a lesson coming to him for a long time now."

"Well," exclaimed Goldie, "I certainly ain't going to stand here and let you kill an innercent kid. I'm going to take out all the clothespins."

Horror twisted Heshey's face. He forgot all about his strength. "Goldie! Goldie! Please!" he yelled and grabbed her arm. "Goldie, you ain't going to spoil everything after all my work? After all I done, you want to spoil my revenge?"

"Just for revenge it's better he should die?"

"He won't die, don't worry. Mrs. Strudel, she'll find him when she collects the garbage tonight."

"Still in all," Goldie said. "Still in all . . ."

"Goldie," Heshey begged. Already he could hear Chink pounding on the basement door with anger and fear. "Don't spoil everything, Goldie. Look, you want I should make you feel good like before? I know a hunnerd tricks, Goldie. Don't spoil it."

"All right," she said finally, giving in. "But don't mix me in it. I wash my hands of the whole business. I wouldn't be so mean to a dog."

Chink was traveling hysterically to the first and second floors, his terror mounting as he found the doors were closed here too. It was a trap. All his courage was leaving him. The prospect of being doomed to a lifetime in the dumbwaiter shaft rose like a black cloud to darken his mind. But every sound he uttered, of fear, of exasperation, of frenzy, was sweet music to Hesh. He placed the ketchup bombs—the grapefruit rinds with the delectable garbage—ready at his side. Chink was still at the second-floor landing. Hesh opened the dumbwaiter door.

"Chinkstink," he called down blithely. "Here I am. Come and get me, you dirty lousy Chinkstink."

"You!" Chink gasped in the middle of his tears. "You did it!" Curses, dirty words, threats! What he would do to Hesh's teeth, his belly, his nose, everything! Who his parents were, what he himself was, and what kind! "I, I, I, I, I . . ." fumed Chink.

"Yare?" asked Hesh pleasantly. "Is that so? Really? You don't tell me? Chinkstink!"

Chink grasped the ropes and started pulling himself up. Hesh darted back and stuck the clothespins through the rings, locking the door. First he would make Chink eat his heart out. For ten, fifteen minutes he would let him eat his heart out. He would be so kind as to give him that little pleasure.

"Let me out, you dirty rat!" Chink screamed from the shaft. "I'm gonna break every bone in your stinking head! I'm gonna knock your lousy brains out! Let me out!"

"Well," said Heshey affably to Goldie, "if it isn't our friend Mr. Chinkstink!"

"And you, Goldie," Chink raged, beside himself, "I'll get even with you if it takes me a million years and I drop dead! You dirty, yellow, stinking rat!"

"Aw, shaddap," Hesh said toughly, his sense of chivalry touched. "You keep your filthy mouth shut or I'll fix you for real."

Hesh could have broken a blood vessel with joy. Defending Goldie he was and he looked at her proudly. But in turning his head he saw a man. It was Max Balkan, plodding up the stairs, holding the railing. Hesh went to him at once.

"Please, mister, please," he begged. "Do me a favor. Don't move, don't say nothing. Just stay here and keep quiet for a minute. It's Chink. He's socking me again."

Balkan's ambition at this time was to find a place to lie down in and sleep. He had no energy to argue with Hesh or to find out what was going on. Bending his knees almost without taking the trouble to will this action, Max sat down on the marble steps and rested his head against the wall.

"Thanks, mister, thanks," Hesh said profusely. "Any time you want a kid he should go for something, call me. I'll go."

He crept up to the door of the dumbwaiter, silently pulling out the pin. Within Chink raged and cracked like a Red Devil firecracker ground with the heel on the pavement on the Fourth of July. Hesh moved back a pace, the ketchup bombs in each hand. Suddenly Chink found the door give. He swung it open. Wham! went the bomb from the left hand. It smacked Chink in the chest and the goo slid down into his lap. Chink's face opened with surprise. Wham! went the bomb from the right hand. This one caught him properly over the eyes. The ketchup dripped down his face. The coffee grounds, oatmeal, and peas clung to him like a Coney Island mudpack. Chink was thunderstruck and speechless, one big splotch of garbage and ketchup. Hesh slammed the door shut and fastened it with the pin before Chink could recover himself. He ran to his flat.

Hesh lay on the floor and rolled in ecstasy. For once! For once! Heshey in his way realized that in this world there were the meek and the proud. All his young life, cringing in the hallways, he had hated the proud and people like Chink. Torment, cruelty, and meanness. Now he had done it! Hesh remembered the spectacle of Chink, the mess all over him as he sat hunched up in the dumbwaiter. He remembered that searching, mystified, almost pathetic expression. Hesh writhed on the floor trumpeting until his mother came running up to him, thinking he had convulsions.

"What's the matter, Heshey baby?" she wailed. "What happened, darling?"

"Nothing. Nothing," he managed to utter. Then he thought of Mrs. Strudel and what Chink would get from her when she finally came to free him. Spasms shook his body. He couldn't control himself and abandoned himself to delirium. Heshey's mother thought her son's last moments had arrived and she uttered piercing screams of anguish.

Outside, Max rested on the steps. Even with all his weariness he had been able to appreciate Heshey's triumph. Good, he thought, good. His bruised spirit raised its feeble head like a daffodil bravely resisting the wind. Hesh was one of his, a compatriot in the army of the meek, his victory was Max's also. There it was, Max said to himself, power, the meek arisen for once among the proud. Power, victory, pride, and dignity, to stand a man—all these things Balkan longed for passionately, and thinking of Heshey and Chink, he also longed for childhood and peace. He rose from the steps, feeling like an unoiled hinge, and made his way to his flat.

Mrs. Balkan uttered one great powerful shriek: "Gevalt!"

They were around him in a circle, like hounds closing in on an animal. Max in the center swayed gently from his heels to his toes. Whenever he had hurt himself as a boy, his mother used to abuse him so severely that Max always ran away and hid. That was what Balkan wanted to do now.

"Well, for crying out loud!" said Ruth, in the low voice of deep wonder. "What in the world happened to you? You been rolling in the gutter?"

"What happened, Maxie?" his father asked, still holding the paper in one hand. "You fell down or something? You hurt yourself?"

"See," moaned Mrs. Balkan softly. "I worry for nothing. Accidents don't happen. Everything is all right. Don't worry. Spit on the floor. Magic . . ."

Rita came rushing through the door from Munves' room. "What's all the racket going on?" she shouted. "It sounds like ten people are getting murdered." Then she saw Max and gasped. "What hit you? A truck?"

"What happened, Maxie?" the old man asked again, pain in his voice. "Tell me, was it an accident?"

"He can't talk!" wailed Mrs. Balkan suddenly. "My God, he can't talk no more! Look, his hands are hanging down and he can't open his mouth!"

"Aw, I can talk, Ma," Max said apologetically. "What's all the fuss about?"

"Fuss! That's a fine how-do-you-do he gives me! Fuss! What happened?"

"I fell down," he said. "It's nothing. Nothing's the matter with me."

"Nothing's the matter!" Mrs. Balkan cried. "Fine, I'm satisfied. You had a good time. Every day you should come home like this." She broke off and squeezed her fingers with pain. "See, I worry, I worry for nothing," she moaned again. "A mother's heart can always tell. Just look at him."

"Aw, Momma . . ." Max said. "Don't raise the roof. Have a heart. I just fell down and broke my glasses. That's all."

"That's all!" Mrs. Balkan shouted. "It ain't enough. He should get his head broken too, he ain't satisfied. Look at him. The glasses busted, the clothes on him torn, he looks like he's going to drop dead any minute, and it ain't enough. He ain't satisfied. Mr. Fumfotch Number Two!"

"Mr. Fumfotch," said Mr. Balkan with disgust. "Maxie got hurt so you help him by hollering?"

"Who asked you?" she asked him viciously. "Hold the paper, read the *Bintel Brief*, shah, shtill!"

"Well," said Rita, "I could eat a Hungarian herring."

Max wished devoutly that they would get it over with. All he wanted was a couch to lie down on. More than anything else in the world he wanted just then to lie, to rest, to sleep, to forget; but at that moment Munves broke into the room as though he had been catapulted. He was exultant and had a mind only for his achievement.

"I've found it! I've found it!" he yelled. "Just think! A contribution to the knowledge on the subject and I found it!"

"What? What did you find?" Mrs. Balkan asked.

"Sealwudu! It's in Somerset! As I said, Rita. I proved it! It can't be anywhere else!"

"A great joy has struck me on the head," Mrs. Balkan muttered in Yiddish and went into the kitchen, exhausted. Crazy! Crazy! The whole bunch of them, from beginning to finish!

Quiet, peace, sleep, Max begged silently, but Munves, quivering with triumph like a plucked string, went right on. "It just goes to show, it goes to show how the most marvelous discoveries sometimes occur by accident. Just as in all science, progress paradoxically comes in the most unscientific circumstances. You remember, Max, how it was. I was sitting at my table, listening to Max, thinking of a hundred and one other things, when suddenly my eyes passed over Sealwudu placed by Kennedy in Essex. I give you my word, I have never studied the details on this particular spot before in my life."

"Please, Munves," Ruth said. "Tell him later, he's tired."

"No, Ruth," he protested indignantly, "I give you my word. I have never studied it before. Just looking at the notation in the glossary gave me a hunch that something was wrong. It didn't sound right from the context. I just had a feeling. And as a result of this . . ."

But at this point Coblenz came tearing into the room, so violently drunk, so hysterical with high glee, that Munves had to notice him and stop.

"Oh! Oh! Bung-a-low!" Coblenz sang. "Oh! Oh! Bung-a-low!"

They stared at him. He capered in a circle, waving his hands and dancing with his knees high in the air like an Indian brave at his ritual.

"He's drunk," Munves pronounced gravely, halting the details of his discovery. "It's a pity."

"Even so," Mr. Balkan muttered gloomily, "what's there to be so happy about?" All this racket upset him and he grumbled. Too much excitement, telephone calls, accidents, Sealwudu, and now a lunatic running all over the house. He wiggled his paper vigorously so that it would make a big rustle, and went across the room in his enormous suit, his shoes causing him to shuffle clumsily. In despair he ducked into the bathroom as a sanctuary and for some moments afterward he could be heard muttering to himself with displeasure: "Nu, nu! Columbus! America! Nu, nu!"

"Oh! Oh! Bung-a-low!" Coblenz chanted happily. "I stuck a pin in the woman's doorbell upstairs where the kids skate all the time without ball bearings. Then the bell keeps on ringing and ringing and Mrs. Fuggle-Wuggle hollers, 'Come in. Come in. Come in, please. Sammy, Sammy, the bell's busted. It's out of order, go downstairs and tell Mrs. Strudel she should come and fix it.'"

Once delivered of this speech, Coblenz set himself seriously to the business of running around the room. His face took on a rapt look and he dashed at great speed from one end of the room to the other, barely catching himself in time to keep himself from crashing into the wall. And all the time he shrieked his strange song about the bungalow at the top of his voice. Munves watched the performance with profound regret, Balkan, who felt sicker, with blankness, and Rita and Ruth were so angry with Coblenz that they kept on sputtering abuse and curses at him. But he disregarded them as though they had never been in the room.

"Sammy, Sammy," he mimicked the woman until he became distorted with fierceness, "go downstairs and tell Mrs. Strudel the bell's out of order. Oh! Oh! Bung-a-low!" And with a final insane burst of speed he was gone suddenly out of the door. The room became for a minute still and empty.

"Like a hysterical butterfly in a subway train," Munves mused, breaking the silence.

"Like a what?" Rita asked him in honest curiosity.

"Like a butterfly," Munves explained. "He ran out of the room like a butterfly that came into a subway train by mistake and finally flew out. I don't know how the image ever . . ." He stopped, collecting his thoughts and dismissing Coblenz from his mind. "Oh, yes!" he cried triumphantly, and the light came back to his eyes. "As a result of a completely accidental glance into a book, I daresay I have made a discovery that will rank importantly with the work done on the subject. I have no doubt that Krapp will make the correction on Sealwudu in further editions of the *Chronicles*, but what I wanted to point out was how completely accidental . . ."

"Oh, Munves, Munves! For God's sakes!" Ruth burst at him.

"What's the matter with you? For heaven's sakes, shut up and get out of here. Can't you see how tired Max is?"

Startled by her tone, for the first time Munves observed Balkan. "What's wrong?" he asked guiltily, immediately recognizing his thoughtlessness and grieving at it. "Don't you feel well? I'm sorry. I'm really sorry. Have you been in an accident?"

"I . . . I fell down," Max said weakly, hoping that this would put an end to it. "I broke my glasses."

"Really, Max, you have no idea . . ." Munves was tied up into a knot with contrition. How heartless he had been, how selfish! "Really, Max, I was so enthusiastic over . . ."

"Come on," Rita called him. "Let's go back to your room. I want to see about Sealwudu in Somerset."

"Yes, certainly, if you want to," he said politely. "If it won't bore you. . . . Max, I can't do anything, can I? Because if there's anything you want, just ask. Just tell me." And he was eager to atone for his selfishness.

"Thanks," Ruth said briefly, speaking for Max with maternal care, for he was in her competent hands and she would have them all realize that. She resented any interference. "He'll be all right, but thanks anyway."

Rita led Munves out. although he hesitated and turned his head toward his friend many times in deep sympathy. "I'm sorry, Max. I didn't realize," he mumbled unhappily, and they went out.

"I want," Max said slowly when all was quiet and everyone gone, "I want to lie down."

"Of course, Max," she said like a mother talking to a baby. "Here." She fixed him comfortably on the couch, resting his head in her lap. Ruth smoothed his hair back into place again and said "Sh, sh, rest, rest," in time to the movements of her hand at his head.

"Look at Munves," Max said softly. His voice was small and he spoke with hopeless resignation. "Look how happy he was with his crazy business about Sealwudu. Even Coblenz, even though he's drunk."

"Sh," said Ruth. "Rest. Rest. You're very tired."

"A mess," he cried feebly. "A nasty mess. I hate it."

"Nothing is a mess, Max. It's just the way things turned out. Sometimes," she said wisely, "things turn out in a funny way. Everything at the same time, all together."

Max felt so sorry for himself, he refused the sense of shame at his self-pity and buried the side of his face in Ruth's belly. His hand stole to her breast and he held it.

"Don't act like this, Max," Ruth said with tenderness. "You got things all mixed up. It was a bad day but you'll get over it and then everything will be all right again. Things will bet straightened out again, you won't feel so disgusted, you'll feel fine. I know."

"I'm not mixed up, Ruth. I knew what I was doing all the time, only things wouldn't turn out right. As if out of spite. I just can't do things. It's true. There's something the matter with me."

"No, there isn't," she said. "You're all right, only twisted up. Maybe this kind of a day is what you needed, in a way. To get you right again. To put you on your feet. You know, Max, in your heart of hearts, deep down, you don't want to be different. You don't mean it, not really. You want to be like everybody else, like normal people, sensible and reasonable and practical. No more crazy business with toilet seats and telephone companies. No more fairy tales about poetry and heroism and peasant shepherd boys. What I want to bring out is that maybe in a way Blenholt's funeral was a good thing for you. It'll make you see how crazy you've been and how impractical your ideas were."

"No, Ruth," he said, steadfast even now. The hand drew away from her breast and he lifted the weight from her belly. "They are good ideas."

"You're being stubborn," Ruth said, smiling as she made to tease him. "You don't want to give in. Now, admit it, Max. Be big enough to admit it."

"No, Ruth," he insisted, struggling reluctantly above her smiles, "you're still wrong. My ideas are right, and that's what makes it so hopeless. It's because I know what I want to do and because I can't. Don't you see, Ruth, I don't want to be like everybody else. It's dingy, dirty, small, and uncomfortable. This kind of house, the dirty dark flats, the cheap neighborhoods with the garbage cans, people hollering in the yards and kids fighting in the hallways—that's no way to live. See, Ruth, I know this. I don't want to go on living and wasting the years I'm going to have. I don't want to waste my life in some small job, making a bare living, sleeping and going to the movies. I want more. I want to live grandly, to have a nice home, cars, servants, power, money. And I want to live with a little majesty and dignity. To live like the men in the old days and in the great tragedies. I don't want to be like other people. I want other people to admire me, to look up to me. When I walk in the streets I want people to say: 'That's Balkan. You know, the famous Balkan,' or something. The way they did when Blenholt was alive."

His voice had been spiritless in spite of the long speech.

"Yes," Ruth said, with a maternal sigh. "I know, Max. I know. But that's just castles in the air."

"That's what hurts. They're Spanish castles. For me, not for other people. Why can't I have those things?"

"Because you can't. Because that's how it is."

"Blenholt had them. I keep on telling myself, if I stick at it, if I don't give in, to you and to everybody else, I'll be like Blenholt some day and then maybe I can have those things too."

"Yes, Maxie. But you're not Blenholt and you're not made like him. While you try to be like Blenholt, while you stick at it, you're wasting your life too. All you do is make yourself unhappy with struggle and disappointment."

"I know," Max said bitterly. "I'm not Blenholt. There's something the matter with me."

"Max," Ruth said, "it's not bad, being like other people. Millions there are and they're happy."

"They're not happy. They just have forgotten everything, they don't think, don't dream . . ."

"Max . . ."

"What?"

"What's the use of talking this way? You're just making yourself feel worse."

"I'm all right."

"Max . . . I hope this doesn't hurt your feelings. I certainly don't mean to offend you at all, but you're so tired and you feel so depressed and morbid, I think. . ."

"What?"

"Let's go to the Miramar. It'll really do you good. You'll rest."

"Ah, Ruth . . . I don't feel like going."

"It's an excellent picture," she said brightly. "You'll like it. Joan Crawford and Robert Montgomery."

"I'm tired, Ruth. I know you're being very kind to me and all. I don't want to seem ungrateful, but would you be angry with me if I said I'd like to be alone? I'd like to sleep."

"Oh! Of course!" Ruth said, rising at once and going for her bag. "I can imagine how you feel."

"Oh, I didn't mean there was any rush in particular," he said. "There's no hurry."

"That's all right," she said, cheerily. "I'll run along. Maybe I'll go to the movies by myself."

"Yes, Ruth. Go ahead and see the picture without me."

"You take it easy, Max, and I'll see you tomorrow. Something tells me you're going to be an altogether different person tomorrow."

"Well . . . how can I be a different person overnight?"

"I'll tell you what," Ruth said in a rush of good feeling. "I'm not going by myself to the Miramar. Joan Crawford's playing tomorrow and we can go together."

"Fine," said Max dolorously. "Fine. That's fine, Ruth."

Ruth went to the door and held it open for a moment. She looked at him and smiled affectionately. She rushed back to him, kissed him and beamed.

"You be good," she said in a mock stern voice.

"It's nice of you not to go to the movies for my sake, Ruth," he said, trying hard to match her kindness. "It's really nice of you."

"Don't be silly. It's nothing. I hate to go to the movies by myself. That's funny, isn't it, Max, but I feel so depressed and morbid when I go alone."

"Well, all the same," Max said, "I mean . . . it's nice of you."

After a while longer she walked out and Max, with the necessity of posturing and pretense gone, relaxed, his features dropping. He rose, walked unhappily around the room, and the feeling of self-pity welled in him and overcame him again. His mind perversely reached out to review in detail some one of the humiliations that he had met during the course of the day's events, and no matter how hard he tried to control his speculations, his mind insisted. Why, he kept on saying again and again, had he not stayed home with Munves and Coblenz? The peace that would have been his now tantalized him. If he had only stayed at home. He sat down on the couch again, his arms hanging at his knees, trying with all his concentration to think of nothing. But it was hopeless.

Mr. Balkan stuck his painted face through the door questioningly.

"Everybody gone?" he asked.

Max jumped a little. "Oh, it's you, Pop. What are you hiding there for?"

"How nice and quiet," the old man said. "What a pleasure the house is." Mr. Balkan stopped for a few minutes and relished the quiet in the room as one breathes the country air. He shuffled to the couch, alongside of Max, the paper still held faithfully in his hand. "Where were you, Max?" he asked kindly.

"At the funeral," Max said morosely.

"That's nice." His father paused. "Was it nice at the funeral? A nice funeral?"

"Well, you know, it was Blenholt's funeral. It was pretty big and all."

"You had a nice time, Maxie?"

"Well . . . you don't go to a funeral for a good time, Pop!"

"Something happened, ain't it, Max?" the old man asked gently, trusting not to rub Max's sores.

"Well, nothing much. See, there was a little trouble at a street corner with a woman with a car. See, she couldn't wait until the people passed, the people in the funeral parade. And the fellows who used to work for Blenholt, they got mad and ripped her tires. You know, they cut her tires with a knife. And then later on, when everybody had forgotten all about her, she came down the hall and tried to make a scene and there was a whole commotion and it was pretty terrible. And then I like a dope had to step in and try to help—well, it was nothing. I fell down and people tripped over me and fell on top of me. And I broke my glasses. And that's all."

The old man heard the recital out with sad acknowledgment, nodding his head and saying "Mn" at the appropriate halts to indicate his sincere attentiveness.

"And now it makes you feel foolish," he said. "Like you did something dopey."

"Now, it's all right," Max said, attempting a show of stoutness. "I'll get a new pair of glasses and then it'll be all over. I'll forget all about it in the morning."

"Sure, sure," his father assured him eagerly. "Try on the glasses from a pushcart on Havermeyer Street. You'll fit yourself better than any eye doctor and it will cost you maybe seventy cents, a dollar."

Max had no feeling to go on with his pretense at courage. He sat silent on the couch. Nor did his father speak, but an unmistakable current of sympathy and understanding flowed between them. With his father, Max felt, as with Heshey, among his own; and as for the old man, it seemed to him that somehow he had always recognized the sorrowful destiny in store for his son, and his fondness for him had grown all the stronger for that reason. Pain he felt for Max because he knew it would take his son time and suffering to resign himself. Mr. Balkan, in his clown's outfit, wanted intensely to say cheerful words to him, to tell him that he understood, to explain how these things were in the world, but he sought in vain for the words. And even if he had managed to articulate his feeling, it was doubtful whether he could have permitted himself to expose his emotion and reveal himself so nakedly to his son. Mr. Balkan was a Charlie Chaplin, a fumfotch, he begged for quiet and read the *Tag*, he craved to float in the still waters of continuous passivity. That was because his wry wisdom had instructed him long ago that in this world pleasure was often only the denial of pain. To close one's eyes and ears, to bury oneself behind a paper, to overlook telephone bells, to hide in toilets from excitement—that was comfort and happiness, and that alone. But now Mr. Balkan, seeing Max and remembering his own youth, wanted earnestly to commiserate with him, to gladden him, to explain that the years brought, at least, peace.

"Doo-dee-doo-dee-dee-doo-doo," he sang unhappily. "Max, when I was a boy in Kiev, in the old country, there was a dog, such a funny dog. The craziest dog you ever did see—all mixed up, you know. One part of this, another part and another and some more parts, but all mixed up. But one part was from a hunting dog somewhere, and he knew it was given him he should hunt. So when he went into the fields, the first thing he would look for the animals in the bushes. He could smell them or something, but he could always find them, and he knew it was asked from him he should get the animal. But he couldn't get it because the hunting dog in him, it wasn't strong enough or something. So he would yip and yip and cry like an angry baby, he would raise an awful holler, because after he smelled out the animal he could never get it."

The old man rambled on, half talking to himself. Max sat silent, immersed, trying not to think of the day's disasters and how peaceful it would have been if he had only stayed, and not succeeding.

"What a sad dog he was," Mr. Balkan sighed. "My, my, so unhappy. Always finding the animal in the fields and always scaring them away when he began yipping and crying. Such an unhappy dog, the saddest I did ever see, always torturing himself..."

He rose and picked up the sandwich boards. "I better go into the streets again before Madame Clara finds out I sneaked in here for a minute." He moved toward the door, shifting the straps and shaking himself to get the signs comfortably fixed on his shoulders. "Such a sad little dog he was," he said. "Such a sad little dog..."

Alone, said Max, alone. He stretched out his arms hopelessly and stared at the ceiling. His perverse mind would not stop; the scenes with Munves and Coblenz, the angry housewife on Rodney Street who told him his mother would have cried her eyes out, the smell of the Lincoln sedan, the abuse from the boys, his quarrels with Ruth, his fight with Chink—all of them flashed one by one to prick him. And all the time he kept on wishing and wishing that he had never set forth foot from the house this afternoon.

At last he went to the phonograph and busied himself selecting a record from the album. Balkan adjusted the disc and went to lie down on the couch again. It was the brokenhearted melody from Puccini's *La Bohème*. How sad it was, how pathetic. Sobs rose but he restrained them. But the warm trickles of water flowed unattended to his ears.

Blenholt's help, the hired cutthroats who had made him what he had been, were on the way home from the cemetery on Staten Island. They were packed five in the car, glumly looking out the windows. The salt smell of the bay and the sea wind disturbed them with its unfamiliarity; the car, too, had been driven into the ferry, and as they waited for the boat to paddle back to Brooklyn, they became restive and ached to get out. They had laid the great man in the ground, the ceremony at the grave summary and speeded after the day's events. They saw the yellow earth shoveled back into the big hole. A hot day it had been and full, and the smell everywhere had been of men's hips soaking underwear pants that were washed once a week.

The big gangster with the thick neck grew irritated with Firpo's fidgeting in the car.

"Hey, what's a matter with you?" he asked grumpily. "The pants burning on you?"

"I wish," said Firpo plaintively, "I wish I knew how the Dodgers made out today."

"Geezus," Thickneck muttered with disgust. "All he knows is the Brooklyn Dodgers and how Casey Stengel is gonna win a pennant with those bums. Go on, ask him, he knows all the batting averages and pitcher's percentages. Wadda schloonk!"

"Fffth to you," said Firpo briefly, producing the extraordinary sound by an involved operation that employed his lower lip and upper teeth.

It was dark in the hold of the ferryboat and the men sat moodily.

"Oh, give me a home," the driver broke out morosely, "where the buff-a-lo roam and the deeeer and the antelo—"

"Shaddap!" Thickneck glared snootily. "Wadda guy! They bury his boss, he sings!"

"He was a great guy," said a fourth individual in the gloom. "A great guy and don't you forget it."

"Well," said Firpo intellectually. "They all go. Sooner or later. Like a light."

"And nobody knows who's gonna be the next to go," confirmed the fourth.

"Well," said Thickneck importantly, "I always told him. 'Boss lay off the sweets,' I said, 'or you're a goner.' 'Never mind, Pip,' he said, 'never mind. I know what I'm doing." Well, now he knows."

"That's nothing," the driver said. "I told him too, he wouldn't listen. He sent Firpo out for candy, and Firpo, the luksch, he goes."

"Hey, Amchy," Firpo said uncomfortably to the fifth individual in the car, "what's a matter you ain't picking on me too? You got lockjaw?"

"Aw, shaddap," Amchy said, depressed. "I'm hungry. I ain't had a thing in my mouth all day. This funeral . . ."

"Look who's kicking," said the driver, bending confidentially to the boys in the back seat. "I got ten bucks on Boojum in the first race and I still don't know how he made out."

"Ten bucks," Firpo said, surprised. "To win?"

"Yare, wadda you think?"

"You guys," Thickneck said, "you smell bad. Here the boss gets put away, and you guys, what are you got on your minds?"

"A great guy," said the fourth individual dutifully.

"Say," exclaimed Thickneck, "you guys'll never see another one like him."

"You bet," the fourth gangster said reverently. "He was like a father."

"Hey, Pip," Firpo asked Thickneck, his brow troubled. "You believe there's a life after death?"

"Aw . . . shaddap. You're worse than my sinus trouble."

"Hah?"

"Haw! Haw! Haw!" laughed the driver suddenly. "Hey, Pip, remember the time the boss got so mad he went and swiped the rug out of the clubhouse and dumped it into the lot? Boy, I can see the puss on him like it was yesterday!"

Everyone in the car laughed but Amchy, who was hungry. Boy, they all remembered that one, they did, and the driver went on with the story about Marge and the little Polish tramp, but Amchy, dour and starved, broke it up.

"Laugh, you schmegeggies, laugh. Have a good time. But did you ever stop to think of the future? What's gonna happen to you now?"

They sobered immediately. Indeed, what was going to happen to them now? Who would own the Garage Association? The Car Washers' Union? Who'd be the new District Leader? The new Commissioner of Sewers? Who'd control the docks at the Market?

"Geezus," Thickneck said in a voice deep with regret. "He shoulda had a noperation."

"Who ever heard of a noperation for diabetes?" Amchy asked contemptuously.

"I had a noperation," Firpo said proudly. "Appendix. They just caught it in time. Another hour and I woulda been in the hot place." He grinned.

"You had a noperation?" the driver asked snootily. "I had one. When I was a kid."

"Wad you have? Ether or spinal?"

"Wadda you mean, spinal? I had ether."

"I had spinal," Firpo said triumphantly. "I know a guy, works in a hospital, he says the injections is much better these days, much better."

"Shaddap," Thickneck said impatiently. "You guys talk another minute about operations and I'll get an attack of sinus."

"One thing about the boss," the fourth individual said, "whatever he said, goes. He was a great guy. You got into a jam or something, O.K., all you had to do was go up and see the boss. He fixed everything up. He was like a father."

"Say," said Thickneck expansively, "we're gonna miss him. Every one of you guys is gonna miss the boss."

"You bet," Amchy said sourly.

"Hey, Firp, you schloonk," Thickneck asked suddenly as the thought struck him, "wadda you do with the little dope I told you to take to his house? The guy with the broken glasses?"

"What guy?" Firpo asked. "I told you, Pip. There wasn't no guy there in the car."

"See that? I'm nuts. I'm screwy. I put the little bastid in the car myself and he tells me nobody was there. You dopey schloonk!"

"Aw, fffth to you."

"Boys," announced Amchy, relishing his pessimistic message as he delivered it, "here's where the fun starts. What I wonder is what you guys are gonna use for money from now on."

At this silence filled the car. Each one, in his own way, sat back on the cushions and began worrying. All of them thought of Blenholt with affection and with genuine dismay at his passing. The future blurred before them for they did not like to turn their thoughts in that direction. Instead they mused on Blenholt and how it had been with him alive and what a gap he was leaving. They remembered his gorgeous appearance, garbed in white linen suit, yellow tie, and blue shirt; his sixteen-cylinder Cadillac with the chromium fittings; the feasts he gave at Joe's Restaurant and the parties at his modernistic apartment with the High Fidelity All Wave six-hundred-dollar radio set. They thought of the sense of highhanded adventure that he brought to their lives, the glorious splendor and their feats of valor and daring. While he lived they could feel powerful and strong, capable of anything they turned their hands to, and yet there was no responsibility or worry, for over them Blenholt hovered like an army of angels. Those days were gone, gone, they thought, the drying perspiration glazing their faces as they waited for the ferry to reach Brooklyn.

"You know, fellows," Thickneck said softly, "Blenholt was a regular king."

Silently they shook their heads in fervent agreement. The boat bumped against the poles of the pier and the ferrymen were banging up the gates of the driveway. The autos in the hold all set their motors turning and the boat shook with the racket.

Rita casually returned a strand of hair from Munves' brow to its proper place on his head.

"Really," she said, "this may sound like a T.L., but I think your research—Sealwudu in Somerset instead of in Essex—I think that was wonderful. I really don't know how you do these things. For one thing, I'd never have the patience."

Munves kept his head down to hide the glow of pleasure. "What's a T.L.?" he asked, modestly disregarding her praise.

"A trade last. Didn't you know?"

"What's a trade last?"

"Well, somebody says something complimentary about you and I trade it after you tell me a compliment you heard about me."

"But who said my compliment? You said it yourself," Munves pointed out severely, always a purist.

"Well," said Rita, laughing, "everyone can't be perfect all the time."

"You want me to say something nice about you? Even though I made it up myself?"

"All right, why not?"

"I think you're very pretty."

"Oh, Mendel," she squealed. "You're so cute!"

Munves flushed and opened a book. Marriage was a good thing, in many ways it had its attractions, and his mind flitted like a bee from the bathtub with the warm water to the vision of himself and Rita sleeping in bed without pajamas. He stole a glance at her fondly. She was chewing gum expertly, the cracks sounding like twigs snapping.

"I wonder," said Rita, wondering dreamily, "when Max and Ruth will get engaged? Or do you think they ever will?"

Engaged? Why hadn't she said married? Munves shied fearfully at the suggestion. Mendel Munves getting married! And what would his sister in Rochester say?

"Marriage," Munves said gravely, "is the normal phenomenon in the course of an adult's life. But, Rita, do you really think that Max is in a position to get married? After all, this isn't something you can enter into lightly. Now, take me. I'm supported by my sister's husband in Rochester. He sends me seven dollars every week. Can I . . ."

"Are you thinking of getting married?" Rita asked roguishly. "I wonder who the lucky girl is?"

That flustered Munves, the academic pose dropped, and he couldn't think of a word to say. Rita was all right. He was imagining things. She had no more idea of getting married at this time than he. Later on, perhaps, two or three years later, he might seriously think of it.

"Rita," he said, his spirits running high again," do you feel like giving me another dancing lesson?"

"I'd love to," she protested.

Across the hall from Munves' room, Max lay in the growing dimness as the sun moved behind the walls of the tenements. But the pathetic song from *La Bohème* was changing magically to the gay tunes of Strauss's *Tales from the Vienna Woods*, and the blithe melodies swelled and filled the room. The room, too, changed. The walls were painted in the most Continental of cream and gold colors and the lighting was now the rosy tint of dreams or half dreams. Balkan, on the couch with his eyes closed, swayed with the music.

A party was going on. Off to one side where Mrs. Balkan was reading the paper by the kitchen light, her lips moving as she formed the words, was the ballroom and Max could hear the cheerful snatches of conversation, the rustle of ladies in satin and chiffon, the soft swish of dancing shoes. Coblenz and Munves stood before him in the room standing like willow trees, in magnificent dark blue evening suits, the tails almost sweeping the floor, and they chattered glibly to Rita and Ruth, both wonderful to behold in French lace gowns. All held cocktails in one hand and cigarettes in the other, their presence the very epitome of the elegant mannerisms of the moving-picture rich. "Shall we dance, darling, cigarette, you never can tell, Oh, I say, really . . ." The butler passed with the cocktails.

They are waiting for the return of M. Sheridan Burlington. He is at a conference at which his steamship lines, Brazilian copper mines, and Midwestern utility holdings are staked against a giant international combine of financiers out to cut the throat of this young upstart who has been bringing them to their knees. If Sheridan wins he owns the world. Loses, and his entire fortune is gone. A tense moment.

"Just think," says Munves, his face drawn with the excitement, "if this merger goes through Sheridan will be the most powerful man in the world. A new Alexander!"

"It makes me shudder to think of it," Ruth says, shuddering a little.

"You're really not worrying, are you, Valerie?" Rita says. "You know Sheridan. Has he ever failed?"

"He is a man who has lost control over himself," Munves marvels. "A strange man. Railroads, banks, newspapers, factories, whole industries. What a colossus! And he goes on, fighting and defeating the Titans of finance until they are begging for mercy."

"He was always one of those persons," Rita says with awe in her tone, "who you know instinctively are controlled by some superhuman force, some destiny that eventually leads them to tremendous success or abysmal failure."

"Do you remember, Valerie," Ruth asks, "how in those early years none of us could understand him?"

"Yes, Valerie, how strange he was as a young man."

"I remember, I remember," Munves says, "in those days he strode the city streets, sunk in gloom because his early ventures failed to emerge. And people in a calloused civilization laughed at him. Absorbed in a million projects which his mind created, he moved through his poverty-stricken surroundings, contained and unknown, withstanding the ribald ridicule of his ignorant neighbors, a mystery."

"He is," Ruth says with a sigh, "still a mystery to me."

"That, I suppose, is the characteristic of genius, the quality of not being understood," Munves explains. "The rabble call him the Mystery Man of the New World. This manner is no affectation on his part but a spontaneous characteristic of his personality quite beyond his control. From the earliest years he had a conception of power and human dignity, and even then the desire for these qualities made him wretched in failure. Often he speculated on suicide."

"Do you recall, Valerie," Rita asks with a gentle smile, "that day Sheridan insisted upon going to the funeral of a man called Blenholt?"

"Ah, Valerie," mused Ruth, "how he admired Blenholt. And how far beyond him he has reached."

"Today," says Coblenz darkly. "But tomorrow?"

"Oh, Reggie," Rita says, "you're particularly disgusting. Are you getting drunk again?"

"Suppose he fails in today's conference?" Coblenz says, warm and dizzy from too many cocktails. "Suppose the Morgans and the Rothschilds win? He has everything to lose, railroads, mines, newspapers, and utilities. Everything. His entire fortune would vanish."

"Oh, you're drunk," Rita says.

"He can't lose," says Ruth, worrying.

"Oh, I wish the conference were over and he were back," Rita says.

They wait. Billows and billows of Viennese waltz music. Balkan floated deliciously in the sky, bouncing from cloud to cloud in time to the music from the strings.

The door opens. Enter M. Sheridan Burlington, dressed and postured to knock a person's eye out. His carriage is suave, his hair is streaked with gray, his face, lined with some mysterious preoccupation, is nevertheless nonchalant and debonair. Behind him are his four secretaries, carrying briefcases and ready to obey Sheridan's slightest whim.

"Sheridan!" Ruth cries.

"Yes, my dear. How well you look and what a pretty gown."

"The conference?" Rita asks, her eyes dreading the worst.

"The conference?" Sheridan asks blankly.

"Did the merger go through?"

"Oh. Of course, the merger."

"Well?" they all cry, on pins and needles.

"Of course it went through. What did you expect?"

"Marvelous! Sheridan! I knew it! Et cetera!"

"The most powerful man in the world today," Munves trumpets. "Nothing like it since the Caesars. Just think, Sheridan. You can start wars and stop them. Order crowned heads of Europe as though they are errand boys. Dictate to dictators. If the caprice seized you, you could paralyze the world!"

"What," says Sheridan at the terrace window doors, regarding the night, "a lovely evening."

"He didn't hear a word of it," Ruth says. "Sheridan, Sheridan, sometimes I think I hardly know you."

"Sir," say the four secretaries, "is there anything else tonight?"

"Nothing. Just see that everything is ready with the seaplane tomorrow."

"Very good, sir," say the four secretaries.

"Are you leaving again, Sheridan?" Ruth asks tearfully.

"Yes, Valerie. A short trip to South America."

"Oh, why must you always be flying off to one place or another?" she weeps softly. "Haven't you won enough money? Enough power? Can't you tear yourself away from your work and spend some time with me? I hardly know you . . ."

"There, there, Valerie. Let's not go into that all over again. Sometimes, indeed, I hardly understand myself. I seem," he says wistfully, his voice miles away in Canarsie, "to have something in me, something not part of me but which nevertheless drives me, and drives me to a destiny I don't know myself. Sometimes I feel as though another person, a stranger, lives in my body and forces my will to obey his imperious demands. Where will it all end, Valerie? Where will it all end?"

"I know, Sheridan," she says sadly, understanding that some mysterious force drives him and that he is not accountable for his actions. "I know Sheridan, I know Sheridan, I know Sheridan, I know Sheridan, I know Sheridan, I know Sheridan . . ."

"For God's sakes!" Mrs. Balkan cried from the kitchen. "Turn off the Victrola! How long you want it should buchert and buchert?"

Max rose slowly from the couch and rubbed the heels of his palms into his eyes. Circles appeared and he grew dizzy. He tried immediately to gaze clearly before him. He steadied in a short time and went over to the phonograph to stop the scratching of the needle.

"All right, Momma," he said, quite at peace.

The telephone rang.

"Maxie," Mrs. Balkan called, the bell bringing it to mind, "a man called Hot Water called you twice today. A Mr. Hot Water."

The bell rang again.

"Answer the bell," she cried. "Take the receiver off the hook."

"It's for Rita," he said. "Don't you want to answer the telephone?" Who's Hot Water? You got the name mixed up again."

"Look at him stand there while the bell rings," she said. "Answer it!"

"Hello," he said in a flat voice. "Yes, this is Mr. Max Balkan speaking . . . Mr. Atwater? I'm sorry I don't understand . . . The Onagonda Onion Producers, Incorporated! Well, hello!" The Onagonda Onion Producers, Incorporated! Max trembled with excitement. His hands grew so moist the receiver kept slipping out. "Yes, indeed, Mr. Atwater . . . Did you really? That letter of mine . . . I'm so glad you do! . . . Oh, of course! Of course! . . . I should be most happy . . . tomorrow afternoon . . . No, no, that's fine, it's no inconvenience at all . . . Thank *you!* Thank *you!*"

Mrs. Balkan came running out of the kitchen.

"What happened, Max? Who was it?"

"I did it! I did it!" Balkan screamed, dancing up and down. "I did it! At last!"

"What did you do? Tell me what did you do?" she begged, wonder consuming her.

"See, everyone laughed at me. I was a schlemiel, a fool, a nut, a kvetch." He was crying in his excitement. "I was a dope. I had crazy ideas. I had no common sense. I *did* it!"

"He's crazy!" Mrs. Balkan gasped. "God in Heaven, help me! All of a sudden he went crazy!"

"My watermelon ice cream idea was nutty, wasn't it? My telephone movie service was crazy? My subway private radio entertainment was crazy? Well, I'll show them this time! I'll show them, Ruth and Rita, Munves and Coblenz, everybody! I'm just at the start!"

Rita came running joyously into the room with Munves trailing. "Momma, Momma," she cried, but her mother was in tears. "Look," Mrs. Balkan said, pointing at Max. "Look. Gevaltenu!"

"See, Pathé News," Balkan gasped at his sister, choking with want of breath, "I'm a kvetch, ain't it? Well, Pathé News, I'll show you! Give me four years and I'll have my first million. I'll be rich, richer than Blenholt! I'll own mines, railroads, factories, whole industries—a Croesus. You wait and see. You all think I'm nutty but you wait and see. Operator, operator, Rutledge 6-1743. Hurry, please," he shouted to the telephone.

"My God, Rita," Mrs. Balkan wailed. "What should we do? What will happen now?"

"What happened, Max?" Rita asked. "What happened here?"

"I'm still crazy, I'm a kvetch, all right, just wait and see. Hello, Ruth? Ruth, this is Max. Max! Ruth, the conference was a success, the merger went through. No, I mean the onion company is taking my crazy idea. See, everyone says I always have crazy ideas, how to make a million dollars telling Rockefeller how to make a new kind of sauerkraut. Everyone laughs at me like Rita. Well, I sold my first one. Let them laugh now! Let Rita call me a kvetch now! Tomorrow I got to go to the Onagonda Onion Producers, Incorporated, to talk business with them. I got an appointment. You know who they are? The Onagonda Onion Producers, Incorporated? The biggest association of onion producers in the world! They're going to take my idea! They like it! I'll be rich, richer than Blenholt! See, I sent them my onion idea just like all the others, only this time they're taking it! My idea, it's to bottle onion juice just like everything else.

Some idea, isn't it? No peels, no odor, no tears. Saves all the fuss. Sell millions and millions more onions every year by making its use more convenient. As I said in my letter. Some idea, ain't it? Well, that's . . ."

He went on, weeping and shouting, hopping on one foot and then on the other. Rita turned to her mother.

"Did they really take his idea?" she asked incredulously.

"I don't know. What can I tell?" she answered, relieved as she began to perceive that it wasn't insanity after all. "What happened?"

"Max sold one of his ideas." Rita was awed.

"It's only the start too, Ruth," Max was crying into the telephone. "Ruth, you'll see. It's only the beginning. One thing leads to another. I'll go from one project to the next. In four years I'll show you my first million dollars! Then I'll go on! I won't stop! You'll see, Ruth. I'll own railroads, factories, banks, mines, newspapers! I'll be the richest man in the world . . . like Tamburlaine!"

"Well," said Rita, impressed to the point of stupefaction, "I'm a Russian kazotzky! Momma," she said, but it was an afterthought, "Munves and me just got engaged." The effect had been totally ruined but not for Mrs. Balkan.

"Ruchel darling!" she cried, overwhelmed by joy, her eyes opening wide with rapture. "My baby!"

Night fell over the sleeping tenements of Williamsburg. In his dreams little Heshey smiled sweetly as he saw again the vision of Chink, squatting in the dumbwaiter, splotched with ketchup and the garbage from the grapefruit bombs. Coblenz whispered in his alcoholic daze, "Latabelle, I love you. Where are you, Latabelle?" His mind went roaming the fields of daisies, seeking Latabelle. Munves rested serene, calm and happy over his contribution to the intellectual progress of the race with his placing of Sealwudu. And engagements did not worry him. They brought one closer to bathtubs and naked couples in bed at night, as Rita managed to show him in a half hour. An engagement wasn't marriage and he still hadn't a job.

Across the hall Mrs. Balkan dreamed of an elegant wedding at McCarren Hall, with bridesmaids and flower girls, the rule being strictly enforced that everyone wear a tuxedo. But her daughter Rita had had a hard day and now slept profoundly, her mouth opened a little. Poor Mr. Balkan, skinny in his winter underwear, was sitting up in the daybed, spitting piously. He had just dreamed a bad dream and it worried him. And as for Max himself, he lay alongside his father pretending he was asleep, but it was all he could do to keep from sobbing aloud. Joy and happiness had been poured into him as though he had been a bottle, and so full was he, he had to choke every once in a while or suffocate. Achingly he longed for daybreak and he had visions of bottles, rows and rows stretching across a map of America, full of Balkan's Onion Juice, No Peels, No Odor, No Tears.

In Washington Cemetery, over in Staten Island, the earth of Blenholt's grave was beginning to settle and there wasn't a sound for blocks.

NINE

Morgan, Rockefeller, Balkan, Rothschild

"O God!"

In the early morning the yellow sun came in splashes of brightness, its full light kept out of Max's room by the flapping of the wash on the line outside in the yard. Max lay still, on his back, and opened his eyes, striving to place himself, to discover why in that half second that carries a person from sleep to awakeness, he had uttered in his mind that profound plea to God. He followed the rusty trail on the ceiling where water had seeped through to the plaster. Afraid and exultant he was, he knew, and he groped uncertainly to recall the reason for his condition. Onions! Atwater! The Onagonda Onion Producers, Incorporated! His body jerked into a sitting position with the full realization.

How had he ever forgotten? Max remembered lying awake in bed all night, dreaming of bottles of onion juice over America and hearing his father cough and spit. He must have fallen asleep early this morning and that accounted for his heaviness. Max smiled happily as his mind went over the details of his triumph last night. He had been near hysteria with joy, dancing and crying and shouting, the saliva bubbling at his mouth. Balkan thought with pleasure of the awed expression on his sister's face. A good girl after all, he thought charitably, sisters and brothers always fought around the house, it was normal, and he forgave her everything. Even kvetch. Then the thought came of Ruth when he had phoned her. She had been speechless. For many minutes Balkan lay on the bed, speculating on Ruth's feeling for him now. In one stroke he had won her respect and it delighted Max to imagine how impressed with him she would now be, how femininely shy and reserved since his projects had vindicated themselves over her objections, and finally how proud of him she would now feel. Oh, good, good! Max chortled, but immediately he grew worried, his face clouding. The water stains on the ceiling, from excessive staring, were now assuming the shape of a man's face, the expression on it grinning. With an effort Max turned his mind away from the picture on the ceiling and wondered why he worried in the midst of rejoicing. He had unconsciously sent up a prayer to God not of joy but of fear, for pity and help. Why? Then it came crashing sickeningly into him that this might fail too, that something might go wrong here as always, that he might emerge only more ridiculous than ever, especially after all his howling and crying. It was impossible! Max sought to bring back the exact words Mr. Atwater had used over the telephone. Very enthusiastic over your letter, he had said, glad to get it, could you come down for a chat tomorrow? And we should like to recompense you for your trouble. Impossible! All the others had sent him formal letters of rejection, some had not bothered to reply at all. Mr. Atwater had called three times! Max remembered with a heartening rush of feeling. Of course! He was just worrying needlessly.

Soberly, Max pushed aside the blanket and sat on the daybed. He worked on his nose, rubbing the nostrils so that he might breathe more easily, and saw his father sitting at the window. The old man was ruminantly paring his nails with a penknife, the yellow sun on his pale face emphasizing his years and his weariness. Max looked at his father for some time. He was in his trousers and slippers, his underwear hanging limply from his chest and arms. It seemed to Max that his father rose in the middle of the night, for no matter how early Max awoke, his father was always there ahead of him, washing his head with cold water and soap or else filing his fingernails close to the skin. Without his gorgeous make-up and his costume Mr. Balkan looked only old and weak and tired.

"It will be a nice cool day," he said, noticing that Max was awake.

"What difference does it make?" Max asked cheerfully. "It's all the same, hot or cold, wet or dry. I should worry."

"Nice when it is cool," the old man reflected, looking out into the yard. "The pavement, it don't get so hot, my feet don't burn."

Max suddenly felt miserable. He was no good. All those fine theories he had—human dignity, power, and heroism—and here he had been letting his father go on supporting him with his ridiculous job with Madame Clara. How tired he was, how old. Remorse made Max wretched and he punished himself with suffering, telling himself that it was no excuse that he had never thought of his refusal to go to work in this light before. Looking back now, caught in deep emotion, Max saw that his faithfulness to his ideals, as far as it concerned his father at least, had been impractical and unreal. There were duties to people, to his father for one, and possibly to Ruth also. People had demands on you, you owed them something, and idealism might be virtuous but no excuse. And there was something wrong with ideals that had made him neglect his father all these years. Feeling welled in Max. Perhaps it was this way with him now because his own victory last night and his warm expectations for today had released him from thoughts that concerned only himself and his own troubles. It was time he realized his shameful treatment of his father. In a painful sweep of sorrow and regret, Max resolved then to do all he could for his father from now on, get him money, make it possible for him to quit working for Madame Clara, even arrange for luxuries and special comforts.

"Pop," he said, "I was kind of crazy last night about that onion business—it seemed too good to be true and I couldn't hold myself in. But on the level, Pop, it looks pretty good, they ought to give me a nice piece of money."

"That's nice," he said, but Max could see that his father was unimpressed, either not believing or not caring.

"Well, what I was thinking—well, I don't need the money. It's not as though I've been bringing money into the house. They might give me two, three hundred dollars. Maybe five. I don't know. It's about time you stopped walking around in the streets for Madame Clara."

"Shah, shah," said the old man softly. Giving away money he hadn't received. Bad luck. "Wait and see, Maxie. Wait and see what happens."

"Pop," Max said, affection for the old man overcoming him, "I want you to take it easy. I want you to stop, to get off the hot streets. From now on I'll do the supporting in the house. It's time you stopped and I began. And I'll make money too. I'm just beginning. The Onagonda Onion Producers is only the first. It takes a little time to get in, but once you've made a start, it goes faster. I'll sell one idea after another now, people will get to know me as a sales promoter with ideas, one job will lead to another and I'll be bringing a lot of money in . . ."

"What are you talking about?" Mr. Balkan cried, a little angry because he was embarrassed. "We'll see, we'll see."

"Don't think I don't realize how rotten I was about never going to work," Max blurted out. "Only I always thought it was better not to do any work at all than to have a job that made me feel sick; work that didn't pay anything or mean anything only made it harder for me to be able to do something important later on. I was always afraid of being deadened, of having my mind dulled for me by this kind of life . . . That was what I always felt, and I still think it's right, but I guess I couldn't afford it. All it meant was that my fine ideas gave me a good time and you did the work."

"What are you talking about?" his father asked. "Are you crazy? Keep quiet, you talk in bunches today."

"Ah . . ." Max said, flushing and uncomfortable because of his outburst before his father. He bent down to lace his shoes and hid his face.

"Work," said Mr. Balkan in a softer voice, talking out the window, "two kinds of work there is, honest and not honest. Standing in a stationery store all day, pressing in a shop, cutting fur—that's honest work and it's no good. When I was a boy I ran away from it. I couldn't do it. It made me sick, too. That's why I went to Yudensky's and became an actor."

He paused and scratched his head contemplatively. Was he comparing sales promotion and commercial ideas with acting? Max wondered. Was he kidding him? His father sometimes had a sly sense of humor and he might be using it now to set Max at ease again.

"The other kind of work is ganavish," Mr. Balkan went on. "You know what 'ganavish' means, Max? To make a living not honestly, by tricks, by schemes, not with the hands. Gamblers, actors, poets, artists. This is good. It is easy, you can have a good time playing, but you need luck. Luck and good tricks. Sometimes," he said, "the craziest tricksters and schemers are the biggest successes, I don't know what it is."

"You mean there's still hope for me?" Max asked, smiling at his father's joke. He felt much better now. Max rose and stamped his legs to straighten the trousers. "So I'm crazy, Pop? That's a nice thing to call your son the first thing in the morning."

Mrs. Balkan came into the room, a glass full of orange juice in her hand.

"All that for me?" Max asked, agreeably surprised. "What's the holiday? Just because I'm going to get a million dollars today from the Onion Corporation you want to get on my good side? You want to get in good with me?"

"He talks from fire and water," Mrs. Balkan said breezily. "Look who's making a million dollars already. Label, you want breakfast?"

"Later, later," he answered. "What's the rush?"

"Later, when is later?" she asked. "He don't eat all day, he makes me sick. How can a person live if he don't eat?"

"All right," Mr. Balkan said. "Make me a glass of warm milk, not too hot, not too cold."

"Paticler. It must be just right. You can get good and fat from a glass of warm milk, neider cold, neider hot."

Max drank the glass of orange juice with great relish, regarding it as a token of respect on his mother's part, for she seldom bothered to squeeze the oranges, holding it a waste to drink only the juice.

"Good," he pronounced, wiping his lips with his tongue. "A whole glass."

"America with the orange juice," Mrs. Balkan said. "The fingers get busted from pressing the oranges, and the pits, go and find them out."

"You know, Ma," Max declared, his eyes shining as the thought came to him, "why should you have to squeeze orange juice? Why shouldn't you be able to go into the grocery store and buy it in cans? You buy everything else in cans, even whole chickens. Why not orange juice?" He pondered the idea.

"Sure," agreed Mrs. Balkan enthusiastically, seriously considering the scheme. "Why shouldn't it be, Maxie? America with the inventions, why shouldn't the grocery have it in cans just like everything else?"

His mother actually approved! That was respect. Any other day she would have laughed at him, made fun, called him Mr. Fumfotch Number Two. Now all he had to do was say something and she was immediately impressed. The first taste, thought Max, that was how they were all going to treat him from now on. Everyone.

"You can sell this, too?" Mrs. Balkan asked Max. "You can get good money for it? Go, try, I'll be the first customer in the grocery to buy orange juice in cans."

"Hey, Pop," Max cried, "what do you think? You think it's a good idea too?"

"Shah, shah," said the old man. "So early in the morning."

"So early in the morning," Mrs. Balkan said. "What difference does it make, so early in the morning?"

What a way to start the day! Max was joyous. First of all there was his appointment with Mr. Atwater and that was enough to send a warm glow over his whole day; then his mother's respect seemed to him to be only the foreshadowing of the way he was to be treated by everyone in the future; and finally he had thought of this really remarkable idea of canning orange juice. No Squeezing,

No Straining, No Pits. A good idea and a dandy slogan. Max thought how universal a habit orange juice was with the American family. Canned juice would have a maximum selling potentiality of millions, the whole country. Just the restaurants and soda counters alone! A cracker jack of an idea! Why hadn't somebody thought of it before? First thing he would do would be to get in touch with the Florida and California Orange Growers' Associations. Better still, and Max's eyes grew vacant with the prospect, why not interest a group of capitalists in the idea, buy up orange groves, open canning factories, distributing agencies, and sell the product himself? A little too ambitious, too fast for him at this stage of his life, but why not? One bold stroke! Max's brain went running with plans and schemes.

"Max," Mrs. Balkan said, "here's your new shirt. I washed it last night and pressed it already for you."

"You did?" Max said. Holy smoke! "Gee, thanks, thanks, Ma."

"What time must you go by the onion company?" Mr. Balkan asked from the window.

"Oh, I got time. He said after lunch, two o'clock."

"Well, don't go too early. You'll only have to wait and get all excited. Don't get worried, take it easy and quiet. No rush."

"Don't worry about me, Pop," he said. "I'll be all right."

Max felt eight feet tall and three hundred pounds in weight. He put the good shirt away to save for the afternoon. "Daddy is a hand-organ man, is he," he sang happily. "Hand-organ Johnny am I, I, I, I . . ." A crazy song he had learned in school when he was ten years old. They worried about him, orange juice, his new shirt with the tab collar, what time he had to go to the onion people. Let Rita call him kvetch now! Max would like to see her try.

"So Rita is engaged," Max said. "Well, mazel tov."

"Engaged!" said Mrs. Balkan, shaking her head and hiding the joy because it would be unbecoming. "What good does it do? They can keep company for years. Where is Munves got a nickel to support a wife and open up a house? A nice boy, educated, knows a million languages, but he needs someone should tell him to wipe his nose."

"Don't worry, Mom," he said. "Munves will get a job soon. They'll get married."

He'd give Munves a job himself. In the canned-orange-juice business, maybe. Five thousand a year, ten thousand. Max grew dizzy for a moment as he pictured himself handing out jobs to all the people he liked and wanted to help. He saw himself sending out checks of ten thousand dollars apiece to his friends. Better still, he would have his attorneys attend to it. "Dear sir," they would write, "enclosed you will please find check for ten thousand dollars in accordance with instructions from our client, Mr. Max Balkan. You may return the money whenever you feel in the position to do so." Max would take care of Heshey, endow the kid, send him through college, carry him through life. He would buy his own mother and father country homes, servants, cars . . . Max grabbed hold of himself abruptly.

"Don't worry about Munves," he said to his mother. "He'll be all right. I'm going to get washed."

At the bathroom door he met Rita in her kimono. Any other day, and Max knew it well, she would have knocked past him to be the first inside, but this morning she waited at the door. "I'm in no hurry in particular," she said. "Go ahead."

"Oh, it's all right, it's all right. I can wash in the sink," Max said. "You go first."

Holy smoke! That was respect! Coming from Rita, too. In a flash Max forgot every quarrel, every bit of unpleasantness he had ever had with her.

"Well," he said conversationally, "how does it feel to be engaged?"

"Oh, I suppose everyone's going to ask me that now. It's a real nuisance." She was quite at home already with her engagement, what was all the holler about? "How does it feel yourself to be on the way to your first million?"

Balkan laughed. "The first million is always the hardest," he said, and, laughing, went into the bathroom.

Nice, nice. Rita was a nice girl. As the lather washed from his hands under the faucets, Max felt a sense of satisfaction in the lather, because somehow it seemed in keeping with his stature as a man of affairs. These small things, they counted, they were the signs of the man. Take Thickneck, the thug, who tried to help him at Blenholt's funeral. You could tell immediately his self-assurance from the way he walked and spoke. Or the moving-picture actors, casually smoking cigarettes on the speeding trains to Monte Carlo. Max soaped his hands again and worked up another lather, feeling sure of himself, confident, a man among men in the world.

Outside in the living room, Mrs. Balkan, who believed that anything was possible in crazy America, asked Rita if it was really true that Max was going to get a million dollars from the onion people. "I can't believe it," she said. "How can people give away money for nothing?"

"It's not a bad idea," said Rita, altogether serious. "After all, wouldn't you buy a bottle of onion juice yourself? You wouldn't have to bother around and smell up all the knives in the house. No odor, no peels, no tears, like Max says. Of course, nobody's going to give him a million dollars."

"I know, a million dollars. You just say a million dollars," Mrs. Balkan said. "But what did Max do he should get money for it?"

"See, Mother," Rita explained kindly, "you don't understand. You're from the old generation. You think that people can make money only from something you do with the hands. Well, this is a new age. Ideas are sometimes better than a piece of goods or a day's work in the shop. Brains are more important than strength. That's why people go to college these days, they should learn to be able to be a professional."

"America," Mrs. Balkan cried. She couldn't understand the whole business. How would people give money for something they couldn't touch or see or smell? "Like Mr. Fumfotch says, Columbus, look what you started. In 1492 what did Columbus do?" she sang gaily, her shoulders shaking happily as she remembered the tune of her early days in the new country.

"Listen," said Rita knowingly, "I know a girl, she won five hundred dollars in the *Evening Post* Famous Names contest!"

"Five hundred dollars? For nothing?" Mrs. Balkan was so impressed she had to stop laughing.

"Well," said Rita triumphantly, "you see?"

"What do you want from me?" Mrs. Balkan protested. From her daughter's tone of voice it seemed as though she were against Max. "I wish him bad luck? I don't want him to get a fortune? From my part, the sooner the better, with all my heart."

"Shah, shah," muttered Mr. Balkan superstitiously at the window. "You talk so much about millions." He spat to break the spell of the bad luck their discussion might cast over Max's trip to the Onagonda Onion Producers, Incorporated. And these things were important too. You mustn't think ahead, no one must congratulate you beforehand, or the whole day's prospect would be ruined. Mr. Balkan knew of many, many cases to the point.

Max in the bathroom had heard every word. They were talking about him already. The feeling of pride, of achievement, of success made him gurgle through the foam as he brushed his teeth.

After breakfast Munves came in. He entered shyly, tender emotion and preoccupation restraining him like a bad headache. How did you act with your girl friend the first morning after your engagement had been announced? The duties of intimacy were new to him and disturbing. Further, the victories of last night with Sealwudu had grown a little stale in his mind and a sharp sense of foreboding and distrust over his engagement had come to take their place. Last night had been wild, with Max crowing like a lunatic and himself hysterical over the proper location of Sealwudu. One thing had led to the other, it was in the air, and without much sense or logic he had lost himself in a state of exultation. Why? Why? Then he had felt that engagements were not so fearsome, as Rita had deftly hinted for his information, so long as you hadn't a job. And his mind had been full of calf smells, hot-water baths, and bodies at night in bed. But this morning, this morning...

"Good morning," he said.

"How are you, Mendel, darling?" Rita cheerfully called out from the kitchen, and Munves quaked within himself as he picked out the note of possession in her voice. Gone, gone, it was all over with him. Marriage!

"A cup of coffee," Mrs. Balkan said. "Mendel, darling, you want a cup of coffee? You had breakfast?"

"Thanks, thanks," Munves protested hastily. "I ate." Her mother disturbed him too and he wondered why. What had she to do with it? Mrs. Mackenzie, he remembered. That was what Max called her, she had told him herself. The Great Campaigner, and he promised himself to read Thackeray's *Newcomes* again. Munves felt weak and overpowered, in a den of lions, and he wished he could find a way to turn.

"Well," called Max cheerfully from the bathroom, bending over his shoes, which he was shining on the toilet seat, "how does it feel to be engaged?"

"Oh, Max!" Rita cried protectively. "You're impossible!" She slammed the door in mock petulance.

Munves winced and sat down. Hopeless, finished . . .

"Mendel," Rita said at once, "you're so brilliant you ought to be teaching at a college."

"You really think so?" he asked feebly, trembling a little. "Well, I haven't even my doctor's degree and these days you can't do anything in a college without a Ph.D. It would take three or four years," he added hopefully.

"Three, four years!" Mrs. Balkan said. "What's the matter with a little business?"

"Business," Rita said disdainfully. "Mendel is a scholar, he's no businessman."

"Well," said Munves, brightening at all this, "I was talking to Gottschalk at the college last year. He was very nice to me, remembered my name and the work I used to do. He said maybe there would be something for me in the fall. In the extension courses. I'll see him the first thing in September. Of course, it's only a part-time job, it doesn't pay anything to speak of."

"Business," said Mrs. Balkan, "is nice too. Everybody don't have to be a school teacher to make a living. You get into a nice business, you open up a store, you can work yourself up." Mrs. Balkan distrusted education. What had it done for her son? For Munves? It was all right for schoolchildren but a regular man who made a living was often so ignorant he couldn't even sign his name, and the more uneducated you were the better businessman you would turn out to be. Take Freddie's father, the one who owned the meat market. Educated people didn't know enough to wipe their noses.

Munves shivered as Mrs. Balkan explained the differences between educated people and businessmen. Nearer and nearer this was bringing him.

"Business," he finally said, smiling depreciatingly, "I don't know a thing about business. What would I do with a store?"

Mr. Balkan had been in the bedroom, getting dressed as he prepared for the day's work. Now he came into the room, in the baggy checkered pants, the suspenders hanging down. "What are you talking about buying a business?" he asked Mrs. Balkan importantly. He remembered about the eight hundred dollars in the bank. This time he had caught her and he had rushed out to seize his victory. "With what can you put a couple into business? Where is the money?" He stood in the center of the room, questioning, proud, gloating.

"All right," Mrs. Balkan muttered, taken aback. "Mr. Fumfotch is here again. Mazel tov. How do you do?"

Munves perked up immediately. He was always worrying and worrying, he told himself, the result of a sensitive temperament easily upset. He couldn't get a job at the college and there wasn't money enough to open a business. They were only talking.

"You know," he said in a spurt of optimism, "in spite of everything all my life I think I wanted to own a store. A delicatessen store."

"A delicatessen store?" Rita asked in amazement.

"A delicatessen store!" Mrs. Balkan exclaimed. "You could make a fortune with a delicatessen store in a good location."

A delicatessen store. With what? Mr. Balkan asked himself. No sense. First she hollered at him because he talked about the eight hundred dollars and now everybody was on the point of opening up a delicatessen store. Routed and defeated, he shuffled back to the bedroom to apply the powder and paint. "Nu, nu," he mumbled. "Columbus!"

"Yes," said Munves, enjoying the sensation he had created. "I have a theory about delicatessen stores. In the old days the wits of the times gathered at coffeehouses and inns. Will's, the Mermaid Inn, and so on. We haven't places like that today, and I often think of a delicatessen store with tables in the back where people can drink tea, eat meat sandwiches, and exchange the gossip of the day."

"In Williamsburg," Mrs. Balkan said, keeping her temper under control and disregarding Munves, "all the young ladies, they don't cook like the older generation. Lunch they eat in the delicatessen stores with the baby carriages outside, and in the night when the husbands come home from work, they throw together pastrami, cole slaw, potato salad, and finished, supper. A delicatessen store these days is a fortune. Good, Mendel, you're a smart boy, a delicatessen store."

"Did you ever see, Rita," said Munves dreamily, "the revolving knives they use to slice corned beef? I'd like to have a delicatessen store with a revolving knife like that. See, the contraption has spikes that hold the meat in place, the knife is protected by a tube of plating so that it is safety proof and you can't cut yourself even if you tried, and you can go as fast as you like. The corned beef moves up automatically to the blade. Those machines are really wonderful."

Munves spoke with a gentle glow in his eyes. There was beauty in everything and all that was required was the perception to recognize it.

"You mean machines you work by hand?" Max asked, coming out of the bathroom.

"Yes, by hand," Munves replied. "You've seen them too?"

"You should see the electric knives," Max told him. "They're really marvelous. Almost human. Do everything but talk."

"Really?" asked Munves. "Well, but in spite of everything I think I still prefer the hand machines."

"I know a fellow," Balkan said importantly. "He was on the coast once and he told me that there wasn't a single Jewish delicatessen store in all of San Francisco. The American delicatessen stores, yes, but not the Jewish kind. One in Los Angeles but not a single one anywhere else. He told me a fellow could make a fortune with a delicatessen store in California. You know," Max said, growing warmer the more he thought of it, "if you opened a store here you could expand and develop a chain. Have certain distinguishing characteristics—new style of fixtures, special services, a catchy trademark and make it stand for something—and you could operate a chain in every big city in the country!" A good idea too, Max thought. Outside of a few of the largest Eastern cities, America didn't know what Jewish delicatessen stores were like. Gentiles liked the spiced meats too. You could always see them in the Jewish stores buying. What ideas he had today! This morning canned orange juice, now the delicatessen chain. As soon as he settled the onion matter, he told himself, he'd get right to work on the others. Balkan's future spread before him like a path in a field of daisies. The feeling of power, of achievement, of moving to fulfill his destiny!

"I was thinking," Munves insisted softly, "I was thinking only of a delicatessen store with tables in the back for tea and talk."

What was all this? Rita wondered. Where did it get her?

"How much money," she asked, "do you need to open up a delicatessen store?"

It was one thing to think about a store and talk. Rita was bringing the proposition too close to home and Munves felt uncomfortable. Here he had been feeling so happy with his thoughts. Why did she have to come and spoil everything?

"Just a couple of hundred dollars," said Max glibly, speaking as the man of affairs in the house, the one who was consulted on business matters. "You buy everything on consignment, on credit. You pay your bills only when the money starts coming in. You could open up a store on a shoestring today."

"But how much?" Mrs. Balkan wanted to know.

"You could start on five hundred dollars," Max pronounced judiciously. "Maybe even less."

Munves began to perspire.

"Where am I going to find five hundred dollars?" Mrs. Balkan muttered hopelessly, half to herself.

Munves began to breathe again.

"Don't worry, Mom," Max said, thinking of onions. "You'll get it. I got a feeling you're going to be a rich woman pretty soon."

The wrinkles on Munves' forehead came back. They had it all settled. All he had to do was sit back and keep quiet. They would take care of everything for him. And he had to open his mouth about a delicatessen store! He had to start it himself! If he could have only managed to keep his mouth shut, how much easier it would be for him now. Munves cursed those extravagant moments when he said everything that came into his head without forethought. Matrimony, as it approached, appalled the etymologist. The routine of his world would be upset. In a tangle of money worries he would lose forever the calm and peace on which he prided himself as a scholar's due. It was all the fault of Sealwudu. If it hadn't been for his discovery last night and the waves of enthusiasm it had created, he would have never been caught, somehow he would have managed to restrain himself. He must have been crazy. Marriage was no joke. You couldn't decide upon it as rapidly as Munves had yesterday. Munves looked for consolation by telling himself that an engagement wasn't marriage, that often long periods took place between engagement and marriage, that he would never get a job with Gottschalk at the college—those goys had everything sewed up for them—that Mrs. Balkan couldn't open up a delicatessen store for him without money. Munves liked his friend Max very much. He understood the philosophical system on which Balkan operated or tried to operate, appreciated its points and had sympathy for his ideals, and wanted to see him succeed in his desire for power and money beyond his wildest dreams. But fervently, fervently, Munves hoped the onion people wouldn't give him too much money.

A delicatessen store, sighed Munves, and his mind began to picture the revolving knife with the spikes that held the corned beef in place, the safety plating and the automatic movement. Munves could see himself turning the blade, slicing neat pieces of meat and watching them fall into a flat pile on the oiled paper. "One pound, missus? Two pounds?" In his vision Munves tossed the packet of meat expertly on the hanging scale. One shrewd eye on the needle. "Forty-nine cents, please. One price to all, no bargaining." The scholars, the wits—famous men, writers, painters, actors—in the back of the store were drinking yellow tea in glasses and talking with the excitement of brilliant conversation ... It wasn't so terrible, running a delicatessen store. He rather liked it. But marriage! Some day, Munves promised himself and hoped it would not slip his mind, he would ask Mr. Cohen who owned a store on South Twelfth Street to give him permission to slice a pound of corned beef on the revolving knife.

Time passed. Mr. Balkan had already applied the white apostrophes in the corners of his eyes under the black circumflexes, and except for the great collar and his insane shoes, he was prepared for the day's work. Ruth had come in, directly after she had finished breakfast at home, and had made up her face, and forthwith she had told Max that his little success with the onions was possibly the worst thing that had ever happened in his life. "This," she had said with maternal wisdom, "is going to ruin you for the rest of your days. You'll never be the same now. If you never had a break with this craziness, maybe you'd forget about it in the end and everything would be all right. This way you'll never get over it, all your life you'll keep on trying to sell another idea, and I hope you don't actually think for a minute that this will ever happen to you again. Lightning," she had said, "never strikes twice in the same place." She knew. A friend of hers once won fifteen dollars in the *Daily News* Crossword Puzzle Contest, and day in, day out, all this friend did was to enter one contest after the other. She spent her whole life on them, had no time for anything else, and the worst part of the whole story was that she had never won a cent since the *Daily News*. "See?" Ruth had said. "You see, I know what I'm talking about."

Max had heard her out good-naturedly for he could tell, somehow, that in spite of everything Ruth said she too was impressed. The legend of Balkan was growing and reaching her too. Ruth had only to notice how he was being treated now by his mother, by Rita, by Munves. There was a difference, Max chortled, dancing inwardly with pleasure, it was all different. When he got the check —two hundred at least, maybe five—a fellow he had heard of once received one hundred and fifty dollars just for a slogan he had thought up for Camel cigarettes—when he got the check, he would bring it first thing to Ruth, wave it before her and smile. Picture in his head: Max bending smoothly before her, holding the check. Ruth reads, eyes wide, unbelieving. Oh, Max, Max. "Never mind, Ruth," he had said easily to her when she had been ranting at him. "You just leave this to me."

He had looked at her knowingly and then Mrs. Balkan had come in to tell her about Rita's engagement, and Ruth had been obliged to grow appropriately convulsed with gladness and feminine stickiness over the news. The silent communion of women in the war between the sexes. In a minute Rita and Ruth had gone off to the bedroom, leaving Mrs. Balkan with a feeling that she was unnecessary, ungratefully discarded. There was much for them to talk about. But in all the fuss over the engagement Munves had somehow been completely neglected. He had sat silently in his corner, trying to look cheerful and pleased even though there had been no one there to look at him. And after a few minutes of neglect his thoughts returned to revolving knives such as were used in the better delicatessen stores.

"Mendel Munves!" Ruth now said, emerging from the bedroom in a show of exuberance. Munves almost jumped, he was that startled after all this time. "Engaged! Well, how does it feel to be an engaged man?"

He looked up, grinning feebly. Engagements were tricky things, the trickiest. To get engaged, there was no great ceremony. All you had to do was to let the word pop out of your mouth and the next thing you knew you were married. Sealwudu, Munves cursed in his mild way, Sealwudu, I hate you, why did you have to come into my life?

"Not," Ruth continued thoughtfully, a little sadly, "not that it isn't about time. How long do you fellows want to be bachelors?"

She looked at Max Balkan. In his own private joy he had to wince. Just as, earlier that morning, he had felt he owed a debt to his father, so now he felt obligated to Ruth. In one glance he could see that in spite of her show of gladness, she was really envious and hurt, that she thought that marriage for her, too, was long overdue, that he was failing her. Ideals, Max thought, the surge for power and significance, to live life in its turmoil, its fervor and variety—those desires were expensive. You always had them at someone's cost and in his new strength he determined earnestly to make up for everything to her. He drew her aside.

"Ruth," he said, "I know how you feel. But it's really silly to be jealous of Rita's engagement. It shouldn't make any particular impression on you. After all, it's just the same with us as an engagement. Sooner or later we'll be married, you know that."

"Sooner or later," Ruth said mournfully. "Sooner or later..."

"I'm going to make money," he affirmed. "This is only the first thing. You'll see..."

"Castles in the air!" she wailed. "This is no way. You can't make a living out of nothing. You got to get a regular job. Here Munves gets engaged, already he thinks of opening a delicatessen business, Rita says. That's the right way. And what are you doing? You're lucky for once in your life and you think it's going to last forever."

Max was going to answer but at that point someone knocked on the door. He was glad at the interruption. Later, when he would be holding the check before her eyes, she would see, she would see... the picture of him bending before her, waving the slip of paper...

"Come in," Mrs. Balkan cried.

It was Coblenz, now looking very respectable indeed in a gray topcoat.

"Mr. Bungalow!" Mrs. Balkan greeted him. "Everybody's in the house now like a block party. Go, Max, run out in street and tell all the people to come upstairs, by the Balkans there's a party."

"I came to apologize," said Coblenz, bending at the hips, "left and right for yesterday. For your sweetheart, apologies, fifty cents, worth a dollar I should drop dead right this minute."

And remembering the pearl peddler, they all had to laugh and laughing, they forgave him, but not Mrs. Balkan.

"Look at him," she cried shrilly. "Mr. Bungalow in a novercoat. What's the matter, it's November all of a sudden?"

"See," said Coblenz, stepping up to her. "America. A wonderful country, a new world, everything goes by inventions—radios, subways, airplanes, talking pictures, phonographs, telephones, everything. See this coat, Mrs. Balkan?"

Mrs. Balkan inspected the garment. "Well?" she asked.

"Spit." He held the coat conveniently within range.

"Spit?" She stared at him, her hands at her hips. "Meshuggeh for good!" she said.

"Go on, Mrs. Balkan," Coblenz urged her. "It's all right. Spit."

"Spit, Momma," Max called out, laughing. "Go ahead."

Mr. Balkan looked at them from the bedroom as though they were all mad. He was always the kind of man who was bothered intensely when he saw furniture or pies or automobiles destroyed in the moving pictures, the heedless destruction of material causing him real anguish. And here they were about to spit on Coblenz's coat. "What's the matter with you?" he cried indignantly through his paint. "A brand new overcoat, perfectly good! Why should you want to spoil it?"

"Spit!" Coblenz commanded.

"I will not!" It was a trick. Mrs. Balkan was used to Coblenz and his crazy tricks.

"Go on, Momma, spit and get it over with," Max told her. "It's all right. He just wants to show you something."

Mrs. Balkan bent delicately over the cloth. "Nu, nu," Mr. Balkan exclaimed, powerless. A tiny drop of saliva on the coat. It remained there in a globule, like a spot of mercury. Coblenz shook the coat. The drop slid off. "See?" he asked.

Mr. Balkan couldn't make it out. Too much. He went back to the bedroom and decided to finish his dressing no matter what turned up.

"America with the inventions," Mrs. Balkan marveled.

"Cravenette," Coblenz announced. "Waterproof. Sheds water.

I bought it in Macy's for twelve dollars and seventy-five cents. Lot of money."

"Macy's? Everybody talks about Macy's. Wherever you go," Mrs. Balkan said reflectively. She had seldom ventured out of Williamsburg. To Klein's, once or twice, yes, but that was near the East Side, familiar territory. The department stores farther uptown she had never visited. "Some day, if I live and everything is well, I must go and see Macy's."

"See, Mom," Max said, "that's an idea just like the ones I get. I bet the man who thought of waterproofing cloth got a million dollars for the idea."

"A million dollars for a coat!" Mrs. Balkan uttered, impressed. "America!"

"Hey, Mr. Morgan," Coblenz said maliciously, "what's the matter you never thought of this? You got a million ideas in your head all the time. Why didn't you get the idea first and make a fortune for everybody in the house?"

Max didn't have to say a word. Coblenz would soon learn that this tone would no longer do. Ruth was the first to speak up, but Rita and his mother followed promptly. They told him all about the Onagonda Onion Producers, Incorporated, in detail: what the idea was, Mr. Atwater, three times, mind you, three times they called! Max was going to the office to get paid. Today he was going.

"No peels, no odor, no tears," Munves chimed in helpfully. "A very good slogan. Catchy."

Coblenz found it hard to believe. "No kidding? You mean to say that Max actually sold the idea of bottled onion juice? Well, Mr. John Pierpont Morgan, I beg your pardon, I beg your pardon on my hands and knees."

While this had gone on, while everyone in the room, except Max himself, had kept on explaining the miracle, Max had tried to restrain himself but in the end he couldn't help himself; he began giggling outright. The finish of all humiliation and petty abuse! Just think. Coblenz had spoken to him in his insulting manner and everyone sprang to his defense. A day ago and they would have joined forces with Coblenz. What a tribute!

"Shah, shah," Mr. Balkan cried from the bedroom, unable to forbear. He had the big shoes on now and had difficulty in getting around in the crowded room. "Don't talk so much. You'll spoil everything. You'll give him a keneinerhurra!" They were ruining Max's luck for sure. The old man spat but they went on.

"Well," Max said finally with the free generosity of a great man, "it's really nothing. You wait. Give me a little time and then there will be something for you to talk about. If you really want to know something, Coblenz, what do you think? Munves and Rita just got engaged.

"I was wondering what you were looking so happy about," Coblenz said to the etymologist. Roped in. Well, good for you, Mrs. Balkan, congratulations. "Well, Munves, how does it feel to be an engaged man?"

Munves grinned, this time with some heart in him. All you had to do was get engaged and people paid attention to you.

"Hey, Mr. Bungalow," Mrs. Balkan called out, "maybe it's time you should get married too? Maybe you'll stop being so crazy all the time? You know, if a man don't get married, it's no good for him. He can get good and sick."

"On the level, Coblenz," Max said in a matter of fact tone, enjoying his new position in life, "you want to take care of yourself. All this business—burning the candle at both ends—that's no good for you. Seriously, you want to cut that out."

"Look who's talking," Coblenz said drily. "Dirty capitalist."

Everyone roared happily at the joke. Max himself tried to hide his smile of pleasure but wasn't fast enough.

"Millay," Munves said cheerfully, taking an interest in the proceedings.

"What, Mendel, darling?" Mrs. Balkan asked solicitously.

"Edna St. Vincent Millay," Munves explained. "'I burn my candle at both ends, it will not last the night, but oh, my friends, and ah, my foes, it gives a lovely light.'"

He beamed with delight. One thing about him if he had to say so himself...

"Educated," Mrs. Balkan said proudly, as she caught on. "See?"

"Hey, professor," Coblenz asked, "who's Latabelle?"

"Latabelle, Latabelle, Latabelle, don't tell me," Munves said, his face drawn in absorption. The scholar sticking his fingers into the dusty shelves of his mind. What was it? Mrs. Wohl had said something about a Lottabelle. "A sickness?"

"Marvelous!" Coblenz gasped with wonder at it. "You know everything?"

"For a minute," Munves said modestly before his success, "I thought it had to do with literature. Keats. You know, *La Belle Dame Sans Merci* ... But one thing about me, if I have to say so myself..."

"Rita," Coblenz said, "let me be the first to congratulate you. You've got a wonderful man and a real scholar." He turned to Balkan. "Will you, if you please, rub my head?"

"Rub your head?" Max asked.

"Yare. For luck. I'm not kidding."

Max, in fine spirits, rubbed his head.

"Wait for me, Coblenz," Mr. Balkan cried as he saw him going toward the door. The old man was fully attired and late. He slipped through the boards (Beauty Treatments By Experts) in a hurry and went to him. "I'm going downstairs too." All this excitement, all the noise, all the people in the house. The streets would be a relief by comparison. He was glad to get out of the house.

"Maxie," he called back from the door, "remember what I said. Don't go too early, you'll only have to wait. Take it easy. Don't get excited. Speak slow, don't mumble. Good-bye and good luck."

As soon as they were gone Ruth rose. "Come on, Rita," she said. "We might as well be going too. Let's get there before the rush."

"Where you going? What's the rush?" Mrs. Balkan asked.

"We're going to Klein's, Mother," Rita said, "We got to get some clothes."

Mrs. Balkan approved. "That's nice," she said. "Good." While the girls were in the bedroom for powder and rouge, she whispered to Max so that Rita might not hear her, "I'm going outside for a minute."

"Aw, Mom," Max said. She was going to tell all the neighbors about Rita's engagement and the telephone call from Mr. Atwater, and she knew that Rita would raise the roof if she knew. It would be all over the house. "You don't have to tell everybody. Wait a while and they can find out for themselves. I don't want you to go."

"Who's telling everybody?" she protested. "I'm just going out for a minute."

She slipped past the door before Rita came back to the living room. Actually Max was pleased by this. Let them all know. His mother would tell the story to them, would impress them, and Max took keen delight in picturing what an effect his success would make on the neighbors. That housewife on the third floor yesterday, who thought that he was hitting Chink when he was all the time saving Heshey—what would she say now? And Chink too? This was the way he liked it. To walk in the halls with everyone gazing at him, pointing him out. That's Balkan. Max Balkan. You know, the fellow who . . . The beginning only, the beginning. Max rejoiced.

"Where's Mother?" Rita asked, as they returned.

Max pointed solemnly to the bathroom door. "We can't wait," Rita said. "Tell her we went already." Rita walked over to Munves. The etymologist grew tense to keep himself from flinching before her. She kissed him on the cheek and his face grew flushed. "Good-bye, darling," she said. "Well, Max, I don't have to tell you, I wish you all the luck in the world."

"I still think it's crazy," Ruth said, a little depressed because she wasn't engaged, she couldn't kiss Max in that casual manner. "But, of course, I hope you have a very successful interview. Naturally."

"Have a nice time," Munves said, faltering as he tried to show his ease in his new state.

"A nice time?" Rita repeated. "Mendel, we're going shopping. To Klein's."

"Well, I meant . . . I hope you get a nice dress."

"Come on," Ruth urged. "Let's get there before the rush gets in first or we'll be killed. We'll be here waiting for you when you come home, Max. Come straight home, we'll be dying to know what happened."

They walked out. "Gee whiz," Munves said sheepishly, "that was a silly thing to say, have a nice time. Sometimes a fellow says the first thing that comes into his head. Well, I guess you got some work to do before you go to the office there. I'll go to my room." He held his hand out to Max, man to man. Balkan wondered at it, finally shook it. "I wish you," his friend told him sincerely, "every success." And Max was alone in the room, they were all gone.

"GA-DA-LA-MON-OP-OLI, GA-DA-LA-MON-OP-OLI." In one great burst he sang the Italian tune *La donna è mobile*, which served in this case to check the overflow of joy. He was a bottle again, the homage of the morning had poured into him beyond capacity. All the time he had been giggling and choking no matter how hard he tried to restrain his glee and to show the proper outward calm. Not a single schlemiel all day. No jokes, no insults. Everyone respected him. They all wished him luck. Even Coblenz had been impressed, had asked him to rub his head.

This was how it would be from now on. Personal dignity to begin with. There would be an end to humiliation and ridicule. Like Heshey yesterday, Balkan felt himself among the proud. The first step on the ladder. The first king had been conquered. Like Tamburlaine. Now there would be time for heroism, for poetry, for the high adventure of life. He was right and had proved it with himself. There was no need to live in squalor, a small man hidden in the tenements. The truly great men rose above their surroundings. Take Blenholt. Take himself now, on the way. Max kept walking around the room, up and back, in that peculiar gait of his which with its delaying circular hip movement resembled more than ever the excited sniffings of a person with a bad nose cold. From time to time he had to stop, to sing the Italian song, to clench his hands, to rub his head, to laugh aloud and utter cries of delight. Max chortled, uncontrolled.

There was still time. He went downstairs and bought a paper. Trying to collect himself, to constrain himself, he read the adventures of the characters in the comics on the next to the last page. Benny was teaching his kittens to swim.

TEN

Latabelle, I love you

"CONFOUNTIT! CONFOUNTIT!" said McCarthy in a whimper. "Holy gee! Holy gee!"

Brannon, a twelve-to-one shot, came in in the second race and it was a great surprise to all the roughnecks and taxi drivers in the cigar store when the news came pegging in over the wire. McCarthy had just dropped three dollars on a sure thing called Moneybags.

"I wouldn't mind, only you know how I play them. Always a long shot. What's the use of getting even money? That's what I always say. So once in my life I decide to play the favorite and then a long shot, he has to come in. It's enough to drive a guy insane."

"Aw, quit squawking," said Coblenz, feeling pretty disgusted over Brannon too. What luck was Max Balkan bringing him anyway? The excitement that morning at Balkan's house had left Coblenz with a mood of depression that looked as if it would last all day. Here, Max was going ahead, making a fortune out of onions. Munves and Rita were engaged, people following the normal lines of human behavior. And all he could do was to go to the cigar store and lay bets in the company of McCarthy, Louis XI, and the other driftwood of Williamsburg. Coblenz had the feeling that he was surely sinking to the gutter. A drunken bum he would end up, with lice all over him. If he lost he would buy the late sporting edition of the *Brooklyn Eagle* and worry over the result charts at Empire City until it grew late enough to buy tomorrow's *Morning Telegraph.*

And if he won, they'd all go to Yusselefsky's for a quart. A rotten, goyish life, no meaning, no spirit, no morale. "Russia," he said morosely, "has four generals, November, December, January, and February."

"Holy gee," exclaimed McCarthy, inspired. "That's a hunch. Janus in the third. Hey, Louis, give me the *Journal*." Beside Janus in the third race the handicapper had noted "Prob odds, 15–1, never beat much." "All the same," Mac insisted. "A hunch is a hunch."

"Hey," said Coblenz, "anybody here jump Brannon?"

"Me, sure, I had him. Hah!" It was Louis XI.

"Holy gee," said McCarthy, "it's enough to drive a guy insane. That cockeyed dope has to pick him. How much did you have on him, XI?"

"Two bucks. Not bad, twenty-six back for two."

If McCarthy had put his three dollars on Brannon he would have had thirty-nine dollars back now. "You dirty louse," he cried, "why didn't you open up? What did you want to keep it a secret for? You're always sucking around. When you know something, why the hell don't you open up?"

"Listen to him! Listen to him!" Louis piped. "As if I didn't tell him! And what did you say? Nuts, you said. Nuts. Good for you, next time you'll listen."

"Hey," Coblenz said, "you got a system? What made you pick Brannon?"

"Aaah, you, too," exclaimed Louis. "You're just as bad as McCarthy. Didn't I say I got a winner yesterday for the third race? Ain't it? And where were you yesterday? You never showed up. Then I don't open up. I suck around and keep my mouth shut when I know something. You guys, you guys . . ."

"All right, all right," Coblenz said. "What I want to know is what makes you pick Brannon?"

"I told you," Louis said eagerly. "It was a cinch. Brannon, he led all the way in the sixth race at Belmont last month, then he stopped in the finish. A mile and a quarter. So I figure him for a seven-furlong horse and that's what he's in today. The mile and a quarter was just too long for him."

"The dirty bastard," said McCarthy bitterly, referring to Louis.

"Aw, shut up," Coblenz said. "Lay off."

"Don't get the impression I'm a sore loser, Coby. That's not the idea. What burns me up is that the cockeyed bastard knew all along that Brannon would win and he just wouldn't open up."

"I told you," Louis muttered. "I told you Brannon, only you wouldn't listen, you said nuts. It serves you right."

"What's that? What's that?" yipped Mac. "You trying to get fresh with me? Another peep out of you and I'll get a radiator cap off a cab and knock it through your head. I'll take nothing from you, you cockeyed bastard."

Louis picked up last Sunday's rotogravure section and began reading with great concern, frail and human.

"My folks, now, they were good Jewish people," Coblenz said reflectively. "They worked for a living."

"Catch me working," said McCarthy in a mournful tone.

"Sure, everybody can beat the races. For example."

"Well, what are you going to do when a thing like that happens? But on and off my system works."

"You got a system too?"

"Now don't get wise with me, Coby. You're my pal, but I don't take nothing from nobody and you know that well enough. What's the matter with my system? It's all right if you play six races a day."

"Sure," said Coblenz. "Take a horse from one to ten, double it, add a million and then run like hell."

"Confountit! Confountit!" McCarthy wept. "All I need is one good winner a day and that's enough. Two and I clean up."

"Ho! Ho! That makes me laugh. Indeed that gives me a good laugh," said Coblenz gloomily.

They sat without further talk, watching the taxi drivers outside toss nickels toward the cracks in the pavements, the toss nearest winning all the coins. The bell rang and one of the hackmen broke away from the game for his cab, running out to a call. McCarthy sniffed contemptuously at the poor dope who worked for a living.

"Hey, Coby," Louis XI said, "I passed your house today. A lady was saying a guy in your house got five hundred bucks just for an idea from an onion company. That on the level?"

"Five hundred bucks!" gasped McCarthy. Holy gee! Holy gee! "You know the guy, Coby?"

"Yare, I know the luksch," Coblenz said, more depressed than ever. Five hundred dollars! He had spent all morning trying to hit the fourth railing on the fence of the school on Keap Street because he knew that if he walked away without a hit he'd never have any luck with the horses today. All that work and Balkan made five hundred dollars just with an idea about onion juice.

"That's nothing," Louis said. "I know a guy, he knows a guy who got a prize in the Irish Sweepstakes. Twelve thousand five hundred bucks."

"Holy gee!" cried McCarthy in tears. "You kidding me, XI?"

"Naaah!" Louis protested. "This guy, he went nuts with the money. Real nuts. He's in Bellevue right this minute."

"Hey, Coby," Mac said, getting a grip on himself and growing more ambitious than ever before in his life, "what good is all this bushwah doing us? What about the next race?"

"Hey, Louis," Coblenz said, "what about the next race?"

"Go to hell," Louis said, turning sulky. "I wouldn't tell you guys nothing. You don't mean nothing to me."

"See, Coby, see him closing up? Listen, you cockeyed bastard, you better talk or I'll break your lousy head in two."

"I don' wanna."

"The hell with him," Coblenz said compassionately. "What's the favorite?"

"Couleedam, nine to five."

"Nuts. We can't make no money with him."

"Hey, Louis, on the level now. What do you know?"

"I don't want to say nothing. If he wins, what do I get out of it? And if he loses, you'll hit me."

"Come on," said Coblenz kindly. "I'm down to my last five bucks."

"I don' wanna."

"What's the matter with Janus, like I said?" McCarthy asked. "A hunch is a hunch."

"Louis, you got a horse in this race? If you don't know, say so."

"I don' wanna say. You'll hit me."

"All right. Louis, I won't hit you. You know that."

"McCarthy, he'll hit me if the horse don't come in. And if he wins, what do I get out of it?"

"Come on, you cockeyed little runt," McCarthy said kindly. "Nobody's going to do nothing to you. You satisfied?"

"Pipper," Louis XI said.

"Pipper, Pipper, Pipper," Mac said, running his eye down the handicapper's column in the *Journal*: " 'Trials smart, might do. Ten to one.' Nuts."

"See?" asked Louis triumphantly. "Nuts. What did I tell you? That's what he always says. Then I suck around. I don't open up when I know something."

"Three furlongs, 7/5, Bel tr fst .35 one-fifth," Coblenz said, reading the latest workouts in the form chart. "Not bad."

"Still nuts," Mac said. "This ain't no three-furlong race. One mile."

"All right. Still .35 one-fifth, that's real running."

"*Louisville Times* picks him to win, Vreeland calls him second, A.P. Consensus third," Mac read aloud, growing impressed. "Well, maybe this horse can do something. Hey, Louis, you sure?"

"Hey, what do you want for ten to one? A guarantee?"

"What's the matter you like him so much?" Coblenz asked Louis.

"Look, like you said, Couleedam is the favorite. He runs a mile last race in one thirty-eight some fifths. All right. Pipper finished third last time out, length, length and a half, but the time was one thirty-seven flat. And it was only his third race of the year. The way I got it figured out Pipper's getting better all the time and Couleedam's been running some time now. Besides, I got a hunch."

"BALDY!" McCarthy shouted.

"Hey, wait a minute," Coblenz said. "You don't have to listen to what this cockeyed runt says."

"What the hell. BALDY!"

The bookie came in and McCarthy bet five dollars on Pipper to win. Louis XI, the seat of his pants hanging pathetically in untidy creases from his thin thighs, shivered when he saw the money change hands. He bet five across, to win, to place, to show, digging the fifteen dollars out of his winnings on Brannon. It was a great deal more than he had intended betting but he felt that he had to impress McCarthy with his good intentions. Coblenz gave the bald-headed bookmaker five dollars, his last, sat back and looked out the cigar-store window at the taxi drivers.

"Out of time, out of space," he said, smoking a cigarette. "Poe. Edgar Allan Poe. There goes my last five bucks."

"Ten to one," Mac said. "Maybe better odds when the prices come over the wire. Fifty-five bucks coming back." The thought held him enchanted. The bookmaker in the cigar store paid off on the telegraphed quotations from the gambling ring at the racetrack, not on the probable odds the newspaper handicappers calculated.

"Look, look, look!" giggled Louis, holding up the rotogravure section. Picture of a lady in a corset. "My, my," he said, enthralled. "Speedies by Vanitie. The Talon fastener makes it 'Speedie' on and 'Speedie' off. Fashions your figure into graceful lines. Five bucks. Number two-two-oh."

"Geeze, what a cockeyed dope," Mac said hopelessly.

"A thing of beauty is a joy forever, it's loveliness never something or other," said Coblenz in a haze. So they paid little Balkan five hundred dollars for his onion juice. The figure was probably exaggerated, but still in all ... What a lucky crazy luksch. It just went to prove Coblenz's main contention: the world was completely nuts. Logical, too, he acknowledged. Nutty world, nuts become the greatest successes. Kid Tamburlaine Balkan would go far if his nutty streak stuck with him. He'd own the world. Ten years from now when Coblenz was a lowdown drunken bum he would turn to Balkan and ask him for a handout. It was always a good thing to have rich friends.

Now Munves was getting married and soon Balkan would be getting married too. Coblenz would end up in the gutter. Coblenz was worried. There was a moral in everything for those who cared to look and had the time, and from Munves and Balkan, Coblenz could tell that he was hopelessly on the downgrade. Pessimism and reckless disregard were all right for kids, for adolescents, but you had to get over it, you had to grow up. It was all right to think that the world stank out loud while you were in school, but a time came into everyone's life when you became a man and were done with childish luxuries. What was being a man? Grown up? Well, a man was sensible, reasonable, practical. He didn't get drunk, he didn't have too many morbid ideas in his head, he didn't go fight City Hall, he kept out of company like McCarthy and Louis XI. "My folks," Coblenz said with resignation, "they were good Jewish working people."

"Gee whiz!" cried Louis, still marveling at the pictures, turning the pages. "Who woulda ever of thought . . ." The wonders of the rotogravures—brassieres, panties, corsets—kept him fast. "What dames . . ."

"Shaddap!" McCarthy cried tremulously. He was at the ticker. "It's corning in."

Louis dropped the paper fearfully, all fun driven from his head immediately, and even Coblenz forgot about his friends and his own fate to wait for the results. It was his last five bucks and he'd be cleaned. The ticks came and Mac pulled the ribbon. Louis XI paled.

"You cockeyed bastard," McCarthy wailed, too sad to be really angry.

Couleedam had won. Pipper came in second.

"Russia," said Coblenz, heartbroken, "has four generals, November, December, January and February."

"Where did Janus come in?" Mac asked excitedly. "I'm going to break his lousy head if Janus . . ." Janus came in fifth.

"Well, hell, second is better than fifth," said Louis weakly. He should have kept his trap shut. This was what he got for trying to be a regular guy with these louses. He inspected the ribbon. "Anyhow," he said for consolation, "Pipper paid only six to one."

"You cockeyed bastard," McCarthy wept. "Five bucks I threw out the window. I shoulda had more sense than to listen to you."

"Aw, quit squawking, quit squawking," Coblenz called, sick at the stomach. Three races today, not a single win, broke. Balkan had put a hoodoo on him when he had rubbed his head. Maybe he took too long to hit that fourth railing on the school fence. He was cleaned.

"I ain't squawking," Mac protested vehemently. "Only what gets me sore is if that little runt don't know what he's talking about he ought to keep his mouth shut." Five bucks!

"Hey, whadda you expect? A guarantee?" Louis asked indignantly.

"Aw, shaddap, shaddap," Mac grumbled. "I got a good mind to take a poke outta you."

"Gee whiz, can you beat that?" Louis cried, consumed with the injustice. "Here I give him a tip and the horse comes in second and he's still got a kick coming. From now on I'll be goddammed if I ever give you guys a winner."

"Winners, I like that! Shaddap!" Mac shouted. "I got a good mind!"

But when Baldy came around to pay off Louis for his second and third place money, it first dawned on McCarthy that the cross-eyed runt was still making money. Louis collected ten dollars on two to one for second place and even money for third, which made his winnings ten dollars on the whole deal on Pipper. McCarthy, seeing the money pass hands, rose uncontainable and bellowed with anger.

"See, Coby?" he cried. "He did it on purpose! That's what it was. He knew Pipper would come in second and he purposely steered us wrong. You cockeyed bastard! You louse!"

He started whacking Louis XI all over the cigar store. But Louis, chased and harried, remained victorious as a prophet.

"Didn't I say he'd hit me if he lost?" he cried over his shoulder as he tried to duck McCarthy's blows. "Didn't I? See?"

Outside there was a commotion too. The taxi drivers had taken time from their game of pitching nickels and were now grouped around a figure. Coblenz recognized his friend Munves. He could have guessed it. If the great scholar realized that the guys here liked to throw insults at him, why did he always insist on passing this way? But Coblenz did not understand that with

Munves it was a matter of courage and principle. He was no coward and refused to be intimidated by these hoodlums.

"What I should like to know," he was now saying, clutching his books under his armpits and gazing earnestly through his glasses at the representative he had chosen to address, "is why it makes you so happy to call me Mr. Pishteppel?"

The crowd roared but the individual remained solemn. He put his hand respectfully on Munves' shoulder and the etymologist smiled invitingly. An appeal to reason. All you had to do with these fellows was to talk intelligently and they would understand you.

"See, professor," the cabman said gravely, "you really want to know the answer?"

"Yes, I should," affirmed Munves.

"Then I'll tell you what I'll do. You can get down on your hands and knees and I—I'll let you kiss my ass."

There was another roar from the gallery. Munves pushed the hand off his shoulder and turned indignantly toward the hackmen.

"It's people like you," he said severely, his eyes glaring with righteous anger at their ignorance and brutality, "it's people like you who make pogroms."

Coblenz couldn't stand another minute of it. He went to the door. "Lay off, you lousy bitches," he said. "Why the hell don't you have a heart?"

"Listen to him, look who's talking?" the representative said. "Smart guy."

Coblenz had won in a short time a great reputation as a drinker and was highly respected in the neighborhood. "How would you," he asked conversationally, "like to get your lousy teeth knocked in?"

There was quiet. The fun was over and the hackmen, turning to business, went back to their positions on the pavement for pitching nickels at the cracks. Coblenz turned to his friend. "If you know these guys are going to get nasty," he said, "why do you have to come past here all the time? Stay away."

"Those hoodlums," Munves said, still indignant, "they're just ignorant. They're all right, they just don't know better. What they really need is somebody to teach them a lesson."

"Ah," said Coblenz, feeling low as it was. Go argue with him. The professor was going to give these bums a lesson. "Go on home, Munves. Read a book."

Munves peered into the cigar store. He could see the ticker, and McCarthy and Louis, both studying the form sheets. "Coblenz," he asked shyly, "could I go inside for a minute?"

No one would ever guess where he had just been. Munves had gone to Mr. Cohen's delicatessen store for lunch, but he had stipulated that he wouldn't buy save on one condition. He had to slice the corned beef himself for his sandwich. And Mr. Cohen had let him, suspiciously, gloomily, very much upset. Sitting at his table with a glass of tea and the sandwich, Munves had chewed his lunch, going over in his mind with the keenest pleasure the details of that operation. How easily the blade had turned, such little pressure had been required. What a sense of satisfaction he had felt in his fingers when he had pushed the hand pedal. How neatly the lump of meat was held by the spikes in the fat, and how gracefully the slices of meat fell into the plate. It had been a great success. Munves needed a broader vision, as he had said, and it was edifying to seek it.

"I should like to see how one bets on the races," Munves explained smiling.

"Social worker," Coblenz said. "You got money?"

"To bet? I don't care to bet money, Coblenz. I just want to see how it's done."

"Not to bet. To lend."

"Yes, I have money," Munves said eagerly.

"How much?"

"Eighty-seven cents. You want it?"

"Ah," Coblenz said, disappointed. "Not enough."

"Well, can I come in?"

"Come in," Coblenz said, going back to the ticker. "Who's stopping you? It's a free country."

Louis XI regarded Munves. "He the guy who got five hundred bucks from the onion company?" he asked, deep respect in his voice.

"Five hundred dollars?" repeated Munves. "Is that how much they gave Max?"

"You ain't the guy?" Louis asked.

"Oh, no," Munves replied. "A friend of mine. I know him well."

"Hey," McCarthy said, hating and envying Balkan with all his heart because of the five hundred dollars, "come over here. Maybe you can break my jinx."

"Who, me?" Munves asked, smiling with pleasure.

"Yare." McCarthy gave Munves the *Morning Telegraph* and pointed to the list of entries. "See, these horses are running in the fourth race. You pick a winner."

"Me?" cried Munves, all amazement. "I wouldn't know one horse from another."

In spite of the low opinion he had of hoodlums, Munves really admired them. Now he enjoyed being among them, spoken to and asked for a winner, for the people here always impressed him as being real adults. They gambled for a living, swore, knew all about women, had men's ways, and were not easily startled.

"Me?" he protested. "What would I know?"

"All you got to do," Mac explained, "is to take any old horse comes into your head. See, it's a hunch like."

"Well," said Munves doubtfully, "all right. It's all the same with me."

He glanced at the list. "What interesting names," he exclaimed. "I wonder whether anyone has ever made a study of horses' names and their derivations."

"Hey, what's this?" McCarthy asked. "You kidding? Come on, we ain't got all day. They'll run the race before you'll get started."

"The hell with it," Coblenz said unhappily at all this nonsense. He was broke and this was only the fourth race.

"Blossom-Time," said Munves, pondering each name with conscientious effort. "Parrel. Fleur de Lis. Model T. Dopey Harry . . ."

"Well," said McCarthy, "whadda you say?"

"I don't know," Munves said helplessly and went on with the entries. "Jimmy Savo. Panflash. Lativitch. Mis—"

"WHAT?"

It was Coblenz, his eyes bulging. "Did I hear you right? What horse did you say?"

Munves was a little frightened for he had never seen his friend in exactly this state. "Jimmy Savo," he muttered weakly. "Pathfinder. Lativitch. Misleading."

"Latabelle!" Coblenz shouted, suddenly gone insane. He had the expression of one who was witnessing a miracle. "Can you tie that? Latabelle!"

"Lati*vitch*." Munves corrected, trembling.

"Munves," Coblenz said very seriously, "you're all right. You're my cheese today. You stick around. You guys want a tip? Bet every nickel you got on Latabelle."

"Ah . . ." Munves persisted gently, "Lativitch."

"I need money," Coblenz said, shaking with excitement. "Hey, Louis, you been cleaning up all day. You want to buy a topcoat?"

"Ah, whadda I need an overcoat for in the summer?"

"Come on, you cockeyed runt. You can save it for the fall. This coat is Cravenette, see? Sheds water. Cost me twelve seventy-five at Macy's only three months ago."

"I don' wan' it. It's too big for me."

Coblenz walked to him menacingly. "All right, all right," Louis said hastily. "Give you three bucks."

"Three bucks! I'll crown you!"

In four minutes Coblenz had worked him up to seven dollars. He patted Munves on the head gleefully. "You're my cheese today, professor. Stick around and don't break my run of luck." He took the money and rushed off for Baldy. At this turn of the situation Munves boldly took a seat among these hoodlums and smiled contentedly. Look what he had done. He hadn't been in the store ten minutes. Everyone asked him for tips. Coblenz was highly pleased with him. This certainly was getting a broader vision. Munves remembered a character in a book by Galsworthy, limited in perspective like himself. This character, deciding to indulge more generously of life, started off by adopting the habit of smoking cigars. With the Galsworthy book in mind, Munves went up to the counter and bought a five-cent Cremo cigar. He smoked happily, first biting off the end as he had seen it done in the movies.

Louis XI was left with the coat, sizes too big for him. "What the hell?" he asked woefully.

"What's this business, Lativitch?" McCarthy asked, looking up the column in the *Journal*. He was not one to let a tip pass. "Haw! Haw! Haw!" he broke out wildly. "Coby's got a hunch. That's a laugh. 'Prob odds 100–1, nothing.' Coby has to call a hundred-to-one shot!"

Coblenz returned jubilant. "Well, boys," he cried, "I placed it. The whole bankroll."

"On the nose?" Louis asked incredulously.

"Sure, to win. And if you guys are smart you'll bet every cent you got on Latabelle. He can't lose."

"Aw, for crying out loud, Coby! He's a hundred-to-one shot!" Louis implored him.

"I know. I know. But he's coming home just the same. What are you guys hanging around for? Go see Baldy before the race gets started."

"Haw! Haw! Haw!" gasped McCarthy, happy to see a sucker roped in. He held the *Telegraph* form chart in his hand while he sought to regain his breath. "It's the first start this season for Lativitch! This horse ain't been in a race all year!"

"Latabelle," Coblenz said, unswayed. "I love you. Munves, you're all right. You're a peach, you're my pal. You stick around and don't jinx my luck."

The cigar seemed to the etymologist at this moment to be a creation of dark doubt. "Lativitch," he corrected his friend uncertainly and puffed on.

"Hey, Coby," McCarthy sputtered with glee, handing the *Telegraph* to him. "When your horse comes in—haw! haw! haw!—when he wins, Baldy will give you only twenty to one. Look at all the money you'll lose when your hundred-to-one shot comes in!" Mac went off into a paroxysm at his joke. The bookmakers in Williamsburg were cautious folk and paid no higher than twenty to one unless the bettor took the risk of sending good money after bad by insuring his possible winnings over the twenty-to-one ratio. For this the player paid a premium of ten cents on each dollar he bet.

"Don't think for a moment," Coblenz returned blissfully, "that I didn't take care of that." He had insured his winnings up to six hundred dollars.

"Well, for crying out loud," Louis muttered, saddened at the waste. "This guy's a coke or something."

"Haw! Haw! Haw!" said McCarthy, having the time of his life. He thought he was going to bust his pants.

Coblenz was now studying the form sheet with great complacence and everything in his attitude showed it. "Look at this horse's times," he said proudly. "One forty-one for the mile; four furlongs, forty-eight seconds; seven furlongs, one twenty-nine. This horse is got class. I can pick 'em. Latabelle, you're the horse of my dreams. I love you."

McCarthy sobered immediately, paying respectful attention to the times. Suppose this long shot came in and he wasn't on him. His life would be ruined.

"Hey, Coby," he asked, "what's the matter you like this horse so much?"

"Latabelle can't lose," he said. "In all my dreams it always seems, Latabelle, I love you."

"He must be a coke," Louis said. He was investigating Lativitch in the *Telegraph* chart.

"Coblenz," said Munves in a dismal voice, "I want to go home."

"I'd like to see you try," said Coblenz fiercely. "You're my cheese. You go away and my run of luck gets broken."

Munves surrendered and suffered for his friend's sake. He was feeling very sick. Nausea.

"For crying out loud!" Louis XI cried, horror-stricken, holding the paper up. "Those times—they were in races in nineteen thirty."

"Nineteen thirty!" McCarthy roared with relief. "This horse ain't been in a race since nineteen thirty! How old is he anyway?"

Surely enough, Coblenz saw the dates for himself. Lativitch's last race had been in October 1930. He must be eight, nine years old at least. He'd fall down on the stretch and break up into pieces.

"Haw! Haw! Haw!" chortled McCarthy, wild with delight. "Whoo! Hoo! Hoo! E-Yah! Hah! Hah! I can't stop. Gimme drink of water somebody. Whoo! Hoo! Hoo! Hah! Hah! Hah!"

"For crying out loud," muttered Louis in heavy grief. "This guy's nuts."

"I want to go home," said Munves miserably. He had thrown the cigar away but the stink persisted to plague him. "Another minute and I'm going to vomit."

"Stick around!" Coblenz commanded. The ticker began pegging. The result of the fourth race was coming in. "Shut up!" he roared and the store became still. In all his life he had never felt so sure of anything as he did now of Lativitch. His lifelong contention was that this was a chaotic, senseless world, and the most logical thing in it was for a horse like Lativitch, a hundred years old, broken down, in his first race in years, to win this race at a hundred to one. Latabelle couldn't lose!

And Lativitch didn't, supporting Coblenz's contention. The price quoted by the ticker had gone down to fifty to one. Baldy would pay Coblenz over three hundred dollars. And while his friend screamed insanely at the outcome, Munves suddenly felt the spasm of retching pass and he was, remarkably, quite all right again. Happy, happy, happy. He looked up at Coblenz and felt responsible for his friend's joy.

McCarthy was shamelessly crying his eyes out.

ELEVEN
Pathé News

You could have knocked Goldie over with a Mack truck. There were Chink and Heshey, sitting on the steps of the third-floor landing, talking and laughing together as though they were brothers, equals, best friends.

"Well," said Goldie, helpless with astonishment, at the last possible degree of wonder, "you could knock me over with a Mack truck."

"Aw, what's got into you?" Chink asked sulkily, the sense of defeat gnawing at him in the presence of Goldie.

"See," explained Heshey smoothly, "Chink and me are pals. From now on."

"When did all this happen? I'm a Russian princess if I can make it out." If she lived to a million years it would remain a mystery to her. What did you know?

Chink turned confidentially to his pal's ear. "Hey, Hesh," he whispered, "you and me want to stick pals, I got one condition."

"What, Chink?"

"No girls, I can't stand the living sight of them."

"Hey, hey," said Goldie. "What's going on here? No secrets between friends."

"Aw, it don't concern you," Hesh said. He was troubled. Goldie had been a good friend to him in those days when he had needed a friend, and a friend in need was a friend indeed. How could he kick her out all of a sudden? Well, who was more important in his life? Chink or Goldie? A fellow couldn't fool around with girls all his life. Heshey cupped his hand over his pal's ear and bent toward him. "Let me handle this my way," he whispered. "I got tricks, hunnerds tricks. Hey Goldie, you want to be pals with me and Chink too?"

"He's got a dirty mind."

"Aw, who wants her?" Chink said, disgusted.

"Hey, hey," cried Hesh. "This ain't no way to act. Somebody would think you were just a couple of kids. Goldie, you want to do me a favor?"

"What?"

"Go inside, tell my mudder she should give me peach."

"I like that! Who was your servant last year, I should like to know?"

"Hey, Goldie, you want to stick pals with me? I know tricks, hunnerds tricks. I don't want the peach for me. For you! I got a trick. You want to feel good, ain't it?"

"Well," exclaimed Goldie, "that's different. Why didn't you say so in the first place?"

She went off to Heshey's mother. Chink turned immediately to his pal, demanding to know what kind of trick this was anyhow. He had said no girls, and no girls it goes, otherwise, no stick pals.

"Listen, Chink," Hesh said. "With your strength and my brains we can beat the whole block. Keep quiet."

He bent over and explained the stratagem, barely finishing in time for there was Goldie already, holding the peach in her hand straight from the bag. She thought of the delightful sensations Hesh had produced on her scalp yesterday.

"So what's the trick?" she asked eagerly.

"Rub the peach in the face," Hesh directed. "First it'll hurt, then you'll like it. Rub hard."

Rub a peach on her face? "What kind of a trick is this?" she asked. "You trying to make a fool out of me? Who ever heard of a trick like this?"

"All right," Hesh cried. "I should worry. For my part . . . Hey, listen here, you Goldie, you want to feel good, ain't it? I made you a fool yesterday? Rub hard, else don't bodder me."

Hesitantly Goldie applied the fruit to her skin. Her face itched in a second and she stopped. "It hurts," she said querulously.

"I know, I know," Hesh said. "Didn't I say it's going to hurt first, hah? First it hurts, then it makes you feel good. Go on, rub hard."

Chink almost busted out loud and would have given the whole trick away if Hesh hadn't jabbed him fiercely with his elbow. Goldie rubbed and rubbed and her face was the funniest thing to see. The skin rasped and itched. Her face felt as though it were on fire. It was like itching powder someone had once thrown down her back at school. When would it start feeling good?

Chink couldn't hold it in. Goldie was furious.

"Well," she gasped, holding her face as it smarted, "of all the lousy, lowdown tricks, this certainly takes the cake!"

Neither of them was able to answer. Roars of delight overcame them and they choked when they tried to say something. What a face she had had on her while she waited for the good feeling to come. Before the sight of them shaking at her expense, Goldie grew so mad she thought she would have a stroke or something. She threw the peach at them in disgust.

"You, Mr. Chinkstink," she pronounced with refined indignation, "you've got a filthy mind and you'll live to see the day when you won't be good enough to kiss the ground under my feet. You'll die a drunken bum. And Heshey, I'm certainly surprised at you. All I can say to you is don't you ever dare to speak to me again as long as you live. I hope you understand that I mean it."

She walked off grandly, her head held high, her behind jutting out majestically. Chink took careful aim and let it have the peach. She jumped forward as though pinched. It was a waste of energy to be polite with some people, some people's children understood their own language only, they could understand nothing better. The hell with them. She marched down the stairway, ignoring them, but before it was too late Heshey yelled out: "Goldie makes pippee in her draws!" and hoped that Chink would be convinced that once for all they were pals. Nevertheless the parting shot had cost him a pang.

"That was good," Chink said approvingly. "That was real good."

"Oh, that's nothing. I got tricks . . . Hey, Chink, you want to know a guy who's got plenty tricks, better than mine? Whadda I'm talking about, better than me? There's no comparison!"

"Who's this?" Chink asked. "Who's this?"

"My friend, upstairs. Mr. Balkan. Guy with glasses. You know him. He had an idea, one single idea, and a company paid him a thousand dollars for it."

"No kidding?" In this very house! A millionaire! And he had been fresh with him, told him he stunk out loud. "Holy crap, I wish I knew that before! I bet he's good and sore at me." Chink bitterly regretted his thoughtlessness yesterday.

"Don't worry, don't worry," Hesh assured him. "I can fix it up. I know him good. All I got to say to him is, that kid Chink, he's a friend of mine, let him alone, and Mr. Balkan, he won't hold nothing against you."

"Aw, Hesh," he cried, "you're a real pal."

"Aw, that's nothing."

"Hesh, you want to do me one more favor?"

"Sure, pal, anything I can do for you, just tell me."

"I want to get even on Mrs. Strudel. That lousy janitor whacked all hell out of me yesterday when she opened up the dumbwaiter. She whacked me hard. All right, I guess I deserved it, but she didn't have to hit me so hard. I want you should think up a trick, something real special for Mrs. Strudel."

Delicate ground. Hesh moved warily. "Right at the moment," he said gravely, "I got nothing in my mind. Oh, I got tricks, ordinary tricks, but I want to get something special, something real good for that pesky janitor. She's getting to be a pain in the neck. I'll think it up, Chink, it'll be good, I give you my personal guarantee. With your strength and my brains," he said.

To be Chink's pal! Heshey had to keep it in or else he would be all over the place. In one day he had managed to rise from the lowly.

And instead of trying to get even with him Chink had actually asked him to be friends with him. He had been the one to bring up the subject, not Hesh. It just went to show, it just went to show . . .

Hesh rose solemnly and held up his arms in the air, the fingers outstretched.

"Hey, whadda you call this?" his pal asked.

"Atlas. You know about Atlas? See, he was a giant, he held up the world on his shoulders. If he went away, the world, it would fall down and get busted."

"Aw, baloney. So whadda you sticking up your hands in the air? You Atlas all of a sudden?"

"Yare. See, I'm holding up the sky," Hesh said, And that was how he felt, too.

"Hah! Hah! Hah! A good one!" Chink cried. Hesh certainly knew tricks. "Hey, Hesh," he said, "whadda you say we go downstairs and knock over the garbage cans for Mrs. Strudel?"

"Okie-dokie, but that's nothing. I'm thinking up a real good one for Mrs. Strudel. You'll see."

"Well, come on, anyway. This'll just be for a sample."

"Okie-dokie. Hey, Ma," Hesh called to the door, as casually as he could manage, "I'm going in street with Chink."

They walked downstairs arm in arm.

Heshey's mother was sitting in the kitchen seriously engaged with her neighbor in a discussion of confinements. The neighbor happened to be the same housewife who had represented to Balkan yesterday the typical injustice of the world. She was the lady who had so horribly humiliated him when she accused him of hitting Chink while instead he had been trying to save Hesh from him.

"Look at him," said Heshey's mother, referring to her son, "now he's going in street with Chink. Children! Yesterday they were fighting like animals, cats and dogs. Heshele almost had convulsions. Children . . ."

"Children," repeated the housewife wisely. "What do they know? One day they fight, the next they make up and they're friends again.

But men, grown up, they should know better. You know Mrs. Balkan's son, Max? He's no child already, he's a man. Yesterday what was he doing if not hitting Chink? I had to rush in and stop him or else he would have killed the boy altogether, made a finish with him."

"Mrs. Balkan's son?" Hesh's mother asked. "You don't know? He got a fortune from an idea with onions. Dollars in the hundreds they paid him, I don't know how much myself. A smart young man. Heshey should only grow up to be smart like him."

"I don't believe it. A nice fellow, if he's so smart, why does he have to go around and hit children?" The housewife began to feel uncomfortable. It came back to her how nasty she had been to Balkan on the landing yesterday. He was probably still angry with her. Hesh's mother went on to tell her in detail of Balkan's achievement and her worries grew as she heard. The housewife resolved to make it up to him somehow. She would try to be in the hallway sometime when he passed and then she'd apologize. "I don't know, Mr. Balkan," she would say. "One thing with me, I can't stand seeing a child hit by anybody. I got children of my own, I'm a mother too. So when I heard a holler, I thought you was hitting him. How should I know better?" It would be all right. Mr. Balkan would forgive her.

"See," said Hesh's mother, "the joys you have from children. You have a baby, he grows up, he makes a fortune. I only wish I was in Mrs. Balkan's boots already. When Hesh grows up," she said dreamily, "I'll make him a pharmacist in a drugstore."

"Don't let him grow up so fast," the housewife said, worry lying heavily on her mind in spite of her talk. "It's better sometimes when they're children than when they grow up. You have a baby, he grows up, he makes a success, like you say. Then what happens? A strange girl, you never saw her or heard her, she walks in and takes him away. They give you no thanks, the children—the worry, the doctors, the hospitals, the dispensaries, God knows what else—good-bye. They forget and after you struggle with them all your life the strange girl comes in and takes him away..."

She stopped uncertainly. Why had she been so mean with

Mr. Balkan? He would have it in for her for the rest of his life. The talk returned to confinements, but she remained uneasy all that afternoon.

Mrs. Strudel, the janitor, unaware that fate hung heavily over her in the mind of Heshey, came at last to fix the bell at the flat above Coblenz—the lady with the skating children.

"Denks," the lady said with the appropriate degree of coldness. "I send Sammy down yesterday you should fix the bell, you come today. In the meantime we can go crazy. The bell is fixed."

"Please don't be so unreasonable," said the janitor, lofty herself. "I got—you can see for yourself—only two hands. Everybody wants the janitor and I can't go every place in the minute."

Down the stairs Mrs. Wohl, the cleaner, could be heard at this moment crying for Mrs. Strudel. "See?" she said with great satisfaction. "I'm the janitor. Everybody is entitled to a piece from me. What do you want?" she asked the old lady.

Mrs. Wohl came breathless. She wanted the key to Coblenz's room. He was outside and she had to get in to clean up the place. "Did you hear?" she asked.

She told them all about Max Balkan and the million dollars the onion company had paid him for his idea. Mrs. Strudel, who knew the story well enough herself by this time, coolly added further details, but the woman whose children skated all over the house remained to be impressed. Great good fortune had a habit of falling now and then on some citizen of Williamsburg—sweepstakes tickets, radio prizes, and newspaper contests. Once when he had been little she had entered Sammy in a baby-picture contest and she hadn't won a cent. She had never taken a prize in her life, not even a five-cent raffle. Why couldn't God be good to her too? Was she a nigger?

"Sammy," she yelled out irritably, "take off the skates. For God's sakes go in street if you have to skate, I got a headache already."

Mrs. Wohl in all her years thought she had seen everything,

but America was a big country and had plenty of surprises left to startle her with every week.

"America with the inventions," she said. "Everything here has to go by magic."

She took the key from Mrs. Strudel and left, but they had all concluded that Max was a wonderful boy and would soon become rich and famous. They secretly resolved to be particularly respectful to him in the future.

Mrs. Balkan was by this time on the fifth floor, still going strong.

TWELVE
A bag of onions

In the wintertime you lie in bed, all is silent and dark, on the ceiling and walls the lights flash from the speeding automobiles in the street, and the sound of men shoveling snow off the sidewalks reaches your ears with a sensation of comfort and coziness. Then you are alone, at peace; the world is unreal, something that happens distantly in a mellow story, and the true reality extends only to the confines of yourself, in the dark, under warm blankets, alone, with the flashing lights on the ceiling.

With all his heart Max Balkan, plodding up the staircase of the tenement on Ripple Street, longed for the wintertime. To be alone, within himself, withdrawn, away from everything that men did and had to do with men. Sad he felt but calm, faint, in a sort of numbness. This was no time for grief but, full of real pain, it cried only for forgetting, for anesthesia, in the same way that a soldier tortured by his wounds demands urgently morphine. Balkan walked with his eyes closed.

The Door

Behind it were Mr. Balkan, Mrs. Balkan, Rita, Ruth, Munves, the world. They were all talking of onions and Balkan in tones grown more intense than ever because they were expecting him back at any minute. Rita and Ruth, returning from Klein's, had heard of the great fortunes Max had received, all the way from the elevator station to Ripple Street, and they had rushed exultantly to find out whether the reports were true. Munves, too, starting with the cigar store, had heard the stories. Wide-eyed with amazement he had pumped up to the Balkan's flat. Even Mr. Balkan, dancing and freezing on the hot pavements on Roebling Street and Broadway, had gathered wind of the hundreds his son had received. He had thrown a handful of the blue advertisement cards down the sewer and had shuffled home. And Mrs. Balkan herself had grown more and more excited as each one came tearing into the house with stories of wealth, clamoring for Max, asking if it was really true that they had paid him a thousand dollars. A thousand dollars! She believed it herself. And now the buzz of their voices, shrill and jerky, two and three talking at once, passed out into the hallway. It was getting late. Where was Max?

The Door

He had to. Balkan opened it. Instantly the hum of noise stopped, Munves and Mrs. Balkan caught with their mouths still opened. They looked at Max searchingly. He let the door close softly and stood helpless before them.

"Well?" In one voice, all regaining control of themselves simultaneously.

Max couldn't say a word. He tried to smile. Failed. The house was achingly still. Max held up a bag of onions, a five-pound mesh bag of onions. He held it before their eyes as one holds a kitten by the neck.

"What . . . what is it?" Mrs. Balkan asked.

"Onions."

"Onions?"

"Onions! Well . . . ?"

"What else? How much did they give you?"

Max tried again to smile, hoping this would make it easier. He was sick in the stomach. His mother's face grew savage.

"How much money did you get?"

"Nothing."

Nothing! Nothing! Nothing! Two hundred dollars, three hundred dollars, a thousand, a million! Nothing! What fools he had made of them all! What would the neighbors now say? Nothing! He was a schlemiel, a yolt, a dope, a kvetch! It served them right for believing him in the first place. What could they expect from him? Was he joking? He was kidding them. Mrs. Balkan, Rita, Ruth paused. It was all a trick. It couldn't be. Impossible. Nothing! The torrents flooded Max, battering him, bruising, smashing. Caught as the dam broke.

"Excuse me," he said.

They waited. What now? Max went slowly to the bathroom, opened the door, and hid. And as his mother and the two girls drew breath to begin all over again, they wondered what was the use, what good it would do them; they changed their minds, muttered, stopped. Each withdrew among her private thoughts and their faces grew solemn as they pondered their troubles. Mrs. Balkan could expect no quarter from the neighbors; Rita had no money to open up a delicatessen store for Munves; and Ruth still had Max on her hands, defeated again, still a lemon, hopeless. Glum silence held the room in its grip for many minutes.

"Doo-dee-doo-dee-doo-dee-dee," sang Mr. Balkan sorrowfully.

"Shah!" cried his wife, so savagely, with such fierceness, that her body trembled as she shouted.

Quiet.

"Rita . . ." said Munves brightly.

"What do you want?"

"Guess where I was today."

"Where?"

"In Mr. Cohen's delicatessen store. He let me cut the corned beef for my sandwich. I used the revolving knife."

"Oi, vay's mir," wailed Mrs. Balkan in Yiddish, and she went into the kitchen, rubbing the tears from her eyes.

The bag of onions rested in the chair neglected.

Protected and hidden by the bathroom door, Max Balkan turned both faucets full force, hoping the noise would drive away the numb jumble in his brain. Achingly he opened the medicine chest and on the back of the mirror he could read again the clipping he had pasted there from Arthur Brisbane:

> If you have a new idea don't be discouraged because others laugh. If they did not laugh, it would not be NEW. Nearly everyone laughed 128 years ago when Fulton's first steamboat, the Clermont, made its first trip from New York to Albany.
>
> The banks of the river were lined with "average Americans," smiling, joking, waiting for "the darned thing to blow up." To their amazement it WORKED and the idea is still working.
>
> Fulton had imagination and what men can imagine they can do.

Max closed the medicine chest softly. How all the neighbors in the hallway had stared at him as he passed respectfully, with awe. The recollection made him flinch. His mother had done her work well. Pathé News, sees all, knows all, tells all. But he hadn't the heart to blame her for he really hadn't wanted to stop her when he knew she was on her way to spread the news. That morning seemed years distant to him now.

What a cheerful, cheerful person Mr. Atwater had been at the Onagonda Onion Producers, Incorporated. When he had finally arrived at his office from lunch and the switchboard operator announced Max to him, Mr. Atwater couldn't wait, he had to rush right out of his private office into the lobby and greet Balkan. "Hello, Mr. Balkan, how do you do, I'm very glad to meet you." Shake hands, smiles, come in, have a seat, cigarette, cigar. Oh, Mr. Atwater, cried Balkan sitting on the bathtub edge, I hate you with the tonic on your hair and the blue-bordered handkerchief in your breast pocket. Why did you have to come into my life? Max had spotted the onion man immediately and identified him: among the proud.

Now Balkan turned on the hot water and the cold water, off, on, off, on, the intermittent streams of water smacking the enamel of the washbowl and relieving his grief.

Mr. Atwater had lain languorously back in his swivel chair, his yellow shoes dangling off the floor. The fingertips had met caressingly over his vest buttons. "Rilly, rilly, it is very amusing—ha, ha —every so often someone writes us a letter that he has just had a remarkable idea that will sell more pounds of onions than ever before. An idea to make onions more popular with the American consumer. Bottle the juice. A wonderful idea. Oh! By the way! Did I happen to keep you waiting very long? I'm so sorry, unavoidable, detained. What was I saying? Oh, yes. Bottle it. We have companies affiliated with us that have been holding the juice for some time now." And the telephone bells rang, the doors opened, the secretaries came walking in and out. Mr. Atwater banged down on the floor, sitting close to his desk, holding the cigarette in the corner of his mouth, his face wincing to keep the smoke away from his eyes. Max Balkan sat in his chair, his knees high, on his tiptoes. Oh, God in heaven.

Max smiled, courageously smiled, Mr. Atwater must never know what a tumult raged in his breast. "Oh, just one minute, Miss Smattersbee," Mr. Atwater had said impatiently. "I have a caller, as you might very well see for yourself. The trouble is," he said, turning to Max again and Max had listened sympathetically, grinning and grinning, "the trouble is, we bottle the onion juice, advertise through the best agencies—have you heard, our slogan? No Peels, No Odor, No Tears. As I say we do the best we can but somehow it is difficult to educate the consuming public to the idea of bottled onion juice. Of course, the first years—well, these things take time, a little time, of course. However, to encourage the popularity of the bottled onion juice we do everything we possibly can. That is the function of a producers' organization. Miss Smattersbee. A bag for the gentleman with the compliments of the Onion Producers Corporation." The bag of onions.

THE ONAGONDA ONION PRODUCERS, INC.
Hope You Will Enjoy These Onions.
Full Of Vitamins C and B

Finished. Balkan was positive that the switchboard operator had snickered when he walked out of the office with the onions under his arm. The whole office must have been laughing at him ever since they got his letter.

Max hated Mr. Atwater. Louse, stinker, bastard. Held down a politician's job, nothing to do, graft. Three times he had to call up on the telephone so that Max could get a bag of onions. If Mr. Atwater had to work for a living he wouldn't have bothered Max over nothing, all this now would have been spared. Yellow shoes, hair tonic, hundred-dollar suits, the blue-bordered handkerchief —go to hell, oh, go to hell. Now in the bathroom Max went to the medicine-chest mirror, too sad to bewail himself. There are times in life when there is nothing more important than to squeeze out blackheads. He worked over the area in the corner of his nostril.

"Maxie. Maxie." It was his father.

"What?"

The door again. He couldn't stay there all night. Balkan opened it slightly and peered out. There were only Munves and his father in the room and he came out, keeping his eyes on the floor, saying nothing and hoping that neither of them would speak.

"Max," said Munves promptly, "don't take it to heart. Don't feel bad over it. Everyone has his bitter defeats. It's nothing."

"It's all right."

Mr. Balkan sat on the couch, reading the *Bintel Brief*, all new, this being a new day. The old man, in his clown's suit and the paint, read awkwardly with his chin on the great collar in order to keep his nose from distracting his attention. His feet hurt and he rubbed them against the leg of the couch. "My feet," he mumbled. "It hurts. Burns."

Max, seeing him read and rest his feet, felt like crying. He remembered his father at the window that morning with the yellow sun shining on his old face, paring his nails in his underwear, limp and loose on his skinny body. The rush of feeling returned. How happy he had been that morning, how sure. In his mind he had promised his father every comfort and luxury. Where, now, were the houses, the servants, the cars? He had been a kid and a fool, and it was time he gave up. All those fine ideals—the desire for the heroic spirit and a dignity in life—they were impossible, good enough for youngsters idling in high school to discuss with important looks on their faces and pipes in their mouths. A grown man could not afford the luxury of piquant speculation, could not play tic-tac-toe with his mind, while someone else paid the cost and made it possible for him to idle, speculating. It was time to end.

"Pop," Max said, "I guess I'm going to look for a job. As soon as I start bringing money into the house, you can stop walking the streets for Madame Clara."

"Shah, shah," Mr. Balkan remonstrated. "What's the rush? What are you talking about now? Where can you get a job?"

"I'll get it. On Seventh Avenue. I can get a job in a dress house."

Twelve dollars a week. Pushing hand trucks with dresses through traffic from jobber to manufacturer, eight to five. Get up, go to work, the subway, wait for the hours to pass, home, the movies, sleep. There was no other way.

"Max," said Munves, trying to cheer his friend, "guess what I was doing today. I cut corned beef with the revolving knife at Mr. Cohen's delicatessen store."

"Well . . . that's nice."

Munves feared to go on. Perhaps he had better stay still. He understood that there were times when a man wished to be alone, and silent. He thought of the delicatessen store, the spiced smell of the meats, the glasses of tea with lemon on the marble-top tables, and the wonderful revolving knife.

"Where's Ruth?" Max asked suddenly. "Did she go home?"

"No, Max," Munves said. "She's in the bedroom with Rita."

Crying, angry, disgusted with him, thought Max. He was more humiliated than ever now, more ridiculous, more laughable. How they would laugh at him now, Rita, his mother, Coblenz, the neighbors in the tenement. Max thought painfully again of the housewives stealing glances at him when he had walked up to his flat. A schlemiel he was, crazy ideas he had, and the bitter irony was that his idea was all right, was perfectly practical, indeed was in use already. Even the same slogan he had thought up. If he had only had the idea a few years earlier! But Balkan drove the thought from his mind. Useless. If he had thought of the idea earlier, something else would have happened. There was nothing for him to do but to surrender, to go to work, to pay his debt to his father, to Ruth, to the world. And Ruth, Max exclaimed. Waiting all these years, waiting for his conversion, waiting for him to get a job, for marriage. Give in! he cried to himself, give in. Forget Blenholt and Tamburlaine, be like the millions of others! How long a fool, tortured with visions among the clouds? How long a dreamer? Reality hit him in the face until he knew he should have realized years ago that his struggle was hopeless.

Balkan went to the bedroom to see Ruth, to tell her he surrendered, he would get a job, they would get married. He felt cold now, with no trace of tears for himself. That was all over. Balkan felt himself a man.

Coblenz came in, crowing and exultant with Latabelle still ringing in his ears and over three hundred dollars in his pocket. But as soon as he crossed the threshold, he stopped, puzzled. All day he had heard of Balkan's millions. A madhouse he had expected and here was Mr. Balkan reading the *Tag* and Munves dreaming with his chair tilted against the wall.

"Hey, Munves," he asked, "what's going on here? A funeral?"

"Oh, hello, Coby," Munves said eagerly. He remembered his exciting experience at the cigar store, at the ticker with Louis XI and McCarthy, the hard-boiled gentry whom he admired so much. At the Balkans' this afternoon he had been neglected in the turmoil over Max and after the treatment he had received with his engagement he missed the attention. Now, Louis and McCarthy had looked up to him with respect, asked him for tips. And hadn't he been responsible for Coblenz's good fortune? "Where did you leave the boys?" he asked.

"Look at him," his pal answered. "'Coby. Where did you leave the boys?' A regular tough guy. Well, kid, Munves, what happened here? Did Balkan get a million dollars or no?"

"Oh," said Munves, feeling for his friend, "it didn't go through. He didn't get the money."

"Nothing? Nothing at all?" After all the excitement all over the neighborhood, Coblenz found it hard to believe.

"Onions." Munves pointed to the bag in the chair.

"That's nice," Coblenz remarked drily. So Balkan got himself kicked in the pants again. The dopey little luksch had to raise a holler so that he'd get smacked all around when the bubble burst. It hadn't been enough for him to go around with his crazy ideas. He had to give them all the impression that the fortune had already dropped into his lap. The poor little dope! He must be crying his eyes out somewhere now, Coblenz thought, feeling sorry for him. "Where's Mr. Rockefeller?"

"Hey, Coblenz," Mr. Balkan said sharply, taking out time from the *Bintel Brief*, "go home, please. Don't bodder around."

"Where's Max?"

"In the bedroom," Munves said. "He's talking to Ruth."

"He feels lousy?"

"Well, it's only natural. He's very depressed."

"Sensitive plant." Crying his eyes out while Ruth held his head in her lap.

"Shelley," remarked Munves.

"What Shelley?"

"Shelley. He wrote a poem called 'The Sensitive Plant.'"

"The professor. Who's asking you?"

The poor little dope. All the time he was yapping about heroism and the poetry of the soul, why couldn't we be like giants, Shakespeare and the Elizabethans, the world was hotsy-totsy, all you had to do was pickle it in spices and rise to the true stature of man, like Caesar or Rockefeller or Al Capone. Now he got himself good and kicked in the pants.

Now the apple-barrel tenement of his soul rebelled and wept, a helpless boat rolling on the multitudinous seas of humankind's cruelty. Oh, the oompah, oompah, oompah of the soul. Couldn't you hear it crying like trumpets blowing over fields of daffodils? Couldn't you see it like a ship sailing the endless seas of Arctic gloom? Ta-ran-ta-ra! Ta-ran-ta-ra! The poor little dope, when would he ever get on to himself?

"Max ought to have a revelation," Coblenz said, "and turn communist. A great cause, uplifts the spirit when it droops."

"Oh, Coblenz," Munves said reverently. "This is no time . . ."

"And how are you, professor?" Coblenz said viciously. "Still playing kitzl, kitzl, kitzl with Rita? Why don't you marry the girl?"

"Please, Coblenz," Mr. Balkan said from the couch. "Go home. You're too smart altogether today."

"I will!" Munves shouted, his eyes aflame. Gratitude! "Rita and I are getting married in the very near future. It's only a question of time."

Mrs. Balkan, hearing the noise, came savagely into the room, ready to take on anybody in her frame of mind. "How do you do!" she cried. "It's Mr. Bungalow again. What's the matter, Coblenz, outside stands a politzmann over your head, you got to come here all the time and bodder everybody? I got my own troubles enough already, thank you!"

Coblenz didn't answer. He regarded the bag of onions. The poor little dope.

"Shah," said Mr. Balkan, always a man of peace. "Shah. Quiet."

"Shah, shrill, the rabbi goes dancing," his wife answered, hopping bitterly before him. Then Max came in from the bedroom, and she turned to him. "Mr. Fumfotch Number Two."

"Momma," he said, "Ruth and I are getting married."

"Mazel tov! Wonderful! You'll live on air! Did you ever see such a schlemiel? The onion scheme you'll live on. Just like that, one, two, three, he's getting married!"

"I'm going to look for a job tomorrow," Max said. "I'm going to work."

"Oh, Max! Max!" Munves called, inspired. "Why don't you and me go into partnership? We could be partners together! It would simply be first rate!" What a marvelous idea! Munves & Balkan, Delicatessen. He could see it on the border of the awning. Munves saw everything, the store, the wits in the rear drinking tea and holding brilliant conversation. Cozy, warm, delightful . . .

"Partners in what?" Max asked mournfully.

"The delicatessen store! Ever since the idea came into my head, I've been thinking about it with affection."

With affection. "Well," said Max, "when are you going to open up your store?"

"Oh, my God!" Mrs. Balkan screamed. "Oh, my God!" It was too much for her, she collapsed.

Coblenz had been surprised. Here was Max, no weeping, no despair, no tears. Something about him impressed Coblenz. There was a change in his friend, he was different. Max actually seemed levelheaded!

"Hey, Balkan," he said, "what's got into you? A pile of bricks hit you?"

"Cut it out, Coblenz," Max said, dejected. "Come around some other time."

"Well," said Coblenz, "don't take it so hard. Cheer up. Why don't you turn to communism?"

"Communism!" cried Mrs. Balkan. "Listen to Mr. Bungalow! Communism!"

"What has communism got to do with it?" Munves sincerely wanted to know.

"It's a new happy ending. You feel lousy? Fine. Have a revelation and onward to the revolution. That's heroism for you and you can feel you're elevating to the stature of man not only yourself but all of mankind. Anyhow, it's a great feeling at a time like this."

"You know," Munves said, disapproving, "you're . . . very difficult. You're a pessimist, that's what you are. A cynic."

"Gee whiz," said Ruth at the door, clearing her nose after the tears, "there's no other word for it, Coblenz. You're a louse, excuse the expression."

"Go on home," Rita said, beside Ruth. "Go home and get crazy in your own house. You're nothing but a dumb drunken bum."

"Please," begged the old man. "Enough already. Go home."

"Mr. Bungalow!" Mrs. Balkan cried. "Rotten through and through. He sees everybody crying, there's trouble, what does he do? To him it's a joke!"

Max sat down. "Oh, leave him alone," he said. "What did he say? Don't make him the goat." Balkan envied Coblenz's pessimism. He envied Munves' gentle insanity. Both were protected by their special faults, both were happy, they had a good time.

Coblenz had been absorbing all the punishment without saying a word, without moving a muscle. Now he rose slowly. He couldn't resist it. It was like being God and the impulse was too strong for him to disobey.

"Mrs. Balkan, you're a wonderful woman and a great mother to your children, you should live to be a hundred and fifty years old," he said solemnly, taking the roll of bills from his pocket. "Here. This is for you."

Mrs. Balkan held the three hundred dollars in her hand, transfixed. Munves and Max could open a delicatessen store! Rita could get married! Everything would be fine. Wonderful! Wonderful!

"Oh, Mr. Coblenz," she protested, "how can I take it?"

"It's all right. I don't need it anyway. As a matter of fact," said Coblenz, "I was just thinking of jumping off the roof."

"It's only for lend," Mrs. Balkan said. "I'll give it back when the business goes good. I can't take money from you like this."

It was like a thunderbolt and Coblenz waved his hand at her, relishing their stupefaction. Not a sound in the house. He had an afterthought, pulled out a five-dollar bill from Mrs. Balkan's hand and left the room without another word, leaving them all still frozen in the attitudes of wonder. The five-dollar bill was for Mrs. Wohl, the cleaner. She had suffered much with him and surely deserved the five-pound box of candy he meant to buy her. Coblenz felt like Adolphe Menjou, in the rain, despised by all and yet a heart of gold. But once on the other side of the door, he felt the first soft pangs of regret. Three hundred dollars. It was true the impulse had been irresistible, but why had he given it all away? He might have kept something for himself.

Mrs. Balkan was overjoyed. As the significance of the roll of bills in her hand seeped through to her consciousness, she uttered little screams of happiness. The delicatessen store became real. She could add a little money from the bank to what Coblenz had given them and the children would be set in business. Rita would get married! It was wonderful. They would have their start. A strange boy was Coblenz, crazy and yet a good heart, strange, but it was wonderful! Munves in his chair was still too dazed to realize what had happened, but he gathered that he was so much nearer to owning his own delicatessen store. To stand behind the counter with the glass showcases, lit by electric bulbs placed inside them, to wear the white starched apron, to turn the revolving knife whenever the notion entered his head. He had forgotten all about the terrors of matrimony for the day. Perhaps tomorrow he would go through torment but all he could see now was his store, and his mind was filled with fond reveries. Mr. Balkan read the *Tag*. Coblenz's act had passed the bounds of reason, and since this perplexed him hopelessly, he could only think of forgetting it, but somehow he was vaguely worried. Max, he knew, had not been helped by Coblenz's generosity, but what it was exactly that caused the uneasy feeling in his mind he did not at this time know. And as for Rita, she immediately regretted her treatment of Coblenz, not only on this afternoon but always. After everything was said and done, he was at the bottom a fine fellow. She would go to him tomorrow, she resolved, and apologize. Married at last!

"You know what?" asked Ruth, still with the appearance of one who has just awakened. "Let's celebrate."

"Oh," said Max heartlessly. "There's nothing to celebrate. What could we do?"

"Oh, let's," exclaimed Munves, aflame and happy.

"Let's go to the Miramar," Ruth cried. "Joan Crawford's still playing."

And that was what they all wanted. For some time Max stood against them but they were too much, he gave in as he meant to give in all the rest of his life. Mrs. Balkan went happily to the kitchen to have supper ready for them all when they returned. A party. A regular party they would have tonight. And while Rita and Ruth were in the bedroom, fussing with powder and rouge, while Mr. Balkan sat on the couch reading the *Bintel Brief*, while Munves blissfully dreamed of revolving knives and spiced meats, Max rested alone in his chair, aching, sore, tired. All over, gone, finished forever. Those happy dreams, those happy days, those happy hopes. The splendor and the glory and the magnificence that he had always dreamed of were something if only in the hoping. And now he would have to turn his back to them, turn his back to Xerxes, Darius, Cæsar, and the giants, turn his back to Blenholt who, as Max himself had meant to, had risen from nothing to majesty in America. No longer could he pay homage to the gleaming ideals of his youth, for from this moment on he knew he was a man, grown up, finished. He looked out into the yard. The chalk was still on the fence. HESHEY ISA BIGE...

"Come on," Ruth cried gaily, and they fussed at the door, chattering and laughing, happy, happy, happy. Joan Crawford awaited them at the Miramar.

Alone in the room was Mr. Balkan and he dropped his paper the better to take in the quiet and the peace of the scene. He stood up, trying to straighten himself out to his full height. He stretched and held his ribs.

"Oi," he sighed. It was time to go back, to put on the boards, to walk the streets again for Madame Clara, Treatments By Experts. But in the gentle haze of muddy reflection he stood for some time near the couch, in his great patched checkered suit with the enormous shoes, in his tremendous collar, the paint and the signs.

Quiet, everything was quiet and for a moment he was taken back again, dreaming of Melbourne and King Lear. Alone, unseen, Mr. Balkan raised his chest. His shoulders went up and he stood his full height, tall and strong. A majestic figure he had become in all of his clown's makeup, noble and with high dignity. Pompously he strutted around in the empty room, in rich pantomime, thinking of his greatest successes, of Hamlet, King Lear, Macbeth, and Tamburlaine. Mr. Balkan grandly lifted his arm ready to declaim, but with the corners of his eyes he spotted his wife. She had been standing at the doorway of the kitchen, her hands on her hips, restraining the guffaws until she was purple in the face.

"Mr. Fumfotch!" she finally burst out and roared joyously.

"Sh, sh," the old man said and picked up the boards.

Then he knew what it was that had been troubling him vaguely before. In his wife's earthly guffaws he recognized the clamorous demands of the world, its insistent calls for resignation and surrender, and he knew now that Max would never be the same again. Much had gone out of Max, aspiration, hope, life. His son would grow old and, aging, die, but actually Max was dead already for now he would live for bread alone. That was the rule and few men were strong enough to disobey it. It had happened to Mr. Balkan himself, he knew, and now it had happened to his son. And regretting the way of the world, Mr. Balkan realized that he had witnessed the exact point at which his son had changed from youth to resigned age. Walking out of the house and shifting the shoulder straps to get the signs comfortably settled, it seemed to the old man that this death of youth was among the greatest tragedies in experience and that all the tears in America were not enough to bewail it.

But all the same the evening sun that day went down on time.

LOW COMPANY

We have trespassed, we have been faithless, we have robbed, we have spoken basely, we have committed iniquity, we have wrought unrighteousness, we have been presumptuous, we have done violence, we have forged lies, we have counseled evil, we have spoken falsely, we have scoffed, we have revolted, we have blasphemed, we have been rebellious, we have acted perversely, we have transgressed, we have persecuted, we have been stiff-necked, we have done wickedly, we have corrupted ourselves, we have committed abomination, we have gone astray, and we have led astray.

O, Lord our God, forgive us for the sin we have committed in hardening of the heart.

FROM THE PRAYER SAID
ON THE EVE OF THE DAY OF ATONEMENT

ONE

It was drizzling, and all the storekeepers of Neptune Beach stood at their doorsteps regarding the gloom reproachfully, as though they were being deliberately persecuted. Mr. Spitzbergen kept on shaking his head in tearful acknowledgment of the weather and its meaning. "No," he sighed bitterly. "No." Shorty, the soda jerker, came running from the fountain, drying his hands on his apron, and he squinted at the sky.

"It won't last, Mr. Spitzbergen," he told his boss at last. "See that over there? Lighter. It'll blow over in no time at all."

"What blow over?" cried Mr. Spitzbergen in pained disgust. "If I dropped dead right on the spot, it wouldn't blow over."

Eager and important, Shorty now trotted back to his place at the fountain, muttering violently. "Jesus Christ, a fellow wants to pass a nice word, what do I get for it? The hell with it, it's the last time I try to be decent." But he muttered low.

"No," said Mr. Spitzbergen in sad resolution, "I'm afraid I am in no danger of getting rich in this business." He went in and sat on a stool, resting his head in his palm. "All winter we keep up a big place, we don't make a penny, we wait for the summer. Comes the summer, thank God at last, and it rains. Eighteen thousand dollars. I put in eighteen thousand dollars—the fountain alone cost me three. And the ice-cream machine?"

“Holy smoke!” exclaimed Shorty, overcome. “What the hell did I do?”

“Yes, yes. He should worry. He cares a lot. He gets his salary, rain or no rain.”

“Well, I’ll be goddammed, that’s all I can say, Mr. Spitzbergen. Why take it out on me?”

“Never mind,” Spitzbergen sighed. “Never mind.”

It was a little after eight, just past the breakfast rush. Then the streets of Neptune Beach had been full of people, moving with worried briskness to the elevated station but pausing at Liggetts or Meyers or the cafeteria, and some of them entered Ann’s, the soda parlor that Mr. Spitzbergen had affectionately named after his wife. These were coffee and buttered toast, or buttered English muffins toasted, or raisin cake toasted. Ten and fifteen cents a head. Most did not even take the orange juice, and with this business you did not get rich in a hurry.

Now the place was damp, dark, and empty, with dismal swirls of wet dirt on the marble floor. Beyond the fountain were the four long rows of tables and chairs, Chromo Art-Metal with futuristic designs on the tabletops, the most expensive of the line, and two of these rows consisted of cozy alcoves, *intime* style, using upholstered settle chairs. The walls were stippled and ornamented in artistic blends of green, red, and yellow. Dividing the parlor into two sections ran a five-foot wall, also Chromo Art-Metal, topped every yard by a great electrical fixture of red, green, and yellow panes, matching the walls. And at the very end of the store, behind a gleaming show window that was lit at night by three 150-watt bulbs and in the daytime by a specially constructed skylight built in the roof just above it, was the ice-cream machine, Mr. Spitzbergen’s pride, his greatest after his wife. Ann’s manufactured its own ice cream according to an exclusive recipe of unsurpassed purity. Known New York Over For Its Ice Cream, the menus said at the very top. The machine cost two thousand dollars.

“Turn out the lights!” Mr. Spitzbergen suddenly cried. “It makes me sick to look at!”

Shorty hustled to the cellar door for the switches.

"Hey! I'll fracture your goddammed skull!"

Shorty's nose went up into the air as he tried to locate the voice. It was Moe Karty studying the *Morning Telegraph* form charts in the back.

"I'm sorry!" exclaimed the soda jerker in mock apology. "I'm awfully, awfully sorry! How the hell am I supposed to know you're back there all the time?"

"Put on the light and cut the crap if you don't mind," Karty shouted, his voice trembling with anger.

"All right! I said I'm sorry, didn't I?"

"Tell me, Moe Karty," Mr. Spitzbergen began earnestly, "how much you pay me I should give you light for the horses?"

"Come on, you lousy shrimp!" Karty yelled at the top of his voice. "Give me some light!" He was just beginning to dope out the day's horses and it was driving him wild to be interrupted.

"Look at him, all excited!" said Shorty, awed. "He can't talk, he's so worked up. B'gee, if that's the way the horses act on you, you want to lay off."

Karty's head went from side to side with exasperation. "God . . . dam . . . you . . . bast— Who the hell's asking you for comment? Put on those lights or I'll—"

"Just see! Just see!" the boss said. "Somebody would think God knows what!"

Shorty had been manipulating the switches so that now a single bulb shone. Karty rustled the racing paper, cooling off and recovering, and he sat down to work at once.

"No, no!" cried Mr. Spitzbergen. "I don't see why it should be like that. What do I get out of it? Mr. Moe Karty, maybe you know how much my electric bill is? You think they give you electric for nothing? Thirty-one eighty! I can show you the bill!"

Karty didn't answer.

"Listen," said Shorty confidentially, looking down his nose, "I can't stand no nagging, that's the way I am, see? The hell with it, they want light, all right, light, only no nagging. One reason I never got married. You think I'm kidding, Mr. Spitzbergen? Dames, sure, that's something altogether different, but no wife for me. All it amounts to is a lot of nagging and grief."

"It rains, nobody comes to the beaches, there's no business, it's all right, only so long Mr. Moe Karty gets light. He can play horses for a living, he don't have to work. A gentleman! I got to struggle for my bread and butter, I got to work like a horse, I got to give him electric. What's the matter, it says like that someplace in a book? It's a law?"

"Aw, can the bellyaching," said Karty from the rear of the store. "Louis Spitzbergen and his bellyaching, he's got a reputation all over Neptune. Listen, if you lost the money I lost last two years, you'd have four hemorrhages and bust a gut."

"I sent you to the racetrack? It's my fault! Yes, yes!"

"Always a squawk. Listen, Spitzbergen, if I had your money, if I had your dough . . ."

"I'm a millionaire! Yes, sure, Mr. Spitzbergen, he's got fortunes in every pocket! You see it?" he asked Shorty. "You see me running with money? I don't!"

"Poor Mr. Spitzbergen," said Karty. "He ain't got a nickel. It's a tragedy. What's the matter with the tenement house on Baten Avenue?"

"Mortgages! You want it? You can have it for a hundred dollars cash."

"All right!" Karty half rose from the table, his little sharp face wizened with nastiness. "I'll give you a hundred cash! I'll pay it gladly, just sign the papers!"

"Never mind," said Mr. Spitzbergen. "Never mind. Don't be so smart."

"See that? See that? A hundred dollars cash! And how about the six-family on Third Street? How about the whole row of bungalows on Featherbed Path? Aaah, what am I wasting time for? He stinks with money, only just try to squeeze a nickel out of him."

Karty sat down in disgust and studied the latest workouts by special wire. Mr. Spitzbergen, frowning, swiveled from left to right and back again, a little happy behind the scowl because Karty spoke the truth, better than he knew, and it heartened him on this dismal morning to think of his bank accounts.

"He's a goner," Shorty said confidentially to the boss. "I've seen them before, just like it. They have their pile, get the racing bug, and they ain't satisfied unless they lose every cent they got or they can get their hands on. I know guys today in jail, perfectly honest guys, honest as you or me, got the racing bug and took money as didn't belong to them. It's a disease."

But Mr. Spitzbergen wasn't listening. He was thinking of his property and worried a little. He was making fortunes out of his houses, it was really true, but that was what worried him. It was too much money, too easily and rapidly earned. No good came out of transactions like these in the long run. Shubunka said it was all right, he said that nothing could happen, but all the same Spitzbergen worried because, as he often complained, it was his nature, he couldn't help it. But what could they do to him? he asked himself. After all, he didn't know anything about it. It was all legal as far as he was concerned. And Shubunka guaranteed that everything was properly handled.

"In case I forget," said Spitzbergen, "if I'm outside for a minute and Mr. Shubunka comes in, call me."

"O.K.," Shorty said, his gold teeth shining as he smiled, striving to please. "See, Mr. Spitzbergen, that's why I take it from him. Otherwise I wouldn't let him get away with it, and don't you think so for a minute."

"What?" asked Mr. Spitzbergen.

"Moe Karty. I wouldn't let him get away with the way he talks to me, only I know it's a disease with him. Listen, would you hit a man with cancer or T.B.? Well, it's the same thing. Mental disease is just like anything else, don't you know? Psychiatry. Delusions, obsessions. Paranoia! Oh, sure!"

Shorty was holding his bald head almost in Mr. Spitzbergen's face as he whispered his confidences. Talked like a crazy man, thought the boss. He had an impulse to slap him on the head, as the others often did, but he felt that this lacked dignity in an employer. He grunted sorrowfully instead.

"As I said, I can't stand nagging," Shorty pronounced. "If a guy wants to horse around with me, O.K., I'll let him have it. Yare, I may not look it, Mr. Spitzbergen. I know what's in your mind, but I ain't afraid of no man. Take nothing from nobody, see? If I had the inclination to tell you one or two things, you'd be surprised!" He swiped the metal covers with the wet rag viciously. "See, never got married. Can't stand the nagging. Forty-two next November, been all over the world, had plenty of girls, don't you know, but no wife for me. I don't want it, that's me!" he proclaimed defiantly, looking his employer in the eye.

"See," said Mr. Spitzbergen, thinking of his troubles and growing unhappy, "all right, he wasn't wrong. After all, I make a few dollars. So what? It goes to the doctors, every cent. My wife."

"Too bad," said Shorty, nodding repeatedly with sympathy. "It's a goddammed shame, that's what I always say, Mr. Spitzbergen. There have been mighty few women her age I've seen as beautiful as Mrs. Spitzbergen. Absolutely a beautiful lady."

"Yes, yes, I wanted a beautiful wife," he moaned. "Sick. All the time. You know Dr. Stein? Bigshot, head surgeon at Mt. Sinai. Fifty dollars a visit! Just a look! The biggest professors, all the hospitals. If I had a fifth—a tenth!—of all the money I spent on doctors . . ."

"Mr. Spitzbergen," Shorty said, "it's none of my business, don't you know, but what's the matter with Mrs. Spitzbergen?"

"Ask the wall!" he exploded. "Go ask the wall! Really, I mean it. Go ask the wall. Yes, yes, the wall knows like the doctor. They tell her nothing is the matter. Get out of bed, they say, you're a fool. Wash your teeth and take care of your family, there's nothing the matter with you, they say. It's a sickness she has, she's sick. . . . Aaah," said Mr. Spitzbergen, "I can't talk about it. I ain't got the heart to think about it. It's like a sewer and the money runs down all the time."

Mr. Spitzbergen winced. This brought him back to the weather and the loss of the beach crowds. All at once he grew desolate. Every one of his troubles came crashing down on him. He no sooner thought of one than another came to crowd its way into his head. The store, his real estate, his wife, Shubunka. There would be trouble there yet, he avowed. It was too good to last. A nasty business, anyway, he didn't like to be mixed up with Shubunka. The man made him feel uneasy. There was something strange and disagreeable about him. Mr. Spitzbergen felt despondent, old and weak.

"A beautiful lady," Shorty murmured respectfully. "It's all like I say, don't you know? Nervous. Neuroses. Illusions. Too bad."

"Please," said Mr. Spitzbergen. "Don't talk. I don't want to think of it. I tell you it's eating pieces out of my heart."

Shorty sympathetically pulled out the milk pump, tilting it carefully so that the milk in the cup at the bottom would all flow back into the can, and he sincerely hoped that Mr. Spitzbergen would be comforted a bit by this evidence of his painstaking attention to his job. He dropped the pump gently into the deepwater basin. "A beautiful lady," he said softly.

"See," said Mr. Spitzbergen, "it was like the other day. A woman I know walks in the store and says, 'Mr. Spitzbergen, how many years are you in Neptune? Fifteen years or more, a good fifteen anyhow. And I remember you, too, when you were in Brownsville, a young man, full of life and energy. Time flies. Now you're wrinkled and gray and you got a corporation.'"

"So what did you say?" asked Shorty, grinning.

"What do you think? I said I felt like a sweet sixteen!"

"Ah, Mr. Spitzbergen!" Shorty protested cheerfully. "You ain't got the right attitude! It's none of my business, of course, but you're the type that worries too much. You want to have some fun. You never took the time to learn how to play. B'gee, if a dame said that to me, I'd kid the pants off her. You take life too serious."

"Too serious," Mr. Spitzbergen admitted sadly. "I should go dancing in ballrooms, yes, yes."

Shorty bent over the counter to him confidentially. "Why not?" he asked. "You should of dated her up. Taken her out. That's the way to take your mind off your business worries for a while. Don't you know?"

"What can I do with her? So I make a date with her. So what?"

"What the hell! You can have a little relaxation. A man needs some recreation once in a while. Spend some money, take in a show, have a good time."

"Yes, yes," argued Mr. Spitzbergen, "but what comes out of it? What do I get out of it?"

The flesh on Shorty's little skull wrinkled all over in tiny cracks. His forehead furrowed. The gold caps gleamed and the saliva was bursting at the corners of his mouth. Mr. Spitzbergen looked at him, wondering, and thought he looked like a goat.

"Ah," he sighed hopelessly, "when it comes down to business I can't do a thing, what's the use kidding myself, you or anybody else?"

"Never mind! A man needs relaxation. Jesus Christ, what do you think I do? Pull sodas all the time?"

Mr. Spitzbergen regarded him thoughtfully. "Rudolph Valentino," he said, slowly shaking his head.

Shorty gleefully pulled the milk pump out of the basin and started to dry it, singing, "Is it true what they say about Dixie? Is it true what they do down there?" The telephone rang. Karty came running up, still holding the *Telegraph* in his hand. Shorty was waiting outside the booths for the bell again so that he could know which phone was ringing.

"If it's my wife," Karty said, "I just had breakfast and went out. But if it's a man's voice, I'm expecting it." He anxiously watched Shorty through the glass windows of the booth and cursed him for wasting time over the mouthpiece in his oily confidential manner.

"It's for you," Shorty said, "Shubunka."

Mr. Spitzbergen climbed in nervously, fumbling with the receiver. Karty's eyes followed him, deep with regret. "I'm expecting a call," he said to the jerker.

"Hell, don't look at me," said Shorty.

"What's Spitz got to do with Shubunka anyhow?" Karty asked. "Who the hell would want to do business with a mope like Shubunka?"

Shorty bent over close to his ear, talking through the side of his mouth. "One thing about me, Karty," he whispered, "I mind my own business, all the time. That's me. I know many a guy today who's in hot water just because he was too nosy about other people's affairs."

"Nuts," said Karty. "Who's asking you?"

"Oh, yare?" asked Shorty wisely. "Well, I could tell you a thing or two about guys who interfered in things as didn't concern them."

"Aaah, you stink," the gambler remarked and walked back to his light. Appalled by the want of decency and warmth in his fellow human, Shorty walked back to the fountain, violently muttering to himself. "Arthur!" he called. "You crazy son of a bitch! Arthur!"

Arthur stuck his mussed-up head out of the kitchen door. "I'm coming," he said. "In just a minute."

"What the hell you doing in there all day anyhow?"

The dishwasher trotted forward. "Honestly, I just got through. I got to clean the range and all those pans and pots good or else Mr. Spitzbergen, he gets sore and hollers at me."

"Cut the crap and get busy on those dishes."

Arthur ran hot water into the second basin and started to clear the counter of the cups and dishes, which he piled neatly, deriving artistic pleasure from his job. Especially it fascinated him to drop the crockery into the water. How softly the dish sank to the bottom when he placed it flat on the surface. What a gentle swirl as the water covered the plate. And what nice bubbles from the soap flakes. Arthur's hands lingered dreamily in the hot water as he placed the dishes one by one into the basin.

"What a crazy mutt," Shorty said. "Asleep on his feet." He shoved the dishwasher aside and dumped all the crockery into the water at once. Arthur watched him with a pang.

"All right, all right," he said. "I'll do it. Where's Mr. Spitzbergen? Gone for the day?"

"Never mind about Spitz. Get busy on those dishes."

But just then the boss's voice rose in a whine and they both turned to see him gesticulating wildly into the mouthpiece as he begged and complained. "Shubunka," Shorty said with a wise nod. "Something's up. Can't stand that guy, gives me the creeps or something like it." He went forward to serve a customer at the street stand. As the jerker left, Karty called the dishwasher for a glass of water.

"What's going on in there?" he asked Arthur.

"Oh, it's Mr. Shubunka."

"What's Spitz got to do with him?"

"Oh, I don't know!" Arthur protested, smiling all the time in his anxious, humble way. "He often calls Mr. Spitzbergen up but what it's all about I really couldn't say. No," he said gently, "I don't know." He saw the form charts. "I've never been to the races. Never saw a racetrack in my life." Arthur spoke in a gasping, thin voice, perpetually eager and impressed by his company, always respectful. Annoyed, Karty looked up at his beaming face, but he took pity and said, "All right. All right."

"They built a racetrack near my home town in Springfield, Mass. Agawam. Perhaps you have heard of it?"

"Nice track," Karty said.

"You've been there? Really? You don't say. My, my. Agawam."

"Sure, I been there two, three times. Always like a mutuel track."

"Some day I must see a horse race," Arthur said with conviction. "I'd really like to go and bet maybe a dollar or two. Do the bookmakers let you bet a dollar?" Karty told him they took dollar bets. "They have tracks in New York City? Of course, of course, I can imagine. You go often?"

But just then Mr. Spitzbergen came out of the telephone booth, slamming the door open with a bang. He mopped and scratched in sorrow, mumbling until he spied Arthur loafing, and he exploded. The dishwasher trotted peacefully to his place, not minding the bombardment from the boss.

"Pay good money," Mr. Spitzbergen exclaimed, "and he don't work."

The bell rang again and Karty was on his feet, reminding Shorty about his wife.

"It's your wife," the jerker told Spitzbergen.

The boss groaned elaborately. "Tell her I just dropped dead," he said.

"He's busy, Mrs. Spitzbergen, don't you know?" Shorty confided. "He can't come to the telephone just this minute. Nature's call."

"Ask her what's the matter," Spitzbergen said.

"She's going to the doctor," Shorty said, delicately covering the mouthpiece.

Hereupon Mr. Spitzbergen collapsed on a stool, speechless. Shorty, taking in the situation in his expert fashion, stroked the phone box knowingly and listened to her give him the message for the boss. Then he walked out silently to his place behind the counter. There wasn't a sound in Ann's in this moment of the boss's sorrow.

"Louie, Louie," moaned Mr. Spitzbergen pathetically to himself, his body shaking in rhythm to the sing-song of his speech, "you wanted a beautiful wife, now you can lay to hell."

"Too bad," said Shorty, commiseration on his face.

"Yes, indeed," said Arthur earnestly. "It's too bad. I'm sorry."

"Who needs you to be sorry?" asked Mr. Spitzbergen distractedly. "Go get me an umbrella, don't be sorry."

Arthur trotted to the kitchen.

"Is Shubunka coming in?" Shorty asked. "What should I tell him if he comes in and you ain't here?"

"Never mind about Shubunka. Mind your own business," the boss said, reaching out impatiently for the umbrella. "Better, when you clean the ice-cream machine, you take good care you don't bust nothing. Very delicate. Keep your mind on the work when you take it apart. Cost me two thousand dollars." He went out, cursing both the rain and the umbrella as he fussed with it.

"What the hell does he do with Shubunka anyhow?" Shorty asked. "I can't stand the greasy mope a minute. Hey, Karty, what the hell does Shubunka peddle for a living? You know?"

"Lay off, I'm expecting a phone call. I can't worry about everything."

"See that guy?" Shorty said to Arthur. "He's a goner. Once they get the racing bug, it's all over. I've seen it often and again. It's a disease."

"You don't say?" said Arthur in his thin small voice of wonder. "My. My."

"Come to think of it, Shubunka's got plenty, too. Funny guy, it's a funny business, too. I can't figure it out, that's all I can say. Never did know what he did for a living."

"Oh, I don't know myself," Arthur said.

"Well, b'gee, what the hell do you know anyway?" Shorty asked thinking of the machine. "Can't even be trusted to clean the ice-cream machine! What a mutt!"

The bell rang, and Shorty went for it, ever eager to greet the world. But Karty was there first. "It's for me, it's for me, and about time, too," he said. He closed the door carefully and spoke in hushed tones. This was the daily special, phoned direct from the track by Joe (Grey Lag) Wack, an extraordinary super-racing service for the nominal charge of one dollar, which merely covered costs of operation. Joe had a hot thing at Aqueduct today in the third race for two-year-old maiden fillies and he recommended it to all his customers. Without reservation. Fifi, a good thing that couldn't fail to hit the first crack out of the barn. And at a lovely price. According to special information supplied Joe (Grey Lag) Wack by his private dockers, the filly had twice broken thirty-five seconds for the three-eights, going handily both times. Moe Karty shook his head at the news. His system never permitted him to bet on a filly, a two-year-old, a maiden or a debutante, and Fifi was all four. He went to the newsstand to see if the *Journal*s had come in. Rain, sloppy tracks, scratches, low odds, not so good, nuts.

"Would you believe it?" Shorty told Arthur. "That guy was once a damned good accountant. Still is, only he don't do the work no more. Lost all interest. It's a disease."

"My! My!" gasped Arthur, his eyes staring at the appalling tragedy. What a strange world, what strange people, what miseries there were in the world, and, strangest of all, how little people knew of them! If a person only knew what was happening about him, how he would be surprised!

It was nine now, and Dorothy, the cashier-waitress at Ann's, walked in with a bank bag full of change.

"Hello," said Shorty, cooing. "Nasty weather, isn't it?"

Dorothy looked anxiously into the gloom of the parlor and started to go forward.

"He's not there," Arthur said, giggling. "Mr. Lurie hasn't been in all morning."

She turned back to the cashier's stand, disappointed. "It'll drizzle like this all day," she said, struggling with her galoshes.

Shorty watched her with absorption, noting deliciously every muscle that moved in her body.

"A pretty piece," he sighed expertly to Arthur. "A pretty piece. Not, of course, that I'd ever touch her. Never laid a finger on a virgin in my life. Not me. Hell, I got principles, don't you know? Besides, she's Lurie's broad. Not that that would stop me. Hell, I'd tumble my best friend if I wanted a dame. But I never started a broad on the downgrade in my life and I never will. Not me!" And Shorty looked as if he meant it.

Arthur giggled.

"Ah, Jesus Christ," said Shorty, disgusted. "Why don't you grow up?"

Mr. Spitzbergen's worst fears were being realized. The rain persisted and the morning was a total loss. Dorothy sat on the high chair at the cashier's desk reading an English novel from the circulating library. "Look here, Mrs. Molesbury, you're a practical woman," says Baron Heshelton, a filthy swine of the lowest type, "you know how I stand, what I'm worth. The girl who marries me—well, I'm a generous man when I get what I want. You're a clever woman and I needn't dot any more i's." "You wouldn't understand," says Mrs. Molesbury. "We don't speak the same language." He marry her daughter? There is something ugly and sinister in the passion of an old man for a young girl, thinks Mrs. Molesbury, and Dorothy, turning the page, told herself it was too goddam bad about it, displeased with her book because she had other things on her mind today and couldn't be annoyed. All the same, she had to read, even if she couldn't concentrate. Why didn't Herbert Lurie show up? His store was nearby but she had to wait until he came in. Dorothy was never the one to start something he might hesitate finishing, and, again, it would make a bad impression. Impatiently, looking often at the door, Dorothy returned to Mrs. Molesbury.

Outside, Moe Karty stood waiting under the awning for the afternoon *Journal* so that he could discover what Tom Thorp and Clem McCarthy had to say about the day's offerings. The newsboy said the delivery wagons were held up by the rain, and as Karty waited he kept on thinking of a wonderful four-horse parlay that he would hit sooner or later if he only lived long enough. Because if you kept at it long enough, you had to hit it, according to the law of averages. Why can't somebody send me a check for a thousand dollars, whined Karty unhappily to himself, why can't somebody send me a telegram? But the *Journal*s did not come, nor did the telegram with the money.

At the washbasins in Ann's, Arthur, the dishwasher, was scrupulously drying every square inch of the dishes, polishing and wiping until each plate felt warm in the hand and good to hold. He played with a dish in the air to reflect the lights.

"Dry as anything," he said to Shorty. "Not a speck of water on it anywhere."

For a moment Shorty watched him work the towel. Arthur took one dish at a time and dried each side separately, moving the rag in thorough circles.

"Fine," said Shorty. "That's nice. You don't let anything get away from you."

Arthur grinned proudly.

"You know what you'll get for doing your work so good?"

"What?" asked Arthur, beaming.

"A good fat kick in the teeth! You waste too much time. It ain't necessary. Here, gimme." Shorty held five dishes in his hand at once and rapidly passed the towel in between, drying the front and back of two dishes at one time, in one motion. He placed the five dishes on the shelf. "Finished, see? You got to know your job or what the hell good are you, see how I mean?"

"Gee, I never thought of that," marveled Arthur. "Let me see whether I can do it. But thanks, thanks." He experimented with a handful of dishes. "This isn't my line. That's why I don't know. Up at home, in Springfield, Mass., my line was smoked fish. I used to drive a delivery Ford truck for a wholesale smoked-fish dealer and I made as high as twenty-four dollars a week. Twenty-four a week, no fooling. I know smoked fish inside and out, but I can't get back in that line because when the depression started the boss, he hired all his relatives. The only thing wrong with me," he said, smiling gently, "is I haven't got any relatives in the smoked-fish line, don't you think?"

Arthur laughed and Shorty smiled benevolently over his cigarette. "B'gee," he said kindly, "that ain't all that's the matter with you if somebody had the inclination to tell you the truth. Been all over the world, myself, never went to Springfield, though, must be a dump. Been to Albany, though. Ever been on Division Street?"

Arthur's innocent face grew puzzled. "Yes, I've been in Albany many times, but I don't think I—you mean the red-light district?" Shorty nodded solemnly. "Oh, yes, indeed!" Arthur cried. "I've heard of Division Street often!"

"That's nothing," said Shorty, squinting an eye masterfully as he dug into his vast store of recollections. "Ever been out on the coast? Well, near San Francisco they have the Pavilion. You'd never believe it if I told you. See, it's like a pier, going out over the water there. A long shed, half a block long, longer. They got rooms like lockers, see, all the way down the pier. Each locker has a girl and a bed and so on, and the doors open in two parts, like a stall door. So the girls keep the top half of the door open, so a guy can go walking down the pier between the rows of the lockers taking a look here and there until he finds something that suits his taste, see how I mean? They got all kinds down there, all kinds colored, nice babies, too, give you a good time." He exhaled wisely. "Chinese, Filipinos, Mexicans, plenty whites, too. You can take your pick. Hell, I been all over the world, Hamburg, Rotterdam, Marseilles, Cairo —all over the goddam world and there's no place to beat the Pavilion for selection."

Arthur was overwhelmed. “You really mean that?” he gasped. “You telling me the truth or just kidding me?”

“What the hell do you take me for?” asked Shorty indignantly. “Think I'd stand here making up a load of bull just to create an impression on you?”

“Uhmy! My!” choked Arthur, convinced.

“Nothing like the rotten dumps they call a cathouse in Neptune,” Shorty said. He was disgusted with the establishments in Brooklyn. “Not,” he rushed to assure Arthur, “not that I'd ever go to them. Not me. I don't have to pay for it when I want it. If you can't get it the right way, decent and normal, why, hell, I wouldn't have it. Nothing doing with a cathouse for me. Rather go to a movie. Can't get no enjoyment out of those places, not me, see how I mean?”

“Oh, yes, certainly,” said Arthur, but his eyes were blank, for he was envisioning the rows and rows of girls on the pier, some colored, some Chinese, some white, exposed by the open half doors. “Gee whiz,” he gasped, “I can hardly believe it.”

At this point Madame Pavlovna, the corsetière, swept into the soda parlor for her breakfast. Shorty promptly dropped his cigarette butt and stamped it out. “Beat it!” he whispered to Arthur. “Stay up the other end of the fountain until I give you the high sign.” He beamed at Madame Pavlovna, the flesh puckering on his skull, his gold caps shining. “How are you this morning? Rotten weather.”

“Veder,” sighed Madame Pavlovna, smiling languidly. “Who cares vat the veder is? Vun day is like another. If you have seen vun day, you may say you have seen them all.”

Without having been given the order, Shorty had already dropped the bread into the toaster. He went up to squeeze the oranges, clearly resolved to give the corsetière his very best personal service. She settled herself on a stool near the double-decked water tray at the far end of the counter, secluded and reserved. Her shop was next door at the sign of the bisque model dressed in the black-lace corset, long a favorite of Shorty's. For three months now she came to Ann's after ten for her orange juice, cinnamon toast, and tea, and always she sat near the water tray so that she might have a discreet word or two with Shorty. Mr. Spitzbergen complained, but the soda jerker pointed out that it was good business.

Madame Pavlovna wore a Russian peasant tunic ornamented with red, gold, and blue cross-stitching. The sides of her skirt were slit to her knees and she wore no stockings. Her face had the soft swollen looseness of women past forty, wrinkled and heavily lined, but always smiling in spite of sadness, in spite of weariness.

"I am not a businessvoman," she said, lifting her eyes to Shorty, "but it is a pity, the veder. People have to make a living. And in Neptune if the veder is bad vat is there then? Neither nice, neither amusing, neither sad, neither nothing at all. Misayrable." She looked vacantly at the street and scratched her chin. "In Nice vun year it rained, all the time it rained and rained, and yet it was charming, it vas pleasant in a kviet vay. The trankvillity, you say?"

"Nice?" said Shorty, placing the orange juice and napkin before her. "That's France, ain't it?"

"Da, da, France," said Madame Pavlovna, her eyes misting a little.

"I been all over France, sure. Paris, naturally. Marseilles? Bordeaux? Sure, everywhere. Been all over the world one time or another."

"Yes, indeed, ven Stefan still lived, ve vent everyplace, all over the vorld, all towns, all countries, all the cities. Oh, let me tell you, the places I have seen, the times I have seen. It vould take me hours to say. I shall never know it again." She bit her toast dolorously.

"It's tough," Shorty said. "It certainly is tough. Believe me, I can well imagine it."

"Berlin, Paris, Bombay, Johannesburg, Melbourne—all over ve vas. In Persia vunce ve vent by camel. Six days on camelback. Over the desert."

Arthur couldn't imagine such a thing. "You mean to say you actually traveled on a camel, Mrs. Pavlovna?" he asked her, sniffling with the shock. Unawares, he had sneaked up to the couple.

"Vat could ve do, my dear boy?" she protested. "It vas a desert, no? Ve had to cross?" She sipped the tea. "Not very hot today, Shurtee."

The soda jerker went up the floor slats, shoving Arthur ahead of him. "Who the hell asked you to throw your two cents in?" he said through the corner of his mouth. "Beat it. Scram!"

"I only wanted to remind you about the ice-cream machine," Arthur explained. "I thought maybe you forgot. Later it'll get busy and then Mr. Spitzbergen, he'll get sore at you. I thought it was a favor like."

"I know damn well what you thought, you son of a bitch. I don't want no interference from you. See, I don't stand for no finagling around when I'm with a dame, that's me. I can take a joke with the rest of them, but when I got a woman on my hands, don't come horsing around." He glared at Arthur's back as the dishwasher went up to wipe the street stand.

"Talking travel, it reminds me of other days, other happiness. I get a cold feeling near my heart, like ice," she said, swallowing the toast. "In the daytime, thank God, it's not so bad, I am active and there is vork to be done. But at night I am all alone, by myself, in the dark. How can I sleep? I think and think, it comes all back to me like a moving picture, alvays the old days, vith my husband, in Russia, traveling, having enjoyment. . . ." She gazed into the distance.

"What line was Mr. Pavlovna in?" Shorty asked, respect in his voice.

"In the ladies' underthings line he vas. Rich. A big manufacturer with a whole factory and a showroom besides on Thirty-second Street. Lost, every cent, gone. I am not a businessvoman, you can see it for yourself."

"The stock market," Shorty whispered.

"Investments," said Madame Pavlovna, shaking her head as she pondered that calamity. "He left me vell off, but how did I know to manage?"

"I know many people today, had millions in 'twenty-nine, ain't got a nickel today. Pardon me." A customer had walked in and wanted cigarettes. "At the cashier's, please. Dorothy, Dorothy. Luckies for the gentleman."

Dorothy had reached the part where Mrs. Molesbury meets Ronald Rider, an old, old beau who had failed to stay for marriage but had gone instead to Australia to raise sheep. A misunderstanding, slight and yet tragic in its consequences. They are now having lunch, both old and gray and much wiser, and after the wine Ronald says, "You're happy, Cecilia? Are you happy with John?" "Very happy," says Mrs. Molesbury, but she thinks to herself, "Happy? Am I? Oh, Ronald! Ronald! Ronald! Why did it have to be the way it was?"

"Two for a quarter?" Dorothy asked brightly.

The man took one pack and she returned to her book. It was very touching, it was sad as anything, you could just imagine how Mrs. Molesbury felt and why she wanted so ardently to protect her daughter from that filthy swine Baron Heshelton. But Dorothy had troubles of her own, and she didn't have to go looking for other people's. It was always hard for a girl to figure whether a man meant business or whether he was just out for a you-know-what. Especially with Herbert Lurie. He had her puzzled. A fine line he had, but maybe it was only a line. She was too good to work in a soda parlor with a rough element, always trying to sneak in a feel when a girl wasn't on her guard. That's what he told her. He sat in Ann's with her at one of the back tables near the ice-cream machine and spoke to her softly, holding her hand, seldom trying anything fresh. And when he took her to the movies all he did was hold his arm in hers, telling her what a wonderful pure love it was he had for her and sneaking a kiss once in a while. Yet all the time Dorothy knew goddammed well how Herbert had had one wife and divorced her and was right this minute living with Flo, no matter what he tried to say about it. Besides, he was a good ten or eleven years older than she was and that kind of made it funny, too. Men like that didn't talk about love without using their hands unless there was something deep in the back of their minds. She was no fool, and Herbert certainly had a surprise coming to him if he thought he was going to get away with anything.

But why didn't he show up? He always came in for his breakfast right after she returned from the bank, sometimes coming out of his dress store and walking with her to Ann's. Dorothy put a stick of Spearmint into her mouth and returned, troubled, to Mrs. Molesbury. "Do you imagine, Phyllis," she was now saying to her daughter, "do you imagine that I haven't known it all—the disillusionment, the pain, the loneliness? All that I have known."

"A sveet child," said Madame Pavlovna, referring to Dorothy. "I never had children. It's my greatest regret."

"Respectable," said Shorty, approving. "That's what I always like about her. Never lets the boys pull a thing on her."

Madame Pavlovna placed the straw-tipped Melachrino exactly in the center of her mouth and the smoke came in clouds. She lifted her head wearily to keep it from her eyes. "Dreams," she said. "Dreams like little clouds in a blue, blue sky. All alone. My life is gone, over, you might say, all finished. No friends, no children, by myself. The old happiness I can hardly remember except in the night ven I sit vith the lights out, alone in my apartment, alone in a vorld of dreams and reveries. It's my only pleasure."

"That's not the right attitude, Mrs. Pavlovna," Shorty said. He bent over the counter. "That's a very negative attitude to take. Tell you what I'll do, Mrs. Pavlovna. What do you say me and you get together sometime? Have a little fun, go out, don't you know? Take in a picture or something?"

"I don't know," said the corsetière, smiling shyly.

"Aw, come on!" Shorty pleaded. "How about tonight? I get off at five. Got the whole night to kill."

"Vell, really," Madame Pavlovna's big body shuddered as she giggled with embarrassment. "It's such a new situation for me. I really don't know vat to say."

The soda jerker was perspiring with eagerness. For three months now he had been working on Mrs. Pavlovna. His eyes were popping as he sensed himself approaching success, but just at that point Arthur at the street stand gasped out, "My! My! Something's up!" It was Karty, running into the store as he sought cover desperately. "Well, what in the world is the matter with him now?" Arthur wanted to know. Karty came tearing around the corner of the fountain, nearly upsetting Madame Pavlovna at the double-decked water tray.

"Hey!" yelled Shorty, with all indignation. "What the hell do you call this, rushing in like this?"

"Please! Sir!" Madame Pavlovna exclaimed.

Karty made for the cellar door. "When my wife comes in tell her I'm not here, Shorty. Get me?" He went running down the board steps.

"I never!" said Dorothy, running up. "What's got into him anyhow?"

"A savage," said Madame Pavlovna, already recovered and languid again. "Did you ever see?"

"Don't mind him," Shorty said. "Most times I always excuse what he does. After all, he ain't perfectly normal. He ain't responsible for what he does." Arthur went up to the stand, looking for Mrs. Karty and relishing the prospect. In the meanwhile Shorty was telling the corsetière all about the racing bug and how it affected some people. "It's a mental disease with guys when they can't take it. If it wasn't for that I'd fix him he wouldn't go running around knocking people off their seats." His lips moved silently with grim significance as he reflected what he would do had Karty been normal. "Hell, the poor slob's in enough grief as it is. I feel good and sorry when I stop to think about it. What the hell, he's human just like you and me, don't you know?"

"Well, all I can say," declared Dorothy, "is everyone isn't in Kings County who belongs there by rights."

Shorty wanted to go on with Madame Pavlovna. He had almost made it when that hopped-up gambler had to bust in as though it were a fire. But he knew Mrs. Karty would be in the parlor in another minute and he felt a little troubled. Shorty cursed his luck, feeling bitter and persecuted, and worrying how he'd handle Karty's wife. She was a warhorse.

"Here she comes!" cried Arthur, jubilantly hopping.

"Aw, shut up," said Shorty, feeling distressed. "Don't raise a holler."

Mrs. Karty stumped into the store, going without a word to the kitchen at the back. She was a tall, strong woman, and walked on legs that knocked at the knees. "Oh, boy!" chortled Arthur with delight. "What she'll do to him when she gets her hands on him!"

Mrs. Karty came back from the kitchen. "Where did he go?" she asked. No one said a word. "What are you laughing at, you crazy dope?" she turned on Arthur. "Get that smile off your face or I'll slap it off."

"Who, me?" asked Arthur.

"Where did he go?"

"Who do you want, lady?" Shorty asked. "We can't have this commotion in a place of business, you can realize that, can't you?"

"Don't you give me no lecture, you goddammed runt. You know goddammed well who I'm looking for. Where is he?" She turned to the others, jabbing her brassiere strings back in place. Her hair was plastered to her head by the rain, and the water ran down in tiny streams on her shoulders.

"Vat do you vant from me?" Madame Pavlovna asked easily, smoking her cigarette and looking away. "I don't know anything about it and I assure you it is a vaste of time to try and find out from me."

"Where did he go?" Mrs. Karty screamed. "That's all I want. Tell me where he is."

"Who?" Shorty asked, his face looking pained. "You want your husband?"

"You know goddammed well I'm looking for that louse!" Mrs. Karty shrieked.

"It's no use getting excited, madam," Dorothy said. "It don't accomplish a thing."

"Mr. Karty came in for breakfast," Arthur said. "An hour ago. See, he isn't here. Look around." The dishwasher gestured to every corner.

"Go to hell," Mrs. Karty said bitterly. "The whole bunch, a pack of bums. Go to hell and drop dead." She went for the cellar door. Shorty tried to stop her. Didn't the sign say For Employees Only—No Admittance? She knocked him aside and pumped down the steps, cursing.

"Jesus Christ," muttered Shorty, conscious of his inadequacy before the corsetière.

"Such a woman," Madame Pavlovna remarked over her cigarette. "Low class. No refinement."

"My, my," gasped Arthur, pushing the hair out of his eyes. He had enjoyed the situation thoroughly.

"Indecent," said Dorothy, holding her English novel. They all waited expectantly for Karty to be pulled up, but in a minute his wife came up without him, her face set in furious anger.

"You see?" Shorty said to her, wondering where Karty had gone but feeling stronger with victory. "We told you the truth. He ain't here. What do you want to come in here and raise a fuss all over the place for?"

"You keep your goddammed mouth shut. Understand?" she shouted at him. "I got enough on my hands as it is." She marched out of the store, mumbling, in a rage.

"Uhmy! My!" choked Arthur. He couldn't get over it. "Really, I never saw anything like it."

"Get the hell out of here!" Shorty yelled at him. The color was returning to his face and he began to feel ridiculous before Madame Pavlovna. "Go on, beat it, or I'll slug you." He remembered the corsetière was still before him. "Little mutt, don't know why Spitzbergen wants to keep him around," he told her. "He's useless."

Arthur went back to the street stand, still shaking his head in amazement. He had been at Ann's three weeks now and the things he saw, the things he saw! Holy smoke, he had never imagined there were people like her!

Dorothy showed plainly that her finer sensibilities were outraged. "Did he hurt you?" she asked the corsetière. "Did you ever see anything like it? What a nerve. How can a woman be like that? That's what I can't get over."

"It vas nothing, child," said Madame Pavlovna. "In my experience I have seen vorse vomen. It vas even amusing a little bit. But Shurtee, tell me, vere did he go?"

Shorty opened the cellar door and yelled for Karty to come up. "He ain't there. He must of slipped out the back door and jumped over the fence. He's probably on the street right now. See, horses," he said confidentially, rubbing his hands. "That's what happens when you get the racing bug. Just misery. It don't make sense."

"Vell, I must be going," said Madame Pavlovna. She smiled distantly as she crushed the cigarette in her teacup. "Here, child." Dorothy took the check and the coins to the cashier's desk. "In Hahvahnah vun time," she told Shorty, "I met a voman in a hotel, she used to beat her husband black and blue. Every night, I don't know vhy. He vas such a little piece of a man and he vould complain bitterly, but nevertheless it vas so comical." Shorty roared at the story, his gold caps showing. She smiled gently. "In Hahvahnah, yes, Hahvahnah . . ." she sighed and slid heavily to her feet. Shorty came running around the fountain, his face drawn with concern.

"I wasn't kidding, Mrs. Pavlovna," he assured her, whispering. "Not a bit of it. I really meant it. How about it?"

"Tonight? To go out? Vere can ve go? Vat can ve do?" she asked timidly.

"Anything you say!" Shorty cried, his eyes flashing, now so close. "You know me. Hell! We can take in a show."

Madame Pavlovna's lids closed slowly. "I don't know. I really don't know. The store. I'm tied down."

"What time do you close? Eight?"

"Half past. A little later."

"Well, hell, that's fine. That's O.K."

The corsetière smiled at him impishly, moving her head to one side. She held his arm and squeezed a little. "Shurtee!" she said. "You terrible, terrible fellow."

"Well, what do you say?"

"All right. Drop in. Ve'll see."

"O.K.!" cried Shorty, trembling with success. She waved him good-bye and he stood there for a moment, transfixed, looking at her and thinking of the night. Barely conscious of what he did, the soda jerker went back to the fountain and started wiping the bread table energetically. Arthur came up at once, grinning.

"Did you make her?" he gasped. "You really date her up?"

"You nosy son of a bitch," said Shorty, waking up, "keep your nose out of my affairs." He stood up to his tallest height and the realization came fully. It was a cinch. That last squeeze and when she called him terrible, terrible. The jerker fished under his apron for his cigarettes and lit one debonairly, looking important as he cupped his hands to shield the light from the wind that didn't exist. He felt like Ronald Colman and exhaled grandly. "Hell," he confided to the dishwasher, "I always like to keep my mouth shut when a woman is concerned, don't you know? I can't stand these guys who are always shooting off their mouths about the broads they got. I get mine and know enough to keep my mouth shut, that's me, all right."

Arthur looked at the soda jerker with keen admiration. He had always heard about fellows working women, but he had never seen it done, never knew anyone who for a positive fact had done it. Out in Springfield, Mass., when he was driving the truck, he often had tried to pick up a girl, but he had never had any luck. The girls always said they couldn't stand the smell of the smoked fish. Some men just could make them, others couldn't. That was the way it was. He stood off, his eyes wide open with respect for Shorty.

"Hell," said the soda jerker expansively, "if I wanted to tell you something I could knock you right off your feet. Can't count the times I've picked it out. As easy as that. Hell, I wish I had a nickel for every time I jumped one."

"No fooling," gasped Arthur. "You don't say."

"Sure, and many's the time I've rolled a man right out of his bed on to the floor and got in myself. Never knew in the morning how he got on the floor, sound asleep all the time."

Arthur couldn't believe it. Patiently Shorty explained exactly what happened on those occasions. "It's all how you do it. All you need is a little practice and guts." He dropped the cigarette butt down the garbage hole.

"Uhmy! My!" gasped the dishwasher. He could see Shorty coming into the bedroom at night, approach the man in the bed, gently turn him out, drop him to the floor, and climb in himself beside the wife. Cozy. Arthur never knew such things happened.

"Yes," said Shorty, "I could tell you a thing or two. But I never talk. When it comes to dames the only smart thing to do is to keep your mouth shut and that's me. Else, don't you know, there's liable to be all kinds of trouble, see?"

"I can imagine," agreed Arthur. "I can easily see."

"Sure," said Shorty.

"Arthur, Arthur," Dorothy called him to her. She had given in. She had to know what was keeping Herbert Lurie. "You want to do me a favor? Go to Herbert Lurie's store and see if he's inside. Don't go in, see, don't tell him I want him or anything. Just see if he's in the store."

Arthur went out of the soda parlor drying his hands. It was aggravating, thought Dorothy, it was enough to drive a person insane. She looked at Shorty, across the store at the fountain, with distaste. The soda jerker was complacently shuffling his feet in a modified tap to the tune of "Is It True What They Say About Dixie?" Cockroach, said Dorothy, almost aloud, fooling around with that old slob in the corset shop. He ought to be good and ashamed. Shorty was watching his feet as he danced, bending over, and now and then he took to clapping his hands. "Do you have to make a racket?" Dorothy asked him in a burst of irritation.

"Hell, don't get sore at me, baby," he said cheerfully. "Everybody's got their troubles."

Arthur came trotting in from the drizzle. "It's a funny thing," he said, very much impressed. "I can't imagine what must have happened. The store's still closed."

It was late. Dorothy wondered what had happened and she nervously hoped for the best.

⁓⁓⁓

Fearful and unhappy, going over his burdens one by one, Mr. Spitzbergen plodded in the drizzle through the dirty narrow streets of Neptune Beach. The sidewalks were broken in all those places where the blocks caved in, and he had to be careful, avoiding puddles. Everything in Neptune Beach was sand. It was a misery. No matter how hard the street cleaners worked, shoveling the sand in mounds along the gutters, more blew in from the beach. On a rainy day you walked in black gritty mud. Nothing was solid, neither the pavements nor the foundations of the buildings. As the sands gave, the sidewalks broke and the houses on their pole foundations never stopped settling. For a landlord it was a constant heartache. There were always huge irregular lines in the walls where the bricks cracked, and few rooms in Neptune were properly plastered. Ramshackle ugly bungalows these were, for the most part, wooden in construction, once covered gaily with gray and green stucco or imitation brick surface, now hideous with time and neglect. These were intended for the summer trade, but the people moved in for the year round, letting out whatever room they could scrape together for the summer boarders.

The sewers, sunken tubs with no drainage, were already full, so that a large pool was found at every corner. The residents used planks for bridges here, but when Mr. Spitzbergen crossed, the board sank under his weight and his shoes grew wet. He felt his feet cold with the water and muttered in his discomfiture. It would have been better to be soaked completely than to have this dampness all over his body. He scratched.

At Baten Avenue he came to his three-story tenement. He glanced at it apprehensively, his mouth open during the inspection, and he went up the gloomy hall. On the top floor Spitzbergen saw a woman sitting on the tiled steps under the skylight.

"You?" he asked, frowning.

She went to the door and waited for him to open it. "The steps is cold," she said. "My can is frozen already."

"Where's Mr. Shubunka?"

"I don't know nothing about Shubunka," she said. "Open the door."

"Shubunka said he would come," he said as they walked in. "Then who sent you here?"

"Peggy Martin, she said I should come. She'll be here later with the girls."

Spitzbergen started and began stuttering with worry. "What's the matter so soon? What's the trouble? I just moved them into the house on Third Street."

"We had a little trouble," the girl said, sprawling on the couch. "A couple of guys came up and told Peggy she couldn't do business no more with Shubunka."

"Why? What guys?"

"Oh, some wise guys. Peggy told them to go to hell and lay off or they'd get theirs. So they got sore. So they started to take the place apart and smashed the furniture to pieces."

Spitzbergen went wild with the news of the disaster. "What did they do? Tell me. How long were they there?"

"Oh, not so long. They took out knives and ripped the carpet and then they busted the sofa. Geez, I got scared and started to scream. I don't like no rough stuff around. It makes me vomit." She looked at Mr. Spitzbergen to see if he understood how she reacted to violence. The easy nonchalance of the girl was unbearably maddening to Spitzbergen.

"My gall is being busted," he said, and moaned as he wondered whether Shubunka would make good the damage. "I am near a nervous breakdown. I should be in a hospital. Where's Shubunka? You seen Shubunka maybe?"

"Geez, what you worrying about?" the girl asked placidly. "Take it easy. You'll last longer, and the longer you last the more fun it is. I ain't seen him in a month."

He looked at her with deep hatred. "Making wisecracks. By her it's a joke." He threw the key on the floor and went heavily down the stairs, a man broken by his burdens.

"When you come back again, then I won't be here," Flo said, still lying in bed although it was past eleven. It hadn't had much effect.

"That's the way it is, so what's the use?" Herbert Lurie told her. He swung his watch chain around his finger, then swung it free again. "We might as well face the music. We don't get along and we never did. It was a mistake from the beginning. I'm glad you're seeing it reasonable." He took the hundred dollars out of his pocket and placed it on the pillow. "It's a hundred dollars. What are you going to do?"

"I don't know," said Flo, not sad, not angry, not wise, but quiet and unconcerned, as though Lurie were the milkman. "I'll figure it out later. Don't worry. I'll be out of the apartment before you come back. You can bring her in tonight."

"Now, don't get nasty," Lurie began. "It ain't necessary to drag her into this. See, that's why things— Listen, Flo, I got to go to the store. It's late already as it is. I want to say good-bye in a good spirit. You been a sport. No hard feelings."

"All right, no hard feelings, don't worry."

"Listen, why don't you go back to Albany, to your family?"

"I don't know. I suppose I will, at that."

"All right. So good-bye. Listen, if you need anything, if you want something, Herbert Lurie is still the name. You can always get me, don't forget that." He hesitated awkwardly near her at the studio couch. "Well, good-bye. Take care of yourself."

As Lurie reached the street he tried to remember whether Flo had said good-bye to him or not and wondered why she had been so quiet about the whole business. A feeling of distress overcame him and instead of going to his store he walked to the boardwalk. It was deserted in the drizzle. So near the ocean, unbroken by buildings, the rain seemed more mournful and colder. Lurie, bundling himself in his raincoat, discovered that the greater drive of the rain here somehow brought him comfort. The concessions that lined the shore side of the boardwalk were now closed, the heavy overhanging shutters fastened down, and without the lights, without the gaudy interiors, the places were ugly, cheaply put together and dismal. Lurie suddenly hated Neptune Beach. The thousands and thousands of people who came by subway in the summer from all parts of the city to lie on the dirty beaches, frying in the sun; the boardwalk itself at night with the unbroken lines of people marching and clumping on the wood flooring, swinging their wet bathing bags with one hand and eating frozen-custard cones with the other; the great lights, the barkers' cries, the raw anxieties of the concessionaires to realize every possible nickel on the day, the constant hum that rose in unvarying strength above the crowds—Herbert Lurie thought of Neptune Beach in the summer when the crowds with their human odors came out seeking a good time almost hysterically. It was a depressing thing to see them. Neptune Beach became loud, hard, selfish, low in every respect, full of clangor. Lurie planned to move out of Neptune Beach with Dorothy.

Crossing the boardwalk, he sat down on a bench facing the ocean, knowing he was long overdue at the store and not caring. As he watched the silent mysterious swell of the water, Lurie thought of Dorothy and of his first wife and of Flo, feeling strangely weak and foolish because of them. When he had married his wife seven years ago, he had been completely convinced and sure with her, believing that their life together would always be happy. But before three years had passed their marriage proved a steady stream of fights, a constant irritation, so that when he met Flo he felt desperately impelled to have his wife divorce him. And how sure he had been with Flo! It had turned out a lucky thing, at least, that he had had to wait for his wife's divorce to take effect—otherwise he would have married her.

Lurie knew that when the news spread about Flo and Dorothy he would feel ashamed before the boys at Ann's. The hell with them, he thought, watching the enormous movement of the black water. They were a bunch of no-good bums, every one of them, greedy for a dollar. They would kill their own mothers if there was anything to be gained. No sentiment, no feeling, not a true friend in the whole bunch, thought Lurie. You chewed the fat with them at Ann's, they played poker together, most evenings in his own house, they went to the racetrack two or three times the season and they were friends, but they couldn't be trusted an inch and well did Lurie know it. They had one of two things on their minds, money or a girl. Nothing else counted.

The thought of Dorothy, innocent and young, working at Ann's, made him wince with pain. He stood up abruptly, resolved that this would be the last day she worked in the soda parlor. Lurie realized that it was late, that his clerk would soon be waiting for him, and he hurried back. As he walked he thought of Dorothy, of her youth and how pretty she was with her blond hair and lovely smooth skin. Lurie thought of their home together, away from Neptune Beach, in Flatbush, maybe. They'd get a three-room flat, he'd sell the furniture and outfit the apartment with entirely new stuff. He grew warm with plans. He might even manage to get out of the retail dress line and leave Neptune Beach altogether. As he swung down the street, Lurie began singing and swinging his arms. Now and again he would suddenly smack his hand with his fist.

At Ann's the lunch rush was beginning. Shorty was working rapidly at the bread table, wiping his knife often, not because it needed wiping but because this was an appropriate gesture, somehow reminding him of his importance as he thought of the night and Madame Pavlovna. From time to time he bawled out Arthur, crossly screwing up his eyebrows until the line almost met across the bridge. Arthur would never be fast enough to team up with as fast a worker as Shorty. And Spitzbergen was out somewhere when he should be behind the counter giving him a hand. The whole job at Ann's was on Shorty's shoulders.

Moe Karty was in the back again, now working on the handicappers of the afternoon papers to see how those experts coincided with his own selections. As for his wife, in the midst of his present concerns she was completely forgotten. At two o'clock the wires opened up on Hawthorne, Agawam, Detroit, Latonia, Suffolk Downs, and Aqueduct, and a man had no time to lose, particularly if he followed Karty's system, which played the favorites at all tracks to place and show when the bookmaker took the bet. One to two, one to three, one to five, and even one to ten were the prices here, so that a player had to bet on as many races at as many tracks as he could to win a fair amount.

The trouble was that Karty never had enough money. He always deserted his system, losing on some tempting long shot. If Karty could ever manage to get his hands on a thousand dollars, not in driblets, but in one lump, he would play a progressive system and clean up a million without a doubt. As it was, the bookmakers were a gang of chiselers. When a horse looked like a sure investment, they knew it, too, and often refused the bet if you wanted to play it cautiously on second or third place. A bettor was practically forced to take on the long shots. Karty pondered on Fifi, Joe (Grey Lag) Wack's daily special. The morning line in the *Green Sheet* on Fifi was eight to one but God alone knew what the official price might finally be. The *Telegraph*'s form chart gave the filly's workouts—special private clockers, nuts!—at thirty-four and four-fifths for the three furlongs, but, geez, this was the first time out and you never could tell. All the same Mower paid six to one first time out and won, and last year Karty himself had caught Brevity in his debut at Saratoga. Five to one. That was money.

Some building workmen were already at their lunch on the stools, fat-hipped in their overalls. Big loose faces with heavy stubbles, hoarse voices talking loudly through food, a great burst of laughter every minute, laughter like a fit. A heavy woman was having trouble with her chocolate parfait, her mind distracted from her work by her son, who wanted a taste. "Goddam you, stop boddering!" she finally bawled out. "Eat your fruit cup." The boy didn't want fruit cup, it was chocolate parfait he longed for. A four-year-old was climbing up the stool at the double-decked water tray with great absorption, trying to reach the tap and turn on the water himself. He struggled for a full minute, straining every muscle, holding his tongue in his teeth with concentration, until his finger finally managed to touch the pedal. Success. "Stop," cried his mother. "Wild Injun! Must bust everything, else he ain't satisfied." She slapped him down. It was too much after such labor. The kid bawled his head off. Shorty, doing the work of two men, looked up from the steam table, reproving but helpless. "Get going with the blue plates," he yelled at Arthur, and Arthur, trotting blithely on his toes, answered, "Just a minute. In a moment." All in all, Mr. Spitzbergen, out somewhere in the rain hunting up Shubunka, would have taken solemn pleasure in the sight.

When Herbert Lurie walked into Ann's Dorothy was back in the parlor, taking the orders of two young ladies, very smart and deliberate over their cigarettes, which they held in the corners of their mouths. Removing the cigarettes reluctantly, picking the paper bits off their heavily rouged lips, they looked at Dorothy as though she were a necessary evil. With a sigh they gave their orders: two grilled Swiss cheese sandwiches on white bread and Coca-Colas with a shot of lemon.

"Hey, Dorothy!" yelled Arthur joyously. "He's here."

"I'll do something to you," she said to the dishwasher. She looked at Lurie. "You, too."

"Keep quiet. Please," said Shorty with delicate offense. "Don't holler around. This is a place of business." He turned to Lurie. "A fine time you picked to come in for breakfast."

"What's the matter, you don't like it?" Ann's gave a specially priced breakfast but it was supposed to be eaten before ten.

"Hell," said Shorty confidentially. "It makes no damn difference to me at all but you know Spitz. It gets him sore, and who does he take it out on? See how I mean?"

"Oh, nuts," said Lurie gaily as he passed down to pick a table. "Don't you hand me an argument this morning."

"Smart guy," said Shorty, looking tough and sullen.

"What?"

"You heard me," the soda jerker said, then in an instant lost courage and shifted his eyes down, pretending he was busy over the sandwiches. "Fry the eggs for him," he told Arthur, still holding his head down. Lurie slapped Shorty smartly on his bald spot. The jerker dropped everything and hopped, uncontrollable with anger. "Jesus Christ! Jesus Christ!" he sputtered wildly. Everyone at the fountain watched the horseplay in silent amusement until the kid with the fruit cup pointed at Shorty writhing and yelled out loud: "Donald Duck!" And it was true. Writhing and sputtering, he looked just like the enraged animal in the cartoon pictures. Everyone roared. In his mortification Shorty opened the cellar door and was halfway down the steps before he recovered himself. He found it difficult to think of Madame Pavlovna with equanimity at this time.

As Arthur passed Lurie on his way to the kitchen, he said, "You must be feeling good today. That's the way it seems to me."

"Scaram, kid," said Lurie. He went up to Dorothy who was

pretending to be working on a checkbook, her back turned on him. He put his arms around her, careful to keep his hands off her bosom to avoid offense.

"Herbert!" she cried. "For goodness sakes. Not here, of all places."

"Hello, honey," Lurie said. He kissed her on the neck.

"Stop!" Dorothy struggled out of his embrace. "Really, Herbert, it don't look nice one bit. What will people think of me?" Lurie stepped back and laughed foolishly. "What's the matter you're so late today? You been to the store yet?"

Lurie stopped laughing. "Yes, I opened up but it can wait. There's nothing doing in the store this time anyway." He paused. "See, I had it out with Flo. That's all over, all finished. We had an understanding."

"Oh, I told you not to do it!" cried Dorothy. "Herbert, why did you do it? I feel terrible."

"Don't be silly. You got nothing to do with it. It had to happen sooner or later. We're both better off the way it turned out."

"What did she say?" Dorothy asked tenderly.

"She said nothing. She felt about it the same way I did. So what are you going to do about it? Cry over it?"

"Oh, I feel terrible. I feel awful. What's Flo going to do now?"

"Don't worry about her. She's all right. She'll go back to her folks in Albany."

Dorothy stood there, as though in a trance, holding her hands together over her checkbook, her face drawn in sorrowful reverie, as one stands at funerals. "It's awful. Just awful. You can imagine how I feel about the whole thing. I'll never be able to look myself in the face again. I don't know how I'll ever look in a mirror."

Lurie looked at her, glum-faced, his jowls feeling heavy and round.

"So?" he asked.

"So what?" she asked with complete wonder.

"Well, what do you say?"

"I have no idea what's going on in your mind, Herbert," she said innocently.

"See, this is a proposal. You said how it might be if it happened

I was a man without responsibilities. Well, so what do you say? I'm unattached." Lurie stood there uncomfortably with his weight on one foot, looking steadfastly at her as he waited for her answer no matter how uncertain and weak he felt.

"It can wait a while," Dorothy said with soft reproach. "After all, there's no rush. You might think of my feelings on the subject."

"Ah," said Lurie with relief, "you'll get over it. Only a little dope like you would worry her head over a thing like this. You're a fool. After all, Flo's no baby. She's thirty-two, old enough to know what she's doing, and she knew what it was about all along." He started laughing. "You're a baby, Dot. You're just a kid."

"It don't make any difference," Dorothy said. "I can imagine how Flo feels right this minute."

Shorty was calling to Dorothy that when she felt good and ready she might bring Mr. Herbert Lurie his morning orange juice. He was sore and had just managed to screw up the courage to call her. While she had been standing with Lurie, he had to run around to the cashier's stand, ringing up the cash.

"I'll throw something at you," Lurie said dispassionately to the jerker.

"Oh, yare?"

"Want to see?" Lurie picked up the sugar bowl. Shorty applied himself to his duties, turning away and muttering. Lurie laughed good-naturedly.

"I better be going," Dorothy said.

"O.K., baby." Arthur brought the eggs, grinning. "What the hell you so happy about this time of the day?" Lurie asked him.

"Who, me?"

"Dopey mutt." He sat down, pleased with himself and happy. Arthur brought up the toast and orange juice. As Lurie began his breakfast, Karty came to his table, nervous and quick, looking at the door for his wife.

"How's the horses, Moe?" Lurie asked. "They tell me they're putting in a bed at Ann's here for you."

"We'll dispense with the comedy."

Lurie squeezed the toast into a lump and dipped it into the egg yolk. "When you going back to work, Moe? After all, you can realize it as good as the next man, this is no life. You're crazy."

"When I'll ask you, you'll tell me."

"O.K. Don't get sore. It's all in fun."

"You can't make no money working with your hands, not in this day and age," Karty said bitterly.

"You're a professional, I thought. You got brains. You got an education. An accountant."

"It's all the same. You sell your time, that's all there is to it. All right, couple of years ago a smart accountant could make seventy, eighty a week, even a hundred and more. That was something. Work my head off for a lousy thirty a week? Not for Moe Karty. Not me."

"What's the matter with your wife's brothers? They're rich, they got a big garage on Bedford Avenue. Why don't they take you in as a partner?"

Karty took a drink of water, his weasel face looking pained at the thought. "My wife's brothers, they stink. That's that."

"O.K.! If that's the way you feel."

"Listen, I know figures, ain't it? I'm an accountant. If I know anything, it's figures. I could make a fortune out of the races, only I ain't got enough money."

"I'd like to believe it. Every time I followed one of your tips I lost."

"Oh, yare?" Karty's sharp face screwed with angry disgust. His Adam's apple bobbed up and down. Look at him, said Lurie, ain't human. "Every tip I gave you lost? How about Flatrock the other day at Agawam?"

"So what? Paid four-twenty. Even money, practically. Nuts."

"See, that's the trouble with you guys. All you want is long shots. That's what makes the bookies rich men. Listen, when you put money in the bank, what interest do you ask for? Three and a half percent and you're glad to take three. Here you win more than a hundred-percent profit on Flatrock and it ain't big enough."

"Get out of here!" cried Lurie, losing patience. "You're crazy! Absolutely nuts."

"What's the matter?" Karty asked, his eyes glaring at Lurie through inflamed lids. "Play it my system and it's as good as an investment in a bank. Interest. That's what it is."

"Your system. I can see how you're cleaning up yourself, your system's so hot."

"See, you got to play with more money, that's all. You need a lot. Like I say. Listen, Herbert," Karty said, speaking low in earnest whispers, "what about the syndicate idea? Five hundred from you, five from Shubunka and Spitz, I put in five and I play the horses on a progressive system with the two thousand. We can't lose. We'll make a fortune."

"Get out!" said Lurie. "Leave me alone!"

"I know plenty guys making a good living on the horses. Only they got the capital."

"You're crazy, Moe. You're absolutely out of your mind. I hate to see you act like this."

"Listen, Herbert. If those guys can make money on the track, I'll clean up. Remember, I know figures."

"Please don't bother me. You're crazy with the heat."

"Well, what do you say? It's the last time I'm asking you."

"Let me alone. Can't you take no for an answer? What the hell do you want from me anyhow? Can't you go to Shubunka? Go to Spitz. I ain't got five hundred bucks to throw out. Maybe they have."

Karty rose from the table, his face covered with bitterness and anger. "Son of a bitch," he said, half to himself. "Throws his money out on broads, goes after anything with a skirt on and wants to marry her. That's all right. I give him an A-one proposition. He don't want it. It's throwing money out."

"Go to hell, you lousy bastard," said Lurie. "Where do you get off talking to me like that? I'll throw this coffee right in your rat face."

"Women on his mind, that's all. Love like in the movies. Kitzl, kitzl, kitzl. A cathouse ain't good enough for him."

Lurie put down his knife and fork and stood up. "Hey, Karty, you said enough. If you want to get out of here in one piece, beat it. I took all out of you I want to take today."

"Son of a bitch," said Karty, moving to his table near the ice-cream machine. "Son of a bitch." He had intended to borrow ten or fifteen dollars from Lurie but the syndicate idea had driven everything out of his mind. Now he wouldn't have more than twenty bucks with which to play the six tracks. That meant he'd have to shoot for better-priced horses again. It was a losing proposition, but what could he do? Karty sat down with the papers, cursing at the stupidity of the men in Ann's. It was clear as daylight. Hadn't he figured it out for them again and again? He knew figures, didn't he? With sufficient capital they couldn't possibly lose, playing for the horse to come in either second or third on a progressive system. Karty turned to Fifi, Joe (Grey Lag) Wack's special. A filly, a two-year-old, first time out, but eight to one on the morning line.

Herbert Lurie had little taste for his breakfast. What Karty said disturbed him sharply because it was true in its way, a reasonable reaction to his marriages, and Lurie recognized it. He smoked his cigarette, wondering whether there was a rush with Dorothy after all. Perhaps it would be better to wait a few months just to see how things turned out. But in his heart Lurie distressingly realized that the longer he stayed away from Dorothy, the more sharply would he feel her absence, the more urgently he would want her, and that nothing would help until they married. Troubled and uncertain, Lurie sat on over his breakfast and chewed his fingers as he thought and worried.

Up in front the noon rush was well over. By this time Shorty was able to think peacefully of the great curves of Madame Pavlovna and what the night held in store for him. He burst into snatches of "Is It True What They Say About Dixie?" but caught himself up in his exultation as he remembered his masculine dignity. Arthur had filled the second basin with hot water and suds until a fine bubbling foam appeared on the surface. Now he was absently drawing pictures in the suds, hastening his work so that the design might be completed before the movement of the water closed the lines again. Karty yelled to him for the time. "Ten to two," Arthur said. "Geez!" cried Karty. He gathered his papers in a bundle and was off for the Garden, the bookmaker, and the Teleflash, which broadcast results from all Eastern tracks.

"It's a disease," said Shorty.

"You ever bet on the races?" Arthur asked. He was very much impressed by gambling, the attribute of the full-grown man.

"Now and again," said Shorty. "Just for the hell of it, don't you know? Nobody can beat the races."

"I never bet on a race in my life," Arthur said regretfully. "Never even saw one, outside of the newsreels."

Shorty had fixed up a pot of tea. "Arthur," he whispered, "take this in to Mrs. Pavlovna. See, just say it's from Shorty and not to forget. She'll understand."

"Oh, boy!" said Arthur, his eyes brightening. He wiped his hands.

"Don't be a kid," the jerker said, speaking calmly, for he was an adult, knew all the answers and took these things in his stride.

"Geez," said Arthur, taking the pot. "Mr. Spitzbergen would get sore if he saw me. He wouldn't like it a bit."

"I'll do the worrying."

"And the machine. You didn't clean it yet."

"Go on with the tea. Spitz'll never know the difference whether I clean it or not. Just tell her Shorty sent it, she shouldn't forget. Remember. She'll understand."

Back at his table Herbert Lurie was reading the *News*. Dorothy was working on her accounts at the cashier's stand but he didn't call her. He remembered that his clerk was alone in the store, suddenly discovered that it became urgent for him to go back, and he rose. As he passed Dorothy at the cashier's he said rapidly, "Back in a minute. I want to talk with you. Going to the store."

Dorothy looked at him tenderly. "Herbert," she said, "I feel funny about the whole business. I don't know what to do."

"Don't worry. It'll all straighten out by itself. Just forget it." Lurie held the back of her neck affectionately in his palm, shaking her head to drive away the worry. He smiled at her. "You're a dope," he said fondly and walked out of the store. But once in the drizzle, Lurie's face grew downcast, the wavering feelings taking possession of his mind again.

Lurie was selling cottons this summer, ninety-eight cents to five ninety-five, culottes, sunbacks, tennis dresses, jacket ensembles, and shirtwaists. The windows were niftily dressed with a large checkered gingham sign suspended from the ceiling saying The Cotton Shop. The walls were papered to represent an old Southern field with the happy darkies grinning among the cotton balls. At the corners two miniature bales of raw cotton were opened with the white stuff spilling on the floor. Lurie looked at the dresses, hanging on the wire stands, pulled back tightly at the waist to give them shape. A fine display, he thought, but he was sick of it. It had been standing there for two weeks, unchanged. Karty was right. All he thought about was women and love. A little disgusted with himself, Lurie entered the store.

At Ann's Arthur returned from Madame Pavlovna's. Shorty went up to him immediately.

"What'd she say?"

The dishwasher giggled. "She said it vas very sveet of you."

Shorty grinned broadly, shaking his head with pleasure. "Is it true what they say about Dixie? Is it true what they do down there?" he sang, and then he stopped all at once. "O.K.," he said. Two men came into the store.

Shorty went bouncing up the flats and put his hands on the counter, leaning over toward them questioningly. They had fat solemn faces. The jerker watched them apprehensively as they kept on standing in their sporty raincoats at the door near the street stand, their hands in their pockets, looking the place over silently.

"Yes?" asked Shorty.

"Shubunka ain't in?" one of them asked, sniffling his nose energetically.

"Who, Shubunka? Oh, no," said Shorty in his soft intimate manner. "See, he don't come here regular."

"Well, that's too bad," said the man, sniffling and scowling.

"Oh, I can give him a message if you want it."

"When we want him we'll find him." The silent one shifted his weight to the other leg. His friend sniffled and declared, "We want the boss. It's Spitzbergen we want. Tell him we want to talk to him."

"He ain't in either," Shorty explained confidentially.

"Nuts," said the sniffler. "He's always in this time of day. Tell him we want to see him."

"Oh, no, he ain't in. See, he's got other investments. Real estate, apartments, bungalows on Featherbed Path, don't you know? And he spends a lot of his time taking care of his property. See, you can't find him in all the time."

The sniffler paused, considering. He looked around. "Who's that?" He pointed at Arthur whose mouth was open as he stared at them.

"Dishwasher," said Shorty, feeling uncomfortable and frightened. "He's the dishwasher."

"Who's the girl?" Dorothy was looking at them, puzzled and scared, too.

"Cashier," cried Shorty. "Say, what the hell?"

"Shaddap," said the man. He turned to his companion, dismissing Shorty before him. "This guy on the level? The boss said he'd be in this time of day. You think he's stalling?"

"No," said the other. "I don't think he's got the guts to stall us."

"B'gee!" exclaimed Shorty. "What the hell would I be wanting to stall you guys for?"

"Pip, pip," said the sniffler. "Look at him go."

"Hold your water," the other told Shorty. "What's burning on you?"

"We'll be in tomorrow, Baldy," the first one said. "Tell the boss to be here."

"Hell," said Shorty, stung by the name. "You don't have to get wise about it. Listen, I don't know who you guys are and I don't care, see? But I don't like to let nobody get away with any baldy cracks, see how I mean?"

The man looked at his companion with a mild expression of amazement, jerking his thumb at the soda jerker. "O.K., kid," he said. "You're all right. Just give him the message."

"That's different, mister," Shorty said. He bent over the counter toward them. "See, if anybody comes in here, wants me to do something for them, why, hell, I'm glad to be of service, that's me. Only they got to be decent about it, see? I don't take no crap from nobody, big or small." The jerker wiped his hands on his apron and played with a glass on the ice tray. "O.K. I'll give Spitz the message."

"O.K., kid, you're all right," said the man. He had been watching Shorty as the jerker told them what a tough guy he was, and now he couldn't resist the temptation. The sniffler leaned over and slapped Shorty on the head. The jerker squirmed and sputtered, shivering like a monkey on a string.

"What the hell you getting all excited about?" the man said, sore at the racket Shorty was making. He spoke with fine offense. "You can take a joke, ain't it? Somebody might think I hurt you or something. Did it hurt I slapped you? Listen, lady," he said to Dorothy, "you see me hurt him or something?"

"Well, that's not the idea," said Dorothy. "A person's got feelings, especially when he's sensitive."

"Aw, nuts," said the man, wondering.

The other pulled his arm impatiently. "Come on and let's cut the bushwah. This don't get us no place." As they went out the door, the man sniffled and said to Shorty, "Don't forget the message. Tell him we'll be in tomorrow." They went into the street.

"Smart guys," said Shorty fiercely.

"Can you imagine?" Dorothy asked.

Arthur came trotting up from the double basins. "I don't like the looks of those guys at all," he said earnestly. "They don't look right to me one bit."

"Think they're a bunch of gorillas or something," said Shorty, scowling through the door in their direction. "They try any of that stuff on me, I'll give them something they won't forget. B'gee! Not for a good long while they won't!" Shorty, moving up the fountain, sought consolation as he thought how he would handle those mugs the next time they came into the store. Biff! Crack on the jaw, butting with his head. Shorty would do it just the way James Cagney laid them low in the movies. While the guy was groggy, slam! bang! A left and a right, two jabs over the heart and a finisher on the button. Those mugs were on the floor. Shorty actually looked at the floor, almost expecting to see them there. Small guy or no small guy, Shorty would show them. “Wise mugs,” the jerker told Dorothy. “I’ll kick their teeth in next time they try to pull something funny on me.”

“Somebody ought to teach people like them a lesson,” she said. “Some people are too smart for their own good.” She went back to her work, checking the slips with the money in the register.

“No,” confirmed Arthur in his breathless manner, “I don’t like the looks of those men at all. Something funny’s going on. Mr. Shubunka and Mr. Spitzbergen and now those guys. What do you think it’s all about anyway?”

“Aw, shaddap,” Shorty said, tough as anything. “What the hell you want to horse around with questions, too?”

Arthur wiped his hands and went walking out of the store. “I was just asking,” he said resentfully. “It’s still a free country, isn’t it?”

“Where the hell do you think you’re going?” Shorty asked.

“I want to get the teapot before Mr. Spitzbergen gets back. Otherwise he’ll get sore.”

“Let me do the worrying about Spitz, see?”

Shorty walked up and down the flats, thinking of Madame Pavlovna, trying to recover his self-esteem.

Mrs. Karty caught her husband at last. Karty was just going out of the Garden for a walk around the block. The smoke and beer smells in the saloon, together with his constant cigarettes, had given him a bad headache and he wanted to lose it in the air, but the minute he stepped outside, he could see his big wife pumping down the street on her knock knees. Karty moved to duck back but he realized she saw him and restrained himself. He walked up to her aggressively.

“Where’s the fire?” he asked her, his nose like a snout. “What’s the matter?”

“Come on home, you,” she said. “You’re in hot water, believe me!” She tried to grab his wrist but he fought free.

"Leave me alone!" he exclaimed. "Where the hell you get off pulling this stuff on me? Go on home, beat it. I got a lucky streak. I can't leave now."

"You'll need all the luck you can lay your hands on!" She shook her head grimly. "They'll fix you, all right!"

"Don't raise a holler," Karty paled with fear. He pushed his wife under the awning of a store. "What's the matter all of a sudden?"

"Matter? All of a sudden?" Mrs. Karty laughed loudly. "It's a pity. He ain't got the least idea! It's too bad about you!"

"Well, for Christ's sakes, what did I do now?"

Her laughter soured at once. "You know perfectly well. You stole the money from the garage."

"Balls!" exploded Karty. He went white. "Who told you that bull?"

"Never mind who told me. It's the truth and you know it!"

"Your lousy brothers told you that?" Karty was gagging. As he spoke the saliva gathered at his mouth and he was spitting. "Your lousy brothers, let me tell you something, they stink! How do you like that? I go ahead for years and do their accounting for a song and this is what I get! Gratitude! The thanks you get! When I got married, sure, they were going to give me all kinds of business. I'm going to make a fortune from my wife's family. Nuts! I'm a rich man! Sure! Just look!"

"You stole the money!" yelled Mrs. Karty. "You can talk from today until tomorrow."

"What am I got to do with the garage? Do I go near the money? Do I handle anything? Why do they want to tell you that bull for? It ain't true, they know it ain't true, and you know it ain't true! So that's that. And now you go on and beat it. You leave me alone. Jesus Christ!"

"You can yell your head off, it won't help a bit! They brought in a new accountant and went over the books. There's a shortage thirteen hundred dollars. So?"

Karty pulled out his pockets for her. "See? I got it! Here, look! I took it! It's in my pockets! Yare, sure!"

"They got it by now!" She pointed to the Garden. "There it is, every cent of it, thrown out on the horses!"

"You're crazy! What's the use talking? Listen to reason. You want to listen to reason a minute? All right. Who are these accountants? What do they know? Suppose they make a mistake? And if there is a shortage, I had to take it? I have to be the only crook in America? What a wife! With a family like yours, what should I expect if not a slob like you?"

"It won't do any good, Moe! Holler until you're blue in the face! Give back the thirteen hundred dollars!"

"Sure!" cried Karty. "I'm running! Watch me!"

"If you're smart, you'll give it back in a hurry. You know my brothers. When they got something in their heads, it's just too goddam bad. You stole the money, you'll pay it back. If not, what they'll do to you I just can't repeat."

"Yare? You tell your lousy brothers they lay a finger on me I'll break in their lousy heads, see? And I can do it, too. Murder is cheap. I know just as many bums they know, and what they can do I can also."

"All right, Moe. I told you, now you know. Better give back the money or you'll be in the hospital."

"All right, so you told me. Now you can get the hell out of here. Now you can go back and tell your fine brothers I said they're lousy. Tell them I said they smell out loud, they're so rotten. Tell them I won't go near their lousy garage again if they paid me a million dollars to go over the books. I'm washed up. And with you, too. You can take back the millions your brothers said they would give me when I got married and give it back to them. Tell them they know what they can do with it."

"Moe," said Mrs. Karty, gritting her teeth as she waited for his outburst to end, "it won't help. Pay back the thirteen hundred dollars."

Late in the afternoon Mr. Spitzbergen came back to the soda parlor, black and wet, scowling profoundly as though this alone would ward off from him further trouble.

"Mr. Shubunka," he asked, "did he come? Did he telephone?"

Shorty greased up confidentially to the boss. "No, he didn't come in all day," he whispered. "Couple of guys, though, came in looking for you. Said they'd be back tomorrow and they wanted you to be here to meet them."

"What did they want? Who were they?"

"Search me, Mr. Spitzbergen. Never saw either of them before in my life. Wise guys."

Mr. Spitzbergen groaned. More trouble, without a doubt. He asked how the business had been all day and Shorty shrugged his shoulders intimately, saying, "Well, you know how it is on a rainy day. Just the lunch rush and not too much of that."

Spitzbergen had opened the cash register and looked glumly at the money. "All right, all right. That's enough. I don't want to hear no more. You cleaned the ice-cream machine?"

"A thorough job," declared Shorty.

Arthur giggled. The boss looked at him, puzzled. Then he noticed Dorothy sitting at a table with Lurie, and he went up to her, boiling. As he left, Shorty whispered through the side of his mouth, "What did I tell you? He'll never know the difference." Arthur said, "Oh, boy!" and marveled at the soda jerker. Some people just had a way.

"Keep it to yourself, Spitz," Lurie told the boss. "Dorothy's quitting tonight."

"What's the matter, all of a sudden quitting?"

"Does it make a difference if I tell you?"

"You quitting?" Spitzbergen asked Dorothy. "For real?"

"It looks like it," she said quietly.

"All right, quit then, I should worry." Mr. Spitzbergen, tired and overburdened, was helpless. "Maybe if they all quit it would be a better idea." He went muttering to the kitchen, to dry out.

"What will I tell my mother?" Dorothy asked Herbert.

"Tell her the truth. What's to be ashamed of in getting married? It's no crime."

"Well, you know. About you. You can imagine how my mother would feel about Flo and everything."

"As they say, what you don't know, it won't hurt you. Who says she has to know everything?"

"Maybe we ought to wait, Herbert. It's all too sudden. It don't look nice, I mean so soon after Flo and all. After all, you got to take my feelings into consideration. I'm a human being, not an animal."

Herbert reassured her, saying it would work out and that there was no necessity for a fuss, but Dorothy felt uneasy. This was not how she imagined it would be when love came to her. Not that she ever thought the movies were true to life particularly, but after all, there was such a thing as romance. And no honeymoon.

"I don't see why we can't take a week off and go away," she said. "We might spend some time in the country. There's an adult camp in the Adirondacks, very reasonable. Only twenty-two fifty a week."

Herbert Lurie again grew disheartened. One moment protesting at the thought of marriage so soon after Flo, the next wheedling for a honeymoon. There was something in her tone that seemed to echo his life with the others—the petty arguments, the everlasting state of irritation, the calloused apathy and indifference to one another. And it seemed a sort of premonition that this marriage, too, might be doomed to sourness and lifelessness. Lurie tried to shake himself out of his despondency by driving all thought from his mind, but he didn't succeed completely.

"Not," Dorothy was rushing to say, "that this is the time and place to be considering honeymoons. There are other more important things to worry about. Except, of course, I don't know what to tell my mother. When my sister got married, it was a ceremony in a hall and they went away for two weeks to Lake George."

"Tell her the truth," Lurie said. "Tell her it's the busy season in Neptune Beach and I can't leave my store just when the rush begins."

"I suppose it's reasonable," Dorothy admitted. "But you know how it looks. After all, not a regular wedding, only a ceremony at

City Hall, and then no honeymoon. It looks kind of funny. You have to admit it, if you want to be fair about it. At least," Dorothy argued, "if that has to be the case I don't see why you want to move out of Neptune Beach to Flatbush just when the season is starting. Personally, I can't see the sense in it. People come from all over the city to the beach in the summer, why do you want to go away?"

"See, that's the way I want it," said Lurie. How could he tell her that he, Herbert Lurie, whom she had seen cursing and fighting with the others in Ann's, wanted to get away from them, from Neptune Beach, from the lowness of the life? How could he tell her he wanted a decent, softer way of living? That he was tired and sick with things as they were with him and that he wanted change? Lurie knew it would be hopeless to talk. She would never understand him, never believe him, wonder what he was getting at.

Lost in thought, Dorothy was absently wetting her lips with her tongue and setting a strand of hair in its place. This was something she did often and in her own way. As Lurie watched the gesture, she seemed especially young and feminine to him. She was just a kid, barely twenty-four. While they kept silent, he noticed again the delicate pink tints of her cheek, the fair skin, the smooth lines of her girlish throat and her soft round shoulders, and she seemed more beautiful, younger, more innocent than ever. He grew heartened. He would take her with him out of Neptune Beach, they'd live away from the people and places they knew, and there would be kindness and gentleness. He held her arm in his fingers, pressing to feel the soft young flesh. She was like a baby.

Mr. Spitzbergen came out of the kitchen. "See, see," he grumbled. "I pay her good money. She sits and talks, the store can fall down."

"Sourpuss," said Lurie. "She's quitting tonight. Cheer up for once in your life."

"What am I got to be happy? Tell me, Mr. Lurie, maybe you know?" He stood in his misery before Lurie.

"I better go back," said Dorothy. "I might as well."

"O.K., honey," he said, sighing happily. He held her hand. "I'm going with you." He had to return to his dress shop.

"Boddering with girls," said Mr. Spitzbergen, following them to the front of the parlor. "A nice business for a grown-up man." Shorty had been looking at the clock on the arch over the entrance to the parlor. At five his relief man came in and he was counting the minutes. Arthur envied him. He had to work all night, this day, but to make up for it he was off the whole afternoon from one o'clock tomorrow. A lady came in for a lime rickey and Arthur had to admire Shorty's suave manner, the sly smile, the apt word or two in the right spots. "See," sidemouthed Shorty to him, "that's how to make them. Of course, I haven't the desire, but if I wanted to I could get that dame in a minute to do anything I wanted her to. Well, hell, look for yourself, you can see how I got her going already!" He smiled, impish with pride.

"What you and Mrs. Pavlovna going to do tonight?" Arthur asked. "Really, I just got the curiosity to know."

"Never you mind," Shorty said, his face growing hard. "I'm not the kind goes around talking about the dames he's put away. See, I can't stand those guys myself. They're despicable, lowest type in the world. If a fellow wants to fool around with girls, O.K., only he ought to have a certain amount of honor about it. See how I mean?"

Shorty looked wise and stern and glanced at the clock again. Not he to lay bare a woman's innermost secrets, not the gallant Shorty. The telephone rang. He went to it soberly.

"If it's Shubunka," the boss said anxiously, "I want to talk to him."

"It's your wife, Mr. Spitzbergen," Shorty said.

The boss threw up his hands. "Tell her I just dropped dead. I never heard good from her yet."

"Geez, it's too bad, Mrs. Spitzbergen," Shorty said, growing close and confidential with the mouthpiece, "but he just stepped outside for a minute. See, things slowed down a little and he thought he'd just step out a moment, don't you know?"

Mr. Spitzbergen, dreading the news, was singing sadly his little song about Louie, Louie, who wanted a beautiful wife and now had to lie in hell. Shorty held his palm over the mouthpiece. "She says she won't come home tonight. She's staying in the hospital for a thorough examination and she won't be home until tomorrow night."

She just had one two months ago! Mr. Spitzbergen started protesting violently to Shorty and Dorothy, explaining all the details. They cost forty-five dollars! X-rays, fluoroscopes, food tests. That wife of his was crazy!

"Hell, what do you want from me?" Shorty cried. "Tell her!"

Mr. Spitzbergen bundled into the telephone booth, his forehead glistening with sweat. "Madame Spitzbergen! You got to support all the doctors in New York City?" he yelled at her and slammed the door. They could hear him popping.

"B'gee!" said Shorty, indignant. "Somebody would think it was all my fault." He looked at the clock. Ten minutes to five. Ten minutes more. Then oo-la-la! Shorty felt overwhelmingly warm with his mastery. Some girls thought him a shrimp, but looks didn't count. Was Clark Gable really good-looking? Take Rudolph Valentino. Looked like an ordinary wop. Had the women crazy. It all depended on your line plus that certain something you either had or hadn't. He had managed Mrs. Pavlovna one, two, three, if he said so himself.

Inside the booth Mr. Spitzbergen was spitting protests and complaints but Shorty was happily planning to order the works at the barbershop, shampoo, singe, face massage, and tonic. He could see himself at the corset shop right this minute, dressed in his new white gabardine with the pinched-back jacket and the side slits. They'd take in a show at the Mermaid, have a bite at the Chink's, and then for Madame Pavlovna's apartment, alone, with the lights out. Shorty thought of the corsetière, big, fat and juicy. Shorty felt it would be like falling into a soft, warm, delicious bathtub; he dreamed of Oriental nights in a harem, and actually rocked on his feet.

But just at that moment the corsetière's clerk came into the soda store. "Madame Pavlovna said you should forgive her," the girl said to Shorty, "but she wants to know will you please excuse her. She's feeling indisposed."

"Jesus Christ!" moaned Shorty, not believing it. "You don't mean it!" He took the girl over to a side. "What's the matter with her?" he implored her. "She ain't feeling well? She got a headache? Then tell her to take a couple of aspirins and she'll be all right. Two aspirins and she'll be good as new."

"No," said the girl stubbornly, "she's just feeling indisposed. That's what she said I should say."

"All right, all right, I'll take care of this myself," said Shorty. He glanced at the boss in the booth and hurried to the fountain. Shorty fixed up an Alka-Seltzer. His relief man hadn't come in but he couldn't wait. Shorty went running out of the store with the Alka-Seltzer and a glass of water, keeping from crying with vexation and disappointment. He went to Madame Pavlovna's. But it did no good. With the greatest weariness she told him it vas impossible, some other time, Shurtee, tonight she vas exhausted. "A stand-up!" shrieked Shorty after he found his wheedling useless. That was what it was, a stand-up. The soda jerker had steamed himself up all day and now he was in a frenzy with frustration.

In Ann's Mr. Spitzbergen stumbled out of the telephone booth brokenly, mumbling weakly. He was soaked with perspiration. His wife was driving him to an early grave, it was only a question of weeks how much longer he would last. He was near a nervous breakdown, he was ready for the ambulance. He slaved to make a living and every cent he made with sweat and blood went direct to the doctors. Mr. Spitzbergen hated all doctors. They were vultures feeding on live flesh. All day it had rained. No customers had come in and the overhead was eating up the place. And where was Shubunka? The apartment on Third Street was smashed apart.

"Where is Shubunka?" Mr. Spitzbergen suddenly screamed. "Why don't he come in? Why don't he call up?"

Arthur grew frightened and scurried behind the fountain.

"Calm yourself, Mr. Spitzbergen," Dorothy exclaimed, showing offense at his rage. "This is no way for a man to act. You'll have a stroke."

"Yes, yes," muttered Spitzbergen hopelessly, groping away from them. "I'll get apoplexy, yes, yes." He was ashamed of his outburst before them. It lacked dignity. He went to hide in the kitchen and read the newspaper. "When Shubunka comes in, call me right away."

The relief man entered jauntily, bouncing on the balls of his feet, and whistling. His was a happy soul, free and self-contained. Without a word he went to the cellar door, hung up his hat and coat, put on the apron and faced the world, his arms crossed over his chest. On the dot of five o'clock.

Karty's eyes looked more swollen than ever over his sharp nose. His stomach had a nauseous feeling after too many cigarettes smoked one after the other without pleasure. He sat on the stool and ordered coffee to kill the sick taste in his mouth.

Karty smacked the marble-topped counter with his hand, wild with bitterness. His face screwed and his eyelids felt warm with water. Where was he going to get the thirteen hundred dollars? His wife's brothers were a pack of bastards, tight with a nickel. They wouldn't dare to lay a finger on him, Karty said, but all the same he worried and wondered where he could raise the money. Where did they get off, thirteen hundred dollars? All he took were some fives and tens once in a while. They were a bunch of crooks, figuring thirteen hundred dollars.

And this had to happen just when he was hitting a lucky streak, too. If it hadn't been for his wife busting in on him, he would have cleaned up today. Four horses had come in for him in an hour and a half: Evangelist at Agawam, Good Trade and Persian Prince at Aqueduct, and Blue Day at Suffolk Downs. Three-sixty, seven to ten, one to two, and four dollars they paid for the show, small prices but safe and conservative according to his system. Doubling up he would have won a hundred today easily. As it was, he had run his twenty dollars up to more than sixty! But his wife had to show up and raise the holler about the thirteen hundred dollars. Thirteen hundred bucks! said Karty, smacking the counter again. He had put the whole sixty bucks on Fifi, the two-year-old maiden filly that Joe (Grey Lag) Wack specially recommended as today's sure thing. The goddam bastard jumped the field at the start and led all the way to the turn where she ran out, finishing out of the money. The great Joe Wack. Every Bet An Investment. "Nuts," said Karty aloud. "Nuts." Now all he had were two or three dollars and he didn't know what he would do for cash for tomorrow's play. When Wack phoned him again he would say to him: "Oh, yare? You stink!" That was what Moe Karty would say to him. "Nuts," said Karty, smacking the counter. "Nuts. Nuts."

The happy-faced relief man was regarding Karty with polite curiosity, his arms still folded across his chest.

"What the hell you standing there looking at?" Karty asked.

The satisfied jerker, without changing expression, bounced up the slats to the other end of the fountain. He strictly minded his own business, never said a word.

"Stinkpot," said Karty, and gulping the coffee he wondered about his wife's brothers and whether they would really try anything on him if he didn't raise the money. They were no better than gangsters, but after all he was their sister's husband, wasn't he?

While Mr. Spitzbergen fretted unhappily over him at Ann's, Shubunka lay flat on his back in his apartment, holding a hand mirror close to his face while he laboriously tweezed out the hairs that grew between his eyebrows over his nose. His was a huge face, his jaws like slabs of meat, black with his beard no matter how often he shaved. His thick black hair, combed straight to the side and back, was heavily greased with Polymol. To save the pillow his head rested on a towel. As Shubunka plucked the hairs, his breath came in soft groans and sighs and his fat, loose mouth twitched a little. This hurt, but he had to pull out the hairs because with his big face, lumpy nose, and gross lips, the black line running unbroken across his eyes rendered him completely ugly, his face on his short thick neck then looking unnatural, like nothing human. Off in the corner the Victor Magic Eye radio was producing the music of "Goody, Goody," desultory tones from an afternoon band.

The telephone rang. Shubunka placed the tweezers at his side on the bedspread but he kept on looking into the mirror, gravely studying his face. Gradually his features broke into a warmhearted benign smile. His eyes solemnly examined his appearance to see how he looked with that expression on his face. The smile disappeared, his face grew reflective and soft, the lips parting a little. The bell rang again. Shubunka now was glaring into the mirror, his brow raised in furrows above the fierce bulging eyes, his teeth showing. Solemnly his eyes noted the expression in the glass. Then his face broke, the angry lines merging into those of a man who has just been amused, at first mildly. But now the joke grows, his cheeks go higher on the bones, the grin grows wider, wider, bursting into uproarious laughter. Shubunka's diaphragm shook and his eyes teared. The bell was still ringing. He rose from the bed and soberly kicked his legs to straighten the trousers at the crotch. Dimming "Goody, Goody" on the radio, he took out an English Oval from the long cigarette box and moved slowly to the phone. He picked it up, waiting.

"Who is it, please?" he asked, his voice flat. His caller told him, and now the voice became high-pitched with leisurely sarcasm. "Well, how do you do? It's nice to hear from you again. Really, it's a great pleasure."

He listened patiently. "I wouldn't say that," he said, his tone still shrill but easy and calm. "No, I would not say that. I'll tell you what you better do. Go down to the house on Baten Avenue. One eighty-three Baten Avenue. Yes." The voice cracked rapidly in the receiver. "No objections," said Shubunka, rebuking softly. "Please." He dropped the French phone on the rest, inhaled a moment in reflection, and, rushing to decision, restored "Goody, Goody" to its proper volume. He went to his clothes closet.

Looking at the rack of ties on the door, Shubunka remembered his father in the East Side when he was a boy. A glazier, a poor man, always in overalls, Shubunka could not remember him ever wearing a tie. Picking a true-striped bow with points, Shubunka recalled how he himself had broken both his legs when he had fallen off a roof while dodging a policeman after a kid gang fight. He stayed in the hospital that time eight months, and when he left it, he never took the trouble to go back to school. From then on, too, he was useless in helping his father on his rounds in the East Side looking for broken windows to repair. As a young man Shubunka had gone into the wicker business, porch sets mainly. But after four years of it he recognized the basic truth of making a living—you couldn't win fortunes working with your hands. You had to sell something. Shubunka moved to Brownsville and opened a candy store on Pitkin Avenue. But people didn't want candy. You had to sell them something they really wanted, something they would be willing to pay for well. Fixing the tie on his short round neck, Shubunka regarded his face, front view, the profiles, looking from all possible angles, and he didn't know whether to be satisfied or not.

The bell rang again. It proved to be a man excited about an arrest and the necessity for bail. Shubunka listened to him apathetically, half hearing him with all the noise from the radio.

"Tell you what to do," he said listlessly, the cigarette dangling. "Call up Charlie Angus and say I sent you. It's very simple. Don't worry about it too much."

The man protested that he didn't like the looks of it right after the place on Third Street was smashed. It looked bad. There were rumors.

"No connection," said Shubunka, patting his straight hair fondly. "It happens. After all, you can't grease indefinitely."

The man went on but Shubunka hung up. Standing before the mirror, he combed his hair into place perfectly. The Polymol grease collected heavily on the teeth of the comb. Shubunka threw it into the washbowl and turned on the hot water. He placed the hat painstakingly on his head, careful not to upset the arrangement of his hair, fixed the handkerchief in his breast pocket, looked at his fingernails. Taking the towel from the pillow, he dried the comb and slipped it behind the pocket handkerchief. He turned off the radio and went to the door, shifting his eyes to the mirror to see how he looked.

Shubunka waddled into Ann's on his bent legs, smelling sweetly from the hair grease and smiling pleasantly, a pleasant, kindly man. Karty, crouched over his coffee at the fountain, immediately swiveled around to him and touched him on the elbow.

"I want to talk to you," he said. "See, I got a proposition to make."

"Not interested in any propositions," Shubunka said blandly, looking at Dorothy. "But talk, all you want, only later."

"No, on the level," said Karty. "It's a proposition you'll like. See, this is something hot."

"Very well. Only later. I'm occupied for the time being. I'll be with you in a minute."

"O.K.," Karty said. "O.K."

Shubunka went up to the cashier's stand and said in his high-pitched voice, "Good evening, little girl. You look very pretty tonight. A picture, really, like a picture." He stood beaming at her.

Something about him always repelled Dorothy. Perhaps it was the heavy fat face with its thick red lips, reminding Dorothy somehow of butcher's meat. It might have been the waddle of his hipless body on those bent legs, or the sweet smell of the hair tonic struggling over the odors of a large body in the summer, or just his ingratiating manner, oily and ponderous. Fine drops of perspiration rested in a line on his forehead. Dorothy kept herself from receding. As his face clouded before her, she forced a smile. "I'm quitting tonight," she said, eager not to offend. "It's my last night."

"You don't say!" exclaimed Shubunka. "You are really quitting? Oh, I am so sorry to hear the news." He paused. "You have a good reason, I suppose?"

Dorothy laughed as if with embarrassment and looked down on the floor. "I'm getting married. It's a sort of a secret."

"How nice!" He extended his arm, tipping the cigarette ash away from them. "How very nice. I am glad to hear it. Mr. Lurie, I presume? A fine man, a little too old for such a youngster like you, I should think. You don't agree? Well, a fine man. I like him very much." He reached out to touch her curls. Dorothy bit her lip and stood firm. "I must give you something. A little something to celebrate the occasion properly."

Dorothy smiled uncomfortably. Karty, who had been watching them all the time from his stool, cursed under his breath, depressed and infuriated because a man with the money Shubunka seemed to have could find nothing to do but fool around with a girl. He couldn't figure out Shubunka and wondered bitterly why the queerest men were the richest. It wasn't fair.

Arthur had come trotting around the fountain and now waited, smiling his stupid grin, until he could speak to Shubunka. When the fat man finally noticed him, the dishwasher told him that Mr. Spitzbergen wanted to see him. "Two men came in the store and wanted to know whether you were in, Mr. Shubunka," gasped Arthur, overwhelmed by his elegant appearance and his indifferent manner. This was a real man. He did all sorts of things, had all kinds of money, and nothing disturbed him. He never batted an eye. Arthur's mouth was open before him.

"Thank you, Arthur," said Shubunka. "Who were the men? What did they want?"

"They didn't say anything. Just asked if you were here, that's all. Then they wanted Mr. Spitzbergen."

"Well," said Shubunka, shrugging his shoulders. "We'll see them again. We didn't miss anything." He went down to a table in the parlor, feeling distressed, for he had been sensitive to Dorothy's embarrassment with him. Arthur went to tell the boss in the kitchen that he was here. Shorty's relief at the fountain went about his business, seeing nothing, hearing nothing. Karty waited, his red eyes nervously following Shubunka down the aisle in the parlor.

"What's going on between him and Spitz?" he asked Dorothy.

"Why ask me?" she said. "I'm sure I don't know."

"Nuts," said Karty.

"Hold your tongue," she said.

Karty muttered balls but the cashier didn't hear him.

Mr. Spitzbergen ran from the kitchen to Shubunka, banging the door. "The apartment on Third Street!" he cried, nevertheless trying to restrain himself. "They busted it!"

"Don't be so excited," Shubunka said gently. He took out his wallet and selected six tens, placing them on the table before Spitzbergen. The soda proprietor calmed down at once. He looked at the money, counting it from the distance, genteelly picked it up and put it in his pocket. Karty at the fountain, seeing the bills, had to keep from weeping outright.

"See," said Shubunka, drawing on his English Oval, "it wasn't very hard. Really, it was simple."

Spitzbergen sat down, sprawling his fat legs out in the aisle. He turned to Shubunka confidentially. "I don't like it, what the girl said. It looks bad. Who were they? The ones who busted up the apartment."

"Really, I cannot say. I really do not know." Shubunka held his palms out in his helplessness.

"What do they mean? They said you can't do business no more."

"We will see," he said. "After all, you cannot stop people from saying what they want to say. You know how it is, Mr. Spitzbergen. People see a nickel, everybody wants a piece. It's like that in every line. But you don't have to pay attention."

"Busting up a house," said Spitzbergen, "it don't look so good. I should say it looks like they mean business. Things like this don't go on every day. Not in my experience."

"It happens. You see, it happens. Don't aggravate yourself."

"Nevertheless," declared Spitzbergen, "I don't like it."

"I don't understand exactly." Shubunka spoke with carefully restrained annoyance. "You have nothing to worry about. I take on all the responsibilities. I pay for the damage when it happens. You don't have to know anything about it. But, of course, if you don't want it, it's your privilege. I can pull out the girls the minute you say."

Spitzbergen felt sure he was bluffing. Shubunka needed him as much as he wanted his money. All the same the soda man realized that Shubunka spoke the truth. If he wanted to pay for the damage, if he wanted to take all the trouble and responsibility, as he said, it was an easy way of making money on the houses, and Spitzbergen decided to change the subject. Frowning deeply, he explained, "I'm a nervous type. You can see it for yourself. My temperament makes me worry all the time." He rose from the table, sighing. "Rotten weather," he said.

"Makes no difference in my line," Shubunka said.

"Hah?" He looked at him for a moment, understood, and walked away, feeling the bills in his pocket. He had to call up the agency for a girl to take Dorothy's place tomorrow. Shubunka smiled wanly over his cigarette. He called for Arthur to bring him a malted milk and got to work with his pencil on a little notebook that he took out of his pocket. When Karty came and sat down, he gestured with the pencil and said, "Just a moment, Mr. Karty, I must clear up one or two little items first."

Bastard, said Karty to himself, making me wait. Arthur came up with the malted, grinning, and it humiliated Karty. "What the hell you standing there laughing at?" he asked the dishwasher.

"Well, I got to bring the malted milk, don't I?" Arthur asked.

"So beat it."

Arthur trotted away.

"I would not say that," said Shubunka, gently reproving. He put the little book of names back into his pocket. "He don't mean harm."

"I can't stand to see his dumb face."

"Can we help what we have, Mr. Karty? God gives us a face, He don't ask questions first." Shubunka smiled expansively, his mouth wide across his broad face. "Poker tonight again?"

"Poker? Oh, I don't know. Who's holding a game?"

"I thought perhaps Mr. Lurie would be giving a little party tonight. Maybe we might have a game."

"He didn't say nothing to me about it."

"Arthur," Shubunka called. He sent the dishwasher into the dress shop to ask Lurie about the game tonight.

"Listen, Shubunka," Karty said, "you know what the progressive system is?"

"The progressive system? What would that be?"

"See, you play the favorites all the time. If the first one loses, you double the bet on the next one so that you make up your losses on the first race when you win. If that dog, he don't come in the second time, so you double again on the third race."

Shubunka swallowed his drink. "Horse racing?" He lit a cigarette and looked away. "Not interested."

"Well, you can listen at least!" Karty cried. "It don't cost nothing to listen, does it?"

"Don't holler, please, Mr. Karty. I ain't quite deaf."

"Listen, I'm an accountant by profession. You know that. Figures is my business. If I don't know figures, I'm hopeless. I studied three years in school. I'm telling you I know what I'm talking about. There's hundred guys today making a good living off the tracks. No investment, no labor, no overhead, no taxes, no expenses. How can you close your mind to a proposition like that?"

"But suppose the favorites don't win. Suppose you double and double and double and no horses win. So what?"

"It can't happen," Karty said. "I got it figured out. I know every angle from A to Z. You think I'd bother you if I didn't take everything into consideration? Listen, it don't happen the favorites shouldn't win all the time. Two out of every six races last year in New York was won by favorites. And that counts in Saratoga and Belmont Park. We'd lay off those tracks, we'd stay away from fillies, maidens, first-time outs, and two-year-olds. We'll play only the best races. With three thousand dollars for a beginning we can make a good income, playing safe and conservative only. Look in the paper. Take any track, any day. See how many favorites come in first, second, and third. Once in a blue moon a horse runs out the money, then we're covered on the next one if we double. Even a thousand dollars would be enough for a start."

Karty finished his speech and drew back from the table to see what effect he had made. Shubunka looked at him apologetically. "All I know," he said, smiling, "is to make a living in America you have to work for it. You don't get money for nothing. Not in this life."

Karty collapsed, his sharp small face hopeless. "Shubunka," he said, "I'm in a spot. I need money bad. What do you say?"

"I'm not in the money-lending line," Shubunka said.

When they needed money, then they came to him. Shubunka, still smiling sympathetically, grew bitter within himself. When he was sick two weeks with the grippe and a high fever, did any of the boys at Ann's try to call him up or pay him a visit? When they went out on a good time, did they take him with them? How many times did they play poker without him, thinking that he didn't know a game was being held? The fact was the only time Shubunka got into a game was when he himself went about organizing one. Shubunka was no fool. He knew that every time he walked into Ann's they all looked away from him, they wouldn't come near him because he was funny-looking, and they hated him, besides, because they saw his clothes and the money he had. They were against him, every one of them. But in spite of them he had built up an organization that made money for him almost automatically. Let them all rot in hell. He had the money and they would come to him whether they wanted to or not.

"I'm not in the money-lending line, Mr. Karty," he said. "I am very sorry. Believe me, I say it with the truth in my heart, I am sorry."

Karty's weasel face grew sharp with anger. "What's the money-lending line got to do with it? All I want is a couple hundred bucks. You'll get it back. With interest."

"I am sorry," said Shubunka, closing his eyes slowly. For a moment he had an impulse to give the gambler the money he wanted, so that he could see Karty's face brighten up in gratitude, so that he would be able himself to glow with his benefaction, so that Karty and the others would see what a fine charitable man Shubunka was, after all. But he knew that any money he gave the racetrack gambler would be lost forever and it seemed too expensive a luxury. "Oh, I'm sorry," he said earnestly. "I feel bad about it, but I'm in no position to lend you any great amount of money, Mr. Karty. You can understand how that is."

Balls! said Karty to himself, standing up. Balls and McCarthy. Shubunka had quite dismissed him but he waited dumbly, feeling useless and low. The fat man held the cigarette in the corner of his mouth, squinting his eyes because of the smoke, while he took two tens and a five out of his neat wallet. He folded the bills carefully into a small packet, still squinting, still aware that Karty was standing before him, and placed the money into a vest pocket. He looked up at Karty, exhaling smoke. "Sorry," he said, feeling guilty.

Arthur came in with the news that Lurie would hold the game tonight at his flat if they wanted one.

"You'll play poker, won't you, Mr. Karty?"

"Balls!"

Shubunka rose with great concern. "Oh, I don't like to see you feel this way! I don't want to see you mad!" He put his hand, the one holding the cigarette, on Karty's shoulder, and looked at him, begging forgiveness. "After all, I can't do what is impossible. You must be reasonable. You'll come, won't you?"

Karty walked away, not knowing what to say. Shubunka puzzled him. He didn't know whether to feel angry with him or not. Queer son of a bitch he was, folding that dough right in front of my eyes, said Karty, telling me he couldn't spare the money when he took care I should see that fat wallet. Dripping with grease. When he touched Karty's shoulder, the hand felt like a lump of dough.

Shubunka went up to the fountain, telling Spitzbergen about the game at Lurie's. "Gambling," grumbled the soda man. "What's this gambling going on all the time?" The fat man told him they'd play a nickel and a dime. "Don't worry," retorted Spitzbergen. "You can lose plenty money playing in a dime game, too." But he would come. His wife was spending the night at the hospital, and after they closed the soda parlor there would be nothing for him to do but worry his head off with his troubles. The game would take his mind off his responsibilities, at least.

Shubunka told Arthur to see Shorty about the poker.

"Oh, I don't know whether he will be available tonight, Mr. Shubunka," said Arthur. "I think he's got a previous appointment."

"But tell him anyhow. We don't want to hurt his feelings. You'll come yourself?"

"Oh, thanks, thanks! Sure!" To be with them, playing poker! Arthur was overjoyed.

"And you?" Shubunka asked the relief man, cordial and polite to the world, acutely conscious at the same time of the necessity of arranging the game himself if he wanted to be sure of having one.

The tight-lipped soda jerker visibly considered the invitation. "I guess I will," he said finally.

"Splendid! That will be splendid." Shubunka counted the players. Karty would come. He would get over it and come. There would be seven of them, counting Shorty, enough without him for a nice quiet game. He turned to Spitzbergen. "I'll have some money for you tomorrow night," he said. "You will be here to meet me?" Karty, taking it in, screwed his face, fighting off the tears. Shubunka was doing it purposely, showing him that he had plenty of money to throw away. Spitz would be there, all right, he thought, he'd be there to collect if he had to break out in a rash of hemorrhages.

Shubunka went up to Dorothy and smiled at her. He took out the neat packet he had made of the bills and held it to her. "A little gift," he whispered. "For the new bride."

Dorothy looked at the money, saw the denominations and protested. She stepped back, holding her hands behind her. Shubunka shifted his weight toward her as he urged the money upon her. His big perspiring face came closer. Dorothy couldn't help it. She gasped and then, recovering rapidly, laughed nervously.

"Come, really, you must," the fat man said eagerly. "After all, I want to give you a little gift. It's my privilege when young people get married. Don't be a silly girl, please."

"No, really," said Dorothy, forcing a smile. Her back was now against the wall cabinets and the face seemed to be on top of her, the thick lips set wide across the heavy flesh of his face in a smile. "I couldn't take it. Not money. It wouldn't be nice."

"You must forgive me for offering a gift of money. I am sorry. But I do not know what would appeal to a young girl. I give you the money and ask you to buy yourself something that would please you. You can understand how it is." But Dorothy persisted. "You won't take it?" he asked, the frozen smile disappearing as he grew uncertain and awkward. His face clouded. "You really won't take it? Please."

"No," said Dorothy. "If you won't mind."

"I am sorry," he said, his expression indeed full of hurt and pity for himself. "Then good-bye. It is too bad you won't take it." Shubunka sadly replaced the packet to his vest pocket. He fixed his hat, careful not to upset his hair, looked at the wall mirror to catch a glimpse of his face when it showed sorrow, and walked out of Ann's.

"I'm closing up," said Spitzbergen morosely, turning over the card.

"Sport!" said Karty with contempt. He had come, after all. "Got a ten showing on top, he ain't satisfied. Goes out the first round."

"You should see my card in the hole," mourned Spitz. "You wouldn't talk."

"He don't go in if he ain't got aces back to back."

"Yes, yes!" cried the soda man. "I should live to see the day I get aces back-to-back."

"Nuts," said Karty, clearing his nose nervously.

"Hey, what the hell kind of a game do you call this?" Shorty asked. "Play poker or let's quit. If you want to horse around, O.K. with me, but if you're playing stud, keep your mind on the game, see how I mean?"

"Tiddle-di-dum, tiddle-di-da, tiddle-di-di," sang Shubunka, drumming peacefully on the table. He threw in a nickel chip. The card that showed was a four.

"I go now?" cried Arthur. "All right, I'm in."

"What the hell you going in on?" Lurie asked him. "You just throw the money away. You shouldn't play poker."

The tight-lipped relief man, the due course of deliberation having passed, gravely placed his chip on the table. Lurie then said he'd take a chance on the next round. "It'll cost me a nickel to see what I shall see," he said, and started dealing out the hand. "Nothing. Nothing. Possible flush. Nothing. Pair of sevens!" It was Karty who drew the pair. "Possible straight." Lurie turned his own card. "Nothing!"

"Just my lousy luck to get a pair of sevens on the second round,"

Karty complained. "Just watch them run." He tossed in a nickel chip and looked questioningly at the others. The relief man closed up without a word. Lurie, looking again at his bottom card, said, "What the hell," and went in. He had a jack showing. The others dropped out, except Shubunka, who kept on drumming to his song.

"Nothing. Pair of sevens." His own card came slowly. "Nothing!"

Karty bet a dime chip and looked at Lurie, who wavered. "Nuts," said Karty. "He's got a jack in the hole all the time. It's just an act."

"Want to change hands?"

"Come on. Play."

Lurie tossed in the chip. "We shall see what we shall see," he said gaily. Shubunka went in, too.

"Like a map of the U.S.," said Arthur, out of nowhere.

"What map?" asked Shorty, distressed and upset.

"The wall. It looks like a physical map of the United States. I used to study it when I went to school in Springfield, Mass." And the truth was the wall was remarkably cracked.

"Neptune Beach," confirmed Spitzbergen. "All over Neptune."

"Nuts," said Karty. "Deal the cards."

Lurie looked at the wall, reflecting. Last night. Tomorrow morning he'd go to Flatbush with Dorothy to look for an apartment. All over. Good-bye, sweetheart, till we meet tomorrow. Good-bye, sweetheart, let there be no sorrow . . .

"Sir, if you please . . . a moment of your time," said Shubunka, kidding. Lurie came to attention.

"Nothing. Still a pair of sevens." Lurie was tantalizingly deliberate over his own card. "Pair of jacks!"

"Jesus Christ!" said Karty, possessed. "Did you ever see anything like that for lousy luck? Wins on the last card. It's enough to make a guy jump off the roof." Never no luck! Hoodooed for life.

"Lucky in cards," said Shubunka, smiling. "You know how the saying goes."

"He must have been doped," said Arthur dreamily.

"I'll crack you one," said Lurie in good spirits.

"Not you! Joe Louis. If I live to be a hundred I'll never understand it."

"A superman never lived," said Shubunka, the English Oval in the corner of his mouth, his fat face screwing to avoid the smoke. "The colored boy was human just like a horse or anything else."

"Hell! What kind of a game is this anyway?" cried Shorty, exasperated. He held the cards in his hand to deal. "I'm going to quit this game. I'm getting out."

"He's got something on his mind," said Lurie with sly malice. "He seems to be all hot and bothered. What got you worked up today anyhow?"

"Never you mind!" the soda jerker exclaimed, standing up. There were no two ways about it, Madame Pavlovna was a common teasing bitch. Hahvahnah, ven I vas in Hahvahnah. Some day Shorty would kick her in the teeth and ask her how she liked it.

"Deal!" yelled Karty at the soda jerker. "For Christ's sakes, deal! Spitz, make it a dime open."

"Not me," said Spitz. "I'll only get stuck."

"Nuts," said Karty. "Just no guts."

"Gentlemen," exhorted Shubunka mildly. "If you please." He was happy, relishing the warm company of the game, and he sang his tiddle-di-dum.

"When I was in the smoked-fish line up at Springfield, Mass., there was a run I had to make to Pittsfield. Once I smelled the smell of boxthorn. Big smell all over the place. So just out of curiosity I stopped the Ford and hunted up the tree. You should have seen it. Such a big beautiful smell and such a little homely tree. It looked shopworn."

"Absolutely out of his mind," marveled Mr. Spitzbergen. "I can't figure him out."

Everyone in the room ribbed Arthur about the smell. "I guess I was sleepy," the dishwasher admitted sheepishly. He applied himself resolutely to the cards as Shorty dealt them.

"What a mutt," said Lurie, but sympathetically. A dizzy kid, he thought, just look at him. He didn't belong. A failure, a dumbbell, a walking tragedy. All his life the poor dope would look around with that innocent expression on his face, smiling and gasping with wonder, and all his life there would be someone around to kick him in the pants. Lurie had a moment of compassion. He wanted to draw Arthur aside, tell him that Neptune Beach was not for him, tell him to go back to his folks, to Springfield. Else sooner or later that wonderful masculinity the dishwasher saw at Ann's and admired so that his mouth was almost continuously opened—the horse-betting, the whoring, the manly curses and hardened actions—sooner or later this life would lead him astray into some wild act of imitation that would senselessly land him in a mess for the rest of his days. A goofy kid, crazy. Lurie had seen many of them before, always ending in some kind of trouble. Get out, he wanted to tell the kid, beat it while the going is good, but the play came to him and he tossed in a nickel chip.

Everyone went in on this hand, even the tight-lipped relief man. Karty held a pair of queens, the second queen in the hole, hidden. He looked around. Spitzbergen was holding a pair of sixes, hoping for two pairs. Karty could read his cautious mind like a book. Arthur had nothing, and the same was true of Shubunka. They were in it just for the ride. The relief man had a king showing, maybe another one in the hole. Anyhow, at least an ace. Karty fearfully tried to read his expressionless face. Lurie had nothing and Shorty was banking on the ace showing.

"Deal the cards," Karty yelled at the soda jerker. "What's the matter with you?"

"I got to see if everybody's in, ain't I?" Shorty snapped back, vicious with his private despair. Hahvahnah! He was thoroughly disgusted with the game. "Pair of sixes. Nothing. Nothing. Plays like a cockeyed mutt. Nothing. Nothing. Nothing. Pair of sixes leads."

"Pass," said Spitzbergen, ever careful.

"Jesus Christ! Passes with a pair showing," said Karty. "You should be home in bed. No guts."

Shubunka and Arthur passed. Defiantly Karty tossed in a dime chip. A nice pile, all the same, he thought. He counted the chips, so many nickels and dimes, greedily. More than a dollar. As Karty threw out the dime chip, Spitzbergen closed up, and the others, too, turned up their cards. Karty's arm went out for the chips.

"Hey, wait a minute! Wait a minute!" Lurie called. "Don't be in such a rush. I'll see you." His dime chip went in. Karty looked at him bitterly.

"You got nothing," he said. "What the hell you horsing around?"

"Well, what the hell you got? I can see only a jack and a queen."

"Show!"

With easy deliberation Lurie revealed a diamond flush. No one had thought of it and it came as a great surprise. Karty slammed the cards down on the table, his nose like a snout with grief. Never the luck! Just plain hoodooed for life! What the hell good was there for him to be playing stud with these guys anyway? He'd never win. And if he did, what good would a couple of bucks do him when he needed hundreds? A waste of time. He'd never raise a nickel with those guys. They never went in unless they had aces back to back. When they didn't, someone had to pull a flush out of the hole! Why hadn't someone called a possible flush?

"Son-of-a-bitch bastard!" he yelled at Shorty. "Why the hell didn't you call a possible flush? You're the dealer."

"Fongoo!" declared Shorty. "The hell with this game. I'm quitting."

"What the hell you beefing about?" Lurie asked Karty. "You got eyes, too, why the hell didn't you spot the flush coming up? Here I was being a nice guy and didn't even raise you when I had you with your pants down, too."

"No," said Karty, white with heat. "That son of a bitch's got his mind on dames all the time. He can't see anything in front of his eyes but a piece. He don't know what the hell he's doing and I got to take the rap."

"Well, I'm quitting," said Shorty, good and sore. He put on his coat and settled with the chips, making Arthur buy them. "See, I like to play a nice quiet game, sociable. If you guys want to play poker, O.K., but no horsing around. There's a limit to everything."

"Oh, don't go, Shorty! Don't go. It's all right." Shubunka implored the soda jerker not to leave. The game would break up. He knew they were all tired, disgusted, wanting to quit, and he tried to hold them together, prolonging the night. Shubunka's face fell with gentle sadness. Soon they would all leave, he would have to go home, alone, listening to the early-morning jazz tunes on the Victor Magic Eye. "Don't go, Shorty. Play a few more rounds," he begged.

"I got a certain amount of patience," explained Shorty, distracted. He couldn't play poker tonight. The fact remained that Madame Pavlovna was a common, ordinary, teasing bitch. "See, I'm willing to stand a certain amount of horsing around, you can see how I mean, but I got no more patience."

"Shorty's going out for nookey," said Lurie, laughing.

"Oh, yare. I don't have to pay for it when I want it. Remember that."

"Not nice," mourned Mr. Spitzbergen. "It ain't decent. Animals."

"Wise guys," said Shorty, going out the door.

"Stinkpot," said Karty bitterly. "Goddam bald-headed stinkpot."

The game broke up. Everyone rose. Shubunka sat smoking in the chair, unhappy and looking pained.

"Twelve people died just from the excitement," Arthur said. He was half asleep. "Can you imagine that? Twelve people dying just on account of a fight." He was still thinking of the Joe Louis–Schmeling fight.

The tight-lipped relief man, smug and free, nothing on his mind, never said a word.

TWO

The tears came down Mr. Spitzbergen's face. Somebody had broken into Ann's during the night and the ice-cream machine lay destroyed, its delicate motor smashed apart, the wires ripped, the metal sheeting bent and twisted. "Who did it?" he asked weakly. "Why should anybody take it into their heads to break it? If he came to rob, all right, I could understand it. But to break up a piece of property for no good reason! What did they get out of it? Who did it?"

"I would just like to get my hands on the guy who did that," said Shorty grimly. "That's all I want."

"Uhmy! My!" gasped Arthur. "Did you ever see anything like it?"

"Two thousand dollars," mourned Spitzbergen. "Gone to hell. I'm a nervous wreck. The hell with it, cut me to pieces and make a finish with me altogether."

"I don't like the looks of it," Arthur declared. "There's something wrong somewhere."

"Einstein!" cried the boss, and now laying his grief to one side he started worrying in earnest. This was clearly the work of a malicious hand and the end was yet to be. "Where have I an enemy in the world?" he asked, really wanting to know. "Who would want to make me trouble?" And as Spitzbergen clamorously beseeched the world to tell him who would do this thing, the realization drove home, fear gripped him and he trembled. Why had he gone in with Shubunka? All his life he had been a solid businessman, working his way up from nothing by years of honest struggle. He had never broken a law, he had never had anything to do with gangsters, he had never even been in a courtroom or a police station. What had possessed him to tie up with Shubunka?

"All I can say," said Shorty wisely, "is I would like to lay my hands on the guy. You want me to phone the police?"

"What police?" cried the boss. "What do they know? They'll only come with their hands stuck out for graft!"

"No police?" asked Arthur. "So what else can you do?"

Spitzbergen exploded with rage and drove them both back to the fountain. It was after seven and the breakfast rush was about to begin. A clear beautiful day it was. Spitzbergen, coming to Ann's on the subway, had examined the sky, his eyes apprehensive, and he had cursed his luck. A wonderful day, but it was no good. Too cold. The crowds would never come to the beaches. And then the ice-cream machine. His whine rose. Shorty bent his head low as he squeezed the oranges and filled up the half-gallon enameled pitcher with the juice. He couldn't find it in his heart to blame the boss today.

"Get a move on, you sleepy son of a bitch," he yelled at Arthur. The dishwasher was boiling the water in the Silex coffee glasses. "Slow as cow flop on an ice-cold day," muttered the jerker. The new girl, whom the agency had sent to take Dorothy's place, walked in. A nice broad, reflected Shorty, quite impressed.

"Show her what to do," said Spitzbergen. "I ain't got the heart for nothing this morning." He went to worry among the ruins behind the show window. Shorty, his gold caps catching the light in his oily eagerness, asked the girl if she had a smock.

"No smock?" he repeated. "Oh, you want to bring a smock. Otherwise you'll spot your clothes." His face grew serious with sincere concern for her dress. He told her that she had to handle the tables in the back, keep them clear and take orders, ring up the cash at the register. "If you don't know what to do, just ask me. It'll take you a minute to catch on, but then it's a cinch. See, there's nothing to it." He looked at her blank face. She seemed completely lost, and he wondered whether she had heard what he said. A lummox, thought Shorty, without a doubt. Her name was Lillian.

"So what should I do now?" she asked.

"Holy cripes," Shorty said. "Come, I'll show you." He led her by the arm and took her to the cash register. "You know how to work one of these things?" She didn't. "B'gee!" the jerker exclaimed. As he showed her, his hands were on her often, and in that narrow area he was all over her, explaining where the checks were filed, what the drawers were used for, what was in the cabinets behind her. Bending down to reveal what lay behind the sliding doors at the bottom, he pushed his hands heavily over her buttocks.

"Oh, please!" cried Lillian, starting. "If you don't mind, I—"

"What?" the jerker asked, honestly puzzled in the midst of his annoyance with her stupidity.

"Well . . . then never mind."

"No. What's the matter? I do something out of step? I don't get you."

"All right, then. We'll skip it."

"Listen," said Shorty with great offense, "if you don't want me to show you the place, if you think I'm trying anything funny or out of place, hell, you just got a swelled head." Indignant, he mumbled to the walls. "See," he said confidentially, "there's the type of woman I can't stand and that's the type that always is afraid some guy or other is trying to take liberties with her. They're always afraid a guy is getting fresh, don't you know? There's women that think all a guy's got on his mind all day is dames and how to put something over on them. They're always looking to get insulted. Well, I got no use at all for that type woman, not me. So if you think I'm trying anything, the hell with it. I got other things to do today and somebody else can help you."

"So it was an accident," Lillian said. "All right. I don't want no fights on the first day."

"Then O.K., sister," said Shorty. As he turned away, heavy with annoyance, his arm skillfully swung out behind him and caught her a hard smack on the backside again. It was clearly an accident.

Shorty did it so well that the new girl herself didn't know whether to suspect him or not. Afraid to cause further trouble, she kept quiet.

"A dumb broad," pronounced Shorty to the dishwasher. "But she's got all the parts."

Arthur giggled. "Don't think I didn't get an eyeful. I saw you."

"Nosey son of a bitch," said Shorty, smiling affectionately. He went under his apron for a cigarette. "Is it true what they say about Dixie? Is it true . . ." He sang, satisfied, as he went about his work.

Outside, the streets were thickening with people. The line of stools at the fountain grew filled. Men came in wearing the sporty cloths of Neptune Beach, English drapes, gabardines, unmatched suits. They wore yellow ties and fancy-colored or striped shirts, relishing novel types of collars. They clicked along in gray or brown suede shoes, the heels an inch high. Shorty scurried from one end of the counter to the other, stirring the orange juice in the pitcher, replenishing the toaster, smearing butter from the big dish, tipping the Silex bowls. He punched out the twenty-cent special breakfast checks. Occasionally a woman with plenty of time ordered the thirty-cent special. Then Arthur had to go running down to the kitchen to fry the eggs, but for the most part his job was to fill the little green beetleware cups with milk for the coffees, pushing them up to Shorty. He cleared the counter as fast as one breakfaster left his stool so that another might find the place ready. Lillian at the cashier's stand fumbled with the change while Spitzbergen hovered uneasily over her, watching her, watching the morning crowd, worrying in the midst of his many other troubles whether he would be realizing everything he could on the rush this morning. There would be no crowds this miserable cold clear day.

The two men Shorty had talked to yesterday now came in and went immediately to Spitzbergen.

"You the boss? You Mr. Spitzbergen?" asked one of them, sniffling energetically.

"So what I am the boss?"

"We want to talk to you. Come in the back and we'll sit down by a table. We got a little proposition for you."

Peddlers, thought Spitzbergen. "Please don't bother me this time of day. My mind's occupied enough. Come back later if you want."

"Look, look," cried the other man. He was pointing at the show window with the wreck behind it. "What happened?"

"Well, I'm a son of a gun!" cried his companion. "What the hell do you think of that?" He turned to Spitzbergen. "What happened?"

The boss's eyes moved fearfully from one amazed face to the other. "Who sent you?" he asked. "What do you want? What's this all about?"

"It's nothing to get excited about, mister," the sniffler protested. "What's the matter you excited all of a sudden?"

"Tell me," cried Spitzbergen, "you know anything about the machine? You got something to do with it?"

"Who? Me? You asking me if I got something to do with that?" The sniffler was genuinely shocked and showed it. "Hey, mister! You're crazy!"

"Never mind," said Spitz. "You ain't fooling me one minute. What do you want?"

"We only got a little proposition. If you want to listen, let's go and sit down over a table like decent people."

The sniffler rubbed his nose and looked archly at Spitzbergen who scowled and hesitated but finally led them down the parlor. As they passed Shorty at the fountain, the man called out, "Hello, Baldy." Shorty looked up angrily and recognized them. "Wise guys," he said, sulking as he worked over the coffee cups.

"Nice kid," the man said to Spitzbergen. "You got an A-one worker over there."

The other was inspecting the place. "A swell joint," he commented. "Just look at all those fixtures. It's a lucky thing those guys, whoever they were, that broke into the place last night didn't get to work on those mirrors, too. Take me, I got a complex. All my life I want to smack up mirrors, I don't know why it is like that."

"You must be a coke," his companion said. "It's bad luck busting mirrors. Don't you know that?"

"You believe in luck?" the first one asked, looking worried. "You got superstitions? I don't know, I'm just crazy about busting mirrors. I can't help it."

"Mr. Spitzbergen," the sniffler interposed, "you believe in superstitions?"

"Hah?" He was nonplused.

"See that guy? He's nuts. He don't care about mirrors. What do you think of that?"

"Crazy!" cried Spitzbergen. "Somebody here should be in the crazyhouse. What do you want?"

"See," said the sniffler, rubbing his nose again as he talked, "it's like this. You ain't doing business with Shubunka no more. That's all finished. You're working with us now." He looked at the soda man questioningly, to see how he would take the news, and his hand was still working on his nose. He waited patiently for the effect to sink in. His companion, who seemed completely uninterested by the proceedings or else took them for granted, noticed Lillian passing and he called out to her cheerily. "Hello, sister, how's it?" She looked at him, wondering, and went her way. "Fresh!" she said. "Don't get sore, sister," he called after her. "What do you say?" Spitzbergen was paling before them because of their easy nonchalance. They were gangsters, he knew it. They would cut his throat for a dime.

"What Shubunka?" he asked. "What am I got to do with Shubunka? He's only a tenant. I got lots of tenants, what's the matter you have to pick on me?"

"Hey, Amchy," the sniffler said. "What do you know? This guy don't know Shubunka."

"So it must of been a mistake," Amchy said. "They sent us in the wrong place."

"Sure, a mistake," Spitzbergen said anxiously. "What do you want from me? I don't know anything about it."

"Well, then, it's too bad, it's too bad. We just wasted his time." But they did not move to go. The two of them sat dreamily gazing at the ice-cream machine. As they stayed there without budging, the soda man began to realize sinkingly that they were joking with him, and he had a queasy, loose feeling in his stomach. There was no escape. The longer he sat there, the more sharply he sensed that they meant his doom. The perspiration came out on his face and panic seized him.

"Listen, boys," Spitzbergen begged. "All right, I know Shubunka. So what is the crime? I rent him apartments. What he does with the rooms, it ain't my business. So what do you want? What should I do? You want me to tell him to get out? All right, I'll tell him today. I'll tell him to take the girls out. I'll be finished with him and with the whole lousy business. All right?"

"Listen," said the sniffler, his whole manner now changed, speaking seriously and to the point, "I want a list of your houses and a list of all the joints you rent to Shubunka. Put down the addresses and apartments. If you hold out, there's a fine. It will cost you two hundred dollars and in the end you'll have to give in anyway. You, Spitzbergen, are a no-good rat. I ain't wasting pity on you, and if you go to the cops we'll put the cops on you. We're doing you a favor by letting you stay in this here business. Instead of renting the places to Shubunka, we'll do the business with you, and we'll pay the rent. Better than this you have no right to expect from nobody. You try something funny, I'll run you out of town. You try and pull something, I'll come back and kick your fat stomach off."

"No!" cried Spitzbergen, trembling. "I don't want it! I don't want to have a single part in the business no more. I'm through with it. I give it up, let the rooms stay empty all year. I'll tell Shubunka to pull out the girls from the apartments and then I am finished and I want you to leave me alone."

"If that's the way you feel, then you're just out of luck, Mr. Spitzbergen. It's too bad, because we need the apartments and we need houses in Neptune Beach and you got them. See, it's a combination now. It's a syndicate on a large scale, same as a chain-store system. All over the city. We even got the madams on a salary or a commission, most of them. We don't want no independent bookers like Shubunka, but we need your joints because that's the way we want it for Neptune Beach and that's the way it's going to be all over the city, and tell me, who the hell are you to be an exception?"

"I want to get out!" cried Spitzbergen. "I'm finished with the whole rotten business."

"So what are you crying about?" the man asked. "I can't figure it out. It's the same as before only now you got an organization paying the rent money. And if you're worrying about Shubunka, it ain't necessary because we'll take good care of him. You're nuts. There's good people behind this combination." The sniffler rose from the table, angry with Spitzbergen but restraining himself. "Come on, Amchy," he said. "This guy don't realize how lucky he is. Listen, you, Spitzbergen, we're doing you a favor and you don't even realize it. Now don't get smart. Don't let nobody tell you we're bluffing because all that will happen is that you'll get what's good for you, and then you'll be sorry and we'll have the houses anyway in the end. We'll be back and when we come we want the list with the houses and the joints. Don't you forget and don't you be smart." He waited for Spitzbergen to answer, but the soda man was sunk in misery and didn't reply. "Well, do you understand?" the sniffler asked.

"It's O.K.," said Amchy. "He understands goddammed good. Let's beat it out of here."

As they walked out, it was easy to see that the sniffler had lost his good humor for the morning. But Amchy remained in good spirits. When they passed the fountain he had to be pulled away from Shorty. He wanted to slap his bald spot and protested bitterly when his partner stopped him. "You got your crack at him yesterday, ain't it?" he asked, arguing reasonably. "What's the matter I can't?" They went out.

"Gee whiz," said Arthur at the double basins, working on the breakfast dishes. "I don't like the looks of those guys at all."

Harassed and persecuted, Shorty finally straightened up. "If I got those guys one at a time in a fair fistfight," said he, "I'd rattle their goddammed teeth. Goddam bastards, who the hell do they think they are? I'd like to meet one of them by themselves on the street some day." The breakfasters at the counter rendered consolation to the soda jerker. Muttering and scowling, he calmed down.

"Shorty. Shorty." It was the boss still at the table. He felt sick. "Bromo Seltzer bring me."

"O.K.," said the jerker, and he went to fix the drink.

Time passed. There now remained of the breakfast rush only the stragglers, mainly wives who went to business, generally their husbands', and these were leisurely, since there were no time clocks for them to punch. They sat on the stools, eating the buttered toast, with one leg crossed over the other. Arthur was absently balancing the dishes flat on the water by this time.

"Free as a bird with nothing on my mind," he said, talking to himself in reverie. "Enough in my pocket to get along on and a little something for extra besides."

"You talking to me?" Lillian asked. Clearing the counter, she piled the dishes before him.

"No, I wasn't talking to you," he said, smiling. "That's just my ambition. Free as a bird with nothing on my mind. You know what I mean?"

"What's the matter? Something is bothering you now?"

"No, not exactly. You don't get the point. It's only my ambition. Maybe you have an ambition, too?"

"Oo!" cried Lillian suddenly, jumping forward. "Lousy bum! I almost dropped the dishes. Such a nasty person."

It had been Shorty again, grabbing her buttocks. "Oh, I beg your pardon," he whispered to her, oily and apologetic. "I slipped, see? Now, Lillian, I don't want you to take offense about this. I realize what I did, but the floor is slippery and I nearly went down on my nose."

"Listen, you!" she said defiantly. "If you know what's good for you, you'll stay away from me. Don't think I don't know what's going on. I'm no dumbbell."

"Look at her getting sore. Hey, Arthur, was it my fault? On the level, did I do it intentional?"

"Didn't see nothing," said Arthur, noncommittal.

"I mean it, Lillian. B'gee, I know it looked bad, but I'd never do a thing like that to you. Hell, I'm just not that kind of a guy, not me."

"Oh, yare?" She walked to the cashier's stand, looking wise. "I want you to know one thing. I got a boyfriend."

"Well, it's nice to hear," said Shorty. He turned on the dishwasher. "Dopey mutt. I mean you. Why the hell did you have to be so goddam ethical and say you didn't see nothing?"

"Because I didn't. That's why."

"George Washington. He cannot tell a lie."

"Stealing a feel," said Arthur. "You should be ashamed."

"No comment from you!" said Shorty, burning up. "I'll take nothing from you! See how I mean?" The soda jerker looked so tough that Arthur receded, turned his back and went back to work. Shorty glanced at the new cashier to see if she had been missing any of this, his lips moving rapidly with grim significance and his eyes flashing with anger at Arthur. Moe Karty came in for breakfast.

The racetrack gambler sat down at the fountain instead of using the tables according to his custom. He had the *Morning Telegraph* under his arm, but it had been scarcely used. Karty had no heart for the races this morning. He had spent the night at the Turkish baths to escape his wife and had slept poorly amid his worries. Now he felt uneasy and depressed as he contemplated the emptiness of the day. Besides, he had nothing but some silver with which to bet. He ordered his onion roll and coffee, frowning through his swollen eyes.

Shorty greased over the counter to him as he brought the roll. "Hey, Karty," he said, "what the hell do you know? I found out last night what Shubunka peddles for a living. You'll never believe it."

"Nuts," said the gambler nastily. "Don't you come horsing around me no more. Last night you were playing poker at Lurie's with your mind on the broads. Wasn't for you I'd be in a couple of bucks right this minute."

"No, on the level, Moe, what do you think Shubunka works at? You can't even guess." Shorty was anxious to make up to him for his faults last night.

"What does he do?" Arthur asked. "I got the curiosity to know."

"Scaram, you nosy mutt," the jerker said, looking important. This was man talking to man. Arthur had no place in the discussion. "Wouldn't tell you nothing." He turned to Karty. "He's a booker. Runs a string of whorehouses and uses Spitz's buildings. What the hell do you think of that?"

"Son-of-a-bitch bastard!" Karty choked on the coffee and stood up on the foot rail to keep it from spilling over his clothes. His sharp little face went bitter with anger. The son-of-a-bitch bastard wouldn't go into the racing proposition with him on a conservative progressive system because it wasn't businesslike enough for him and all the time he ran a row of whorehouses!

"Geez," said Shorty, puzzled. "What the hell you getting so sore about it? Hell, I don't like the idea so hot, either, but hell, what's it to you personally?"

"Aw, shaddap," Karty said. "When I ask you you'll tell me."

As soon as Arthur heard the news, his face had grown long with concentration, but now he brushed his hair away from his eyes and chortled out loud. He had figured it out at last. Shorty looked at him. "Where were you last night you found out about it?" Arthur gasped. "Where did you find out about it?"

Shorty, who never paid for it when he had the urge, started cursing in great anger and took to whacking the dishwasher down the floor slats. Arthur protected his head with his arms and laughed riotously during the scuffle.

"Lay off," Karty yelled. "The kid's got right, ain't he?"

Shorty hastened back to explain how he picked up the news. There had been a friend who told him. "See," he said, anxious to preserve his reputation, "what gets me sore is the insinuation I'd go to a cathouse. Hell, Karty, if I have to buy it, then I don't want it. Can't get no pleasure out of it that way. But what gets me sore is the insinuation he goes around passing."

"Oh, nuts," Karty said. "Nuts. Nuts. The kid's got right."

The telephone rang. Shorty cut short his protestations and ran to the booth. The call was for Karty, and growing fierce with resolve the gambler strode to the telephone. It was Joe (Grey Lag) Wack, this morning specially recommending a two-year-old called Apogee in the third at Aqueduct. Yesterday's special, Wack was man enough to admit, failed to come up to expectations, but Apogee was a sure thing calculated to make up for all losses sustained on Fifi and offered to the clientele with that thought in mind. A real good long shot. Twenty to one or better. "You don't say!" said Karty pleasantly. "Is that really so?" Yes, said Joe (Grey Lag) Wack, and he advised that the two-year-old be played across the board, to win, to come in second, and to come in third, and that the win money be insured. "Well, that's nice," Karty said. "I'd like to tell you something. You stink out loud!" He banged the receiver on the hook and walked out, warm with the feeling of satisfaction. But after all what did this get him? He had the Telegraph under his arm, all set for a day of doping the horses and betting, and he didn't have a dollar. And the fear of his brothers-in-law oppressed him.

"Hey, Shorty," he said. "You got a couple of bucks on you? I'm short."

"Hell!" cried the soda jerker, his hand unconsciously going to the money in his pocket. "That's tough. I know how it is. I'm busted myself. Don't get paid for two days yet." He looked sorry.

"You lying son of a bitch," Karty said, half to himself. "O.K. I'm not begging you for nothing. Only don't you come sucking around when I'm in the dough."

"Jesus Christ!" Shorty implored him. "I ain't got a dime myself! If I had it I'd be glad to give it to you."

"Balls," said Karty. "Oh, balls and McCarthy."

At the end of the fountain, at his double basins, Arthur pondered long, giggling nervously to himself. But finally, when Lillian came by him, he screwed up his courage and brushed against her, his hand going out behind him to her backside. If Shorty could do it, why couldn't he? Arthur barely felt the touch when the new girl whipped around, surprisingly fast for her heavy body, and smacked him on the face. She hit him hard. His jaw stung and felt cracked. The dishwasher could do nothing but grin foolishly in front of her. Lillian drew herself up haughtily.

"Don't you try to get away with anything like that on me," she glared. "You won't get away with it no more. I'll give you what's coming!" Shorty up the counter was roaring with easy, happy laughter. "You, too!" Lillian shouted. "You try any more accidents and I'll get my boyfriend after you. Just wait and see."

"Hell!" said Shorty, abruptly turning serious. "What the hell do you want from me? I suppose that's my fault, too!"

"Gee whiz, Lillian," Arthur said, really apologetic. "I didn't mean nothing. It's just the way it happened."

"Oh, yare?" She marched off, her double chin trembling with emotion.

The bell rang. It was Mrs. Spitzbergen at the hospital, and without calling the boss, Shorty told her he was out for the moment. She said just to tell him she was all right this morning. The examination was still in progress and they couldn't judge the results at this time.

"Mr. Spitzbergen," Shorty called to him far in the rear of the store. "Your wife just phoned. She said she feels all right this morning."

"That's fine!" groaned the boss, without much force in him. "Now I can go dancing in a ballroom." All this time he had been considering the visit of the two thugs in the morning, and at last he had permitted himself to grow a little heartened. After all, it wasn't so terrible. What they said was true. As far as he was concerned, it meant only a change in tenants. They would pay the rent instead of Shubunka. Shubunka. What worried the boss now was that the booker owed him two weeks' rent on the joints and it remained a question whether he would see the money tonight as the fat man had promised. Spitzbergen's eyes traveled sadly until they met the wreckage of the ice-cream machine. "No," he muttered to himself, nodding vehemently. "No. I am afraid I won't get rich in a hurry in this business." Why had it been necessary to smash up the machine?

Karty was talking to the dishwasher. "Listen, kid, you got any dough on you?"

"Who, me?" asked Arthur, flattered to be chosen. "Gee whiz, I'm sorry, Mr. Karty, but I don't get paid until the day after tomorrow. I'm broke but I'll lend you when I get paid."

Karty's face fell as he wondered where he might be able to raise some money. Spitzbergen was hopeless. There was no point even in trying. Lurie might give him some money, but the dress man didn't get into his store until late and Karty didn't want to wait. He would even try Shubunka if he could reach him. Karty didn't know what to do, where to turn. All he could hope for was that his wife had been exaggerating the news of his brothers-in-law. But he knew them and could find little to cheer him here.

"What's the matter?" Arthur asked sympathetically. "You got something hot today?"

"Yeah," said Karty. "I got something good and I'm broke. It's lousy. What gets me sore is I'll have my hands on all the money I'll want tonight and I ain't got a buck now. Listen, maybe Spitz'll give you something in advance on account. Why don't you ask him?"

"Oh, geez, I wouldn't do that. He'll only holler at me and get sore. He wouldn't like it."

"So what's the difference he wouldn't like it? What do you care? You got a right to the money. All I want is four, five bucks."

"Geez, I'm sorry, Mr. Karty. But I can't ask him."

"Aw, nuts," said the gambler. "Nuts. Got to eat my heart out for a lousy couple of bucks."

He went out of the store to hunt up Lurie, even though he knew the dress store wouldn't open for an hour. Maybe Lurie's clerk was in the place and he might get a buck or two from her. He had the *Morning Telegraph* under his arm, barely opened. The clip that held the pages together to thwart newsstand readers hadn't even been broken.

The morning rush at Ann's was over. Shorty was working on the new girl, trying to get her down into the cellar. "On the level," he said, his face wrinkled on its skull with eagerness, "I got to show you where Spitz keeps the dirty towels and aprons. It's part of the job. See, when the laundry man comes, you got to get the things together for him."

But by this hour Lillian was too smart for him. She balked, standing dumbly on her feet, her double chin quivering with resentment, but at the same time she was afraid she might be neglecting her duties. Spitzbergen might fire her. "I won't go," she said. "If I must, Mr. Spitzbergen, he'll tell me. Else I won't."

Shorty glanced at the boss in the back, holding his temples in the heels of his palms as he mournfully went over the list of his trouble.

"All right, sister," said the jerker. "You do whatever you want. And if you get fired, that's your hard luck, not mine. Sooner or later you'll get wise to it I'm not trying anything funny on you. I want to tell you, you got me wrong."

"Oh, yare?" asked Lillian.

"Well, I won't force myself on you. Time will tell, time will tell."

She went to the cash register while Shorty philosophically lit a cigarette to hide his disappointment. Arthur came up and told him about poor Karty, what a spot he was in, broke with a hot, sure thing today. The soda jerker puffed wisely, saying nothing because all that applied to the subject had already been said and by him, long ago. "And look at Mr. Spitzbergen back there," Arthur said. "Those guys certainly told him bad news today."

"Hell," said Shorty, exhaling the smoke, "everybody's got their own troubles in this world. That's the way it is."

In Shubunka's mirrored apartment the Victor Magic Eye radio played "Love Is Everywhere" while the fat man stood at the telephone, collecting the signs of his impending doom and not taking the time or the trouble to believe in them. The English Oval dangled from his lip. As his man spoke to him excitedly, with fear in his voice, Shubunka looked at the mirror often to catch the reflection of his face as it expressed the calm reaction of a man hearing his peril and paying no serious attention to it. "All right, all right," he said. "You go to Charlie Angus again. Give him the names and the jails where they are locked up and it will be all taken care of. I cannot understand the fuss."

The man sputtered into the mouthpiece. He didn't like the wholesale arrests. These weren't the regular raids the detectives staged to create an impression with their superiors in order to keep the routine graft quiet. "If they can pull the cops like that, it looks bad," he complained. "They got the pull. They're the big shots."

"Who are they? Who are they behind it?"

Shubunka's man named a big shot, so renowned throughout the country that Shubunka had to laugh. "You saw him? Just tell me that, did you see him?"

"No, I didn't see him. You know he don't go running around. But it's the dope. It's all over the town."

"Bluff," said the fat man. "It's a bluff. If everybody who said he sent them really worked for him, he has an army then. Any snot-nose wants to make an impression only has to say he sent him. Then everybody is supposed to lay down with the scare. It happens all the time."

"All right, you can laugh. But they mean business. They got it too good organized it should be the work of a couple outside bums. They got a syndicate now. They're putting the house managers on a salary now instead of the old fifty-fifty cut with the girls. They got a bail-and-lawyer fund. Each girl is got to pay them ten dollars a week, the madams five, for the bond fund, and besides, the madams is got to pay two hundred and fifty dollars security for each girl and one hundred and fifty for herself. They're raising the two-dollar houses to three, and the four-and-five-dollar joints will be boosted, too. They mean business, all right, and it just looks too goddam bad for us."

"Bluff," said Shubunka, hearing his man out. "I heard it before, the whole story. All you got to do is hang on and they will run away."

He placed the phone on its rest, a little worried in spite of his talk. These hijacking practices were part of the business. They had happened often before and Shubunka had always ridden through them easily, given a little patience and time. A couple of cheap bums were always on the make. They would decide that the time had come for them to go up in the world and then they would try to chisel in. Their only stock in trade was bluff. They had no capital, no approach to the men at the police station, they didn't understand the business and lacked ordinary ability to conduct a going concern. All they knew was to smash up a few joints, make threats, even shoot a little. Then they were finished, exhausted of their learning and talents. You held on. You paid a few dollars here and there to the gunmen of Myrtle Avenue. You stalled for time while you counterattacked with the strong-arm men. It was a simple situation in the line and Shubunka knew well how to handle it.

But all the same he didn't like these methods. His was a business, practically legitimate, the oldest in the world, they said, and it wasn't as though he was breaking a law. Booking was almost as respectable as bootlegging had been. Everyone knew it was going on and only hypocrites, envious of him and his kind, had anything to say against it.

And as Shubunka greased his thick black hair with Polymol in the bathroom, he thought warmly of his organization. Eighteen houses, using most of Spitzbergen's properties and the buildings of one or two other landlords besides. He had over forty girls whom he changed on regular weekly schedules from one joint to another so that the cops and the varying fancies of his clientele were both satisfied. Shubunka always paid his bills. There was no one in Brooklyn to whom he owed a cent. He was a solid, honest businessman, and it displeased him to think that strong-arm tactics were a necessary part of his trade.

A pity, he sighed, fixing the bowtie with the points, but where there was honey there would be flies and you needed a flyswatter. Shubunka picked up the telephone and called an Evergreen exchange for a pool parlor on Myrtle Avenue. When he gave his name, they told him that none of the boys he wanted was in. Perturbed a bit, he called another Evergreen number, to a candy stand this time. Here again no one he wanted was in. It seemed for a moment that he just caught a man's voice saying "Shubunka? He's marked lousy." But he couldn't be sure.

A shadow of perplexity clouded his face. Shubunka, in his wonder, took the time to study his expression in the mirror, watching the slow doubt deepen in his face. "I do not understand," he said softly to the mirror. "I cannot understand. Where could they all be?" But he remembered it was early. Of course. The hoodlums hadn't stirred from their beds at this hour. It was natural, what could you expect? Reassured, the fat man fixed his pocket handkerchief and worked his hat on his head, careful not to upset the perfect hair-comb. He turned off the radio.

Downstairs at the street door, he stood for a minute to watch the children playing in the sunshine. A clear, cool day with lovely clouds in a blue sky. All the women had their babies in their carriages in the sun. They sat on folded chairs, knitting and talking. Smiling agreeably, Shubunka went from carriage to carriage, peering beneath the hoods to look at the babies and to compliment the mothers. They smiled back at him, controlling their uneasiness. It was unnatural for a man to leave his apartment so late in the morning for business. A strange man, they always said among themselves, strange in appearance and in his habits. Shubunka went to Neptune Beach, waddling sadly on his bent legs. He had noticed their discomfiture before him and it distressed him.

At Baten Avenue Shubunka stopped the policeman. "What is going on, Johnny?" he asked. "You know, you cannot say it is quite all right."

"I don't get what you mean," the policeman said, looking up and down the street for the sergeant. "I don't like to be standing chewing the fat on the street corner. It don't look good if anybody should come along. You know that." All the same, he remained where he was, his face showing annoyance. At no time did his eyes meet those of the fat man. Shubunka handed out a ten-dollar bill every week to each cop on the beat. In addition, he took care of the plainclothesmen in the district together with the precinct captain. As he reminded the cop of this, the policeman shook his head impatiently, displeased by the bald exposure. "I know all about it," he said. "You don't have to repeat it. So what?"

"So would you not say I am entitled to a certain amount of consideration?" Shubunka asked.

"Well, we never made any promises. All we ever said was we'd try and see what we could do. You got anything against me personally? Did I do anything to you? I ain't responsible for anybody outside myself."

"I cannot see the sense in paying out good money when I do not get anything in return for it. It don't make sense. What do you think about it, Johnny? Am I unreasonable, perhaps?"

"Figure it out for yourself. I never came to you. You came to us in the first place. You know I don't like to be standing here talking. I can't tell who might be coming along." The cop was massaging his face gently with his fingers. "Look," he said, his eyes on the pavement, "you know how it is. We got to follow orders. Whatever they tell us, we got to do. Now we don't start nothing from our end. We're quiet, you can count on that. But what the hell can we do if the guys higher up want to start something? If they feel like it, what the hell can we do?" He waited a moment and then without another word went off.

Shubunka smoked his cigarette, his eyes calmly following the patrolman up the street. "Little snotnose," he remarked aloud. "I can fix him." He walked into the three-story tenement house and went waddling up the flights on his bowed legs, growing warm with the effort. As the perspiration came, fear suddenly gripped him. He could now recognize behind the cop's manner a lack of respect, which meant that as far as he was concerned the handouts were finished. The policeman almost plainly told him that the money was now coming from other quarters, that Shubunka was no longer needed, that he had been displaced. On the top-floor landing he held his heart. It had begun to beat violently. Shubunka, in a panic, wondered whether he might be having a heart attack. The panic now heightened, sweeping over him until he trembled. He gasped, his eyes rolled helplessly, and he stood stock-still as if he had suddenly become paralyzed. But the peculiar fact was that as he stood there, holding the hall railing with one hand and clutching at his heart with the other, Shubunka in his mind's eye could easily envision his appearance in this attitude, as though he were looking at himself in a mirror. Moreover, this heroic posture pleased him, bringing him comfort.

Relieved, he sighed. Moving brokenly, almost staggering, he reached the hall steps and sat down on the marble to rest. From time to time he groaned. Shubunka sat there for many minutes, under the sunshine from the skylight. Then, quite collected, as though this had never taken place, he rose from the stairs and knocked on the door.

The damp laundry smells of towels and linen filled the room. Peggy Martin was in the kitchen washing a pair of stockings in the sink. She was a shriveled little woman, barely weighing ninety pounds, so it became remarkable how energetically she rubbed the stockings together to work up the suds. Women's clothes hung untidily from the chair backs. In one corner of the kitchen lay three or four pairs of old pumps and shoes, the laces of the latter trailing fuzzy with dirt and dust on the floor. There were opened cans on the drainboard. The pans were left on the range, unwashed and greasy, and the dirty dishes were piled on the table. A dozen flies circled busily around a coffee cup at the bottom of which a thick layer of dried sugar remained. Shubunka sat down at the kitchen table, pushing the coffee cup and its flies away to the other corner. Peggy Martin barely looked up from the sink.

"Clean up, my house manager," the fat man said wearily. "You run a filthy establishment."

"What do you want from me?" she said, brushing the hair back angrily with the dry side of her hand. She applied herself to rubbing the soap into the stiff heels of the stockings in almost fierce absorption. "You might as well know right now, Shubunka. We ain't working with you anymore. That's finished."

The fat man was acting the part of a burdened sick man to whom another bitter betrayal had just been revealed. "So they scared you, my house manager. They came with their bluff and their bull stories and you believed them," he said sorrowfully. "Well, it is to be expected." He shook his head, hurt but nevertheless not surprised by her.

"They came today again. They said you were quitting the business. They said I got to work for them or else. So what could I do?"

"I see," said Shubunka. "I see. The first little snotnose who comes along, you believe him. It is all bluff. They cannot handle the business. Do you think all you need to do is know how to fight and break up houses? In a week's time you will be running back to me, on your hands and knees, begging me to let you work again."

"Never mind that line. There's plenty good people behind this combination. They'll have the whole city organized."

"Of course, sure, oh, sure. That is what they always will tell you. All right. I won't say another word. I won't interfere. It is your privilege to do whatever you like. I cannot force you. Only just think, my house manager. For four, five years already I have been bringing you girls, finding you houses, buying the protection, taking care of the police, sending you lawyers and bond. All that time you never had a complaint and it cost you only ten percent while you went half and half with the girls. It was all so simple, so easy. Remember it. Now the first bum comes along and he tells you a story full of bluff and you get scared."

"Jesus Christ, Shubunka, don't lay it on. You act like I wanted it. I'm on the spot myself, just like everyone else. Do you think I like this? They're putting me on a salary. Ninety bucks a week and I got the expenses. I got to bond all kinds of fancy money every week and then there is the security. Do you think it's a picnic for me? I can't do anything about it. They smashed one joint apart and they told me they'd take this place to pieces also and put me out of business. If I wanted to get funny, they'd take care of me, too. They got the cops or else how come all the raids in the other houses? So what do you want me to do about it? My life's precious to me!"

"I see, I see," said Shubunka, no longer the mastermind but an old, old man buffeted severely by fate. He sat there at the dirty table, his head drooping, and his expression showed that he knew well this was the ungrateful way of the world. It was bitter and low, humans were always miserable in their relations with one another, but it was an old tale, he knew it and could not be shocked. Now he was stripped of all vanity, all affectation, only a simple man left to his grief. Feeling so sorry for himself that actual tears came to his eyes, the fat man looked intently into the greasy enameled tabletop to see if he could discern the appearance of his face in the dim reflection.

⁓⁓⁓

"No," said Herbert Lurie to the superintendent. "We don't care for this flat. We'll take the one in front."

"It's sixty-five dollars in the front," the agent said. "But if *you* like it better, it's whatever you want. You're the boss."

"What's the difference, Herbert?" Dorothy asked. "We might as well save the money off the rent."

The rooms here faced the sunless backyards, drab and dreary. "It's gloomy. I don't like it," Herbert said, and they went back to the other apartment. These rooms were on the street side, looking out at the Brooklyn Museum of Art and the green shrubbery of the Botanical Gardens. It was as though you lived in the country. Standing in the furnished apartment on Eastern Parkway, Lurie thought that this was what he had been seeking all along. On that sunny day, everything seemed fresh, gay, and clean. You might have been a million miles from Neptune Beach with its dirty, badly paved streets, its ugly broken-down houses, the constant wet and sand from the beach. Here were no people rushing wildly to grasp a good time, shouting and fighting in the streets.

"What sixty-five dollars is he talking about?" Lurie asked Dorothy. "He'll take fifty-five and a month's concession."

"Oh, I'm sorry. It's positively the lowest price," the superintendent protested. Lurie got to work on him and in five minutes he paid the ten-dollar deposit. The rent would be sixty dollars with a month's concession, since they were taking the year lease. The agent went down to fill out the receipt for his deposit.

"Well," he said. "You like it? You satisfied?"

"It's nice. It's really very lovely, only what will my mother say when she hears it's a furnished apartment? She don't think it's respectable for a couple to start off in furnished rooms. When my sister got married they fixed up three rooms."

"Well," said Lurie happily, looking out the window, "I like it. I think it's swell." Going up to him, Dorothy put her arm on his shoulder, leaning on him fondly.

"It's real luxurious. You really have a view here. I hate to admit it, Herbert, but I guess you were right after all. I like it very much. I can almost forget about the bathing I'll miss at Neptune."

Lurie laughed and hugged her tightly.

"Herbert!" she cried. "Please!"

"What the hell? I'm your husband, ain't I?"

"Not yet!"

"Honey, what do you say?" he asked, growing earnest and begging. "Let's run down to City Hall and get married today."

"We said tomorrow, so let it be tomorrow."

"What's the difference? Everything's all ready. We could move in tonight."

"I can't, Herbert, so stop pestering. I haven't even got my birth certificate."

"O.K., honey," he said. "Only I got a hard job waiting. You know how it is."

He laughed. Dorothy broke away and went through the flat. There was a bedroom and living room, the closet kitchenette hidden in the wall. She pulled open the panels and toyed with the gadgets for cooking. It was compact and neat. She liked it, but wondered whether the cooking smells wouldn't fill the living room. In many ways she couldn't understand Herbert. Why did he want an altogether new flat when he had a perfectly good one already in Neptune Beach? And what was the rush, too? She'd go to visit Herbert on the hot days, Dorothy thought, and change in his store for the beach. It wouldn't be so bad.

"Herbert," she said. "The store. It's time you were getting back. Your girl comes in at eleven and you got to open the store."

"Oh, nuts on the store," he said in gay spirits. "The girl can wait until I come. It can wait today. I want to take a walk through the park. What do you say?"

"It's impossible. Herbert, do you realize it's ten-thirty?"

"What the hell? A guy don't get married every day!"

Herbert grew conscious the remark was inept. He regretted it the moment he made it. They went downstairs. In the lobby the superintendent handed him his receipt. Lurie told him they would probably be back that night with their bags.

* * *

There was a little card on the door window of Lurie's dress shop that said: Out For Morning Will Be Back 11 O'Clock. Karty cursed his luck, the tip of his nose nearly touching his upper lip as he screwed his weasel face to keep back the tears. Hoodooed for life. Everything went wrong. The gambler felt the change in his pocket. He had exactly eighty-five cents and after that what? Unfair, he cried to himself. Why me? What had he ever done to find himself in this fix? Not a friend in the whole wide world to go to. The only prospect Karty could find before him was to return to Ann's and try Spitzbergen. But it was hopeless before he started. Bitch, he muttered in rhythm to his stride as he walked, bitch, bitch.

Suddenly darting from the sidewalk across the street, dodging past the autos, a man came running up on Karty with such a rush that he fell on top of him and they both nearly went down to the ground. Karty had no time to see who it was. He barely managed to raise his arm to shield his face before the man started to belabor him heavily about the head with his open palms. The man swung freely, bringing his hands up from the ground, panting with each effort. Karty bundled his head in his arms and hunched his shoulders, but it was little help against the beating. He fell to the pavement and looked up. It was his brother-in-law, Harry. The man had his foot raised in the air, ready to pump it down on the gambler, when Mrs. Karty came running up to the spot and fiercely banged into her brother, knocking him off balance.

"Leave him alone!" she cried. "Murderer!"

"I'll give him," said her brother, his breath coming in wheezes. "This is only the beginning. He's got plenty more coming to him." He pushed her off him and went on with the blows.

People started running from all parts of the street until a large crowd collected about them. They watched the proceedings with avid interest, taking in the performance with pleasure, but not interfering. A nine-year-old boy gravely sucked at his ice-cream sandwich as he contemplated the scene before him. "It's a shame," said one woman to another, as the brother-in-law smacked Karty on the ground. "Such a big man hitting him. He ain't his size." They looked on.

Mrs. Karty hung on her brother's arm, yelling at him to stop, but the man mauled the gambler. From time to time he would interrupt his work on Karty to pull up his pants, shiny and stiff with grease. This was necessary because he was a fat man with his belt coming around just under his belly; and further, Karty, in protecting himself, was keeping his head between the garage man's legs, pulling on his trousers constantly to shield himself in that position. The brother-in-law whacked away at him laboriously with the satisfied, preoccupied expression of a man who is doing his job. His shirttails swirled in the air and he panted.

A bald-headed intense old man had been watching the fight from his second-story window directly above them. He could not believe it was taking place and felt outraged at the shame. "Why don't they stop them?" he cried, overwhelmed by the inaction of the crowd. "Why do they stand there?" Confused, he drew his head in as he groped to do something, but the next moment he jerked it back again. "Police!" he screamed. "Police! Police!" It did no good. The brother-in-law continued to clout Karty mercilessly, as if he were performing a necessary duty.

More people came swarming to them and the crowd swelled. "What's up, kid?" one of the newcomers asked. The boy, thirteen or fourteen, scratched his head sheepishly and said, "It's her husband. He caught this guy fooling around with her and now he's beating him up. That's why she's trying to stop him. You can figure it out for yourself."

"I guess the rat's got it coming to him," the newcomer said and they both went back to the fight.

"Harry, Harry, stop!" Mrs. Karty screamed, pulling on her brother. "He's got enough already! You'll kill him!"

"No," said Harry, his voice strangely unexcited. "First I got to learn him he should know." He went on punching and slapping. Karty dug his head desperately between Harry's legs, trying to receive the blows on his shoulders. He pulled on the pants as hard as he could and wondered when the man would finally stop.

Deep in the crowd a woman was fighting her way free. She had her little girl on her arm and now the child had wet her Kiddie Pants. She was disgusted with the kid because this cut the show short for her. "Let me out!" she cried irritably, striking her way with her free arm. "Lousy kid," she said to the little girl. The child was sobbing quietly, rubbing her fists into her eyes until they had wide circles of dirt around them.

The bald-headed man on the second floor could restrain himself no longer. "People should be ashamed!" he called down. "Is this a civilized people?" No one paid any attention to him. He left the window in a burst of fury but soon returned with a pot of water. He swooshed it so that it fell in a wide curve all over the crowd. The hum of the mob ceased. They ran a few paces and looked up at the bald-headed old man. He still held the pot in his hand and the crowd began to curse and yell at him. He took advantage of the occasion to deliver a lecture, impassionate and burning, on the decencies of human life. Everyone quite forgot the fight to hoot and yell up at the intellectual.

"Enough already," said Mrs. Karty. She punched her brother on the shoulder and he stepped back, satisfied. Karty rose, blinded and gasping. His clothes were twisted and splotched with dirt. He bled from the nose so that it was difficult for him to catch his breath. His Adam's apple bobbed violently as he sucked and wheezed. The dirt on his face formed in thick black swatches, but behind the dirt could be seen fat welts from the fists of his brother-in-law. Karty pawed the air as he groped his way to escape. He was holding his head well back on his neck to stop the blood coming from his nose and it was hard for him to see. As he turned his back, fighting off his wife, and made to leave, Harry ran up, caught him by the coat collar and shook him to a halt.

"Leave him alone already!" shouted Mrs. Karty. "He's got enough. You won't be satisfied until he lays dead?"

"This is only for a start," he told the gambler, paying no attention to her. His tone was almost conversational, so calm and determined was he. "This is only for a sample so you can see what there's in stock for you. Now we will talk."

The three of them moved away from the crowd, Karty's coat held tightly in Harry's fist. A few of the spectators followed them, but these soon lost interest and went back to the crowd where there was further excitement to entertain them. On the second floor, insulted and harried by the crowd, the intellectual had gone back for another pot of water. When he reappeared everyone dashed away wildly, tripping and knocking one another down in haste. But the gesture developed into a false alarm. The bald-headed man didn't throw the water. Finally victorious over the mob, he held the pot high and his flashing eyes dared anyone to say him nay again.

The brother-in-law shoved Karty into Ann's, still holding him by the coat collar, talking in a steady determined stream. Mrs. Karty ran behind them, tripping over their heels. She was pushing and punching her brother, crying at him to leave Karty alone, but the big man ignored her and shoved the gambler before him.

"Hey, what the hell do you call this?" Shorty exclaimed from the counter with profound offense. "This is a place of business. We can't have no commotions in here."

The man went on, pushing Karty through the parlor, acting as though he had never heard the soda jerker. Spitzbergen came running from the kitchen, his face black with fear in the expectation of further trouble. He had thought at first it was the two thugs coming back for more damage. "What's this? What's going on?" he asked, seeing who they were almost with relief. "I don't want it. This ain't a drugstore. Take him out."

"It's all right, Spitzbergen," the garage man said. "You leave it to me. There won't be any trouble. All I want is a place to talk to this louse. Then we'll go. There will be no trouble." He drove Karty past the soda man into the kitchen.

"No!" protested Spitzbergen after them. "Is this a place for talking? It ain't my business here for people to come in for talking. I don't pay rent for it."

"What's the matter? What can we do? We ain't going to eat up the walls." He looked at Spitzbergen with deep annoyance and shoved the gambler into the kitchen. Mrs. Karty bundled in behind them. The door banged shut.

"No!" yelled the soda man, near tears with helplessness. "Why should it be? How much does he pay me for it?"

"Uhmy! My!" gasped Arthur, open-eyed. "It must of been an accident."

"An accident, nuts!" said Shorty wisely. "What did I tell you? Karty probably got the hell knocked out of him. He had it coming to him a long time, too. See, I let him pull anything over on me around here. Hell, I figure him for a bug. If a guy's got the racing bug, it's the same thing as a disease. That's what I always say, don't you know? Well, some guy probably took a different view of the matter, and when that hopped-up gambling fiend spoke out of turn or something, why, wham, Karty got what was coming to him. I never seen it to fail. Anybody bets on the horses, he goes to the dogs and that ain't no wisecrack. There's more truth than poetry in it. Yare, I seen it happen often and again."

The last word. Shorty, looking important and all-knowing, fished under his apron for a cigarette. Arthur heard the soda jerker attentively but all the same he almost envied Karty. A real man, full grown, gambling and all. Here it was the dishwasher's short day. He'd be off after one o'clock and what would he do with his time? He'd take in a matinee at the Mermaid, drop in at Ann's for his supper, go home and listen to the radio and then go to bed at ten. There was something childish about the way he did things and Arthur longed for man's estate.

Lillian, the new cashier, had sat on her stool at the register all the time, taking in the whole performance. The full flesh under her chin hung loosely as she kept her mouth open with amazement.

But in a way she was grateful for the incident. It had been a relief from Shorty's maneuvers and she had been able to relax her guard a moment.

Inside the small kitchen Karty immediately sat down on the only chair, grateful for the rest. His wife wet her handkerchief at the sink and was applying it to his nose to stop the blood. "Give me your keys, Harry," she said. Her brother slowly took the ring out of his pocket, staring contemptuously at Karty all the time, and she applied them on Karty's spine at the neck, holding his head back so that his gaze rested on the fly-specked ceiling. "See," she wept to him, "what did I tell you? Why didn't you make good? You would of saved yourself the whole goddammed business."

"Let me alone," Karty whined, shoving her away from him. "Don't you bother me no more. I'm through with you. I don't know you."

"Maybe you like it, Moe," the brother-in-law began. "Maybe you had a good time. Maybe you want some more?"

"Go to hell, you bastard. Don't think I'm going to forget this in a hurry. You'll get yours for this."

"I'll get it. All right. That's fine. I'm satisfied." His fat palm shot out and slammed Karty on the cheek, half knocking him off the chair.

"Bastard," Karty cried.

The brother-in-law raised his hand again but Mrs. Karty caught it in the air and hung on to it with both hands, clamping it fiercely against her chest. "You stay out of it. Nobody needs you," he said, pushing her away. Mrs. Karty suddenly became infuriated. In a spasm she rushed against her brother, slapping his face in a frenzy. "Louse! Bastard! Leave him alone!" she screamed. "You want to kill him altogether for a couple of lousy dollars?"

The noise was too much for Mr. Spitzbergen outside. He took to knocking on the door. Mrs. Karty grew quiet again and worked on her husband, still calling abuse on her brother in a steady stream as she washed Karty's face and straightened his clothes. Karty kept on pushing her away but she persisted in helping him.

"Listen, Moe," said the brother-in-law, "what you got today is only to show you we ain't forgetting the whole business and it will pass over. This is no fooling. What we want we'll get and if the thirteen hundred dollars don't come back tonight by the latest, the next time it won't be with hands you will be hit."

"Balls," said the gambler weakly. He listened with his head held back because of the nosebleed but his eyes constantly watched the fat palms, flinching with every movement they made. "Balls," he repeated. "You're crazy."

"Crazy or no crazy, bring back the thirteen hundred dollars or you'll spend a year in the hospital."

"Where do you get off with thirteen hundred dollars?" Karty's nerve had gone and he begged and whined. "I didn't take the money. I don't know anything about it. It's all a frame-up."

"It's not to argue." The brother-in-law spoke all the time with such hard determination and certainty that his voice sounded oddly impassive. The racetrack gambler was frightened more by this tone than he had been by the beating. "I don't come to you discussing it. It's all settled. You stole the money and you got to give it back. Every penny of it. I'm just telling you what's what. Listen, Moe Karty, if the money ain't in the garage by tonight, we'll come for you with monkey wrenches this time in our hands. We'll fix you. We'll smash you, nobody will know you for months to come, and when you come out of the hospital you'll be a cripple for life. No, we won't send you to jail, a hospital will be better for you. And if you think we don't mean what we say, every word, if you think it's a big bluff, then you're making the biggest mistake in your whole rotten life."

He scowled with disgust over Karty. "Horses," he muttered. "Gambling on horses. An educated man, a professional. A stinker for a husband." He grabbed his keys from Karty's neck roughly, so that the gambler's head bobbed and he put his hands before his face, crying out with fear at another attack.

"Go already, bum!" Mrs. Karty said. "You did enough."

"A fine husband you got. Education. By rights you should throw him down a sewer and wash your hands with him." Hitching up his greasy pants, he glowered at Karty and walked out. Mrs. Karty applied the cold compresses to the bleeding nose.

"Leave me alone!" Karty cried, pushing her away. "It's stopping already."

"See, Moe?" she whispered. "See what trouble you're in? I can't do nothing with them, they're like an ox. You can't talk to him. He came to the house this morning looking for you. He couldn't wait."

"Go away. Go to hell. Leave me alone." Karty held his head in his hands, bruised and swollen. He felt sick. His body seemed to have lost all its strength so that it became a genuine effort to move any part of it. He rested limply. A heavy, dizzy sensation weighed his head and it was difficult for him to see clearly. He tried to focus on the black pots on the gas range but his gaze was fuzzy and wavering.

"Where can I get the money?" he whined. "What do they want from me? I ain't got a dollar to my name. Thirteen hundred dollars!" He laughed bitterly. "Sure, thirteen hundred dollars. I'll go pick it off the trees."

"Pay it back, Moe," his wife said grimly. "Pay it back. Otherwise they'll kill you. You know my brothers."

"Where? Where am I going to find it?" he burst out at her. "Where can I go? What can I pawn? Who will lend it to me?" He looked at her with deep hatred. "Go to hell! What the hell are you standing around me for? Go ahead, beat it! Leave me alone! All you ever brought me was trouble. I never saw a good day with you yet. From the very beginning it was only trouble."

In the narrow kitchen Karty began to kick at her from his chair. She suffered the feeble blows dumbly, standing at the door. "Moe," she said. "Moe." But Karty's paroxysm of rage continued. "Moe, pay back the money," she said, tearful and miserable.

She went out and walked through the parlor to the street, clearing her nose in her grief, her knees knocking as she walked. In the kitchen Karty's hysteria passed, but to take its place fear sank in. He felt cold and shivered convulsively. The ruthless manner of his brother-in-law now came back to him and he knew with terrible clearness what would happen to him if he failed to raise the money. What could he do, wept Karty, turning to stare helplessly at the walls of the dingy kitchen? Where could he go? How could he escape? It was a miserable world. He sat motionless on the chair, gathering the strength back and trying to collect himself.

Madame Pavlovna, smiling languidly and shuffling with her feet pointing outward as she walked, came into Ann's in her Russian tunic, a little late for her. She went to the cozy stool near the double-decked water tray, climbed upon it, and wrapped her wine-red bedroom slippers around the pole of the seat as a little girl would, and she looked at Shorty with the timid expression of a child who fears a scolding, begging forgiveness. But Shorty was adamant, he was. He looked at her briefly, his eyes flashing with silent contempt, and he went deliberately to the other end to serve a customer who had just come in for a Coke. The corsetière pouted, the loose lines of her puffed face turning impish.

"What is this pro-gress? What is this pro-gress?" It was Arthur, declaiming solemnly with his finger cutting lovely circles in the foam that he was creating in the second basin. His hair was down over his eyes and his face wore its distant look. "What," he asked defiantly again, "is this pro-gress?"

"Vat, my dear boy?" asked Madame Pavlovna, at a loss. "Vy do you say this strange thing?"

The dishwasher looked up ruefully. "Oh, good morning," he said. "It's nothing. I was talking to myself. It's in the picture *The Shape of Things to Come*. See, a man stands up on a platform and says, 'What is this pro-gress?' See, that's all it is."

"Vell, vat is the meaning?" she persisted. "Vat means this pro-gress?"

"I don't know," grinned Arthur hopelessly. "It just sounds good. It's crazy but I like to say it, I don't know exactly why."

"Strange," said the corsetière, mystified. "A strange boy."

The little old woman with the white shawl over her head came in for her money. Regularly twice each week she appeared at the store, holding her hand wrapped in a neat handkerchief—the sign of her trade. She was a beggar. "She's here again," Mr. Spitzbergen wailed. "Now everything's all right again. Give her a penny." He turned away, frowning, but all the same it brought him a certain degree of warm feeling to realize that he was not, after all, a hard man, tight with his money and unfeeling as stone. Spitzbergen was still seeking reassurance over the visit of the two thugs and was still trying to convince himself that the end of the world hadn't come for him. But every time he grew a bit heartened, his gaze passed to the ice-cream machine and he shuddered. The two weeks' rent money Shubunka owed him seemed hopeless. He would never see the fat man again.

"A beautiful day," sighed Madame Pavlovna. "Nice veder."

The soda man couldn't understand her. He started as though she had directed a personal insult at him. "Nice weather? It's rotten! It's ruining me. Too cold! Maybe it's different with a corset shop, you don't have to worry, I don't know. But for the soda-parlor business, it's a finish."

The old woman in the shawl stood dumbly, holding out her napkined hand. She might have been a piece of furniture in the store. "Arthur," the boss said. "What's the matter? Give her a penny."

"Who, me?" asked Arthur. He beamed with pleasure and ran to the cashier's stand. He always took great relish in operating the cash register whenever he could. He fussed over the keys. No Sale, he pushed and banged the black button at the top. The cash drawer slid out as if by magic. Arthur picked out the penny and put it into the cloth. The little old lady ambled out of the store, no change of expression, not even the slightest, taking place on that weary face. "See?" Arthur told Lillian behind the cigar stand. "What is this pro-gress?"

"Crazy," she muttered faintly. She remained in the narrow aisle behind the stand because it offered the best protection.

"See, see," said Madame Pavlovna when Arthur came back to his place. "A new girl."

"Oh, yes," the dishwasher said. "Dorothy quit. She's getting married to Herbert Lurie but it's a secret."

"A sveet child, it's good for her. I'm glad." The corsetière was examining the new cashier. "Sveet, too. A little stout, vouldn't you say?"

But Arthur had ducked away, grinning. Shorty stood there now, grim-faced and unyielding, meaning strictly business today. "Order. Please," he said. "What'll you have?"

"Oh, Shur-tee," Madame Pavlovna said. "You're making fun. You don't mean it."

But he did. The soda jerker wouldn't say a word. He picked up two slices of bread, dropped them into the toaster, and went up to the pitcher for the orange juice, slapping his fingers on his apron smartly to wipe them. Mrs. Pavlovna recognized the end of their intimacy: generally, Shorty squeezed fresh juice for her, today he was pouring from the common pitcher. It was over.

"Arthur," said Spitzbergen, "go inside the kitchen and tell Mr. Karty he should go home. What does he want to do? Live in there all day? Then let him pay rent."

The dishwasher dropped his towel and went trotting down the parlor. Karty was half asleep on the chair, leaning his head against the wall of the kitchen. "Give me a glass of water," he said. Arthur sympathetically fussed over him, and when he brought the glass from the sink he helped him by holding the water to his mouth.

"You had an accident, Mr. Karty?" the dishwasher asked. "Something happened?"

"Yeah," said the gambler, feeling a little better. "Arthur, you want to do me a favor? A big favor?"

"Anything you say, Mr. Karty! If I can only do it!"

"I'm in a spot, Arthur. I need a couple of dollars."

"Gee, I told you. I'm broke. I don't get paid until day after tomorrow. I'm sorry."

"So ask Spitz to advance you a couple of bucks on account. Tell him you need four, five bucks right now. He'll give you."

All at once Arthur took pity on the gambler. He had never seen him in this condition before, and the intimate, begging tone he now used contrasted strangely with his usual nasty way. For some reason this affected the dishwasher strangely. It made him feel close to Karty, and he experienced a powerful urge to help him, but hesitated before going up to the boss.

"Gee, I can't, Mr. Karty. He'll only holler at me and I won't get the money anyhow. It's useless to try."

"Aw, gee! Aw, gee!" Karty wept, punching the wall. "Jesus Christ, I'm in a hell of a hole. I'm in a jam and I can't get a single guy in the world to help me. Aw, go to hell, Arthur. You, too. I thought I could count on you."

"Geez, I would if I could! But, holy smoke, he just sent me in here to tell you you should go home. And now you want me to ask him for an advance. All that will happen, he'll holler and get sore."

"Then get out!" cried the gambler. "Then what good do you do standing here? Then beat it."

"Well, then, O.K. I'll ask him. All right. I'll ask him. But it's only a waste of time."

Unhappy with his duty, the dishwasher went out of the kitchen. Spitzbergen was waiting for him at the fountain. "Well?" he asked, his brow contracted with displeasure. "I don't see no Moe Karty."

"He's feeling sick," said Arthur. "He wanted to rest for a minute, so I said O.K., but only for a minute. He's pretty knocked out."

"Who made you the boss all of a sudden?" Spitzbergen growled, but he had to restrain himself. Madame Pavlovna was still in the store and he didn't want to spoil the effect of the beggar woman on her now. "Not that it makes a difference if he stays in there or not," he mumbled. "Only who's he to give orders around here? The place still got a boss. I ain't dead yet." He moved away. "Snotnose," he added. Arthur followed him.

"Mr. Spitzbergen, I wonder if I . . ." He stopped. While he wavered with fear, Arthur hated himself because he recognized his lack of spirit. If he were a man, with man's ways, he would not be afraid. He would simply come straight out with it and ask him for the money. It wasn't as though he had no right to it. "Mr. Spitzbergen," he began with determination, "I want to ask you . . ."

"Don't you bodder me!" the boss exclaimed, turning his back on him. "What do you want from my life, too?" He went to the back of the store and sat down. He had troubles enough of his own and they weighed heavily on his mind. Those gangsters this morning. Spitzbergen took out a small piece of pencil and started preparing the list of houses he rented to Shubunka together with the account of his other real-estate holdings. He had to worry for the whole world.

Arthur stood blankly, angry with himself at the display of his cowardice, at his fright before the boss. He was still a kid. He lacked the self-respect a man had. He went in to Karty, near tears with himself, and told the gambler that Spitzbergen had said no.

"Shur-tee!" wheedled Madame Pavlovna over her tea. "You terrible man. Shurtee, I vill be angry vith you in a moment. I vill lose my sense of humor, and then vat vill be?"

"If it's all the same to you," said the soda jerker formally, "I'd rather have nothing further to do with you."

"Shur-tee! I vas really sick. You are unkind. I vas so sick I could hardly stand on my feet. Vy must you be so unreasonable? You are acting terrible to me, Shurtee, and it isn't like you at all. After all, how much longer do I have to be patient vith you?"

"See, Mrs. Pavlovna, I don't know what your opinion of me might be, but I want you to know one thing. See, no lady ever gave me a stand-up before and I want to say I was really very much hurt, see how I mean? You may not think it to look at me, but I got feelings. I'm sensitive, that's my temperament, even though I hide it."

"Poor little Shurtee. But he misunderstood me. He gets hurt for no reason."

"That's what you say now," he said, sulking.

"Shorty! Come over here quick! I want to see you." It was Mr. Spitzbergen at his table. The jerker ran over to him. "What do you call this?" the boss asked. "I'm paying you good money to give Mrs. Pavlovna a good time? It ain't necessary you should stand talking all the time."

Son of a bitch. Nothing doing in the store, he ain't happy unless I'm working my pants off all the time. I got to sweat. "Listen, Mr. Spitzbergen," Shorty said confidentially, "you got to pull the customers in, ain't it? You got to give them what they want or else they don't come back, ain't it? They can find other places. The way you act somebody would think I get enjoyment talking to that fat dame. I ain't doing it for fun, it's just for the business, don't you know?"

"Never mind," the boss grumbled. "You talk in riddles. All I know is you don't need it." He went back to his list of apartments.

The soda jerker made an elaborate operation of avoiding Madame Pavlovna and letting her know that as far as she was concerned he had lost all interest. He wiped two or three tables, fixed the menus into their clasps, examined the sugar bowls critically to see if they were filled. As Madame Pavlovna watched him, understanding and patient with him, smoking her Melachrino, she smiled reproachfully. You naughty boy, she said, you naughty boy. Shorty, nothing fazed, went over to the cashier at the cigar stand. She hadn't budged an inch from her haven.

"See, you and your mind," he said. "You got a notion I'm trying to put something over on you all the time. See that fat broad over there? I'd give ten bucks right this minute to get her off my hands. I can't lose her in a crowd. Listen, sister, if you think I got that on my mind only, then, hell, why would I be ducking that dame? See? You certainly got the wrong impression of me, that's one thing I can say for a fact."

Lillian's mouth quivered and her big eyes gazed at him with sullen suspicion. "Don't be smart," she said. "Just leave me alone and mind your own business or else you'll get what's good for you. I want you to understand I got a boyfriend."

"That so?" Shorty asked pleasantly. "I'm glad to hear it. I'm shivering in my pants with the scare already. Listen, I could tell you what you can do with your boyfriend, only I'm a gentleman for the moment."

"I know. Never mind. You think you're smart."

"See, you got me all wrong, sister," Shorty said in a confidential burst. "I'm not at all the guy you imagine. Hell, the way you act, somebody who knew me would think you're nuts. If I say so myself, when it comes to the dames, I don't have to chase no woman, see?"

"So what do you want from me if you're so hot? I don't send for you. I can live without you."

"Nasty kid," said Shorty, giving up hope. Ingratitude. "All I came over for just now was to tell you you're off after the lunch rush today. See, you're off until seven in the evening. Then you stay till twelve, thereabouts. See, I come over to help you out and you give me an argument. She don't send for me! I don't have to come near her! Listen. Suppose I was a different type of a man, that's what I want to know, with a different temperament? How do you think I'd take it when you got nasty?"

"Well, how should I know?" Lillian asked, her tone softening. Maybe she had misjudged him after all. "You got to admit, it certainly looked bad with all those funny accidents one after the other."

"All right," said Shorty, honor satisfied. He lit his cigarette the better to create an impression of magnanimity. "You don't have to apologize."

"Who's apologizing?" she asked. "Who put that idea into your head?"

"All right," he said. "We'll let it pass."

Lillian was anxious to have him understand fully she wasn't apologizing, but the soda jerker cut her short. He moved away, majestically waving the match in the air to extinguish the flame. He went to the counter and wiped the sandwich table, conscious of his mastery over Madame Pavlovna, for all this time she had remained on the stool, long after her breakfast, waiting patiently until he took it into his head to return. She crossed her legs, picked the cigarette paper from her rouged lips, and grew serious.

"Listen, Shurtee," she said, "how long can this situvation last? It's growing a little boring, don't you agree? I'm getting tired vith you. You're acting like a little boy."

"Well, it's just too bad then. Somebody would think I'm holding you or something."

"Let's make up, Shurtee. It's so tiresome."

"Gee whiz, Mrs. Pavlovna. You don't know me. Once I make up my mind, that's final!"

"Such a silly quvarrel," sighed the corsetière, climbing down from the stool. "In Salsburg, vun year, I met a voman. Her whole life was ruined, positively shattered, just because of a little silly quvarrel. People are so stubborn." In her languid dreaminess Madame Pavlovna was now shuffling to the door, her wine-red slippered feet pointing to the sides as she move her heavy body. "Poor Shur-tee," she said, as if to herself. "Poor Shur-tee. I hurt his feelings and now he is angry vith me. A pity. A pity, but he vill get over it and then everything vill be all right." She was out of the store.

The soda jerker bit his lips, vexed. The skin on his skull tightened with reflection as he wondered whether he had been adamant just a moment too long. Hahvahnah! Ven I was in Hahvahnah! "Arthur!" he yelled, to relieve his anxiety. "Lunk-headed mope. Arthur! What the hell you doing in that kitchen all the time?"

The dishwasher came trotting down the aisle. "I got to clean the range, ain't it? What are you hollering about?" He poured the water into the basins. "I was talking to Mr. Karty for a minute. He told me I got to bring him back a bowl of soup.'

"Poor slob," said Shorty, ever a man of compassion even in the midst of his own troubles. "But that don't give you no call to stall around in the kitchen all night. There's a pile of dishes and you ain't going to leave it when you quit." He went to the steam table to see if the soup was hot enough. Arthur started to work on the plates. From the intense look on his usually blithe face, it was clear that he was puzzled and absorbed in thought. Shorty had his troubles, too. Had he been too severe with the corsetière? He ladled the tomato soup into the bowl and gave it to Arthur. The dishwasher filled up a plate with crackers and set off for the kitchen.

"Stop!" cried Spitzbergen, looking up just in time from his work at the table. "Where you taking the soup? Mr. Moe Karty again? Maybe it ain't enough we give him rent free, we got to supply him with board, too?"

"Oh, he'll pay for it, Mr. Spitzbergen," Arthur exclaimed, "What did you think?"

"It's not your business what I think. Just be sure Mr. Moe Karty stops by the cash register when he goes out." He returned to his list, sick with the whole business of the joints and the gangsters, but he had investments and it was his duty to look after them.

And what about the ice-cream machine, pondered Spitzbergen? What about the two weeks' rent money? He gloomily watched Arthur's back as the dishwasher gazed carefully into the bowl to keep the soup from spilling on his trip back to Karty. The soda man was too overwhelmed to take out the proper time and effort for Karty and his outrages upon him today.

Shorty's fears, at least, proved needless. In five minutes Madame Pavlovna's clerk entered with a note for him.

My Dear Boy:

Please stop this siliness of your behaviur. I did not intend to cause you any offend. By my indisposision last night. You are being a ridiculus childe. Think it over and let us be freinds again. Perhaps you will be free tonight?

Ever yours,

(Mrs.) Sophia Pavlovna

P.S. Please excuse terrible spelling.

As the soda jerker read the note his eyes seemed to bulge with absorption. He dried his hands on his apron, told the girl to wait for the answer, and ran over to the cashier's stand for a pencil and a little paper bag on which to write. Lillian flinched at the onslaught but Shorty had no time to remonstrate with her. He brought the little candy bag to the counter, and as he worked on the reply the beads of perspiration appeared on his brow.

Dear Mrs. Pavllovna:

A freind in name is no freind in deed. As the provurbe is. I thought you are my freind I was wrong about it. Live and lirn that is my mottoe. While I thought you are my freind you were appairantly just having your flinge with me to you I was just the soda jerker at Anns. Well, we all make mistakes all the time I made mine about you.

Yours truly,

The Soda Jerker

Arthur looked at the clock on the arch over the parlor for the first time at Ann's with a reluctant feeling at the approach of one o'clock on his off half day. A little scared and yet tremulous with anticipation, what worried him was not Karty's plan but the fact that in an hour and a half he would be quitting. The thought of leaving the calm security of Ann's depressed him. Free as a bird, with nothing on his mind, that was his ambition, and for one who sought adventure and excitement there could be no peace, which was also a desirable quality. Shorty told him not to stand moping. The dishes, stacked up on the washstand, needed drying and the noon rush soon would be upon them. The soda jerker was gaily singing the song about Dixie, in excellent humor.

Two men came into the soda parlor. They settled on the stools but when Shorty came up to get their orders, they said they wanted a drink of water, that was all. A young lady near them at the fountain looked up over her strawberry frappé, scratched her nose contemplatively, and wondered at them. The one with the prizefighter's broken nose returned her stare flatly and she dropped her eyes to the frappé hastily. "Nice baby," he commented, still staring at her. His companion, a thin man in dapper clothes, pulled his arm and said, "Cut it out." The girl swallowed the last mouthful and hurried to pay her check, leaving the glass of water untouched in her rush. Shorty looked at the two men, saying nothing in apprehension. They peered into the parlor.

"Shubunka ain't in by any chance, is he?" the prizefighter asked.

"Oh, no," said Shorty, shaking his head solemnly. What this Shubunka business was all about he didn't know, but he knew enough to stay as far away from it as he could.

"You expect him in today?"

"I don't know nothing. I'm just the soda jerker here. You better talk to the boss or somebody."

"What's the matter with you?" the dapper man asked. "You ain't got the power of speech? We want to see Shubunka."

"Hell," exclaimed Shorty in his best intimate manner, "I'm doing the best I can for you fellows. What's the use of me saying anything about Shubunka when the goddammed truth is I don't know a thing about it. I'd just be putting you guys wrong if I opened my mouth on the subject, don't you see?"

They thought it over. Shorty, gaining confidence, bent toward them to explain fully how he felt on the matter of giving incorrect information just for the sake of congeniality, but the broken-nose man cut him short. "Nuts to you, mister. You know where you can shove that crap. Where's the boss?"

Shorty, paling as he repressed himself, pointed sullenly to Spitzbergen in the parlor. As soon as they left he had a great deal to say but he told it to himself, his lips moving rapidly. "Wise guys," he muttered, and he looked at the door. He had his own affairs and Shubunka was nobody in his life. Madame Pavlovna had another note coming to him and he expected it any minute.

The two men sat down at Spitzbergen's table before the soda man knew they were there. He looked up from his list, frowning and afraid. "What do you call this, please?" he asked. "Is this a way to butt in on a person?"

"Hold your horses," the dapper man said. "Where's Shubunka?"

"Shubunka!" Spitzbergen nearly wept the name. "Who sent you now?" He went white and shifted his heavy weight on the chair as he squirmed.

"See, it's all right," the prizefighter said. "You know all about us and what we want. It's O.K. We're doing this just as much for your peace of mind as for our own sakes. You don't want Shubunka around the place and we promised you protection. That means chiselers besides the cops. We want Shubunka."

As Spitzbergen studied their faces, he grew more nervous with the minutes. These were strong-arm men. They came to smash and kill. "Not here," he begged. "I don't want no trouble here. I got my full share already. This soda parlor cost me eighteen thousand dollars and I can't afford to lose my investment. I'll be a ruined man. If you have to make trouble, all right, only don't do it here."

"We ain't making trouble for nobody yet. We ain't going to start anything here," the dapper man said. "You don't understand our meaning. All we want right now is Shubunka."

"I ain't got him. This is a soda parlor. It's a store. Don't start nothing here."

"Did he come in today?"

"No! No!"

"You expecting him in here sometime today?"

"Maybe yes, maybe no. It all depends. I can't tell in advance. It's when he wants to take it into his head."

"Where does he live? What's the address?"

"I don't know."

"You got his phone number?"

"I ain't got it. He never told me."

The prizefighter paused to inspect him critically. He glanced at his companion, seeking to confirm his doubts. The dapper man couldn't understand Spitzbergen.

"What the hell are you stalling us for?" he asked. "You don't get the point. We're here to help you. You don't want Shubunka coming around to bother you. He'll only be a nuisance to you as well as us."

"I ain't stalling. I can't tell you what I don't know. That's how it is, you can believe it or not, I can't help it."

"You been doing business with him a long time. It ain't natural you don't know nothing about him."

"He always paid me my money. That's enough. If he don't want to say, I don't have to stick my nose in so long he pays me the money. I don't go where I don't belong."

The prizefighter tapped the table thoughtfully, making no headway. "So what?" he asked his partner.

"Don't worry. We'll find him."

"The boss said we got to see him in the morning. It's getting late. You want to try the joints?"

"O.K., we'll look around. We'll find him. The day's young yet."

"What you going to do with Shubunka?" Spitzbergen asked fearfully. "After all, I don't see the sense of making trouble when it might not be absolutely necessary. Sometimes it's better to use your brains a minute instead of hitting in a hurry."

"Nothing'll happen to him if he's smart and knows what's good for him. But if he wants to be stubborn, you know how it is. We can't help it."

"All I want is I shouldn't be involved. I'm not mixed up in it."

"We'll do all the worrying necessary."

"I put eighteen thousand dollars into the store," the soda man begged. "The fountain alone cost me more than three thousand. The ice-cream machine is smashed already. I can't afford further losses. Please don't stay here. Find him some other place."

"So we're sorry about the machine," the dapper man said. "We couldn't help it. It was orders. People don't show respect until you do something. You, yourself, you wouldn't listen. It couldn't be otherwise. But we're sorry."

Thank you very much! They were sorry. Spitzbergen's gloomy face grew horror-stricken. What kind of people were these? They calmly admitted they had caused the damage, without fear, as though it were the most ordinary matter of course. What kind of people had he associated himself with?

"All we advise you," the dapper man continued evenly, "is after tonight don't go walking with Shubunka. Don't stay in the same place with him. If he comes near you, you go away. When you see him, run away like it was a contagious disease, because we can't be responsible for accidents. They will happen no matter how much care you take. What he'll get might happen to you. Then everybody will be sorry but it will be too late. In the hurry you can't watch everything and sometimes a bullet flies by itself even if you don't mean it."

The two left Ann's. Mr. Spitzbergen, trembling with fear at their departure, regretted bitterly that he ever lived to see the day on which he first took up with Shubunka. This was not his business. He had made a living with his real estate and with the soda parlor all his life. If he had used his head to begin with, he would have had enough sense not to leave his own ways. No matter how much money he might make with the new combination, the worry wasn't worth it. Spitzbergen was a man with a wife and responsibilities. It was no part for him to get mixed up with gangsters, racketeers, lawbreakers. He wanted desperately to get out of the whole mess before it was altogether too late. With Shubunka this might have been possible, but with these he would never live to see that happy day. Spitzbergen, hearing the casual news that a fellow human might well be murdered, felt intense sorrow for his own misery, and he bewailed the fact that he might never see Shubunka again or the two weeks' rent money he owed him.

Back in the kitchen the tomato soup seemed to revive Karty, and he argued with Arthur in determined, energetic tones, his red eyes glaring with the desire to convince.

"Gee, I don't feel like it!" Arthur protested. "He'll find out about it and then he'll holler at me like anything."

"How will he find out?" Karty cried. "He won't know nothing about it. He don't figure up the cash register until the night and by that time we'll put back the money."

"But suppose we lose. Then what?"

"I'll put it back. I'm telling you! I'll have plenty of money by tonight. See, that's the lousy part of it. I'm broke now but I'll have all the dough I want tonight. Besides, we won't lose. Not today. I got the card figured good. See, we'll slip the money back into the register and nobody'll know the difference. It's a cinch."

But Arthur still hesitated. "Gee whiz," he said. "Mr. Karty, you might almost call it stealing. That's what it practically amounts to."

Karty rolled on the chair with hopeless irritation, the lines of his sharp face screwing near tears. "Jesus Christ, I told you. It ain't stealing. He owes you twelve bucks for a week's pay, ain't it? You asked him for an advance and he's just a stingy louse for not giving it to you. So it's the same thing like an advance, ain't it? If nobody's going to know about it, what difference does it make? It's your money. It's coming to you. So what do you want?"

As Arthur stood awkwardly before the gambler, his weight on one foot and scraping the floor with the other, he told himself that what Karty said was totally reasonable. The whole trouble was the dishwasher was still a kid. He was afraid. "Gee whiz," he said, "that's all right, but just the same I just don't feel like it. I don't know why it is."

"Aaah, you're just an ordinary mope. I'm disgusted with you." Karty turned his eyes away, gazing with deep contempt on the black pots on the gas range. "Here I want to do you a favor, sort of. Here I figure I'll take you out to the racetrack and show you the horses, the betting and all, and you act just like a kid. I don't have to do it. I got plenty of dough. I can lay my hands on it, too, right this minute, only I don't like to give certain parties the satisfaction of knowing I'm broke for the time being. I don't like people to gloat over me. You see what I mean? But if you don't want to go to the track, it's O.K. with me. I ain't forcing nobody. You told me just the other day you wanted to go to the racetrack, ain't it? So I'm taking you, but if you changed your mind it's perfectly O.K. with me." Come on, you cockeyed bastard, give in, implored Karty, wiping the bubbles of saliva from the corners of his mouth. Give in. If he could only get his hands on some money! He'd clean up at the track today. Bad luck in one thing meant good luck in the next. That's how it always was. Things evened up. The beating he took this morning meant he would clean up in every race. It never failed.

"Come on, Arthur," he said as casually as he could manage. "You do this for me and we'll have a swell time at the track, and we'll come home with plenty of dough, besides."

"Gee, I don't know," Arthur said, laughing uncomfortably. "Gee, I'd like to go to the racetrack with you, oh, sure. But I don't like this funny business."

It couldn't fail, Karty thought. They'd clean up today. And all he needed was two or three hundred dollars. Even a hundred. If he could win a hundred at the track today, he could bring that to his brothers-in-law and they'd give him time for the rest. Come on, you little son of a bitch, Karty silently begged, weeping inside of himself. Give in. He looked at the frying pan hanging from the hook over the range. He wanted to bang Arthur on the head with it, bang his head off with it, and he would have done it, too, he longed to do it, but he restrained himself because he knew it wouldn't help. What tantalized Karty most was that he was positive he would win today. He knew, as a gambler knows his hunch, that he would be able to run a two-dollar bet up to hundreds today. And all he needed to keep his wife's brothers off was a hundred dollars.

"Come on, Arthur, you're a good kid," he said. "You're just a little scared. Hell, it's time you grew up. These things don't mean anything. Every man has to take a chance once or twice in his life. After all, if you don't take a chance in the first place, you'll never get anywheres. You'll always stay where you are." He slapped the dishwasher on the shoulder, and Arthur, grinning sheepishly, said, "We'll see how it turns out. If it works just right, maybe we'll do it. But I don't know."

"O.K., kid, now you're talking!" Karty said, hopping off the chair and trying to hide his jubilation.

At this Arthur grew frightened again. "I didn't promise!" he cried. "I just said maybe. It's not definite."

"All right, all right," said Karty. He gave the dishwasher a quarter. "Go out and get me a *Telegraph* and then pay attention to me. When I give you the high sign, then we go to work." The gambler pushed him out into the parlor.

"Gee whiz," said Arthur faintly, at loose ends. "Gee whiz."

Outside, the noon rush was beginning. It was just before twelve o'clock. Yesterday's building workmen hadn't come in and Ann's remained quiet, but the mothers with their children were already on the stools, eating chocolate parfaits, sundaes, or frappés, while they fed their children cheese or tomato-and-lettuce sandwiches. In the parlor Lillian held her checkbook to her bosom while she haltingly took the orders of the two smart young ladies with the bored airs. These had barely noticed the change in waitresses for they were all the same, a part of human existence, tiresome but necessary. Lillian, nervously on guard, looking up and down the aisles for attacks from all possible sources, was too flustered to be insulted by their manner. She waited for their orders. Mr. Spitzbergen, who had put on an apron, wasn't helping Shorty at the counter, however. Fearing for the safety of his fixtures, he stood at the doorstep and watched the street to see if by any chance

Shubunka might be coming. There were thugs everywhere, no doubt. All he needed was for the fat man to come in. Then they'd smash up Shubunka and the place with him. Later they would be sorry. Spitzbergen, a cautious man, was watching the street.

As for Shorty, he had scarcely noticed the prolonged absence of Arthur or the failure of the boss to give him a hand during the rush. The corsetière's clerk had just come in with a note. While Shorty served the women on the stools, he was mentally composing his reply and this was no soft job. From time to time he reread Madame Pavlovna's note, hoping for inspiration.

My Dear Boy:

Your little note hurt me terribly. I confess you have misjugged me crually. I am disappointed in you. You say I am not your freind this to me who alone and by myself all the time understand so well the full beaty and valu of freindship well you are mistaken my Dear Soda Jerker. That is all I can say at this time. Will you let me prove to you what my feelings on the subject is? If you should care to call on me tonight you will realize better than words can expresse how crually you have misjugged me.

Ever yours,

(Mrs.) Sophia Pavlovna

P.S. It has one l. I cannot say I think your stasionary in the very best of taste!!!

"Arthur, you mopey mutt," Shorty cried as he spied him coming back from Karty's table down in the parlor. "Ring up those checks." Two women were at the cashier's stand, but Lillian was still waiting for the orders of the two young ladies in the alcoves, *intime* style, who could not make up their minds. "She's slow as mush on an ice-cold day," the jerker commented, distracted.

Arthur hesitated so long over the cash register, he was afraid his confusion would be showing too plainly and that the plan would be spoiled. He half hoped that Karty would notice this and call off the whole scheme as too risky, but the racetrack gambler, flushed with new hope, was nervously studying the form charts in the *Morning Telegraph.*

"Well, you want I should wait for the answer?" Madame Pavlovna's clerk asked impatiently. A crazy business, she thought. Grown-up people, passing notes. It was a shame.

The reply was too much for Shorty. In the rush he could not take time for exactly the correct tone he wanted. He called the girl close to him. "I'll tell you what to do," he said. "You tell Mrs. Pavlovna that I'm busy, the rush, and I ain't got the time to write. But say he's considering the matter. You understand?"

The clerk looked at him, swallowing contemptuously. "Oh, all right," she said.

⌣⌣⌣

Shubunka left Peggy Martin's house on Baten Avenue, well nourished by the dramatic conception of himself that he carried in his mind's eye. He moved in jerks and stops down the stairway, and outside the door he leaned heavily against the ironwork which protected the large panes. He looked at the sky a minute or two, the whites of his eyes showing. The heavy slabs of his jaws sagged. His breath came after gasping effort and occasionally he held his hand to his heart. The attack. Betrayed on all sides, deserted, without a friend, Shubunka took comfort in the drowsy numbness that had possession of his mind. Two little girls came up vying with each other in the creation of strange noises which they produced by compressing their cheeks over the saliva in their mouths. Now they took time from their intense preoccupation and incredulously sucked their thumbs before the appearance of Shubunka. He shook himself free enough of his mental cloudiness to step from the stoop. "King Kong," one of the girls said. "Just give a look. Ain't he just like King Kong?"

Now it pleased his fancy to overlook this hurt from the child and he pathetically approached them. His huge face broke into the genial, warm-hearted smile, the thick lips curving wide. "Hello, little girls," he said kindly. "How are you?"

They sucked their thumbs and retreated a pace. Shubunka took out a nickel.

"An ice-cream cone?" he asked, still smiling. "Maybe you would like an ice-cream cone. Here, go buy it."

One girl stuck out her hand for the coin but the other promptly slapped it down. "Don't take, Ettie," she said sternly.

"Why?" protested Shubunka, hurt. "Why do you stop her? Let her have the ice-cream cone, my little girl."

They sucked their thumbs, gravely staring at him. A housewife passing by looked suspiciously at the fat man and stopped, watching him three yards away. Shubunka glanced at her, smiled feebly as he sensed her suspicions, but it did no good. She kept on staring at him and he pocketed the coin, walked away to the corner. "Funny business going on," declared the woman. She chased the girls angrily down the street. The brow of the fat man tightened in furrows with pain. Not even the children. His mind bathed in the warm waters of his grief.

As he walked down the street in his sad absorption, on his way to another of his houses, he caught a glimpse of Johnny, the cop, coming out of one of the side streets. The policeman saw him, knew that Shubunka had seen him, but nevertheless darted back behind the building and hurried out of sight.

Shubunka started. His mind cleared. Driven from the refuge of his self-dramatization, he wavered uncertainly as the full meaning of the day's events flooded into his mind. The behavior of the policeman, the many sudden raids last night and this morning, his man's reports on the telephone, the joint-smashing, Peggy Martin's desertion—all these incidents and their significance came back to him with terrible clarity. The feeling of panic returned to him, now heightened immeasurably because he felt he had been wasting precious time. Shubunka suddenly ran on his bent legs to the drugstore on the corner.

The pool parlor on Myrtle Avenue told him the gunmen he

wanted still weren't in the place. Shubunka wouldn't believe it but the rack man insisted. He called off the list. "Where's Tetro? Mickey? Sklar?" The rack man at Myrtle Avenue told him indifferently that none of them had been seen in the room all day. Cramped in the booth, the fat man perspired and fretted. He dropped a nickel in the slot and called another Evergreen exchange. But the candy-stand man gave the same answers. Shubunka regretted that he had thoughtlessly given his name when the man had asked who was calling. But the implications grew clearer to him as he paused to reflect at the telephone. Whether or not it was the big shot his man had mentioned over the phone this morning, whoever was behind the combination was powerful enough to drive him out, Shubunka now felt convinced. There was no mistaking it. Abruptly he asked himself why he was still sitting there? He had to move rapidly!

The fat man fumbled with the folding door, and in his panic to get out he stumbled and fell on the floor. The druggist came running out of his prescription room, concern on his face. He tried to help Shubunka to his feet but the fat man pushed him aside. "You all right?" the druggist asked. "Listen, don't run away if you don't feel all right." But the fat man hurried out of the store without answering him. He looked up and down the street for a taxi. Almost hysterically, he was now rushing back to Baten Avenue where the traffic was a bit heavier. Cars passed but no cab appeared. While he waited the frenzy mounted. Shubunka kept clenching his fists and twisting his head in all directions. His body was wet with sweat. Finally a taxi came down the other side of the street. Shubunka rushed out across and piled in.

"The Williamsburg Savings Bank," he panted. "Hurry. I'm in a hurry."

"O.K.!" said the hackman, shifting gears resentfully. "I'll get there as fast as I can."

Resting sprawled on the upholstered seat in the cab, Shubunka tried to control his panic as he considered the possibilities. He would have to leave town immediately. Whoever these people were, they were powerful and ruthless. He knew they would waste little ceremony in clearing him out of the way. He would go to Troy where he had a cousin in the wholesale produce business. His plans could be formed later, but at the moment the important step for him was to get his money out of the bank and leave. Shubunka sat upright in the cab. He didn't have his bankbook with him or the passkey for the vault.

"Stop the car," he shouted at the driver. "Stop. I forgot something."

The hackman rolled the cab to the curb. "Jesus Christ," he muttered, shaking his head. "After all the excitement. They're all like that. Where to now?"

What was the rush? The interruption served to jolt Shubunka back into himself. The hysteria left and he grew calm and collected. These hijacking tactics were no novelty to him, he told himself. He had been familiar with them for years. This wasn't the first time. How ridiculous he had been! Why fall into panic? Suppose these men were a little stronger, a little more determined? He could match them. If the thugs on Myrtle Avenue had been scared off, he could import. There was no scarcity of gangsters in America, and New York had no monopoly. And as for the cops, as soon as the collections faded, they would come back to him, their caps in one hand and the other outstretched. Shubunka felt like laughing at himself. How stupid he had been, how childish. How could he have let himself grow lost with fear. This was the business. It had its own problems. You either met them or you didn't, but there was no need for the trembling. He would beat this bunch as he had the others, and if he lost there would be plenty of time then to run away. They didn't kill people so quickly, for nobody, no matter how hardened, liked murder.

"Well, make up your mind," the hackman said. "It's your funeral. The flag's down on the clock."

For the first time Shubunka noticed the man's nasty manner. "I would not say that," he remarked easily in his high-pitched voice. "That's not a nice way to be. Some day you will meet the wrong person and then you will get hurt a little. You would not like that."

The driver jerked his head around, scowling, but he saw

Shubunka's cool expression, broke off whatever it was he was going to say, and turned his head straight forward again. The performance pleased the fat man hugely. It was a sort of omen. He took an English Oval out of the long box and told the driver to return to Neptune Beach. Bluff! That was it. The biggest bluffer always won in the end.

By this time the building workmen in their overalls were sitting on their fat hips at the fountain in Ann's. The soda parlor resounded with their hoarse laughter. The afternoon rush was on. Shorty, scurrying behind the counter, worked with distracted features today, his mind composing a letter which ran: Very well. Every person deserves a second chance. I shall give you yours. However, it would be an error on your part to deceive me again. Please remember the proverb. Once bitten, twice shy. That is my slogan for tonight. Nifty and to the point, if the corsetière knew how to read between the lines. Shorty felt a wave of satisfaction with himself. "Arthur!" he yelled. "Bacon." The dishwasher, today no longer absent-looking but with a preoccupied worried air about him, wiped his fingers on the dishtowel and went to the back.

As he passed Karty, the gambler caught him by the trousers at the thigh, holding him to the table.

"I gave you the high sign twice, Arthur," he whined. "What's the matter? You got no guts?"

"It wasn't right. Lillian was too near the stand," Arthur complained, knowing he lied.

"Bull. I thought you said you'd go in on this with me. It's after twelve already. When are you going to get set?"

"I want to wait just before the relief fellow comes in. Then it'll look better. I just want to wait a while."

"You'll wait too long," cried Karty, his voice rising. "You'll put it off little by little and then it'll be too late. That's what you want. I know what's in your mind."

"Sh!" whispered Arthur fearfully. "They'll catch on. Let me go. It looks suspicious already."

Son of a bitch, lousy rat, going back on his word. "Listen, Arthur, you lay down on me now, you're putting me in a spot. I'll slug you for it. Don't forget it. It's too late to change your mind."

"All right. All right." Arthur wrenched free and went to the kitchen where the pot of bacon was warming on the range.

Karty's stomach had a sick feeling. His head ached. But he went back to the fine print of the racing charts. He'd have to play the long shots today. Aqueduct was a good track for favorites but Karty knew as well as he knew anything in his life that today the long shots would come in for him. It was a hunch. Whenever he had had bad luck, good always followed immediately, to make up for it. It couldn't fail today. In the sixth race he had already doped out a beauty, Gillie, and the morning line had him at twelve to one.

Spitzbergen, still standing on the doorstep, was caught unaware when Shubunka came up to him. He had been looking up and down the street, expecting to see him waddle, but he had not been prepared for the taxi. When the soda man saw him, he almost wept with the peculiar irony of the situation. Normally the fat man would never have dropped in during the afternoon. Just today, when he was least wanted, he had to take it into his head to appear. The man with the broken nose and his friend had hardly gone a half an hour and they might very well still be in the neighborhood.

"Go away! Please, Mr. Shubunka, go away from the store!" he begged, unconsciously backing away from him. "I got eighteen thousand dollars invested in my store. If anything should happen I'm a ruined man."

The fat man smiled reproachfully. "You should be ashamed of yourself, Mr. Spitzbergen," he said. "A couple of snotnoses should not make you frightened." He brushed his way past him into the soda parlor. Spitzbergen, worried over the effect he might make on the lunch rush, had to lower his voice. He ran ahead, trying to get in front of the fat man and to push him out again, and in spite of all his efforts the workmen halted their noise to look at them.

Spitzbergen now remembered the rent money. Perhaps he might manage to get it now. Glancing at the door in terror, he was hurriedly pushing Shubunka forward. "The kitchen," he begged. "Please, the kitchen." At the door he ran back to the street to see if anyone outside had noticed.

At the commotion Karty raised his head. When he saw Shubunka he stood up from the table and went out to touch him, but then he noticed Spitzbergen's excitement and decided he had to wait. The sight of the fat man, so early in the morning, brought a sudden rush of hope.

In the small kitchen the two big men took up almost all the space.

"You saw the ice-cream machine?" Spitzbergen wept. "You got a good look maybe. Snotnoses. Yes, yes. They're only trying to make a scare, otherwise everything is perfect. I can see it for myself."

Shubunka was examining the kitchen, the cigarette dangling from the corner of his mouth. "Not so clean, Mr. Spitzbergen," he remarked. "Germs. Bacteria. When it's dirty all kinds diseases are possible, especially when it's food you handle." He rebuked him gently. "You should take better care, Mr. Spitzbergen. It don't make a good impression." Painstakingly in that dirty hole he flicked the ash into the sink.

The soda man heard him out with wonder. "The man," he said, "is out of his mind! He don't see what's happening."

"Roughnecks," said the booker, as if bored by the subject. "You musn't pay attention. It happens all the time, only you let it aggravate you."

"He's crazy!" wailed Spitzbergen. "He's a raving lunatic! They bust my machine, he tells me not to pay attention! Listen, Mr. Shubunka, that machine is a piece of property. It cost me two thousand dollars."

"Keep quiet, please." As he stared at him impassively, the soda man's eyes flinched. His fit of fury passed and he waited, now suddenly turned sober-faced and embarrassed. "What good will it do you to make a noise?" Shubunka asked. "Tell me. You could holler your head off. It won't help anything. See, Mr. Spitzbergen," he said, his tone turning kind and reassuring, "you mustn't take life too serious. It don't pay. You get nothing for it."

"Never mind," he said. "Never mind. Pull the girls out of the apartments, close up the flats, do what you want, only I'm finished with the whole rotten business. No more. I suffered long enough and money ain't the only object in life when it brings so much heartache."

The fat man held out his arm and tapped him on the shoulder to stop him. He smiled with genial understanding. "You're not fooling me, Mr. Spitzbergen. Not for a minute. Those snotnoses came to you and got you scared already and you went over to them. All right. I know how it is. You're a family man with responsibilities, you do not like something if it looks dangerous. And you are right. It's perfectly reasonable. Nobody could ask you to do different. After all, what difference does it make who pays you the rent money, me or somebody else? Eighteen months already I been doing business with you. Now you see something better, you throw me out like an old shoe. It's reasonable. Anybody else in your place would do the same thing. It is your privilege to do whatever you think is right." Shubunka spoke his speech in all sorrow, calm with the understanding of the way of the world. He seemed pained by Spitzbergen's betrayal but not surprised by it. And as the ingratitude deepened the lines of his big face, Spitzbergen, standing before him, grew apologetic.

"Listen, Mr. Shubunka," he said, his eyes staring at the cigarette butts on the floor, "you don't take into consideration how it happens. I'm a man standing under a knife. All I want is to get out. Believe me, that is only what I want. I don't like to do with hold-up men, with gangsters. It ain't my line. But what can I do?"

"I know how it is," Shubunka's shrill voice whined. "Eighteen months you got your money and never was there a complaint. Some little snotnoses come in and bust up a machine, make a big bluff, and you run away. All right. Who says you must do different? I don't want from you nothing." His voice trembled.

"I can't fight them. It's not my business. My hands are tied. Listen, Shubunka, they were in the soda store looking for you. You think I ain't got you on my mind, too? It makes no difference what happens to you? You think my heart is a stone? Believe me, Shubunka, when I heard they wanted you, I ... I didn't know what to do, I was so excited. All day I was standing at the door like you saw me, waiting for you so I could tell you they wanted you. Yes, yes, believe me."

"See," said Shubunka, his voice low and sad, "it don't frighten me. Let them come and see me. What can they do? Hurt they won't, because they know they'll get three and four times what they give me. It is bluff and let them go to you with it. It don't fool me."

Spitzbergen scraped his foot uncomfortably. "What can I do?" he asked helplessly. "It's my nature. I can't stand it. Other people, they're stronger. They can be like iron. I can't ..."

"Like an old shoe," said the fat man mournfully, smoking his cigarette.

"Mr. Shubunka ... I don't like to ask you at a time like this ... but after all, business is business ..."

"Say it. Do not be afraid of me. I do not bluff you."

"Well, after all, I got expenses. The taxes. The interest. The rent money. You promised me the rent money today."

Shubunka passed his hand over his eyes with weariness. "The rent money. Yes. I said tonight, didn't I? I have not got it with me. You will get it tonight." He held his cigarette in his fingers, looking around for a place to discard it. He went to the sink, held the butt under the tap, and deposited it carefully in the garbage pail. "Stinks here," he remarked, going to the door. "Damp. Mr. Spitzbergen, you're a fool. You worry too much. These people, what can they do for you? What protection can they give you? There's laws for landlords, too. If I wanted to, I could bother you. I could send in roughnecks, too, to break and smash. But this is not my way. I don't know it. Let the others have the pleasure. In a week you will come back to me. Just wait and see." He went outside but the soda man ran after him.

"Mr. Shubunka," he called. "A favor, please. Do me a favor. With the rent money tonight—you don't have to bring it in yourself. Send it in with somebody." Spitzbergen's trouble-stricken face beseeched him.

The fat man laughed with bitter humor. His heart was not a stone in his breast. He was a friend and he wanted the money. "All right. Don't worry. You'll have the cash tonight." Spitzbergen let the door of the kitchen bang shut in front of him. He hadn't the face to go outside and be with Shubunka any longer.

Karty, huddled over the dope sheets on his table, hated the fat man. Giving money again to Spitz! His fingers pinched his bruised cheek cruelly as the thought gnawed at him. Spitzbergen had a smell with his money. He didn't need a cent more, but Shubunka ladled it out to him again and again, while all the time the gambler had to look desperately for a dollar.

"Hey, Shubunka," he said, choking down the tears. "Sit down. For a minute."

"Very well." He spoke absently, a man shocked into a haze by the baseness of things. No one was ready to lift a finger on his behalf, but when it was others who needed help, they came to him.

"Shubunka, I'm in a hole," Karty said, bending his chest low over the table with anxiety. "I hate to talk like this but I can't afford to be particular no more. I need money bad. You can't imagine how bad I need it. If I don't get it, I can't tell you what will happen to me."

"I know," the fat man said, his eyes roaming helplessly. "You think I'm a child? I can understand it."

"Look, I'll tell you. I ain't ashamed no more. I took a couple of dollars from my wife's brothers. All right. I took it. I admit it. Now those stinkers want to kill me if I don't pay it back. I took a couple of dollars only. They're a pack of louses. They say its thirteen hundred dollars. I can't get it. Today one of those bastards got me right out on the street. Look at my face. See what he did? And I'll get more. Shubunka, I need money. You don't know those bastards I got for brother-in-laws. They'll murder me for a dollar." The gambler's voice whined. He sobbed and made sucking noises as he caught his breath. "Shubunka, I'm coming to you because you're my only hope. If you don't help me, it's all finished. I'm wiped out like somebody would step on a cockroach. Shubunka, take pity. Have a heart. Help me out."

The booker looked at Karty's swollen eyes, at the red lids, the skin welts on his small weasel face. The gambler was groveling before him. They come to me, cried Shubunka. When they're in trouble, at least they can always find me. I can help but where can I turn? Where can I go? Who is my friend? Everyone betrays me, everyone runs away from me, but when it is someone else, they come to me gladly. "Mr. Karty, you do not understand the situation with me," he explained. "You come to me like I was a god. You look at me and say, Shubunka, he is all right. He is good off. Plenty of money, no worries. Yes, I can imagine it, what is in your head when you see me. But it is not true! I am alone. I have nobody, nobody in the whole world. When people can use me, then I am their friend, but when I need something they do not know me. They throw me away like an old shoe. Ask Spitzbergen. Maybe he will tell you something about it. I could send you other places, too. Yes," the fat man said, shaking his head piteously, "like an old shoe . . ."

"Shubunka, it ain't got nothing to do, what you say. You got money. I need it. Three hundred dollars. A hundred, even. If I give them something they'll leave me alone until I can catch my breath again. All I want is a hundred dollars!"

"You do not understand how it is!" Shubunka wailed. "Why do you refuse to understand how it is with me? I can't help you."

Bitch! Bastard! Wallet full of money. "Shubunka, then I'm asking you for ten dollars! Give me only ten dollars!"

But in the vast reservoir of pity for himself Shubunka could find no feeling to spare on the gambler. He looked at the green, red, and yellow stippled walls of the parlor while the man before him begged and wept. The fat man was conscious only of the strange existence of himself in his body and Karty and the walls were one in being outside of him, beyond his own urgencies, beyond his own satisfaction, useless to him and unnecessary. Karty could have never been born. Wrapped up in himself, the fat man barely heard him.

"Five dollars, then. All right, give me five!" Karty's bloodshot eyes popped as he begged. "I got a right to ask you for five lousy bucks, ain't I?"

"Ugly," moaned Shubunka in his sadness. "Ugly colors. They hurt the eye."

Karty could not restrain himself. He rose jerkily, pushing the table away from him so that it fell on top of the fat man's thighs. His fury broke. "Bastard!" he screamed. "You lousy son-of-a-bitch bastard, you ought to get your lousy eyes pushed out with an ice pick! You listen to me and let me talk and all you do is crap around while I'm eating my heart out! You're a goddammed lunatic! You're crazy! They ought to put you away!"

"Mr. Karty," protested Shubunka softly. "Mr. Karty, don't raise a holler. It isn't nice. There are people in the store."

The customers on the stools at the fountain all interrupted their chatter. They held their spoons and glasses in midair and their mouths remained open, fixed in that attitude by the noise. Those at the *intime* alcoves rose from their chairs to see better over the partitions. "What is it?" piped a boy's voice. He sensed the excitement and wanted to know. "Tell me, mother, what is it? The men are fighting?" The mother pushed him back on the stool, dying to know herself, but polite and refined. Inside the kitchen Mr. Spitzbergen heard the racket and trembled. He was afraid to come out into the parlor. Arthur, clearing the dishes at the counters, gazed with absorption on the scene, hoping that in some way the argument might serve as an excuse to let him out of his bargain with Karty. Shorty, doing the work of two men again this afternoon, was wrenched from his amorous speculations. He scowled ferociously at the two in the back. "It's nothing," he told the customers. "Just two guys having an argument. Don't pay attention to them." They had a nerve. This was a place of business and their behavior was unseemly. They were old enough to know better.

Shubunka drummed with his fingers patiently. Karty, conscious of the effects of his outbursts, sat down shamefacedly, wanting to cry with the hopelessness of his condition. The soda parlor returned to its normal hum. Everyone went back to his food, resuming the thread of his conversation, forgetting the incident, calloused by the frequency of its type in Neptune Beach. Shubunka waited silently a moment longer. He took his wallet out of his pocket. Karty, watching every movement the fat man made with intense interest, could not control the trembling of his body. Shubunka squinted to get around the smoke of his cigarette. He picked out a five, folded it in his neat way and left it on the table. Without a word he rose, sighed and walked away from the gambler. In spite of every worry, in spite of every indignity and disappointment mankind showered upon him, he was noble, benevolent, and forgiving. He waddled to the door. "A little excited today," he commented to Shorty at the fountain. "He should learn how to control himself. It isn't nice." He saw Lillian. "The new girl?" he asked and looked at her kindly. He thought of Dorothy. What a lucky man Herbert Lurie was.

At the table Karty cried to himself. Five lousy bucks. The bastard had hundreds and he gave him five bucks. He had plenty of money for Spitzbergen. Every day he handed it out to him. Didn't he see him practically beg Dorothy, too, to take the twenty-five dollars? What could Karty do with five bucks? His bastard brother-in-law wanted thirteen hundred.

Karty glared at Arthur. Now was the time. He tried to catch the dishwasher's eyes but Arthur was working, staring resolutely into the water at the double basins. This was the time. Lillian was away from the cashier's stand taking orders at the alcoves. Spitzbergen had locked himself out of sight in the kitchen, and Shorty had his hands full with the lunch crowd. Arthur looked up for a moment, saw the gambler staring at him, and quickly dropped his eyes. But it was too late. Karty had already stood up and was walking deliberately down the aisle.

Not now! Arthur silently begged. After the fuss he had just raised, everyone in the store would be looking at him. Not now! But Karty glared fiercely at him. He dropped the dishes and went running around the counter to the cash register. Karty pushed the five-dollar bill through the opening in the glass pane. Arthur was unable to meet his eyes. He plugged the ten-cent button and punched the black knob. The cash box flew out and he gazed for a moment, seeing the cubbyholes with the change and the bills of different denominations in a blurred haze. With trembling application to the task he counted out ninety cents in coins, pulled out three one-dollar bills, took a ten from the other compartment, and hiding it among the others, placed the money flat before Karty.

"Wrong change," said the gambler. "You made a mistake."

"What?" Arthur looked up at him, his face deep with wonder.

"Wrong change," Karty whispered, standing rigid. "Another ten."

It wasn't fair! Arthur wanted enormously to shout out his protests but he had to repress himself. They had bargained to take only ten dollars. Now the gambler had him in a position where he couldn't argue. He was squeezing him for another ten.

"No, no," Arthur whispered, looking around as openly as he dared. "The change is right. It's no mistake."

"Take out another ten!" Karty whispered fiercely. "Take it out!"

"Don't stand there! They'll catch on! Spitzbergen'll come out. Move away!"

"Get that money! I won't leave the spot until I get that money!"

"She'll come back! Go on, Mr. Karty, go away from the stand."

"You son of a bitch!" Karty's voice was rising. Arthur, contracting within himself, kept on looking at the top of the cashier's desk, afraid to look up. "Get that money or I'll kick your teeth in!"

He waited. Arthur's eyes pushed him away but he stood there. It seemed to the dishwasher that everyone in the store was looking at them. Lillian would be back at the stand in another moment. Another customer might be leaving the counter to pay his check. Shorty might notice what was going on. Spitzbergen would be coming out of the kitchen. Arthur didn't want to do it, but, trembling with fear, he took out the other ten and handed it to Karty.

"I'll be at the el station," the gambler said. With agonizing slowness he folded the money and placed it in his pocket. As he left, Arthur hurried to the refuge of his counter, covering his face as he mopped his head with the apron. The building workmen at the counter broke out into a burst of laughter and Arthur jumped. He returned gratefully to the dishes in the basins.

Shorty had been revising his note to Madame Pavlovna. "Dear Mrs. Pavlovna," he was writing in the cool recesses of his mind as he labored. "Very well. I have made my decision. I shall forgive you this time on the condition that it don't happen again. Please remember the proverb: Once bitten, twice shy. That will be my slogan tonight. I am the type of man who gives every person no matter what his offense might be a second chance. Very well. It is settled and we will forget about our quarrel. Yours for a hot time tonight, Your Friend." Shorty planned to underline the word "hot" three times. He was happy as he piled the vegetables on the blue plate. The telephone was ringing but he could not attend to it now.

To Arthur the clangorous persistence of the bell was a recurring stab, meant especially for him. In the pauses between the ringing, the enormity of his action at the cash register welled within him until his fear approached frenzy. He dropped the dishes and went to the booths. It was only Mrs. Spitzbergen. She sadly told the dishwasher to give her husband a message. The examination had proved negative in all respects. She would be home soon. Relieved and heartened, Arthur went up to the kitchen to give the boss the news.

"Did he go from the store already?" Spitzbergen asked immediately.

"Who? Karty? Mr. Karty?" Arthur's heart stopped.

"What Karty? Who needs Karty? Did Shubunka go out of the store?"

Arthur had to take time to reflect. He barely knew. "Yes. He went out. Five minutes ago, I think."

The boss grunted and went to the door. Arthur half forgot to give him his wife's message. "Mrs. Spitzbergen just called up. She said I should tell you she's all right. The examination was negative. They still don't know what's the matter with her, she said. She'll be home soon."

"Fine!" bawled Mr. Spitzbergen in a fit. "It's a great relief! Now everything flies off my mind. It's all I need. Just so long as my wife is with the doctors and the hospitals, everything will be hotsy-totsy with me. Go," he told the dishwasher. "Don't stand here. I don't need you." Arthur ran down the aisle. "Forty-five dollars," groaned the soda man. "Forty-five dollars and nothing is the matter. Money thrown out for nothing." But his mind wasn't on his wife.

When Arthur reached the fountain, he noticed that his relief boy had already come in. He looked at the clock. It was one. Arthur ran down the cellar steps, changed his clothes, and hurried out of Ann's as though it were a jail.

Soon after, the two thugs again appeared at Ann's, and now their faces were grim with many disappointments. Spitzbergen trembled at once. He began sputtering excuses and protests but they cut him short.

"You know where Shubunka is," the one with the broken nose declared. "If you're trying something smart, we'll take care of you."

"Why come to me? Where does it say I have to know where Shubunka is all the time? I ain't his father and mother!"

"Don't stall. You're just wasting time. Where's Shubunka?"

"Here! Look! Look!" Deep in the parlor, Spitzbergen began pointing in all directions. He opened the kitchen door. "Do you see him? Look and see if I keep him in some place hidden. Find out for yourself." He ran heavily to the cellar. "Look in here. Maybe he's downstairs. If you don't believe me, you can search the store for yourself. I don't stop you."

The thugs looked at each other. It was clear Spitzbergen meant what he said, and they wondered where the fat man could be. Up the block a man had told them he thought Shubunka was in Ann's. "So what?" the prizefighter asked his partner.

"Listen, gentlemen," the soda man interrupted, the perspiration shining on his face. "Your men came into the store today and said I shouldn't work for Shubunka no more. All right, so I don't work for him. They say they want a list of the houses with the girls. All right, I make the list. What do you want from me further?

Please, gentlemen, it's no place for you here. I'm a businessman. I don't want trouble. Not here, please, gentlemen."

"Did Shubunka come in today?" the man asked.

Spitzbergen went on, ignoring the question. "Try his houses. Find out where he lives and go to his home. He don't stay here. He comes in once in a while, whenever it comes into his head."

"All right. So I'm asking did Shubunka come in today?"

"Listen, gentlemen, you shouldn't come in and bother me—"

"He wants to know if he came in today," the dapper one said nastily. "He asked you a question so why don't you answer?"

The soda man caught himself up. His face looked blank. "What?" he asked.

"Hey, you. You over there. You seen Shubunka?"

Shorty looked at them. He hadn't even noticed them come into the store. "Well, b'gee, Shubunka. Let's see," he said. He recognized the men and swiftly tried to read Spitzbergen's face for the correct answer. "I don't know yes, I don't know no. There's people coming and going in here all the time and it's hard to say. Might of dropped in at that and then again on the other hand he mightn't. It's hard to say, don't you know?"

The dapper man caught Lillian's elbow and brought her to Spitzbergen and his partner. The girl stared at them fearfully.

"You seen Shubunka?" he asked.

"Leave me alone," she whimpered. "I don't know nobody called Shubunka."

"She's a new girl. Just came to work this morning," the boss said. "She don't know a thing."

"I wasn't asking you for advice," the dapper man said. "Listen, sister, you been in the place all day. You seen a fat guy come in today?"

"I don't know anything about it," she wept. "Leave me alone."

"A fat guy. Looks like an ape or something. He's got busted legs and when he walks, he walks funny. Tell me, you seen him today?"

"Maybe yes. Maybe he come in. I don't know. Yes, a man like him come in, I think."

The dapper man released his hold on her and she fled to the

safety of her cashier's stand. "By rights I ought to slap you in the puss," said he bitterly. "You ought to get what's coming to you, you fat slob."

"She don't know what she's talking about," Spitzbergen cried. "You got her scared. She don't know nothing. And if he did come in the store, so what? So what can I do? He ain't here now."

"Listen," the prizefighter said in a businesslike tone, "you're holding out on us and that's a mistake. Tell us what you know because if you don't we'll take good care of you. You're wasting time. The ice-cream machine don't mean a thing if you want to get wise. What we'll do to you will be a holy shame if you try anything wise. So if you know anything, tell us now."

Spitzbergen broke down with fear. Much as he wanted the two weeks' rent money, he confessed completely. He told the thugs that Shubunka had suddenly taken it into his head to drop in this morning and that he might come back tonight as well. But it wasn't Spitzbergen's fault. What could he possibly have done about it?

"Tonight," said the dapper one. "That's too late. That's no good for us."

"Well," said the other, "at least we know where to find him if we don't get him soon."

They went to the door without further ceremony but at the threshold the dapper one recalled something and he went back to Spitzbergen. "I'm doing you a favor," he said. "By rights I should slap your teeth in." Spitzbergen began to shudder with the shock when they left. It also pained him deeply that the rent money seemed impossible now.

"Aw, gee whiz, Mr. Karty, I'm sore," said Arthur in the train. "You said only ten dollars. Why did you make me give you another ten?" They were on the way to the Atlantic Avenue station for the one-thirty train to Aqueduct, and the gambler was absorbed in the selections of the afternoon papers.

"Ten dollars wasn't enough. So what's the difference?" Karty asked. “It makes no diff. We’ll put back twenty instead of ten and nobody will know.”

“But now it’s like taking money. It’s like stealing. See, if I took ten, all right, it’s my own money, like you said, because I got it coming to me. But taking money that ain’t mine, I don’t like it. It’s stealing.”

“Aaah, nuts!” Karty cried. “Give me peace. I got a good mind to lose you and go to the track by myself. I don’t need you.” And the truth was that if Karty hadn’t recognized the necessity of keeping the dishwasher in his confidence, he would have left him long ago. As it was, he was still half inclined to get rid of the kid. “Listen, Arthur,” Karty said, trying to sound kindly. “I got plenty on my mind. I lost my temper. See, we’ll go to the track, we got to clean up, then we’ll put back the money in the cash register. Now you satisfied?”

“Gee, it sounds reasonable,” Arthur said. “I got to admit it.”

“So keep quiet and let me dope out the horses. O.K.?”

And as the express fought its way on the rails to the Long Island station, Arthur went over the gambler’s argument in his mind and was comforted by it. He was just afraid. He was still a kid. A man took a chance once in a while. Gee whiz, some day he would think of how scared he was today and laugh at himself. After all, what had he done? It was nothing. There were people like Shubunka, like Karty, like Shorty, who did much worse things, gambling, going with women and so on, and they never batted an eye. The prospect of spending the day at the racetrack for the first time in his life became suddenly exciting again. He had forgotten about it when it was the most important part of the day. To see the horses running down the track, to watch the men in the gambling ring, to see the bookmakers with their rolls of bills! Arthur had heard all about it and today he would be actually seeing it. He couldn’t wait for the train to get to the station. But then all at once his face fell as the thought struck him.

“Mr. Karty!” he cried. “What if we don’t clean up today?”

“We’ll clean up! We’ll win! Don’t worry. I got a hunch and it never failed me yet. Why should today be an exception?”

"But all the same, what'll we do if we lose? I want to know."

"I told you! I said I'll have plenty of money tonight, didn't I? I'll put it back. The way you talk, you do no good and all that happens is you'll jinx my luck. So shut up for a minute!"

Karty went back to the dope sheets, promising himself he would lose the dishwasher in the crowd at the track if he kept on crying. Sunfeathers, fifty to one on the morning line for the first race, seemed promising in spite of what the experts said of the colt. Never shown nothing, said the *Journal*, and the *Telegraph* noted for him: Trailed all three starts. Nevertheless the colt had done the five furlongs in a morning workout in 1:01. Karty was an accountant. He went by figures. A two-year-old that ran the five furlongs in 1:01 could win this race today, and fifty to one was the price he needed. For a moment his resolve weakened when he recalled that Sunfeathers was a two-year-old and a maiden. But today a system was a burden. His hunch couldn't fail him, and no matter what Sunfeathers cost him, Gillie in the sixth would make up for it with plenty to spare. A sweet horse. Twelve to one and ripe for the brackets. The motion of the train, together with his excitement, blurred the type before his eyes.

The lunch rush at Ann's was slackening when Madame Pavlovna shuffled in for an afternoon cup of tea. Smiling her blissful, distant smile, she went down to the cozy nook at the double-decked water tray, heavily rolling the weight of her hips on top of the stool. She looked at Shorty, her chin well in, the eyes impish and coy. Aren't you ashamed? her expression asked, and the soda jerker, embarrassed, wiped his nose with his hand.

"Shur-tee!" she whispered. "You terrible, terrible boy! Vot you need is a spanking."

"O.K.," Shorty said, trying hard to recover his presence. "I will forgive you and forget. Everybody deserves a second chance and I will give you yours tonight. But please remember the slogan: Once bitten, twice shy. B'gee, what do you want? A cup of tea?"

Madame Pavlovna started giggling. It seemed as though she couldn't stop. The soda jerker grinned sheepishly. "See," he confided, "one thing about me, I'm sensitive about going where I'm not sure I'm wanted, don't you know? Some guys I know, they can force themselves on anybody. Not me. I would rather die. On the level, Mrs. Pavlovna, I would rather die than people should think I'm forcing myself on them."

"Who in the vorld vould ever think you vere pushing? I can't understand the psychology," the corsetière protested. "A nice young man with such a charming personality. It is impossible, Shurtee, positively impossible." But as she protested, her gaze wandered. She lapsed into soft languor again. She noticed Lillian mutely surveying the scene from her cashier's stand, resentment in her attitude. "A sveet child," the corsetière murmured. "But vy is she so angry vith the vorld?"

"Lummox," Shorty pronounced. "No brains. I don't know why Spitzbergen keeps her. He ain't got his mind on the job these days. Too much preoccupied with his other investments and then there's something fishy going on with Shubunka. People coming in all the time asking for him. You know Shubunka? A queer duck, the queerest you ever saw, I can't figure him out. Oh, yes! But so far as she's concerned, lummox, that's it. She and Arthur make a fine pair. They ought to get married. If Spitz had his mind on the store they'd both be fired."

"Oh, Shurtee, you are too unkind." She wagged a finger at him. "You have no charity."

"See," the soda jerker bent forward, the gold caps gleaming, "I got no use for the young dames. Chickens. They got no experience, see what I mean? Never seen nothing, never been nowheres, don't know nothing about life. If you want to know what I like, it's a woman, don't you know? Real woman, not one of those things. The right side of thirty, been all over the world, got sophistication, knows her own mind." He winked at her slyly. "That's the type for me. The kids can have the others, it's perfectly O.K. with me. B'gee, Mrs. Pavlovna, you might be thinking I'm throwing bouquets at you! You might think I'm trying to get on your good side!" His face wrinkled as he laughed and squirmed with his compliment.

"Shur-tee!" cried the corsetière. "You're positively enchanting! I don't know vat to do vith you!"

The soda jerker turned solemn abruptly. "No, on the level, Mrs. Pavlovna, don't you know? Now you take a young kid. What the hell does she know about life? You know? She's just a kid. A man don't feel right in her company, he don't like to take advantage! He don't know what to do. A real woman, on the other hand, she's familiar with life. She knows what to expect. When, you know, things come to a certain turn, why, hell, she's prepared to meet the situation. And if she feels O.K. about it, then, hell, O.K. And if she don't have the inclination, well, hell, that's another story. But you always know where you are. See what I mean?"

Shorty's face was close to her, earnest and anxious. The corsetière puzzled out his meaning, and as she caught on she brushed his face with the tips of her fingers, let a giggle or two escape, rolled her head wickedly from side to side, her eyes wide open as she smiled knowingly. Shorty stood back erect, elated with his success. For a moment neither said a word. Madame Pavlovna covered her face with the teacup and Shorty, now in full possession of the situation, took out a cigarette. She understood what he was after, all right, and he hoped sincerely that she also understood him when he said once bitten, twice shy.

"See," he said, exhaling the smoke in fancy curves and slants, "what the hell, we're both grown-up people."

"I think I better go," said the corsetière, turning shy. "The shop." She wiggled off the stool.

"Then it's O.K. about tonight? Eight, a little after?"

"Vatever you say, Shurtee." She was almost limp in his hands. "Drop in then and then ve shall see."

The soda jerker escorted her to the door as though she were a fragile piece of crockery. They couldn't find it in them to say a word. But as she left him at the doorstep, Shorty's reserve broke. He dropped the cigarette on the ground, danced his modified tap step, clapped his hands and sang, "Is it true what they say about Dixie? Is it true what they do down there?" She understood what he meant! There would be no mistaking him tonight. Shorty thought of Madame Pavlovna, her great curves, the full, soft body. The image of the bathtub returned and his eyes closed heavily as he indulged himself in his dream.

On the way back he stopped at the cashier's stand. It was nearly two and he reminded Lillian that she was off until seven. "Hell, make it half past seven. Eight if you like it. What's the difference? The night rush don't start until after the movies anyway and the boss, he's in a coma all day."

For the first time Lillian relaxed her vigilance when Shorty was near her. She had seen him in close conversation with the corsetière and she felt that his attentions might be exclusively directed elsewhere. Perhaps she had been wrong about all those accidents. "Thank you," she said. "It's nice of you you reminded me."

"Hell, that's nothing at all," said Shorty. "See that woman in the store? Madame Pavlovna. Runs the corset shop down the block. A fine woman. Respectable. Been all over the world. You'd be surprised at the life she's led, the things she's seen, the places she's been to. She's been all over the world. All over! Me, too. Sure, don't you know?"

"Yes," said Lillian gravely.

"Always after me," Shorty mentioned. "Yes, that's the way it is. But hell, that's the only type of woman I can stand. Experienced. She's got that certain something. Sophistication, you might say, only that don't do it justice. I can go for a dame like that, that's me." He looked at the clerk, tearing himself away from his thoughts. "Hell," he said grandly, "I guess you can beat it right now. Cold day, no crowds, nothing doing in the place and the boss is unconscious anyway. It's O.K., kid, I'll take the responsibilities. Go on, skip."

A kind man. "Listen," she said, "I don't want to make a bad impression on my first day. If it was accidents, all right. I'm sorry. Excuse me. It just looked bad to me."

"That's O.K., sister. As a matter of fact, I think you got the right idea. A girl's got to be careful with everybody, it don't make no difference who, see how I mean?" Stern admonition, he gave it in the wisest of tones. "First thing you know, a girl loses her reputation and then, hell, that's the beginning of the end, the beginning of the end."

Lillian agreed and came out of her stand to leave for the afternoon. Shorty, gracious and important, started back for his place behind the fountain. He resisted the impulse to let his hand fly out backward, just ignored the temptation and felt a mighty man for it. He felt good.

"Make it eight," he told her. "It'll be O.K. I'll take the responsibility."

She walked out of the store. Obviously a mistake on her part, but after all, it had been her first day and she couldn't be too sure.

No one remained in the store except the dishwasher. Shorty let loose his restraint. He stepped and danced on the floor slats, clapping his hands and singing the Dixie song. The soda jerker created a racket in the store but Mr. Spitzbergen did not hear it. He was sitting in the kitchen holding his head. It ached.

Dorothy and Herbert Lurie were in the dress shop. Lurie had sent his clerk out for her lunch so that they now had the place for themselves. In the morning, after taking the flat on Eastern Parkway, he insisted on the walk through the park. Now, laughing to hide his awkwardness, he was chasing Dorothy from one dressing booth to the other as he wrestled with her. Dorothy protested, alternately offended at his liberties, serious and angry, and then giggling to make up for her severity with him. After all, he would be her husband in another day and it wasn't so terrible.

"Really, Herbert, I must go home now. I got so much to do. My mother will be wild."

"It can wait. We'll move the stuff in tonight. You got plenty of time. It won't kill you to hang around, and your mother will get over it." He caught her and squeezed as hard as he could. Dorothy pushed against his shoulders. Then they both became aware that someone was in the store watching them. It was Shubunka, standing at the entrance, his huge ugly face sad and smiling at the sight of their innocent frolic. Lurie's hands released her and she stepped back decently.

"Oh, do not stop," the fat man urged. "Do not let me stop you. I am sorry. I am in the way. I should not come in."

"It's all right, Shubunka. I'm glad you dropped in," Herbert said, sobered.

"I was just leaving anyway," said Dorothy, going for her bag. "I'm late as it is."

Shubunka still smiled. "A pretty sight. It warmed the heart to see. Young people, I envy you. This is how it should be. When," he asked, "is the happy day, if I may ask?"

"The wedding? It's tomorrow," Dorothy said. In spite of herself she had to turn her back to him.

"Wonderful. That is very nice. I must wrack my brains," he said playfully, "and decide on something you would like for a present. Mr. Lurie, I wanted to give your bride some money to buy a present that might appeal to her. And what do you think? She would not accept it. She got insulted."

"I wasn't insulted," Dorothy said. "Only I don't like to take money. You can understand it. It's a very ordinary attitude."

"She's sensitive," Lurie said proudly. "She's just a kid."

Dorothy pouted. "That's what you think," she declared and went to the door. "So you'll be at my house for supper?"

"O.K., honey. We'll bring the stuff in tonight. I'll be seeing you."

"Good-bye, dear," she said, and turned to go but Shubunka hurried to her.

"I want to wish the future bride every happiness," he said, sorrow and regret deep in his voice. He sounded oddly mournful as he delivered his benediction. He held her hand, patting it and feeling it while she squirmed, smiling to hide her distaste. "Every happiness in the world. The best of luck I want for you." Dorothy politely drew out her hand, thanked him and left.

The fat man gazed after her wistfully. Here people were getting married, there was comfort and companionship and love. Why not for him, too? He went back to Lurie in the dress shop, gazing at the racks of dresses in reflection. His eyes came to the triple wall mirrors set in an alcove, and the fat man moved slowly as if without intention so that he might see himself in the glass. His eyes sneaked the view of his profile, full length. The heavy jowls, the thick lips, the lumpy nose, that heavy face on its squat neck, the dumpy shape of his large body resting on its short bowed legs —the sight depressed him. He told himself bitterly he had the appearance of a monster and unhappily he looked away.

"Moving in so soon?" he asked. "You have an apartment already?"

"We took a place on Eastern Parkway," said Lurie, expanding with his good spirits. "Right across the Museum. Thirty-two forty. You know where that is?"

"Thirty-two forty," said the fat man. "Near the park. I have been there often. A good neighborhood. Quiet. Mr. Lurie, you are a man to be envied from the bottom of my heart. I would change places with you any minute. You have a wonderful girl. A wonderful wife. You will have a home; perhaps, I suppose, in time, children, a family. That is how it should be. A man should be with his own and have his own." His voice trailed sadly.

"Shubunka," said Lurie, cautious in spite of his gaiety, "if it's all the same to you, it's a sort of a secret. Nobody don't have to know what isn't their business. I'd appreciate it if you didn't broadcast the news. You're about the only one who knows about it."

"I can understand. The boys at Ann's. Yes, I know what you mean. No feeling. No heart. They live their own selfish way and they have no room in their heart for another, for his hopes and desires, for his disappointment and tragedy. They are hard as stones, their hearts."

Shubunka pondered the truth he spoke, stealing again to the triple mirrors. Didn't he know how they were? Spitzbergen, Peggy Martin, his great friends on the police force, everyone? Weren't there thugs this very minute looking for him? The world was a miserable place in which no man had brothers. He tried his profile on the other side, hoping for solace, but it brought him none. He was ugly and monstrous. There was no hope for him. Lurie's girl came back from her lunch.

"I haven't had a thing in my mouth since the morning," Lurie said. "I don't want to rush you but I'd like to get a bite."

Shubunka awoke from his lethargy. "Mr. Lurie!" he exclaimed. "I should like to buy you your lunch today. A kind of a celebration. Let us go to Pundy's for a meal together. I should like it very much."

"Ah, hell, Shubunka, it ain't necessary," Lurie said, embarrassed. "Let's go to Ann's for a sandwich and that'll be fine."

"No, no. The idea appeals to me. We must make a little party. Let me take you to Pundy's." And insisting, he overwhelmed the dress man until he yielded. Feeling foolish with the fuss, Lurie told his girl he would be out for an hour, and they left the store. Once outside, Shubunka examined the street apprehensively but there was nothing he could see to fear.

It was a long walk to Pundy's, on the other side of Neptune. This was an elaborate seafood establishment, the lights were dim and the waiters wore heavily starched monkey jackets. Lurie always felt uneasy amid the splendors of the place and he regretted a little that he had promised to go with Shubunka.

To reach Pundy's they took a shortcut that led through side streets, over sandy lots and garbage dumps. There were few people to be seen on these queerly curved narrow streets, which were lined by the poorest wooden-frame bungalows. In many places the streets barely were paved and here they had to plod through beach sand, loose as it was on the shore except for a few clumps of weeds. The sand worked into their shoes and they walked uncomfortably. Lurie, oppressed by the empty dreariness of the neighborhood, took heart as he reflected on his marriage and his escape.

As they plodded, the fat man told him of his loneliness, his unhappiness, and the blank monotony of his days. To look at him people would think he hadn't a care in the world. But this was a mistake. He had enemies. Every dollar he earned was won through the bitterest of work, and what money he had, proved singularly unsatisfying to him. "Money is not everything," he mourned. "Mr. Lurie, it is not a new thing to say, but it is as true as gold. You cannot buy some things with money." There were gaps in his life and Shubunka slowly unfolded to the dress man the intimate details of his discontent. His shrill voice, halting with the exertion of walking on sand, was gentle but profound with sorrow.

At the other side of the lot they were crossing stood a whitewashed city garbage incinerator. In the cool sunshine it looked neat and pretty, set off on its well-kept lawn far away from other structures. As Shubunka and Lurie approached it, two men abruptly came around the corner and looked at them thoughtfully. The one with the prizefighter's broken nose dropped his cigarette on the sand and stepped on it with great deliberation. He went up to them.

"You're Shubunka," he said quietly. "It's no use saying anything. We're looking for you."

Shubunka's whole manner changed as he turned upon them. "Good afternoon, gentlemen," he said blandly. "I was expecting you. It is a pleasure to meet you."

"Who's the guy?" the dapper one asked. "He one of your boys?"

"What's this?" Lurie asked. "You know these guys, Shubunka?"

"Don't worry, Mr. Lurie. This is a private matter. It does not concern you. Just stand aside for a minute and then we will proceed." The fat man addressed the thugs pleasantly. "He has nothing to do with it, gentlemen. A friend. We were going to lunch together. Perhaps you would join us. No?"

"This guy's nuts!" the dapper man cried, overcome with amazement. "Hey, you, what's your name?"

"Lurie. Herbert Lurie. I run the dress store on the Avenue. What's this? A stick-up?"

"He ain't in it," the prizefighter said. "Leave him alone. Listen, you, you get up against the wall and stay like that. What you don't hear, the better it will be for you. What you don't see, the less you'll have to forget. If you're a smart boy, you'll make believe you were never here. We got business with the fat guy, not you. But if you get in the way, that's your lookout, see?"

"Oh, please," protested Shubunka, waving the English Oval at him gently. "I would not talk like that to him. It is not necessary. Mr. Lurie, you must excuse me. You see how it is? Sometimes you must do business and you never know what class of people you must meet." Lurie went to the whitewashed wall, a little afraid, and wondering.

"This guy's a pansy!" the dapper man cried. He couldn't understand Shubunka at all and it seemed to excite him strangely. "Can you imagine that? A pansy!"

"If you please!" said Shubunka. "If you please! Why is it necessary to be insulting?"

The prizefighter, ignoring his partner, stepped close to the fat man until their faces almost met. "There's a knife in your stomach, fat guy," he said. "It's after two. You got eight hours to get out of town." Shubunka looked down coolly. The man had the knife with its point hidden in his vest, his thumb flat on the blade. "This is no kidding around," he said. "If you're smart, you'll know we mean business."

"Well, I can imagine," the fat man said easily, exhaling the smoke and gazing into the distance. "No one in his right senses would say you did not mean what you say."

"Jesus Christ," the second thug burst out, infuriated. "I'm going to take a smack out of him right now! I can't stand him. He gets me sore just to look at!" He moved forward but his companion caught him and jerked him to a stop.

"You know what the boss said. You try that and you'll get good and slapped around yourself."

"Jesus, I don't care! I just can't stand his lousy face! I don't like it."

"Oh, sir," exclaimed Shubunka. "How wrong it is to quarrel with a man's face. After all, can I help it? As one reasonable man to another, I ask you, is it my doing that I have this face?"

"Jesus!" The dapper man nearly wept with emotion. "I'd give my right arm to smack his face in!"

"For Christ's sakes, cut it out!" the other said. "You give me a pain." He turned to Shubunka. "All I'm saying now is you got eight hours to beat it out of town. That's orders. Don't forget it or it will be the last mistake you ever make in your life."

"Just a minute, please. Let us see. Perhaps we can talk for a minute and straighten this out. It never hurts to wait a minute anyhow."

The prizefighter reflected and made to listen but the dapper man said, "We can't do no talking. The boss said we couldn't tell him anything."

"Well, what is this all about?"

"It's a combination now," said the prizefighter. "All over the city. They don't want no independents in the business. They're taking over."

"Organization," mused Shubunka. "It is always a good thing. But what a pity we cannot straighten this out by ourselves."

The prizefighter glanced significantly at his companion and the other reluctantly dropped his head. "Listen," said the man with the broken nose, "we want to give you a break. It don't make no difference to us either way. If you give us ten thousand dollars we will do to the other fellow as we were supposed to do to you."

"Oh, I'm sorry!" said Shubunka, smiling. "I do not carry ten thousand dollars in my pocket."

"Listen, if you give us ten thousand dollars, we'll make you the biggest man in New York."

Cheap thugs! Snotnoses! Ten thousand dollars were behind this great citywide combination. He could buy off these big shots for a couple of thousand dollars. Shubunka laughed shrilly. The two thugs looked at him, mystified until they understood his contempt. "I am satisfied the way I am," Shubunka told them. "I do not want to be the biggest man in New York. I am a simple man and I will without a doubt remain the way I am. Nobody can bluff me. I been in business eight, nine years already and you—"

He was choking. The prizefighter had him at the throat, holding the cloth of his coat tightly rolled up in his fist. His face was so close to Shubunka that the fat man felt the spit spattering into his eyes. The thug was in a fury and slapped the fat man heavily on the cheeks. Lurie at the wall stepped forward impulsively but the dapper man held him off, his left fist cocked ready to strike, his other hand going for the pistol in his pocket. Lurie, white-faced, stepped back to the wall, helpless. The prizefighter kept on cracking Shubunka with his palm and finally shoved him backward. He fell to the sand, jarring his head as he hit the ground. He lay still, his eyes opened in fear, rigid. The hat fell off his painstakingly combed hair, which now grew disheveled.

The prizefighter wiped his hands and straightened his clothes as he collected himself. "I ought to kick your teeth in," he said. "If you got what was coming to you, I'd break every bone in your body. I ought to pump you full of holes right this minute because that's what you'll be getting tonight anyway if I see you." He threatened quietly, glowering over Shubunka's form.

The dapper man was hopping. He held his gun out in his hand and begged to kill the fat man.

"Put it down," the prizefighter said. "Put it down."

"No, Bull, I want to do it now and get over with it. I can't stand it and he's got it coming to him."

"Put it away," he repeated. "The boss said not unless he don't leave town. I don't want to get in dutch."

"He don't have to know, Bull. We can say he got wise and we had to give it to him. Come on, Bull, let me give it to him."

"I said put it away. If he's a wise guy, you'll have your enjoyment tonight." The dapper one acted as though he were heartbroken and replaced the gun in his pocket. "Remember, you fat slob," the prizefighter said to Shubunka, "I said eight hours. We see you after ten, you're a goner." He turned to Lurie. The hard nastiness left his voice. Almost kindly he explained. "You don't want to get mixed up with this, brother. See, you don't know nothing about this. You never even saw me and you weren't here. Understand?"

Lurie stood up against the wall, too frightened to speak. He was worried over the expression on his face, fearing that by some chance the thugs might be dissatisfied with it and would slug him. He tried desperately to look as scared as he could. The two thugs scowled, looked around to see if they had been watched, and made to leave.

Shubunka on the ground suddenly roused himself. Waves and waves of terror overcame him. He had been a fool. He would be murdered. He had misjudged them completely on the ten-thousand-dollar bribe. It was a common shakedown, for they would have taken his money and then gone ahead with their boss's instructions. He hurried feverishly to his feet and rushed down the sand to the two strong-arm men. Grabbing the prizefighter by the coat, Shubunka swung him around with great force.

"Please! Sir! Listen to me a minute," he begged, panting. His jaw sagged. The eyes were wild. The fat man rocked, trembling on his legs. "You cannot do a thing like this to me! It is not right! Eight years I worked to build up a business. Eight years! How can you come to me like this? How can you take what I have done and kick me out? What am I? A dog? You have no right to do this! It is not the way for one human being to treat another!"

The thugs stared at Shubunka incredulously.

"Look, here is my watch," the fat man cried. He swung it before them on the chain. "Here, take it. Please, I beg you, take my watch. Let us be friends! Let us act like human beings should act with each other. Here, please, take it. It cost me fifty-five dollars wholesale and I give it to you for a sign of our friendship." He forced the watch into the prizefighter's hand, closing the fingers around it. The thugs stood awed by the spectacle. The prizefighter said, "Jesus Christ!" For a moment he held the watch dumbly in his hand, almost unconscious that he had it. Coming to himself, he looked at it with great curiosity and then suddenly threw it on the sand.

"No! Do not be like that!" Shubunka screamed, his voice shriller than ever with frenzy. He bent down for the watch but straightened hastily again, fearing that the thugs would leave while his back was turned. "It is not right to throw the watch away! You should accept it. It was a sign of our friendship. We must not be like animals to each other! We are human beings all together in the world. Please! I beg you. Take the watch!"

Shubunka gesticulated passionately, his face turned ugly with the intensity of his paroxysm. Tears streamed through the fine sand on his face. His bowtie had been twisted into a knot and it hung ludicrously over his chin so that he seemed to have some odd kind of beard. He hopped fitfully on his short bulky legs, his motions grotesque with clumsiness. The strong-arm men hadn't said a word during his convulsive outburst, staring with wonder. But now Shubunka approached them and grabbed the lapels of the prizefighter's coat to keep him close as he begged him to accept the watch.

The thug recoiled with the jerkiness of one who had been burned. "Get your lousy hands off me!" he cried nervously. He paled and fought fiercely to dislodge the fat man. But Shubunka held on with all his strength, as though this was the most urgent duty in his life. The dapper man ran up to help. Swinging up with his hands on their shoulders, he fell between them to put his weight on Shubunka's wrists in order to pry his hands loose. But the fat man persisted with insane resolution. After a moment the dapper thug dropped to the ground and began chopping at close quarters with his fist, striking him on the forehead and on the cheeks as he twisted his head to escape the blows. The three men fought for many minutes until in the end the dapper one managed to reach Shubunka's jaw with a hard punch. The heavy man sank to the ground. It was over.

The two stood off with him at their feet. "Jesus!" gasped the prizefighter. "Crazy as all hell!" They looked at him another moment and hurried away, wondering.

Shubunka lay exhausted in the sand, his arms outspread. He was sobbing violently, sucking back his breath in great wheezes. At the whitewashed wall Herbert Lurie stood weakly, leaning against the building for support, feeling deathly sick.

THREE

SHORTY CLEANED HIS TEETH with cellophane as he respectfully listened to Mr. Spitzbergen's gloomy philosophy. The soda parlor, gaudy with mirrors, artistic fixtures, and ornaments, had the depressing afternoon stillness. Cold weather, no crowds, no business. In the dim parlor sat Arthur's relief boy concentrating on his lunch. The boss, drawn by his misery closer to his fellow man, spoke on equal terms to the soda jerker, bereaved, desolate, and human.

"Ten years ago, good times it was, I could of sold my place for thirty thousand dollars. I could of made a fortune from speculating in real estate and selling out. But a man never knows what he wants, what's good for him, what he should do. Fate hurries him like a witch into mistakes and heartaches. Nobody does what's good for them. Take the Jews. When they were slaves in Egypt, Moses came to them and begged to take them out but they didn't want to go. Ah," he sighed regretfully, "it's the same in every line."

"Mr. Spitzbergen," declared Shorty solemnly, "that's more truth than poetry, what you said."

"Hah?" Goat. Talked in riddles all the time. "Yes, yes. It is a world only for tears and we're all better off when we die, goddammit. Only the trouble is we never know how well off we'll be then, either. Death, too, you know, it ain't no picnic! Otherwise plenty people, believe me, they would take their life." He shook his finger at the jerker with sad foreboding. It was just a thin hair that separated

Spitzbergen from suicide, and the soda jerker nodded in careful awe. Madame Pavlovna's clerk came in, sneering with disgust, and she handed Shorty another note.

"Parm me," said Shorty to his boss, the awe dropping from his face, concern flooding in to take its place. Was this another stand-up?

"Parm you," muttered Spitzbergen vacantly. He had nothing to keep him occupied. Up to his neck in troubles and the worst of it was he couldn't lift a finger to help himself. "Rotten weather," he scowled at the clear beautiful day, and he decided to go over the morning receipts, checking the stubs with the cash in the drawer. A man couldn't stand idle, for it wasn't his nature. He pushed in the No Sale button.

Shorty's wrinkled face blossomed with joy. No fear here! He had her so steamed up that she couldn't wait for the night.

My Dear Freind Shorty:—

I was standing alone in my little store when all of a suden the thought flew into my mind what is he thinking what is going on in his mind here is he here I am two people there own thoughts and hopes and personalitys so close to one another and yet so far apart it is truely strange. Life is so mysterius! It was my ernest conviction. I wonder and I wonder the beaty of existence the sadness of life always it perplexes me. Do you understand my Dear Shorty it is so hard for one to expresse herself in thoughts which are so mysterius and strange. So au revoir until tonight. Ever thine,

(Mrs.) Sophia Pavlovna

P.S. Please forgive this letter, throw it away I am only an old foolish woman writing stupid notes forgive me I cannot help it.

Poetry. B'gee. Shorty was deeply touched by the expression of her emotion for him. He thought the note was beautiful. Boy, did he have her steamed up for tonight! He looked at the clock. Crawling cripes, it would be years and years. He set to work on his reply.

Madame Pavlovna's clerk chewed her gum contemptuously at him.

"What's the matter here?" cried Spitzbergen as he worked over the cash register. "What's going on here? It looks like it was a progrom or something." Everything was in disorder. The dimes were among the nickels, there were pennies with the quarters, and the bills were in a mess. The checks on the needle had been clumsily pierced, one on top of the other, so that large holes appeared, destroying the figures. A man could make nothing of such cash-keeping. "What do you call this?" he asked, frowning with annoyance.

"The cash on the bum?" Shorty asked, looking up from his note. "She got the money all balled up?"

"Looks short!" the boss cried. "Checks on the file and nothing in the box! A fine how-do-you-do!"

"Lummox," said the jerker sympathetically. "It's probably O.K. That dope must of got the bills all mixed up in the boxes, but the money has got to be there. She's too dumb to know enough to take what don't belong to her. It's O.K."

"Thank you very kindly," began the boss sarcastically, but just then his wife walked into the store, which had been affectionately named after her. Madame Pavlovna's clerk halted her chewing long enough to gaze upon her, and the boss, forgetting to lose the frown, nevertheless took pleasure in the appearance of his wife. A beautiful lady. She wore a black sheer dress with a white lace collar, the red lacquered hat, ornamented with black cherries, matching the red handbag. Powdered and perfumed, imperious, refined and aristocratic, she barely took the trouble to look at her husband in greeting but walked at once to a seat in the parlor. "Bring me glass buttermilk, Shorty," she said, and the soda jerker acted as though it tickled him pink to serve her. He knew well that Mr. Spitzbergen loved her to distraction. The boss closed the cash box and hurried after her anxiously.

"Anna," he said, his eyes solicitous, "how are you? How do you feel?"

"Please! Don't ask me questions. My mind is upset. I came

straight from the hospital here. I'm worn out. Louie, you'll never know what I went through yesterday and today. Fire and water. It was a torture and still they don't know what's the matter with me." She peeled her black gloves off her fingers. "Thank you, Shorty, thank you. I'm dying with thirst. Ain't had a drop in my mouth all day. The Examination." Shorty's wrinkled skin drooped on his face with commiseration.

"You don't say, Mrs. Spitzbergen?" he breathed. "Well, I can imagine. I know. Once spent two weeks in the hospital myself. Worse than hell, believe me."

"Oh, you couldn't imagine!" she wailed, a little offended because he said he could. She wiped the buttermilk off her lips with her tongue and closed her eyes at the memory of the ordeal. "You couldn't imagine if you tried for years. Stomach pumps, salts, different kinds, it makes me nauseous to my stomach to think of it."

Her face suddenly screwed threateningly and her hand clutched her bosom. Spitzbergen roared at Shorty in terrible concern. The little soda jerker, overwhelmed to think that he might be the cause of an attack, trembled and stuttered apologies for his stupidity. In a moment, however, Mrs. Spitzbergen recovered. Shorty gasped with the relief.

"Go," commanded the boss sternly. "You done enough damage here already."

"Leave him alone, Louie," she called weakly. "It ain't his fault. How should he know I'm nervous?"

"I'm sorry," muttered Shorty, uncomfortable and angry because his good intentions had gone awry. He went back to the fountain. Fat horse! A hypochondriac, that was what she was. Self-esteem restored, he gazed into the distance, seeking inspiration for the right tone in his reply to the corsetière. The clerk, noticing his concentration, had to shake her head. Her nose wrinkled with disgust.

"A lot the doctors know," mourned Mrs. Spitzbergen. "I'm through with them, Louie. I got to admit it, you're right. All they know is how to suck the money. What good do they do? A thorough examination, forty-five dollars, two days in the hospital, everything, and they can't find out. Negative, they say, everything is negative, they can't help. But I know. I got my insides, no? Who should know if not me? I don't need a doctor when it comes to pain and I can't sleep in the nights and it hurts. Listen, Louie, from today on it's finished. I can die right on the spot but no more doctors. Finished."

He stuck out his paw and touched her arm shyly. "Good, good, Anna," he murmured gratefully. "You're smart. Stay away from the doctors. They suck money and it'll go away by itself anyway. God gives, God takes away. Doctors don't help."

"Don't touch, Louie. You'll spot the dress. Stingy. It hurts him only it costs money. My suffering don't count."

"Anna!" the soda man wailed. "It hurts me when you talk like that! It ain't true! What do I sweat and struggle for if not for you? Who do I give the money? What do I want if not for you?" His begrimed face creased in pain. He wanted to touch her again but he recalled his stubby fingers were wet and cracked with dirt. He held his hands in the air before her. "Anna, I got troubles. Everything is on my mind. It's like a machine shop in my head. The store don't make out. The weather is bad, one day rain, the next cold. The season don't come out and if we can't save a few dollars on the season, what can we do in the winter? Look," he wept and pointed to the wreckage of the ice-cream machine. "Look, Anna. Two thousand dollars!"

For the first time she saw the ruin and she gasped "Oh, my God, Louie, tell me quick, what happened?"

"See," he wept in sad triumph, and in his fashion he explained about Shubunka and his enemies, how he had rented the flats, not knowing or caring what was being done with them so long as the rent money was paid. After all, this was business and a businessman didn't have to know too much of what was going on, or he'd never make a living. Mrs. Spitzbergen, eager and concerned, wanted to know what the rooms were used for, but her husband put her off, ashamed before her, saying that he didn't know. All he knew was that gangsters and gunmen were mixed up with Shubunka and that he didn't want to be involved. She listened to him in great sympathy, in marked contrast to her manner a few minutes before, and as the soda man gave the details of his burdens, he found himself growing comforted beneath her warm gaze. She knew that something illegal had taken place, that her husband wasn't guiltless, but she readily excused it. A righteous man had no place in business and she could not hold him to practices that would lead only to losses.

Now she held his cheek in her palm. Her fingers felt cool and pleasant on his stubble, and he held her hand in his against his face, softly pressing. He told her how he now had to rent the rooms to Shubunka's competitors when all the time his only desire was to be free of the whole mess. True, the apartments wouldn't be standing empty, he'd have money with which to pay the interest and taxes, but he wasn't altogether money mad. When it came to strong-arm men he didn't want any part of it. It wasn't his line. And Shubunka owed him rent for two weeks. Lost money.

"Don't take it to heart, Louie," she soothed him. "So you lose a few dollars. The apartments are rented, everything will be all right, we should only live and be well. Don't worry, Louie."

Hearing his wife warm with affection and solicitude for him, Spitzbergen felt the weight lifting from his shoulders. It was good to have a wife, solace and comfort. If a man had a friend in a hard world, his aching loneliness, his fears and his uncertainties disappeared. Let Shubunka think of him as a hardened businessman with no feeling of loyalty and humanity, let Karty hate him because he held on to his money, let Neptune Beach give him the name of miser. At least he had his wife and to her he would always be a good man, honest and hard-working, meaning no evil, wishing peace and happiness for everyone. "Anna," murmured Spitzbergen, "you're like a doll, you're so beautiful and understanding and good. Anna, you're all I got in the world. Without you I would take my life." His eyes solemnly met hers, flinching a little at the naked expression of emotion.

Mrs. Spitzbergen spat indignantly at the mention of suicide. "I must go, Louie. I ain't seen the house for two days now." She rose, slipping on her gloves. A doll, said the boss, heartened by her beauty. He dug into his pocket for the money, rolled the rubber band off the bills and took out a five.

"Buy a hat, Anna. Buy something nice for yourself. The hell with the doctors, spend the money on yourself instead."

"No more doctors," she declared, putting the money into her bag. "It's a finish. I'm through with them."

"Good, good, Anna. It's sensible. We'll take the money we save from the bloodsuckers, and who knows, if the season makes out and God is good, we'll go to Florida two, three weeks in the winter."

She was going to the door. "Yes, Florida, Louie," she said over her shoulder. "Every summer it's the same story. Florida. I know you, Louie, you don't fool me." And they both laughed pleasantly at the joke. "Go tear him away from the business. You could kill him first." As she left, Mr. Spitzbergen was beaming, that troubled, sorrow-lined face actually drawn up in the expression of laughter.

"A beauty!" exclaimed Shorty. "I always said it. I been all over the world in my time, and it's mighty few women I've seen as beautiful as Mrs. Spitzbergen in her age. Hell, I can tell a good-looker when I see one." He stood with his hands on his hips, the face serious with authority.

"Yes, yes," said the boss uneasily, his face clouding. His wife had gone and he returned immediately to the attitude of business, apprehensive and gloomy. "Thank you very kindly, Mr. Shorty." He didn't pay him good money for compliments. The soda man snorted, recollected his misfortunes and his worries, and went back to the cash register. But the corsetière's clerk had gone back with Shorty's note and the jerker failed to make any notice of the boss's incivility, for he dwelt in the warm halls of his dreams. Dear old Hahvahnah. Tonight was the night pour l'amour and that meant oo-la-la in the French language, the language of love. He had just sent off his note:

My Dearest Sophia:—

Thank you for your exquizit wonderful letter I enjoy it so much it was potry. You are my dear a wonderful woman sen-

sative and sofisticat not like the usual run of women a man must put up with in every walk of life. In the corss of human existance you can understand what I try to expresse. Are you thinking of me? I am thinking of you every minute and I am longeing for the moment when I can see you when I can talk to you and when I can ?????

Yours forever,
Thomas

P.S. Do you mind my freshness in calling you Sophia I hope you do not mind.

Mr. Spitzbergen at the cashier's stand was perspiring. He banged the box out for the fifth time and went over the bills in the compartments, comparing them with the checks on the needle. "Looks funny!" he cried. "Goddammit, what's the matter here? Shorty! Come over here!" The soda jerker, business before pleasure, presented his absorbed expression before the boss. "Shorty!" yelped Spitzbergen. "The money ain't in the box! Just a few dollars here!"

"Must be a mistake," said the jerker. "It couldn't happen." He began to grow uncomfortable. Was the boss suspecting him? He examined the register under Spitz's weeping eyes. There had been over forty-three dollars punched out on the machine according to the tape. Spitzbergen started the day with about fifteen dollars in change in the box so that all told there should have been about sixty dollars there now. Shorty went over the bills in the compartment. Thirty-four and then the change. "B'gee!" exclaimed Shorty, amazed and trying to seem properly amazed before the doubts of the boss. "It certainly looks short!" They couldn't account for the twenty dollars.

"Did you pay anybody out today?" Spitz asked, trembling at the definite news of his loss. "Did any money go out today?"

"Only for the pies. Two thirty-four." He found the pastry bill. "That's all that went out. See, that lummox, she got everything balled up."

"I can't understand it!" Collecting himself with an effort, the boss started to go over the accounts again. "Watch me. See if I make a mistake," he said. The two counted the cash carefully. Shorty then bent down to the cabinet and pulled out the adding machine. He called off the figures from the checks while the boss pressed down the buttons and worked the handle. What discomfited Shorty was that the boss was always looking over the adding machine at the checks to make sure that the jerker was calling off the correct figures. The sum of the checks coincided with the register tape. There was no mistake. Everything tallied except the cash. It was twenty dollars short. Mr. Spitzbergen, perplexed and worried, gazed at Shorty until the little man squirmed.

"What do you want from me?" he begged. "I ain't the cashier. I been working my pants off behind the counter all day. You didn't give me a hand and I had the whole job myself. Jesus, I couldn't of got to the register if I had the intention."

"Who's saying you did it?" the boss said, looking black. "Nobody accused you, what are you making excuses for in advance?"

It looked bad for him, protesting so soon. "Geez, it's a new girl, Mr. Spitzbergen. I don't want to say nothing against nobody, but after all, what the hell do we know about her?"

"The new girl," said Spitzbergen, pondering.

Wrong tactics again, groaned Shorty to himself. First he protested, then he shifted the blame to someone else. Cripes, cried Shorty, he had nothing to do with it and here he was getting himself into a spot. He rushed to redeem himself. "Not," he said, "that I think for one minute that kid did it. See, I wouldn't talk like this about nobody, it makes no difference who. Besides, she's a good dumb kid. She wouldn't take a dime. Hell, I know human nature. I can read a person's character like a book. That girl Lillian, she didn't take the money. It's a mistake somewhere. When she comes back, she'll straighten out the whole mess."

B'gee! He had told her she didn't have to return until eight tonight! Now Spitz would surely be suspecting him. He'd be waiting on pins and needles for her and when she finally showed up it would look bad for him when Lillian told the boss Shorty was responsible for her lateness. The soda jerker, resenting the vicious nature of fate, felt himself a persecuted man and cursed himself for being too goddammed willing and helpful to live. "Just a good-natured slob," he mused bitterly. "That's me. It's the last time."

"What?" asked Spitzbergen, glum and glowering, suspecting the whole world and catching up Shorty at once.

"Nothing! Nothing! I didn't say a word. Honest!"

"What nothing? I'm deaf all of a sudden?" He turned away in hopeless disgust. That was his life, stealing from the till, smashing expensive property, failing to pay rent money. Everyone stood ready to do him harm. A misery. The world was only for tears, and we were better off when we died. "I am ready for a hospital," he wept. "Call me an ambulance. Some day I'll take gas and get finished with the whole goddammed life."

"Jesus Christ!" cried Shorty, near tears himself. "What do you want from me? I told you I don't know a thing about it!"

"Yes, yes. He don't know from nothing. Nobody knows. The money went away by itself like magic." What could he do now about the twenty dollars? He didn't even know where the new cashier lived. Grumbling and mumbling at man's inhumanity to man, the soda man went to the telephone to call up the agency, but it would be hopeless. He'd just have to wait until tonight and see whether she would come back to work.

While he was in the booth, Mrs. Karty, the gambler's wife, walked in on knocking knees. Yesterday she had given the impression of a tall, powerful woman, and it shocked Shorty in the midst of his own troubles to notice how slight she really was in spite of her size. She looked wretched in her sleeveless dress, with her straight short hair pushed back on her head so that the ends stuck out over her neck unevenly.

"Shorty," she said, "tell me, please, where's Moe. Don't hide from me. Don't tell me lies."

"B'gee, Mrs. Karty, I don't know. I would if I could, on the level."

"He ain't been home two days now. He ain't had a warm meal in his mouth. He's nervous, weak, he has no strength. He'll kill himself with his aggravations, you'll see. I got to find him, Shorty. Tell me where to look. He ain't in the Garden. I can't find him no place."

"I'm sorry. I don't know. He went out of the store twelve, one o'clock. I ain't seen him since." The jerker gazed at her with genuine sympathy, and Mrs. Karty, seeing he spoke the truth, turned sadly and went into the street, still looking for her husband. A tragedy, thought Shorty, it was really too bad, but that was horses and you had to expect it once a man got the racing bug. He looked up at the clock. Crawling cripes, the hands had barely moved.

Mr. Spitzbergen came out of the telephone booth, more perplexed than ever. The man of the agency had assured him that Lillian was completely reliable. She had references which were as good as a bond. Otherwise they would have never sent her down as a cashier. The manager had been cheerful, and Spitzbergen, hating him for his light-heartedness, nevertheless was inclined to dismiss Lillian from his suspicions. "Louse, he should worry," he muttered, referring to the manager. "It hurts him a lot somebody steals money from the register." Who could have taken it? It was still possible the money had been misplaced and that Lillian would set the shortage right when she returned. The boss, heavy with his sorrow, went back to the cashier's desk and searched through the drawers and corners for the missing twenty dollars.

Shorty, feeling a little surer of himself, looked at the clock again and patted his wallet pocket. He always carried a package of Trilbys around with him, from affection and from a sense of precaution, for a man never knew when and in what place an emergency might arise.

"I always play dem on der nose! I always play dem on der nose!" cried a big man in the row below Arthur. He had a rolling waist that overflowed his belt, wore no jacket and chewed nervously on his cigar stub, for he was impatient for the race to begin, and he worried and fretted. He turned several times to his companion, repeating his system of betting on the horses to win only. "My watch right?" he asked, and looked at the wood clock on the field.

The first race, said the clock, started at two twenty-five. "I got past two-thirty already," he said. He looked off to his right, toward the paddock for the horses to appear on the track.

"Listen," said the old man next to Arthur. "Listen. How old do you think I am? Could you guess my age?" He was a thin old gray man, wrinkled and skinny to the point of boniness, and Arthur thought he looked a hundred. He smiled helplessly at him and protested he couldn't imagine. "Sixty-four!" pronounced the old man with huge satisfaction. "Sixty-four!" He seemed proud.

Karty came running up the steps of the stand and sat down next to Arthur, grim and silent with the excitement.

"Did you place the bet?" the dishwasher asked. "Tell me what you did so I can know what's happening."

"Sunfeathers. Number Eight. I played him three dollars to show," said Karty, smoking his cigarette in rapid puffs. His gaze was joining the fat man's in the row below them, looking for the horses, to the right. "Twelve to one. Thirty-six for three."

"Three dollars to come in third! You said you were going to play him across the board," Arthur said. "What made you change?"

"He's sixty to one. You think I'm crazy? I don't go throwing my money out on sixty-to-one shots. I'll be plenty satisfied if he comes home with the show money."

"Oh, it don't make a difference to me!" the dishwasher said. "I just got the curiosity to know, that's all."

Karty smoked his cigarette, looked at the paddock, studied the form sheets for the second race, all at once, his movements jerky. Arthur, bewildered and yet beaming with pleasure, decided to trouble him no longer but feasted on the scene. On the other side of the track, where the stables were, the owners of horses had parked their cars. The sun hit the windshields so that flashes of light blinded Arthur when he looked out on the field to see the funny barber poles, the curving rail, and the hedges on each side of the hurdles. Instead, he gazed on the paved walk below him where the thousands of race-goers ran about, pushing their way, tripping and falling in their hurry. No one stood still. Each man was in constant action, going to a place near the rail, hopping in the air to look over people's heads for the horses, rushing back to companions from the betting ring or deciding on last-minute wagers and chasing back to the shed in a fury lest he be too late. To Arthur, sitting high in the stands, the crowd seemed to become a single unit, in constant motion but according to a definite pattern and design, like an ocean swell and fall, and this was so because the people streamed to their destinations in the same channels: rushing to the gambling ring and rushing away from it, in motion to the stands and to the rail. Arthur marveled at the sight of the men smoking fat cigars which they rolled ceaselessly in the o's of their mouths until the brown spittle gathered on their lips and they had to spit. Everyone smoked cigars and everyone spat, seldom taking the time to step on the mess as decency commanded.

"Would you believe it? Would you believe it?" It was the skinny man, aged sixty-four, now pulling on the dishwasher's coat to force him into attention. "That's no bull story!" He glared at Arthur.

"Oh, I can believe it!" Arthur gasped, impressed, wondering what it might have been he wouldn't believe.

"Two million dollars!" the old man went on. "Those years, nineteen twenty-five, twenty-six, seven. Two million dollars. You hear a lot of bull stories around these places but I'm no bull-thrower and never was!" As he thought of any such possible accusation, the old man grew indignant. "Never told a bull story in my life. There's plenty people get a kick out of talking big, not me. The hell with that.... Two million dollars. Lost every cent of it on the horses. All my life on the tracks, don't know nothing else. No trade, no job, no line of work. Couldn't be bothered!"

"My! My!" gasped the dishwasher. Karty took time from his anxiety to discover what Arthur was doing.

"Nuts," he said, nasty with nervousness. "Nuts. Gives me a pain."

The bugle blew and Karty convulsively flipped his butt, striking a spectator a few seats away from him in the row below. The man glared at Karty but immediately directed his attention to the horses. The fat man, who always played them to win, had risen with a jerk and was now kicking his legs violently to straighten his trousers, worried and absorbed. The horses, behind the red-coated leader, bobbled on their thin legs, snorting and blowing, twisting their heads roughly. The jockeys were pulled and yanked as they coaxed the colts. They were precariously high over the saddles, holding on to their perches by squeezing their calves against the horses almost at the withers and they were bent double over the manes. But they tried to appear unconcerned in spite of the skittishness of the two-year-olds.

"Dere he is!" the fat man cried with emotion. "Dat's the one! Number Six. Hey, Kumpell! Ride him! Ride him good! Kumpell, boy, bring him home!" He turned to his companion. "Lousy jock, dat monkey, can't get a horse away from the gate, especially wid der young dogs." He shook his head and grieved.

Sunfeathers looked big and quiet in spite of his youth, the veins on his head giving him a tired appearance. In contrast to the others who were fighting for the reins and cantered high, Sunfeathers plodded forward, his head bobbing regularly with the motion of walking, his eyes big and calm, looking like a workhorse.

"Geez," said Arthur, "he looks half dead already."

"Shaddap!" Karty snapped. "You'll jinx my luck. Can't tell nothing by the way they look. Sometimes the quiet ones win, sometimes the crazy hopped-up dogs all in a lather, they come in. It don't make a difference. Hell, all I want from this dog, he should come in third. Nobody's asking him to do the impossible."

Sunfeathers wore red blinkers and Arthur noted also the jockey's colors—white with red dots and red cap—so that he might be able to pick him out during the race. The horses were now going up to the barrier which, for the five furlongs, was set at the end of the curve at Aqueduct, for the home stretch here was long. The fat man in the row below was now standing on the bench, watching the horses and impatient, although it would be five minutes or more before the horses left the post.

"My people fixed me up an income," said the old skinny man. He had gone on talking no matter whether Arthur listened or not.

"What? What?" asked the dishwasher, cordial and wanting to be attentive.

"Not a bad income. Not tiny," he confirmed. "You could live on it but they gave it to me on condition that I stayed away from the track. Well," he protested, his eyes brightening with the thought of it, "they might as well of buried me!" He looked at Arthur for sympathy. The boy shook his head in rapid comprehension and then turned to stare at the post. It was hardly visible around the bend. Most of the spectators were now standing on the benches trying to catch the break when it occurred. The fat man below them was intent on the barrier but muttered continuously as though it might be a lucky charm: "I always play dem on der nose! I always play dem on der nose!" Because of the curve all the crowd could see was the line of heads, and every time they seemed finally straight and ready, some colt or other would have to bob out, and it was tantalizing. A sigh came from the throng in the stands. "Bury me!" shrieked the old man, still sitting, paying no attention to the race, reflection making him angry. "Bury me! Listen . . . let me tell you something. I'm sixty-four years old and for more than forty of them I been following the horses, all over the country, from track to track, north and south with the season." He muttered to himself. Further below, an eight-year-old boy came running back to his mother, who was knitting quietly. "Number Three is a beauty," the kid piped. "He looks fine, mother. He'll win the race all right." She patted him on the head for his loyalty and turned to her friend. "I got this watch on the coast. When the horses were at Santa Anita. Like it?" She interrupted her knitting long enough to hold out her arm for inspection. Arthur was impressed by her detachment and by her child. What kind of people were these? What sort of lives did they lead? It was fascinating for him to think of them. "Bury me!" shrieked the old man, settling in his mind many old scores with friends and relatives. "They wanted me to stay—"

The stands seemed to shudder as the colts flew out. Arthur jumped on the bench but could see nothing. The racers were hidden behind the curve and he could scarcely discern the bobbing horses and the backs of the jockeys. The old man remained silent, hunched up within himself, wrapped in the attitude of a man deep in prayer. He was lost among the thousands, hidden among all the people who danced on the benches. "How did Number Seven break?" the old man called, his tone sounding sheepish as he forgot his indignities and worried over his horse. "How did Devil's Pace get away at the gate?"

Arthur couldn't tell, for the horses formed one indistinct mass, colors and jockeys becoming parts of a group and undistinguishable. The dishwasher recalled the colors of Sunfeathers, white with red dots and red cap, but the silks meant nothing at this distance because all the boys seemed to be wearing white, which was the color of their pants, and as they rode, so close to their colts' necks, this was all that could be seen of them. "I don't know," Arthur told the old man who crossed his knees tightly, folded his arms and bent double over the bench, tightening with trepidation. Unable to make anything of the race, Arthur turned to the crowd. The people here, too, were unaware of their luck in the race but kept their eyes fastened on the surging, fighting lump of horses in the distance to their left, and as their eyes watered with the strain, they bit their lips, made movements with their mouths as they prayed and cursed and blessed. A man, holding his coat over his arm, his collar open, came crashing down the wooden steps. He had lost his balance as he went tumbling down for a better view. No one interrupted his gaze long enough to help him, and, indeed, the man himself seemed more intent on catching a glimpse of the horses through the crowd than on regaining his feet. "Mother! Mother! He's leading!" the loyal little boy was shouting, but she went on with her knitting. She had no concern with the race. All she waited for were the lights flashing the winning numbers on the result board.

Now the racers came around to the stands, spread out on the rail. The crowd tried to distinguish the different colts, and Arthur, spying the red blinkers, yelled in glee, "That's Sunfeathers leading!" He looked at Karty for his reward, but the gambler's sharp face tightened with sorrow. "Too early," he wept. "He got away too fast. He'll never hold it."

"Who? Who's leading?" the fat man called, turning his head to Arthur.

"Sunfeathers. Number Eight."

"You're crazy!" the fat man burst at him. "Whad der hell is der madder wid your eyes?" He went back to the race. "That's Six! Come on, Kumpell! Bring him home. Kumpell!"

"Who's leading? Who's leading?" begged the thin old man piteously from his bench.

"Sunfeathers," said Arthur, looking apologetically at the fat man's red neck.

"You're crazy! It's Six!" He glared with hatred.

The colts were running nearer them now and everyone could see that it was really Sunfeathers. The fat man grew profane and called Kumpell a string of filthy names, one after the other, beside himself. But as the pack came up, Number Six seemed to be improving his position, and as if to atone for his outburst, the fat man now began yelling: "Come on, Kumpell! Bring him home! Whip him! Give him der stick! Hit him! Kick der bastard in der belly!"

"Who's leading? Who's leading?" came the thin voice of the old man, huddled into himself as he grew unhappy over Devil's Pace, his choice.

"Sunfeathers," said Arthur.

The fat man turned confidentially to Arthur. "He'll never last," he said with solemn wisdom as he shook his head. "He'll never last. Dat dog won't hold it." And Sunfeather's lead began to disappear. The pack of colts came closer and closer to him. Karty was ready to cry. Too often had he seen his horse take the lead for four-fifths of the way only to finish a bad last in the last sixteenth. The fat man was yelling his head off for Number Six, but Karty closed his eyes, wept within himself and begged his horse to stay up.

"Who's in front now?" asked the old man. "How's Devil's Pace? Where is he?"

"Sunfeather's still leading," Arthur called. He made a conscientious effort to find Number Seven, Devil's Pace, but the pack close to the leader was thick and he didn't want to take his eyes off Karty's choice. He ignored the old man in spite of his qualms.

"He won't last," breathed the fat man. "He'll never make it."

"Nuts!" wept Karty. "Nuts to you." He wanted to run down to the track and push his colt by the rump. It was agonizing for him to watch. The horse seemed to be running in slow motion. The pack kept coming up and the finish seemed miles away. The horses fought each other to the judge's stand, three or four of them running almost in perfect stride, but when Arthur stepped off the bench at the end of the race, he was positive that Sunfeathers had won and he told the old man so. The fat man below them wanted to sock Arthur and raised his fist into position. His companion pulled him away and they gazed impatiently again at the result board. The old man whimpered with disappointment. The neon-light PHOTO appeared and a roar rose from the crowd, as bettors took hope or lost it.

Arthur, looking down at the mass on the lawns and the paved walks in front of the rail, now saw insistent streams trickling through the crowd as men fought and shoved their way back into the gambling ring. Except for these men struggling toward the big shed, most of the others stood still, their eyes on the glass-enclosed judges stand. A small knot of men pushed around the judges house. They were packed tight, and a line of heavy, tall Pinkerton guards in gray uniforms held them off, pushing them back.

Arthur wondered why those men were rushing back to the shed before the winners were posted. Karty, sunk among his worries although he felt certain his horse had come in at least third, explained that these men were going to bet with the bookmakers on the results of the picture. The crowd stood suspended, anxious and irritated, waiting for the numbers, and finally the lights went on. The crowd roared, happiness and disappointment intermingled into an enormous outcry. The lights flashed: 7, 8, 6. The fat man, who always played them on the nose, sat down heavily on the seat, overwhelmed. So close, and yet so far. He mumbled brokenly, sniffling hard to clear his nose and to recover himself. As for the old man, he took the news calmly enough. His horse, Devil's Pace, had won, and he appeared satisfied, as an eater would be after a rich meal, but nothing more. Arthur, exulting with the success of Karty's choice, had to admire the old man for his restraint. He turned to Karty.

"Geez," he said, "you certainly know how to pick them!"

But Karty was hardly overjoyed. "Played it like a mope," he complained. "Wanted to play this dog across the board and went and got cold feet when I saw the prices. If I'd a had two across, I'd of won almost a hundred bucks, first shot out of the box." As it was, he would collect only for the third-place award, even though Sunfeathers had come in second. He was pushing out to the aisle, secretly rejoicing in spite of his frown, for his hunch was true and he could use it. He would clean up today.

"Where you going, Mr. Karty?" Arthur asked.

"Got to collect off the bookie. Going down to the shed. Thirty-nine lousy bucks coming back when I might of had a hundred, and a jump race coming on next. Oh, nuts."

He went muttering down to the paved walks. On his way to the shed he passed the enclosure and took a moment to watch the swells. Here the race-goers were casual and smiling and chattering. The men wore odd jackets and handled their ladies with gracious ease. Stinkpots, just like everybody else, said Karty, they're only human, too. He looked bitterly at the women in their bright knitted frocks, their expensive hats, the rich jewelry. Smelled nice, he thought, smelled like the toilet in Roxy's Theater. Talked loudly. Blah, blah, blah, muh deahr! Lindah muh darlin! How choo choo devine! Bitches, he said, for their manner seemed to him arrogant and unfeeling. What did they care about him and his troubles? They had money and so far as they were concerned Karty could go to hell. Flat-chested, narrow-legged, skinny bitches with their noses stuck up in the air all the time. What they needed was a good hot jazz. Karty scowled, but the ladies barely noticed him.

As the gambler hurried to the shed to collect his winnings, he reflected all the way on what he would like to do to these society swells. His bile rose as he thought of their money and their indifference. They were in and he was out. Here he was eating his heart out for a few lousy hundred dollars. Here he stood chasing himself all over the place in order to keep his wife's lousy brothers from sending him to a hospital. They had no worries. The most important thing they had to do in the world was to stroll over the lawns, holding their programs and gushing their stupid line of chatter to each other. Choo, choo, devine, blah, blah, blah. The whole goddammed mess was unfair. What had they done to deserve all the money while he had to bust his gut for a buck? What made them so much better than he? What right to their fortunes did they have that Karty lacked? Bitches. It was lousy. It made a guy sick in the stomach to think about it. Karty, talking to himself, felt like crying. O.K., you bitches, he said. Some day I'll get my pile, too. I'll hit that four-horse parlay sooner or later and when I have all the jack in the world you'll come running around fast enough. Then you'll want to know me but you can suck my goddammed can all day then.

Comforted a little, he dug into the mob under the shed and stood on line before his bookmaker, waiting to be paid off. The next was a steeplechase. Only suckers bet on jumpers but Karty's hunch was riding high. He'd put twenty bucks on the favorite, Ferryman, at eight to five, maybe better if he waited for the price to go up. A long shot in a hurdle race was suicide.

Back in the stands, the old man, aged sixty-four, collected from the betting agent in the aisles. Arthur beamed over him, happy and proud to watch a man casually take ten dollars in winnings from an envelope and to feel part of the gambling scene.

"We won thirty-six bucks, my partner and me," the dishwasher said. "Sunfeathers. We bet on him to come in third and got twelve to one. Would have won more, too, only we bet on him to show."

"Never want to fool around with long shots," counselled the old man wisely. "The path to a bettor's grave. Listen, son, I know a man in the madhouse today, playing horses for a high price. Don't pay a bit!" He stowed his money into his pocket. "Always play the favorite. Or better still, son, lay off the horses altogether. You can beat a race but you can't beat the races. That's the truth." He squinted into the distance.

"Biggest thrill I ever got in my life," gasped Arthur, bubbling with enthusiasm. "I never saw anything like it."

"Biggest thrill, ay?" He rubbed his chin. "Biggest thrill I ever had in my time was that day in Albany. Nineteen seven. Ever hear of Chester Gillette?"

"Who? I don't know about racehorses. See, I ain't familiar in that line."

"They burned him in nineteen seven. The *American Tragedy* feller. Man wrote a book about him once. Well," he spoke with easy nonchalance for all of his importance, "I sat in the very same electric chair a couple of hours after they burned him. Yes, just for the hell of it."

"You don't say!" gasped Arthur. "Really?"

"That's nothing. I once wore the cap of the man who assassinated McKinley. Wore it a minute or so. You bet!" Proud and glorious, the skinny old man returned to his copy of the *Telegraph*. Crossing his legs, he was picking a winner. Arthur was overwhelmed. A real character, familiar with historical figures. For all he knew, the old man might be someone well known in sporting circles. And here he was sitting right next to him! Arthur, choking with happiness, noticed that the lawns were now empty of people. It puzzled him until it occurred to him that they had probably gone to the big gambling shed off to the far side of the stands.

"Can anybody go into the betting ring?" he asked the old man. "See, even if I don't go to bet?"

The old man looked at Arthur. "Sure, you can go," he said, "but what the hell for? People fighting around in a madhouse. That's what it is, a madhouse. You get just as good prices from the agents here in the stands and you're more comfortable. I can't understand how people will go to all lengths, make themselves heated and sweated just because they think they can get a few cents more on the odds. Don't make sense!" He rustled his paper smartly and went back to work for a winner. In spite of what he said, Arthur still wanted to go to the gambling ring. He excused himself apologetically and went down the steps.

The dishwasher caught his breath before the jam. Men were squeezed together with the compactness of a subway rush, but where the passengers stood patiently still on a train, here everyone was in motion. Lining the walls of the vast shed were the stands of the bookmakers. On each platform one man sat on a high stool taking money and calling off the numbers on the bettor's tickets, a second man worked with the hand slate, erasing figures with the ball of chamois and substituting new ones, a third man behind them noted the odds and the ticket number on the large pad. There must have been eighty or ninety of these stands. Around each of them stood a group of bettors anxiously watching the fluctuations in the odds, making notations on their programs, waiting for the price to rise so that they might place their bets to the highest fraction. Arthur was working his way into one knot with great difficulty, but just when he finally was on the point of reaching a good position, a group of men swirled against him in a sudden eddy. He was caught up by the momentum of the crowd and, struggling and protesting, he soon found himself outside on the grass again. He grinned ruefully.

Arthur found he had to walk to the very end of the shed where the throng was thinner, in order to make any definite headway. The press was greater to the sides, toward the rows of bookmakers, so that a sort of aisle was created in the very center. Standing on his toes here, he peered over shoulders and looked at the prices on the slates. But at that distance and in the dimness of the shed, the figures were illegible. The bookmakers sat on their high stools, holding the thick layers of bills in their hands. There must have been thousands in every fist. Clutching the money tightly, they called constantly to the crowd: "Don't jam around, boys! Let 'em get in! Come on, boys, get your money in! Quit the stalling around and bet!" Runners tore through the crowd and whispered changes in the prices. The man with the chamois, which was tied to the slate by a string, rubbed out the odds, making changes. Hereupon the crowd moved immediately, as if impelled by an electric shock. Some surged forward to make their bets before it would be too late. Others left hastily, seeking better odds from layers down the line. One man, rushing past Arthur, bumped into him heavily, almost knocking him off his feet. Arthur looked for him, but he was gone, sucked up in the mob. The dishwasher made his way toward the end of the shed, resting against a vacant bookie platform that had been pushed to the wall.

Near him stood three uniformed armored-car guards, calmly watching the turmoil. They wore their pistols in holsters at the side. Arthur gazed at them apprehensively. He had never seen revolvers before. The thought that these were real, carried real bullets and were genuine instruments of death, scared him a little, and suddenly the whole atmosphere of the gambling shed became oppressive. Arthur wanted to go home, to leave this hard, unfamiliar place. He grew aware of the smell in the shed and groped for a moment until he could analyze it. It was the heavy odor of thousands of cigars. Arthur found it unpleasant. One of the guards was watching him curiously. Uncomfortable, alone, frightened, the dishwasher walked away from the stare to the fringes of the crowd on the lawn.

For the first time he noticed the faces of the bettors and the bookmakers. As they ran with bills in their hands, the men seemed to be utterly absorbed in the business of winning money, their faces grim and vicious, wholly concentrated on the odds. A Negro, a towel over his hips with the ends stuck into his back pockets, had a pail of water near Arthur. He ladled out drinks for nickel tips. One man, drinking from the big spoon, swirled the water angrily over the floor, spilling it on the shoes and trousers of those about him. But he did not take the time to notice, nor did the men upon whom he had spilled the water. They held their programs in their hands, scowling at the odds and muttering curses as they calculated. The time was growing short. Off to the side, one man had just made his bet and now struggled to get out of the dense throng about the bookmaker. The press of men, holding their money in one hand and their ticket numbers in the other, swept against him in their frenzy to reach the bookie before the odds dropped. "Let me out!" he cried. "Let me out." But it did no good. The man rose on the platform, put his hands on the shoulders of the men before him and fell forward, forcing a path. But no one noticed his efforts. No one was upset by his fall. The odds were on the slate and the bettors wanted only to take advantage of them before it was too late.

The bookmakers collected money, called off numbers, and had no time to wipe the spittle which collected over their chins.

The horn croaked, resounding through the great shed to indicate that the horses were approaching the starting positions. The hum of the crowd rose at once. The rush of men was intensified to the force of fury. Discountenanced by the scene, Arthur impulsively ran out to the lawns. He pushed his way up through the mob to his place in the stands, relieved to quit the ring. He would not go back, he promised himself. Arthur discovered he was hating the place and its people, the grim preoccupation with the bills they always had exposed in their fingers.

Up in the stands Karty was already waiting for him. "Where the hell have you been?" he cried, his anxiety over the horses pouring out on the dishwasher. "If I lost you in the crowd you'd think I did it on purpose and you'd get sore."

"I just went down to see them bet. I'm sorry I'm late." Arthur felt strangely unmoved by the excitement, and cold. He no longer took pleasure in watching the people and the scene. He looked around for the old skinny man but he had disappeared. The dishwasher wanted intensely to go home. It depressed him to think that there were still four more races. Away from Neptune Beach, from the soda parlor, he grew lonely and afraid. The twenty dollars he had taken from the register now returned to loom in his mind and filled him with terrible foreboding. Free as a bird, with nothing on his mind, that was his ambition. Why had he begun with the whole business? Why couldn't he have remained in Neptune Beach, at the Mermaid Theater, happy and at peace? Arthur sat down on the bench. "Mr. Karty," he said, "I want to go home."

But the gambler hadn't heard him. The horses, deep in the field, were getting in line for the start. Karty had twenty dollars on the nose of the favorite, Ferryman, a gray gelding. The price remained at eight to five and he stood to win thirty-two dollars. His system never permitted him to play steeplechasers, suckers' paradise, but today he rode his hunch and couldn't fail. All the same it was so easy for a horse, no matter how much the favorite, to stumble on a hedge, and the gambler fretted.

"Mr. Karty, I want to go home," murmured Arthur miserably. "We got enough to put back into the register, so let's take the train."

The horses leaped out. Karty jumped on the bench, his eyes glued on the four racers. The gray gelding was easily the best, full of strength and run so that it was clear from the stands that he should win. The horse fought for his mouth and went twice to the front, but the jockey, standing up in his stirrups, took him back to follow the pace. "Let him run, you bastard," Karty yelled. "Let him run!" He hopped on the bench, cursing with tears in his eyes, but the jockey ran his race well and Ferryman took the lead as soon as the horses reached the last hurdle. Karty prayed for the gelding to make it safely. Ferryman went over easily and won nicely in hand, two lengths in the lead. Karty was overjoyed. He pounded Arthur on the back in hysterical glee. His hunch was perfect. They would clean up hundreds today. Two races in a row. He was sixty-eight dollars to the good already. "See?" he cried, his weasel face screwed in tears with gladness. "What did I tell you, Arthur? One after the other! I'm hitting every race today! My hunch can't go wrong on me!"

Happy for once in his grief, the gambler went jubilantly down the stands to collect his money. For the third race, Joe (Grey Lag) Wack had recommended Apogee, twenty to one on the morning line. Nuts to you, Joe Wack, said Karty. He had the race all doped out. The Fitzimmons entry, Drawbridge and Dizzy Dame, was his choice. They couldn't fail to click for him, one or the other, and they might be as good as ten to one, maybe better. He would play them ten bucks across the board. Two horses, backed all the way, he couldn't fail. Exhilarated for the first time in two weeks, the gambler took on new life. He gaily skipped over the steps on his way to the gambling ring.

Out on the field a white flag fluttered. Unnoticed by the crowd, one of the jumpers had fallen on the fifth hurdle. The horse had broken his neck and they were waving the white cloth for the low-slung wagon to haul the jumper off the course. When someone explained this to Arthur, the news somehow depressed him further. He sat on the bench, gazing dumbly before him and taking no further interest in the proceedings. The windowshields of the cars across the track flashed back the bright rays of sun.

⌣⌣⌣

For many minutes after the two strong-arm men had left, Shubunka lay in the beach sand on that deserted lot off Neptune Beach, lying still except for the sobs and the tears. With time the hysteria lessened, and sober coolness and quiet came over him although he still sobbed deeply. But now he cried as a baby does, enjoying his tears, deriving comfort from them. How cruel to him those thugs had been. Hardened, without human feeling, how they hounded him! What a wretched life he led, what a miserable world it was. As he lay sprawled in the sand, he went over, one by one, the details of his persecution, overlooked the fearful implications in them, but wallowed instead in his tears and self-pity, taking a kind of pleasure in his hopeless misery. Shubunka reflected soothingly how Lurie, still standing against the whitewashed incinerator building, must be touched by the appearance of his unhappiness and what pity for him the dress man must be now feeling.

At least there had been someone to witness the calloused injustice that had befallen him. The tears dried on his face, tightening the skin with the stickiness. Shubunka looked up at the blue sky, lost in a melancholy that was now gentle and nourishing. Billows and billows of clouds against the pale blueness of the sky, clouds in wondrous formations, noble and rich and majestic. Shubunka found their beauty aching. The spectacle somehow filled him with intense longing for other places, for faraway lands and the hills and valleys of the country. The clouds brought deep regret to him for his years, which now seemed to him to have been wasted, for his preoccupations, for his whole low way of living. Some other world, he begged silently, some other life, other people, other ways, joy and peace. The fat man on the ground fervently wanted a new life. A little round island of a cloud was floating away swiftly and Shubunka's eyes followed it in sad absorption.

"Come on, Shubunka," Lurie said. "Let's go back." They were the first words he had uttered in a half hour and his voice broke from his throat unevenly, first too low, then shrill. The fat man on the sand barely heard him. "Come," repeated Lurie. He stepped away from the wall, feeling sick and weak. Violence was always ugly, but the savage nature of the episode oppressed him heavily. Lurie recalled the brutal inhuman expression of the thugs and the mean hardness of their demands on Shubunka. He remembered the fat man's frenzied outburst, the raw pleadings, the slobbering tears, a thorough exposure of a man's innermost emotions, repulsively naked and quivering like a nerve when the flesh around it has been pinned back. This was Neptune Beach, Lurie cried to himself, lacking dignity, lacking spirit and feeling, concentrated wholly on desire and the process of its satisfaction, abject and mean.

"Come," he said again impatiently. "What's the sense of staying here all night?"

He helped the fat man to his feet. Quite recovered, Shubunka brushed the sand off his clothes. Combing his hair with his fingers he looked for his hat. His fingers grew greasy with the Polymol. Methodically he wiped them on his handkerchief. His face showed no shame before Lurie, no embarrassment, as though this was common and to be expected. He picked up the watch and examined it critically, worried that some grains of sand might have fallen into the works. He blew at the case with absorbed concern. Lurie took his elbow and they started back to the Avenue.

"You must forgive me," Shubunka said slowly, still cleaning the watch. "It was hardly excusable. I am very sorry."

"O.K. Skip it. It didn't make any difference," Lurie said.

"No, no," protested the fat man. "To involve you in my affairs on such an occasion as your marriage. Not such a fine celebration, after all, not quite what I had planned, Mr. Lurie, but you must forgive me. I cannot control my emotions. I am very sorry."

"It's O.K.," Lurie said wearily. He shook his head helplessly, unable to understand Shubunka. He was always putting on his show, always worried over the impression he was creating, no matter how real and serious his troubles might be.

"No," said Shubunka. He took an English Oval from the white

box and lit it thoughtfully. "No, it is not right this way. But I want you to forget it. Forget the whole business. You have other matters to concern you. Go to Dorothy, fix up your place, get married and be happy. Don't think twice of me. It is worthless to bother yourself."

"You better beat it," the dress man said. "You better leave town. Those guys weren't kidding."

Shubunka stopped him on the street, putting his hand on Lurie's chest. He looked amazed and aggrieved at his companion's advice. "But why?" he exclaimed. "It is not right. It is not human. People should not be like that to one another. I worked eight years building up an organization. Why do you say it's right for them to take it away?"

"I'm not saying it's right. It's none of my business. You can do what you like. Only I think you'd be smart to get out of town." Lurie grew disgusted with him, willfully misunderstanding for the sake of pity.

Shubunka's face fell as he sensed Lurie's condemnation. When they resumed walking, he looked at him wistfully. "You hate me. You are angry with me," he said, his high-pitched voice sounding like a whine. "You are right. It is a rotten business I have built up and I deserve no consideration. My money is blood money. I know, I know."

"That's got nothing to do with it. I ain't got a thing against you." Lurie felt tired as he spoke to him.

But Shubunka persisted. Lurie was right in condemning him. For the first time the booker revealed his occupation to him. He explained how these many years he had expanded his business, increasing the number of houses and girls and growing prosperous off the money the prostitutes won from the merchants and workers of Neptune Beach. These were grocers, fruit peddlers, barmen, counter salesmen, soda jerkers, candy- and cigar-store proprietors, butchers, storekeepers of all kinds, mainly middle-aged men, worried and clumsy in their movements. Often they ran out of their places for a half hour, still in their dirty, smelly working clothes, and then they returned grimly to their business. Pathetic they were, and it was a hard man who lived off their dingy lust. Shubunka did not spare himself. He told Lurie of the girls who begged him for work, how they came to him anxiously, preferring the security of an establishment to the hazardous income of the streets. The fat man told him how they were ignorant, young in years but old, deserving a better life, but abused and exploited because they were ignorant and helpless. Shubunka went on with the stories of their inevitable sicknesses, the casual medical treatment they received, their frequent recourse to drugs and to perversion, the courts and the jails in their wretched short lives. He did this to them, he affirmed, he was a monster. He ate and slept in luxury off their flesh. "Yes," he wailed, "it's right, Mr. Lurie. You should hate me. You should find no pity for me. The worst I get is the best I deserve."

"I'm not a hypocrite," Lurie said, depressed. "I'm not angry and I don't hate you. Business is business. It's the same goddammed thing in my line, only a little less lousy. All I'm saying is you better leave town. That's all."

But Shubunka was not satisfied. He returned to the story of his own meanness, giving cases and instances. Lurie grew completely disgusted with the man as they walked on, for he recognized clearly the relish he took in his mortification. Rubbing it in, he said, having a good time. A queer son of a bitch. He ought to be put away in a lunatic asylum. He turned his head and tried not to hear. They were now approaching the Avenue but the fat man continued, his shrill voice talking in a constant stream. Lurie cut him short.

"I got to go back to the store," he said. "What are you going to do? What good is all this you're saying? Where will it help you?"

On the street Shubunka held out his hands in hopeless desperation. "Let them find me," he moaned. "Let them kill me. I'm a monster. I'm rotten. I don't deserve to live another minute. They will be doing me a favor." A passerby overheard him and stopped, wondering. Lurie returned his stare until he felt obliged to leave.

"Get out of town, Shubunka," he said. "Take a bus and go to Atlantic City or to the mountains for a few months. Don't be crazy."

"Mr. Lurie, don't talk that way to me. Not you. Please! You are not like the others. You have feeling. You can understand a man.

Help me, Mr. Lurie. Do something for me. Don't leave me alone."

"There's nothing for me to do. I couldn't help you if I wanted to. You got to beat it, that's all. Take a bus." In spite of himself his tone grew cold and he sounded untouched by the fat man's difficulties. His manner became impersonal, revealing his disgust for him. Shubunka paused as he noticed the contempt in his tone. He stopped his whining and pleading and grew angry.

"He tells me to go away!" he cried, sharply pained, as if by another betrayal. "Take a bus, he says. It's very easy for him. Why? Why should I run away and give in? Why should they take away my business? He says it to me!"

"Don't holler, Shubunka. What do you want from me? I don't say nothing. I'm just telling you for your own good, go away."

"Like everybody else!" the fat man wailed. "He's just like the other people. All he has in his heart is for himself. He, too, could see a man die and he wouldn't help."

Lurie took his arm, trying to restrain him, but Shubunka went on weeping and muttering. People were stopping to look at them. The dress man felt uncomfortable. He had to return to his shop. Shubunka's troubles were not his concern and there was nothing he could do anyhow. It was a painful situation. "Listen," he said. "Listen, Shubunka. Stop and listen." It did no good. Shaking his head and frowning, Lurie broke away from him. But as he walked away he felt guilty. In a rush of contrition he stopped and went back to the fat man on the corner.

"Listen, Shubunka. O.K.," he said. "You tell me what the hell you want me to do and I'll do it. Just tell me what you want."

The fat man's excitement disappeared immediately. His face became quiet and beseeching. "Mr. Lurie, I'm all alone," he begged. "I have nobody to go to. No wife, no family, not a single friend. I need help. All I need is to wait a while. It is not sensible for me to run away. I can't give up a business just because somebody makes threats on me. I must wait and see how it turns out. If they're too big for me to fight there's time for me to run. But I got to be here to take over if they can't manage."

"So what? So what? What can I do about it?"

"I need a place to stay. I must get away from my apartment and I can't stay in Neptune Beach. Here they'll find me. I got to go somewhere where they won't know. Mr. Lurie, you have a place on Eastern Parkway. They won't find me there. Let me stay in your place for a week."

As he looked imploringly at him, Lurie could not meet his gaze. "What for?" he asked. "What good will that do? If you need a place away from Neptune Beach, you can find plenty others. I'm getting married tomorrow, Shubunka. I want to move in. I'm putting in my clothes tonight. It's a crazy proposition. You can find plenty other places."

"No, Mr. Lurie, they'll find me. You must help me or else they'll find out no matter where I go and it will not be safe."

"I can't do it! It's no sense. You don't need only my place. Look, Shubunka, you can take my apartment in Neptune Beach. I'll give you the keys. If you want, I'll go rent another furnished flat for you on Eastern Parkway. Why must you want only my rooms?"

The fat man rolled his head. "You don't understand, Mr. Lurie. You don't see how I mean. I'm all alone. I got no place to go. Nobody wants to help me. Why don't you understand how it is with me?"

"It's crazy!" Lurie said. "Don't holler. Talk low. I don't know what you want from me. I don't want to get mixed up in it. It's none of my business. I'm getting married and I don't want trouble. But what good will it do if I give you my place?"

"See," wailed Shubunka, "he don't want to get mixed up in it. He don't want to help. It's my troubles and now he don't know me!"

"Don't holler," begged Lurie, feeling miserable with the situation into which the fat man was plunging him. "Tell me, what's the sense? That's all I want to know. Where's the sense in the plan?"

"He wants to get married. All right. He don't want troubles. He wants everything for himself. What hurts another he don't care." Shubunka was crying, the tears coming down his face again as he lost himself in pity.

"Listen, Shubunka," cried Lurie. "Don't holler. Listen . . ."

"Oh, don't bother me. You're just like the rest. No heart, no feeling, no sympathy, no understanding. For all you care, I could go to hell. All right. Let them find me. Let them murder me. What difference does it make to you? You get married."

"Listen, Shubunka . . ." But the fat man was uncontrollable, weaving on his feet, rolling his eyes and refusing to heed Lurie's protests. He went on. "O.K.," Lurie finally said. "I can't do nothing about it. I want to do something but I can't. So O.K. I got to get back to the store." The dress man hurried off, without looking back, muttering dismally to himself, feeling angry with Shubunka and conscious of a sense of failure toward him. As the fat man saw him leave, his complaints stopped at once, the pitiful expression disappeared and he grew sober and collected. His audience had gone. He walked to the trolley to go home.

When Lurie reached his dress shop, the girl told him that Dorothy had called and wanted him to phone back as soon as he arrived. Distressed with his scene with Shubunka, Lurie now felt a rush of annoyance at the news. He went to the telephone and called the number.

"What's the matter, Dorothy?" he asked.

"You sound angry? What did I do you should be grouchy against me?" Her voice was aggressively petulant, irritating him.

"I'm not angry. It must be the telephone connection. What's the matter?"

"Where were you? I called up for an hour."

"I went out for a bite. I went with Shubunka to Pundy's."

"That man gives me the creeps. I don't know how you can stand him, Herbert. He's positively revolting."

"So what are you calling up for? What's the matter?"

"My mother," said Dorothy. "She don't like the idea of furnished rooms. She says she don't like the whole business. She wants us to get a three-room apartment and fix it up."

"So we paid the deposit. She'll just have to make up her mind and like it."

"My mother says we should try to get the deposit back. We can find something else maybe in the same house unfurnished."

"We can't get the deposit back, Dorothy. Besides, it'll take time to furnish a house. We want to get married tomorrow."

"Well, you don't have to holler at me, Herbert. I can hear you just as good."

"So I'm sorry. I didn't mean to holler. All right. But we can't give up the flat. We'll lose the deposit and then we'll have to wait. I don't want it at all."

"My heavens, Herbert, I can understand. But my mother, you don't know her. I been arguing with her since I got home this morning. If she makes up her mind, that's the end of it. I can't do a thing with her. I got my hands full. I'm afraid we'll have to give in to her."

"No," said Lurie. "It's too bad about the old lady but we're going ahead like we said. See?"

"My heavens, Herbert! I can't say I like your attitude at all today. What's got into you?"

"I didn't—"

"I want you to know, Herbert, I can't stand people who yell at me."

"All I want—"

"After all, Herbert, when it comes right down to the facts in the case, I owe something to my mother, too. She's letting me do everything I wanted. The least I can do is give in to her about the apartment. If she wants us to have a home of our own, after all, I think she's only got right."

Herbert winced. He covered the mouthpiece and cursed. "Look, Dorothy," he said, controlling his vexation. "I got a customer in the store. I got to attend to her. Look, we'll talk it over when I come around for your bags tonight."

"My heavens, Herbert. You're impossible. I won't have the bags ready tonight because my mother says she don't want me to live in furnished rooms. Can't you get that through your head?"

"I got to tend to the customer, Dorothy. I—"

"Of all the nerve!" she screamed. "Go ahead, Herbert. Go ahead and hang up on me!"

"I ain't hanging up on you, Dorothy!" he pled. "I got a lot on my mind. There's a customer—"

He heard the click. Dorothy had hung up. "Goddammit," Lurie

cried and slammed the receiver on the hook with force. The girl stared at him with fright. "Oh, it's O.K., Helen," he said. "It's O.K."

Shubunka walked from the trolley to his house, perplexed, bitter and uncertain. The afternoon sunshine was brilliant now but weak in force. He had to close his eyelids to avoid the glare. At this time the streets here were empty and quiet in the sun, the housewives taking up their baby carriages when they went to their flats to cook supper. Shubunka grew immersed in the sunny melancholy of the scene. Lonely, he said aloud as he walked. Lonely, I am all alone. There is no one to see me, to help me, not even Lurie. He kept on talking to himself.

At his doorway Shubunka noticed at once a man smoking a cigarette, smiling as he watched the lumbering walk of the fat man. Taking fright, Shubunka kept his eyes away from him and tried to brush past, but the smoker touched his elbow.

"What's the matter?" Shubunka asked, paling. "You want something?"

The man smiled pleasantly at him. "See, here we are. We got the address," he said softly. "Hey, you packing your bags? You getting ready to go?"

At this Shubunka backed away as though the man might be planning to attack him at once. As he retreated, the door gave, swinging open so that he nearly fell. He uttered a gasping cry of fear. The man with the cigarette laughed good-humoredly. "Don't get scared of me. I'm not out to do anything to you. Hell, I'm just here to remind you in case you forgot. See?" He flipped the butt neatly into the gutter and hitched his trousers to leave.

"Please, mister," Shubunka called. "Tell me. One moment. Who sent you?"

"It's O.K., brother. It's O.K.," the man said genially. "Don't you worry about that. See, we don't like trouble no more than the next guy. All we want is for you to get out of town. We just don't want you around."

"Please, mister, I would like to talk to the boss. Perhaps there is some kind of arrangement we might make. Maybe a little money would help just as good. Maybe I could work for him. He needs men to watch over."

"Don't talk to me," the man said. "Hell, I'm just the hired help. I got to follow orders just like everybody else. I got nothing to do with that."

"So who could I talk to? Give me a telephone number. Give me something," Shubunka pleaded with the man. "Come on upstairs. We'll have a little drink. You like a drink perhaps? Come on upstairs. We'll have a little talk." Oily, perspiring with eagerness, he held the man by the coat collar and forced a smile to his lips.

"Oh, nuts! Nuts! What the hell kind of a phony are you anyway?" the man asked, turning angry abruptly. He slapped Shubunka's hand off his coat roughly. "Keep your lousy paws off me, see? Get the hell out of town. That's the only thing I got to say to you. Jesus Christ!" He went down the stoop. "Pack your bags and beat it. See, we'll be around and don't you forget it." He walked down the street, disturbed out of his good spirits by the fat man. Shubunka watched him until he disappeared and then went glumly to his apartment.

The rooms were dim and dreary. Shubunka sighed. But in spite of all pressure upon him, in spite of all sadness, he was first dirty. He bathed and changed his clothes, moving methodically, performing a necessary duty. The sun filtered through the shades. The house was clean. Alone in the apartment, Shubunka longed for a visitor, for a telephone call, for anyone. He sat down on the bed and started cleaning his fingernails, wondering what to do. And as he sat, he found himself waiting for that visitor or that telephone call. Normally the bell was always ringing with calls from women wanting to be placed, from his man reporting, from Charlie Angus, his bondsman, or from the madams registering complaints. He grew filled with foreboding that no one was calling him now. It was as though he were dead.

The silence oppressed him, compelling him in the end to turn on the Victor Magic Eye radio. A Hawaiian band played its sad twanging music and Shubunka hunted for something else. Organ strains, reminding him of funerals. He turned it off. A talk to a women's club by the president of a theological school. "We live in a frightful world," said the voice, resonant and profound, "where titanic forces lay mastering hands upon us. It is not merely our lusts, our greeds, our laziness, our ignorance with which we have to reckon. There are malignant forces—call them trends, lags, obsessions, or call them plain devils, and they are viler, more brutal, more dangerous than we at our worst." Shubunka, losing interest, gazed vacantly into the mirror, standing for many minutes before the glass, watching himself. He opened his mouth and closed it, swallowing the saliva. "Thank God that we need not ascribe all our baseness and brutality in our feelings and motives and opinions to ourselves," declared the voice. "No, bad as we are, we are better than our devils. There are Satans who drag us down—the national spirit, business usages, social customs, family ways, the outlook of acquaintances. Something worse than we does possess us."

"Holler, holler," Shubunka told the radio. He went away from the mirror and turned the dial. Boys of the Ranch. "She'll be coming round the mountain when she comes, when she comes." Their voices filled the room with mechanical brightness, but no one called, no one telephoned, and Shubunka remained disheartened. He picked up the French phone and called Charlie Angus, but the girl in the bondsman's office would say nothing except: "Who's calling? I must have the name, please. Who is it?" Shubunka told her it was all right but the girl persisted. And when he gave his name, Mr. Angus was out. He just stepped out a minute ago but the girl said she would have him call back the minute he returned to the office. "You are lying to me," Shubunka said sadly. She hung up. He called the pool parlor on Myrtle Avenue. "I can't say my name over the telephone," he told the rackman, "but tell Sklar it's from a friend. Tell him he'll know who's calling." Sklar finally came to the phone.

"How are you?" Shubunka asked him. "How are you feeling?"

"Who is it? Shubunka? What the hell do you want?" The voice was impatient and angry.

"I just wanted to say hello. That was all. Don't you like it no more when I call you?"

"Hey, Shubunka, lay off me from now on. I don't know you."

"Why?" the fat man asked plaintively. "Only tell me why all of a sudden."

"Because you're marked lousy. That's why."

The phone clicked. "She'll be wearing red pajamas when she comes, when she comes," sang the ranch boys. They had him covered on all sides, said Shubunka. The gunmen, the madams, Spitzbergen, his bondsman, the police. Shubunka lay on the bed. Everyone had deserted him. There was no one to whom he might even go begging for help. As the hopelessness of his situation forced itself upon him, he thought of his father as a glazier on the East Side. He thought of his poverty, of his work in the wicker business, of the counting of pennies and nickels when he had his candy stand on Pitkin Avenue in Brownsville. Shubunka remembered his beginning as a booker, when he had three houses and ten or fifteen girls. He thought of the eight years of building up, his increasing power with the police, his expansion to eighteen houses and forty girls. Every week he had been collecting between four and five hundred dollars, netting eight thousand dollars a year for himself in clear profit. His bankbooks were good to read. Shubunka, in his loneliness, relished too keenly the position he had won through his wealth and through that alone. "No," he wailed aloud. "I won't go. Let them kill me. Let them shoot me. I won't give it up."

Alone, always alone, thought Shubunka. If there were only someone to whom he might go. Now he thought of Moe Karty and how piteously the gambler had begged him for help. Why didn't I give him the few dollars he wanted, the fat man asked the ceiling? He felt sharp remorse. A human being, just like himself, was in misery, had come to him and begged for help, and he had turned him away without a second thought. Shubunka forgot his own grief to think of Karty. He would see him tonight, he promised, he would see him and give him whatever money he wanted. It was the least one human could do for another.

⁓⁓⁓

Shorty's eager flashing eyes were now tightly closed, his wrinkled face was rigid and composed. The hot Turkish towel was folded neatly over his forehead, a considerate oval granted so that he might breathe. The barber bent over and neatly clipped the hair showing at his nostrils. This was La Mode, the shop on the corner. The soda jerker was half asleep on the chair from the pleasing fingers of the barber, who was shaving and massaging his cheeks with the electric contraption. Very soothing. Shorty loved it and always ordered the massage. It was a quarter past five. The soda jerker had forgotten Spitzbergen, the loss of the twenty dollars, Lillian and the late hour at which he had told her to return tonight. His drowsy mind had room only for the great curves, the juicy, plump, and Oriental attractions of Madame Pavlovna. The barber removed the towel, slapped witch hazel over his skin, awakening him. His head bobbled gently when the barber's chair was pushed back into its upright position.

"O-le-o-lay-dee, o-lee-o-lay-hee-dee, o-lee-o-lay-hee-ree-dee-di," Shorty sang, stretching in the chair.

"Some fun, eh, kid?" said the barber morosely. He was working Wildroot into Shorty's fringe, a little distastefully, for he had been standing on his feet all day and the night was yet to come.

"Listen," said Shorty, rubbing his eyes, "I want to ask you guys one thing: Is it true what they say about Dixie? Is it true what they do down there?"

"O.K.," mourned the barber. "You win. I give up. Pick up all the marbles."

"He's happy. That's good," pronounced the man in the next chair. He owned the fruit market on the corner and had sneaked out for an hour during the afternoon lull. His shoes were damp and deep with store dirt and his grimy pants lay stiff upon him. When he talked, his voice had a peculiar sound, rasping, without body. "I am always glad to see somebody happy in this world. It gives me satisfaction," he said. "People get happy, they spend money, prosperity comes back. One, two, three, what do you think?" He stared dubiously at his face in the wall mirrors. It didn't please him and he looked distressed.

"He's got a piece all lined up, I bet," his barber told the fruit man. "That must be what he's so happy about."

"O.K. I got no objections. Listen, put something on," he rasped. "Make a good smell, you know. Cologne." The fruit man felt sheepish on the subject of perfume but he wanted what he wanted. "I am glad to see somebody get whatever his little heart desires. If it makes you happy," he said dolorously, turning in his sheet to Shorty, "then I'm happy, too. I always take enjoyment in other people's pleasures. I'm not so lucky myself."

"O.K., brother," said Shorty, very important. "Only you don't have to believe everything you hear. That guy's full of it."

"Oh, yeah, oh, yeah," said the second barber. "I can see it all over his face. It's the only time he's happy."

"Hey, Shorty," said his own barber, "how the hell do you make 'em? Give me the secret of your success. You'll pardon the expression, but you ain't Clark Gable, not exactly. How do you lay 'em down?"

"O-lee-o-lay-dee, o-lee-o-lay-hee-dee, o-lee-o-lay-hee-dee-hee-dee," said Shorty, self-satisfied and masterful. "The hell with you cheap punks. Don't you come sucking around me, and what is furthermore I don't want none of this here talk floating around where I'm concerned. It might get somebody in trouble, maybe me, maybe some innocent dame, and brother, maybe you. See what I mean?"

"Nuts!" cried the barber. "You know where you can shove that."

"No, on the level," said the soda jerker, turning confidential. "You never want to talk that way about dames. What the hell, a guy ought to have a sense of honor, don't you know? Kiss and tell, that's no way for a regular guy."

"Make me smell nice," begged the fruit man. "Put on the tonic."

"Listen, Shorty," said the barber, "what the hell do you go around fooling around with dames for? A runt like you can't do nothing for a broad. You ain't got nothing to make it interesting with. Now if you was a considerate guy, you'd do your piece a favor tonight and send me to take your place."

Shorty bolted upright in the chair, deeply offended. "Why, you son of a bitch," he cried, "don't you know size ain't got nothing to do with it?"

"Lay down," said the barber. "Lay down and hold your water."

"No fights, boys," said the fruit man in his sandpaper voice. He patted his hair and looked into the mirror as he spoke. "It ain't respectable. Besides, I always feel disagreeable when I see an argument going on. All I want in the world is happiness, enjoyment, and a smile on everybody's face. That is my sincerest wish." He finished virtuously. His barber tightened a towel over his scalp and brushed the cloth until the hair on the fruit man lay flat against his skull. When the towel was removed, the fruit man thought he looked knobby as anything.

"Ignorant bastards," said Shorty, still fuming. "Of all the ignorance."

"Listen," said the fruit man's barber, "what the hell you getting all worked up for? Can't you take a joke?"

"Hell, I can take a joke as good as the next guy," the jerker said, indignation cooling. "Only what call is he got to pass remarks? See, hell, there's certain things a guy ain't got a right to pass off in conversation. Can't you dumb mugs understand that?"

"My friend," said the raw voice. The fruit man had risen from his chair and had touched Shorty's arm beneath the cloth. "Let me tell you something, my friend. I am an older man than you. The years bring experience. Right? There is no school like the School of Experience. Right?" He waited for confirmation.

"So O.K.," Shorty said.

The fruit man bent his sweet-smelling head close to the jerker. "It ain't worth it! Believe me, I know what I'm talking about! What's the use of eating your heart out over nothing?" He fixed Shorty with his eyes imperiously. The jerker started to say something but the man cried: "Uh!" and nudged him to a stop. "Blood pressure!" he said. "You get a high blood pressure from aggravating yourself. You go out like a light." Shorty wanted again to speak. "Uh!" said the fruit man.

"O.K.," said Shorty, overcome. "O.K."

"See? A little word goes far." Quiet triumph. He fished in his greasy pocket for a bill and handed it to the barber. Patting his slicked, tonic-wet hair he looked fondly at his white jaws in the mirror and absently said: "She'll work a whole lot easier for her three dollars, my friend, than you did for the sixty cents."

"You bet," said the barber bitterly and gave him the change.

The fruit man turned to Shorty. "All I want is happiness in the world, enjoyment, a smile on everybody's face. That's my satisfaction." He walked out.

"A cathouse," said the jerker. "It's disgusting. It turns my stomach. I can't stand them places. Listen, what I say is a guy if he can't get it normal and free, the hell with it, he ought to take in a movie show instead. See what I mean?"

"Look who's talking," said the barber. "Listen, just because we kid around making you feel good, don't think we believe that bull you hand out about making broads. You never got a hunk of nookey for nothing in your life yet and you ain't getting better-looking with the years. If it wasn't for the cathouses you'd be a terrible sight."

"Oh, yare?" Shorty screamed, hopping to his feet out of the chair, his legs apart because of the footrest. The apron swirled up and he brushed it away from his face. "If I wanted to tell you mugs something I'd knock you off your feet! Hell, listen, if you knew what I got lined up for tonight— Nuts. I don't talk. That's me. I never talked about dames before in my life and I ain't going to start now. But I want you fat dopes to realize one thing: When I feel the inclination, I don't have to pay for it!"

He sat back, resolved to have no further discourse with the barbers. The hell with them. His head jerked around in a gentle circle as the man brushed the fringes on his scalp. The movement served to lull his mind again. He'd get dressed in that white gabardine with the fancy back. They'd go to the Mermaid and take in a show after a bite at the Chink's. And then for her apartment with the lights turned off. Oo-la-la. Dear old Hahvahnah! Shorty was just about to yodel again but he caught himself in time. He wouldn't give these ignorant clouts the satisfaction.

The sun at the Aqueduct racetrack had shifted so that the flashing beams from the autos across the field no longer blinded Arthur. He sat unhappily in the stands, having stayed there for the last three races without stirring. He took no further interest in the motion of the crowd, in the running of the horses, in the gambling and the excitement. The show was over for him. Unfriendly premonitions filled him. Free as a bird, with nothing on his mind, that was his ambition. He longed to see Shorty and Spitzbergen again, to work in the usual routine at Ann's. He wanted to be home, away from the track, at peace and quiet. The thought of the twenty dollars he had taken from the register rested heavily on his mind.

"Mr. Karty," he begged, "let's go home. Let's take the train already."

"Leave me alone!" the gambler snapped. His swollen eyes glared at him for a moment. "You're hoodooing my luck." And Karty's had changed a little, too. In the third race he had played the Vanderbilt entry for thirty dollars, spread across the board. Dizzy Dame came in third at three to one, so that Karty lost nothing on the venture, but what dismayed him was that Apogee, the choice of Joe (Grey Lag) Wack, won the race at the juicy price of twenty to one. It was tantalizing. Karty choked as he thought about it. Here he had been following the handicapper for weeks, losing heavy money on his selections. When he finally put one over, Karty was away, roaming the fields of daisies. Had he played Apogee instead of the entry, he would have cleaned up three, four hundred dollars in one blow. He would have quit then and there, he told himself, while the luck lasted. On the level, he would have quit. With four hundred dollars in his hands, all his troubles would have been over. His wife's brothers would have given him months to make good the rest. With time, probably, their rage toward him would have cooled and they would have been satisfied to get the four hundred.

What's the use moping about it, Karty cried to himself? He was hoodooed for life. Never no luck. In the fourth he had dropped twenty dollars. Sir Quest. The horse had been leading by yards for five furlongs and then dropped to last in the remaining one and a half. It was disgusting. A reasonable bet, seven to two, Sir Quest had been pulled. No doubt about it. It was clear as daylight. Crooked work, a faked race, and Karty had to suffer for it. The fifth race was better. Karty had played Thorson, a thirty-to-one shot, three, five, and ten across the board, and the horse had come in third, netting him thirty-two dollars on the deal. By the time of the sixth race, Karty was eighty-odd dollars to the good. With the money from the cash register, he had a hundred dollars all told. He had enough to quiet the garage men for the time being. Lay off, he told himself. Quit while the quitting is good. His hunch was broken. He had run his luck as far as it would go today and the smart thing for him to do now was to catch the train, give his wife's brothers the hundred, and live in peace for a while. And he would have done this, too, said Karty, only for Apogee. Twenty to one! He would have had hundreds. The money was practically in his hands and he had let it go. Karty tried to drive the recollection from his mind, but it returned again and again to gnaw at him.

"Let's go home, Mr. Karty," Arthur called. "I got enough. We made enough money. Let's put the money back in the register and be through with it, Mr. Karty."

"Jesus Christ, leave me alone!" the gambler shouted. "I got enough on my mind without you bothering me. I'm aggravated enough!"

His anger frightened the dishwasher into silence, but Karty kept on sitting on the bench, his sharp weasel face screwed up with uncertain reflection. By rights he ought to go home. He had a hundred in his pocket. But Apogee! And now Gillie was coming up for the sixth race. The time was growing short, for the horses would be lining up before the stands any minute now. Karty pondered, rubbing his sharp nose, wavering and troubled. Gillie was his hottest thing today. He had doped out the four-year-old for a sure bet and now he went over his attractions one by one. Ten to one he was on the morning line, probably better now in the shed. A fine classy colt, used to good company, he had been entered in the fastest stake races this season but just hadn't hit his stride. Karty knew figures. The horse, which as a three-year-old, could crack 1:37 for the mile, would cop today's race against the cheapest sort of opposition. Not an outstanding horse among them, nothing in Gillie's class, and the four-year-old was ready to crack the wire. In previous exercises he had two morning workouts of 1:45 for the mile and a sixteenth, today's distance. Coucci was riding, and even if the jockey had been having poor luck lately, he was a reliable boy and was due for a winner anyhow. The weight at one hundred nine pounds was a feather, giving him five and six pounds advantage over most of the others. A sure thing, ready to come home, but Karty sat undecided, for in spite of everything he could think of in Gillie's favor, the fact remained that he had a hundred dollars in his pocket and this would be enough to hold off his brothers-in-law. His stomach felt raw and nauseous from lack of food and too many cigarettes. He crossed his legs tightly to drive away the sick feeling in his stomach, and held his lips in his fingers, kneading them in nervous irresolution.

Down below in the stands a man and his wife were arguing bitterly. "It's my money, goddammit," the man cried. "I earned it. I worked for it and I can do what the hell I want with it, can't I?" he tore away from her grasp and went down the stairs. "Buys a dress for sixty-eight bucks. That's O.K.," he said over his shoulder. "That's fine, ain't it? But I can't fool around with the horses, hah? It's my only pleasure. Don't I deserve something out of the money I work for?" He went out of sight. The wife sat down, looking cautiously around to notice whether anyone had been watching.

"I don't want to be a pest," Arthur whimpered, "but I think we should go home, Mr. Kar—"

The bugle blew. The gambler jumped up involuntarily. The line of horses was making a curve from the paddock out upon the track. It would be too late in another few minutes. His indecision broke, and without a word to Arthur, without another moment of reflection, he ran wildly down the steps to the lawn, smashing into people, shoving them aside, fighting to get to the shed before the horses reached the post. Panic seized him. In his feverish haste he was conscious only of one enormous force, and that was the urgent necessity of laying his bet on Gillie before the horn blew. Reaching the shed, he found the paths to the bookmakers clogged by jamming and shouting men. Karty ran down the short grassy slope, picked up momentum and battered his way in, using his shoulder as a ram. Three or four men went down to their knees and a hole lay open. The gambler rushed through it but one of the men who had been knocked over followed him in angry pursuit. He grabbed Karty by the collar and punched at the back of his head, absorbed with rage, keeping silent as he socked. Karty wrenched his way free and ran ahead without looking back at his assailant.

Inside the betting ring four thousand gamblers were rushing wildly to make their bets before the wild clanging of the bell announced that the horses had left their posts and that no more bets could be taken. They sought the best odds and had to fight their way into the bookmakers' stands. Karty did not wait to shop for prices. He squirmed through the crowd at the nearest platform, ducking his head, squeezing through holes, coming up, finally, under the bookie's nose, grimly triumphant. A dozen gamblers had their money stretched out and called off their numbers and their choices. The bookmaker pleaded with them. He could handle only one at a time but they insisted and kept on calling off their horses. Karty grabbed the rail and pushed himself high on the platform, inches in front of the bookmaker.

"A hundred on Gillie," he panted. "To win."

The man with the thick roll of bills in his hand stopped his cries to the mob and looked at him. His mouth drooled saliva like a baby's. "Hey, George," he said to the man with the slate, "this guy wants a hundred on Gillie to win. O.K.?"

"A hundred?" He looked at Gillie's price on the slate. "Sure. Sure. What are you wasting time for? Take his number."

The man with the bills called off to the clerk behind him with the large pad. "Twelve hundred to a hundred on Gillie." Karty held his ticket up to the lawyer's eyes.

"Look at him," said the slate man, now beginning to worry when he heard the twelve hundred dollars he would have to pay out if the horse won. "Repeat his number and take a good look at him."

Karty waited impatiently. "O.K.," said the one with the bills. Karty struggled to get out but the pressure from the mob grew intensified. Hearing the fuss over Gillie, most of the gamblers made a last minute switch to the horse. They knew, too, that the price would soon drop before their onslaught and each one grew panicky at the thought of missing a good thing. "No more twelve to one!" cried the man at the slate, worry making his voice unpleasant to hear. "Don't take no more bets." He rubbed out the figure with the chamois and lowered the price to ten to one. A deep sigh of sorrow swept out from the men massed about him.

Karty finally managed to reach the lawn. He looked across to the barrier at the far end of the field. The horses were just then deliberately moving into their stall positions. After all his rush he wept with impatience at their slowness. He might have shopped around for better prices. Twelve hundred to a hundred, he thought as he walked back to the stands. If Gillie came home he would have the thirteen hundred that he needed. A coincidence! A hunch! It couldn't fail or else what accounting could there be for the queer coincidence? Karty was flushed with his luck as he sat down next to Arthur. He clapped the dishwasher on the back. "Cheer up," he called to him gaily. "Don't be a Jonah! You'll queer my luck."

"Let's go home, Mr. Karty," wept Arthur, sunk in aching despondency. "I want to take the train."

"Nuts," Karty said. "After this race we'll go, and not a minute sooner." He stood up on the bench waiting for the alignment of the horses. Karty picked out Gillie by the pink shirt with the black stripes worn by the jockey. "Come on, Cooch," he prayed. The black horse was shuffling in and out of his stall. An assistant starter was tugging at his bridle to keep him quiet, and as the horse fretted, Karty fretted. But Arthur sat hunched up over his knees on the bench, his face held sadly to the side, one hand resting his chin, the other on the top of his head. He saw nothing of the horses or of the hopping crowd.

The horses burst out of the stall gates and went flying down the backstretch in a bunch. Karty yelled for Cooch to come on at the top of his lungs. At the first turn the horses had already strung out in a line. The favorite led by two lengths, the second horse was a length before the third and the others lined out behind. Gillie was in sixth place, five or six lengths behind the leader. A whoosh of surprise went up from the crowd at the unusual runaway so early in the race. Karty turned to the man beside him and said fervently, "They'll all bunch up when they hit the home stretch. They'll come together." The spectator barely heard him. "Holy smoke," he was saying, "Holy smoke. Never saw anything like it." The horses were galloping around the wide bend now and as they approached the home stretch it seemed to Karty that they were beginning to bunch up. A rush of gladness went through him with the hope. "They're closing up!" he yelled to the man. "They're bunching up! Come on, Cooch!" The man shook his head regretfully. "It's only the way it looks from here," he said. "It's the angle." And he spoke the truth, for as the horses came down the stretch, Karty could see that they were still running in the same order, lengths apart from each other. Coucci raised the whip and Karty could see the horse charge. It was too late. Karty knew the horse would never catch the leader or make up any considerable ground. The sight blurring before him as the tears rose, Karty watched the finish, the horses still spread out. Gillie was in sixth place. The gambler sat down brokenly and cried.

The crowds now poured through the narrow doors that led underneath the stands to the railroad platform, and as they went they dropped racing programs, cigar butts, tip sheets and newspapers. Karty sat and sobbed. "Come," said Arthur. "We'll miss the train." As he watched the people leave, he wanted impulsively to hurry out with them, as though he might be left alone on the racetrack. His anxiety would have driven him to leave Karty and go home alone but the gambler had the train tickets.

"Mr. Karty, come," he begged. "The train will go without us." But Karty listened to him hopelessly. He might as well stay where he was. Where could he go? Why should he go back to Neptune Beach? There his wife's brothers would find him and beat him up. In time, however, he yielded to Arthur and they followed the stragglers to the train over the paper-strewn walks.

Inside the car Arthur watched the gloomy faces of the gamblers. It was hard to tell from their expressions whether they had won or lost, for they all looked disgruntled and absorbed in their private affairs. Some of the men worked, scowling over their notebooks, recording the day's play and the characteristics of horses they were interested in, storing this information for wiser betting in the future. Others went over their money, their fingers moving in their pockets and their lips silently calling off the count. All looked tired with the glaze of dried perspiration and dust on their faces. They gazed out of the windows and unhappily switched the cigars in their mouths from corner to corner.

Arthur felt oppressed and scared. As the Long Island train continued its desultory trip back to the Atlantic Avenue station, the fear mounted. By this time Spitzbergen had probably discovered the shortage. By this time there might even be policemen waiting for him at Ann's or at his boarding house. Arthur was afraid to go home. What would they do to him now?

"Mr. Karty," he said, "when are you going to get the money tonight? I want to put the twenty dollars back in the register and get finished with the whole business. I'm sick of it. I'm sick and tired."

"You son of a bitch, what the hell do you want from me?" Karty snapped, his weasel face glaring with hatred. "Spitzbergen's got enough dough. It won't kill him if we don't hurry up with the lousy twenty bucks."

"Oh, Mr. Karty!" Arthur cried. "You promised we'd put the money back!"

"Aw, nuts!" Karty leaned back in the dirty red plush seat and closed his eyes. Spitzbergen had plenty of money. Shubunka always ladled it out to him like beans from a pot. Hadn't he himself seen him give the soda man a pack of tens yesterday? Hadn't he heard the fat man say he'd give him more money tonight? It wasn't fair! The miser had all the money in the world while Karty had to tremble with fear because he needed a few hundred dollars. "Listen, Arthur," the gambler said, his voice suddenly turning friendly, "I lost my temper. But we'll have the money. Plenty of it. Tonight. Don't you worry. Just stick around and you'll see. I always keep my promises."

Arthur caught himself in the midst of his new fears and looked questioningly at Karty. Did he really mean it? Would they put back the money tonight? Would he be able to drive the whole rotten business from his mind at last? The dishwasher looked at the dreary streets of Queens through the dirty train window and hoped that Karty would keep his word. Free as a bird, that was his ambition.

Karty's red eyes grew intense as he formed his plans. He took time from his absorption, however, and sobbed. If he had only followed his first intention and stayed away from Gillie! He would have had enough money now to lose all his troubles. A hundred in his pocket, but he hadn't been satisfied. Cursing his luck and weeping, he pulled himself away from his grief to think of the night. Spitzbergen had enough money for the world. He was a dirty, bellyaching miser. People like him didn't deserve to have money when they didn't know how to use it. Money wasn't made to be put away in a bank.

"Don't worry, Arthur," the gambler said through his tears. "We'll have money enough tonight. We'll grab a bite, take in a movie and then we'll have all the money we want. Just stick around and see if we don't."

It was past seven-thirty now. Mr. Spitzbergen at Ann's looked at the clock over the arch, checked the time with his watch, and grew more worried by the minute. "Where is the girl?" he asked. "Why is she so late?" Shorty's relief man, even-tempered, self-satisfied and calm, returned the boss's stare with perfect control of mind. "Snotnose," said Spitzbergen, angered. "What's the matter I can't ask questions in my own store?" The relief jerker dispassionately turned his back and polished the shiny water boilers. The soda parlor was empty. Not a soul in the place, moaned the boss to himself. Cold weather, no crowds, no business, only troubles, troubles on all sides. Lillian had surely taken the twenty dollars or else why was she so late? A man could stand no more. "I'm a wreck," he said to the walls. "I'm a nervous wreck. Go, call an ambulance and let them take me away." The jerker crossed his arms over his chest and looked out to the street, free in mind. The telephone rang. "If it's for me," screamed Mr. Spitzbergen, "tell them I just dropped dead! I give up."

It was Mrs. Spitzbergen. "She says for you to come home early tonight," he relayed to the boss. "She says she wants to have a little party tonight."

"Parties! Yes, yes, parties. That's all I need now," he muttered, but the sourness left his expression. "Give me the telephone." The relief man climbed out of the booth and the boss took the receiver. His wife told him she would like to have supper with him for once. "After all, Louie," she said tenderly, "I never see you. I can't tear you away from the business. It's years since I ate a meal with you."

"What's the matter, a party all of a sudden?" he asked, fearing new troubles.

"It's nothing the matter. It ain't no party, only like you say. Just you and me. We'll have supper for once together in our lives."

The suspicion left his voice. "Anna, Anna," he moaned. "I got such aggravations. First Shubunka and the rent for the apartments, then the machine, and now a new cashier, she went and took twenty dollars from the register. Twenty dollars. Like you tear up a piece of paper and throw it down the sewer."

"Don't take it to heart," his wife said. "You'll find the money. You'll get it back. People can't steal like that. But even if it's lost, it ain't worth the worry. What can you do?"

And Spitzbergen poured out the full burden of his grief to her. His wife clucked sympathetically, telling him that he worked too hard, that he worried too much, and that life was too short for all the heartache he went through. As she soothed him, his voice grew softer. "Yes, yes, Anna," he moaned. "It's true what you say. But what can I do with myself? It's my nature to be aggravated. I can't help it."

"So come home early, Louie. We'll have a bite together."

"Maybe yes, maybe no. The store. All day it's been quiet like a cemetery. I got to take care of the business after the movies. And the thieves, too. I got to stand and watch, otherwise they'll take the whole store away. But maybe by eleven."

"Eleven is too late. Who eats supper eleven o'clock? Come nine, half past."

"All right, Anna. I'll be home ten o'clock. A little earlier if I live and be well."

He hung up, feeling comforted, but the moment he stepped from the booth into the yellow glare of the soda parlor, it was as though he had left one world and had gone into another. Here he could no longer beg for sympathy and cry. He was a man of property, of capital, and it was his stern duty to protect his wealth. He looked up at the clock again. "Where is Lillian?" he asked. "Why don't she come in?" The soda jerker, arms folded, bounced on the balls of his feet up the slats of the floor out of the boss's range, not one to be affronted needlessly. The boss stared at him, muttering venomously.

Lillian stepped in twenty minutes before eight, with the virtuous air of one who does not watch the clock, of one who intends to give full service. Spitzbergen was on top of her at once.

"Give back the twenty dollars or I'll call a policeman!"

She stared at him, wonder and fright mixed in her eyes. "What did I do? What do you want from me?" she asked breathlessly.

"She don't know! That's a hot one! She knows nothing about it!" Mr. Spitzbergen's perspired face lined with his many burdens, broke into ugly laughter, ugly, for while the appropriate sounds came, his face retained its mournful, angry expression. "You took twenty dollars from the cash register. Don't make believe you don't know anything about it. It wouldn't help you. That's why you came in an hour late, because you took the money and you know it."

"Mr. Spitzbergen, on my word of honor!" the girl wailed. "Believe me to God, I didn't take it. Shorty told me to come in eight o'clock. It's not even a quarter to yet. I didn't take no money, I should drop dead right on the spot."

"Shorty told you eight o'clock?" The soda man paused, impressed. As he thought about it, the soda jerker's behavior had been sort of suspicious this afternoon when he learned about the shortage. And why hadn't he come in for supper tonight? But the bald-headed jerker had been at Ann's over a year now. Why should he suddenly want to take money from the box? It didn't make sense. Nothing made sense, Spitzbergen told himself impatiently. He returned to the girl. "Go to work," he said. "I got other troubles on my head. You ain't got a monopoly on me. My head feels like it's a machine shop. Go to work, but remember one thing, please. If the money ain't back in the register before we close the store tonight, somebody will not sleep in their bed tonight. They'll be in jail."

Lillian was sobbing, her cheeks wet with many tears, the mascara on her eyes running in streaks down her face.

"Mr. Spitzbergen, I didn't take the money," she said. "It's not in me to do such a thing. I'm insulted. I'm not a thief."

"For God's sakes!" screamed the boss. "Don't cry!" He went to the cellar door. The crowd would be coming in and he had to help the relief jerker behind the counter. "Somebody steals twenty dollars from me, so she cries! Fine! It makes me feel fine. All I want is somebody to cry over me." He removed his coat and put on the apron, tying the strings around his wide belly. "Believe me," he bewailed himself to the walls, "sometimes I want to close up the store, throw away the keys, and run away. Believe me, sometimes I want to throw away every penny I got. Free and finished. No more responsibility on my mind. Nothing to aggravate me. I'm a nervous wreck. A poor man is always happy and in good health. What good does my real estate do me? What good is my store? I work like a horse. My reward is a bundle of worries on my head."

He took his place behind the fountain, his hands on his hips, gazing with concern at the door, waiting for the evening rush to begin. The weather was rotten. The season started badly, it would continue bad, it would end bad. God was no longer over America. Twenty dollars were missing and it was as though you threw them out into the ocean. Spitzbergen knew he would never see them again. The gangsters were pulling pieces out of him. And with Shubunka, he would get into trouble both ways. If the fat man didn't appear, the soda man would lose his rent money. If he did come in tonight, there were gangsters all over, they would see him, and the place would be wrecked. Standing on the boards, Spitzbergen took to shaking his head violently, keeping from outright wails only because of a sense of propriety. "No," he cried, "no, I won't get rich in this business in a hurry."

"What?" asked the relief man politely. "You speaking to me?"

"What what?" the boss asked. "What do you want from me, too? I ain't got enough. Find something, please, and bring your share also. Everybody's got a right." The relief conscientiously wiped the marble counter. "So put on the radio. Make music," the boss grumbled.

The soda jerker switched on every light in the parlor. The room became flooded with the garish lights from the red, green, and yellow fixtures. The glare was reflected by the similarly colored walls and by the Chromo Art-Metal tabletops with their futuristic designs. The relief turned on the radio to its full volume. The metallic tunes of a jazz band poured over the store. When the time came for the chorus, the singer screamed in the tones of a giant. Spitzbergen's ears cracked with the racket, his eyes were dazzled by the lights, but that was what his customers wanted at night, romance, bright colors, and music. It was business and he supplied the radio and the lights without a murmur, even though the electric bills were enormous.

Lillian dried her tears and regained her composure as she sensed that the boss's suspicions of her had lessened. She hated Ann's. Rotten people, always bothering her, getting fresh, and now, out of a perfectly blue sky, they told her she had stolen twenty dollars. A terrible place, she thought. She would get out of it as soon as she could find another job. She gazed carefully at the relief soda jerker. Would he try any tricks on her? But be looked too fishy and stuck-up to start anything.

The movies still held most of the people who came to Ann's but couples were already trickling into the store, chiefly boys and girls, these, sixteen and seventeen years old. They came in in pairs, sunburned and tanned from days spent on the beach. Their hair was slicked, they wore white shoes and dressed in sporty clothes. The couples sat cozily over the tables in the alcoves, shouting and shrieking to one another above the radio. They began mock fights, ended them abruptly, delivered their particular lines of talk to their boy and girl friends, and took good care not to spot their clothes. They were, for the most part, the children of boarders who came to Neptune for the season, and they wanted a good time. "Oh, you nasty man!" a boy screamed in falsetto tones and was rewarded by a roar from his friends. He flapped his hands and sat down, elated with his success. "Margy, Margy, you're terrible!" a girl cried out, swinging her bag playfully. "Don't you tell them another word. I hope you understand what I mean!" "Come on, Margy," the boys nagged, fiddling around. "Don't listen to her, she's just nuts with the heat anyhow." "I'll slay you! I'll walk out and leave you flat! I'm disgusted with your antics entirely!" the girl yelled shrilly. "So-o-o-o-o-o," clucked a boy, imitating Ed Wynn. The parlor roared. Another fellow rose up before him. "Wanna buy a duck? Wanna buy a duck?" he quacked. "You're not petite, you're not so neat," bellowed the singer on the radio. "There's nothing so sweet about you." But in spite of the singer's giant voice, no one in Ann's heard him. They were engrossed in their own affairs and they couldn't be disturbed.

Lillian ran up and down the aisles, taking orders and delivering them. At the fountain the relief and Spitzbergen were rapidly manufacturing the concoctions the young people called for: waffles in syrup, Romeos, Neptune Delicious, Ann's Specials, caramel nut sundaes, Devil's Temptations, Parisian Fruit Frappés, Broadway Heavens, Hollywood Pot-Pourris and the Hot-Cha-Marajahs. Whipped cream, fruit syrups, nuts, bananas and pineapple cubes, marshmallow, chocolate sprinkles, and cherries—they plastered them on the balls of ice cream in the odd-shaped metal containers and the customers loved them. Spitzbergen wiped the sweat off his forehead with his arm. He was working hard and he frowned, but the night would be good to him if it continued as well as it had started. If only Shubunka wouldn't bring in the rent money himself and attract the thugs. Even when you finally made a nickel, moaned the soda man, you had to sweat and shiver for it. Shorty's relief man worked on, unruffled by the rush, his face absorbed in his duties and showing his competence. Even though there was no dishwasher to help this evening and he had to do the work of two men, nothing upset him, never a muscle quivered with resentment, never a flicker of his eyes.

As the evening rush heightened, two men walked in, the sniffler and his friend, Amchy. They sat on stools near the door. Spitzbergen, looking up from the tray of gay concoctions, recognized them immediately. He almost knocked the relief man down as he brushed by him in the narrow aisle.

"Please," he begged, "what do you want now? It's my only time for a little business. Don't come in now."

"Pip, pip," said the sniffler cheerily. "Look at him all excited. Mr. Spitzbergen, we're your friend. We mean only good for you."

"So what do you want, you're my friend? You're my friend, so go away in peace. Let me make a penny. It's coming to me, ain't it?"

"The list of houses. The list of joints. Jesus Christ, what's he all in an uproar about?" The sniffler seemed offended at the lack of social courtesy.

Spitzbergen ran down the fountain to his coat pocket behind the cellar door. He had worked on the list all day, careful not to make a mistake, careful to have it complete, because he knew there would be a fine of two hundred dollars and he knew these thugs would seize on every pretext to squeeze money out of him. The sniffler looked into the parlor and was mightily impressed by the racket, the lights, and the number of customers. He rubbed his chin thoughtfully and told his partner this was a nice dump.

"I bet you could make a nice nickel with a dump like this, ain't it?" Amchy said.

"A good business," the sniffler pronounced. "With a location like this in Neptune Beach a man could make a fortune."

They both looked solemn and Spitzbergen, holding out to them the paper with the addresses, quaked in his shoes. The lines on his face deepened with apprehension, "Here, take it and go," he begged. "Here's the houses. Take it."

"A nice joint," the sniffler said. "You should be making a good living, Mr. Spitzbergen."

"You don't know from it!" the boss exclaimed. "My worst enemies shouldn't have the aggravations I got. Troubles, troubles, always troubles. I am lucky to make expenses."

"See," said Amchy. "What you need is a little protection, maybe. You got good protection, you don't have so much trouble." His eyebrows lifted slyly. Mr. Spitzbergen paled.

"No!" he screamed above the bedlam in the store. "No protection money. I don't have to pay you money. I won't do it. I'll close up the store and go on relief first."

"O.K, O.K.!" called the sniffler, offended. "Just take a look at him bust. Somebody would think God knows what happened. We don't mean you harm. We want only for your good." He glanced nastily at the soda man and grabbed the list from his hands. "If you're holding out on us, remember there's a two-hundred-dollar fine. You'll have to pay it same as everybody else, there's no exceptions."

Spitzbergen watched them suspiciously but his fears were relieved. They were just making fun with him. They got him worried just because it suited their taste. "Listen, boys," he said beseechingly, "I don't mean nothing by it. It's just my nature. Worries on my head all the time. I'll go crazy, it's only a question of time. Look at the day I had today. A man can't stand no more. Take the list, please. I'll do whatever you want. Only go away. This is a place of business. I'm a man with responsibilities. I got to make a living."

The man sniffled with absorption. Studying the list, he wasn't listening to the boss. As for Amchy, his gaze had fallen upon Lillian and he speculated dreamily on the possibilities. "A swell piece," he confided respectfully to Spitzbergen. "You got a nice-looking number over there."

"Hah?" His furrowed brow glistened with perspiration. Shubunka might be walking in any minute now and then the place would be smashed in the slaughter. Spitzbergen trembled for his eighteen thousand dollars and begged the men to leave. "Listen, boys, all I want from you is you should go away. Please."

"Hospitality! That's what I call real hospitality!" the sniffler cried. "A fine way of talking to people. What's the matter we can't hang around? We ain't good enough for this dump?" He looked at Amchy in the midst of his indignation and smiled with the fun. They knew, and relished the thought of it, that Spitzbergen well understood why they were waiting. It delighted them to see his pretended ignorance of their motive and they played his game with real enjoyment. Shubunka was coming in. Spitzbergen had told their boys the news himself, and they had to wait for him. The soda man read their smiles and realized their intention. His brows contracted and he mopped the ice-cream covers with tearful helplessness. He couldn't do a thing to help himself. In the meantime, Shorty's relief, for all his competence, was far behind with the orders. Fretfully Spitzbergen left the men to help him.

"A nice piece," said Amchy dreamily, referring to Lillian.

"Listen," said the sniffler, "this guy Shubunka sounds like a coke to me. It'll be trouble in that direction. You'll see. He don't look like the kind to take a hint."

"So it'll be too goddammed bad for him," his companion said distractedly. "I ain't going to worry about him. We got to make an example of him or else there'll be trouble all over town."

"Well," he said, sniffling and sighing as he closed the subject, "it's a job for Bull and Two-Bits outside tonight. They'll tail him until ten o'clock and after that, like you say, it'll just be too goddammed bad. That's all. See, those mugs, they like it, you could almost say. But take me. I got no use personally for guns and shooting. Rough stuff. It's out of date, behind the times. I like organization and smart handling. Businesslike, see? What the hell, if you can't operate like any ordinary business, you never last long."

"Hey, this joint certainly coins the dough. Just look at the people in the back. Fifteen, twenty cents a head. Not so bad."

"Don't believe everything you see. They sit around all night over a fifteen-cent check. Not so hot, if you ask me," the sniffler commented wisely.

"Well, it ain't bad. We might shake this guy Spitzbergen down for something, you and me."

"Aaah, I ain't got the time or the inclination. Leave me alone."

"No, just you and me, see? On the side."

"Nuts. I ain't got no use for it." He swiveled on the stool and looked at the door. There was no Shubunka, but outside across the street, he could discern the prizefighter and his dapper friend, stepping on cigarette butts as they waited for the fat man to appear. Amchy had grown bored with the subject of protection for Spitzbergen and was distantly watching the movements of the waitress. But Spitzbergen, working with the relief man, was all on edge. This morning they had broken the ice-cream machine and soon they'd wreck the place altogether. He fervently prayed that Shubunka would not appear tonight, ever though this meant the loss to him of some two hundred dollars in rent. He was willing to forgo it. Money was no object. In his profound anxiety Spitzbergen had to laugh ironically to himself. Just tonight his wife wanted to have a party. Yes, yes, parties, he wept to himself. There was no enjoyment possible for him in this world.

Back in the parlor the screams of the boys and girls grew louder as they upset water glasses and ducked out of range to avoid spotting their clothes. "Cut it out, Norbert!" a voice screamed angrily above the uproar. "You think it's a joke?" "I'm in Heaven!" shrieked the soloist on the radio. "I'm in Heaven and my heart beats so that I can hardly speak, when we're out together dancing cheek to cheek." Spitzbergen and the thugs and the two across the street waited for the appearance of Shubunka.

A little before nine the fat man waddled into Ann's. He wore no hat and the wind had pushed his hair, stiff with the Polymol, into odd slants over his head. His fleshy face was intent with pain and he moved on his bent legs as one who is numb, not seeing, not hearing, not understanding. Spitzbergen, working near the double-decked water tray, shivered at his entrance so that the shiny ice-cream cup fell out of his hand. His eyelids closed with fear. He wanted to yell out, to implore the fat man to leave immediately, but it was as though he were paralyzed. At any moment he expected to hear gunfire, the sounds of panic in the parlor, the noises of mirrors and glass being shattered. Spitzbergen couldn't endure the suspense. In an uncontrollable spasm he opened the cellar door and hurried down the steps. The relief man looked at him with gentle wonder.

"What did I tell you, Amchy?" said the sniffler, his voice thin with amazement at the sight of Shubunka. "That guy's a coke or something. He don't look normal. Hey, you!" he called to the fat man. "Hey, Shubunka, you must be insane!"

The fat man went up to him, his face sad and blank. "Why do you say that?" he asked. "What is the matter?"

"You're nuts! You got a nerve! You only got till ten o'clock to get out of town and here it's almost nine!"

Shubunka stared at the two. "Listen, gentlemen," he said, speaking slowly, "you cannot ruin me like this. It isn't right. It is not human. Why do you do this to me? What harm did I do you?"

"You better beat it out of town," said Amchy, his voice going sing-song with determination. "There'll be guys tailing you every minute until you scram. It's orders. Be smart. Don't act like a dope charged up all the time."

"Listen, gentlemen, take pity on me. I worked eight years. It is not fair to ruin a man like this."

"You're a no-good rat," the sniffler said. "I ain't wasting pity on a slob like you. We're doing you a favor by talking to you in the first place. Beat it. We don't want you in New York."

"Let me keep the houses," Shubunka begged. "You got houses plenty enough. It won't kill you if I keep a few. Let me have something. I'll pay. I'll give in a hundred dollars every week. I'll pay you commissions. I'll give you a hundred and fifty dollars a week. Only let me keep the houses."

"The boss said nothing doing. Don't stall. There's guys waiting for you. Make up your mind in a hurry to scram or else it will be too late," the sniffler said. They rose from their stools, standing before him so that the three blocked the door. The tight-lipped relief man took a moment from his work to inspect them but there was no reaction on that face. He never said a word or batted an eyelash even though the youngsters leaving and entering had to worm their way through the three men, looking resentful.

"You need collectors," whined Shubunka in his shrill voice. "You need helpers. Give me a job then. Let me work for you. Let me talk to the boss. Take me to him or give me a telephone number. I know the business inside and out. I am a good man for the trade."

"Collectors get thirty-five, forty dollars a week. It's no job, but it's O.K. with me. The boss, but, he don't want nothing of the kind. You're too high-hat for the job. Sooner or later you'd make trouble." The sniffler argued reasonably. "We can't help it. That's the way it is. You have to leave town or else we got to take care of you. Be smart. Listen, Shubunka, I'll do you a favor. It's getting late. I got a car outside. We'll ride you out of town before it's too late."

"Nothing doing," said Shubunka hopelessly. "I will not go."

"It's all right!" he insisted. "We ain't going to dump you on the road. Don't be afraid of that."

"I am not afraid," moaned the fat man. "I will not go. You can kill me. You can shoot me. I cannot leave. Eight years I worked up a business. It isn't fair. You cannot do it to me."

Amchy shook his head and muttered with impatient irritation. "Jesus Christ," he said. "What the hell do you call that now?"

"This guy's a coke, all right," the other said, exasperated. "He's a goner. We're wasting time here. We can't do nothing with him. He's hopeless. Listen, you no-good rat, I'm talking to you for the last time. It's after nine o'clock. There'll be guys waiting for you all the time. They'll kick your fat belly off. They'll fill you full of holes. They'll slug your fat head in. Beat it! For Christ's sakes! I don't like to see a guy slaughtered when it might be avoided. Take a train. Catch a bus. Anything, only get out of New York. It's suicide!" He looked at Shubunka, his expression pained. "Jesus Christ," he muttered to Amchy, "that guy don't even hear me. The dumb slob should be in an asylum."

They walked out of Ann's, angry and puzzled. Shubunka stood at the fountain in a haze. The radio blared the jazz music. Inside, the parlor was roaring with the laughing, quarreling racket of the boys and girls. "Let them kill me," moaned the fat man to himself. "Let them murder me. I don't care. It makes no difference to me what happens. I won't leave." With his hair twisted on his head and standing out stiffly at ends, he was motionless in his pity, his face in rapt despair.

Spitzbergen finally stuck his head out of the cellar door. He sighed heavily with relief when he discovered the racket going on peacefully in the store.

"Mr. Spitzbergen," the relief man said impassively, "I need a hand here. I can't catch up with the orders."

"Don't bodder me!" growled the boss. He saw Shubunka standing at the door and went up the slats to him, looking into the street as he moved, still worried over the gunmen. The relief's nose twitched slightly with anger but he went back to work methodically. Lillian had to repeat the orders again and again, making mistakes. The heckling from the insistent youngsters upset her until she trembled nervously with each step. "Hurry up, please," she cried. "They're waiting an hour already." "Take it easy, sister," said the relief ponderously. "I'm only human. They can wait." "My heavens," she wept. "My heavens." It was her first night.

"I don't like to say it, Shubunka," said Spitzbergen warily, his eyes on the door, "but please. You're blocking the door. Please go away. I can't have no disturbance here. I got to make a living. You can understand how it is."

Shubunka stared at him with baleful eyes. "He sees a man going to the electric chair," he murmured, "what worries him is the door is blocked. A human being lies in misery and he is afraid he will lose some business."

"Mr. Shubunka!" pleaded the boss. He was hurt. "Don't talk like that! What good can I do? How can I help? I'm a man under a knife myself! All the time! Please. Go already."

But Shubunka did not hear him. He was lost deep in melancholy reflection. "Where's Moe Karty?" he suddenly cried in his high voice. "Where is he? He's in trouble and I can do something for him."

"What's the matter Moe Karty all of a sudden?" asked the boss, mystified.

"Where is Mr. Karty? I must see him. I must talk to him."

"What the hell do you call this?" Spitzbergen asked, overcome. "I ain't got Moe Karty. I didn't see him since the morning."

At this, sharp pain pierced the fat man's face. He looked away from the soda man and muttered to himself, remorseful and repentant. He remembered how urgently the gambler had begged him for a few dollars this morning. He remembered the terrible panic in his sharp screwed-up face. "I could help him," Shubunka whispered bitterly. "I could do something for him and I would not lift a finger. Good for me. Now it serves me right. My troubles come to me and I cannot go to anybody."

"Mr. Shubunka, what's the use talking Moe Karty and standing here?" the soda man reasoned, glancing rapidly at the street. "What good does it do you? Be smart, Shubunka. Use your head. Go away. I don't want to see anything bad happen to you. It would hurt me, believe me, I would feel miserable if those gangsters lay their hands on you."

"No," wept the fat man, stumbling to the street. "I will not go away. It is not right. Let them do what they want with me. I don't care. I don't care what happens now." Spitzbergen rushed up around the counter and touched him on the shoulder. His face creased apologetically.

"Mr. Shubunka," he said, "I hate to ask you under the circumstances, but you promised. The rent." The fat man looked as though he hadn't heard. "The rent," repeated Spitzbergen anxiously. "For the apartments."

Shubunka shook his head in sorrowful acknowledgment. It was a rotten world. "See," he muttered, "a man goes to the electric chair and another human being watches him and it bothers him only what touches himself. Don't worry, Mr. Spitzbergen. You'll get the rent. Somebody will bring it to you whether I'm still in this world or not."

"Who?" asked Spitzbergen, his face going black with grief. "Who will bring it to me?"

But Shubunka was going down the street, without answering, engrossed in himself, and the soda man feared to follow him further. He went back to the store, a broken man. By this time the first shows were over at the movie houses and the store was growing packed. The youngsters had left for the most part, their places taken by older couples, solemn-faced, yawning, sleepy after the pictures. These ordered ice-cream sodas, malted milks, and dishes of ice cream, and they looked resentfully at the outcries of the boys and girls who remained. After nine the customers at Ann's preferred quiet, for drowsiness and romance. The relief, taking time from his work, switched off the ceiling and wall lights so that the parlor was softly lit by the electrical fixtures on the Chromo Art-Metal partition and by the little lamps on the tables in the alcoves. The shiny table surfaces reflected the red, green, and yellow lights upon the customers so that their sleepy faces looked sick and distorted. The blare of the radio was turned down to a whisper. Almost every seat in the parlor was taken and many sat on the stools. Spitzbergen surveyed the scene but was not satisfied, the scowl heavy on him. That was settled once and for all. The rent money was gone. He would never see it. The soda man wiped the sweat with his arm and went back to work.

Soon after, Mrs. Karty came into the store, still looking for her husband. Circles of black dirt lined her neck, her straight hair was pushed untidily over her head and she still wore the black sleeveless dress. In spite of her bulk she seemed thoroughly exhausted.

Mr. Spitzbergen would waste little time on her. He told her brusquely that he hadn't seen Karty since the morning. "Please, don't stay here, Mrs. Karty. I got enough troubles myself. Believe me. We got to do a business here."

"Where is he?" she whimpered, cracking her knuckles. "Why don't he come home? They're looking for him already. My brothers, they're riding in a car for him and when they find him they'll cripple him. Please, Mr. Spitzbergen, help me find him."

"What does she want from me?" the soda man wailed to the walls. "Mrs. Karty, I don't know nothing about the whole business. I got my own troubles. I don't keep Moe Karty in my pocket. I don't know where he is. Please, go away!"

But Mrs. Karty sat down on a stool, resting her head in her hand. She muttered and wept to herself in a steady monotone. Her husband had been away for two days now. He hadn't had a warm meal in his mouth. He was skinny and sickly and nervous. He had no strength and would break down altogether. And now her brothers were riding through the streets of Neptune Beach looking for him! Mrs. Karty broke into sobs. Lillian, registering the cash, took pity on her and went for a glass of water, but Mr. Spitzbergen grew more and more irritated by the disturbance the gambler's wife was creating in the store. It wasn't good for business.

"Please!" he begged. "I can't help you here. Please go away! I got to make a living."

Mrs. Karty stirred sadly and went to the door. It was hopeless and she had to resign herself. She would never find her husband in time. Her brothers would break his bones.

Lillian came up with the glass of water to find her gone. Spitzbergen glared at her. "What do you want, too?" he howled. "I pay you money you should bring water to all kinds women who come in the store? Don't be so generous. Please."

The new cashier stuttered before his wrath. "I only wanted—"

"Never mind! Never mind!" the boss shouted. "And don't think for a minute I forgot about the twenty dollars. You'll make good for the money before we close the store tonight or you'll go to jail. I'll call a policeman."

Lillian whimpered and cried, protesting her innocence. The telephone had been ringing for some time now. The relief man, going to answer it, shouted out to the boss it was his wife again. She wanted to remind him to come home early for the little party tonight. Spitzbergen laughed loudly. Yes, yes, parties! That was all he had on his mind. He went to the telephone to tell his wife he was sorry but he would be late tonight. In the dimness of the soda parlor a crooner sang with affectionate gentleness: "Love is everywhere. Its fragrance fills the air."

Outside, the two men no longer stood waiting across the street.

The glamorous blonde raised her saucer eyes and said in her tinkling voice: "Don't touch me. I'm not fit to be near decent people." She blew the cigarette smoke defiantly, a woman of the streets, down and out with her shabby fur piece, but yet proud. The handsome gentleman in the full-dress suit gazed at her, pity and regret in his expression, and he said: "You're coming to my home. I won't hear another word said. We're going." The waste of her loveliness appalled him, he couldn't stand it another minute, and besides, he knew already that he was destined to a passionate love with her. Over her objections he brought her to his home. A mansion in the country. They drive under the porte-cochère, there are eight servants, mystified by the appearance of the bedraggled woman but respectful, and the derelict of the streets is tossed plumb into the lap of luxury, soft cushions, chaise longue, silk bedclothes. Wistful expression: gratitude but still pride.

A pretty piece, said Shorty to himself unhappily, sitting in the Mermaid alongside of Madame Pavlovna. Where was all this getting him? He was already out a dollar fifty-five cents for the Chink's including the tip (twenty-five cents, for the benefit of the corsetière, tossed on the tablecloth with a casual flourish). Admission to the Mermaid came to seventy cents. Two twenty-five, a lot of money, but hell, said the soda jerker, that was him. Chicken feed. He didn't pinch nickels like some people he could mention by name. All the same, there had been little progress and it disgruntled him.

At the Lotus they had sat over their pineapple chop suey, dainty and refined in the soft light of the rose lampshade. All through supper Madame Pavlovna had told him the story of her early years with her husband, how they met, how they lived at the University in Moscow, their excursions into the country. A touching tale, full of longing and pathos, deep sighs, her voice going soft and tearful with the memory so that she spoke as though she were suffering from a severe nose cold. Shorty had listened with enthusiastic sympathy, his face glistening, the gold caps showing, in an effort to be sociable, but he had grown impatient. The talk was getting him nowhere in a hurry. When he had touched her knee under the table, it meant nothing with her mind on that trip with Stefan over the Black Sea and the pale moon making a ribbon on the waters. He had given up, hoping for better opportunities, and now at the movies he pressed his leg against hers, his eyes glued on the fascinating blonde, innocent of evil. Madame Pavlovna shifted uneasily in her absorption, as one stirs in a dream.

"Close," she murmured. "Stuffy. There isn't a breath of air, no, Shurtee?"

"Hot," said the soda jerker. "An excellent picture." He kept his leg pressed against her. She had read between the lines of the notes he had sent her and he would just like to see her try and pull something over on him tonight. Two dollars and twenty-five cents. Hell, a lot of money in any man's language, if he said so himself!

A thousand men and women of Neptune Beach sat in the leather-covered chairs of the Mermaid Theater, tired after the day's work, their faces glazed, their mouths opened with concern and absorption in the affairs of Joyce Darline, the glamorous blonde derelict. Joyce, it is discovered, has once been a sensational actress, the toast of New York (champagne glasses, grinning sleek old men in top hats, bubbles, bubbles as the recollection comes). But she has one fatal flaw. Everyone with whom she has become associated immediately encounters misfortunes: death, accidents, domestic troubles, financial ruin. Joyce has been shunned by producers and former friends (shoulders, guilty looks, shoulders) who fear her sinister influence. Down, down the scale she goes (penthouse to cheap boarding room); beauty changes to lined despair (bum sitting in bare joint, legs apart, looking miserably at her whiskey glass. Gulp! Haah!). She forgot her calamities in drink. "That's my story," she says, sighing insouciantly over her cigarette, a veritable picture of loveliness. "Now you can leave me like the others." But the handsome gentleman, wearing full dress day and night, bears a stern visage. "We'll see about that," he declares. "First we have to get you back in shape again, shan't we?" "I'm warning you," she says, affection peeping through her air of indifference. In spite of all degradation, in spite of her lowness, love plays its magic over her heart. "You'll be no exception. I'm a hard-luck piece to anyone who ever knew me."

A thousand people shifted their weight in their seats, stirred to their marrow by this depiction of human souls in action. Will the handsome gent get his? He is an architect, working on skyscrapers exclusively, at this very moment designing what is to be the masterpiece of his career. Will his efforts succeed in spite of the evil spell of Joyce Darline? And the blonde, what will happen to her? It was a problem. A woman in the row before Shorty scratched her head, perplexed but still refined: as she scratched, her little finger stuck out sharply at the proper angle. Across the aisle, however, a man had found the picture too much for him. He had had a heavy day at the shop and could find no energy for Joyce. His head was tilted back and he snored gently.

"A sveet face," murmured Madame Pavlovna. "Slight. A person could see right through her." The corsetière wore a light blue Chinese gown, going straight to her ankles with slits at the sides. It had a high collar, worn close to the throat, and was heavily embroidered with Oriental dragons. She was elegant tonight, careworn and sophisticated, dressed for the theater and a night out with her gentleman friend. "A nothing of a girl," she said.

"Well," whispered Shorty confidentially, "you know how it is. Hollywood movie stars always reducing, half the time they spend in hospitals. Too weak. It ain't natural and it ain't beautiful, see what I mean? Because only nature is beautiful. Take me, I don't know why, but I can't go for these skinny dames, I don't care if it's Myrna Loy or Bette Davis. I like them full and normal, a real woman." His little face was ardently turned close to hers.

"Oh, Shurtee!" gurgled the corsetière. "You're making fun of me again."

"Oh, no!" he protested, but a middle-aged gentleman in the row behind tapped him gravely on the shoulder.

"Please," he said in frigid indignation.

The soda jerker turned around to inspect him cautiously.

"Well, b'gee!" he cried, his tone low but majestic. "Where the hell do you get off telling me what to do? Hell, I paid my admission just as good as you or anybody else, see how I mean?"

"You don't have to get excited," said the man. "All I want is quiet. I can't hear a word that's going on."

A dozen spectators were now watching the argument with keen relish, and Madame Pavlovna, a lady, nudged Shorty. "Don't bother," she said. "It's a vaste of time to bother vith some people. It gets you no place."

Shorty turned forward again, feeling magnificent. "No," he said glaring, "that guy's got no call to talk to me. Hell, I don't take nothing from nobody and I don't care who it is." His anger cooled and he bent close to the corsetière's ear. "See," he said, "I don't care what a guy says to me when I'm alone. What the hell, don't you know? But when I'm with a lady I won't stand for insults, see what I mean? It humiliates the lady as much as me, and hell, I won't stand for it! That's me. Not," he added modestly, "not that I'm such a tough guy. Hell, I been licked often and again."

"Oh, Shurtee," Madame Pavlovna reprimanded him. "You are terrible."

"I can't help it," the jerker said. "I got a temper."

All this time the middle-aged man hadn't said a word, afraid to cause another commotion in the theater. Shorty returned his gaze to the gorgeous blonde, happy and proud, secretly conscious of his mastery over the gentleman in the row behind him. He had shown Madame Pavlovna what sort of guy he was. Looks were deceiving. Sometimes the strongest, toughest, gamest men were the smallest. Small size, big heart. What the hell, said Shorty to himself. He dropped his arm, as if absently, on the corsetière's heavy thigh. The satin didn't make a sound but his fingers felt rough on the fabric and he feared they might catch the threads. He sat tensely in his seat for the next few minutes.

But Madame Pavlovna didn't flinch a muscle. Shorty was overjoyed. His hand felt uncomfortably warm and it perspired abundantly but he kept it on the thigh, now moving the fingers a bit so that he could feel the thick folds of flesh beneath the satin. The corsetière followed the picture wholeheartedly. Joyce Darline, now restored to stunning loveliness, is rehearsing in a play that the handsome gentleman has bought for her and will produce. A slight shade of distress is now visible on his face, for his new skyscraper is going awry, he is losing money left and right, and the end is not in sight. "Drop it all. Send me away," begs Joyce. "You can see for yourself I spoke the truth. I am not fit for decent people." "No!" replies the hero. "I shall see this thing through no matter what the cost." He is resolute, but in that wonderful mansion, with its eight respectful servants and expensive furniture, he strides about, worried and preoccupied. He loves Joyce Darline but he faces ruin. A hopeless tangle. Shorty's fingers worked to the little roll of flesh at her knee. He pinched it fondly.

"Oh! Shur-tee!" gasped the corsetière, looking around at once to see if anyone had noticed them. "Really . . . I don't know what to say . . . I am surprised . . ." She drew herself away in her chair and seemed enormously insulted.

B'gee! Shorty, in his white gabardine suit with the fancy back, winced with disappointment. Was he going to have trouble with her after all? Was she going to put on a teasing act again? Hell, if she tried anything on him tonight, gentleman or no gentleman, he'd take a poke out of her, that was what he would do for a fact. He was all steamed up. It wasn't fair. After all, she understood what she was going into tonight and if she didn't have the inclination, she had no right to accept his offer.

"Who? What?" he asked, all innocence and sweetness, biding his time. "What's the matter?"

"You know, Shurtee. Don't make believe." She looked at him, gently rebuking.

"On the level, Mrs. Pavlovna," he perspired at her. "I ain't got the least idea of what's in your mind."

She patted his hand knowingly and carried it slowly into his own lap. "Oh, that?" he cried, amazed. "Well, b'gee, Mrs. Pavlovna, why didn't you say so? If that little thing annoys you, hell, it's O.K. with me." He shifted angrily over to his corner of the seat, away from her, stared hard at the screen, and gave the appearance of one who has been very unfairly misunderstood. The corsetière, watching him ruefully, began to grow remorseful. She had hurt his feelings again. He was so sensitive. Shorty, offended and pained, moved his lips silently, still gazing at the gorgeous blonde but quite clearly miles away, absorbed in his own thoughts: here he had gone out of his way to show the lonely widow a good time; here he had been stood up once; he had forgiven her, had taken her out for supper and a show, spent money like water, and the first move he made was purposely misunderstood and she got sore. B'gee! The corsetière could read his mind for herself.

"Shurtee," she whispered, smiling, "don't get angry with me. Only it's not nice, you know. In public. People all around."

"O.K.," the jerker muttered gravely. "O.K. Anything you want, it's O.K. with me."

"Shur-tee!" She stretched out in the darkness of the movie theater and held his hand. He made to remove it, still angry, but she kept it, pinching and squeezing his fingers until she restored him to good humor.

"See, Sophia," Shorty explained in an outburst of confidence. "I'm sensitive that way. I can't stand it when a woman thinks I'm trying to get fresh with her. You can understand what I mean."

The noise finally proved too much for the middle-aged man behind them. Afraid to remonstrate openly with Shorty, he now rose from his chair. Exploding in mild cries of indignation, he strode up the aisle for another seat. Shorty turned around and glared. "Why," he said, "I got a good mind to poke that geezer in the eye."

"Don't bother vith common people," the corsetière said. "It's a vaste of time." They returned to the picture. The handsome hero smokes his cigarette in bitter contemplation. He is a ruined man. The evil spell has worked again. His plans for the skyscraper have gone to smash. He has borrowed every cent on which he could lay his hands, for the production of Joyce Darline's play, and now she has disappeared, leaving him with the complete wreckage of his life. In a spasm of despair he flings his cigarette away. There is a knock on the door. Fixing his white bowtie, he goes to open it. It is Joyce Darline, the gorgeous blonde. She had just discovered the essential secret of her fatal flaw. "I have always lived for myself. I have been selfish, Gary," she says, her saucer eyes tearful but determined on restitution. "Only by living for others can I lose my fatal flaw."

His eyes brighten with delight, his arms open, she falls weeping on his stiff-shirted chest. "Oh, my darling. Oh, my darling," says the hero. He is happy, for he knows now that all will be well again. His eyes gaze over her wonderful hair into the distance, dreamy with plans and hopes: the play will now be a terrific hit, his skyscraper will now win him back his fortune and position as the leading architect in the world. They would be getting married soon, one or two babies, who knows? Shorty, once for all, dropped his hand on Madame Pavlovna's leg again. The picture would be soon over and he wanted to make sure of clear sailing tonight. His arm was rigid on the satin. The corsetière, sophisticated and careworn, looking like Marlene Dietrich, smiled softly at him, and with an expression of feminine mystery returned her gaze to the screen. B'gee! cried Shorty to himself. Now he certainly had her without a shadow of a doubt. Nevertheless he was prudent enough to keep his arm rigid, trying no tricks too early. But later, in her house with the lights off, o-lee-o-lay-dee, o-lee-o-lay-hee-dee, o-lee-o-lay-hee-dee-dee-di. Waves and waves poured over the little soda jerker, bathing in his warm drowsy dreams.

Joyce Darline is on the stage. A splendid audience, full-dress suits, ermine wraps, and perfect coiffures. "Can't you see, my dear Eric," she sighs, brushing her lovely blonde hair over her head in despair, "it is impossible, utterly, utterly impossible." Eric kisses her hand. Off in the wings stands the handsome gentleman, his eyes blurring with love and happiness. The curtain comes down. Wild applause. Bow, modest and shy. Trip, trip, trip. Off the stage she goes, into her lover's arms. A thousand people in the Mermaid Theater stared glumly at their embrace, relieved. A nice picture. Had a moral. They rubbed their eyes.

"Hell," said Shorty in Madame Pavlovna's ear, "what about a cocktail after the show?"

"Oh, Shur-tee!" giggled the corsetière, her continental manner succumbing. The soda jerker wiggled joyfully in his seat. And the night was still young.

Also in the audience at the Mermaid Theater were Moe Karty and Arthur. At other times the dishwasher took pleasure in the movies because his mind was then lulled to a sort of sleep so that for two hours in the darkness the vacant monotony of his uninteresting life became suspended and he lived adventurously with the actions of the hero and heroine on the screen. Now he moved restlessly on his seat, taking no part in the enjoyment of the gorgeous blonde as he tried to forget about the twenty dollars he had stolen from the cash register at Ann's. But he did not succeed. More than the money, what troubled him was the abrupt strangeness of the events and places he had experienced today. Different from his usual contented routine, the day oppressed him heavily with vague fears and uneasiness.

"Mr. Karty," he whispered. "Let's go outside already. I don't like the movies. Let's get the money and put it back like you promised. I'm worried."

The gambler touched his elbow reassuringly. "Don't worry, Arthur," he said, his voice beseeching, for he, too, was worrying and he wanted the warmth of company. "I'll be all right. Only I can't get the money right away. It's too early. We have to kill some time."

"Gee, I don't like it. I don't like the waiting. It's making me nervous, Mr. Karty."

"A little longer, Arthur. Just have patience and then I'll see my friend with the money he owes me. Just wait."

The gambler looked at the screen, his weasel face screwed up with the aching distress. From time to time he almost broke outright into tears, and at those moments he had to seize his face with his hands, twisting his mouth and his nose cruelly to keep back the sobs and wait for the spasm to pass. They would get him tonight, they would. When his wife's brothers made a threat, they were bastards enough to keep it, and for the lousy few dollars they would break his head open. Karty knew them well. Why, he kept on asking himself, why again and again, torturously, why had he decided to throw away his hundred dollars on Gillie in the sixth race? Why hadn't he followed Joe Wack's advice on Apogee at twenty to one? All his troubles would now be over.

The gambler sat in the movie house, envying the blank, unconcerned expressions of the other spectators. Why me? he cried. There were so many people in the world, why did all the misery have to fall on him? He looked at the people on the screen, well dressed, good-looking, living in comfort and contentment, in beautiful homes, with luxurious motorcars, among friends, happy-faced and smiling. The movie actors moved about serenely. They drank cocktails and smoked cigarettes, unburdened and casual. Why couldn't he be like them, he asked fervently? Why couldn't he be like everyone else in the world? Alone among the thousand spectators in the dark theater, Moe Karty covered his face with his hand and cried silently to himself.

The newsreel was now appearing on the screen. A man, who had won fifty thousand dollars on a sweepstakes ticket, was being asked for his reaction to the news, and he sat uncomfortably in his best suit while his wife beamed fondly from her place at his side. Fifty thousand bucks, wept Karty. Look at that. Other people had all sorts of good luck. Never him! Hoodooed for life. The lucky ticket-holder on the screen opened his eyes wide and told with reverence how he first caught the good news. "We was all playing pinochle, see, and I said to my friend, 'Mike, why don't you go to the radio and see what is?' So he went, so we played cards, calm just like any ordinary day, and so all of a sudden Mike, he comes running into the living room and he says, 'Gee whiz! Al! Golden Roubles win!' Everybody dropped the cards, they yelled and screamed, a whole commotion. And I was calm. No, I mean it, I took it like a glass of water."

A thousand people sat in the Mermaid, heard the details of the man's great good luck, and not a face changed its grave expression. A lummox, wept Karty. Look at him. An ignorant common laborer, no education, no nothing. Well off, too. He wins fifty thousand dollars! "Well," said the winner, looking up to his wife, "what have you got to say on this occasion, Lena?" Before the camera, her pudgy face broke into an awkward smile. "Well," she said, "all I can say is I feel like giving a scream." "O.K.," said her husband graciously. "Then give a scream. Two of them, if you want." "Well, all right." She looked foolish but screamed dutifully, once, twice.

"Come on," Karty said, unable to sit quietly any longer. "Let's get out of here."

"Are we going for the money, Mr. Karty?" Arthur asked eagerly. "Now?" He followed him up the aisle, waiting for his answer but the gambler said nothing. Once on the street, the dishwasher pulled him by the sleeve. "Mr. Karty," he begged. "Tell me, I want to know. Are we going for the money?"

"You'll see," he said. "You'll see." But it was too early, hardly ten o'clock, much too soon for his plans. The gambler wondered whether he would still have the courage when the time came. He was desperate.

Arthur's suspicions grew that he was lying about the friend who owed him money. He fretted nervously and kept on asking Karty where they were walking to and whether he really meant to replace the twenty dollars. "Pretty soon it'll be too late," he cried. "It'll be hard enough to put back the money in the cash register. Later Mr. Spitzbergen will catch me and then he'll holler at me and get sore. Mr. Karty, I'm worried. I'm scared."

"Aw, shaddap, Arthur. You give me a pain. Don't worry so much about Spitzbergen. He's got enough dough. He don't need your sympathy. I'll take care of everything, so don't nag me."

"Where you taking me? I don't know where we're going and I want to know."

Karty pulled his sleeve from the dishwasher's grasp. To stall for time, he had taken to the back streets of Neptune Beach. Arthur followed him, sick with impatience and uncertainty. As they walked, he could see the people in their underwear tops sitting on the stoops of their shabby stucco houses. The buildings here were chiefly two-family structures, with double porches, one for each floor. With the summer season the boarders came. A family of four or five individuals squeezed into the two rooms their landlord managed to scrape together from his own use. The two families then on each floor used a common kitchen and bathroom. Sixteen to twenty individuals they were, and during the evening hours when everybody was home they overflowed to the porches and the streets.

The mothers fanned themselves on the porches in their housedresses, talking energetically to one another of the misfortunes and disasters in their families—operations, deaths, business losses, and scandal. They drank soda water and affirmed to one another that they had made sacrifices to come to Neptune for the sake of their children. The sun and the seawater here built up their bodies and gave strength for the winter in the city. Their husbands virtuously looked up from the stoop steps in assent. They were tired after the day in the shop in the city and after the terrific jams of the subway crush on the Sea Beach, West End, or Brighton Beach expresses. They arrived home after six, were out on the streets at seven, and they were due back at their places by eight in the morning. They caught the night air almost grimly.

The colors of the stucco houses, brown and green and gray, had run with many rains and the buildings were splotched and ugly. The stucco itself had cracked into crazy streaks on the walls. In the little dirty area alongside of the stoop, set aside for a garden, a ring of clamshells surrounded the scraggy broken bush. The rooms were dark and empty but the radios had been turned on. A confusion of melodies, speeches, and wisecracks raucously poured out into the street so that no single program was distinguishable. But no one seemed to mind, for no one really listened to the music or the speakers. It was as though they needed the metallic racket of the radios to serve as a base on top of which they might shout out their own conversations.

The streets here, badly paved and narrow, were thronged with automobiles bumping to the boardwalk, to the Avenue or to the garish delights of the seashore amusements and shows. The autos drove through the streets, but the children, whom their mothers had brought to the seashore after many sacrifices, darted recklessly between them, playing their games. Like everyone else in Neptune Beach, they, too, were determined to have a good time, for that was why they had come.

As Arthur walked through the racket of the radios and the kids at their games, seeing the apathetic people out on the sidewalks, a heavy sense of foreboding grew on him until he impulsively seized Karty by the arm, bringing him to a stop.

"I won't stand it no more!" he said. "I'm not going to walk around here all night. You're lying to me, Mr. Karty. You're just telling me bull stories. If you don't find your friend right now I'm going back to the soda store and tell Mr. Spitzbergen about the money. If I tell him then I won't get in trouble."

"Shaddap," Karty begged. "Keep quiet, Arthur. I'm going where I have to. What do you think I'm doing? I'm going to this guy's house for the money, see?" It was too early, three, four hours too early. They just had to wait.

They continued walking. Now the gambler was taking Arthur out of the heavily congested section of Neptune, farther away from the shore, where the houses were few and the sidewalks disappeared entirely. To keep the sand out of their shoes, they walked in the gutters. It was desolate here, with no one on the streets and no lights except for the occasional lamppost. Arthur was biting his lip as he debated in his mind whether Karty really meant what he said. Absorbed in his fears and doubts, he suddenly grew aware that the street before him was white, lit up by the headlights of a car. As he turned around, the lights dimmed at once. Arthur could not be sure, but now it seemed to him that the black sedan had been following them for blocks.

"Mr. Karty," he said, his voice trembling, "they're following us. Geez, I got a feeling they're following us on purpose."

The gambler studied the car, his body growing taut. "It's your imagination. You're just nervous. Why should a car be following us?"

"It's policemen! Spitzbergen found out and sent policemen after us!" Arthur was in panic. "What'll we do now? Tell me, Mr. Karty, what should we do now?"

"Just make believe nothing's the matter. Keep on walking and they'll go by us. It can't be the cops. How would they know where to find us. Besides, it's ridiculous."

Arthur stumbled on the broken pavement, uttered a cry of fear, but plodded ahead obediently. The sedan was abreast of them but they looked directly forward, as if by ignoring the machine they would escape all harm.

"Hey, you, Moe! Stop."

It was Harry, and with him were his two brothers, big men, heavy with paunch, their faces forbidding and businesslike. The car came to a halt. Karty, perceiving them, started running wildly toward the sandy lot, but the car door flew open and the two brothers were after him at once. They hurled themselves at him and the gambler went down to the ground as though he had been tripped. Arthur stood fixed to the spot, frightened and mystified. These weren't policemen. Then what did they want from them? And they weren't hold-up men because they knew Karty.

The two brothers dragged him back to the car, Karty slumping in their grasp so that they half carried him. The gambler held his hands before his face, fearing an assault on the street. He made a hideous picture in that position, for the brothers were continuously jerking his elbows as they moved to the auto and his hands bobbed convulsively, now revealing his fear-stricken features and then covering his face again. He uttered little cries for mercy, but the men seemed in no way open to pity. Their expressions remained businesslike with determination, as though this were some ordinary task. Harry sat at the wheel, disgust on his face as he watched them pull his brother-in-law. "Throw him in the car," he called. "Come on, throw him in already."

One of the brothers now tried to get a hand free for the door but Karty fought them violently, with all the strength he could find in his thin body. In boiling frenzy he punched at them, scratched their faces and kicked at their legs. They dodged his blows without countering, intent only upon throwing him into the car. Karty finally managed to raise himself high in the air and kicked out with both feet. He struck the one at the door in the face and wriggled out of the fingers of the other. Crying and panting, he turned and ran again to the lots, stumbling in the sand. They cursed and went after him. This time when they caught up with him they hammered him on the head, their fists slanting down with machinelike force. Karty sunk to his knees, his face upraised as he sought to tell them that he would have the money soon, that he would make good if they only gave him a little time. But the brothers, breathing hard, and angry at his resistance, did not stop to listen but drove away with their fists until the gambler fell on the sand unconscious. They paused for a moment to watch him, sprawled, and they seemed satisfied. Even with the headlights turned off, the moon was bright enough that night for Karty's body to stand clearly outlined on the white sand. They picked him up, his head dangling, and dumped him to the floor of the car. Harry stepped on the starter.

Then it was that Arthur suddenly started into action. The realization came to him that with Karty driven away he would lose his last chance of returning the money to the cash register. "Please!" he cried out. "Don't take him away. Listen, please, he's got to see a friend for me. If you don't let him I'll get in trouble. They'll put me in jail." In his fear he was clawing at Karty's body in the sedan, trying to drag him out. They shoved the dishwasher aside.

"Keep your hands off!" Harry said. "We don't want no interference from you."

"Harry, what's the matter he talks about jail?" one of the brothers asked. "What's he saying?"

"I should have troubles like I know what he's talking about," Harry said. "It's not for us to worry about."

"So what should we do with the boy? We don't need him but he can make trouble if it goes into his head like that."

Harry stopped to think. The motor of the car hummed. "Pull him in the car, too," he said finally. "We'll take him with us. We'll learn him he should know to keep quiet."

The brother grabbed Arthur by the shirt at the collar and forced him into the back. He sat wedged between the two, dangling his feet awkwardly in the air to avoid kicking Karty. Arthur sobbed in terror. The mess he was in was growing worse and worse. His hair fell into his eyes and he pushed it away. "Where are you taking me?" he begged. "I got to go back to the store. If I don't get back to the soda store they'll put me in jail. Please! I didn't do anything to you."

One of the brothers dug his elbow sharply into his side and raised the back of his palm as if to smack him. "Keep the mouth!" he snarled. "Nobody wanted you in the first place. Now you're here, don't make a noise, don't hear nothing that ain't your business. Keep quiet and you'll have a nice ride in a car. But if you open your mouth, you'll go to the hospital, too."

Arthur slumped back into his seat, despairing and hopeless. It was all finished with him now. Sick and weak, he kept his feet suspended because of Karty, but the effort made him ache. The car bumped through the deserted streets into the bright glare of the Avenue. People were walking in their shirtsleeves, drinking soda water at the candy stands, talking to their friends, laughing and shouting with their hands in their pockets, following the normal procedures of men and women. It was fantastic! The scene seemed unreal to Arthur, the lights, the people sauntering, their unconcern with the black sedan speeding through the street.

The car drove on for a half hour, out of the hard gaiety of Neptune Beach into Williamsburg. This was a business district, near Bedford Avenue, and at this time all the stores were dark except for their dim night bulbs. The sidewalks were empty. Towering mute and black, with the iron shutters permanently closed over the windows, the begrimed old buildings rested patiently for the morning, the day's activity over. Harry drove the sedan on to the sidewalk and blew his horn before the huge garage doors. A sleepy Negro opened the small wood frame cut out in the door. He held one foot on the sidewalk, blinking before the rays of the headlights.

"Open up, Lawrence," Harry called. "It's us."

The Negro shut the frame and started pushing the big doors

open. Harry drove inside. "You can take a walk for an hour," he told the night man. "We don't want you for an hour."

The Negro seemed surprised and kept on looking at them. "Boss, I got no place to go this time of night," he protested in complaint. "Everything's dead here."

"Go on, Lawrence," Harry said. "Take a walk and come back in an hour."

"O.K.," the night man said reluctantly. "O.K." He closed the doors and they were alone in the dimly lit garage.

The brothers pulled Karty out to the running board of the car. He was stirring now and they let him rest. The telephone rang, the bell resounding fearfully through the emptiness. "Go," Harry said to one of the brothers. "Answer the telephone."

The brother couldn't imagine who would be calling up at this time of night. "Who could it be?" he asked. "Who needs us now?"

"Go and you'll see," Harry said. The brother left, and the two others stared at Karty, contempt and anger frozen on their faces. The gambler was moving on the running board, groaning and crying feebly. His eyes were closed but he rubbed his scalp slowly with his fingers, and once or twice he scratched his head in the midst of his absorption with his pain. Arthur still sat in the car, slumped and dazed. The huge garage seemed empty in spite of the trucks that formed neat rows along the walls. These were the vehicles of butter-and-cheese companies, herring firms, wetwash independents, small bakeries and similar establishments. The trucks were old and black, soaked with the smells of their trades, so that a queer mixture of odors filled the air above the dominant smell of gasoline and oil. The floors were black and shiny with grease. The chipped whitewashed walls, the bricks showing red in many spots, were lined with the rows of radiator pipes, completing the desolate aspect of the garage. Karty's legs began to roll off the edge of the running board. He caught himself in time and sat up, leaning weakly against the door of the car. The brother who had gone to the telephone now returned.

"It's Bella," he said. Harry and the other brother shook their heads sternly. "She's looking for that louse." He indicated the gambler. "I said we don't know nothing about it, but it looked funny. She knows I'm not in the garage this time in the night and she wanted to know why."

Harry bent over the gambler and held his head up by the chin, studying the face.

"He's all right," he grumbled. "Stinker. This world's too good for him. He should be lynched."

"The boy is in the car yet," the brother said. "You want him here?"

"Take him in the office," Harry said. "Close the door and show him if he knows what's good for him he should make no trouble."

The man squeezed through the narrow door and pulled Arthur out by his coat lapels. Arthur kept his hands before his face in the position of a man who is about to catch a high ball, the palms outspread. "What do you want from me?" he whimpered. "I didn't do nothing to you. Leave me alone."

"Take him away," Harry said. The brother held on to Arthur's collar all the way to the little office at the side of the garage. Harry tugged at his greasy pants under his wide belly and went to the gambler. He pulled Karty to his feet, holding him by the coat over his chest with their faces inches apart. The little man's eyes were still closed and he stood limp in Harry's grasp.

"Well," his wife's brother asked with terrible quiet in his voice, "where is the money?"

"I ain't got," Karty mumbled. "Give me a little time. Two hours. An hour."

"Promises! Lies!" Harry shook him violently, rage overcoming him so that he ground his teeth and his eyes glared. "Stinker with the lies!"

"Don't hit, Harry," the gambler begged. "For God's sakes, don't hit. It's true. I'll have the money soon. I ain't lying. You'll see."

"Rotten faker! Don't tell me stories. It won't do you good. What we said will happen. I told you you got to make good the money tonight and now we'll send you to a hospital." He glanced at the brothers. Without a sign these came up, holding small but heavy wrenches in their hands. As they closed up on the gambler, he screamed and jumped in Harry's grasp. In spite of his exhaustion he fought with tremendous energy, catching the surprised garage man off his guard. Karty hugged him with his arms, getting his head so close to his that the brothers would have to hold off with the wrenches for fear of hitting Harry. Harry cursed and worked on Karty's fingers, trying to pry them loose from his neck, his elbows in the air in that clumsy posture. The two men swayed.

Harry's brothers dropped their wrenches to tear the gambler away. As they forced his hands apart, Karty's fingers scratched the fat garage man until lines of blood appeared on his neck. The brothers were forcing Karty to the floor. He dug his head between Harry's thighs, as he had done that morning, to shield it from their blows, and as he dug with his head he pulled on the pants to keep close. The brothers picked up their wrenches and started to slam the little gambler on the shoulders. Karty shrieked in pain and in fear. Harry, towering above him, writhed to shake him off, but he held on desperately, pulling and hanging on to the pants and digging his head in. The garage man was continually losing his balance, so that he had to struggle to keep his feet. He cuffed madly at Karty with his fat palms. Often he stopped the blows from the wrenches and cursed with fury. Karty shrieked at the top of his lungs, but the doors were closed and the streets were deserted. Inside the little office Arthur was crying, shaking with terror.

Suddenly the beating ended. The two brothers stepped back. The belt of the fat garage man slipped underneath his belly. Clutching at the pants in his desperation, Karty had finally yanked them down so that his head was partly covered by the greasy cloth and Harry stood exposed in his full-length underwear. Harry kicked viciously at the gambler. "All right," he muttered. "All right, you stinker. Leave go." Karty kept his head covered until he grew convinced that the blows had finally stopped. He crawled away to the running board of the auto and sat down. The brothers watched him uncertainly, and as they watched their fury cooled. They became conscious of the wrenches in their hands and threw them to the floor. Harry pulled up his pants, tightening the belt securely. The fight was over.

"Don't hit no more," Karty begged from the car, breathing with great effort. "I ain't faking. I'll get the money. I know a man with money. He'll give me and I'll make good."

Their anger dissipated so that they felt aimless and unsure the brothers looked at one another. "It's all a lie from start to finish," one of the brothers said. "Just like every goddammed thing that ever came out of him. It's a trick to get out of the garage."

"What do you say, Harry?" the other brother said. "Maybe he means it after all. The object is to get the money. If we don't have to cripple him, it's just as good so long as the money comes back."

"I don't know," Harry said, frowning.

"The minute he gets out," the first brother said, "he'll run away and then go find him."

On the running board Karty weakly kept on shaking his head. "What's the use talking?" he sobbed. "Where could I run away? I ain't got money to run away. I ain't got friends. Give me a little time and I'll make good. I'm talking the truth. I'll bring it to you tonight."

"Who?" asked Harry. "Who'll give you money?"

"A man. In Neptune Beach. He's got plenty money."

"Why should he give you money?"

"I'm telling you. He owes me money. He'll give me. You'll see. What do you care why?"

The three men stood silently, debating in their minds whether or not the gambler was telling the truth. Their faces were absorbed, scowling and hard as they reckoned dollars. Karty was bent over on his knees and he held his head in his hands, sobbing and exhausted. In the gloomy light of the garage, Harry gazed at his brothers and then shook his head, still frowning.

"Take out the boy," he said. "Bring him here."

The brother went off and Harry leaned over to the gambler. He jerked his head up roughly so that he could look into his eyes. "All right," he said. "We'll let you go. We'll give you a chance. We'll wait here until you bring back the money. But remember, if it's a lie, if you're faking and the morning don't find you here, we'll look for you. We'll get you and there will be still time to fix you. Don't forget it."

"I don't like it," the first brother insisted. "It's a trick. Nothing good will come out of him. Send him to a hospital and forget about the thirteen hundred dollars. It's lost money."

"So we'll see," said Harry. He glanced nastily at his brother. "I want the thirteen hundred. The hell with him. It'll be still time with the hospital. It don't run away."

The brother muttered, disgruntled. Arthur was brought forward, trotting in a daze, his hair in his eyes. "I'm going to vomit," he said. "I can't help it. I'm sorry. I'm going to vomit."

"Take him outside he should vomit," Harry said. He shoved the dishwasher to the door. "Go," he said to Karty. "We'll let you out in one piece this time, but remember, we'll be staying in the garage until you come back. It ain't finished until you make good. Nothing will help until then."

Karty sat a moment longer on the running board. Slowly, he picked up one of the wrenches from the floor and put it into his pocket. The brothers watched him curiously but did nothing to stop him. The gambler went to the wood-frame door. Arthur was at the curb, sick and retching.

There were eight blocks to the elevated station and once they reached it, it would take them almost an hour to arrive at Neptune Beach. Karty pulled the dishwasher by the arm and they walked down the street together.

"Don't worry, Arthur," he moaned. "Don't worry. It'll be all right yet. Everything will be all right. Just wait and see."

At the garage frame door the three brothers stood with their hands in their pockets, solemnly watching them as they disappeared to the station.

The sniffler sniffled apologetically in the presence of his boss and put his paws on the red-checkered tablecloth in the grill room.

"Gee," he said. "I think Shubunka wants to hold out. That's the way it looks like to me. I saw him in the soda parlor tonight."

"Can't we get him off our minds?" the boss asked irritably. He had a drooping face, full-lined, with sad eyes and a perpetually wrinkled forehead. "I don't like to keep him on my mind. Settle it one way or the other."

"Yes, naturally. It'll take a little time. Sounds like a coke if you ask me. He don't act normal."

"Well, tell you what you do. Take Bull and Two-Bits and see what they can do about the matter. See that we don't happen to be bothered again from him. This business is not a picnic exactly, even with that guy off my mind."

"They're on the job already. They'll see what they can do about the matter. But what it is, it's I can't understand that guy Shubunka. He fascinates me. He don't want to beat it."

The boss grunted impatiently. "I suppose he's a wise guy."

"Oh, we'll take care of it. He just don't want to clear out."

"Why didn't you fix him up before? I told you I wanted the matter in Neptune Beach all cleaned up by this time."

"I thought I could go around and talk to him." "You can't talk to some of these guys. They're stubborn. Get after them! Step on them! Make any arrangement you like only clean the matter up in a hurry."

"Oh, we'll take care of him!"

"So O.K." Looking weary and worried, the boss drummed nervously on the tablecloth.

Outside, the taxi waited. Herbert Lurie was in the hall of Dorothy's apartment house, his two suitcases at his feet.

"So make up your mind," he told her. "I can't let the cab wait indefinitely."

"Oh, Herbert!" Dorothy cried. "You're impossible! Why do you have to be so unreasonable? Sometimes I really think there's something wrong with you."

"See, that's the way I am. I'm sorry."

"I can't give in in everything. If I let you have your way at the start, I'll just be a rag in your hands all my life."

"All right," he said. "So?" His right foot scraped uncomfortably on the tile floor, as though he were stamping out a cigarette. All afternoon, with Shubunka gone, Lurie had been depressed in his cotton shop. A cloud of despondency had settled upon him. What it was exactly that had troubled him and why it had come, he hardly knew, but he had found little taste for his work that day. At five o'clock he decided not to have supper at Dorothy's louse and he had his clerk say he was called to the city on business. "I didn't make it up," he had to tell her later when he saw her. "It was the truth. I wasn't sore. I didn't do it for spite. I had to go to see a manufacturer."

In his store he had felt spiritless. His experience with Shubunka and the strong-arm men at the lots on the way to Pundy's this afternoon upset him for many hours. Brutal, inhuman, and unfeeling they were, and the sight of their raw impassive faces continually returned to oppress him. With Shubunka, too, he somehow felt guilty in refusing him his help, his company, his sympathy. His only impulse then was to get away from him, to drive him and his troubles out of his mind, and that day in the dress store he realized with a pang his own hardness in driving Shubunka into loneliness when the fat man needed warmth and aid. No one had good in his heart, not even he himself in spite of his innermost distaste for Neptune Beach and its calloused men. Lurie felt shame for himself at his treatment of Shubunka. Ugly and distressing as he was, no matter how rotten his calling, no matter on what misery of women and stupid lust of men he had been living these years, Shubunka was still a man, sensitive to hurt, unsatisfied in spite of his wealth, clamorous with unhappiness in this world. He was a human being in trouble and Lurie had shut his mind to him, he couldn't be bothered.

"Hey," called the hackman from the street. "Make up your mind."

"Hold your horses," Lurie called back through the door. "If you're in a hurry, you don't have to wait."

The taxi man didn't answer but turned down the flag on his clock and started the motor going.

"Herbert, it's ridiculous standing in the hall all night. It's late. It's after ten," Dorothy said. "Why must you be so stubborn?"

"Because it's how I want it," he said. "We're getting married, not your mother. If I want a furnished flat, that's the way it's going to be. I'm sick and tired of Neptune Beach, Dorothy. I hate the sight of the neighborhood and the faster I get out the better I'll like it. We took the rooms, ain't it? We paid the deposit. What's the sense in backing out the last minute?"

"I can't see what's the matter with Neptune Beach in a hurry? And besides, my mother's got right. At least that's what I think, Herbert. We can give in to her at least this one time. After all, she's still my mother. There's no sense in antagonizing her, is there?"

Lurie winced as he thought of the hour he had spent upstairs with Dorothy's parents and the married couple, long apprehensive faces, insisting and bargaining as though the marriage were some sort of business deal in which they were afraid of being cheated. They looked at him distrustfully, sitting straight in their chairs against the wall in the dining room. Somehow they had learned or suspected about his first wife and Flo. His appearance, too, was against him, for they disliked the prospect of a man ten years older than their daughter. If it hadn't been for the dress business and his reputation in Neptune as a man who could provide for a wife, they would have had none of him at all. For a moment Lurie speculated whether this might be the case with Dorothy, too. In the hall he gazed at her searchingly.

"What are you looking at?" she asked, growing self-conscious under his stare. "What's the matter? Something's funny?"

"No," he said rapidly. "Nothing's the matter." Outside, the hackman raced the motor. Lurie bent down and took the bags. "So what do you say? Look, Dorothy, when two people are in, well, you know, if they have a real feeling for one another, little things shouldn't stand in the way. I want to get married tomorrow. I want to get out of Neptune Beach. If your mother still wants it, we can break the lease later and find another apartment. We could manage something to please everybody. Come on, Dorothy. Come with me." He stood before her, his arms pulled down by the suitcases, almost pleading.

"My heavens, Herbert," she cried before his argument. "Don't go. Send the taxi away. I don't want to have a fight over a little thing, either, but I made up my mind. I won't give in this time." She kept her hands on her hips and her face was determined.

"Look, I'm going to the flat. That's final. If you like it, you can take a cab and come later. I'll wait for you." He went forward, dropping one bag as he opened the door. He held it with his knee and turned, waiting.

"I won't come," she said. "You'll be staying in the house for nothing."

"Still in all," Lurie answered, "I'll be there if you change your mind." For another moment they stared at each other. Finally he picked up the other bag and went down the small stoop. Dorothy went to the door after him.

"You'll be sorry, Herbert," she said. "This quarrel will have serious consequences you won't like."

Lurie stowed the bags in the cab. "If you change your mind," he said, "I'll still be there." He climbed in and the hackman impatiently slammed the door. As they drove away, Dorothy remained on the stoop, glaring angrily at the taxi. She strode back to her apartment, muttering to herself, and asked who the hell Herbert Lurie thought he was anyway. John Pierpont Morgan?

At her flat she flung the door open. "See?" she shouted at them. "Mix in! Tell me what to do! He went away after all."

Her parents and the married couple took the news calmly. "I'm not aggravated," her mother said. "It will do him good. Let him know he's not the boss altogether. I'm still in the world."

Riding in the cab to Eastern Parkway, Lurie pulled out the collapsible seat in front of him so that he could rest his legs on it. He felt tired. His argument with Dorothy was the depressing finish to a bad day. Shubunka's piteous wails and his misery, his own sense of failing him, the uncomfortable hour in Dorothy's home, and now his uncertainty over her—all these thoughts persisted stubbornly in his mind. Thinking of Shubunka, he regretted again that he had refused him the use of the apartment. Even though the demand seemed unreasonable to him, it meant something to the fat man as a sign of human sympathy and understanding. This was what he really wanted, and as it turned out, Lurie would have no use for the place, either. This brought him back to the question he had asked himself in the hall with Dorothy and had solved by driving it out of his head. What was he to Dorothy?

A sickening feeling of humiliation and shame overcame him. Once again, he felt, he was plunging into marriage recklessly, not because of the girl but from some impelling desire within himself. It was as though he thought a new wife would mean a new world for him and an end to the dingy, lifeless ways he knew. It was as though any new wife would do. He recalled again how excited he had felt when he met Flo, how certain of her he had been. Lurie tried to reassure himself about Dorothy. It was a trifling argument which he would probably have overlooked entirely on any other day but this. She was a young girl and her mother's influence was still strong. The disagreement meant nothing.

The taxi stopped. Lurie carried the bags up to his flat. When he entered his rooms, he immediately went to the windows. The Museum of Art across the street seemed majestic and massive, but behind it was a vast expanse of space. He opened the window to look out. Trees, grass, a pleasant breath of air instead of the salty dampness at Neptune. The streets here were wide, with a little island of trees and shrubs dividing the thoroughfare into two lanes. Quiet and orderly, this was not like Neptune Beach with its throngs on the streets, shouting, laughing, and fighting in their underwear tops. Even though it was still early, the traffic was fairly light. The red and green lights of the signal towers, the street lamps and the lights of the cars studded the darkness. Looking down on the scene from his window, Lurie took pleasure in the night. It seemed beautiful and soft.

Longing to be part of that quiet and order, Lurie left the window. The house was empty and he realized there was nothing for him to do. If he unpacked his suitcases, he might well have the whole job to do over again. He let the bags stand on the floor. Sitting down on the couch, Lurie hoped that Dorothy would come, would remove his fears, would make possible for him the way of living he had longed for all his life. He watched the door.

⌢⌢⌢

At the garage near Bedford Avenue, the three brothers sat in the little office, rubbing their chins with their hands as they waited for Karty. It was past eleven now. Their sister had called up twice since Arthur and the gambler had left, and at these times they had assured her that Moe was all right. They spoke sincerely, trying to set her at rest, for there was nothing to be gained by worrying her needlessly. But now they sat and waited, knowing only that thirteen hundred dollars was money which they had earned by sweat and heartache and that they wanted it back.

"We made a mistake," the first brother said, gloomy. "We shouldn't of let him go. We'll never see him again."

"We'll see," said Harry. "Only wait."

"After all," the second brother argued, "what would it help if we cripple him? It don't bring back the thirteen hundred dollars."

"It's a fake! You just say what Harry says," the first one insisted, his voice droning with the certainty. "Once for all, it's a trick. We should show people like him they should know."

"All right, all right," Harry shouted. "We'll wait and see. He'll bring back the money because he knows what will be in stock for him if he don't."

This silenced the other two. In the yellow light of the office, they waited for Karty to return.

⌢⌢⌢

"See," exclaimed Shorty eagerly, "take me. All I can eat for breakfast is a cup of hot coffee, that's all." He gazed gravely at the corsetière to drive home his meaning as he put the cup of tea down on the little oval table before the sofa. "I don't know how other people stand it. I can't! Not that I got a sensitive stomach or anything. Hard as nails, can eat pickles just before retiring, don't you know? But I can't eat anything in the morning. Can't work, can't think clear when my stomach is full. Makes me sleepy, see how I mean?"

"You don't say?" marveled the corsetière, stirring the tea.

"I can't help it," the soda jerker cried. "I'm just particular about certain things. Don't like certain foods—spaghetti, fish, sauces. Can't bear them. That's just for instance. Take underwear, if you'll pardon my mentioning it. I always wear silk. Listen, times when I was broke and starving, down and out, you might say. Had to have silk underwear. Can't stand cotton or anything else! I got a peculiar skin that way!"

"I can't believe it!" exclaimed Madame Pavlovna, solemnly shaking her head.

"Oh, sure!" The little soda jerker drew back with offense that she might think he didn't mean it. "Take sleeping. Never wear pajamas. It rubs my skin raw."

"So vat do you do, Shurtee?" she asked, really at a loss,

"Sleep in the nude!"

"Naked? Naked! I don't understand such a man." She was helpless with astonishment and finished her tea. Shorty felt proud.

"Well, it's a kind of insanity with me. It's not something to go around bragging about. See, most people are insane, more or less, in one thing or another. There's no definite line," he told her, wagging his finger, "between when a man's sane and when he's insane. Everybody's got some little twist of personality that's peculiar and funny. Sure," he murmured wisely, "you never can tell. Everybody's got some neurosis or other. Illusions, obsessions, complexes, inferiority and superiority complexes, and what not else? Paranoia! Not," he added, "that I know anything in particular about psychiatry, the study of mental diseases. Hell, I ain't no psychologist and I don't want to go around making an impression."

But no matter how modestly he disclaimed all education, Madame Pavlovna remained awed. Shorty, grinning, rose from the couch. “Mrs. Pavlovna,” he said, “would you mind if I removed my coat? Warm.”

“Please. Make yourself thoroughly comfortable.”

“Listen,” the soda jerker said, “there’s no reason in the world why you shouldn’t be cool, too, don’t you know? Why don’t you take off that heavy gown and get into something light?” His gold caps were gleaming with concern for her comfort. The corsetière cast down her eyes.

“It isn’t like it vas really so hot,” she murmured. “Do you really think it would be all right, Shurtee?”

“Sure! What the hell? We ain’t kids like. We’re people of the world! Ain’t it?”

“Very vell,” she said finally. She rose, still keeping her eyes to the ground, and went into the bedroom. When she shut the door, she could not restrain herself any longer. She giggled.

Shorty folded the pinch-backed coat with great care and placed it neatly over a chair, the silk lining at the armholes showing. He went to the mirror, fixed his tie, inspected his conservative black-and-white cord suspenders. Not bad, but he didn’t need looks. It was all in the line and the way you handled a dame. Plus that certain something. Look at Rudolph Valentino and Clark Gable. After the show, they had dropped in at Heineman’s Bar and Grill for cocktails. Madame ordered an Orange Blossom, knowing and chic. Shorty, who told her he personally couldn’t stand the taste of gin in anything he drank, had a Bacardi, and when the bartender raised his eyebrows at the pair for ordering cocktails at that hour, why, b’gee, Shorty glared right back again, and if he didn’t like it he knew goddammed well what he could do about it! As he thought of it, the soda jerker muttered in the mirror, looking tough.

But hell, thought Shorty, the evening had cost him over three bucks and that was no chicken feed when you came right down to it. He looked at the door, imagining he heard it move. The corsetière was femininely taking her time. Hell, said the jerker, he wasn’t rushing her. He could do these *affaires de cœur* (affairs of the heart) in style, slow, easy, debonair. He looked at himself in the mirror, his face drawn in sophisticated dignity, feeling like Ronald Colman in a full-dress suit. Shorty started. Staring intently at the mirror, it seemed to him as though he had cockeyes. He shifted away uneasily from the glass.

Dreaming of his naked women and glancing at the door, Shorty passed the time by looking through the heavy yellowing album with its enameled covers. Pictures of Madame Pavlovna, Stefan, relatives and friends, saved over the years. Brown pictures, people in their best clothes, looking strangely quiet and innocent and composed. B'gee! exclaimed the soda jerker. Was he going nuts? Most of these here also seemed to him to have cockeyes. He examined the faces carefully and it was true. It must have been the bad photography of those days but the eyes weren't right. He grew uneasy. The album had an odor musty with age and he put it down.

The corsetière lived in four rooms above her store on the Avenue and she had furnished the living room lavishly. On one wall hung a tapestry, a representation of an eighteenth-century young man in short pants and slippers making love to a full-skirted broad with a parasol against a garden background. Goddammed beautiful, said Shorty respectfully. Real taste had the corsetière, a woman of refinement. The samovar rested on the round table in the corner. That was Russian. Tea. Russians always drank tea. Shorty grew impatient and kept his eyes on the door.

He went to the floor lamp and switched off the lights so that the room was illumined now only by the apple-green light which shone through the imitation quartz of the lamp on the end table. He surveyed the effect with admiration. Romantic. It was a pity she had no radio in the place. Soft lights and low music, that always brought them around, it got them nuts, a combination not to be despised. In another corner stood an old-fashioned box phonograph. Shorty opened the cabinet and studied the records. There wasn't a single one with which he was familiar, not a jazz song in the lot. "On the Volga," solo by Richard Tauber. He put it on the disc and listened critically. Too loud, but would do. Dreamy and sad, O.K.

Standing alone in the room he reviewed his prospects nervously. They'd fool around on the sofa for a while, murmuring passionate nothings into each other's ears. When the moment came, Shorty would rise, gaze at her significantly and then at the bedroom. Her eyes down, she would leave the sofa. "Just a minute." Shy and tender. And then Shorty would go in. The door closed and then, don't count your chickens before they hatched, the jerker told himself, superstitious. You could never be too sure. He could think of case after case when everything seemed just right and at the last minute the whole business fell through. He was grave with anticipation.

The door opened and for a few moments Madame Pavlovna stood on the threshold, one hand on the wall, smiling her warm, distant smile. She wore a black chiffon negligee tied at the side with a green sash. Her short hair had been fluffed over her head, and she had powdered the swollen lines of her face. Looked nice, smelled nice, thought Shorty, what a piece. The corsetière noticed the soft music and the dim lighting, and she smiled wickedly.

"Goddammit!" cried Shorty with tremendous conviction, "I have been all over the goddammed world one time or another and I've seen them all. But I can truthfully say I have never seen a woman as beautiful as you are right this minute."

Madame Pavlovna turned her head to the side and her eyes roguishly reprimanded him for his compliment. "You are terrible," she said, "simply terrible. Shurtee, I don't know vat I vill ever do vith you. How do you like the negligee?"

He sucked in his breath. "Gorgeous!"

"So. Pretty. It really is. I bought it in Brussels. Nineteen twenty-eight. I love it." Her eyes swam. "Those days," she sighed, patting the chiffon as she settled grandly on the sofa. "I can remember those times. Vere vasn't ve? All the places in the vorld and ve lived only for joy and good times. Over. All over."

Shorty sat down and bent confidentially close to her, ready to relieve her burdens with his cheer, but the needle scratched. "On the Volga" was finished. The soda jerker jumped up and removed the record.

"You got something modern?" he asked. "A waltz or something light?"

"Mostly classical," she replied. "I love the old songs. Genuvine music fills the heart. Othervise tinkles."

"Oh, sure! I agree with you in every respect. There's nothing like the classics. That's what I always say. I don't know nothing about music but I can recognize good stuff when I hear it. But what I mean, just for a change, don't you know?"

"Look in the bottom then. Maybe you vill find something you like." Superior and bland, she idly dangled the green sash.

Shorty pulled out a pile of records from the lowest shelf in the cabinet. Jazz, but old. He had never heard of them. "Chickahominy Blues," "Tiger Lily," "The Cap in My Hand," "Yodel Day." He wished she had a radio in the dump. He finally found "Alone," by Irving Berlin, and put it on the disc, turning the volume indicator to its minimum. The tearful melody flooded the room and he sat down close to the corsetière.

"Sad song. It brings back memories," she said. "It reminds me the olden days."

The little soda jerker had to sit up straight against the back of the sofa so that he could put his left arm around her shoulders. He crossed his legs, and with his free hand he was now pushing back the bobbed hair. "I can imagine," he whispered. "Believe me, I can understand how it is. I'm not like one of those people you see around. I got feelings, too, don't you know?" He had difficulty in breathing and he feared she would be able to hear his heart pound. It wouldn't be sophisticated if she realized his emotion. After all, he was no kid about these things and women were an old story to him.

"Oh, Shurtee," said the corsetière, "you are a friend indeed. Kind and gentle."

"Nothing at all," he protested. "B'gee, Sophia, I'm only human myself."

"All alone by the telephone," wept the singer in his nasal voice, hitting the chorus again, "waiting for a bell to ring."

"It isn't alvays you find a gentleman he should understand a voman's nature," she said. "People in my experience are not so sympathetic as you might think, Shurtee. Vomen mean only vun thing to most men. Believe me, I know."

"Take me," insisted the jerker. "I ain't got no use for that class of men. They ain't got a sense of honor and they don't realize that womanhood is sacred. After all, I know how it sounds, but it's only the truth. When God created woman, he made something fine and beautiful, different from men, see how I mean? And a guy who don't appreciate that fact, why, hell, he's just common and dumb."

The right hand slipped from her hair, he wiggled himself closer on his crossed legs, and the hand carefully went through the slit of the negligee. Once there, the hand paused tactfully for a moment, feeling nothing except rayon tightened against her body, the brassiere. He didn't say a word, barely breathed, waited, and the corsetière sat motionless, too.

"Feel-ling so blue!" wailed the phonograph through the stillness of the room. "Wondering where you are, and how you are, and if you are all alone, too."

"Oh, Shurtee!" she said almost inaudibly. "Isn't nice." She stiffened and picked feebly on his hand with her fingers.

"Oh, it's O.K.! It's O.K., Sophia," he whispered. "That ain't nothing to think about." She lapsed into uncomfortable quiet. His hand remained there and it was clear sailing ahead. B'gee. Shorty liked a woman who didn't let too easily, who argued a little and put a man off. It wasn't respectable to be too willing. The fingers pressed gently on the rayon.

"The needle," said Madame Pavlovna. "It's scratching."

B'gee! The soda jerker stood up, tried to smooth his trousers unobtrusively and walked straight to the phonograph. He lifted the handle. The hell with it. It was a nuisance. Now he would have to start all over again from the beginning. Nuts.

He sat down and rested his arm against the top of the sofa, feeling her chiffon in his fingers for a start. "Excellent material," he confided. "Real good quality. I can always tell." The arm slipped down and he was wiggling in close. "Oh, Sophia, I can't resist you," he cried suddenly with great passion.

Turning her face to him with his left hand, he stabbed with his mouth to kiss her. His face dug too deeply so that the lips pressed back and the teeth clicked. The corsetière broke out in a fit of smothered giggles while she twisted her head, trying to dodge his mouth. Using one foot on the floor for leverage, Shorty now half rose above her and hugged violently, pushing her head back on the sofa top with his mouth while he kissed her. Madame Pavlovna couldn't control her spasm of laughter. Shorty felt her rock beneath him. He couldn't tell whether she was laughing at him or just because of the situation. His face grew wrapt with emotion. He dug his free hand heavily into her abdomen, squeezing the roll of flesh with all his power.

The corsetière shrieked amid her laughter. Shorty kneaded the flesh, his teeth grinding together. She fought clumsily to get out of his grip, and now she began gurgling and coughing. "Stop! For God's sakes, stop!" she gasped. "I'm choking to death!" But it wasn't until she began to hit him with her hands in a frenzy and there was no mistaking she was in earnest that the soda jerker let go of his hold. He leaned back, one knee on the sofa, white-faced and panting. Madame Pavlovna held her throat, disregarding him completely as she waited to see what damage had been done.

"All I can say," she told him coldly, "is I am certainly surprised at a man of your character. I never expected a scene like that from you."

But Shorty himself in his confusion was all offended innocence. "Why, what did I do, Sophia?" he begged. "No, on the level, tell me, I'd like to know. What was so terrible about it?"

"This is no vay for a gentleman to act vith a lady. Ven you act like this it only goes to show exactly vat is in your mind. It tells volumes of your opinion of me. Vat you think of me obviously is I am a low-class type. I am sorry, my dear Shurtee. I am sorry to disappoint you. You only made a mistake." She drew within herself with majestic dignity.

"Oh, Sophia!" he cried. "You don't understand how it is! I realize my behavior wasn't of the very best type but you are a woman of the world. You're not a baby. You should understand a man can't help himself in certain circumstances. After all, Sophia, I am a man with a certain temperament," he whispered, his eyes glowing intense. "When I'm with a beautiful woman it is practically impossible for me to resist. I can't control myself. You can see what I mean."

"Listen, Shurtee, vun quvestion, please. I vant to ask you, you believe in a Platonic love affair?"

"Sure!" cried the soda jerker. What the hell? She was carrying her refinement too far and it was time to give in. Shorty grew worried.

"See," she went on blandly, now quite recovered, "it's a beautiful relationship between a man and a voman, and it means vithout the hands, no sexual intercourse, only two souls in harmony. It means a fine friendship, talking, books and literature and music and poetry. That is a relationship vich I vant. If anybody has other ideas on the subject, let him go home. It's time."

Shorty rose from the sofa, dismay in his face. "Sophia," he cried in pain at his betrayal, "you don't mean it! That's no way to treat men. After all I did and yesterday! I thought you understood what I said in my notes!"

She rose grandly and handed his coat to him. "I am very sorry. It vas obviously a case of misunderstanding on both sides. You made a mistake and I made a mistake. It is late. Please." She was before him, the white coat with the armholes showing held in her hand by the collar.

Shorty went wild with anger as he gathered that she really meant what she said. The cheap, dirty bitch! he cried to himself. Playing with him again, teasing him first to get a rise out of him, steaming him up on purpose and then going cold as a Frigidaire on him just to see him in a fix. The notes had been clear enough. She knew what he wanted in the first place and if she hadn't wanted it, then she had no business accepting his invitation. It was too late to change her mind. But she had known exactly what she was about all the time. It was a cheap, dirty, deliberate trick. Well, he swore, she wouldn't get away with it this time.

"Sophia," he begged, "please don't be that way to me. Come on, Sophia, be nice. After all, you shouldn't treat me like this. Come on, Sophia, let's have a little fun together, you know, and then I'll go home. Aw, Sophia, come on. Be a good sport."

But the corsetière was cold and adamant. She held the coat resolutely, her face never for a moment losing its hardness with pity for the little soda jerker. "I am sorry," she repeated. "You are obviously not the type individual I vish to associate vith, and I am obviously not vat you thought. Please go. It's late."

The cheap, dirty bitch! When she was in Hahvahnah! Pulling that teasing stuff on him again. Well, she wanted to see him get all steamed up and watch him hop and now he'd show her. He wasn't begging her any longer. Screwing up in rage, Shorty slapped the coat out of her hand and it fell to the floor between them. She stood rigid in fright. The next moment he rushed forward and seized her about the shoulders. Thrown off balance by his sudden push, she screamed and clung to him for support. They wrestled awkwardly, struggling with each other and at the same time trying to keep their footing. Shorty worked her to the sofa, and when they finally lost their balance they fell heavily on the cushions. Mrs. Pavlovna had to bear his weight, striking at him clumsily from her position beneath him. But Shorty, panting and determined, sprawled above her, twisting his head to avoid her blows and pressing her down with his elbow. His hands worked feverishly to get under the negligee at her legs.

"Stop!" the corsetière suddenly screamed, furious anger in her voice. "You're tearing the chiffon!"

Shorty continued and she struggled with him. A long ripping sound was heard. At this she grew fierce and uncontrollable. She raised herself from the sofa with extraordinary strength, exploding into a burst of cries and curses. As she rose, she lifted Shorty outspread in the air. The grim concentration in his face now changed abruptly with the fear of falling. He twisted in the air and went down on his side on the sofa. Madame Pavlovna, now thoroughly enraged and out of patience with him, seized him by the cord suspenders across the chest and swung him to the floor, his body swishing in a curve. Beside his short form she seemed a giantess. Shorty couldn't catch his breath. She had him fixed fast with the fringes of his hair in one hand while she slapped his face with strength, each blow stinging until the tears came to his eyes. She went on whacking him, tripping and falling over him, dragging him to the door as she belabored him. Here she almost picked him up bodily and threw him into the narrow hall. Once again the door swung open. The white gabardine coat with the fancy back flew over his head.

The corsetière towered over him, her chest heaving. She drew her negligee carefully over her and looked down at him with enormous contempt.

"Cockroach," she said, and slammed the door.

Shubunka lay flat on his back in the gloom of his apartment. The room was lit only by the gauzy rays of the street lamp outside which were reflected in queer crossing lines by the mirrors. Occasionally an auto sped by through the deserted street below, and its lights flashed in broken horizontal bars on the ceiling. The fat man lay with the towel on the pillow to protect it from the Polymol on his hair. His mind still seemed lost in its numbness, dulled and unperceptive, stunned by his critical position and yet strangely unaffected and cold. He could concentrate only on the ceiling, waiting for the next auto to appear so that he could follow the bars of light in their odd conformations, broadening and thinning, ever changing as the car approached and then drove out of range. The lights held his mind, but somewhere, no matter how deeply hidden, the consciousness persisted with him that it was after eleven, that he should have been gone, and that men waited somewhere to do him harm. But the fear was subdued and stripped of force.

In that peculiarly lit room, with the distant murmur of the radio, Shubunka lay alone, feeling himself somehow noble and tragic. It seemed to him that the world must be watching him as an actor is viewed by his audience, with intense sympathy, with pity and concern, with avid apprehension at his inevitable downfall. Certainly this was the way he wanted it, and every movement, every thought in his head, the expression on his face, was conditioned by its conceived effect upon this invisible audience. Shubunka relished their pity and the tears, imaginary as they were, for he had no others to turn to.

He was alone. Everyone he knew had casually thrust aside his imperious pleas, having no room for anyone outside of himself. They had abandoned him completely. Even the telephone had not rung all day. At this time of the night his house managers usually called up in a steady flow, complaining that the girls he had booked for them were late, or had failed to show up at all, or were unsatisfactory for some other reason. Formerly Shubunka had handled these complaints in his cool, apathetic manner, the English Oval dangling from his lips as he told the madams what to do. He had been unruffled then, easy, enjoying his sense of importance and yet his indifference. Now, on the bed, the fat man thought of his old power and position. He thought of the respect he had forced out of the men at Ann's in spite of their distaste for him. And he thought again of his boyhood and early years.

Shubunka remembered the poverty of Rivington Street in the East Side, the steaming, relentless heat of the tenements in summer, in winter the wretched cold when the only heat for the whole flat came from the kitchen stove. His mother would buy five-pound bags of coal at a time, standing in her shawl on the frozen streets while the iceman weighed the bags in the basket scale at the end of his wagon. They used the coal with painful caution, banking the fires often, freezing most of the time so that the bag would still have coal left when they looked into it again.

Shubunka remembered many meals of dry rolls, bought seven for a nickel, eaten with salt for flavor, for his father had been a poor man, a glazier everlastingly looking for broken windows to mend. The old man walked through the streets, working his way uptown to Washington Heights, the wooden board slung by clothesline rope over his shoulder to hold the glass panes, his portable stock in trade. In later years his left shoulder grew permanently deformed because of the constant weight.

Shubunka's home had been small rooms strung out in the fashion of the railroad flats, so that only the front and rear rooms had windows, light and air. Bare, broken board floors, wallpaper that hid thousands of roaches and bugs, a common toilet in the backyard for the thirty or forty people in the whole building.

Shubunka lay on the bed and remembered the cruelty of the streets, the gang fights, the cops, the day when he fell off the roof dodging one of them. Eight Ball, the boys called him, or Nigger or Coke or Dopey Schmugguggle, because of his odd gait, his squat bulk, the unnatural heaviness of his features. "Pee-Yew! Stinks like a wagon full of herring!" the boys cried whenever he approached. "Shtunky Schmugguggle's in town again!" And they ran off, as if frantic, hopping in a wide circle away from him, holding their noses. Nor did this change when he was in the wicker business or in Brownsville. People came into his candy stand and groped with their hands for the change on the counter, while they looked at him, their amazement politely restrained. On the streets the children stared at him outright and passersby stopped to turn back. The boys at Ann's showed their revulsion for him no matter how hard they tried to cover it because he was, after all, a man of money.

And women? Not the wretches he handled as a businessman deals in merchandise, but some girl who could bring him a home, a family, companionship? For all his ties and shirts and suits and the Polymol, Shubunka desperately had to drive the thought of women away from his mind. The humiliation and the pain became too sharp even for reflection.

For eight years he had built up his organization, and now they would take everything away from him. There would be no more money, no fine suits, no respect no matter how unwillingly wrung. Without the prestige of his money, he had nothing and he might as well be dead. He could not run away and it made no difference whether they shot him and killed him.

And it comes to me, the fat man said calmly, staring at the patches traveling on the ceiling, it is only what I deserve. He told himself he had no right to be spared for he, too, had been faithless and had spoken cruelly, had robbed and done evil, had lied and exploited and persecuted and crippled. He had committed all the sins, not heeding their significance, arrogant and presumptuous within himself. When Karty, the poor gambler, came to him for money, it had pleased his fancy to turn him aside, and now the fat man regretted bitterly that he could not find him, give him the money, make him happy. Evil was rewarded by evil and his punishment would be just.

Shubunka smoked his cigarette lying on the bed, solaced by his reflections, for they contained the right elements to draw pity and understanding from his imaginary audience and he knew it. He watched the end of his cigarette glow with life as he inhaled. Outside, men lay in wait for him, he faced ruin and death, but he was composed and resigned, a man going to his just end. The image of himself in his mind's eye soothed him.

The telephone rang.

A sweet sound after the day's lonely stillness. Shubunka lay long as the bell rang again and again, taking great relish in the piercing impact after each interval of silence. In the end he went to the phone.

"Hello," he said, his shrill voice listless. "Who is it?"

The man sniffled on the other end of the wire and Shubunka, recognizing him immediately, shook his head to clear it free of its cloudiness, and he listened with deep concentration. The dramatization was abruptly ended. All Shubunka knew now was that they were calling him, that his houses might still be his, that there was still hope.

"I want to talk to you," the sniffler said. "Come and meet me down at Ann's soda parlor."

"One minute," the fat man said. "Tell me. What's it all about?"

"We don't want trouble, Shubunka. Like you said. Maybe we can fix it up. It all depends. But come down and we'll talk."

"One minute, one minute," Shubunka called. He held the phone and wondered whether to trust him. It might be a trick of some sort. "I don't like it. Frankly, it sounds puzzling to me."

"Listen," said the sniffler, "you said you wanted a job making book for the boss. So O.K., so I was talking to the boss and I say he don't want to get out, he wants to work for you. So the boss says, what the hell, if he wants a job, forty, fifty bucks a week, if he ain't too high-hat for the job, it's O.K. with me. See, all the boss wants, he wants the situation in Neptune cleared up in a hurry. He's all out of patience. Just so long you don't try no monkey business, and handle the houses good, he says he ain't got objections. So what do you say? It's what you wanted."

There was no answer and the sniffler grew impatient. "Listen, I hope you realize I'm doing you a favor. We been organizing all over New York. You're the first guy that's getting a break like this. All the other independents had to get the hell out of town. If you don't want to, O.K.! O.K.! It don't make a difference to us."

"Listen, mister, please," begged Shubunka, still doubtful. "Tell me, who is behind the combination? Who sent you?"

"I can't talk over the telephone! What the hell do you think?"

"Your boys said after ten o'clock they find me they'll make trouble. You cannot blame me if I'm suspicious a little."

"What could we do in the soda parlor? Don't worry about it."

"Nevertheless," said Shubunka.

"So, look, you can understand. You can get the idea. We don't like trouble when it ain't absolutely necessary. If there's some other way of settling an argument, it's O.K., that's how we want it, too. If we can straighten this out with a job, the boss, he says he's got no objection. Come on down to the soda parlor. We'll give you a list of the houses you'll handle. Out of Neptune Beach, naturally. You'll take care of the collections and the girls. It's forty, fifty a week, depending, but you can make more when you see how we work it. There's ways when you get used to it. That's all I can say on the phone." The sniffler paused. "So what do you say? Listen, I don't have to beg you. I ain't going on my hands and knees waiting for you all night to make up your mind."

"All right," said the fat man. "But why can't you come up here to my apartment? We can have a drink."

"Take it or leave it! I'm getting tired. You can come down to Ann's and settle the whole business right now. I'm hanging up."

"I'm coming! All right! All right! I'm leaving the house right this minute!"

Shubunka replaced the phone and went looking for his hat in feverish haste. The call had heartened him immeasurably, giving him new life and strength. To hear a voice again, speaking in friendly tones, to find someone taking pity on his misery, someone wanting to help him! In his wave of emotion Shubunka lost all pretense and affectation. He was anxious only to get at Ann's, see the men and arrange for his work. It would not be all over. He was not finished. His job with the combination would not be quite the same as his old standing. There would be less money, less prestige. But it was better than to be cast off entirely. Hope and gratitude flooded him. In time he would manage to rise again, within the organization or outside of it, in any case a stronger man. It would be all right! The sudden change in his status affected him to the point of tears of relief and happiness. At the door, in his hurry, he stopped and ran back to turn off the radio.

Shubunka ran down the stairs, leaning against the hall walls to steady himself on his bent legs. At the door outside he looked up and down for a taxi. At this hour his block was empty of people and few cars drove through the street. Shubunka was perspiring in fear lest he be too late, lest he arrive at Ann's and find the men gone, lest he lose his last chance. He started running to the corner, turning his head to watch the traffic behind him for a cab.

The dull exploding sound of a revolver shot abruptly broke the stillness of the street. The fat man, in startled terror, tripped in his flight and stumbled to the pavement, rasping the skin off the heels of his palms against the rough surface.

A black sedan was speeding down the block. As it approached directly alongside of Shubunka, the car lurched in a wild curve to the curb. In rapid succession five more gunshots echoed and reverberated through the street, filling it with the roar. Shubunka could hear the impact of the bullets on the sidewalk, chipping the stone and send two or three pieces flying against his face. An entire window to his right came down with a loud crash. His mouth was open, and breathing heavily he sucked up the street dirt until his tongue felt fuzzy with the grit. Saliva dripped from his lips. He held his head close to the ground until long after he heard the car swishing down the street. It was over but he lay trembling for many minutes.

Now the windows of the buildings that lined the street grew lit in a crazy-quilt design. People in nightclothes peered anxiously into the darkness, uttering confused shouts of wonder as they blinked with sleep. Three or four men were hoarsely yelling for the police at the top of their voices, and down the far end of the block a woman was senselessly wailing in resounding screams. A man on the fourth floor of one of the buildings was shouting indignantly that the trouble with New York City was that it was lousy with goddammed racketeers. "They got every goddammed judge and politician all fixed!" he yelled as more and more lights and people appeared. "The cops want to do their jobs and they could clean up New York in a week. But what the hell can they do when the goddammed gangsters have all the political pull?" His voice thundered down the street but no one listened to him.

In the confusion they could not locate the actual spot of the shooting. They were all looking for a body but they fixed their range remarkably too far distant from Shubunka, unable to imagine that the action had taken place directly below their windows. The street was full of cries and shouts and the piping demands of children.

Shubunka picked himself up from the ground, huddling against the wall of a building as he stumbled around the corner, out of sight. He was unhurt. The first premature shot, fired when the car was too far away for sure aim, had mercifully startled the fat man into pitching impulsively close to the pavement so that none of the other five shots hit him. As he hurried away, Shubunka suddenly became aware that his palms smarted. In the slanting light of a street lamp he could see the pimples of blood on the heels of his hands. He brushed them against his trousers.

The first shock of terror had worn off, and to take its place the full raw meaning of the attack became clear in his mind with brutal intensity. They meant to kill him and they were in deadly earnest. There was no way in which he could turn them off now. Shubunka had always felt, deep within him, that no serious harm would come to him and that the men really meant only to scare him out of town. The abrupt realization of his danger now stunned him. But above his great fear lay dismay and bitterness at the betrayal by the man at the telephone, for now Shubunka felt truly abandoned and alone in the world.

FOUR

FROM THEIR POSITION in the darkened doorway of a store across the street, Karty and Arthur could see the movements of the people in Ann's and its gaudy interior, lit up at the fountain by the rays which gleamed from the metal equipment, the mirrors and the shiny surfaces of the cabinets and showcases. To Arthur, at this distance, the scene, glaringly brilliant amid the darkness of the other stores on the Avenue, became strangely unfamiliar, far away and unreal, as though he were seeing it in a dream. Nevertheless, he longed to be back in its warmth. He turned to Karty as they sat on the step of the doorway.

"Gee, it's late. I don't want to bother you no more, but I wish you would tell me what we're waiting here for. I don't understand what it's all about it. I don't know. When are we going to get back the twenty dollars?"

"Don't worry, Arthur," the gambler said, exhausted and broken so that his voice sounded as though he were sobbing even now. "See, I got to wait until my friend shows up. He said he would be around soon. If I go away now, after waiting all this time, then we'll miss him altogether and then you wouldn't like it neither. See, Arthur, you don't want to go away, do you?"

"Yes, but it don't sound right to me," the dishwasher cried. "I got a funny feeling about the whole business. It's all a dumb bull story."

"It's the truth, Arthur. It's no bull story. You just wait and see,"

Karty begged, but it was not the truth, much as the gambler himself wished it might be. They had traveled in the empty elevated trains, bleak and desolate at that hour, from Williamsburg back to Neptune. The train had crawled, making many stops and lingering between them, but all the same it was only eleven-thirty now and Spitzbergen didn't leave the place until it closed for the night. This would be at two, even later, perhaps. Karty wondered how the time would ever pass, how he would manage to keep Arthur quiet, and whether he would retain his courage. But he was desperate.

They sat in the doorway of the store with their eyes fixed on the bright illumination within Ann's. Arthur could not help himself as he waited for Karty's friend to appear with the twenty dollars he owed him. He kept up a constant stream of complaints and protests, mumbling tearfully to himself and crying out at intervals to the gambler. Soon Spitzbergen would be tallying the day's receipts with the cash in the box. If the friend didn't arrive in another few minutes, it would be too late for the dishwasher to slip the money back into the register and then they would have to go to jail, even if they finally had the money. It had been the most miserable day in his whole life, he whimpered, the cash register, the races, the losses, the garage, and now the agonizing wait for the mysterious friend.

Arthur bitterly bewailed that moment in the little soda parlor kitchen when he had allowed Karty to talk him into the whole mess. And all he wanted right now was to replace the money, to go home to his boarding house, to sleep and forget the day. Let those boys at Ann's keep their tough ways and manly talk. He no longer envied them. He didn't want them for himself. Arthur wanted only peace and quiet and no troubles. "Free as a bird," he wept aloud. "Nothing on my mind. That's what I like. Gee whiz, Mr. Karty, I'm sorry I ever got mixed in this rotten business. I hate it. I'm nervous and disgusted."

"Don't get discouraged, Arthur," Karty pleaded, putting his hand on the dishwasher's shoulder. "You can imagine how I feel about it myself. Don't get the impression I enjoy it. I'm in the same boat, too, only worse, much worse. I'm sorry I ever got you in this jam, but I'll get you out, Arthur. Then everything will be O.K. again. You'll see, Arthur. I won't forget you for this. I'll take you to the track again when we'll have no worries and then we'll have a real good time. You'll see, Arthur, you'll see."

"I don't want to go to the races," the dishwasher sobbed. "I hate them. I don't like it."

"Then we'll do something else. We'll have fun, Arthur. We'll have good times. You'll see."

"No good times!" he wailed, brushing away the thought with his arm in a gesture of misery. "I don't care about having fun. All I want is to get rid of the whole mess now. To get my mind relieved, that's all I'm wishing for."

"Oh, I'm sorry, Arthur. It's my fault. I got you in this jam and I don't blame you for the way you feel. But it will be all right, Arthur. It'll all be O.K. soon." The weasel face was tightened with grief and repentance.

Arthur paused in his weeping and touched the gambler on the elbow. "Oh, it's O.K., Mr. Karty," he mumbled. "I ain't got nothing against you. I'm not blaming you. What's the use of making you feel bad, too? It don't help."

Wishing heartbreakingly that he were back in Springfield, Mass., driving the smoked-fish truck, Arthur tried to control himself, for he sincerely did not want to add himself to Karty's burdens. The gambler was as miserable as he was, even more, as he said. Arthur made an effort to drive away the tears and to compose himself, but just then he could see Spitzbergen in front of his store. The apron was off. He was wearing his coat and hat. That meant he would be soon leaving.

"He found out!" the dishwasher cried. "He's going to the police! He never goes home so early. He knows already. Now we're really in for it! It's the finish for us!"

Karty had risen, trembling, his eyes on the soda man. His right hand went impulsively into his pocket for the wrench and he waited for Spitzbergen to step out of the store. He had not heard Arthur, forgetting for the moment that the dishwasher was still there. Arthur looked up in dismay, unable to understand the sudden change in him.

"What are you doing?" he called. "What the matter now?"

Karty continued to ignore him. He could now see Shorty, the soda jerker, enter the parlor. At this, Spitzbergen took to raising his arms in the air as he always did when he was complaining and crying. The soda man wasn't leaving the store. Karty sat down again on the doorstep.

"It's O.K., Arthur," he said. "Don't worry. He didn't find out nothing. He don't know about it yet."

"I don't like it!" Arthur cried. "Where's your friend? You're not waiting for any friend. It's Mr. Spitzbergen you're waiting for! I know! I can tell."

As Karty moved restlessly on the step, the wrench in his pocket jarred against the stone. Arthur heard the hard noise and grew frightened. He could sense further trouble, and as the moments passed he became panicky with foreboding.

"What you got in your pocket?" he asked, his voice thin with fear. "Tell me. I want to know. What you got there?"

"What? What's the matter, Arthur? You're getting nervous and imagining all kinds of crazy things. I ain't got nothing in my pocket."

"I heard the noise. You can't fool me no more. I heard it."

"What? I must of kicked the stone with my foot. See, that's what it must of been. My foot."

In his anxiety to soothe the dishwasher, Karty began kicking the step with his heels with patient persistence. Arthur listened carefully to the sounds he produced in this way but was not convinced.

"It wasn't like that," he whimpered. "It sounded like a piece of iron or something."

"You imagined it, Arthur. Honest, you did. In your nervousness you imagine all kinds of things. I ain't got no piece of iron in my pocket."

Arthur, still uncertain, was rolling his head in helpless misery. "I don't want no more trouble today," he moaned. "I can't stand no more. I got all I can stand. Where's your friend, Mr. Karty? Why don't he show up already?"

"He'll come, Arthur," the gambler said, patting his shoulder reassuringly. "You'll see, Arthur. He'll come."

His eyes were on the soda parlor. Spitzbergen was in a sweat with Shorty, but his hat was still on his head and he would be leaving soon.

"Listen, Spitzbergen, you got me in the wrong mood," Shorty snapped, sulking and looking tough. "I ain't got the patience to argue with you. All I want to say right now is I didn't take no money, I don't know nothing about it and now leave me alone. I got my own troubles just like everybody else."

"See, see," shouted the boss, spitting in his anger. "See how excited he gets all of a sudden. Look at him. He can't stand to hear about it. They take twenty dollars from my cash register and I ain't got no right to mention it even! No, I dassen't say a word! I must like it, I must say it's fine, it's O.K., sure, thanks. What's the matter, it flew away by magic, the money?"

"I refuse to say another word about it. It don't concern me, so leave me alone." The jerker sat down on a stool and swiveled around so that his back was turned to the boss. What the hell did he have to come back to the soda store for, he asked himself? "Goddam son-of-a-bitch bastard," he muttered, disgusted with the world, suspicious and conniving all the time. He was disgusted enough to say the words out loud. Spitzbergen jerked back, his arms sweeping up with surprised anger, fuming in an inarticulate jumble. "Draw one!" Shorty commanded the relief defiantly. "And if it ain't good and hot, you know where you can shove it!"

"My, my!" whispered the tight-lipped one, going for a cup. He raised his eyebrows in mock alarm at Shorty's fierce expression.

"Nuts to you, too!" snarled Shorty.

The relief whistled complacently and busied himself with the Silex pots.

Spitzbergen glared at Shorty's fancy gabardine back with helplessness. "Lillian!" he screamed. "Lillian!"

The new cashier, clutching her order book close to her bosom, came running forward, wide-eyed with fear. "What's the matter now?" she whimpered. "If he said anything, it's got to be a lie. I didn't take a cent, I should drop down dead right this minute!"

"Never mind!" bawled the soda man. "Who told you to come in eight o'clock? Answer me that."

Lillian looked at Shorty's back and stuttered. "Who?" shouted the boss. She pointed at him. "He told me," she said, her voice breaking.

"So?" the boss howled. He had worked himself up to a fine point and now screamed at the soda jerker's fancy coat with grim triumph. Replacing the cup, the soda jerker swiveled around.

"So what?" he asked. "So I told her to come in eight o'clock. What's the crime in that?"

Mr. Spitzbergen groped helplessly, caught off balance. "No crime?" he asked. "It's not a crime? Who, tell me, please—since when you the boss?"

Shorty dismissed the boss and glanced bitterly at the cashier. "O.K.," he said to her, shaking his head in sad wisdom. That was women. They were all alike, all a bunch of bitches without a single thread of appreciation or gratitude in them. "O.K., sister. At least now I know what kind of a broad you turned out to be."

Spitzbergen was beside himself. Almost choking with futile fury, he glared first at Lillian and then at the soda jerker's back. The money was gone from the register and there seemed to be nothing he could do about it.

Lillian quailed, her eyes big and the double chin quivering before his wrath. The boss took to slapping his sides with his hands, repeating the gesture again and again. "I give up," he gasped. "I'm finished. The hell with it. Let everything in the store go to hell. I'm going away. Do what you want with the store, only leave me have my life."

He seized his hat and pulled it straight on his head with fierce energy, but he waited, unsatisfied, and his fury grew cool. He was reluctant to leave the place. The rush in the parlor had by this time died down to a half-dozen couples sleepily whispering over the tables while their mouths sucked soda through the straws. Cold weather, no crowds, otherwise the place would have been roaring for hours with the home-going bathers who stopped at Ann's for ice cream on their way to the New York trains. Rotten weather, muttered Spitzbergen, distracted. The papers said hot for tomorrow but what did the papers know? His glance fell on Shorty's relief man. The tight-lipped one was leaning happily against the wall, his arms crossed over his chest, placid and content. Snotnose, the boss said, pay good money, he stands and feels good. "Hey, you," he called. "You got nothing to do? Everybody died here? You finished for the night? That's very nice. I'm glad to know it."

The relief picked up a rag and started mopping the metal work, easy and calm. Spitzbergen, glaring at him, kept on turning around on his feet, his hat still on his head. He had to go home but he didn't like to leave the place alone. He could see them in his mind pillaging the register the moment he left, neglecting the customers, ruining the whole business. They were a gang of thieves. Each one of them thought Spitzbergen had a little money and was therefore entitled to tear as much out of him as he could. Spitzbergen always liked to lock up himself, but his wife had phoned twice in the last hour and it was almost twelve. Parties. That was all he had on his mind.

"Please, Mr. Spitzbergen," Lillian said. She had been standing there in front of him all the time, holding the checkbook as she waited to be dismissed. "I don't care what you think, but I didn't take the money from the register. It's an insult to my character. If you knew me, you would never think I could do such a thing."

"Leave me alone!" he roared. "Don't you think for a minute I forgot the twenty dollars! You'll make good yet or you'll go to prison."

"Mr. Spitzbergen, I didn't take it!" Lillian wailed. The tears came down her cheeks in remarkable profusion. "I don't know a thing about it."

"Then it's too bad. Then I am very sorry. You're the cashier, no?

I pay you money to watch the money in the box, no? Who took it if you didn't? A ghost? By magic? Don't worry, you ain't seen the finish of it. You'll go to prison!"

"Oh, Mr. Spitzbergen! Oh, Mr. Spitzbergen!" She was bawling at the top of her lungs and the couples in the rear were already standing up to look at the racket. The boss grew furious with irritation, twisting his head from the customers to Lillian.

"Shaddap!" he cried. "For God's sakes, shut your mouth! Get out of here. Go away. Don't make such a holler."

He pushed her away. Wiping her eyes with her handkerchief, she went sadly to her place behind the cashier's stand. The couples finally sat down at the *intime* alcoves, and the boss glared with hatred at Lillian for having caused a commotion in a place of business.

"Cry, cry," he said, his voice carefully held low. "You can cry your head off. You can knock your head against the wall a hundred times. It won't help you. Make good or you'll go to prison. You'll see if I'm bluffing."

"Insulting," she blubbered. "I'm insulted. I got a good character or how do you think I got my references? You got no right to insult me like this."

The boss turned his back to shut her up before she began all over again. Enough and more he had suffered today. Lillian sniffled and in great concentration cleaned her nose with the handkerchief. A crazy place. She hated it. She wouldn't stay another day. The minute she could get another job, she promised herself, she would leave this miserable hole. All day it had been the lousy soda jerker, pinching and grabbing at her. Now it was the boss himself saying she had stolen twenty dollars. He was going to put her in jail and what proof could she give that she hadn't taken the money? After all, as he said, she was the cashier, she was responsible. She sobbed, unable to stop. She had arranged for her boyfriend to meet her at twelve and take her home when she quit work. That would protect her from Shorty, but what good could he do for her with the boss? Lillian looked at the clock. Twenty minutes to twelve. At least she would be getting off soon. She'd be able to go home and forget this rotten place for a few hours. Could Spitzbergen really put her in prison, even if she hadn't stolen the money? The sobs broke out afresh.

"Quiet!" yelled the boss. He shuffled impatiently on his feet. He had to go and it was a blessing in disguise. Another hour in the soda parlor today would be enough to send him to the hospital. He was on the verge of a nervous breakdown. He was a wreck. He smacked his brow below the hat and stumbled to the door.

"Hey, you," he called to the relief. "Lock up good. Make sure everything is all right before you go, and don't be in such a hurry, too. Don't close up the store like it was a fire."

The tight-lipped one acknowledged the order without a word, glancing peacefully at his employer.

"Snotnose," said Spitzbergen, dissatisfied with the response. "And you, too, mister," he said, wagging his finger at Shorty's gabardine back, "I'll show you to get fresh. I'll learn you how to keep the mouth. Don't think because I'm going home so I'll forget all about it. I won't forget. I'll take care of you, too. I'll show you I'm still in the world yet."

Shorty had been hunched up over his coffee for ten minutes, engrossed in his thoughts, but now he turned on the stool. "See, Spitzbergen, I ain't in no mood for arguing tonight," he told him, clipping the words in repressed anger. "You feel like getting sore at me, it's O.K. You can enjoy your pleasure. I don't care, but I didn't do nothing to you and you would realize it if you wasn't so excited." Speaking his piece, he swiveled back again, and the boss wagged his finger at him, shaking his head in rhythm, at a loss for further words. On the doorstep he glared at them all. A lousy life, a stinking world, he would be better off dead. Thieves, gangsters, rotten weather. Only miseries. He had a monopoly on them.

"You, too," he finally cried. He pointed violently at Lillian at the cashier's stand. "It's not a finish yet with the twenty dollars."

Lillian broke into a new spasm of tears and sobs. The boss raised his hands high above his head and slammed them down again in despair. "The hell with it! The hell with the whole goddam business!" He wept. He was walking out of Ann's to the station, slapping his sides in his gesture of bitterness, thinking of his burdens and overwhelmed by them. It had been a terrible day but the worst of it was that all his days had been like it and would continue in the same fashion.

Across the street, Karty, the gambler, was tremblingly pulling Arthur to his feet by the coat collar.

"What are you doing, Mr. Karty?" the dishwasher begged, amazed and afraid. "I don't understand what it's all about! I can't make it out!"

"Come, Arthur! Come with me! You'll see," Karty whispered, shaking with emotion. "I'm only doing what I have to."

"I don't want further trouble! I can't see the sense in following Mr. Spitzbergen. I don't know what you're doing!" But brushing the hair away from his eyes, he trotted obediently after the gambler to the station stairs.

Inside Ann's, at the cashier's stand, Lillian was lost in a fit of tears. She rested her head on her hands over the desk and couldn't stop. Mr. Spitzbergen was going to the police station to put her in prison.

Under the gentle light of the deserted lampposts, while the wind idly worried newspapers and sent their scattered sheets flying over the badly paved, sandy streets of Neptune Beach, while huge, ugly cats, with faces like fists, cried and wailed with misery over unfruitful garbage cans, on that still night of terror Shubunka stumbled in crazed panic, his mind numb, knowing only that there were men on the streets seeking him out so that they might murder him. Where could he go to escape them? The fat man slobbered at the mouth, his lips open as he breathed heavily with exertion and fear. In his mad flight he had gone senselessly back to Neptune Beach. He had taken no time for thought on his direction, but had run on his bent legs, absorbed only in movement and haste no matter where it was he fled. Forgetting the trolley line in his enormous dread, he had hurried on foot all the way from his home to the Beach, trembling at the approach of every automobile. When he heard the car, he would dart into hallways, down the steps leading to the apartment-house yards, or, when he was caught exposed, he would huddle fearfully against the shadows of some building, shivering and perspiring until the auto passed. Then weakly recovering his strength, he hurried onward, stumbling and groping, his mind hazed but filled with the tremendous desire to run, to hurry and to escape the thugs pursuing him in the big black car.

Shubunka was now coming to the boardwalk, anxious to be mixed among people for their warmth and their protection. Here the streets were flooded with the glaring lights of hot-dog stands, the amusement contraptions, and the sideshows. The sudden clanking roar of the wood cars tearing down the steep inclines of a scenic railway filled the air, startling the fat man until he was able to locate the noise. The streets and the boardwalk were brilliantly lit but they were empty of people. It was growing late and there had been no crowds of bathers from the city today, so that the few strollers here were residents of the neighborhood. They took the night air for a half hour before going to bed. But the concessionaires persisted stubbornly, begging them to play the balloon games for merchandise prizes, to buy frozen custard cones, waffle ice-cream sandwiches, hot potato chips and knishes. They banged their counters monotonously with spoons, glaring hatred at the passersby because they would not stop. The swish of balls rolling up the alleys came from the skee-ball establishments, but the players here were the Filipino owners themselves, hoping to entice players. Banging and jerking around in its circle, the cars of the Whip were empty and forlorn. The Ferris wheel lumbered dispiritedly high above the ground, the cradles unoccupied. The weight-guessers, the health-talkers, and the fortune-tellers sat moodily at their stands, unhappy with bad business. For all its clanging noise and brilliant lights, the boardwalk was abandoned.

Shubunka abruptly halted. There were no people here, no comfort, only the bleakness of electric bulbs shining in dusty circles amid the emptiness. Why had he come back to Neptune Beach, he asked himself? It was the worst place in the world for him to be now! The thugs would surely be looking for him here! He had to hurry, to go somewhere else before it was too late. Shubunka grew frenzied with haste but as he turned his head and shifted from one start to another, he wondered which direction to take. Where could he go now? Whom did he know and who would save him? He rested weakly against the railing of the boardwalk. Before him lay the houses, and stretching in front of them was Brooklyn, the city and the world. Within the darkened buildings were people sleeping, thousands and thousands, and there was not one among them who had heart for him, who even knew of his despair or would come to his aid. Spread out before him lay the world, hardened and unfeeling, black as the night itself. Where could Shubunka go?

Through the desolate alleys of Neptune Beach sped the big black sedan looking for Shubunka. On its windshield were reflected the bright cigar ends of the strong-arm men. They were the sniffler and his friend Amchy, the one with the prizefighter's broken nose and the dapper individual who hated Shubunka at the sight of him. Crestfallen and angry, the sniffler drove the car while the others kept their eyes dutifully on the sidewalks, examining the pedestrians for the fat man.

"What I say," Amchy told them, "is we should dump the car. It's no sense taking chances. Somebody might of seen us and they might be tailing us right this minute for all we know. I don't like to take risks when it ain't necessary."

"Aw, shaddap, shaddap," cried the sniffler, impatient and worried. "Who the hell let out that first crack anyway?"

"Search me," said Amchy. "I didn't. I waited." He glanced virtuously at the other two.

"So I did it," the dapper one admitted, looking surly. "So what about it? I couldn't help it."

"Jesus Christ," the sniffler broke out, slapping the wheel with his hand and staring straight ahead on the street. "He ain't got the least bit control. Gun crazy! All he wants is to shoot. He don't care about nothing else. What the hell's the sense taking a crack when it's too far and you can't be sure? Tell me that."

"So I couldn't help it! So what about it?" the dapper one retorted. "I couldn't wait. I can't stand the sight of that guy. He gets me nuts just to look at."

"Aw, lay off," the prizefighter told the sniffler, "What's the use yapping now about it?"

"No," he insisted, really enraged. "It's not the thing itself, but it's the principle like. What it is, it's why shouldn't a guy have the least bit control over himself? He acts like a dope charged up all the time. He's a wild man."

"So what are you so sore about?" the fighter asked. "It's his hard luck. What's it got to burn you up? I don't see how it concerns you so hot."

"O.K.! That's fine! I'm glad you like it, a nice ride in the evening. It don't concern me the least bit. I only got to talk to the boss. I got to tell him, 'Oh, no, we didn't get him, see. See, Amchy, he can't stand the living sight of him, he don't like him so good, he couldn't wait and shot too soon so that fat bastard could duck.' The boss, he'll say, 'That's swell! That's simply hot!' I'll get a bonus!"

Satisfied after his speech, the sniffler wriggled restlessly in his seat and stepped harder on the gas pedal. The car raced through the streets. Moving uncomfortably on the upholstered cushions, the boys clutched their cigars firmly in their teeth, silent in gloomy reflection, for the sniffler had spoken the truth. They had bungled the job and the boss would be angry with them. The only way in which they could make up for their failure was to meet Shubunka before the night was over, but it seemed a hopeless task to find him on the streets once they had scared him at his home.

"Let's try the soda store," the fighter said. "Maybe the lunkhead went there."

"Why should he go to the soda store?" the sniffler asked. "What's the matter, he's brainless? Just because he looks like a clunk, it don't necessarily mean he ain't got a head on him."

"He must be a coke, like you said," remarked the fighter. "I can't figure him out myself, but what the hell, he might be just crazy enough to go there. At least we can try. It's better than nothing."

"It's hopeless," the driver mourned, but he turned the car toward Ann's.

"I think we must of got him anyway," the dapper one said staunchly. "It looked to me like we got him, I don't know."

"Yeh! Yeh!" snorted the sniffler angrily. "Sure we got him. We got him fine. He had all the time in the world to duck. I can just imagine how we got him."

The dapper one fell back in his seat. Going thirty-five, forty miles an hour, using revolvers instead of sawed-off shotguns, they hadn't had a chance with Shubunka warned by his first crazy bullet. He knew it was his fault and he kept his peace. The men sat silently as the car rumbled through the streets back to the Avenue.

"What I say is we should dump the bus," Amchy finally repeated. "It's no sense taking chances for no good reason. We can dump the car and pick up another bus, and we're just as well off. The way it is we're taking a chance. Somebody might be tailing us for all we know."

"Aw, shaddap!" roared the sniffler, beside himself. "I'm all out of patience!"

He brought the car to a screeching halt at the soda parlor, banging the door when he got out with an elaborate show of irritation. But inside Ann's he could learn nothing to satisfy him. The tight-lipped relief man, his arms folded across his chest, showed neither fear nor interest when the sniffler asked him for Shubunka. The thug looked at Shorty and the cashier with blazing anger but as he glared the fury cooled. He was a reasonable man and had to realize that there was nothing to be gained by cowing them. Shubunka wasn't in the store. He went back to the street.

"Sure, he's in the soda store!" he ground out to the fighter. "He's sitting there and saying, 'Here I am, boys. You looking for me maybe? Then what the hell you wasting time for? I been staying here in the store all the time just for you to put in an appearance.'"

Offended, the prizefighter viciously flicked his cigar ash. "Hey, I ain't taking nothing from you!" he called. "Where the hell do you get off pulling that crap on me?"

The sniffler got into the driver's seat and turned his back on him as he stepped on the starter. He ignored them all in his bitterness. "Lousy charged-up coke," he muttered. "Got to go chasing all over the goddammed town for him when I could be home in bed right this minute." If they didn't settle the situation in Neptune before the morning, he knew he'd have his troubles with the boss. "We'll get him," he said quietly, glaring through the windshield. "We'll find the bastard and when we do he'll be sorry he put us to all this extra trouble."

The sniffler shifted into first and tore up the block. They would try the joints, they would go back to Shubunka's house, they would trail the streets of Neptune Beach all night. Sooner or later they'd find him.

"I don't like it," Amchy said, absorbed in his worry. "We should dump the car. I still say it."

"See, that's all he's got on his mind!" the driver cried. "I got to do the talking to the boss. It's me who has to explain. All he wants is we should change cars." He couldn't understand him and shook his head violently.

The car sped through the streets.

⌒⌒⌒

What were they after Shubunka for, Shorty wondered? The last two days those gangsters had been all over the place. Smart guys, out for nobody's good, but the way he felt now they could just as well find the goddammed fat mope, beat him up and do anything they liked to him. He didn't give a hang. It was a rotten world and he was no longer feeling sorry for anyone beside old Number One. It didn't pay. Here he was, a nice fellow, anxious to do everybody a favor, a regular guy. He worked his fingers to the bone for Spitzbergen in the soda parlor, half the time doing the work of two men. He tried to cheer up Mrs. Pavlovna, that fat bitch, and show her a good time. He fixed it up for the new cashier to take an extra hour off in the afternoon. What did he get for all of his efforts? In each and every case a kick in the teeth. No more! declared Shorty. He was through with it. From now on he wasn't anybody's good-natured slob for nothing.

"Fill it up!" he told the relief man. "Good and hot, that's the way I want it, see?"

The relief's eyebrows went up, and, taking up the cup, he whistled grandly down the scale in mock alarm.

"Nuts!" cried Shorty. The tight-lipped one went down the board flats, bouncing on the balls of his feet. "Son of a bitch," said the little soda jerker, and glared darkly at his back. A goddammed lousy world. No cause and effect. It made no difference what kind of fellow you were. No matter how hard you tried to do the right thing, all you ever got for your efforts was a kick in the teeth. It paid to be a bastard. Take Shubunka. In spite of whatever trouble he might be having with those gangsters, all the same he was always full of jack, wore expensive clothes, and did what he liked. He could have a broad whenever he felt like it. And what did he do to deserve all the luck? He ran a string of whorehouses! That was how you got along, the soda jerker affirmed, now growing distracted. The radio murmured its sleepy waltz tunes. No! he cried almost aloud, he wasn't going to a house tonight! The relief placed the steaming cup before him on the counter.

The soda store was now almost empty, with two or three couples lingering over their ice cream in the parlor as they whispered ardently but sleepily across the futuristic tabletops. At the cashier's stand, Lillian still sat on the stool, watching the door for Spitzbergen to reappear. Her tears had now stopped, but occasionally she became unable to restrain herself and broke into hiccupping sobs again. The boss was out calling a policeman. He might even put her in jail and how could she prove that she hadn't taken the money? Lillian looked at the clock. Ten to twelve. She'd leave at twelve, her boyfriend would meet her outside on the street to take her home, and then she would never go back to Ann's again. The sobs came again.

Over his coffee Shorty hated the world and Madame Pavlovna, and thought for solace of his naked women. In his haze the little jerker was now six feet tall, wore a full-dress suit, one hand in his pocket, debonair and handsome as Ronald Colman, who, after all, was about the same age. He is walking down the cream-tinted halls of the mansion, smoking his cigarette and looking majestic. As he approaches the door he exhales smoothly in reflection. Should he or shouldn't he? But what is the difference? After all, what is the difference? To make her happy costs him so little. With a resigned shrug he discards his cigarette and enters. From the pile of silk and lace on the bed in the center of the large, high-ceilinged room lies a hot piece, beautiful as all hell, her shoulders showing bare and rosy over the covers, plump, juicy, all the parts. She gazes at Shorty, dying with longing and passion. Her burning eyes devour him. "Ah, Vincent," she murmurs breathlessly, "my darling Vincent, I can hardly wait another minute. All evening on the terrace I been following you and you been so heartless to me." He looks down at her from his height, one hand still in the pocket, magnificent and bored-like. "Very well," sighs Shorty. "Very well." Ecstatic with joy, she leaps up on the bed to embrace him. As the covers fall away from her she is revealed nude. Not a goddammed stitch on! And as she hugs Shorty her warm fluid body presses against him.

"B'gee!" wept Shorty. "Oh, b'gee!"

"You speaking to me?" asked the relief.

"What? Who?" The soda jerker came up from his vision. "No, I ain't talking to you. What the hell would I be wanting to talk to you?"

The relief whistled, and Shorty, overcome by his misery, squeezed on the stool as he crossed his legs in the narrow space next to the marble fountain. Lillian was still sobbing and he noticed her with annoyance. No, he affirmed to himself, keeping back his own tears, he wouldn't go to a cathouse tonight. He watched the cashier with distaste but as the minutes passed his expression slowly changed. He climbed down from the stool and went to the cashier's stand.

"What are you all upset about?" he asked softly, his manner confidential and sincerely concerned. "What are you crying about?"

Lillian looked at him suspiciously, her eyes red and swollen.

"It's all your fault," she blubbered. "If you didn't tell me eight o'clock, Mr. Spitzbergen, he wouldn't of got the idea in his head."

"Gee, I'm sorry. How was I to know this would happen on this night? It was just the way it turned out, don't you know? I had only the best intentions in the world. See, he was all upset with those guys who came into the place all day, and I figured his mind was all taken up and, what the hell, you might get the benefit since there's nothing doing in the place anyway until nine. See, that's why I told you, Lillian. I can't help it if somebody has to steal some dough and he should think you did it. Hell, the way you act, somebody would think I told you eight o'clock on purpose."

"So it ain't your fault," Lillian wept. "So what good does it do me now? I didn't take the money from the cash register."

"Hell! I know you didn't, Lillian! You ain't that kind of a girl. I can tell human nature."

"So what good does it do you can tell human nature? He's calling a policeman. I got to make good the twenty dollars or he'll put me in prison."

"Lillian, look," said Shorty, bending close to her, "you don't want to worry about that guy Spitz. He's just a lot of noise. Bluff, see? All he's trying to do is scare you. What the hell, he can't do a thing to you. I know!"

"That's what you say. It's easy for you to say it because it's my troubles, not yours. Everybody don't worry when it's somebody else's troubles." But nevertheless Lillian's sobs stopped and she felt comforted and relieved a little by the jerker's kindness. She looked at the clock. Five minutes more and then she'd go home with her boyfriend. Then she would forget the whole mess. It was hell here. The double chin trembled as she collected herself. "What's the matter you know he can't do me a thing?" she asked.

"Listen," he whispered into her ear, his little face tightened with concentration. "Listen, Lillian, you want to know something about Spitzbergen? You so worried he'll call the cops. You want to know why he can't? You want me to show you how you can forget about the whole matter?"

The stout cashier gazed at him in suspicious wonder. "What's the matter you're so anxious all of a sudden?" she asked. "It don't seem so natural. Excuse me if I'm hurting your feelings, but it's kind of funny you're so anxious."

Shorty fell back from the stand and drew himself up in indignant protest. "Hell!" he cried. "That takes the cake! Lillian, I'm surprised at you for taking this attitude. I thought by this time you'd realize what kind of a fellow I was." He bent close to her again. "See, I feel sort of responsible, you know. After all, I think it's part my fault Spitzbergen thinks you took the money. So I see you aggravated and worried, and hell, Lillian, it makes me feel sort of lousy, see what I mean? So I want to show you you really ain't got nothing to worry about. That's the only reason."

The cashier continued to gaze at him doubtfully. "I don't know," she said. "It's almost time when I quit. It's almost twelve. I don't know."

Shorty threw up his hands and stepped back to the fountain, sputtering at her ingratitude. "Then O.K.! O.K.!" But in another impulsive moment he was back at the stand. "Listen, once for all, you want me to prove it? You want me to show you why Spitz can't do you nothing? If you want it, then O.K. If you don't, it's O.K. with me, too. I don't have to beg you to do you favors."

He paused for his answer. Lillian worked her finger in her ear to clear it of wax and, capitulating, said, "So?"

"Come with me."

Without looking back to make sure she followed him, the little jerker in his white gabardine suit stamped to the corner of the fountain, going for the cellar door. Standing placidly at the water boilers was the tight-lipped relief man, watching the maneuvers with a discerning eye. The radio moaned its soft love song. Lillian held back.

"Where you think you're taking me? What are you going to show me? It still looks fishy to me."

Shorty held the cellar door open. "Then O.K.," he said with cold decision, "it's just the way you want it. You feel like worrying all night about Spitz getting the police after you, you feel like aggravating yourself with prison, I don't give a hang if that's the way you want it. Only I can show you something to prove he can't call the cops. He can't, see."

Lillian looked at Shorty, at the relief, at the clock. It was almost twelve. She could leave right now but it would be good to sleep in peace tonight if she could be sure Spitzbergen was bluffing. She passed in front of the soda jerker and went down the steps. The relief man let out a chuckle and Shorty glared at him, his face distorted with anger, his lips moving as he uttered silent curses. He went to join the new cashier. The tight-lipped one whistled joyously and the door closed. He wiped the metal covers with a knowing air.

In the damp bare cellar, lit by the yellow rays of the bulb that hung from the ceiling, Lillian searched dubiously for the evidence that would assure her Spitzbergen was in no position to call the police. What could it be? Was it all a trick just to get her downstairs? All Lillian could see were the long slender tubes that carbonated the water, an old coffee boiler, boxes of ginger-ale bottles, and empty cardboard cigarette cases. Standing against the wall in one corner were an old maple sideboard, a round dining table, and a dirty sofa.

"So what is it?" she asked. The cashier firmly held the railing post at the foot of the stairs. As Shorty came down after her, he crowded her so that for the sake of appearances she was obliged to walk forward and lose the support of the post. But as soon as he stepped into the cellar she went back and grasped the banister again, her eyes wide with apprehension.

"Look," said Shorty. He seemed unnaturally pale and breathed hard. "You know what Spitzbergen peddles? It's against the law, see? He wouldn't like it if the cops heard about it or got too nosy."

"I don't see the connection. It's all a fake. What if he peddles? It don't concern me."

"Oh, yes, it does!" he whispered, eager and perspiring. "See, a crook can't call a cop when he's in trouble. He's afraid, too, don't you know? Now you can put two and two together and figure it out for yourself. If Spitzbergen tries anything on you, hell, he's in no position to throw stones at glass houses, see how I mean?"

He was talking nonsense! "I don't see," she said, troubled and dubious. "I don't know what you're talking about. What does he peddle it's so terrible?"

Shorty ran to the old sideboard, mysteriously silent, pulled out a drawer and waited for Lillian to come up and see for herself.

"Just take a look," he said. "Then you'll know."

The cashier moved slowly to him, regretfully leaving the post. She peered into the drawer. It was empty, absolutely empty. "For God's sakes!" she exclaimed. "What do you call this? You must be crazy or something!"

"What?" asked Shorty. He looked for himself and grew covered with apologies. "I pulled out the wrong one. No wonder you thought I must of gone insane." The soda jerker started pulling out all the drawers as he searched for the illegal merchandise that Spitzbergen sold. As he worked, he kept talking to her in a rapid flow, afraid to hesitate and give her time to leave. It was after twelve and she was off for the day. Then, abruptly, he stopped his searching and leaned against the sideboard.

"You want to know something, Lillian?" he asked. "I think you're a beautiful girl."

Lillian gaped at him for a moment, puzzled and growing scared. "Crazy!" she gasped. "What's the matter with you all of a sudden?"

"No, on the level, I seen a lot of girls in my time, but you got something about you, I don't know what it is, Lillian, but you're really a good-looking girl."

"So all right!" She was near tears. "I don't want compliments now! I want you should show me!"

"You know something," he said, pleading with her, his face earnest. "You and me could have a lot of fun together, see how I mean? We could have good times. I'm a regular guy. I don't hold on to a nickel. I like you. On the level, I got a real feeling for you."

"It's twelve o'clock. Listen, I got to quit at twelve o'clock. My boyfriend is waiting outside for me. If you want to show me something, show me. I ain't got all year."

Shorty stepped forward to touch her on the arm but she fell back in a panic, going to the wall of the cellar. He stood before her, his arms stretched out against the wall at her sides so that she could not escape.

"I'm not going to do anything," he begged. "Gee, Lillian, I'm not going to do a thing. Why can't you act like a nice kid? I like you, Lillian. No kidding. I got a real feeling for you. We could have a lot of fun."

Backed against the wall, hemmed in by his arms, Lillian stared at his pleading face in terror. It was all a fake. She knew it now. Spitzbergen didn't sell anything illegal. The skin on Shorty's face was tightened in wrinkles and in furrows, and the saliva had gathered into a sticky paste at the corners of his mouth so that when he opened his lips, lines of the stuff hung in front of his teeth. He was ugly and repulsive. Lillian would have screamed but she controlled herself.

"Look, you, my boyfriend's upstairs, waiting for me on the street. I want you to know that so you can't say I didn't give you fair warning. He's waiting to take me home. It's no fake. I ain't fooling. You try something fresh with me and he'll take care of you. He'll fix you if you try something funny. You better let me go before you get yourself good in trouble."

"Oh, Lillian, you got me wrong! I'm not trying anything on you. I wouldn't think of doing a thing you wouldn't like. Only why can't you be nice?"

"Let me go then if you're such a fine gentleman. You ain't got nothing to show me here. It's time. I want to go."

"Oh, Lillian, be a good kid. I'll take you out. I'll show you a real good time. On the level, I'm no piker when it comes to spending dough on somebody I got a feeling for. We'll have a swell time. I'm nuts about you. I like you."

Shorty pressed closer and put his arm on her shoulders, trying to embrace her gradually, but Lillian fought him off in frenzy. Crying, with the tears running down her cheeks, she punched out at him awkwardly and kicked at his shins. Shorty would not give in before her blows. He pressed in, pushing her closer to the wall, and hugged her with all the strength he had. The cashier sobbed and writhed helplessly in his grasp, her face distorted with disgust.

He fiercely clung to her. She could not dislodge him no matter how hard she struck at him, and she could not escape him. He had her fixed against the wall. She rubbed the skin off her elbows on the bricks but would not stop fighting him. Lillian would have screamed but she would have been ashamed to have people find him on her. She struggled to the banister, inching to the stairs, but Shorty held on, his face twisted with grim intensity, so that she had to drag him as she moved.

Suddenly the soda jerker let go. Lillian almost tripped with the abruptness of the release. She ran at once to the stairs, saw that Shorty was not following her and stopped on the fourth or fifth step. She looked down at him, flushed with hatred and humiliation, stooping her head in order to avoid the sloping ceiling.

"Don't you think for a minute you're going to get away with it, you filthy thing," she cried, her voice determined but still breaking in sobs. "You'll regret it. My boyfriend is waiting outside. He'll break every bone in your rotten body for this. You just wait and see."

"Aw, nuts. Nuts," Shorty called to her dismally. "Go on. Beat it. You were in a hurry to go, so go. Get out of my sight. Leave me alone."

"Louse!" she sobbed and went to the door.

Shorty sat down on the dusty sofa, neglecting his white suit. He felt sick and disgusted with himself and everything. It was lousy. That goddammed teasing bitch, Hahvahnah. It was all her fault. She got him all steamed up and he couldn't help himself. Shorty told himself he was a good fellow, had only good intentions, but everyone was unfair to him. No matter what he did he always got a raw deal. He sat on the sofa in the yellow light of the cellar and felt low and mean, unable for a long time to collect himself and go home.

When the tight-lipped relief saw Lillian burst from the cellar door, his eyebrows went up and he chuckled in careless delight, a happy man.

"Louse! You, too!" cried Lillian, hating Ann's and everyone connected with it.

"What did I do, baby?" the relief asked innocently. "Don't take it out on me."

Without answering or turning to look at him, she grabbed her purse at the cashier's stand and rushed to the street for her boyfriend.

⁓⁓⁓

In the little office of the garage near Bedford Avenue, the brother who had held out against letting Karty go slapped the top of the desk forcefully. "Lost!" he shouted, clamping his jaws tightly together in rage. "Neither the money, neither him, nothing! You'll never see him again. Thrown out." He glared at his brothers. "Leave him go! Let him out! You wanted it! Now we can stay here all night. It's after twelve already and where do you see him?"

Harry kept on looking glumly out the window, his hands in his pockets. The other brother sat philosophically and held his chin.

"Don't get excited over nothing," he said mildly. "What did we lose if we let him out?"

"No," said the angry one. "A man shouldn't steal money and do what he likes. There's still a God over America. We should learn him good he should know for all time. He takes thirteen hundred dollars and we stand by and say, 'O.K., that's nice, Moe. Go home.' We're cripples. We don't do a thing." The thought of it choked him and he had to stop. Overcome with vexation and anger toward his brothers, he had to turn his back on them to avoid fighting.

"Don't worry," Harry told them, his tone resolved and hard. "Don't get excited for nothing, like he says. If he brings back the money, it's fine. If he don't, we'll still know how to find him. There's always a day to learn him."

The three brothers, their heavy faces like slabs of meat, waited in the little office, struggling hard to control their impatience.

⁓⁓⁓

Sighing and groaning softly to himself with his many burdens, Spitzbergen rested on the wicker seat of the train on his way home. It was a joke for laughter. After a day such as his had been, he was going home for a party. In the midst of his bitterness, his face clouded deeper as he thought of his wife. He had kept her waiting almost two hours and she would be furious with him, especially after she had gone out of her way to prepare a special meal for him. He slapped his thighs weakly, hopeless and overcome. Everything was rotten and a man couldn't forget his troubles even when he went home. They persisted in the mind and nagged and tortured you so that it was much better to go to work. When you were active you had less time to worry. Spitzbergen glanced around, down to the far end of the train. He was almost positive that he had caught a glimpse of Arthur and Moe Karty on the station at Neptune Beach when he was waiting for the train to pull in. He must have made a mistake. Why should the gambler be going any place with Arthur? The soda man again lapsed into his troubled drowsiness, trying to forget his black day in the rocking motion of the train.

In the enclosure of the unused motorman's seat, two trains before Spitzbergen, Karty and Arthur were huddled with their knees against the door which had been slammed back flat against the driving apparatus before them. The dishwasher held his head in his hands and moaned to himself in monotonous despair. "I don't know what we're doing. I don't see the sense in it. What do we have to follow Mr. Spitzbergen for? What good will it do if we follow him?"

"Please, Arthur. I'm only doing just what I have to. I got it all figured out. It'll be O.K. and then you'll see. I know how you feel and I don't blame you. But just be patient a little longer, that's all I'm asking you."

"Ah, you! You and your bull stories! You lied to me about the friend and you're lying to me now. I don't know what you're doing. I wish I was finished with the whole business. I'm going crazy with the aggravation."

The dishwasher went on muttering unhappily to himself, disregarding Karty since he had lost all trust in him. Arthur stared out the black window and brushed the hair away from his eyes, sobbing and wondering what would happen now. What a hopeless mess he had pushed himself into since the morning! What a sap he had been, feeling jealous of Karty and Shorty and Shubunka. They could have all the tough talk and ways. Arthur didn't want them. So he was a kid, so he didn't know nothing, so it was better. You had nothing on your mind and that was something money couldn't buy. He wiped his nose with his finger and regretted bitterly for the hundredth time that he had ever listened to Karty.

"It's O.K., Arthur. It's O.K.," said the gambler, patting him on the knee. Karty at this time feared to lose the dishwasher's company and hoped the boy's nerve would not break altogether. He knew that without him his own courage would leave and he would never go through with his plans. And he had to, for the vision of the three brothers grimly waiting in the garage for him was constantly in his mind. They had beaten him up twice today and the third time they would finish him altogether. They were brutes, bastards, animals, but they would cripple him for life. Hidden by the motorman's enclosure in the empty train, Karty sinkingly realized that he had already been putting off his plan, had been stalling for more time, hesitating and postponing, and he knew that if he didn't act soon, it would be too late forever.

The local train drove ahead on the rails at the lowest speed, for there were many stations here and the intervals between the stops were four- and five-block runs. But slowly as the train moved and many as the stops were, for Karty the train was rushing to its destination and the ride could never be too long. The deserted streets from the station to Spitzbergen's house were lined by one-family homes and Karty understood that he would have to stop the soda man there or never. "It's O.K., Arthur," he wept. "It's O.K." He was hoodooed for life.

The train lumbered up the platform and ground to a stop. Karty looked out the window. Under the dim light of the station lamps he could read the street on the blue-enameled board. Avenue J! This was Spitzbergen's station! So soon! Karty was jolted to his feet and he dragged Arthur up by the coat shoulders.

"Come on!" he whispered fiercely, his weasel sharp features and swollen eyes contorted as he trembled. The blood rushed away from his head and he felt sick in the stomach.

"I don't know where we're going," the dishwasher wailed feebly. He stumbled out of the booth, not looking where he was being pushed. "Where are you taking me? I don't want more trouble. I'm going crazy with nervousness. I can't stand it. I'm sick and tired of the whole business."

The sliding door would jam back into place and then it would be too late. Karty hurried behind Arthur and shoved him forward. The door was already closing and he had to jump between it and the pole, struggling to keep it open while he tugged at the dishwasher to force him through to the platform. Once outside in the night air, Karty pleaded with him.

"I don't believe a word you say no more," Arthur moaned. "Bull-thrower. That's what you are. Always tells me bull stories." But he followed the gambler down the long narrow platform. The train rumbled away and they were left alone, the strong gusts of wind in the wake of the local blowing at their hats so that they had to grab them.

To their left lay the empty tracks, gleaming with the reflection of the platform lights and humming with the movement of trains far in the distance. The green and red signal lights twinkled in the windy darkness of the night. Before them Karty could see the short, plodding figure of the soda man as he went with his burdens to the station house which led to the street. The gambler felt cold with the breeze and yet he was perspiring. He buttoned his coat tightly but it did little to help his shivering. Spitzbergen climbed down the steps, holding on to the railing as he went.

The concrete floor of the little station room was swept bare. An old-fashioned barrel stove was a little behind the change booth and its turnstile. Within the box the elevated railway agent could hardly be seen. There was a small yellow bulb at the money hole and the man was resting his head in the shadows, napping with the lateness of the hour. Beyond the railings was a newspaper stand, but this was boarded up. Directly opposite, across the room and to the back of the booth, were the toilets, a narrow tiled area blocked out in the wall leading to the door. Between the ladies' and men's rooms stood a long wooden bench. Karty, following Spitzbergen down the stairs, was just in time to catch the soda man going into the men's washroom. A lucky chance! the gambler cried to himself. The toilet was better than the streets. It was perfect.

"Come with me," he whispered, his eyes intent on the head of the sleeping agent in the booth. "Follow me, Arthur. Now we got to see Spitzbergen."

The dishwasher stared at him hard, trying to drive the haze from his mind and discover what Karty's motive could be. "I won't go," he said, wavering with doubt and fear. "I won't go in. I won't do another thing more. I'm finished with the whole business. Let them put me in jail. I don't care. I can't stand it no more."

Karty jerked his arm savagely. "Keep quiet! Please!" he begged, his swollen eyes tense on the sleeping train agent. "He'll hear you! He'll see you, Arthur!"

"I won't go in," the dishwasher repeated dully. He pulled his arm away from the gambler and sat down on the bench. "You can do what you want but I'm all finished. I don't want to get mixed up in any more trouble. I got enough."

It would be too late! "So all right, Arthur," the gambler hurried to tell him. "Then sit down. Don't go away. Just sit down and keep quiet." He looked at the agent's head again, and then, taking out his handkerchief, stepped resolutely into the washroom.

Spitzbergen was on the point of leaving. His black, trouble-lined face deepened into a worried scowl as he looked at the man behind the handkerchief. It was Karty. What was the racetrack gambler doing here with him?

"What do you call this?" the soda man exploded. "What is this all of a sudden? Somebody here must be crazy!"

Karty removed the handkerchief with which he had been pretending to blow his nose in a feeble, senseless effort at concealment from Spitzbergen. Now encountering him at last, he was at a loss to know what to do or say. "Quiet, please. Don't make a holler," he begged, gesturing futilely.

"What's the matter I should talk low?" Spitzbergen asked, apprehensive and wondering. He didn't like the gambler's appearance. "You been following me from Neptune Beach. I saw you on the platform with the dishwasher. You been following me, ain't it?"

"Yes, Spitzbergen, I been following you," Karty answered, still standing uncertainly before him.

"For what? What's the matter?"

"Spitzbergen, please, I'll go down on my hands and knees. I need money. I got to have money. You don't know how bad I need it." The gambler shook his face tearfully for emphasis. "I'm in an awful hole, Spitz. I got to have the dough tonight, or else I'll get murdered. It's no fake. I mean it. Please, Spitzbergen."

"What the hell do you want from me?" the soda man cried. "I'm Rockefeller all of a sudden? I got money to give away? I'm not a philanthropist."

"Spitz! Please! I'm begging you!"

"Ah, go to hell! A fine how-do-you-do this is! He needs money, so he comes to me. I'm a bank. He follows me on the train and holds me up like a gangster. He gambles on the horses and when he needs money he comes to me! What's the matter with you, Mr. Moe Karty? They'll put you in Kings County yet."

"Spitz! Please! Never mind about Kings County and the horses. That don't matter now. I need the money."

The soda man stared at Karty, and as he stared he grew softened. The little gambler seemed hopeless and wretched, his nasty manner gone altogether as he begged and cried helplessly in his misery. Before the sight of his complete desperation, Spitzbergen could not find it in him to be too hard and his anger broke.

"Listen, Moe Karty," he said quietly, almost kindly. "I don't know what you want from me. I ain't got fortunes to give away and you should know it. I'm in all kinds of troubles myself. I ain't got a nickel to throw away. And even if I had, what do you want from me now? I don't carry money with me in my pocket. I got to go home. My wife is waiting for me. What hurts you I am sorry for, but I got my aggravations, too, and I can't help it. Let me go please."

"No!" said Karty. He backed against the washroom door and blocked the soda man's way. His face was white. "You ain't going until I get the money. I can't go away from here without money or I'll get crippled."

The scowl on Spitzbergen's face deepened but in spite of his irritation he restrained himself and paused. "Moe Karty," he reasoned, "don't be a foolish man. You got troubles, it makes you crazy. It won't help you to bother me. What can I do? I ain't got the money. So go out of the way, please."

"You got money. In your pocket. You got a roll. I know."

"What money in my pocket? What are you talking about?"

"Shubunka gave you money tonight. He paid you rent for the houses. I know. I heard him say it to you. Don't you think you can fool me with lies. All over Neptune they know you and your money and your bellyaching. You got plenty. You hold on to every nickel you got like it was the only one, but you got plenty."

"Moe Karty!" exclaimed the soda man, losing patience. "Please! Not another word! I don't like to be like a stone when another has troubles, but after all there is a limit to everything. I ain't got a penny. Let me pass!"

Spitzbergen moved forward to the door but the gambler went for him, grabbing with his hands at his pants pocket where he knew the soda man kept his money rolled up in a rubber band. Crying and cursing, he tried to seize the roll, his hand digging into the pocket. Spitzbergen, thoroughly enraged, whacked heavily at his neck with his right hand while he held the roll in the other.

"Bastard," he panted as though he were asking a question, "what do you think of this all of a sudden? A crazy man! Out of his mind!"

In the narrow room of the toilet, the yellow light gleaming at the tiles of the walls, the two men struggled clumsily over the money, which Spitzbergen still managed to keep in his pocket. Karty slobbered and talked fitfully as he fought. In the end the soda man smacked him away to the door. The gambler's head cracked against the metal sheeting and for a moment he paused, dazed. Spitzbergen drew himself together and straightened his clothes, breathing heavily. He glared angrily at the gambler, at the same time examining his face with concern lest the head blow had been too hard. The gambler was all right. Spitzbergen snorted and made to push him away so that he might pass.

But then, abruptly starting to action, Karty had brought the wrench from his pocket and began slamming the heavy man with the strength of a maniac. He pounded him on the face and the shoulders with it. Under the attack Spitzbergen grew so amazed and frightened that he failed to counter but stumbled blindly back to the wall, holding his hands up to protect himself from the blows of the wrench. He was too dumbfounded to cry out for help for some time, but twisted his head and ducked, hunching his shoulders, trying to escape. Was Karty meaning to murder him? He suddenly opened his mouth to scream, but, gasping and breathless, his cry had little force. His right cheek felt as though the bone had been broken. The little gambler would never stop. He was entirely insane. Spitzbergen was jammed against the wall so that when he tried to dodge the wrench he struck his head against the tiles. Karty was killing him! He began to grow weak and found he could not fight back. The gambler was overpowering him! He really meant to go on until he had murdered him! "Help! Police!" he gasped.

At the cries Karty grew violent with fear. He dropped the wrench and grabbed the soda man by the throat with both his hands, strangling him in frenzy to keep him quiet. Karty had him pressed against the wall and leaned against him, his legs apart, a yard away so that he brought his weight as well on the heavy man as he choked him. Spitzbergen squirmed and made retching noises. His hands were feebly scratching at Karty's face, and soon they fell to his shoulders, which he began patting slowly and listlessly as a man would in talking to an old friend. Then the squirming stopped, the choking noises stopped and the hands fell down to his sides, softly slapping the wall with the swing. Karty felt the weight on his arms increase and discovered he was holding him up. When he stepped back and released his grasp, Spitzbergen began to slide gently against the wall, his legs doubling up beneath him until he touched the ground. Karty stood back in panic. Before him the soda man was sitting on the floor, his hat still on his head, his face resting on his knees, as though he had suddenly fallen asleep. Karty began trembling.

Had he killed him? The gambler grew rigid, clenching his fists and holding his arms stiffly at his sides, to control the twitching of his body. His eyes were fixed on the hunched-up peaceful figure. Overhead he could hear a train rumble, on its way to Neptune Beach, and the room shuddered jokingly with the heavy weight above. Had he really killed him? Was it so easy to kill a man? It wasn't possible! Karty bent close to his face and peered under the hat. Spitzbergen didn't seem to be breathing! What was he standing here waiting for? Why was he looking at Spitzbergen? Springing to action the gambler rushed to the door and pushed it open halfway before he remembered. The money!

He could hardly bring himself to touch the soda man. Spitzbergen's legs were squeezed close against his body so that the pocket with the roll of bills was hard to reach. Whimpering with distaste and fear, Karty forced his hand in and clutched for the money. He held it finally in his fist, and with enormous relief went to the door, but he had to go back once again. He had forgotten the wrench. Grasping for it on the floor, it slid from his fingers tantalizingly until he was able to seize it.

Outside, the waiting room was still empty except for Arthur and the sleeping form of the train agent. Karty looked carefully into the booth but the man's head was still peacefully reclined against his palm. He had been napping all the time, unaware of him, of Arthur, or of the episode in the washroom, for at that hour, there had been no passengers from the city. No one had entered, and the train from Neptune had not yet passed on its way to the city.

"Where's Mr. Spitzbergen?" Arthur asked, his eyes wide with suspicion and terror. He stood up from the bench. "Why don't Mr. Spitzbergen come out? It's funny he should be inside so long."

"Come," Karty cried, ignoring the question. "We got to go fast."

"But where's Mr. Spitzbergen? Tell me why don't he come out?"

"Keep quiet, Arthur! For God's sakes, don't wake up the agent! He's still in the toilet. He's O.K. What do you think? Come on!"

Karty had run up on the steps and was pleading with the dishwasher from the distance. He bled a little at the face and the clothes were twisted on him. And, unawares, he was still holding the roll of bills tightly in his fingers. When Arthur noticed the money, he could no longer restrain himself. He remembered the metallic noise he had heard at the doorway of the store across the street from Ann's. In a burst of fear he ran into the washroom, saw Spitzbergen sitting so unnaturally against the wall, and broke out in a spasm of tears. He ran up to the gambler on the stairs.

"He's dead!" he gasped hysterically. "You killed him! Why did you do it?"

"For God's sakes, Arthur, keep quiet! He'll hear you!" Karty shook him violently, as frightened and desperate himself as the dishwasher. The two men went racing up the stairs.

"He ain't dead," Karty moaned as they stood impatiently on the open platform. "He's O.K. You're just nervous, that's all. You're imagining things."

"Oh, he's dead. He's dead," Arthur cried. "You killed him and now we'll both go to the electric chair and they'll kill us."

They waited for the train. Karty felt the money in his pocket. It couldn't be more than twenty or twenty-five dollars in singles. Shubunka hadn't paid him, or, if he had, Spitzbergen hadn't taken the money with him. The whole plan had been useless from the beginning. He didn't have enough to bring his wife's brothers in the garage and now he didn't dare to think of what would happen to him because of Spitzbergen. Even if the soda man wasn't dead, he had recognized Karty and they'd put him in jail for years. But he was dead. Karty had to get away, out of New York.

Arthur wailed quietly, rocking on his feet and squeezing his fingers.

"Stop it, Arthur," the gambler begged. "Please, Arthur. People will catch on just by looking at you. They could tell. Please Arthur, stop it."

"He's dead," wept the dishwasher, waving him away hopelessly with his arm. "Why did I ever listen to you? You told me bull stories. You're a bull-thrower, that's all you are. I listened to you and now they'll give me the electric chair."

"He ain't dead, Arthur. He ain't dead. You'll see, Arthur. It's just your imagination. You're nervous. He ain't dead." But Karty was in terror, too, and it was just a matter of hours before he would break into hysteria himself. Alone on the elevated platform, they waited for the train to New York. They would take a bus, Karty told himself. They would leave town. It would be O.K. if they just waited a little and didn't lose their nerve. They would find some way out of the mess. "He ain't dead," he repeated again and again. "He ain't dead."

In her apartment in Neptune Beach, Mrs. Karty sat up, listening to the radio as she waited for her husband to come home. All day she had gone through the streets looking for him, at Ann's, at the Garden where he laid his bets with the bookie, and at the garage near Bedford Avenue. He was a sickly man, underweight and with a nervous disposition, and he hadn't had a warm meal in his mouth for two days. He would drop to the pavement with weakness. Mrs. Karty regretted the day she had ever encouraged her husband to go to work for her brothers. They were coarse people, crazy for money, without feeling or pity. In spite of all his failings, her husband was an educated man, a certified public accountant. He had met a rough element at the garage. In time he had learned to play cards and gamble on the horses. If he hadn't been mixed up with her brothers, if he hadn't gone crazy over the gambling, they could have lived a wonderful life together, for even in the depression an accountant could make good money. It was all over. God alone knew where Karty was this minute, shivering in fear of her brothers, without a decent meal, without sleep or rest.

Mrs. Karty couldn't endure waiting any longer and for the tenth time that night she called the garage. Her brother, Harry, answered the telephone at once. It was queer. At this time of the night Lawrence, the colored night man, should have been the only one in the garage, and she wondered what kept her brothers there tonight. Something was going on and she spoke in tearful tones to Harry. He reassured her. They were all in the office. Moe wasn't there and they weren't out looking for him. They had business of their own to handle in the place tonight. Patiently he convinced her they were not seeking her husband.

Mrs. Karty hung up, sighing unhappily, but with a measure of comfort. If her brothers weren't looking for him, then he must be all right. Relieved, she turned out the lights, stopped the radio and went to bed.

⁓⁓⁓

The tight-lipped relief man whistled gravely at Shorty on the stool before him at the fountain. "There's a party waiting for you on the street," he said. "Looks like an interesting night for somebody." He clearly took great relish in the situation. Shorty had to face the outside.

Pulled from his thoughts, the jerker glared contempt at him. "Fongoo, you skinny son of a bitch," he said bitterly. "What the hell's the matter with you anyhow? What's the joke? What's so goddammed funny about it?"

The relief held out his hands dispassionately and sucked air to clean the cavities in his teeth. "Nothing funny," he remarked. "You don't see me laughing, do you?"

"Ain't human," Shorty said. "Like a fish. Must be a fairy or something."

"My! My!" said the relief, and his eyebrows went up in mock alarm. "Such indecent language. I'm ashamed of you indeed." He bounced primly down the floor slats, a man not wishing to be involved in unnecessary complications. The store was quiet. The way things were he'd close the place at one o'clock or a little after. Spitzbergen would never know the difference.

"Unnatural," muttered Shorty softly to himself as he glared at his back. "Go take a flying French . . ." His voice trailed. Outside waited Lillian and her boyfriend, and Shorty realized he couldn't stay in the soda parlor all night hoping they'd get tired and leave.

He hated the relief heartily. Look at him, he thought, got no desires, got no inclinations, hardly alive. Never got into trouble. That was the best way of doing things, three-quarters dead, because then you had no inclinations and you were never disappointed, never got kicked in the teeth. Take Shorty himself. Everybody's good-natured slob. Laughed at the right time, was sympathetic at the right time, never said the wrong thing, always wanting to do somebody a favor so far as it was possible for him to be of service. All he asked of life was a piece now and then and what happened? It was disgusting. Down the deep end of the fountain, at the double water tray, the relief gazed significantly at the street and whistled.

"Son of a bitch," Shorty exclaimed. He jumped off the stool and glared at him, resplendent in the white gabardine suit. He'd show that fish-faced cluck, and besides, he couldn't stay here all night. The soda jerker walked out of the store defiantly. At his departure the relief whistled grandly down the scale. He moved up to the street stand, resting his elbows on the marble counter, and took in the show. Outside Lillian pointed out Shorty to her boyfriend.

"So do something," she cried, her voice plaintive. "We've been waiting here twenty minutes already. He insulted me, Paul. He's a nasty, filthy thing."

Paul had a young face, round and full, unused to violence. He was a heavy man with thick thighs so that the trousers there were tight on him. He stepped in front of the little soda jerker and pulled him aggressively by the arm.

"Hey, you, listen here," he said, the chubby face solemn. "You can't do certain things and hope to get away with them. I hope you realize that. You do something, you're going to get it. That's the way it is."

"Give him, Paul," Lillian called behind him. "You give him so he'll learn better manners. He's a dirty, filthy thing."

Shorty studied the boy carefully and looked tough. "Fongoo!" he said.

"What?" he asked. "I didn't quite get that."

"That's what I said, clear and distinct. So what can you make of it?"

Paul turned to his girlfriend, puzzled, eager to take advantage of the pause. "Hey, Lillian, you know what fongoo means? Is it a dirty word or something?"

"I don't know," she said impatiently. "So what are you waiting for? We stood around waiting long enough. Don't talk. Hit him. Learn him good manners. I told him he lay a finger on me, my boyfriend would fix him. So you my boyfriend? I'm getting angry with you."

"Oh, don't worry," exclaimed Paul. "Whatever's coming to him he'll get. I just want to make sure what he says. He wants to call me names, he'll get it with interest."

Reluctantly the fat boy cocked his fist, ready to sock the soda jerker. It was evident he didn't enjoy his task but it was also clear he could very easily bang up Shorty. At the street stand, resting on his elbows, the relief man observed the proceedings, a satisfied smile on his face. The world was his oyster but he himself got mixed up in nothing. A man passing by stopped to watch the performance. To avoid the appearance of impolite curiosity, he ordered a Coke. And when the relief brought it to him, he sipped, lingering pleasantly over the glass.

The fat boy stood fixed in the posture of a prizefighter, uncertain under the staring eyes of the men. Shorty waited tensely, holding his fists ready at his side, making lip movements of contempt.

"Oh, for Heaven's sakes, Paul," wailed Lillian. "Give it to him already. What are you waiting for?"

"All right, Lillian," he said obediently, and he swung.

Shorty weaved away from the blow, ducking, and as he came up he caught the fist, holding it tightly.

"Just a minute," he said. "Don't get so reckless with your punches. If you want to fight it's O.K. with me, too, see how I mean. Just because you're over my size, don't get a swelled head. Looks are deceiving. I can handle myself, too."

"Don't listen to him, Paul," she shrieked. "Go on. Hit him. He's a nasty, filthy thing and I told him I got a boyfriend, so don't listen."

The fat boy looked at her helplessly and permitted Shorty to hold on to the grip on his fist. "Look, Lillian," he argued, "it don't hurt to wait a minute."

"Hey, mister," Shorty called to the Coca-Cola drinker at the street stand. "When you get into a fight, you like to know what you're fighting about first, ain't it? You don't want to waste your time over nothing, ain't it?"

The man shifted on his feet and smiled uneasily. "Sure," he said. "Naturally."

"See?" asked Shorty with vicious triumph. "See?"

Paul didn't know what to make of this turn in the situation. "I'm sorry," he protested, his fist still in Shorty's grasp. "I don't see what it's got to do."

"So what are you standing talking?" Lillian cried. She was banging him on the shoulder with her bag. "This makes me out a fine person! Here I told him I got a boyfriend, so you're my boyfriend?" She was boiling with exasperation.

"Sure!" Shorty cried. "Listen to her! She don't want you to listen and she's got good reasons! Get yourself into a jam and don't take a minute to find out what it's all about. That's got sense."

Paul wavered stupidly on his thick thighs. He was afraid to turn around and face his girlfriend. At the street stand the relief and the drinker watched the two intently, their faces clouding as they feared disappointment.

"So what is it?" Paul asked weakly. "All right, I'll give you a chance."

Shorty pulled him to a side while Lillian glared bitterly at them. "Look," the soda jerker said in a confidential whisper, "if it was coming to me, if I deserved it, then O.K. What the hell, don't you know? But you can understand how some dames are. Not that I'm saying anything against Lillian. She's O.K. See, she's respectable and refined, but naturally she's likely to be more sensitive about certain things than the average girl. See how I mean? See, when they're refined they don't like nobody should get away with anything on them. So that's O.K. But she thinks everything is an insult. Naturally, she's sensitive. After all, you know it as good as me, when a person looks for something, she'll find it even if it ain't there."

The fat boy pushed the hand off him. "Talk," he said, "You can talk your head off. It still sounds kind of funny to me."

"No, on the level. What the hell. I admit I was kidding around. Sure, why not, I'm old enough to be her old man. But perfectly harmless, don't you know? Hell, if you knew what kind of a guy I was, you'd understand that in spite of everything I got a clean mind."

"Well," said Paul, "I can't make up my mind. By rights I still think you ought to get it."

"Hell, listen. Ain't there been times when you kidded around with a girl? You know, just fooling around harmless, meaning nothing dirty and then all of a sudden she gets insulted and makes out you're trying something. Ain't it happened to you, too? Sure!"

"Hey, Lillian," he called. "He says nothing happened. He says he meant it harmless."

"Oh, for crying out loud, Paul! It's disgusting. Don't listen to him. He's a dirty liar. He's a dirty, filthy thing. I can't even tell you what he did to me. All day and then just before. I can't even mention it."

"So?" asked the fat boy.

"See, it's just like I said! There she is, still thinks I tried to get away with something! She's sensitive and sees bad intentions even when they don't exist. Hell, you can figure it out for yourself. It must of happened to you, just like this."

"Oh, hit him, Paul," she begged. "Hit him. He insulted me. For God's sakes, what's the matter with you?"

"After all," he protested to her, "I can't hit a man for nothing. There's two sides to every question."

"Oh, for Heaven's sakes, you make me sick. You're a dope." Now she grew conscious of the gaze of the two spectators at the stand and her embarrassment increased. "So if you don't want to do nothing, so come. So let's go home. I'm disgusted with you entirely."

"No," said the fat boy, "I ain't finished with him yet."

"Oh, come on, you make me sick." She was pulling on his sleeve. He resisted her but not with too much force.

"Hey, you, listen you," he said to Shorty. "By rights you ought to get it right here and now. I'm letting you get away with it this time but don't you try another thing. You get funny again and the next time I won't listen to any arguments." He shook his head with self-contained anger and succumbed to Lillian as she hopelessly pulled him away. "Don't forget it, either," he called.

As they went down the street, the men at Ann's could hear Paul insisting that there were two sides to every question and he couldn't hit a man unless he was absolutely sure in his mind that he deserved it.

"You my boyfriend," Lillian was wailing. "A fine boyfriend I got. The whole world can insult me right and left and he don't care, he wouldn't lift a finger." They went up the Avenue to the elevated station, arguing hotly.

The man with the Coca-Cola placed the glass regretfully on the counter. "Nothing with nothing," he murmured. "False alarm." He walked off. The tight-lipped relief man was disappointed too. He began clearing the counter of the chewing-gum and Life Saver racks, preparing to close up an hour earlier than he should. Spitzbergen would never know the difference and, besides, there was no business anyhow. As he worked, he glanced at Shorty, the eyebrows raised on his forehead.

"What are you standing moping at?" the soda jerker snapped. "Who the hell's asking you to look at me? What's the goddammed attraction?"

The relief whistled grandly down his scale and pulled the window gently down, locking up. Self-possessed and satisfied, he bounced along the flats.

Shorty stood outside the soda parlor in his white gabardine with the fancy back. So he got away with it. The boyfriend hadn't beaten him up. But it was lousy. The way he felt he might just as well have been kicked around. He didn't care a hang what happened to him. Nothing was fair and no man got a decent shake in the world. Feeling bitter with the injustice of his fate, the little soda jerker walked moodily to his trolley line.

⁓⁓⁓

At none of the joints they visited could they find any trace of Shubunka. Every time the sniffler started the motor again, the dapper thug, resting in the back seat, grew uneasy and restless, tactfully keeping quiet in order to escape notice. But the sniffler made a point of twisting around in the driver's seat and glaring at him.

"He couldn't help it!" he muttered. "He can't stand the sight of him. A wild man. A lunatic."

"Aw, lay off," said the prizefighter. He was growing sleepy and wanted to call off the search. "Listen, we might as well quit. We can't catch that coke if we stand on our heads."

"Sure! That's fine," the sniffler said. "'See, we got tired, boss,' I'll tell him. 'We felt sleepy and so we figured we might as well quit.' He'll say, 'That's swell.' I'll get a bonus. A fine bunch of guys I got to work with." He drove the car through the empty streets, consumed with anger.

"So where do we go looking for him now?" the dapper one asked, his voice meek. "We tried the houses. I don't see the sense just driving around."

"Aah, you got ideas, too. Intellectual!" the sniffler exclaimed. "Everybody chips in with a comment. That's all we need now. Listen, you charged-up fiend, I'm doing you a favor by not stopping the car right this minute and taking a crack at you. And don't you forget it, too."

"O.K.! Then O.K.!" he retorted, angry but yet restrained. After all he had been in the wrong with that crazy revolver shot and he knew it. If they didn't find Shubunka tonight, they'd all put the blame on him. The boss would be sore and he'd get it, not the sniffler.

"What I say is," said Amchy, coming out of his doze, "my point is, so long we're riding around we should dump the car and look for him in a different bus. It's too risky. Somebody might of spotted us and the cops might be tailing us right this minute for all we know. It makes sense. You got to admit it."

That proved to be the last straw for the sniffler. He exploded over the wheel. Everyone had ideas on the subject but no one of them could do a thing to help. One wanted to change cars, another wanted to give up altogether, and the third was an irresponsible lunatic. The way the three of them worked together they would soon pick up Shubunka. A fine bunch. The whole burden rested on him alone. He it was who would have to report to the boss, to him had been assigned the situation in Neptune Beach, and while Shubunka was still around the boss would be angry with him. The sniffler muttered violently, his eyes on the road.

"So O.K.," cried the prizefighter at last, showing offense at the outburst. "So don't get all burned up. We'll find him yet or we'll know the reason why."

"That's satisfaction, all right," the sniffler exclaimed, cooling down. "I'll tell the boss we know the reason why and he'll say, 'O.K. That's simply swell.'"

Cursing softly to himself in quiet fury, he wheeled the car around the corner without slackening speed. The three thugs were jolted out of their seats on top of one another with the sudden lurch. The car sped on.

* * *

"I didn't want to come," Dorothy said. "Only my mother made me. It's no picnic to travel at this hour without anybody for company. You can imagine for yourself. But my mother persuaded me. She didn't want you to go away mad."

She stood before him in the furnished flat on Eastern Parkway, one leg in front of the other, petulantly refusing to take off her hat. It was a white piqué bonnet tied at the back, and it made her look ridiculously like a Puritan maiden. Lurie took his eyes away from her, his gloom unrelieved by her arrival. She hadn't brought her suitcases. It was clear to him that she had come only to make sure the marriage would not go awry at the last moment. He thought of her parents and the solemn-faced married couple in their apartment in Neptune. Anxious, they must have been, worried, as a businessman worries when he feels he has bargained a little too sharply and the deal might fall through altogether.

All evening alone in the furnished flat he had thought of Neptune Beach, trying to analyze his repugnance to the neighborhood and its calloused, unfeeling, calculating ways. He had thought of the people at Ann's: of Shorty and his burlesque shows and perpetual concern with his naked women; of Spitzbergen who fretted over each penny, driven into a constant state of tears by his passion to make money; of Karty and the miserable gambling life he led, petty and raw, searching nervously for dollars with which to bet. Lurie had been thinking of Arthur, a kid who did not know what it was all about, who gaped enviously at the manliness of the men in Ann's and who would surely end up in some disaster. His own treatment of Shubunka and the experiences with him this day returned to vex him. Lurie felt guilty, but nevertheless the fat ugly booker and all he meant was loathsome to him. The life in Neptune Beach was poor and empty, mean, without beauty or aspiration. And standing before him was Dorothy, looking like a Puritan maiden, looking stupid and ridiculous, seeming dishearteningly to Lurie to be a part of the life at Neptune Beach. He no longer could doubt it. There would be no escape with her.

"You hollered I should come," she said. "So I'm here at last and he don't say a word to me."

"I'm glad you came," he said quietly. "I'm glad it's turning out all right."

"A dollar eighty-five cents," she mentioned crossly. "It cost a dollar eighty-five cents for the taxi and what was the point? What good can I do here without the bags? He took it into his head to get sore and just to give him satisfaction I got to spend two dollars for a cab." Dorothy began walking around aimlessly as she talked. "This is a very bad way to start. From now on I'll just be a rag in your hands. Every little thing your heart desires, you'll just mention it and I'll have to give in. It's a bad way to begin married life."

"All right. What's the use of arguing? You might as well keep quiet." He looked at his suitcases, unpacked. "You can bring your clothes in the morning. Then we'll go to City Hall and get married. It'll be O.K. Don't walk around so much. Sit down."

"Furnished rooms. Move out of Neptune just when the hot weather starts. Get married tomorrow. Everything in a hurry. It's like a fire was going on and you have to rush or something."

"Oh, Dorothy, cut it out!"

"Listen, Herbert, I want you to know I got a temper, too! Don't think you can holler at me like that. I'm not a rag in your hands yet. I'll stand for many things but I'm not a nobody at all." She drew herself up before him, her face flushed under her Puritan hat. "I must say you have certain qualities I don't like at all. Do you think I came all the way from Neptune so you could holler at me?"

"I wasn't hollering at you," Lurie said. "If you thought I was hollering, I'm sorry. I didn't mean it."

"All right. So you're sorry. All day you're sorry. I came down after you. So what do we do now? Just tell me what to do. You tell me. I have to do whatever you say. That's the way you want it. You're the boss. I'm just a rag."

Herbert Lurie stared at her, hating her in the silly bonnet and at the same time trying to drive away that hatred. They hadn't even been married and here they were arguing and nagging each other. It would be the same story all over again, and with a sinking rush of clearness he could envision what their life together would be. Dorothy would be no different from Flo or his first wife. Lurie had to restrain an impulse to break out. He wanted to tell Dorothy that their marriage would be all a mistake, that he regretted his promises and wanted to be released from them. She had no affection for him. He meant to her only a responsible husband who owned a fair business. Somehow, if it hadn't been for the time he had spent with Shubunka and the reflection the day's movements had caused in him, he would have gone ahead, sure in his fool's paradise that Dorothy would be surcease to Neptune Beach and all it meant to him. Lurie opened his mouth again, drew in his breath, but he stopped. It had been a bad day. Shubunka and the thugs might not have cleared his mind for him as he supposed, but rather they might have depressed him into a dismal view of everything. It would be better to wait.

"Come on home," she said. "So I came and now we can go home."

"Listen, Dorothy," be began, "I think maybe we should—"

There was a knock on the door. Lurie stopped, puzzled. Dorothy looked at him.

"Who could it be at this time of the night?" she asked. "You told somebody to come?"

"I didn't call nobody. I don't know who it is."

He went to the door. It was Shubunka. He was hatless, his stiff hair wildly disheveled in a weird arrangement on his head. The neat clothes now had swathes of dirt and at the right knee the trouser leg was open in shreds. On his fat cheeks was a web-like design where the dirt from the sidewalk, grown wet with his saliva, had dried. But what impressed Lurie most was the black terror in his eyes. Lurie had never seen him quite like this, not even on that sandy lot near the incinerator building this afternoon. There had always been something false, something artificially dramatic and faked with him. Shubunka always acted, but now he seemed to be a man completely engrossed in fear so that no room was left for affectation. The fat man remained lumpishly outside the door as Lurie and Dorothy stared at him in wonder.

"Well, of all things!" Dorothy finally gasped. She turned to Lurie. "How did he ever get here? Who put it into his head all of a sudden to come here? You told him to come or something? What for?"

"I didn't tell him anything," Lurie said. In spite of the argument they had had on the street corner this afternoon, Shubunka had come. "I didn't call him, Dorothy."

"Then how did he know where to find you? It looks suspicious. We just moved in today."

"I told him the address. I told him where we were going to live. But I told him not to come here."

"It's mystifying," she cried belligerently. "I can't make head or tail of it. Why should he want to come here? Why did you have to tell him not to come? What did you two do when you went to lunch anyways? Something's going on. I want to know what it is."

"Nothing's going on," Lurie said. "It wasn't any plan or anything. I'll tell you what it's all about later if you want to know. What's the matter with you? What's there to get so excited about?"

Shubunka had been standing in the hall all this time, staring helplessly at Dorothy, but now he stepped into the room. He turned to the girl. "Please," he begged. As Lurie went forward and closed the door, Dorothy's suspicions increased.

"What's he going to do here? Are you leaving him here? Is he going to stay here all night or something?"

"Please," said the fat man, his eyes pleading with her in his misery.

"What's the difference?" Lurie argued. "If he wants to stay here overnight, he's got a good reason and it's O.K. with us. We don't need the place tonight."

"Why?" Dorothy was completely bewildered. "Why should he stay here? What's the sense? I always said something was the matter with your head, but what do you call this now? It's craziness altogether! Why should he stay here?"

"Because he wants it." Lurie went to the door. "Come on home. It's late. Let's get going."

"No!" she cried, her face twisted near tears with exasperation. "You're crazy! There's something wrong with your head. I gave in to everything you wanted but I won't give in now. It's out-and-out craziness. Herbert, what's the matter with you anyway ?"

Shubunka stepped to her and put his hand on her shoulder. "Please, Dorothy," he begged. "I have always been nice to you at the soda store. I never had a bad word with you. Do me this favor. Let me stay here tonight. It will not hurt you to let me have the flat for one night and it will mean a great deal to me. You don't know, Dorothy, what it means to me. It's life and death to me."

She wriggled her shoulder away from his hand. As it fell off she could see the pimples of blood on his swollen palm. "What happened?" she asked. She first noticed now his disordered appearance, the dirt on his face, the torn and smeared clothes. "I don't want to get mixed up in any of his troubles. Herbert, tell him to go away. I can't stand the sight of him. He's revolting. He makes me sick. If he ever stayed a night in a house I could never live there again. Something's the matter with him. It's none of our business. After all, we don't want to go looking for trouble. I don't like him and I don't want the whole business. It looks funny to me from start to finish."

Shubunka fell back, pain showing in his face. It was real pain, nothing faked, thought Lurie. He discovered he had suddenly lost all affection for Dorothy.

"Come on home!" he said. He held the door open for her to pass.

"No!" she screamed. "I don't go until he goes! I won't give in this time. I don't see why you have to have your way in everything. All the time I have to give in to you. Well, I won't stand it this time. I won't have him in the house. Now you'll just have to do what I want. I made my mind up."

She was talking so loudly that Lurie had to close the door. "You're unreasonable," he said. "What difference does it make to you if he stays? I don't know exactly why he wants the flat, either, but if he wants it so bad, it don't concern us. We don't need the apartment tonight."

"No, see? I don't want him in the house. He's revolting. I'm not giving in no matter what you say. That's all. Tell him to go away."

"Listen, Dorothy, please," begged Shubunka. "I'm in trouble. Outside in the streets gangsters ride around looking for me with revolvers. They got me once, by my house. Six bullets they shot at me. They're still looking for me. I can't go no place. They will find me in Neptune Beach. I got to hide. Please, Dorothy, I beg you, let me stay."

"Let him stay," Lurie said. "It won't do no damage to anybody. I don't see why you have to be so stubborn."

"No! Once for all, no! Listen, Herbert, I want you to understand this much. I stood enough from you. I'm all out of patience. What means more to you, him or me? Either you tell him to go or I'm through with you. See, if you want to make an issue out of it, I'm willing, too. I'm sick and tired of you and your crazy tricks. Make up your mind once for all. It's just like you want it. Either he goes tonight, or you and me, we're finished." She was grinding her teeth in fury.

"It's ridiculous," said Lurie.

"Well?" she screamed. "Make up your mind. I stood about enough."

Shubunka had gone to the window and now looked down the street. He could see the treetops rustling quietly in the wind of the night. The double-laned thoroughfare below had few cars. Across the street the huge, dark Art Museum rested against the emptiness of the park. It was still and peaceful. The fat man wanted to stay in the apartment. Away from Neptune Beach the thugs would never find him here. He would have time to collect himself, to go to the banks for his money, to leave town for his cousin in Troy, or, if he changed his plans, to fight the combination.

But as Shubunka looked through the window he could see a sedan drive slowly down the narrow lane directly off the street across. Shubunka gasped with fear. Had they trailed him here, too? It was not possible. He watched the sedan carefully, hoping for it to pass on, but when it reached the wide lawns and darkness of the Museum building, it stopped. It wasn't possible! Shubunka cried to himself. It must be a different car. They could not have followed him here. But he fell back from the window with a sinking feeling.

"Look out the window," he whimpered. "See they found me. I can't go outside now. I have to stay. They are gangsters. They have revolvers. They will kill me. I cannot go down."

"Baloney!" Dorothy cried. "It's baloney. Don't you tell me that. I know you and your crazy shows all the time. I'm not bothering with you. Listen, Herbert, I can't stay here all night. Listen, Herbert, this means a finish. It's not just tonight and him. It's everything that happened. If you want to be crazy altogether, we better not get married. I'm through. You understand what I mean?"

"I can't tell him to go," Lurie said. "It's trouble. I know it. Those gangsters would kill him if they saw him."

"I don't care if it's true or if it's not true. It don't make a difference with me. Tell him to go out."

"No," said Lurie. "I won't tell him."

"So, all right! So good-bye and good luck. I'm through with you forever. It's better it happened now than later. You and me are all finished. The hell with it. You're absolutely out of your senses." She slammed the door and went downstairs. Lurie watched her go, could hear for some moments her wooden heels clicking on the marble steps of the hallway, and discovered that he felt satisfied and relieved. He turned to Shubunka.

"It's O.K.," he said. "You can stay if you want to. You can stay in the flat as long as you like."

"What is happening?" the fat man wailed in his confusion. "What does she mean, Mr. Lurie? Is it really true or is it just a little quarrel?"

"It's nothing. Don't worry about it."

"Oh, I am sorry, Mr. Lurie. What did I do to you?" It impressed Lurie oddly that in spite of his terror with the sedan downstairs, Shubunka showed such intense dismay at Dorothy's departure. Was he putting on a show again?

"It ain't your fault," he told the fat man. "You ain't concerned in it. You stay in the flat as long as you want. It's O.K. now."

But in his great fear and misery Shubunka could now think of nothing but what he had done to Lurie and Dorothy. He rocked brokenly on his legs, murmuring and crying constantly. From time to time he would stop to bewail himself in loud shrill tones for having been the cause of the quarrel. Lurie could not understand him and his intense concern. Was Shubunka putting on a show again in spite of his appearance a few minutes ago? It seemed hardly believable at this time.

"Cut it out," he said. "What are you worrying about us? That's O.K. You got more important things to worry about. I'll go and you can stay here."

"It's too late. They're waiting for me outside. They have found me. They will kill me and I had to go and drive her away." He trudged to the window and looked down, tears on his heavy cheeks, lost in grief.

Lurie went to the window to see if a car was really there. He had to shake his head, unable to solve the enigma of Shubunka. He had always thought the man was mostly fake, willful acting and pretense, but seeing him as he had when he first came into the flat, it seemed to him for the first time that there was something genuine in Shubunka's strange manner, something that gnawed everlasting at him, rendered him unhappy and different. For the first time Lurie perceived that there was a reason to the man, that he acted logically within his circumstances. And Shubunka's irrelevant absorption over the quarrel with Dorothy puzzled him all the more. Unwilling to consider his concern affected, feeling that Shubunka was sincere, he wondered what here distressed him so keenly at a time when his own life was so perilously near an end. Across the street, near the dark Museum grounds, the car was still waiting.

"How do you know it's the same car?" he asked. "And even if it is, they'll go away in the morning. They can't stay here all the time. You can get away in daylight. Then you can leave town. It will be all right yet."

"No," he moaned, his voice lifeless, "it is all over. I know it. And what did I do to you? Why did I have to bother you, too, when it will do no good? I have no right to interfere. I am no good. I should get all that is coming to me. It is right for me to suffer now. A man who has done what I have, who has lived as I have, deserves to be alone in the world, with no one's pity, with kindness from no one. I have no right. Go, Mr. Lurie, go find her. Let her have it as she wants it. I will go. I deserve all that is coming to me." He sobbed helplessly, tears blinding his eyes, sniffling and overcome. It was as though he realized now clearly that he could have no more hope.

"For God's sakes, stop it," Lurie said. "What is the matter with you? I'm going. You'll be all right."

As he went to the door, Shubunka rushed in a sudden outburst before him. He blocked Lurie away with his own body and ran into the hall, slamming the door behind him. He went rushing down the steps, slobbering and lost in hysteria.

"Cut it out," Lurie yelled. He went after him in the hall, but as soon as he caught hold of him, Shubunka knocked his hands off his shoulders. They began to struggle down the stairs. Lurie grabbed his coat at the collar, pulling him back, but using all his strength in his wild spasm Shubunka fought free, striking at him and pushing him back on the steps. In that awkward position above him, Lurie could not get a sure grip on him. He was constantly tripping and falling over the fat man. Shubunka was weeping in his unnatural shrill voice as he ran, protesting that to have everything he had built up in the last eight years taken away from him was as good as death and he preferred it. At the same time he wailed that he was no good, a monster, a man who had lived on human flesh, who deserved no pity and all suffering. He reviled himself. A man who had lived as he had deserved no mercy from any human. Lurie could not stop his sobbing entreaties. He persisted in grappling with him but Shubunka always managed to wriggle free, intent upon his own destruction. There was no pulling him out of his insane paroxysm. When they reached the lobby of the apartment building the fat man tore away and went running heavily to the door. Lurie felt sick. He halted, deep in the hall, afraid to follow him for the bullets that were to come.

Outside, against the ironwork that protected the glass doors, Shubunka stood panting and sobbing, his arms outstretched, his eyes closed.

"Kill me!" he whined. "Go ahead. It is right. Shoot me. Murder me. It is only what I deserve."

He waited for the barrage of bullets but the car remained still. The night wind blew across the bare pavements and the leaves on the trees rustled, producing their mysterious sighing sounds as if they understood and this was their gentle lamentation. At this hour one or two autos sped up the street, but except for them the Parkway was deserted. Waiting in agony for the bullets, Shubunka opened his eyes.

"Kill me," he begged. "It is a favor. I want it. What are you waiting for? Shoot already and make a finish of it."

He began waddling across the wide street, his arms still outstretched, still talking weakly in his gibberish of hysterical outcries in which he reviled himself. As he left the curb, Lurie came forward to the door and paused. Fear of the attack for himself and yet tremendous pity for the clumsy man filled him. Even now it seemed that Shubunka insisted upon a spectacle but Lurie this time could not grow disgusted with him for it. It seemed to him somehow normal and right for Shubunka.

He had waddled across now, near the darkness of the great lawns of the Museum.

"Kill me," he murmured. "Shoot already. Please."

"Oh, George! Oh, George!" A girl's voice piped with fear. It was a couple, staring at him from the car in scared wonder. The boy took his arm off her shoulder and sat up, tightening within himself.

"Don't worry, Edith," he said, breathless. "It's nothing." He was as frightened and puzzled by the strange sight, and feebly screwed up his courage. "What do you want?" he asked Shubunka. "What is it?"

The fat man's arms fell to his sides. It was not the thugs. In an instant his mad paroxysm was over. The hysteria died away and he felt cool and self-possessed again, feeling a little ridiculous, too. He could think of nothing to say to them but stared at the couple helplessly and uncertainly.

"Oh, George!" whimpered the girl. "Oh, George! Drive away!"

The boy stepped on the starter in fumbling haste. His presence of mind was returning and he turned to her. "He's harmless," he said, speaking now with some anger. "He's only a halfwit."

"Never mind, drive away!" the girl cried. "Just let's get away from here."

"They ought to keep people like him locked up," the boy said. "Scaring people at this time of the night. Why doesn't somebody keep an eye on him? He could get himself in trouble."

As the car drove off, the gusts of wind it created tossed Shubunka's stiff hair about on his head. He stood still. Lurie came up quickly from the street but he had to pull his arm in order to bring him out of his reverie.

"What happened?" he asked. "What was it?"

"Wrong car," Shubunka said. "It was not the gangsters. I made a mistake."

He was calm now, almost apologetic after all the fuss and the wild cries. Looking at him and seeing the human despair in his heavy face, Lurie grew filled with pity for him.

"Look, Shubunka, leave New York," he said. "It's useless. In the end that's what you'll have to do, so you might as well go now. Take the subway. Go to Grand Central and take a train. It's the only way."

"Leave New York," murmured Shubunka, his high voice sounding distant. "Then all right. Then all right."

There was no longer hope in him, force or even self-pity. He knew it was over. He would take the train for Troy where his cousin in the wholesale-produce business lived. He had to go there. Without another word to Lurie he moved away and went waddling slowly on his bent legs down the Parkway to the subway station, wrapped in his own thoughts and troubles, collected, walking with the tired tread of a man who might be going to his place of business in the morning.

Lurie's eyes followed the short squat figure until it blurred in the weak light of the street lamps. He turned and went back to his flat. Going up the hallway, deep in reflection, Lurie found that the mood of despondency that had oppressed him all day had suddenly lifted. Perhaps this was because of his quarrel with Dorothy and the end to plans of marriage, but his strange easy-heartedness, it seemed to him, went beyond the relief here. For once now he felt satisfied and resolved. His old inner distaste for Neptune Beach and the people there had gone. Witnessing the resignation of Shubunka as the man walked to the subway, realizing that he, too, had conscience and recognized in his own peculiar way the justice of his fate, above all, feeling with pity his complete wretchedness, Lurie knew now that it had been insensible and inhuman for him, too, simply to hate Neptune and seek escape from it. This also was hard and ignorant, lacking human compassion. He had known the people at Ann's in their lowness and had been repelled by them, but now it seemed to him that he understood how their evil appeared in their impoverished dingy lives and, further, how miserable their own evil rendered them. It was not enough to call them low and pass on.

And for himself, this evening, with Shubunka's appearance, Lurie felt somehow clear and sure. His old desire to leave Neptune Beach and escape with Dorothy now became useless and without point. Lurie entered the flat, picked up the suitcases and turned off the lights. He decided to go back to his rooms in Neptune.

The new day broke hot and steamy. From all parts of the city—from the East Side and Washington Heights, from Williamsburg and Brownsville, from the Bronx—the thousands and thousands poured to the beaches in their light summer clothing, swinging their bathing-suit bags gaily and smacking one another with them in the trains and trolley cars. They were playful and free. They had left behind them the baking rooms of their tenements to seek relief and joy on the dirty sands of the beaches. All day they would bathe in the water, fry in the sun, rest in healthful mudpacks, eat their lunches of sardine sandwiches in their bathing suits. In the evening, before they returned to the baking rooms, they would stroll along the boardwalk, munching hot dogs and frozen-custard cones. They would buy rides on the Whip, the Thunderbolt, the Canal of Romance. Amid the joyful jangling clatter of the side-shows and the merry-go-round calliopes, they would be a part of the tramping, shouting millions enjoying life at the seashore. Waiting to reach the beaches, they ran around impatiently in the cars, unable to sit quietly. The trains moved much too slowly for them, for they must hurry to seize their good time. The concessionaires and storekeepers of Neptune waited on their doorsteps, nervous with anticipation of the crowds.

The late morning newspapers carried the account of Spitzbergen's murder. The *Mirror* and the *News* published front-page photographs of the dead man, sitting peacefully against the tiled wall of the washroom, his hat down over his eyes. The people on the Avenue read the newspaper accounts aloud to one another, sighing and clucking regretfully and secretly animated at the notoriety so close to home. And avidly reading the details of his murder and his fame, it was as though they were seeing Spitzbergen as he was for the first time in spite of the many years in which they had known him. The newspapers seemed to pull the soda man into their consciousness out of the background of Neptune Beach, which they knew but did not see.

The account told how Spitzbergen, fifty-four years old, owner of a soda parlor and real estate in Neptune, was found strangled in a men's washroom on the Avenue J station at two in the morning. A receipt from a pastry company led to his identification and to his wife who was waiting for him at her home. She had arranged a little party for him. The paper told how Spitzbergen was first supposed to have died of natural causes but the autopsy by the Chief Medical Examiner revealed that the death was "a typical case of manual strangulation," as he called it, the death caused by the fracture of the larynx. The Examiner added that the murdered man had a bruise on the right cheek and a hemorrhage inside the mouth. The police theory was that the assailant had struck him with a blunt instrument before strangling and robbing him, and that the robber evidently hurried to get away since he left the victim's watch, a pair of eyeglasses, and a diamond ring. The detectives believed that the murder was committed by lush workers whose habit it was to rob late travelers, and they promised to round up all subway suspects immediately.

But while the neighbors in Neptune shook their heads over the morning editions with solemn respect, Karty and Arthur had already been picked up by the police at the Fortieth Street bus terminal. Trembling and hysterical, they had attracted the attention of detectives waiting there. They were brought to the West Thirtieth station where they were questioned on their motives for leaving town. Unstrung and wild, they soon confessed to the murder of the soda man. The afternoon papers told, how, according to detectives, Karty had threatened repeatedly to "kill himself if Arthur ever squealed."

The storekeepers of Neptune Beach put the papers aside and grew prepared for the rush. It was too bad about Spitzbergen, but after all, business was business and a man had to make a living.

It was a blazing sun, pouring thickly over the atmosphere, which was heavy with dampness. It was like a steamy blanket. Their clothes were damp and chafing on their bodies. Going inside the stores, they scratched their chins thoughtfully and said it was a pity the soda man wasn't alive to enjoy the wonderful weather.

CODA

I'VE BEEN WORKING RECENTLY on a more or less autobiographical article, describing, among other remembrances, my arrival in Hollywood from Brooklyn thirty-five years ago, and I wrote that one of the first things that struck me when I came here was the sight of the Los Angeles streets, which I had seen so many times in the backgrounds of the old two-reel comedies and through which, by a quirk of fortune, I now found myself passing—those streets with their unfamiliar Western trolley cars, their semaphore traffic signals, the palm trees, the lawns and bungalow dwellings, and the rolling line of the hills always in the distance behind them. After I finished my article, thinking of the old Laurel and Hardy comedies, the ones with Larry Semon, Harold Lloyd, and Harry Langdon, I went back in my mind another thirteen years or so (which now put me in my early teens) and I thought of the movie houses in Williamsburg where I had first seen the comedies; and since the moviegoing then played a remarkably large part in my life, as it did in the lives of the rest of us there, this chain of recollection—the Los Angeles streets, the old-time two-reelers, and then the Williamsburg movie houses—brought back quickly to me the whole feel of my old boyhood neighborhood and the way it was in those times.

Within a short radius of the street where I lived, a very poor street in this very poor section of Brooklyn, there were no fewer than seven movie theaters. On Grand Street, three or four blocks to the north, were the Grand, the Garden, the Plaza; they were decorated in a flowery, trellisy blue-and-pink style, with bowers and arbors, the three theaters owned by the same family, I think—you could see the boy bicycling endlessly from theater to theater with the cans of film, so that the same feature could be played, in rotation, at all three houses. To the south were the grander theaters, the Marcy, the Commodore, and, later, the Republic. But the one that was the most important to us was the Hooper, on South Fourth Street, an exceedingly ugly, squat, one-story yellow-brick structure. The management here somehow got the pictures we craved to see—dramas, melodramas, pictures of high life, with great scenes, with Bebe Daniels, Norma Talmadge. The bill was changed every day or every other day, I can't remember which, and almost all of us, children and grown-ups, foreign-born and American-born, went regularly to the Hooper twice a week, and a good many of us went even more often.

It has been noted that the movies had their great rise because, by an accident of timing, they came into being just as the flood of immigration was at its height, and that, by an even luckier accident—those mysterious coincidences of timing that seem providentially to take care of these things—they were silent pictures, without soundtracks, in this way making it possible for the foreign-born to get past the barrier of language. (You could hear the mothers in the dark whispering to their children: "What does it say? What does it say?" and the boy or girl, tugged and prodded, their eyes still fastened on the movie screen, would swiftly whisper back, reading out the subtitles.) So it has been said that the movies did their share in educating and Americanizing the masses of immigrants, but I don't think that was the reason people went so avidly to the pictures, to become Americanized. The audiences at the Hooper had an intense European theatrical tradition and they hungered for drama, but I don't think it was this factor either that accounted for the extraordinary appeal the movies had for us. No, what these pictures did—with their virility and vigor, their command of life, their consistently positive statements—

was to act against the fear that came down to us almost unconsciously from our parents, a fear that came out of Old World oppressions, from the difficulties of life in the new world, from the hardships our parents and grandparents had undergone in transferring themselves and their families from the Old World to the New—it was as though the feat of emigration had used up their strength and courage.

I remember the dark, fearfully cold winter nights on our street in Williamsburg. We were hemmed in—if you wandered eight or ten blocks in any direction you were promptly laid low by Poles, Irish, or Italians. The street was extremely narrow; it was lined on both sides by the unbroken walls of the tenement buildings, each one five stories tall, and so the street became a tight, closed-in canyon and you hardly saw the sky and seldom noticed the stars. The wind smashed through the canyon of the tenements like a malevolent force. It was a setting that gave rise to superstitions and strange fancies. We used to splash water down a twenty- or thirty-foot stretch of sidewalk, wait a few minutes for the water to freeze, and then have ourselves an icy slide—we would take running starts and go skittering down the twenty or thirty feet like demented wraiths. And while we played in the dark on those forbidding wintry nights, numb with the cold and wind, always keeping close to our homes, I sometimes had the fantasy—I wonder how many others have ever had this notion—that it was all a conspiracy to deceive us: that this was all there was, there was no outer, wider world, that our elders systematically made up a geography and invented similar myths so that we wouldn't lose heart and despair.

Late at night, when my father was home from work and was having his supper, he would want a pitcher of seltzer water—"Jump downstairs for me," he would say to me, handing me the pitcher, "and go to Yozowitz's [the candy store]"—and I remember what a struggle it was to get myself through the darkened hallway; there was one spot in particular, just behind the turn in the stairway, the space near the letterboxes, a black abyss of the unknown, and, coming back from the candy store, I would go through a crazy ecstasy of fright, spilling globs of seltzer out of the pitcher, until I finally worked past this bad, black area. (Fifty years ago, and this bad dark patch of the letterboxes behind the stairs still appears in my dreams.) My mother gibed at me, scolding and reasoning with me to allay my fears, arguing as an older sister would in league with her brother—she wasn't a great many years older than I was. Her name was Sara Molly. "What are you afraid of?" she would plead with me, holding me by the hand and looking into my eyes. "The worst they can do to you is shoot you." But the truth is she was just as fear-bound as I was. She stayed close to the door of her house, to the stores on our street—she had never even seen Macy's. It was to her and to most of her neighbors a faraway place, something to be talked about.

Back in those times, the way it was, a man couldn't bring his whole family with him when he came to America. He would come by himself or with an older son; they would save up money—working in sweatshops, living in hovels, denying themselves—until there was enough to bring over another member of the family and then another; and one by one, over the period of time, they would finally be all gathered together again on this side of the ocean. For this reason it happened that my mother, when she was thirteen years old, had had to travel across Europe from her small town in Russian Poland to the port of Rotterdam in Holland; she wore a tag pinned to her coat, saying who she was and where she was going and who would collect her, and she traveled with another child of her own age, the two of them holding firmly to each other as they made the long journey by themselves. In Rotterdam my mother apparently had been terrified by some soldiers, whatever it could be that had happened there, and after the fright with the soldiers, after the horrors of the three-week voyage in the steerage of the ship, she wouldn't venture forward again, to Macy's or anywhere else, no matter how brave she pretended to be when she told me not to be afraid and remonstrated with me.

We stayed close to our street. Living in one of the tenements on our block was a boy some years older than I was and so not part of the group I spent time with. He didn't talk to us, we had nothing to do with him, but we watched him from the distance. His name was Cannonball Lishinsky. He was slender, light on his feet, long-legged and jaunty, with a certain light in his eyes, a wild resolution. He sallied forth and took his chances—he went to the Broadway Arena, a neighborhood fight club (not on the Manhattan Broadway, on our Brooklyn Broadway, under the el; the fight club was not far from a dance hall called the Lorraine where, although we didn't know it then, the bouncer employed on the premises was the young Al Capone). Lishinsky fought in the four-round preliminary bouts, open to all comers at those clubs, and, when he came back, still keeping our distance, we watched him in an awed silence—the skin horribly mangled on his face, his forehead pounded and discolored, the grin still on him, the light in his eyes a little wilder and more desperate.

My father took me with him one night when he had some deliveries to make. My father had a newsstand, a candy stand, in one of the big office buildings on the Battery in Manhattan, and at Christmastime some of the rich men in the building gave him orders for five-pound boxes of chocolates—Page and Shaw, Park and Tilford—which he then had to deliver after work. He took me along with him that night, really for the sake of the company, not to help him with the packages, and in this way I got to see Flatbush, a section of Brooklyn just a few miles away from us in Williamsburg but like a place in another country. Flatbush then was a kind of village to itself. I saw the blaze of lights, the Christmas decorations, the gleaming, well-stocked butcher shops, the ruddy faces of the tradespeople as they dealt with their lady customers—all of it new to me, remote and seeming unreal.

Our high-school gym had a set of flying rings rigged from the ceiling, and I was soaring on them one spring afternoon, swinging high in the air from ring to ring, until my hand slipped and I crashed to the floor, jamming my wrist, dislocating the bone. Mr. Brown, the gym teacher in his gray coat-sweater, grabbed me by the arm, getting in front of me and pulling me along with him to the gym office, all the while tugging furiously at my wrist to shove the bone back into place. In the gym office, he split the top of chalk boxes, fixed me up with a temporary splint, and then sent me home. My mother had to get me to the doctor, but she also had the problem in this emergency of taking care of my father—that is, she had to keep me out of sight when he came home, so that he would be able to eat his supper. She sent me to the Hooper (Norma Talmadge, Conway Tearle), and when I came back, everything had been explained, everything was peaceful, my father had eaten, and my mother was already finished dressing. We set out together.

The doctor's office was across the river on the Lower East Side, and in order to get there we first had to walk the eight or ten blocks from our tenement to the Bridge Plaza, a wonderful expanse open to the sky and filled with a miniature multitude of people bustling and coming and going in all directions. We took the trolley across the bridge and, once on the other side, went walking again, along the length of Delancey Street, past Rivington Street, Hester Street, Orchard Street, Old Broadway, those old, old worn streets redolent of struggle and aspiration. It was a warm evening. In these localities, where the dwellings were poor and confined and people tried to live as much of their lives as they could out of doors, the sidewalks swarmed with life and movement, and as my mother and I passed through the throngs a contagion took over and exhilarated me. I knew there was a world for the exploring, wonders of places and people and experiences to be sought out and savored.

My mother took my arm. It was the first time we had been out together in this way; it was an expedition. I walked along that evening, fifty years ago, free and happy, immersed in the fragrance of my companion, so soft and alluring in her long, tailored suitcoat, with her hair coiled on top of her head, as it was worn in those days and often now too, with her fine young cheekbones—that beautiful young woman whom I astonishingly see now again in the faces of my grandnieces and grandnephews.

DANIEL FUCHS
Hollywood, California
October 1971

NOTE

THIS VOLUME REPRINTS the three Brooklyn novels that Daniel Fuchs published between 1934 and 1937, when he was in his mid to late twenties. By then he was no longer living with his parents in a Williamsburg tenement but with his wife, Susan, in a Flatbush apartment building, on a block full of schoolteachers and scholars, at Parkside and Ocean Ave., just across the street from the Brooklyn Museum and Prospect Park. He wrote mainly during summer breaks from teaching fourth-graders at P.S. 225 in Brighton Beach, where, from 1930 to 1936, he was a "permanent substitute" teacher—not a salaried employee but a full-time freelancer, earning six dollars every day the school was open, working without contract or benefits. ("Six dollars a day didn't go far," he later remembered. "Of course, prices were different then. We paid $42 a month for a good one-room apartment. Bread was 5¢ a loaf. Newspapers, 2¢.") He would outline a novel during the school year, work up scenes on weekends and holidays, then write a complete draft in June, July, and August. "I wrote *Blenholt* in three weeks," he said. "Once I sat down to it, the work went fast."

Fuchs's first novel, *Summer in Williamsburg*, was published by The Vanguard Press, New York, in 1934. *Homage to Blenholt* followed from the same house in 1936, and *Low Company* in 1937. The books were also published in London, by Constable, in 1935, 1936, and 1937. Because there had recently been an English book also called *Low Company*—it was the autobiography of a jailed gentleman bank robber—Constable published Fuchs's third novel under the title *Neptune Beach*.

When the books came out, they were disappointments to the author. "They failed, had no sales, attracted few reviews," Fuchs wrote. "Some years afterward, I was with a friend, talking about the old days in Williamsburg, and I told him about the killing I saw on South Third Street. My friend said what a good story it was, why didn't I write it? Of course I had."

The Broadway impresario Jed Harris read and admired *Blenholt*, and in January 1936 he phoned Fuchs out of the blue and asked him to do a stage treatment of it. He wanted the adaptation to center not, like the novel, on Max Balkan, but on the secondary character Munves, and talked with Fuchs at length about the Munves subplot, "reviewing certain incidents with full understanding and appreciation, other incidents in original ways I had not thought of." Although Harris flattered Fuchs, brainstormed with him, stole a month of Saturdays from him in work and excitement and talk, he never read Fuchs's dramatization, in fact had lost interest in the project shortly after he proposed it. He strung Fuchs along, because he delighted in Fuchs's company and because it pleased him to build castles in the air.

"I had finished the dramatization during the Easter vacation," Fuchs remembered some fifty years later. "Toward the end of the summer of that year, with the approach of a new fall school term, when my wife and I were living in the country, I received a communication, in a plain brown envelope, from the Board of Education officially informing me that I was at last granted an appointment as a regular teacher. I was told that since I had taught for seven years as a permanent substitute, my probationary period was considered completed and I would start with permanent tenure from the outset. I was further informed that my wages were to be calculated on the basis of the accrued seven years' annual increases and I would therefore start on eighth-year teacher's pay. I decided not to accept the appointment.

"I was tied down to a publisher's contract which I had signed when I was twenty-three years old and couldn't get out of. (The Author's Guild had made a study of these contracts, had listed thirty-two different abuses, and said my contract was the only one they had seen with all thirty-two of them.) I suddenly found I wanted no more to do with the publisher or the novel I had been working on that summer.

"I put all of it behind me—the teaching, the novels, the disappointments. I struck out on my own and was successful from the beginning. I wrote story after story. I broke up my unfinished novel into stories. The letter from the Board of Education had inflamed me. There was in exhilaration in me, something of the joke that flickered in Jed Harris, on which he subsisted, and which perhaps had carried over to me. The money that came in delighted me; it was a preoccupation and pursuit as enjoyable as any other.

"The stories I wrote for *The New Yorker* put me in a company I admired with all my heart and brought me esteem. The ones I did for the large-circulation magazines were even more rewarding. . . . One day I read of a horse-trainer who as a boy was a pigeon-fancier. I got the notion of a group of cab drivers who band together, buy a racehorse, and turn it over to train to one of their number who has tended pigeons all his life. *Collier's* called the story 'Crazy Over Pigeons.' My original title was 'The Day the Bookies Wept,' and this was the title RKO used on the movie, in 1939, with Joe Penner and Betty Grable. It was the first thing of mine to be filmed, the first connection I had with Hollywood and the motion-picture studios. . . ."

Fuchs went west, on assignment from Metro, in the spring of 1937, and worked as a studio screenwriter for most of the next three decades. One of his earliest projects was an adaptation of his own *Low Company*; it was eventually made by Monogram Pictures and released, under the title *The Gangster*, in 1947. (The movie was directed Gordon Wiles, and the cast included Barry Sullivan [Shubunka], John Ireland [Karty], and Harry Morgan [Shorty], with Akim Tamiroff as Nick, the Spitzbergen figure.) When Fuchs resumed writing fiction in his forties, publishing four brilliant stories in *The New Yorker* in 1953–54, certain critics took notice; all of them welcomed his return to "serious writing" but some rebuked him for his "misspent years" in Hollywood. Around this same time Irving Howe, writing for *Commentary*, published a long and influential and hand-wringing piece about Fuchs ("Escape from Williamsburg, or The Fate of Talent in America"), and soon the Brooklyn novels were again being checked out at libraries and ferreted out in used-book stalls.

In 1961 Arthur Rosenthal, the director of Basic Books, republished the Brooklyn books in one volume, under the title *Three Novels*. In 1965 the novels were reissued individually, in rack-size mass-market paperback editions, by Berkley Jove. Seven years later, the three-in-one omnibus was reprinted by Avon, under the title *The Williamsburg Trilogy* (although the books do not form a trilogy, and one is set in Brighton Beach). Scattered reprints followed, some of them strictly for the academic-library market. *Low Company* was translated into Polish, *Summer in Williamsburg* into French.

In 1989, four years before his death, Fuchs wrote: "A man sits in a room, writing novels. Nothing happens. They don't sell—four hundred copies apiece, the last one a few more. The reviews are scattered. Twenty-five, thirty years later they are resurrected and brought out again. I am rediscovered.... It turns out I am a cult with a respectable following somewhere in the country—and none of this through any doing on my part or with my knowledge beforehand. How does it feel to be a cult? It's flattering. I like it. I don't know what to make of it. At bottom I know the books are not first class and I privately wonder about the acclaim. The books are fine. I wrote about the restless Americanized sons of their immigrant fathers, and the novels have a good tenement-house yeastiness and sense of life in them, but I won't reread them (I have never reread them) because the flat print of the pages will only sicken and disappoint me. It's always like that. It is the usual author's lamentation, the author's perpetual dissatisfaction with what he's written. Critics and bystanders who concern themselves with the plight of the Hollywood screenwriter don't know the real grief that goes with the job. The worst is the dreariness in the dead sunny afternoons when you consider the misses, the scripts you've labored on and had high hopes for and that wind up on the shelf, when you think of the mountains of failed screenplays on the shelf at the different movie companies; in all my time at the studios, I managed to get my name on a little more than a dozen pictures, most unmemorable, one [*Love Me or Leave Me*] a major success. It's the same when you write for publication, on your own. You have the same record of misses, the bouts of wretchedness, the typed sheets of paper going flat in your hands—'The *cafard*,' Graham Greene has called it. 'The despair of never getting anything right.' Of course, the difference is that in the movies you get paid when you fail and there is that to carry you over. I must say, in my case, there was never a rebuke."

This Black Sparrow edition of the Brooklyn novels is based on the texts of the Vanguard editions. In our copyediting and design we have silently corrected typographical errors in the originals, regularized the spellings of certain words across the three books, and brought consistency to the treatment of section breaks and other display elements.

Fuchs's preface first appeared in *Three Novels*, the Basic Books omnibus of 1961. The piece we have chosen as a coda first appeared, as "The Silents Spoke to the Immigrants," in the Brooklyn–Queens–Long Island edition of the *New York Times* for October 17, 1971; Fuchs reprinted this essay, under the title "The Williamsburg Bridge Plaza," in his miscellaneous collection *The Apathetic Bookie Joint*, published by Methuen in 1979.

Jonathan Lethem's piece began life as a one-paragraph contribution to the "Lost and Found" column of *Tin House* magazine (Fall 1999). We would like to thank Mr. Lethem for expanding his comments into an introduction for this volume, and for being in the room with us, as it were. Thanks also to Jacob and Thomas Fuchs, the sons of Daniel Fuchs, for their continued trust in Black Sparrow; to David Godine, for his enthusiasm and largesse; and to the reference staff of the Boston Athenæum, for their always cheerful bibliographic assistance.

CHRISTOPHER CARDUFF
Editor and Publisher
Black Sparrow Books